MORTIMER'S
DEEP

Simon Taylor was born in 1950 in Fife, Scotland, where he grew up and was educated, studying German and French at St Andrew's University, later returning after two years in Germany to edit *The Anglo Saxon Chronicle, MS B.*

Simon Taylor is a Scottish Tourist Guide; but during the winter months he has also worked on editing and translating the enormous medieval work, Walter Bower's *Scotichronicon*, with a heavy involvement in Volume 5 (published by Aberdeen University Press, 1990), as well as writing *Mortimer's Deep*, which is his first novel.

Both the *Scotichronicon* and *Mortimer's Deep* share their roots in the Augustinian monastery on Inchcolm, the island in the Firth of Forth, where Walter Bower was abbot 200 years after the 12th and 13th century setting of *Mortimer's Deep*.

Simon Taylor lives in Edinburgh.

MORTIMER'S DEEP

SIMON TAYLOR

BALNAIN BOOKS

Text © 1992 Simon Taylor

Printed and bound in Great Britain by Billings, Worcester.

Published in 1992
by Balnain Books
Druim House, Lochloy Road,
Nairn IV12 5LF
Scotland

The publisher gladly acknowledges the financial assistance of
the Scottish Arts Council toward this volume.

British Library Cataloguing in Publication Data
A catalogue record for this book is available from
the British Library

ISBN 0 872557 15 5

Acknowledgements to:

John Boswell's *Christianity, Social Tolerance
and Homosexuality* (Chicago 1980)

Peter Daniels, who put the translations of the medieval
poems into verse.

Contents

Part 5 SCHEMES

Part 6 AMBUSHES

Part 7 SIMON DE QUINCY

Appendix

Dedicated to:

Sigrid and Laur and Mark

PART ONE
YOUTH

*How does a youth improve his life? By the keeping of thy
  words.
With my whole heart I have sought Thee; do not push me
  away from Thy commandments.
I have hidden Thy words in my heart lest I sin against
  Thee.
Blessed art Thou, O Lord; teach me Thy statutes....
I have found as much delight in Thy testimonies as I have
  done in all riches.
I shall follow all Thy commandments, I shall contemplate
  Thy ways.
I shall meditate on Thy statutes, and I shall not forget
  Thy words.*

Praeconium legis divinae Psalm 118 Beth

SUMMER, 1224

The sea was now luminous blue-green, now slate-grey, as the sun shone or was darkened by the fast moving clouds. Inchcolm too was forever changing colour, from dark green to bright emerald, while the Priory stones changed from dull brown to warm beige as the shadows came and went. It was as if a veil was being drawn and lifted, drawn and lifted, by a giant, invisible hand.

A stiff wind was blowing out of the west. It was all the oarsmen could do to keep the Bishop's barge on course for the island. Master Martin de Dunfermline sat in the bow enjoying the cool spray on his face and watching excitedly as the buildings of St Columba's Priory grew gradually larger.

Ever since he had returned from Paris the previous winter he had wanted to make this journey. Several times he had asked permission from his master, Bishop Hugh of Dunkeld. Hugh never said no, but at the same time always found some reason to postpone the trip to an indefinite future.

Then came the scandal caused by Prior William. One night shortly after Whitsun a messenger had arrived at the Bishop's palace at Tibbermore, bearing a letter which had been signed by almost every canon of the Priory of Inchcolm. It was a long list of complaints against their Prior: he kept a woman in his apartments, he ruled them more like a tyrant than a loving father, and he distributed among his relatives and friends silver and victuals belonging to the whole convent. The letter ended on a threatening note which could not be ignored: they would rather return to the world than continue to live under the excesses of Prior William.

One of the problems at Dunkeld had been old Archdeacon Henry. For a long time now he had been unwell, neglecting his duties as the eye of the Bishop, and so the usual visitations of the churches and monasteries in Dunkeld's care had almost ceased. No official from Dunkeld had been on the island in the last three years.

Now Archdeacon Henry had been forced to resign. The Bishop had a new eye, keen and foxlike, Archdeacon William of Ednam, who was leading the investigation into the charges against Prior William. With him were several clerks from the Bishop's chancery, one of whom was Martin de Dunfermline.

Martin's thoughts were light and dark together. His excitement and his purpose revolved not around Prior William, but his predecessor, who had ruled the island community for five years, Prior Simon de Quincy.

For as long as Martin could remember, Simon de Quincy had stood at the edge of Martin's young life, like a hill which a child is forbidden to climb, beyond which he cannot pass, but which casts its shadow over everything.

Martin had spent his childhood in the Abbey of Dunfermline. He had been given to the monks as a baby by Queen Ermengard, the wife of William the Lion, King of Scots. His mother had been one of her ladies-in-waiting, Affrica was her name. She had died at his birth, unmarried. Nobody seemed to know who his father was.

Most child oblates would, if sufficiently whole in body and mind, become brothers of the monastery in which they grew up. However, as soon as Martin was able to understand, it was made plain to him that this was not to be his future.

"Why not?" the little boy would ask.

"Because it is not God's will, nor the will of Simon de Quincy," was the reply.

"Who is Simon de Quincy?" was the next question. "Is he one of God's angels?"

This caused much laughter amongst the monks of Dunfermline, so little Martin would repeat it often, thinking himself very clever, until one day Brother Ralph the novice master gave him a thrashing for being blasphemous.

For a long time laughter and a beating were the only answers Martin received. Like all children he provided his own answer to a question the world would not. Simon de Quincy lived on the clouds, above the world of humans, just beneath the world of God. It was his breath which moved the trees at night when little Martin lay on his pallet in the novices' dormitory and watched their branches like giant arms at the window, and it was his voice which he could hear in the waters of the burn roaring in the glen beneath the monastery.

One day, when he was about five, he was taken to Abbot Patrick's chamber. Beside the Abbot was a man dressed in the habit of an Augustinian canon with white hair and a black beard.

He had a pale, unsmiling face, which reminded the little boy of the marble statue of St Laurence in the Abbey church, his favourite statue. The stranger was Simon de Quincy, Subprior of the Priory of Inchcolm. Martin did not remember much about that first meeting except that he reminded him of St Laurence, and that he did not smile. Afterwards the little boy had to revise his vision of the universe.

At regular intervals throughout the rest of Martin's childhood Simon would appear at Dunfermline and Martin would be summoned to meet him. He would take the boy for walks round the gardens or down into the glen between the Abbey and the royal castle. Simon would question the little boy about what he was doing and learning, and what he hoped to do in the future. Sometimes he would even smile.

Martin lived for such times. Nobody else in the world paid him the attention that Simon did. The only other person who showed any interest in him was Queen Ermengard, but he saw even less of her than Simon, for it was rare for the court to come to Dunfermline in those days. When he was taken to her presence in the old, draughty tower of Dunfermline castle, she would look sad and distracted. He clearly remembered her saying that it was a great pity he did not look more like his mother. It was, she said, his original sin. These words had haunted the little boy, and with the unshakeable certainty of a child he knew that if he had resembled his mother more, he would have found greater favour with the Queen, and his future would have been very different. As it was, his future lay with Simon de Quincy and the Church.

When he was sixteen he was informed that he was going to study at a great university in Paris. His expenses were to be paid by Simon, and the only condition was that, apart from returning to Scotland a Master, he was to write to Simon twice a year with an account of what he was studying and how he was living. He gladly fulfilled this condition and always received in reply a brief acknowledgement accompanying a gift of a new cloak, writing materials or silver.

When the time came for him to return to Scotland, Simon informed the young man that he would be joining the household of Bishop Hugh of Dunkeld as a clerk. Simon also told him to come and visit him at the Priory of Inchcolm, where Simon was now Prior. By the time Martin reached Scotland, however, Simon was dead.

The boat was now drawing near to the island. Martin gazed up in amazement at the fine buildings which seemed to rise out of the very sea itself. A high, sturdy tower, an elegant chapter house, a solid yet graceful church: he had not expected such grandeur in a small, isolated Priory. His amazement would have been even greater had he known that much of what he was admiring was the work of Prior Simon.

The hearings began the next day in the chapter house which Martin had admired from the sea. Its exterior, however, had not prepared him for what lay within. Finely carved ribs sprang from behind the benches to meet in the centre of the roof in a magnificent flower-like boss; and the walls were covered in scenes and figures skilfully drawn and painted in brilliant colours. On first entering Martin was overwhelmed by the rich colour and the beautiful lines; then with a growing sense of horror he realised that the scenes depicted the martyrdom of the saints in Rome at the time of the Great Persecution. They were portrayed in such detail that he had to look away.

Martin's role was to record the proceedings and to assist Archdeacon William in drawing up questions and weighing up evidence. Bishop Hugh had taken the whole affair so seriously that he had allowed Martin to bring with him an episcopal secretary to help him. William also had with him his own clerk, Master Robert de Raperlaw. His role at the hearings was similar to Martin's, as well as being the Archdeacon's amanuensis.

This meant that Martin was not going to be overtaxed with work, unless something very untoward happened. Besides, Archdeacon William would want to work with him only when absolutely necessary. The Archdeacon did not like Martin, he tolerated him because he had to, and Martin knew this perfectly well. It did not disturb him in the slightest. Martin had great faith not only in his abilities as a clerk and scholar, but also in his ability to charm Bishop Hugh, in whose favour he felt very secure. Thus his hope was that he would be able to conduct his own, private investigation, relatively undisturbed, into the affairs of Simon de Quincy.

The first day of the hearings went very slowly, and at the end of it there was little to record except the names and background of each of those who wanted to give evidence for or against Prior William. The Prior himself took up much of the time, denouncing his accusers.

The accusers, chief of whom was one Brother Henry, insisted that the hearing proper could not begin until the King's representative, Sir Gervaise Avenel, had arrived. This led to a long argument, interrupted by the bell for Nones. It was decided to adjourn until the next day. The Archdeacon spent the rest of the day praying that Sir Gervaise would hurry up.

Martin made the most of this time. He had singled out the precentor, Brother Roger, as a kindly man who might be able to help him for he had been a canon of the Priory for over ten years, five of which were spent under the priorship of Simon de Quincy.

Brother Roger was standing staring into space beside the book cupboard in the cloister when Martin stepped quietly up to him and touched his sleeve. He jumped, looking as though he had seen a ghost. "St Columba preserve us, what a fright you gave me, my son!" he exclaimed. "What can I do for you? Would you like to see our collection of manuscripts. We have a fine collection, including —"

"Thank you, Brother Roger," Martin cut in. "Perhaps some other time. I simply wanted to ask you something, not about Prior William, but about his predecessor, Simon de Quincy. I wanted to know what kind of a man he was."

At the mention of Simon's name Roger looked as startled as he had done when Martin first approached him.

"It's just idle curiosity, really," Martin added hastily, sensing Roger's confusion. "I knew him when I was a boy, and he showed me some kindness."

"Then you were one of the chosen few," Roger muttered, almost to himself. "Listen, if you want to find out about Prior Simon, may his soul rest in peace, you should go and talk to Prior William. He knew Simon better than anyone."

Martin pulled a face. "I cannot see Prior William saying very much to me about anything. Is there no one else?"

Roger was silent for a moment. "There's an old brother in the infirmary, Michael's his name, precentor before me. I've not seen him for years. He was badly injured in the fire." Here Roger paused to clear his throat. "He's blind, and I've heard his wits are not very sound. He must have known Simon longer than any of us. Now, if you'll excuse me, I have work to do."

"Certainly, brother, and many thanks," Martin said. "But perhaps you could tell me the way to the infirmary?"

There were two ways of entering the infirmary. One was by a small bridge that led off the gate house, just inside the main gate. This went across the corner of the latrine pit, through the infirmary latrine, and into the room of the cubicles. Nobody liked using this entrance, especially at low tide, because of the latrine pit. The door to this bridge was either guarded by Malcolm the gateman, or kept locked.

The main entrance to the infirmary was at the eastern end of the north side. This meant leaving the monastery by the main gate and going down the harbour path almost to the end of the infirmary building. This entrance led into the kitchen and apothecary room, where either the infirmarer himself, Brother Peter, or his servant, Fergus, was always to be found, cooking for those on special diets, brewing potions, mixing ointments, or, as was frequent in the case of Fergus, snoozing beside the great fire that was never allowed to go out. All visitors were supposed to come this way, past these guardians. No dragon watched over gold more assiduously than Brother Peter over his infirmary.

It was to the main entrance that Master Martin was directed.

Finding it locked he took the knocker, a coiled serpent made out of iron, and knocked out a playful rhythm. Silence. He knocked again, more loudly, less playfully, his ears straining for a sound within. "This is absurd!" he muttered to himself. "It's more like a castle than an infirmary. How are the sick supposed to gain access?"

He knocked again and sparks flew from the serpent's back. At last he heard a noise within, and a small eye-door shot back to reveal one bright, malevolent-looking eye.

"Who are you and what do you want?" a voice snapped.

Martin was taken aback by the hostility of his reception. He was not used to finding doors closed in his face. He thought for a moment, then, using his master as a battering-ram, said loudly, "Open in the name of your Bishop. I am not prepared to discuss his business through an oak door."

The eye stared at him a moment longer, then the eye-door slammed shut. A bolt was pulled back and the door swung slowly open.

As Martin stepped into the kitchen and apothecary room he felt he had stepped into a chamber of Hell. On his right flames roared and leapt in the great fireplace. The heat stung his face. The air, filled with smoke, steam and a bizarre mixture of smells, both acrid and sweet, made him catch his breath, and turned his stomach. Dizzy, he put his sleeve over his face, and for a moment thought he was going to faint.

He quickly collected his wits about him and introduced himself, using all his titles. The plump, rather pompous looking brother who stood before him, both eyes now glinting malevolently in the light of the flames, introduced himself as Brother Peter, infirmarer and canon regular of the Priory of St Columba, adding in an insulting tone, "for more years than you have been on this earth, young man. Now we know who you are, tell me what is your business. And hurry up about it. I haven't got all day." He turned his back on Martin and crouched down at the fire to stir several pots that were bubbling over.

Martin could hardly breathe in the disgusting air. On the other side of the room from the main door a small window opened out onto the grey, still sea. He walked over to it and drank in the cool fresh air. He coughed and spoke.

"Brother Peter, you have before you a representative of your Bishop. By your lack of courtesy to me you dishonour him. I have come to speak with one Brother Michael, an old brother who I believe is in your care."

Peter sprung up from the fire with surprising agility and glared at Martin. Mentioning the Bishop had opened the door for him, but it did not seem to be getting him much further.

"What, may I ask, do you want to see Brother Michael for?" he said. "He's a perfidious old fox who has led a shameful life. What would a Bishop's representative, as you call yourself, want with a man like Brother Michael?"

Martin decided to try a different tactic.

"Brother Peter," Martin said, lowering his voice and bringing his face closer to Peter's in conspiratorial fashion, "this is strictly between you and me, but Brother Michael might be able to furnish important evidence in the inquiry into the conduct of Prior William. Exonerating evidence," he added carefully, knowing full well that Brother Peter was one of the few brothers who was prepared to testify in Prior William's favour.

"Is that so?" Peter said, narrowing his eyes. "I'm pleased to hear that the Bishop and his clerks are interested in exonerating evidence. I thought you had been completely taken in by Brother Henry and his pack of troublemakers. Exonerating evidence, eh? I wonder what that could be." "So, if you would be so kind as to take me to him," Martin went on, ignoring Peter's prying remark.

Peter again turned away to attend to the pots on the fire, leaving Martin to his uncertainty and his nausea. Martin cursed him under his breath and waited patiently, gazing out over the sea. It seemed to Martin as though he was in some giant, motionless ship.

Finally Peter stood up and without looking at Martin muttered, "Follow me!" then disappeared through a door beside the fire.

Passing through a dark, empty chamber, used for blood-lettings, they came to the room of the cubicles. Peter went right along to the last cubicle, the one nearest the latrine. An old man, his back to the door, was standing staring out of a tiny window looking out over the sea.

"I don't know what he's looking at," Peter said contemptuously to Martin, as if the old man was not there. "He's as blind as a mole." "It's my good friend, Brother Peter," the old man said hoarsely, without turning round. "What torment have you brought me today? Another of your foul potions?" "I have brought a young man to see you," Peter said, adding insultingly, "He says he's from the Bishop, and that he's got some questions he wants to ask you. And may I remind you, Brother Michael, that it is my potions that keep you regular." "Yes, I've never been a very regular canon," Michael replied with a chuckle. "I could have done with those potions when I was younger." Martin smiled at the old man's comment. His wit, however, was lost on Peter, who said, "Well, I'll leave you now, I have important matters to attend to in my apothecary room. Goodbye." And with a curt nod he disappeared back down the lobby.

Martin saw a tall, rangy man, his broad shoulders somewhat stooped with age. His bushy hair, pure white, stuck up around his tonsure like a crown.

"Goodbye, Brother Peter," Michael said as the footsteps died away. "Poor Brother Peter," he sighed, "will never be able to rest until he is in his grave." Then he turned at last from the window and came over to greet his visitor.

No one had prepared Martin for what he now saw. Brother Michael had no eyes, but in their stead sockets of scarred and twisted skin spread over the upper part of his face.

"Do not be afraid, my son," the old man said gently, hearing Martin's horror in the silence he had heard all too often. "It is fire that has ravaged me thus. It was a miracle that it did not take my life." Martin, overcoming his fright, asked the old man for his blessing and introduced himself. Trusting in the smiling mouth and the kind, soft voice, and speaking quietly in case Brother Peter had crept back from his hell-hole to eavesdrop, Martin said, "Brother Michael, I will be frank with you, I have not come to you as part of the official inquiry but on a personal quest. I have come to ask you about your late Prior, Simon de Quincy." The old man let out a little cry, staggered slightly and sat down heavily on the bed, as though someone had pushed him in the chest. His breath came in short, sharp bursts. For a moment Martin was afraid for him.

Martin sat down beside him and took his hand. It felt like holding something dead, but the action seemed to calm the old man, and turning towards Martin he whispered, "Why?" Martin launched into his story. He saw no reason to hide anything. He knew that there were moments in his life which, like key-stones in a building, carried far greater weight than all the rest, without which all the rest would be jumbled and meaningless. He knew that this was such a moment, and that it demanded he reveal himself entirely to the old man.

When Martin had finished Brother Michael sat for a moment in silence. Without a word he put up a trembling hand and ran it over the young man's face. It tickled and Martin found himself fighting against laughter.

Finally Michael spoke, his voice hoarse and cracked, "Yes, I have a story to tell you, young man, — what did you say your name was? — yes, Martin, but I do not know if you have the time to listen to it." "I will make time, Father," Martin replied, using the term of respect, "for it is very important to me." "It is very important to me, too, my son," said Michael, "for I need to tell it to someone before I die. There was no one. Now God has sent you. His mercy is limitless, praise be to God." "Amen", Martin replied, breathing a great sigh of relief.

Suddenly footsteps could be heard coming towards them from the direction of the kitchen. Without knowing why Martin sprang to his feet, almost as if he was pulling away from some guilty act.

Brother Peter came bustling into the cubicle. "I really must ask you to leave, young man. It is almost time for Vespers. I take it you have finished your business. You don't have to go out by

the kitchen. I'll let you out through the latrine. This way please."
Jangling a big bunch of keys he motioned Martin to follow him.
Martin decided to comply with Brother Peter, for the time
being at least. He quickly took leave of the old man, promising
that he would return the next day. Then, addressing Brother
Peter, he said in his most deferential tone, "In fact, my inquiries
are not quite over. I'm turning up some important material, so
I will have to come back — tomorrow, perhaps, depending on
how the hearings go." "We'll see," Peter said self-importantly.
At this point they were crossing the little bridge over the latrine
pit. The sea swirled below them and Martin was seized with a
desire to pitch Brother Peter over the low railing into the filthy
water. He looked down with great satisfaction at the flailing
figure splashing about amongst the Priory's excrement, frightened to call for help in case he swallow some. He chuckled to
himself at this demon-inspired vision, then made the sign of the
cross to show contrition.

Peter unlocked the side door which led into the gate-house.
Martin was taking in every detail. He had not known about this
way into the infirmary. Already he was planning visits to Michael
without having to subject himself to the foul air of the kitchen
and the foul temper of its denizen. The air of the latrine would
smell sweet by comparison.

"Goodbye, Master Martin," Peter growled as he ushered
Martin out into the gatehouse, past the inquisitive look of
Malcolm the gateman.

"May God be with you, too, Brother Peter," Martin replied,
his tone mocking. It did not matter, because Peter had slammed
the door in his face.

The next day there was still no sign of the King's representative.
In desperation Archdeacon William dispatched a messenger to
Edinburgh, where the court was lodged.

Martin was delighted with the turn of events. As soon as Prime
was over he made his way to the infirmary. He stopped at the
gatehouse and chatted with Malcolm, one eye on the door which
led almost directly to Brother Michael.

Malcolm was a lay brother, 'a servant in a habit' as he called
himself, which meant that every day in church he was expected
to recite a few of the most important prayers. This was the only
Latin he knew, but he spoke French, the everyday language of
the Priory. Otherwise he could not have carried out his duties
as gateman, questioning all who came to the Priory, as he had
done for many years now, always with great enthusiasm and
good-nature. For he liked his fellow-humans, and no matter
what cruel and unpleasant things might be happening within
the Priory, it always greeted the stranger with the friendly face
of Lay Brother Malcolm.

Malcolm's mother tongue, in common with all the servants

and lay brothers, was Scottish. Very few of the canons and higher Church officials could speak this language, which they regarded as barbaric and uncouth. So Malcolm was surprised and pleased when Martin addressed him in it.

Martin had learnt Scottish from the servants at Dunfermline Abbey. They had always shown more interest in him than the monks had ever done, and were delighted when the little boy had wanted to learn their language. The monks disapproved, which only added to Martin's determination, and the servants' delight.

As Martin was taking his leave of Malcolm he casually asked if he could slip into the infirmary by the back way, as he wanted to see Brother Michael, without disturbing Brother Peter.

Malcolm chuckled and gave him a sly look. "Naebody wants tae fash Brither Peter," he said, "but aabody daes." Then nudging Martin cheerfully, he went on, "Aaricht. An gin ye gie a wee chap on the door here efter, A'll let ye oot." Martin thanked him kindly and pressed a silver penny into his hand.

As on the previous day Michael was standing at the window facing the sea. He turned as Martin hesitated in the doorway.

"Tell me your name again, young man," Michael said in greeting. Martin did so, stepping forward and taking the old man's hand. Today he did not shrink back from the sight of the broken face. "Ah, yes," Michael was saying. "My memory. A demon seems to have lodged there. I try to remember yesterday and I cannot. Then without even trying I remember my youth as clearly as if it was yesterday.

"But I do remember why you have come. You want to hear the story of Simon de Quincy, do you not?" the old man said, nodding in reply to his own question. "Well, there is a price you must pay. Yes, I have given it much thought and prayer, and I have decided you must pay a price." "What would that be, Father?" Martin asked, wondering what in Heaven's name the old man was going to demand of him.

"You must hear my story too, Martin. That is the price. Do not be too alarmed. You will find our stories run together after a while, like a dog worrying a sheep." "That is a strange way of putting it," Martin exclaimed.

"They are strange stories," Michael replied. "Stranger still, it is the sheep that has survived to tell them."

BROTHER MICHAEL

"I was born in the year of the rebellion against King Malcolm the Maiden on his return from France, the year of our Lord 1160. My father's name was Flathbertach, my mother's was Margaret. My father was chief steward for the lands of Aberdour, recently come into the possession of the Norman knight Sir William de Mortimer, on the death of his father-in-law Duncan, the old laird. My mother was a very beautiful woman, and it was from her that I inherited my looks, which were to be both my blessing and my curse.

I grew up in a house just to the east of the castle. It was bigger than the other houses in the village, because my father was an important man. I had two brothers who survived infancy: my elder brother Gillecolm, named after my mother's brother, who later succeeded my father as de Mortimer's chief steward; and my younger brother Duncan, named after the old laird. It was decided when Duncan was only a baby that he would join the Church. However, this was not God's will, for when he was twelve he was killed by a bear.

I was baptised Duscath after my great-grandfather, who had been a chief in Atholl. His daughter, my mother's mother, had been brought back to Aberdour by my grandfather, either willingly or as booty, for he had been in Atholl as a soldier in one of King David's campaigns.

As with my two brothers, from an early age my own future was carefully planned. I was to join the household of my father's lord, Sir William de Mortimer. There I would be first a page, then a squire, then, if I became proficient in the arts of war, on foot and on horse-back, a knight. A pity, because even as a young boy I had a great thirst for learning and longed to enter the Church. Whenever I could, I accompanied Duncan on his daily visits to Father Abraham, the village priest, who was to teach him to read and write. In fact I was a far more willing pupil than Duncan, who wanted only to roam the woods and hunt birds and animals.

In my childish innocence I once asked my father if Duncan and I might exchange destinies, me joining the Church, him taking my place in de Mortimer's household. My father was not a cruel man, but he was inflexible. Once he had made up his mind about something, there was no changing: his decisions were as immutable as divine decrees. With a threatening frown he told me never to mention such a thing again.

So at the age of ten I left my father's house and became part of de Mortimer's household. De Mortimer's liege-lady was at that time the queen-mother, Countess Ada de Warenne, so we spent much time at her castles in Crail and Haddington. My lord was also often obliged to attend the royal court, mostly in Dunfermline, Forfar or Perth. By that time our King was Malcolm the Maiden's younger brother, King William the Lion. I scarcely saw my family after that, for only rarely did Sir William come to stay in the rickety old castle at Aberdour.

My fellow pages and squires became my brothers and de Mortimer became my father. I hated them all. They were rough and heartless, for they thought that to show affection for anyone but the god of war was a slight to their manhood.

However, I found a second mother, who consoled me much in my sadness and my loneliness. It was not de Mortimer's wife, the Lady Anicea. She kept herself aloof from such lesser beings as pages and squires. No, it was my lord's liege-lady, Countess Ada de Warenne, widow of Earl Henry, and mother of the King.

She was a tall, formidable woman, about fifty years old, with a stern face and eyes as fierce as a hawk's. Her great love had always been power. In the reign of her eldest son, Malcolm the Maiden, she had been his chief adviser, and when he was ill, which was often, she had ruled in his name. She knew however that if her younger son William succeeded to the throne, it would be the end of her influence at court. This was why she was so desperate that Malcolm marry and produce an heir. She always denied the story that she had sent a woman into Malcolm's bedchamber to tempt him, but I never quite believed her. It was the sort of thing she would do.

However, despite her hopes and her efforts, Malcolm died childless. William succeeded, and one of the first things he did was remove her from court. She did not rant and rail against her son nor scheme against him. She went with dignity and honour, taking with her her chief vassals, and of course, Sir William de Mortimer. At first it was through these nobles she kept in touch with the court, for she saw to it they did not neglect their duties of attendance on their monarch.

The Lady Ada had left the court, but it was not long before the court began to come to her. At first it was her youngest son, David, who later became Earl of Huntingdon. You will remember him, Martin, for he died only recently, rich in years and honours.

He valued his mother's advice more than his brother the King. By the time I joined de Mortimer's household, four or five years after King William's accession, Earl David frequently visited his mother at one or other of her castles. Tall and handsome, and always splendidly dressed in white, he shone like the sun and dazzled a young page like me.

The Lady Ada showed me special affection and would always insist that I wait on her when my lord was in attendance.

Laughingly she would say that it was because I was so fair in looks, and sometimes after dinner, when I was pouring out her fourth beaker of wine, she would stroke my face and say that when I grew older I must promise to be her knight. 'Promise, Duscath, that you will love no other lady than me', she would whisper. My heart would swell with love and pride at her words, and I swore to God that I would love her only and she would be my spur to many a noble deed.

The great favour she showed me aroused envy amongst my peers. However, sometimes I would be asked to put in a word with her for this or that squire or relation. It was my first taste of power in the world, but I was too young and timid to use it. I never asked the Lady Ada any favours, either for myself, my family or anybody else. Perhaps that was another reason why she liked me.

At the age of thirteen, as I was strong and tall in body and could wield a sword passably and ride a horse without falling off, I was made a squire to Sir William de Mortimer. That was at Easter in the fateful year 1173. At harvest-time of that year King William and his nobles joined in the war between the English Kings, Henry the Elder and his son Henry the Younger. Ignoring the advice of several of his nobles and his mother, he joined in on the side of King Henry the Younger. A huge Scottish host gathered at Caddonlee in Lothian and prepared to march on Northumberland. My lord de Mortimer became part of the King's council of war. Never before had I seen my lord in such good humour.

It was my first taste of war, and its bitterness still fills my mouth like gall, and in my nostrils there is still its stench. I was unprepared for the things I was compelled to see and do. I had no protection against the demons that attend on war, and they almost drove me mad.

It was not a war of army against army, armed men against armed men: it was armed men against defenceless villages, women and children, cattle and crops, the very roots of life. 'First destroy the land, then one's foes,' was the advice to King Henry the Younger from his allies. I was a young squire who was being trained in arms for glorious deeds of which my Lady Ada would be proud. Instead I found myself amidst a slaughter of innocents.

It was in the second summer of the war. Several castles had fallen to us, but Carlisle and Prudoe stood fast. At Prudoe there was a rumour that a huge English army was approaching from the south, so we abandoned the siege, after devastating the fields and orchards, and headed north to Alnwick. The massive castle there was still in the hands of William de Vesci, a loyal supporter of Henry the Elder. Once Alnwick was taken, we could then safely turn and attack the approaching army.

As soon as we arrived before the mighty walls of Alnwick

Castle, King William himself took charge of the siege. He kept with him most of his household and retinue of barons, as well as a company of Flemish mercenaries. The rest of the Scottish host was sent out in three contingents to harry the surroundings.

One contingent was put under the command of Earl Duncan of Fife. He was a mighty chief, wise in counsel, but merciless in war. He marched to Warkworth, which lay on the coast a few miles to the south east. De Mortimer accompanied him, taking me along with him. The castle at Warkworth was small and unimportant, one of the few that our army had managed to take the previous year. Now it was back in the hands of the enemy. To stand once more in front of this castle, which had so recently been our prize, and was now heavily defended against us, to hear the taunts and jeers of the garrison, all this drove Earl Duncan and his men into a frenzy of fury. The castle might be defended, but the village was not. It was here that they vented their fury.

Warkworth village lies on a long, gentle slope which runs up to the castle at the top. At the bottom is the parish church of St Laurence. Over three hundred villagers had taken refuge there. Earl Duncan turned his back on the castle with its jeering garrison and gave the order to burn the village and the church and slaughter all those who escaped the flames. With a blood-curdling shriek the foot-soldiers threw off their cloaks and, naked, swept down upon the village. There was little enough to plunder and burn, only what had been built up during the past year, for the previous summer also our army had razed Warkworth to the ground. Then, however, the people and the church had been spared.

De Mortimer watched everything with a cold, fierce eye. He led his own men slowly down through the already burning village, ordering them to stay back from the church and kill all who broke through the inner ring of Earl Duncan's men. 'Kill them outright,' he commanded us. Then, his face contorted in a scornful grin, he added, 'It will be an act of mercy. You will be saving them from the Scots.'

Me, he commanded to stay with him, and hold my axe at the ready. Already the church was burning. Terrible sounds filled the air: war-whoops; the crackling of the fire as it took hold of the roof; the splintering of wood as the church door was hacked to pieces by a score of battle-axes; and behind it all, at first scarcely audible, but soon drowning out all other sounds, the screams of the doomed people of Warkworth.

Suddenly a great roar went up from Earl Duncan's men. No longer able to endure the smoke and flames the villagers were starting to spill out of the burning church. Pale and trembling, I prayed to St Laurence for a miracle. De Mortimer struck me violently on the back of the head: 'It's time you tasted blood, young hound. Look, here comes the first hare.'

Towards us a little girl ran screaming, her hair and dress on fire. Behind her a woman, her dress in tatters, ran after her, calling her name. The little girl was crazed with pain and fear. The woman was trying to catch her to put out the flames and comfort her.

Before I knew it de Mortimer grabbed my hand which held the axe and with fearful strength forced it down on the skull of the little girl. It cut into it like ripe fruit.

Blackness came over my mind. I do not know what happened next. When I returned to my senses I was still standing holding the bloody axe over the crumpled body of the little girl. Her clothes and hair were still smouldering. Near her lay the woman, silent and motionless, her hands outstretched, above her heart a gaping wound. I turned away and vomited onto the grass. De Mortimer gave a grim laugh and told me to clean my axe and go over and wait for him by the horses.

God leaves nothing unpunished. The very next day King William became a prisoner of King Henry the Elder and the war between them was over. While the Scottish host was still rampaging through the countryside, a group of Henry the Elder's barons led by Odinel de Umfraville and Randolph de Glanville captured King William and his retinue in a surprise attack.

I had returned to Alnwick with de Mortimer the previous evening from the massacre at Warkworth, so I was captured too, as was my lord.

I gave thanks to God and St Laurence that we were prisoners, for thus the land and the people were rid of war and its horrors. My soul, however, was not so easily rid of them."

MONT ST MICHEL

"As soon as it was known that King William had been captured, all the Scottish barons surrendered and the Scottish host, now leaderless, returned to Scotland. King William and his barons were brought to King Henry the Elder at Northampton. Their feet were shackled beneath their horses, but despite this humiliation they remained haughty and cheerful, and there was much banter amongst them, and between them and their guard-escort, which was made up of nobles of equally high standing from the realms of King Henry the Elder. Captive and guard were mostly related by blood or marriage, and had it not been for the shackles on one half of the party, and their absence of arms, it could easily have been mistaken for some huge family gathering at Easter or Yule.

I rode in silence behind my master, deep in thought. By this time we knew we were on our way to Normandy. There the jousting would be first class, and there, too, were relatives to feast and hunt with.

It's just a game to them, I thought disgustedly. We leave behind us thousands of peasants dead or maimed, their fields and cattle destroyed, while my master and his companions look forward to good jousting in Normandy.

The one member of the Scottish nobility who seemed downcast was King William himself. A huge, brawny man with a mane of red hair, he had a deep, booming voice and a laugh you could hear even when a banquet was at its loudest. He usually dominated any gathering as much by the size of his person and his voice as by his kingship.

Now he sat strangely silent. At Alnwick he had left himself unguarded while his army rampaged through the countryside around him. A band of Yorkshire knights had simply ridden up and taken him. It was checkmate with all his pawns still on the board, and he had only himself to blame.

From Northampton King Henry accompanied us down to the English coast and across the Channel to Barfleur. He informed King William that he and his barons would be kept prisoner in Falaise Castle until every spark of rebellion in Henry's realms had been stamped out. King William himself would remain in chains until safely within its walls.

It was the height of summer. We rode from Barfleur to Caen in one day, although it is usual to do it in two. King Henry was a furious horseman. Moreover he was still at war with his son and King Louis of France, who at that very moment were threatening Rouen.

We rode from dawn to dusk in the blistering sun. Purgatory could not have been more punishing. However, I welcomed such hardship, for, like the constant activity of the journey, it helped relieve my spirit of the terrible thoughts and visions that plagued it.

Falaise is a rich and handsome town, which lies half a day's ride south of Caen away from the coast. At the upper end of the town, where the land rises up then plunges down steep cliffs to the river, there stands Falaise Castle. Huge curtain walls surround a grim and massive keep, casting a shadow on town, field and wood.

Inside the castle it was cramped and uncomfortable. The squires slept out in the dark corridors, which even in the heat of summer were damp and draughty.

Ralph and I were the only members of de Mortimer's retinue whom he had been allowed to bring with him, apart from Father Roger, his chaplain, who had happened to be with us when we were captured. There was no need of servants, for everything was provided by our warders.

For over a month none of the Scottish prisoners were allowed to set foot outside, which was a bitter blow to them. But with the war still not over, and the armies of Henry the Younger and King Louis only a few leagues away, King Henry would have been foolish to allow otherwise.

The castle governor apologised to his prisoners for this and in compensation increased the supplies of meat and wine. So that they would not become too bored he brought in bears and bulls for dogs to bait in the castle courtyard. Also he ensured that there was never any lack of women from the town to entertain the noble prisoners. Still they behaved like caged lions, and the castle walls echoed to many a fight and flyting. Had they been allowed their swords, much blood would have flowed.

At Michaelmas peace came at last. King Henry the Elder won a total victory over all his foes and could afford to be magnanimous to the vanquished. All those who had rebelled were restored to the lands and positions which they had held fifteen days before the outbreak of war. All, that is, except King William. He had to do homage to King Henry and give up the chief castles of his realm to English garrisons. Until this was effected, he and his nobles had to remain prisoners at Falaise. Now, however, the doors were opened and the festivities began in earnest.

For most of the Scottish nobles the castle now became the hunting-lodge which they had so long looked forward to. Relieved of affairs of state, far from the complaints of tenants and the demands of their courts, given the run of the countryside, they could now devote themselves to their chief joy, hunting. Many of them had family in the surrounding country who stood surety for them if they wanted to stay away overnight. It was a great hunt which seemed to last for ever. 'If this is prison,' my master cried, 'then freedom be damned!'

King William thought otherwise. He fretted and kept himself apart from his roistering barons. He could not forget that he was now less of a king than he had been before. His kingship and his power were more precious to him than anything else in the world, and now they had both been diminished.

I too could find no joy in the greater freedom granted us. I was a prisoner, whether I was surrounded by walls or by the rolling plains of Normandy. Not only was I a prisoner of my lord and of his commands, I was also a prisoner of my dreams.

At night as I slept a demon would bring before my mind's eye all the terrible things that I had witnessed during the war, above all the massacre in the churchyard. I would feel again the pressure of de Mortimer's hands gripping my arm and forcing the axe down on the little girl's skull. I would see again the brains spilling out onto the grass. I would wake up with her screams still ringing in my ears, to find her screams were my screams, and the horror as fresh as on the first day.

My fellow squires taunted me. I would often wake up to find Ralph slapping my face. 'Stop your accursed noise. Is no one to get any peace because of your nightmares?'

They made me sleep in the castle chapel in the hope that the demon would have less power in such a holy place. Also there were fewer people nearby whom I could disturb. But it was all to no avail.

Not long after the peace was concluded and the gates of the castle opened, Father Roger, chaplain to de Mortimer, spoke to me. He was a small, plump, sour-faced man who knew by heart all the bloodthirsty passages from Scripture, and could work around them fine sermons, to the delight of de Mortimer and the other barons. Absolution tripped easily from his tongue and his penances were light. But his bland and easy absolutions could do nothing for my stricken soul. Obviously he had been given orders to try something different.

'Well, my son,' he said one bright autumn day, 'we're going on a pilgrimage. I will take you to Mount St Michael, the greatest shrine to St Michael in the whole world. He slaughters demons by the thousands, so he'll make short work of your one. Then we'll all get a bit of peace. All very well putting you in the chapel to sleep,' he added grumpily. 'But what about us poor priests who have to sleep next door? Yes, St Michael will put things right.'

So Father Roger and I set off for Mount St Michael. I was glad to be away from the castle. It was as if the devil that tormented me drew strength from its dark, dank walls.

I had no clear idea where it was we were going, some shrine or other on the coast where St Michael had appeared hundreds of years ago. The anniversary of this vision was approaching and pilgrims were flocking to the spot from all over Normandy and Brittany, and even France.

Although I was surrounded by people I felt very alone. Father Roger hardly spoke to me and made sure no one else did. Whenever other pilgrims asked us our purpose he would pull a long face and tell them I was possessed. 'Pray that St Michael will drive the demon out,' he would say in his resonant voice. Awe-struck they would look at me, make the sign of the cross and draw back slightly. If they stayed to talk with Father Roger they always kept well clear of me. I began to understand what it must be like to be a leper.

The last night of our journey we spent in the episcopal city of Avranches. From here we could clearly see our goal, which looked like a huge, threatening castle towering above the flat coast. It was in fact an Abbey perched on the summit of a rock as high and steep as that of the Castle of the Maidens, but which unlike that castle had no easy slope on one side. Such a rock in Scotland would surely have been strongly fortified to dominate the surroundings. Yet this rock was dedicated not to earthly power and warfare, but to God. For me this was the first miracle of the Mount.

From Avranches there are two ways which lead to the Mount. One is for the rich, longer but safer, crossing the great River Sélune by the bridge at Pontaubault. The tolls on this bridge are the highest in Normandy.

The other is for the poor or mean, or those who cannot bear to add another league to their journey. It soon leaves the fields and the woods to cut across the salt-marshes which stretch away to the horizon. These marshes are criss-crossed by a hundred rivers and burns. The narrower, deeper ones have little bridges of wooden planks over them. The wider, shallower ones have to be waded through. This includes the main arm of the River Sélune, which can often be treacherous.

As we were setting off from Avranches on the last morning of our journey Father Roger informed me that we would be taking the route across the salt-marches. I knew he had plenty of money with him and could well afford the toll. But Father Roger was mean. I did not care. At that time death seemed to hold less terror for me than life. Besides, I was a good strong swimmer with no fear of water.

We were still several miles away but in the clear autumn sunlight against the crisp blue sky we could see almost every detail of the Mount. I was astonished to realise that what I had thought was living rock high up near the summit, above the trees and houses at its foot, was in fact the walls of the Abbey, soaring many hundreds of feet into the air. At this sight even my despair, which had been sitting on my heart for so long, shook itself and became lighter.

After crossing several rickety old bridges, and wading through several muddy burns, we arrived at the bank of the River Sélune. It was about three stone throws across. Its surface was very agitated and it moved swiftly. Although the days of our journey had been dry and bright, there had been heavy rains the previous week. It was clear the river was still in spate.

A small chapel marked the main ford. In this chapel pilgrims would say a prayer and make an offering for a safe crossing. Beside the chapel, and higher than it, was a large cross, erected by an Abbot of the Mount many years before to commemorate the miraculous rescue by the Virgin Mary of a pregnant woman who had been swept away while trying to cross the river. Around the large cross were other, smaller crosses, in memory of those who had not been so fortunate.

The greatest danger was the deep pools that the eddies hollowed out in the soft, sandy river bed, always shifting under the influence of the tides and the currents. Dangerous also were the crumbling river banks, which could go from under you if you were standing on them, or throw you back into the river if you tried to climb out.

As we approached we could see a small group of pilgrims gathered around the door to the chapel. They were arguing with each other about whether or not they should cross. Excited voices rose into the morning air above the loud gurgling of the river.

'And they charge you a fortune to cross,' an old man shouted shrilly in broad Norman. He was wearing filthy clothes and supported himself heavily on a staff. I could smell him from where I stood, mould and urine.

'We know that, old man,' an exasperated voice shouted from the other side of the group. 'Why do you think we're all here?'

'Because it's shorter,' someone else shouted, in the French of France. 'My journey's been long enough, all the way from Paris —'

'I thought everybody was rich in Paris. Where's your horse?' It was the old man again.

'I had to sell it to buy bread. Daylight robbery the price you Normans charge!' A mocking roar went up from the crowd.

'But what are we going to do?' The plaintive voice of a woman cut through the mirth. 'It worries me that there are no guides here.'

I had not noticed her until she spoke. She was standing on the edge of the group. Her face was thin and pale. Wisps of lank blond hair escaped from under her tattered coif. She held by the hand a little girl who seemed oblivious to what was going on around her, staring into the distance towards the Mount.

'Yes,' another voice shouted, 'why are there no guides? There usually are. That's a bad sign you know, no guides. A bad sign.' Several people muttered and shook their heads at this.

'They're all still drunk from last night,' the old man shouted.

'Or they've all been swept away,' the woman said. There was a lot of laughter at this, although the woman had not meant it as a joke.

'As long as we all keep together,' the old man went on, 'we'll easily manage across. I've been over this ford many times. Each person must tie themselves to the next by a rag or a rope or something. And before every step you must test the ground with your staff. You don't need some lazy, good-for-nothing guide to tell you that.'

'How deep will it be?' the woman asked.

'Up to about mid-thigh,' the old man replied, touching his scrawny leg just below the groin.

'What about my child?' the woman wailed.

'I'll carry her on my shoulder,' a deep voice boomed, a giant of a man who had been standing looking down on the company and who up until then had been silent.

'May St Christopher bless you,' the woman cried. Then she added, looking uncomfortable, 'but I don't know if she'll let you. She's — she's very afraid of men.'

'Well, tell her I mean her no harm,' he boomed back with a good-natured smile.

'It wouldn't do any good,' the woman said quietly. 'She's dumb, and since she lost her speech there is no reasoning with her. She was not always so,' she added almost desperately. 'She could speak once, oh, how she could speak! She would chatter away from morning till night and could understand things far beyond her years. But then —' she hesitated, looking down uncomfortably at the sand, 'then it all changed. That is why I am taking her to the Mount, to beg St Michael to heal her and give her back her speech and her carefree soul.'

'But I mean her no harm,' the giant repeated, almost as if the woman had not spoken. 'I wouldn't harm a flea. Look, little girl, I will help you across the river.' And smiling from ear to ear he moved towards her with outstretched arms. The little girl screamed a terrible, piercing scream that sent flocks of water-birds rising into the air from the river banks. The giant shrank back.

'Has a demon got into her?' he asked amazed, crossing himself, a deep frown on his good-natured face.

Even after he had withdrawn the little girl kept screaming, as if she were being tortured. She would not be comforted and buried her head in her mother's skirts.

'I told you she was very afraid of men,' the woman explained with a helpless shrug of her shoulders.

'A good hiding would sort her out,' the old man growled.

'No,' the woman cried, putting her hand up as if to protect her daughter, 'no, I've tried that, I've tried everything. Only God and his angels can help us now.'

'Well you'll just have to carry her yourself or go up to Pontaubault,' the old man said. 'She's too small to cross safely on her own.'

'But I can't afford it,' the woman cried. She was almost in tears now. 'I haven't a sou left. And I'm too weak to carry her all that way across.' Then, looking at Father Roger, she added quietly, 'She's not afraid of clerks, my little girl.'

Father Roger turned pale. 'Madam, are you suggesting —'

'She's very light,' the woman added hastily.

'A well-fed nag like you should manage no bother!' someone shouted from the back of the group. It was the man from Paris.

31

Everyone roared with laughter, everyone, that is, apart from myself, the woman and Father Roger.

'Have you no respect for the cloth?' he shouted, going bright red.

'We'll have a lot more respect if you carry the little girl across,' the Parisian shouted back.

Father Roger looked around speechless. The woman was on her knees, begging him, while the rest of the group looked at him expectantly. What could he say? Serves him right, I thought to myself.

'All right, I'll take her,' Roger muttered. 'But don't blame me if we both drown,' he shouted. The woman kissed his hand and the group cheered.

The woman gently led the little girl up to Father Roger. She eyed him suspiciously but did not scream.

'Come on!' the old man shouted. 'I'm not standing here all day. Let's get moving before the tide turns and the river gets even deeper. All those who want to cross, start roping yourself together. Those who don't, the bridge is that way,' waving his staff in the direction of Pontaubault. 'About five miles,' he added maliciously.

A few of the group said that they would wait, they wanted to pray first in the chapel. 'They're just waiting to see if we make it,' the old man said, spitting onto the sand. 'We'll show them, won't we, Father?'

Father Roger glared at the old man, as if to say, 'This is all your fault, you old fool.'

Finally we were ready to move off. Father Roger kilted up his tunic. The woman lifted her daughter onto his broad, round shoulders. He tottered slightly as he found his new balance. The little girl seemed completely at ease now. She looked around until her eyes fixed on the Mount, then she kept staring at it, looking neither right nor left.

The woman walked beside Father Roger. She held out her hand to steady him but he pushed it bad-temperedly away.

I stepped into the cold water, which was soon up above my knees. The river was like a giant, invisible hand, pushing relentlessly from the side, trying to sweep everything away that disturbed its course to the sea.

The line of pilgrims crept slowly across, wavering, sometimes stopping, as the old man carefully tested the ground ahead of him with his staff. At last he reached the other bank. He let the giant climb out first, so that he himself could be helped up the steep, slimy side. Then three, then four, clambered up onto dry land and gave thanks to God and the Blessed Virgin for their safe crossing.

Suddenly there was a great shout and a splashing behind us. Three young horsemen on huge chargers were crossing just upstream from us, laughing and waving cheerfully. The little girl jerked her head back towards them, a look of terror on her face. She at once started to kick and scream.

'Keep still, you little wretch!' Father Roger shouted. He put his arms up to steady her but it only made her worse. Like a wild animal she started to bite and scratch, digging her nails into the soft flesh of Father Roger's face. With a roar he flung her from his shoulders, losing his balance as he did so and toppling over into the river. We hauled him up by his robes, but the little girl was already out of reach, screaming, splashing, being carried away from us by the strong currents.

The only person on dry land capable of saving her was the giant. He was already running along the river bank.

'Save her, save her!' the woman was screaming.

Just as he was drawing level with her, he tripped and went sprawling face first into the rough grass. He lay where he had fallen, groaning and clutching his foot. The little girl was getting further and further away. She had stopped screaming because now she was fighting for her life.

I had been watching all this like someone in a dream, not really believing that it was happening. Now, in a flash, I knew it was real, and I knew what I had to do. I undid the rope at my waist, pulled off my tunic, thrust it into Father Roger's hands, and dived into the river.

The cold on the upper part of my body was like a knife in my vitals, but the pain lasted only for a second. I swam as hard as I could towards the girl, the current bearing me more swiftly than my own swimming. I could see her up ahead, then suddenly she was gone, only to reappear, gasping and spluttering, a little further away. Her dress was hampering her movements, and the river was deepening. She could not last much longer.

'You must not die, little girl, you must not die,' I kept saying to myself, over and over again, almost like a chant, strengthening my determination. 'You must not die, you must not die!' Then the words changed of themselves: 'If you die, so will I.' And I knew that if she drowned I would let myself be taken down the same road, to that place where there would be no more nightmares or despair.

A final lunge brought me to her. Desperately she grabbed hold of my neck, clinging so tightly that at first I thought she would strangle me. I pulled with all my strength towards the bank, half walking, half swimming. I glanced into the little girl's face, which was pressed right up against mine. Her eyes were tight shut but her lips were moving vigorously, as if in prayer, although she was not making a sound.

Hands reached out to us from the river bank and we were dragged up onto dry land. Exhausted I threw myself down onto the coarse grass. Amongst the hubbub I heard a little voice beside me say, 'Where's my mummy?' The little girl had spoken. 'It's a miracle!' someone shouted. 'The mouth of the dumb has been unstopped!'

Stupefied faces surrounded us as we lay on the river bank, the little girl clinging to my hand. People were crossing themselves and giving thanks to God. Everybody looked so serious. Why? The little girl was alive, I was alive, and for the first time since that terrible war, since the slaughter in Warkworth, it felt good to be alive. I had rescued the little girl. I had saved a life. I felt whole again. So why was everybody looking so serious?

Then I saw what they were seeing: two thin, wet, shivering bodies, neither of them fully grown, lying there like two stranded fish. It looked so funny I started to laugh. Soon I was helpless in the grip of my laughter, which was shaking me violently. I did not care. I writhed half choking, half screeching, abandoning myself to this great flood which swept through every chamber of my body.

Somewhere far away I heard my name being called. The voice was unpleasantly familiar, sharp and angry, and belonged to Father Roger. He did not see the joke. This only made me laugh even more. Suddenly a stinging pain on my face checked my wild laughter. I rubbed my cheek and looked around.

'The demon has left the girl and entered the youth,' someone whispered, and everyone crossed themselves again.

'The priest said he already had one demon,' someone else said.

How funny you all are, I thought to myself, with your muttering about demons. You should be rejoicing that a little girl has been saved and returned to her mother, and that I am able to laugh again. But I stopped myself laughing. It was obviously upsetting people.

By this time the girl's mother had arrived and was cradling her daughter in her arms. She was making short, gasping noises, half sobbing, half laughing. Then she lifted her head from the head of her daughter, her face radiant with tears and smiles. She was not afraid to laugh.

'Thank you, young man,' she said softly, 'May God bless you wherever you go.'

'It was a brave thing he did,' a voice said from the crowd, 'demon or no demon.'

'Enough of this talk of demons,' the woman cried. 'The water has purged them all — and this lad's courage. Let us give thanks to St Michael at his shrine. And let us put these two youngsters into some warm clothes before they catch their death of cold.'

The three horsemen, three well-dressed young squires, stood by looking sheepish. People were accusing them of causing the near disaster by their foolish shouting, and by coming too close to the group as it was crossing the river.

Father Roger gently rubbed his face. Both his cheeks were

bruised and bloody and his nose was badly scratched. He glared at the little girl, who stuck out her tongue at him and took my hand.

'The least you can do,' the woman was saying to the horsemen, 'is to let us ride on quickly to the Mount.' The crowd muttered its agreement. The young men were only too happy to make amends. One of them offered me his mount. He also lent me his cloak. Father Roger had dropped my tunic while scrambling out of the river. Another of the young men did the same for the woman and the little girl. Father Roger insisted that he ride with me. The young squire frowned, unsure about the extra weight. Father Roger brushed him aside imperiously, saying that a horse that size could carry four grown men and still ride till sunset.

'What about me?' a voice boomed out, just as we were leaving. Hobbling up came the giant. 'Help me, I've broken my foot. I can't walk.'

'You can walk better than I can,' the old man grumbled.

'No, I can't,' the giant cried, and to reinforce his point he keeled over onto the grass.

So on that bright October morning three horses rode across the salt-marshes towards the Mount St Michael, carrying much joy and heart's ease, carrying a hero and a miracle.

Those whom we passed, and who stopped to stare, saw quite a different sight. They saw on one horse a poor woman and her little girl, wrapped in a rich cloak; on another a shivering youth, grinning from ear to ear, also wrapped in a rich cloak, with a fat, sullen priest sitting behind him. While on the third, as in all the best romances, rode a giant.

Crowds of people swarmed like ants around the base of the Mount, which now towered splendidly above us. As we approached them the giant started to shout, 'A miracle! A miracle! St Michael has vouchsafed a miracle!'

'Shut up, you fool,' Father Roger hissed. 'Do you want us dragged off our horses?'

The giant was enjoying himself too much, shouting and pointing and being the centre of attention. The crowd surged forward, hungry to know more.

'Clear a way ahead!' Father Roger shouted. 'You will hear everything in God's time. But we must get warmth and food for these young people. Their lives are in danger!' It was the first time he had shown any such concern for either the little girl or myself. It was he who wanted warmth and food, as well as peace and quiet.

The giant roared, 'There he is, the fair youth, he snatched her from the river. I have never seen a swimmer like him, more like a seal than a man.'

All eyes were on me. People clapped and cheered desultorily and I waved, feeling very foolish.

'But what about the miracle?' someone shouted from the crowd. Disappointment was written on the upturned faces. The giant went on cheerfully, 'And there, behold the young virgin! She stepped into the river deaf and dumb, she was pulled out able to hear and speak!'

The crowd found this much more to their taste. They surrounded us, wanting to touch our garments. They even started tearing strips off our cloaks. The little girl screamed and the crowd fell back. Father Roger made the most of the respite, 'You must let us through. They are dying of cold.'

It was true, I had begun to shiver uncontrollably. My joy, which had buoyed up my spirits until now and kept exhaustion at bay, was receding fast in the face of cold and fear.

The crowd, touched or frightened by the little girl's scream, let us through. They still followed us eagerly, full of curiosity, but kept a respectful distance. We were on the Mount itself now, riding up through the village, often having to duck, so low were the projecting upper storeys of the houses, so narrow was the street.

The path rose up steeply. Soon we left the houses behind us. To the right we looked out over the vast empty flatness of the salt-marshes, and down onto the tops of the giant trees at the foot of the Mount. Above to the left towered a wall of dressed stone like a cliff-face. I had never seen such a high wall. We were so close to it we could see each individual block, carefully shaped and placed to form the vast foundations for the Abbey in the air.

'There's no more room,' some pilgrims shouted. 'They're not letting anyone else into the Abbey.'

Others fell back, awed by the sight of our horses, then confused when they saw the motley ragged riders.

'Clear a way!' Father Roger shouted. His voice was becoming hoarse.

As the horses picked their way through the crowd in front of the gate, the people that had followed us from below started to arrive behind us with shouts of 'A miracle! A miracle!'

At these words everybody stopped moving, as if frozen by a great icy wind. Our horses could go no further. A human will push another human out of the way. A horse will not. It will either wait for the person to move, or, if spurred on by the rider, trample them blindly.

'Get off, leave the horses, get to the gate!' Father Roger shouted. We all slipped off our mounts. The little girl was crying. The giant was groaning with pain as he put his weight on his foot. As we reached the gate another miracle occurred. It swung open, revealing a long corridor which disappeared into the gloom. We stumbled through; behind us the gate clanged shut and the noise of the crowd outside faded into the distance. We stood in a quiet twilight. We had reached the Abbey of Mount St Michael.

The four days we spent in the Abbey were among the happiest of my life. Because of the rescue of the little girl, and the miracle of her regaining her speech, I was treated as a special guest of the Abbot. This meant that Father Roger and I were given a little room in the Abbot's lodgings. We did not have to stay in the crowded guest-house with the other pilgrims or seek a place to stay in the village below.

The day after our arrival I was sitting at the open window of our chamber. It was another clear, bright day, and the world stretched out beneath me like a great, green wall-hanging laid out to air. I was alone with my thoughts, which were as bright and clear as the day.

I was startled by a knock at the door. It was a servant who said that he had come to take me to a Brother William, who wanted to see me. I had no idea who Brother William was, but, my curiosity aroused, I followed the servant gladly into the dark lobby.

For all that the Abbey was surrounded by brightness there were many corridors and stairways the light scarcely penetrated. In places it was so dark I had to grope my way. Torches and candles were forbidden, however, even at night, so great was the fear of fire.

I followed the servant down endless corridors, up staircases, both straight and twisting, through vaults and chapels. In the darkest places the servant told me to hold on to his belt. It reminded me of crossing the River Sélune, except that now it was a river of darkness that we had to traverse. Sometimes our way led us out into the open, and from the bowels of the darkness we were suddenly in the glaring sunlight on a roof high above the world. But there was no time for my eyes to get used to the brightness and take in the view, for immediately I was plunged back into the subterranean gloom.

Finally we came to a winding staircase much wider than the others we had stumbled up, and well lit with slit windows filled with opaque glass. 'How can we still be going upwards when we are already so high?' I asked myself in amazement.

At the top a large heavy door studded with bronze and gold barred our way. My guide seized the huge door handle, which was a ring held in the jaws of a lion. The door opened. He stepped through. I followed.

Stepping into the room behind that door was like stepping onto a cloud. It was huge, almost the size of a church, and light flooded in through a long line of windows that filled one wall. They were glazed with the finest white glass that was almost transparent, and the whole wall seemed like a wall of light.

Because of the brightness I could not at first make out the

details of the room, but I was immediately struck by a strange murmuring, almost a humming, like the sound of bees in a hive.

It was the scriptorium. There must have been thirty monks, bare-headed, each one standing at a copying desk, each one quietly speaking the words he was copying. It was these words, softly murmured so as not to disturb his neighbour, that filled the room with such a strange and pleasant sound.

As I stood staring in wonder at the room the servant tugged at my sleeve and beckoned me on. Our journey was still not over. I blushed as I felt many eyes watching me from scarcely turned faces, and heard the murmurs dying away then rising again after I had passed.

The servant approached a small silver-haired monk standing by the window in the far corner, slightly apart from his brothers. He too was speaking softly but he was not copying. Instead he was dictating to a tall young brother stooped over a copying desk too low for him. I could not believe my ears: he was dictating not in Latin but in Norman French.

'Brother William de St Pair,' the servant said quietly, 'I have brought the youth as you requested.'

The small monk beamed. 'Thank you, Brother Dennis,' he said, addressing the scribe. 'You may rest now.' Then turning his kindly eyes on me he said, 'I was wanting to ask you a little about what happened yesterday, the incident at the ford. Many are calling it a miracle. I have spoken with the little girl and with her mother. I have sent to their village for evidence that the little girl was indeed dumb, as is claimed. But whether or not she was does not alter the fact that you were a very brave lad, was he not, Brother Dennis?'

'A very brave lad,' Brother Dennis echoed in a bored voice, without looking up from the manuscript he was reading.

'Yes, he was very brave, and such bravery deserves a reward. I have decided to give you the greatest reward that I can bestow. Humble and poor as I am before the Lord, the reward is one that even princes covet. Do you know what it is, young man? What is your name, by the way?'

'Duscath, father,' I replied.

'Duzkaz', he repeated, twisting his mouth to show how outlandish it sounded to him. 'What a strange name! It sounds like one of those weird names our neighbours in Brittany love to plague us with. We had better make sure brother Dennis knows how to write it down? Always assuming that you know how to write it down,' he added, raising his bushy eyebrows.

'I can read and write,' I said proudly.

'Excellent. Well now, about your reward. I am going to include you in a great book that I am writing about Mount St Michael. I have gathered together all the stories of this sacred and wonderful place, from old documents, from the mouths of old brothers and from the old folk that live in the villages around.

Stories, legends, miracles. Your story will be among them. The story of your bravery for sure, for that is clear for all to see; the story of the miracle too, if that is what it proves to be.

'Now, I want to know everything about you, because unless I know everything, I cannot decide what to include and what to leave out.'

So I told him about my parents, my village, Father Abraham, de Mortimer and the war. I even told him about what had happened at Warkworth. It was easy at first, as if I was talking about somebody else. Then right beside my face I saw the face of a little girl. It was pale and frightened and the eyes were tight shut. Was it the face of the little girl at Warkworth, or the little girl in the river? I had to know, but there seemed to be a veil between me and her, and I could not make out her features although I could feel her breath on my cheek. I tried to brush the veil away from my eyes and found myself wiping away tears. I broke down and covered my face with my sleeve.

Making soothing noises he led me out of the scriptorium by a small door. We seemed to walk for a long time, down corridors and staircases. The darkness was comforting and in it I gave myself completely to my tears. Eventually I stumbled behind Brother William into the huge church, filled with light and incense and murmuring voices.

He led me before the altar, and told me to repeat everything he said. This was his prayer.

'Oh Lord, blessed are you in giving, blessed are you in taking away. You gave this youth the strength to strike the innocent, and with that same strength you gave him the bravery to save the weak. His spirit was broken by the first blow, and made whole again by the second.

'St Michael, whose sword arm is raised only against evil, bless this boy and bless his arm, that it may, like yours, only be raised for good. He knows the misery that evil brings in its wake. Lest he ever forget this, may he always feel the breath of your wings upon his soul.'

'Amen,' I whispered, and vowed that one day I would make a special sacrifice to St Michael, although I did not then know what it would be.

The rest of the days in the Abbey passed easily and comfortably. I spent a lot of time with the little girl. Her name was Eleanor. Every day she would bring me a little gift — an apple, a sweetmeat, a straw doll. We would walk down to the village together and she would tell me stories of her home, her mother, her grandmother, her cousins, aunts and uncles. She would describe each of them in detail. It was as if she had absorbed everything about them into her stillness, and now that the dam of her silence had burst, everything poured out.

Sometimes however she would fall silent, frowning, as if she had stumbled upon some sadness that she had forgotten was there. When I asked her about her father, she just shook her head and said she had to find her mother.

Little girls can be very burdensome to youths, but she was never so to me. I rejoiced with her in her new-found speech. In her presence I would feel the new wholeness of my heart, whose healing had started on the river bank, and had received its blessing with Brother William's prayer. In Eleanor's presence I knew this is what my heart had been healed for."

TOURNAMENT

'When I returned to Falaise, renewed in strength of body and spirit, the castle was in turmoil. Word had just arrived of a great tournament at Valennes-sur-Sarthe near Le Mans. All the Scottish nobles were invited. Even King William was being allowed to attend.

I hated tournaments. Half your waking hours were spent burnishing and repairing armour, the other half running around the tournament field in a great cloud of dust, dodging horses and keeping your lord always in sight.

However, this time I found myself looking forward to the tournament. My new-found strength of spirit seemed able to turn everything into an exciting adventure.

The very next day after my return from Mount St Michael, I was riding behind my lord in a huge convoy towards Le Mans. The roads were thronged with bands of knights hoping for rich prizes and victory at the tournament, the first since the end of the war.

It was a long day's ride, at a pace very different from the one I had become used to with Father Roger. It was exhilarating galloping down the paved roads across the rolling wooded plains of Normandy and Maine. I amused myself by singing some of the pilgrims' songs I had heard at the Mount. I could sing them quite loudly with no danger of being heard above the sound of the horses' hooves. My heart would rise like a lark at the thought of the Mount and the bright cloud of the scriptorium even now filled with the busy hum of scribes. It was a world far away from galloping chargers and rattling armour. It had taken root in my heart, and was growing there like a fragrant flower.

Sometimes during our journey, when our pace slowed, my lord would ride beside me and talk affably with me as though talking to a fellow knight. I found this both flattering and alarming, as usually he addressed me as civilly as he would a dog. At last I had done something to please him. Not only had I been rid of my demon, but also by my deeds I had brought honour to his name.

We arrived at Valennes just as the sun was setting, and hastily pitched our tents in the cold wind that was blowing rain from the west Finally, all my duties done, I wrapped myself in my cloak and sank down exhausted on the ground at the foot of de Mortimer's pallet. Sir William's last words to me before he fell asleep were, 'Duscath, you're a fine lad.'

I was like a dog used to receiving from its master nothing but blows and rough words, which is suddenly is petted and praised. I felt happy, but on the alert, wondering when my old master would return. I felt safer when I was being treated badly.

The next day the sun rose behind heavy clouds above the forest to the east. Rain was pouring down in sheets. The huge jousting field stretched out bleak and sodden before us. It was already turning to thick, black mud under the horses' hooves and the heavy boots of the knights.

Down the long sides of the field, at intervals of ten yards, stood the refuge cabins. These were rough wooden huts, which could be bolted from the inside, where the knights could go to rest, or have their armour adjusted, repaired or changed. It was forbidden to attack a knight once he had reached a refuge hut, or to force an entry if the door was bolted.

In the middle of the long north side was a pavillion, where the ladies of some of the combatants, wrapped in furs, sat sheltered from the rain.

At the far end of the field, like an attacking army, stood the serried ranks of the French, Norman and English knights. From the pavilion the signal was given. The knights surged forward from either end, sending up a wall of black mud over the squires and the grooms. The earth trembled as if in fear. The squires, like a small army of foot soldiers, slipped and slithered behind them in the wet, churned up field, each one of us keeping his lord in sight. The shock of the meeting in midfield was like a clap of thunder.

By the time we reached them, the mêlée had resolved itself into a hundred single combats. For a moment I had lost sight of the de Mortimer boar and blue chequered banner. I saw his horse trotting riderless away from the fray. I whistled to him and he veered towards me. Catching his reins I led him quickly off the field, tethered him to a post, then plunged back onto the field to find my master.

The great boar emblazoned on his back was unmistakable amongst the ranks of fighting knights. He was locked in single-combat with a knight in the following of Sir William de Tancerville. The Norman knight was tiring fast I stood by and watched de Mortimer deliver a final blow to his adversary's helmet. The Norman's legs buckled under him. Down he went, face first into the mud at my lord's feet.

De Mortimer tugged off his helmet and looked round, his face dripping with sweat and aglow with the light of triumph. He saw me beside him and in the ecstasy of victory embraced me. It was like being squeezed by a mail-clad bear. I could hear my bones crack. He shouted into my ear to get one of the judges to witness the surrender. 'If I haven't killed him, that is,' and he gave a great roar of laughter.

By the time I returned with one of the judges de Mortimer's prisoner was sitting up, leaning against his squire, who had pulled his helmet off. From a gash above his left eye blood poured down his face. He had just enough breath in him to speak the words of surrender. Then de Mortimer ordered me to take his sword and horse and to follow him. The captive was now free to crawl away and lick his wounds. The only condition was that he present himself at de Mortimer's tent that evening to discuss ransom.

Almost all the knights remaining on the field were fighting on foot now. We picked our way carefully through them, mud up past our ankles. De Mortimer was leaning heavily on me, as he had strained his leg during the combat and now that the battle-rage was no longer on him, he could scarcely walk. He kept his helmet off, so he would not be attacked.

We struggled to the nearest empty refuge cabin. I helped him down onto one of the straw pallets and said I would fetch a surgeon for him.

'No, you won't,' he said. 'Not letting one of those butchers near me. Just a strain. Rest here a while. Then back to my tent and prepare for the next bout. Now shut up and bolt the door. Hurry!' he added urgently.

I had come to read my lord's eyes as you would read the sky for weather. There was nothing you could do to change whatever was approaching, but at least you could be prepared. Anger, scorn, violence, even murder, all of these I knew well. But the look in his eyes now unnerved me because I had never seen it before, and I did not know what it was.

I did as he said. In closing the door I closed out most of the light, as there were no windows in the cabins, just slits at the top of the walls beneath the eaves. The sounds of the tournament, which was still raging outside, filled the air.

'Duscath, come here,' he said, his voice softer though no less urgent.

I approached the pallet. He was sitting up. He told me to take his armour off. I did, leaving him only in his hose and linen tunic. Dimly I could make out that it was stained with blood on the chest and arms, where the chain mail had bitten into him during the fight. .

'You are wounded, my lord,' I said. 'Please, let me fetch —'

He smothered my words with his arms, again taking me in a rough embrace, forcing my head against his chest He stank of sweat and urine. I tried to pull away, but he held me tighter. I began to be afraid, although I still did not know of what.

'Stay with me and do as I say,' he growled, 'or I'll slit you open.' He let me go and picked up his dagger which lay beside him on the pallet. 'From your groin to your throat, understand?'

I nodded in mute terror. Like a flash of light on the dagger's blade I understood what I had seen in his eyes. It was the look of lust.

He ordered me to strip, then always with one hand on the dagger, he made me do vile things. He was like a wild animal slaking its thirst at a filthy pool. He had no thought for me, often hurting me, and would press his dagger up against my throat or my belly to force my compliance. I cried out for him to stop, but it only made him madder and more vicious.

Finally he gave a great shout, like one of the battle-cries that were still rising all around us. His body juddered, then went completely still, and for a moment I thought he had died. The dagger lay on the grass beside his limp hand.

I was numb with cold and fear. He was lying on top of me like a corpse, pressing me into the soft, grassy floor of the hut. My body was covered with filth and mud. My soul was even more soiled.

If he is dead, I said to myself, as thought and feeling gradually returned, I will clean and dress myself and him, then run for the surgeons. No one will ever know, and I will be free of this accursed man forever.

Even as I rejoiced at this, he groaned and rolled off me onto the earth. 'Filthy little animal,' he growled. 'Drag your lord down into the mud, would you? No better than an infidel dog. Get up and put some clothes on. I'll decide what to do with you later.'

All that day I was frightened, guilty and in pain: frightened at how my lord was going to punish me for what I had made him do; guilty because already in my confusion I had forgotten that I had done nothing to provoke him, nor had I consented in any way to the sin; and in pain because every part of my body hurt, as though I myself had been wounded in the tournament after a long, hard fight.

I could look no one in the face. I was sure my sin was written in my eyes. I blushed when anyone spoke to me and could not hear their words for the rushing of shame in my ears. It was as though my very blood had been wounded.

My lord did not fight again that day. His leg swelled up, preventing him from putting any weight on it. After we had left the hut, he made no reference to what had passed between us.

Nor, however, did I see again the friendliness that he had shown me on our journey from Falaise, the brief sunburst before the storm clouds covered his countenance.

The tournament lasted three days. The other side won, having taken more prisoners. The champion, who all agreed had fought the best and bravest, was an unknown knight in the following of Sir William de Tancerville called William the Marshall, the same man who more than forty years later was to become Regent of all England.

We rode back along the paved road to Falaise, where I had passed only a few days before. The world had looked fair then, and I had been happy, with the memory of Mount St Michael fresh and sweet in my spirit, and my lord smiling upon me. Now the world looked grim and grey. I felt like Adam and Eve driven from Eden, and like them I had lost my innocence and was covered in shame.

From that time on, whenever my lord had drunk too much wine, which was most evenings, and if there was no one else in his chamber, he would order me to his bed. There he would spend his lust on me, afterwards kicking me away from him, telling me that I was a sinful wretch and that I should go back to the Devil who had sent me. I would crawl away to my pallet and lie awake thinking of how I might escape. Death often seemed to me the easiest way, but what then? Then there were the terrible flames of Purgatory, or even Hell, that awaited sinners such as me.

In my desperation I made confession to Father Roger. I was forbidden to confess to anyone else. Father Roger told me I had an accursed beauty, which I flaunted shamelessly, and the flesh of our lord de Mortimer was weak, no match for such temptation. I said I did not know what to do apart from leave my lord's service. Father Roger replied that this was impossible unless de Mortimer himself consented, and this he would never do.

'Do you find pleasure in his bed?' Father Roger asked.

'No!' I cried.

'Then that is your penance,' he replied, adding, as he dismissed me, that he wanted to hear not another word on the subject.

King William remained a prisoner at Falaise until Advent, when a Great Treaty was made between him and King Henry. In it King William agreed to become his liege man, and to deliver the five chief castles of Scotland into his hands, to be garrisoned by the English and paid for by the Scots. King William was then allowed to cross over to England. However, most of the Scottish nobility, including my own master, were kept as hostages until the Scottish castles were safely in English hands.

King William was allowed to return to Scotland in the February of the following year. Soon afterwards word reached us in Falaise that we were at liberty. By Easter we were back in Scotland.

Peace was now established between the kingdoms, as well as within Scotland itself. The revolt in Galloway was over. With the help of the English garrisons order had returned to the burghs. The King and his barons were at liberty once more. For the poor, terrified creature that was Duscath mac Flathbertaich, however, his spirit was at war with his body, and the Babylonian Captivity was just beginning."

FOUNDATIONS

"Three years it lasted, my captivity, while my body developed into manhood, and my spirit was broken and afraid. Then came the year of change. When you are old, Martin, you will find that the years run into each other, like clouds piling up at the edge of the world. But there are years which you remember like flashes of lightning, which burn themselves into your memory, because after them nothing is the same. Such a year for me was 1178, when I had been in this world eighteen summers.

The royal court had been at Forfar since Easter, with most of the Scottish nobility in attendance, including Sir William de Mortimer. Usually the barons visited their own lands after Easter, but this time they remained with the King until Whitsun to be present at the foundation of the royal Abbey of St Thomas the Martyr at Arbroath.

This was to be a great occasion, the first house of God that King William had founded. It was to be given to the Order of Tiron, whose monks already served the great royal Abbey of St Mary, Kelso, founded by the saintly King David. These were monks who would remain loyal to the King, not like some others, such as the Augustinians, who could not be trusted. At least this is what my lord de Mortimer and his fellow-barons said, often cursing them and making lewd jokes about them. My lord de Mortimer held most clerics in the utmost contempt, although he had to watch what he said in public places.

We left Forfar at dawn on Whitsun, a great procession of nobles and prelates, King William at our head, and made our way eastwards to the sea. The Abbey was to be built on raised ground to the north of the village. A cluster of wooden huts for the masons, and deep foundation trenches marking out the proportions of the church, showed that work had already begun.

A large trestle altar was set up on the site of the future high altar. At it two Bishops, Jocelin of Glasgow and Andrew of Caithness, celebrated a mass of dedication. It was a bright, clear day, but the cool sea-breeze made us all shiver and draw our cloaks closer about us.

When the mass was finally over, the altar was cleared to become a desk at which the great foundation charter would be signed and sealed. The throne was placed behind it so that the King could sit and oversee the whole proceedings. The King's herald read out the charter, first in Latin, then in French, and finally in Scottish. Most of the earls and barons were unable to write, so each put their cross, and beside it one of the royal scribes wrote their name.

I was cold and bored. From where I stood I could see right down the coast and far out over the white-blue sea. It was empty of boats, just as the fields were empty of peasants: everyone for miles around had gathered to watch King William make his great gift to God and St Thomas Becket, the churchman who had refused to bow down to the authority of an earthly lord, and who, only a few years before, had been cut down at the high altar of his cathedral. Now his was the final victory. Kings knelt down before him and dedicated Abbeys to him.

King William had chosen to dedicate his new Abbey to St Thomas because since his capture at Alnwick during the English War he had held the saint in special honour. Everyone knew that St Thomas had delivered King William into the hands of King Henry the Elder. Had not that very day King Henry done public penance at St Thomas's tomb?

The King's herald called out the name of the chief baron in the land, Sir Richard de Moreville, Constable of all Scotland. A shudder went through the assembled multitude, eye-brows were raised, and anxious glances were exchanged. I turned my attention back to the trestle table and the great charter. It was his brother who had been St Thomas's chief murderer. Sir Hugh de Moreville had led the band of killer-knights into the cathedral at Canterbury and up to the high altar, where Thomas Becket was praying. It was he who had been the first to plunge his sword into the holy man's body.

Many churchmen saw Sir Richard's presence here as an insult to the honour of the saint, and had strongly counselled against it. King William had dismissed such counsel as superstitious nonsense, and as yet another tiresome example of Church meddling. John Scot, the ambitious Archdeacon of St Andrews, had quarrelled with the King at Yule over this very issue. His tall frame, lean, death's head look and his burning eyes, got from much fasting, had once been a common sight at court, reproaching the sinful excesses of the great. But at Yule he had returned to St Andrews and had not been seen since.

The crowd held its breath as Sir Richard approached the table. He made his cross, planted his seal in the hot wax and returned to his place. That was all. There was no thunderbolt, no darkening of the sun, nothing to show the saint's anger.

I looked away, having lost interest again, and noticed a small cloud of dust moving towards Arbroath from the south. Someone is in a hurry, I thought. Then my eyes strayed back out to sea and my thoughts were of the quiet cloister, away from the sordid turmoil of the world.

My musings were interrupted by the beat of hooves. The horse that had been at the heart of the dust cloud was galloping through the village towards us, setting all the dogs barking. From the livery I could see that the rider belonged to the household of the Bishop of St Andrews. He dismounted and handed his sword and dagger to Walter the Usher.

King William was already standing, towering impatiently over the last witness, Sir John de Lundin, who wasted no time in signing and sealing. The messenger was then ushered over to the King.

No one heard what his message was, but only the deaf would have failed to hear the King's reply. It was as if he had been bitten by a snake. Over went the table, scattering parchment, ink and clerks, as the King lunged towards the messenger, who nimbly stepped back, keeping his head so low that it almost touched his knees in a comic gesture of deference and self-preservation.

Everything was in an uproar, and I lost sight of King and messenger as the nobles and men-at-arms rushed forward.

Furious, the King swept back to Forfar. De Mortimer had ridden off with him and commanded me to follow immediately.

Already as we rode along the dusty track away from the broken ceremony and the trampled grass, rumours were flying.

'This is all King Henry's doing,' Ralph the squire declared with his usual great authority. 'I heard de Lindsey say that King Henry had ordered the Archbishop of York to send to the Bishop of St Andrews —'

'But there is no Bishop of St Andrews,' Robert the shield-bearer cut in, delighted to have caught Ralph out so easily.

'I didn't mean the Bishop, you fool, I meant the Cathedral Chapter.'

'Then why didn't you say the Cathedral Chapter?' Robert came back at him. Ralph scowled and it looked as though a fight was going to start.

Suddenly a little voice piped up. It was Serlo, one of the pages. He rarely spoke, so all heads swivelled towards him. 'I heard one of de Lundin's pages say he heard the messenger say Archdeacon John Scot has been elected Bishop of St Andrews, and that's why the King is so angry.'

'Don't be ridiculous!' Ralph jeered. 'They'd never dare do that without the King's permission. Besides everyone knows that the King has promised the bishopric to Hugh the Chaplain.'

Even Robert and I had to agree with Ralph on that point.

'Well,' I said, 'he was certainly angry about something.'

'Very well observed,' Ralph said with a sneer.

By the time we rode into the bailey at Forfar the King and his counsellors were in session. Rumour had hardened into fact. Little Serlo had been right, for all Ralph's scorn and everyone else's disbelief.

Without the King's consent or knowledge the Chapter of St Andrews had elected John Scot first Bishop of the realm. This was a double insult to the King. Firstly he hated John, his self-righteousness, his criticism of court morals, his total loyalty to the Holy Father in all matters. Secondly he had already chosen a successor to old Bishop Richard: his favourite chaplain Hugh, the very opposite of John in all things. Besides, how dare a Cathedral Chapter elect a Bishop without consulting the King. The ghost of Thomas Becket was abroad.

The King descended on St Andrews like a whirlwind, while flustered clerks, harassed servants and grumbling barons swirled in his wake. By the time I struggled into the town with de Mortimer's baggage train, John Scot, the new Bishop-elect, had fled the wrath of the King, and was on his way to the Pope to appeal against the flouting of canon law. Meanwhile preparations were almost complete for Hugh's election as Bishop of St Andrews in John's place. The royal wind blew and, like grass, the Cathedral Chapter now bent towards the King's Bishop, Hugh.

Hardly had I arrived in St Andrews than word came from Crail that the Lady Ada was on the point of death. De Mortimer was the only one of her vassals who was with the King, so he set off at once, taking me with him. The King gave us a message for his mother that he would come to her as soon as Hugh's election was over.

It was a hard ride into the teeth of a cold east wind. I arrived exhausted and empty, as if the wind had blown my spirit clean of all feeling. So the tears which overwhelmed me as I stood beside the crumpled figure of my lady took me by surprise.

She was dressed in the habit of a Cistercian nun. The white wimple surrounding her thin, drawn face made her look even more severe than usual. She was unable to speak. She put out an emaciated hand for me to hold but quickly withdrew it as a spasm of pain racked her body. She closed her eyes and turned her face away, so that I would not see how distorted it had become.

'Goodbye, my Lady,' I said softly through the tears. 'Thank you for all your kindness. I will pray for you always.' I made to go, but her hand grasped mine again, pulling me towards her with surprising firmness. In that grip I knew the old spirit of my lady was still there. She was trying to say something. I bent over and put my ear close to her mouth, trying to ignore the sickening smell of decay.

'Get away before it is too late,' she whispered. That was all she said. Again she was racked with pain, and again she let go my hand and turned away. She seemed to fall asleep. One of her ladies-in-waiting came up and led me away. She died during the following night.

The King had ordered that, if he did not reach Crail before his mother died, her body was to be brought to St Andrews for burial. The Countess had wanted to be buried among the nuns of St Mary's Priory in Haddington. The King could not leave St Andrews at this difficult time, so the wishes of the living overrode those of the dead.

Scarcely had the spirit left the Lady Ada's body than I was sent packing to my lord's castle at Aberdour. I travelled alone along the coast of Fife and Fothrif, my only companions my troubled thoughts. Why should I not attend my lady's funeral and join in the ceremonial mourning? It was clear to me that my removal to Aberdour was Sir William's way of showing respect for the Countess, his liege-lady. Yet I knew that my grief was deeper and more real than any one's at court. Her son the King was glad to be rid of her, while her liege-men had spent the years of her last illness seeking favour and position elsewhere.

For the court I was either a sinful wretch, who caused my master to stain his soul with foulness; or a worthless whore who would lie with anyone if my master did not keep a jealous eye on me. I had long since been incapable of thinking anything different about myself. Yet my lady Ada had thought I was worthy of being saved. Even on the point of death she had thought that. I owed it to her memory to start thinking that myself.

I reached Aberdour at dusk. I had to present myself to the Lady Anicea and deliver my message from her lord, that she was to take a small body of men-at-arms and without delay repair to St Andrews for the funeral.

She was at table when I arrived, a tall, slender, beautiful woman, with fine red hair done up in two thick plaits which hung over her shoulders in loops. Opposite her, on a small stool, was a handsome young man whom I had not seen before. He had fair hair and a beard the colour of ripe barley. His name was Raoul. He was strumming a lute and singing softly when I entered the hall, a love song from Provence. She signalled him to stop as soon as I told her the news about the Countess.

'Are you to accompany me?' she asked, forcing the words out

of lips that were tense and unsmiling. She despised me. I did not blame her.

I blushed and replied, 'No, I am to await my lord's return here.'

She nodded, then dismissed me, saying that I would find food in the kitchen if I was hungry. It would have been an insult to any other squire, not to invite him to sit at table with her. To me it was no more than I deserved. I had no desire to share meat with someone for whom my presence was unbearable. I ate in silence in the kitchen. When everyone had retired I threw myself onto a pile of straw in the corner of the hall and wept myself to sleep.

The next day the Lady Anicea set off for St Andrews. The minstrel Raoul helped her onto her horse and mounted his own. They rode off laughing and singing.

I had several weeks in Aberdour, with little to do except turn up at mealtimes, when a disgruntled servant would throw down food for the few retainers and guards who were left. Sometimes I would eat in my parents' house, where I would hear my father grumble about all the mouths he had to feed, or my mother describe her latest ailment. I preferred the castle hall, where conversation was as dull, but where at least I did not have to pretend I was listening.

Every morning, after Mass and prayers for the soul of Lady Ada, I practised archery or went out riding in the hills. I could not remember the last time I had spent so much time alone. It soothed and comforted my soul, and when I was alone my tears could flow freely for my lady.

In the afternoons I would hurry over to the cottage of Father Abraham the priest. He was a canon of Inchcolm, but he lived in the village and looked after the church of St Fillan's. He was a good, kind man, the salt of the earth. I had known him since I was a child. He it was who baptised me, buried my grandparents and Duncan my brother. He had taught me to read and write a little Latin. In fact any child eager to learn, who could slip away from their work for an hour or so each day, could be taught whatever Father Abraham knew.

I realise now that Abraham's knowledge was not very great, but to us children he seemed as learned as Bede. Besides it was not the breadth or depth of his knowledge that mattered, but his willingness to share it with us, and surely that is greater than all the learning in Christendom.

I had scarcely seen him since entering Sir William's household. Although he had aged a lot in recent years, and was in poor health, he was still his old self, eager to talk and teach. We read the psalms together and I asked him many questions about his life.

He had been among the first group of canons on the island, when life was more building than praying. The early community was poorly endowed and so unable to employ many craftsmen. All the brothers had to have building skills, not like nowadays. After the main buildings were erected on the island, Abraham was sent as priest to serve St Fillan's, but first he had to build it. The ancient church, built by St Fillan himself hundreds of years ago, fell down one windy night, just after Sir William had paid homage to Countess Ada for the lands of Aberdour. Even Sir William must have been shaken by this omen, for he gifted the church to the Priory, with promises that he would help them rebuild it. In the end the canons did most of the work and met most of the expenses themselves, and poor Abraham bore the brunt of the toil.

I had always been fascinated by the new Priory on the island, although I had never been there. We grew up together, as it were, and that made it special to me. The pious King Alexander forty years before my birth had built a church there to give thanks to St Columba for rescuing him from shipwreck. They say he had wanted to found an Augustinian Priory as well, but he died soon afterwards, and for many decades there was only the church, served by a canon from the Abbey of Scone.

Finally in the reign of King Malcolm, about the year of my birth, Bishop Gregory of Dunkeld and Countess Ada brought the Priory into being. The Countess vowed ten celibate men to the service of God and St Columba in the hope that her son Malcolm would give up his own celibacy and take a wife. It was to no avail, for Malcom died a virgin, but the community, which followed the Rule of St Augustine, took root and flourished.

Thus a new world was created on the edge of my own dull one, a world that brought many churchmen, grand and humble, solemn and jovial, to our village. They seemed to be different beings, moving to different laws. As a child I would look out over the sea and watch with excitement as the new buildings rose into the sky and changed my horizon for ever."

The old man fell silent. When he spoke again, it was to ask Martin to leave him, but to promise to return the next day. This the young man did.

At that moment Brother Peter the infirmarer arrived, jangling his keys. "Come along," he said officiously, "you've been with Brother Michael quite long enough. Look at him, absolutely exhausted." Then pointing towards the latrine he added sternly, "I'll let you out the back way."

Martin was angry. Yes, he had been with the old man a long time, longer than he had intended, he realised. But what business was it of Brother Peter? Biting his tongue, he silently followed the infirmarer out over the latrine bridge.

-

51

JEDBURGH

"It was a day of perfect calm, a rare day when the sea held its breath and the only movement was the islands, the rocks and the shore trembling in the heat haze. The Priory church was cool and pleasant, but Martin was impatient for Nones to end, so that he could once again hurry over to the infirmary and Brother Michael.

Malcolm the gate-keeper greeted him with a broad smile, jangled his keys merrily, and opened the back door to the infirmary.

It was pitch black in Michael's cell. The shutter was still over the window. Martin peered into the gloom. Questioning the darkness he said, "Are you there, Brother Michael?"

A trembling voice replied, "Martin, my son, I am so pleased you have come. I thought you had forgotten me. It seems an age since you were last here."

"Forgive me, Father, but I was unable to come yesterday. But how could you think that I had forgotten you! I'm in your spell, don't you know that?"

The old man chuckled with delight.

"It's wicked to tease an old man like that, you know, and a man of God, too!"

"Then why are you sitting here in the darkness?" Martin went on, encouraged by the old man's mood. "Outside God's world is full of light and warmth. To turn your back on it is a sin. Not even the oldest of bones could be chilled on a day like this. Come, I will take you down to the beach. There we will sit and you will tell me more of your story."

The old man did not reply at once. All that could be heard was the buzzing of flies, and the distant clamour of the gulls.

"If you first bring me a cup of that concoction Brother Peter makes from the juice of eye-bright. It clears my memory."

Sitting on a large, smooth rock by the south beach, half shaded by the oak trees which overhung the shore, and out of sight of the Priory, Michael resumed his story.

"Now how far had I got when we last saw each other?" he asked.

"You were at Aberdour after Countess Ada's death," Martin said gently.

"Ah yes. After about a month Sir William returned. During the days which followed I had little time to dwell upon my grief. There was always an uproar when he descended upon his Aberdour lands, especially when he had been away for some time.

My father, who was responsible for seeing that my lord's dues from the village were properly gathered, nervously followed Robert the chief steward around as he inspected the granaries and stores. Meanwhile Sir William sat in his hall, roaring and cursing at the thousand and one things not to his liking, and meting out his justice. The gallows were never idle when Sir William was in the castle.

Now it was more chaotic because Sir William was leaving within the week. The King had summoned him to Jedburgh, and this time Sir William wanted me with him.

Each night I was so tired I would fall asleep before my head even touched my cloak. Often that week I was roughly wakened and pulled into Sir William's chamber. I begged him not to touch me, but that seemed to make him even more lustful. I stopped myself going mad by cutting myself off from my body. Perhaps you do not know what I mean, Martin. I pray you will never need to know what I mean. I could feel nothing, not even when my body answered Sir William's pleasure. This was a great blessing, because there were times when I felt too much with Sir William, when his lust set me on fire, in spite of myself, and flames would engulf us both.

The week passed. We set out for Jedburgh. We were on the road early, before the heat. It was a day like this, with not a breath of wind to freshen the air. I crossed the water at the Queen's Ferry with Sir William and a few others, while the bulk of his company went by Stirling with the horses. We unloaded the baggage and left it with a guard by the shore for our horses to pick up, then we hired mounts and rode to Edinburgh.

The sun was still high as we came through the West Port and made our way up the steep wynds to the castle. We were lodged in the hall in the outer bailey. Scottish barons and their retinues were not allowed any further into the castle because it was still held by King Henry's men.

I remember gazing out from the battlements that evening, after Sir William had gone down into the town to some brothel or inn or other, and the other squires with him. I was searching for this very spot where we are now. The island and Priory of St Columba are much more difficult to make out from Lothian than from Fife. From Lothian they melt into the opposite coast. But finally I saw it, a light brown patch amid so much green. I stared and stared, until the Priory seemed to dance before my eyes.

I saw in my mind's eye a Mass being celebrated for my Lady Ada. Her body had been lying in the earth now for over a month. How much of her dear face would still be recognisable? How much would the face of death have taken its place?

I was filled with such horror at the thought that I had to close my eyes. I found myself praying with all my spirit. In the warm summer's evening, hovering like a bird above the world, my broken soul reached out to God, and for an instant found peace, not in the numbness that was my usual refuge, but in the full awareness of all the ugliness of the world, and the wretchedness of my soul.

A wonderful light lay upon the land like a halo, staining the sky the colour of red glass. It went right through me and there was no darkness in me. It was a miracle, Martin. For the first time in my life, and when my soul had most need of it, I had been granted a vision of God's grace.

God granted me a further boon that night. Sir William was so drunk that he was carried back senseless from the town, and my night was undisturbed.

The next day we rode up over the Lammermuirs and down the Leader towards Melrose. It was heavy and close and the grey-black clouds hung so low that it was like being in a vaulted chamber. I thought to myself that it might as well be a vault, I felt so trapped. All the wonder of the previous evening had fled, leaving me even more downcast than before.

We had just crossed the Tweed when the storm broke. With a great crash of thunder water burst from the clouds. It was as if a loch had formed on their thickness and the bottom had cracked open, letting it pour down on the world. Soon I was soaked to the skin and shivering.

I heard Sir William shout that we would press on to Jedburgh. We quickened our pace, but soon had to slow again as the road became a river of mud. On we stumbled, blinded by rain and mud thrown up by the horses' hooves. The tree-tops were dancing wildly as the wind became stronger, and lightning tore the sky apart. We struggled through another river and then somebody cried out, 'That's Bonjedward, we're almost there.'

Just then a blinding flash burst on me from the side. I felt my horse go from under me. I felt myself lurch forward. I didn't hear the thunder.

The next thing I remember was candle-light flickering on a ribbed ceiling. I was warm and dry. Occasionally a shadow would pass over, but I was too drowsy to care who or what might be casting it.

I must have fallen asleep again, because the next time I opened my eyes daylight filled the chamber. With great effort I lifted my head and looked around. Beside me sat a young man in a black habit. He looked at me and smiled.

He was so beautiful that I thought I had died and was in an ante-chamber to Heaven, with an angel to attend me. He had deep, brown smiling eyes, fair hair, high cheek bones and a broad nose.

'How are you, Duscath?' he asked softly. He spoke in Inglis, hesitating over my name, which sounded strange in his foreign tongue.

I smiled back at him, thinking it odd that Inglis should be the language of the angels. There would be trouble when the Normans found out. Then I remembered he had asked me a question, and was probably expecting a reply.

'Tired', I said, 'but well enough.' My Inglis has never been very good, but I was happy to form the same sounds as my angel.

'My name is Edgar,' he said. 'You are in the infirmary of the Abbey of St Mary Jedburgh. Your horse threw you when the lightning struck close by. You hit your head and you've been asleep for two days. Your companions are all well, and are lodged in the castle with the King.'

He paused. Painful memories started flowing back.

'Sir William de Mortimer has a servant posted in the lobby. He wants word as soon as you have come to. Is there any message you wish to send your master?'

At the mention of my lord's name my stomach knotted. I had been jolted violently back to earth. If de Mortimer was around this could hardly be Heaven.

'Don't bring Sir William,' I said in desperation. 'He must not know where I am. Please hide me!'

'Calm down, calm down. He will not be coming,' he said soothingly.

'I must get up, I must get away!'

I was completely beside myself, Martin. But my arms and legs might just as well have been made of lead, for I could not move them at all.

I passed out again and awoke with the dull pain of leeches on my arm. I tried to move it to ease the discomfort, but it would not obey me. I was now very frightened.

'Help me, please,' I cried out. 'I can't move. My limbs have died.'

'Duscath, don't worry. Father Edwin is here. He is skilled in the art of healing.'

I recognised the voice. Soft, Inglis. Yes, it was Edgar.

'Why can't I move?' I whimpered. I felt as helpless as a little child.

'Duscath, I have examined you carefully over all your body and I can find nothing amiss.' This was a different voice, also Inglis, older, harsher. I turned my head and saw a wizened face with a large nose and bright blue, youthful eyes which looked out of place amidst the wrinkles. He too was dressed in the black habit of an Augustinian, which hung strangely on his small body. Only later did I realise this was because he was hunch-backed.

'It may be some humour at the root of it, or some grief or soul-hurt. Regular bleeding will ease the former, confession and God's mercy the latter. But you must eat. Do you have an appetite?'

His cool, matter-of-fact voice calmed me. His tone was one of confidence and authority. The leeches, sated on my blood, let go my arm and were put back in their jar. My stomach answered his question with a growl. Yes, I was starving. I was propped up on bolsters and Edgar fed me gruel made with roasted oat-meal and eggs. Manna could not have tasted better.

For days I lay there. I never fell into a faint again, but still I could not move. Yet my memories of that time are sweet, like being wrapped in a warm cloak of love and care. Edgar was my arms and legs. It was almost as if he became my body. It could have been shaming for me, but strangely it was not. Father Edwin, too, in his own way happed me in love. Every day he would come to me, take my useless hand in his, and hear my confession.

At first I was resolved not to tell him everything. Yet what had I to lose, condemned as I was to languish in my prison of paralysis? And he had such kindly eyes. Every sin I confessed to him he forgave totally, telling me clearly why. Each such reasoned absolution gave me the strength to step further into my guilt. Then suddenly he asked me,

'Edgar tells me you are afraid of de Mortimer. Why?'

'I have been commanded not to tell,' I replied, feeling my body tense at the mention of my lord's name.

'Neither man nor woman can come between penitent and priest. Earthly commands melt like wax in God's heat. Never forget, my son, that I am under orders myself, for the Holy Trinity forbids me to reveal to any living soul what is confessed to me. You have nothing to fear but God's wrath at an incomplete confession.'

So I told him, not only about Sir William's abuse of my body, but also about my own abuse of myself and about the strange breathless excitement aroused in me by some men, and about the delight I felt in the presence of Brother Edgar and even in the thought of Brother Edgar. I knew that in some devilish way the Hell of Sir William and the Heaven of Edgar were two ends of the same rope, and that to break the rope would be to break myself. And here I lay, broken.

'You are indeed blessed, Duscath,' Edwin said, 'for in your sin lies your salvation. When you are well you must leave de Mortimer, for what he is doing to you is evil and imperils your soul. You must leave this sinful world, where the snares of the Devil are many, and men and women destroy themselves and the world in pursuit of power and glory, which must always elude them, because all the power and glory belong to God alone.

'However there is another world, within this world and yet outside it, beyond it, a world of love whose eyes are turned heavenward, and whose sole purpose is to praise and serve the Holy Trinity. It is the world of the cloister, and it is to this world that you must go.

'From what you have revealed to me I say that you are well suited for the world of the cloister, for you are drawn by your heart and your love to your own sex more than to the other.

'That love, purified through prayer and time of its baser elements, will shine forth like gold and be pleasing to the Lord. It will lead you to form spiritual friendships, and spiritual friendships between two brothers or two sisters in Christ are the knots which should hold a convent together, for those who dwell in friendship dwell in God, and God in them.'

I listened spell-bound to his words. Did this mean that there was a place in Creation for me after all?

Before me I saw the towering walls of the Abbey of St Michael, the magnificent church like a crown, the great room full of light and whispering scribes. It was a vision from which I had often drawn comfort. Yet between me and the world I had glimpsed so briefly in the Abbey there had yawned a great chasm: my lord was so powerful he would never let me go from his world; and I was such a sinful wretch I would never be allowed entrance into that other world. Now, as if by a miracle, Father Edwin's words were a bridge over that chasm. For the first time the future lost its grim and threatening aspect. For the first time I saw clearly the way I had to go.

There were so many questions I wanted to ask, but before I could ask even one Father Edwin was shuffling towards the door.

'I'll be in to see you tomorrow. Make sure you look after Brother Edgar.' He gave a little chuckle and was gone.

Martin, how can I express the joy I now felt? My whole body tingled with it, even my lifeless arms and legs.

That night I had a shameful dream. An incubus had taken the form of Edgar and had caused me to spill my seed in my sleep. The next day I could not look at Edgar without blushing. I longed to confess to Father Edwin, for I knew that he alone could untie the knot of my confusion and shame.

Father Edwin always came to see me late in the day, as the sun's rays were probing the dark corner of my chamber furthest from my bed. That day the golden light crept so slowly along the wall and past the door that I thought it would never reach the far corner, but at last it did, and Father Edwin appeared.

'Father,' I asked, after I had unburdened myself to him, 'how is it that the feelings were so sweet that I can still taste them, like honey on my tongue, and yet my body did such a shameful thing?'

'You are young,' he replied, almost in a whisper, 'and full of passion and seed. A tide is rising in you. It is hard to turn tides before their time has come, but it will come and the tide will turn. Never doubt that.

'Remember always what I told you yesterday, that God dwells in special friendships. If that friendship is sometimes stained by too much passion, well, there are worse things that can happen, and the stain can be cleansed by a contrite heart and a willing spirit.

'There are many churchmen who believe that the spilling of seed which cannot sprout children within wedlock is a crime worse than murder. I have seen Abbot Osbert of Kelso foam at the mouth while preaching this. But the voice of love is whispered in the cloister, quiet but strong. It has not been drowned out by voices such as Abbot Osbert's, at least not yet.

'Duscath, my son, contain your bodily passion as much as you can. Cut it back to the root so that spiritual passion will grow in its stead. But do not despair when you stumble and fail, as you must sometimes do because you are human. Always confess, but be moderate in your penance, and be careful in your choice of confessor.

'Be careful, also, in your choice of friend — infinitely careful and prayerful. But when you have found him, press him to your bosom, as Jesus did John. Take his hand, cherish that which is good and holy between you, and with your combined strengths tread down what is evil. I will say no more at present. Please, continue with your confession. If that is your worst sin, your penance will be light.'

"Martin," Michael said, turning his face towards his young listener, "beware of these words. They have meant much to me, both of joy and sorrow, but now they are dangerous. Our present fathers in Christ all think as Abbot Osbert did then, and who am I, a mere canon, old and blind, to question them? Father Edwin spoke in a different time, with a different voice. God alone will judge who speaks the truth. I have already said too much, God beshrew my blethering old tongue."

Martin was able only to stammer a reply, "Brother Michael, I am — I am — honoured that you have revealed yourself so openly to me."

He was not even sure what he was saying, so shocked and confused was he. He was also afraid. By God's wounds, was it not drummed into every novice nowadays that the Devil himself lurks in special friendships?

Martin decided he must steer the conversation towards the shore he had almost lost sight of, towards Prior Simon. He said, his voice matter-of-fact, almost casual, "Father, when did you first meet Simon de Quincy?"

"I do not wish to speak of Simon at this point," the old man said firmly. "One thing leads to another. You must be patient if you want to know the truth. The truth is like a spider's web, made up of a thousand strands. Now I wish to finish what I was telling you about Father Edwin and Brother Edgar. But if you have better things to do?"

"It is not a question of 'better things', Father," Martin replied, trying not to sound annoyed, "but time presses. I do not know how long I will be allowed to remain here on the island."

"Trust me, Martin," Michael said. "And trust God. He will not take you away from me until the web is complete."

Martin was not so sure, but he saw that it was useless to argue. Sighing inwardly, he said, "Father, please go on with your story."

"Well, not long after Father Edwin left me Edgar came in to ask how I was. At the sight of him my heart leapt for joy and I no longer felt shame.

You see, I was no longer afraid of his beauty. The Devil thrives on fear, but if we are strong and sure and unafraid we stand in God's hand and the Devil cannot touch us. I was no longer racked with shame and despair at the movement of my heart towards Edgar; the Devil was powerless, and I was free. At least so it seemed to me then.

I told him that I felt very well, and that I thought life was coming back into my limbs. I could feel the blood throbbing in them, and I could move my fingers and toes.

Yet even greater than my joy at finding the use of my limbs again was my joy at finding Edgar. I could not learn enough about him, and till the bell called him away to Vespers I plied him with questions about his life.

He came from a family of free tenants who held lands from the Scottish King near Berwick. The English Wars had laid them waste and the whole family had fled to Edinburgh for safety. That was where they were living when his father was killed fighting with King William in Northumberland.

After the war he and his mother and his two sisters had returned to what was left of their estates. His mother had been forced to marry a local Norman lord, one of the de Moubray's, King Henry the Elder's man. This was during the time of chaos when our own King was a prisoner in Normandy.

Edgar had been given the choice of becoming a squire in his step-father's household or entering a monastery. His step-father had a whole brood of sons by a previous marriage, all older than him, and he had no stomach for the fight that was sure to follow for his ruined inheritance. But he had a keen hunger for learning and God's word. So it was that he became a novice at the great Abbey of Jedburgh the winter before I met him.

'Are you happy?' I asked him with bated breath.

'How do you measure happiness? The food is scant, the clothing rough, and just when my sleep is at its sweetest the bell calls me to a cold, dark church. The novice-master is strict, but I learn well, so I rarely get the sharp edge of his tongue, or his stick.

'There is a spirit of love in this place which touches even the hardest of hearts. There is peace and calm everywhere. I hardly knew the meaning of these words before. Also we never get the poor coming to complain that we are cheating them. We rarely get involved in litigation. My father spent half his life fighting his enemies in the wars, and the other half fighting his neighbours in the courts.

'Best of all, birth makes no difference here. Goods are distributed according to our needs only, not our blood. Christ is here amongst us. Over the years I will get to know Him better and better, and that gladdens my heart more than anything else in the world.'

I drank in his words. It seemed to me a paradise, a shelter from all the storms that had raged around and within me for as long as I could remember. He did not tell me of the storms that could rage within the cloister and tear the tranquility to shreds. Perhaps then he did not know.

The bell rang for Vespers.

'And just when conversation is at its sweetest,' he said with a wry smile, 'the bell calls me to church. Lord is telling me I talk too much. Goodbye, Duscath. You are making me forget my duties. I was supposed to have weeded the herb garden before Vespers.'

He took my hand and squeezed it, then hurried away. For the first time since my fall my hand did not flop down like a dead bird, but hung trembling in the air.

By the next day I was able to sit up and, leaning heavily on Brother Edgar, I took my first steps. My legs had grown so thin and weak that I thought I might never be able to walk again without a sturdy arm like Edgar's to support me. I accepted this with a calmness that surprised me, and thought already I must be becoming more holy. Sancta simplicitas!

'Take me outside, Brother Edgar, please. Just a few steps!' I was hungry for the sun and the fresh breeze.

At first he hesitated, worried at what Father Edwin might say.

'Well, you could always ask him,' I suggested. 'He can't be far.'

'I daren't disturb him,' Edgar replied with a frown. 'When he's in his workroom preparing his potions and his lotions, he is only to be disturbed on matters of utmost urgency.'

'Well he's not likely to find us then, is he?' I could already taste the sweetness of the summer air. I was determined to go outside.

Finally Edgar relented. We shuffled along a dark lobby and through a heavy, creaking door into a blinding brightness that made me shrink back and cry out. It was as if my brain was seared again by that lightning which had taken me away from Sir William and my previous life. How long ago was it? Days? Weeks? Years?

I clung to Edgar, suddenly afraid, and begged to be taken back to my chamber.

'Come on,' he said, 'we've got this far. It'll be all right. The light takes a bit of getting used to, that's all. You've been cooped up in the darkness for too long. There's a seat over there under that tree. I'll lead you to it. You can keep your eyes shut if you want.'

So, blinded and half crippled I was led by Edgar into a sunny summer's afternoon. There are many things I have to thank Edgar for, but for nothing more I think than for taking me into that garden and into that day.

My eyes did indeed quickly get used to the light, and I had never seen colours so vivid, or smelled flowers so sweet, or heard sounds so clear as on that afternoon. The song of birds cascaded from the branches and rose from the reeds, and the river murmured below us. The stone-work itself was golden-brown and dappled with leafy shadows.

I believe, Martin, that we build protective walls against the beauty of Creation, otherwise it would so overwhelm us that we would do nothing but stand and gape in amazement like children at a fair. However, on that day I had no walls to protect me for they had all crumbled in the darkness of my chamber and my disease.

There was something else, as well. There was the God-given presence of Edgar, to whom I clung. In his person there seemed to gather all the new beauty of the world. I felt it was through him that all the sights and sounds and smells of that magnificent day were reaching my senses. His smile was the light of the sun striking the river, his voice the sweet singing of the birds, his eyes —

Oh, Martin, on that summer's day in the garden of the Abbey of St Mary Jedburgh I tasted Heaven.

I was back in my chamber long before Father Edwin pushed open the door and shuffled in. He found me sitting up holding a cup of water. He did not look in the slightest surprised, but felt my brow and asked me to move my arms and legs. He examined my whole body, muttering to himself.

Finally he said, 'Well, young man, your recovery from now on will be rapid and complete. You will soon be leaving us.'

I should have been overjoyed to hear him say these words, but instead a chill went through me.

'But there is still so much to talk about,' I said. 'I have still much to confess.'

'Your life cannot just consist of confession, Duscath my son,' he said with a smile. 'There must be a time too for sinning, or else there would be nothing to confess.'

'I also have so many questions still to ask,' I went on unabashed. 'About special friendship, for example. Please, tell me more about that. I have been able to think about little else.'

'Before you can understand friendship, Duscath,' he said, serious again, 'you must learn to make friends with yourself. Our Lord says, "Love your neighbour as yourself." People often

61

think it is loving your neighbour that is the difficult part of this command. But there are so many in this world who hate themselves, and if you have not learned love within the school of your own heart, how can you practise it towards others?

'Greater than both these loves, of course, is the love of God, but they are all three so intertwined that if we lose one we lose them all.

'Now you ask about friendship with others. Listen carefully, for these are not my words alone, but the words of that great and holy teacher Ailred of blessed memory. He himself was inspired by the Holy Spirit, but he was also drawing on a deep and ancient well of wisdom.

'There are, he says, three sorts of friendship: carnal, worldly and spiritual. The real beginning of carnal friendship springs from an emotion which hungrily follows every passer-by with lustful eyes. By way of the senses it brings into the mind images of beautiful faces and bodies. By gesture, nods, words, compliance, spirit is captivated by spirit, spirit is inflamed by spirit, kindled to form a sinful bond so that the one will do or suffer crime for the sake of the other. This type of friendship is entered into rashly, and is tested by no great act of judgment and is in no way governed by reason, that great gift from God. Such friends can part as suddenly as they came together.

'The second type of friendship is worldly and arises out of a desire for worldly advantage or possessions. It is very prone to deceit and intrigue, for it contains nothing certain, nothing constant, nothing secure, but everything changes with fortune and follows the purse.

'Spiritual friendship, on the other hand, should be desired only for the sweetness which it brings with it. It is born of a similarity of life, morals and pursuits. It is full of love and wisdom. In fact, it might almost be said that true friendship, is nothing else but love and wisdom.'

'Can one type of friendship not lead into another?' I asked, straining to catch every word and the meaning of every word. 'Or must they be forever sealed off one from another?'

'That is a good question. It is easy to see why we should be attracted to those who are beautiful to look at, well-built, sweet in voice and distinguished in behaviour. This attraction can move not just to love but also to lust. If this happens, well, it is not the end of the world, or the end of the chance for spiritual friendship to grow. If we were all perfect beings, untainted by the sin of our first parents, we should love the virtuous more than the beautiful, which is to say, the morally attractive more than the physically attractive.

'Always remember, however, that our feelings are not ours to command. We must accept that we can be attracted towards someone against our will, while towards others we can never experience a spontaneous affection, however pure in heart they are.

'Remember also that if we are moved solely by our feelings, it is not love. But if our feelings pull us towards a person who is both beautiful and good, then use them as a guide, as a horse for your journey, as a staff for your way. Never forget, though, who is guiding whom, who is riding whom, who is supporting whom. So do not shun a person because you are physically attracted to them. On the other hand, do not seek their company only because of that physical attraction.

'Friendship brings with it great joy, Duscath, even a friendship which includes lust; but my heart leaps when I think of the far greater joy of a friendship which transcends lust. No, not transcends it, transmutes it. Let your mind dwell on this greater joy.

'What could be sweeter, what could be more strengthening, than to have someone whose conversation is as sweet as a song in the tedium of your daily life? Or to have someone on whose breast you can pour out your innermost thoughts? To have someone who can weep with you in your troubles, rejoice with you in your happiness, question with you in your doubts? To have someone whom you lead by ties of love into that secret chamber of your mind where alone with your beloved friend you can rest from the din of the world in the embrace of charity and the kiss of unity, with the sweetness of the Holy Spirit flowing between you?'

Edwin was trembling with the beauty of his words. Staring at me, his eyes wide and moist, he seemed to be looking into my soul, or not seeing me at all.

A sharp knock at the door startled us out of our lovely vision, and we heard Edgar's voice, soft but urgent.

Father Edwin murmured to me, 'Go and let your friend in.'

I walked shakily over to the door and opened it.

'Father, Duscath, forgive me, but —'

Edwin put his finger to his lips to silence him.

'Brother Edgar, Duscath and I are discussing a matter of utmost importance, and I would like you to join in. I beg you — no, as your superior I command you — to wait until we have finished.'

Edgar tried to speak, but Father Edwin silenced him again.

'My son, Duscath will not be with us for much longer, and our discussion is more important than your message. Believe me.

'Now, sit and listen. Duscath and I have been talking about the different kinds of friendship, and how a baser friendship can lead to a more noble one, more pleasing to God, to a friendship which we call spiritual. I know we two have talked about these things before, but it is amazing how certain circumstances, and company, can sharpen our hearing and our understanding.

'I was telling Duscath that once a friend has been chosen and tested, and it is most important to test a friend before admitting him to your heart, you must join yourself to him in such a way that you mingle soul with soul, making one soul out of two.

'There is nothing unseemly in such a deep and intense friendship. Look at Jesus himself. Out of all his disciples he allowed only John to rest his head on his breast. Not that he did not love the other disciples, but it was a sign that with John he had a special and more intimate friendship. The virgin head upon the virgin breast. One might even call it a heavenly marriage.'

At this point a loud clattering outside the door broke the spell Father Edwin had cast over us both, and loosed Edgar's tongue.

'Reverend Father,' he cried, 'Sir William de Mortimer is demanding to see Duscath and —'

Before he had time to finish his words the door crashed open. In strode Sir William himself followed by a flurry of monks and servants. My limbs froze. I could not tell if it was from the return of my disease or from pure terror.

I had been so wrapt up in the small world of the infirmary, Edgar, Edwin, the state of my body, the state of my soul, that I had pushed my earthly lord far from my thoughts. Foolishly I had believed that this had pushed him also from my life. Now here before my eyes my foolishness had become flesh, and it was terrible, like a sword in my heart.

Father Edwin moved towards him like a swan protecting its young. 'Sir, really,' he hissed, 'there is a boy here seriously ill. With all due respect you must not —'

'Am I to be kept waiting outside like some peasant until my squire deigns to grant me an audience?' He shot a grim glance at Edgar.

'I was in the process of bleeding him, my lord,' Father Edwin said, less harshly, pointing to a jar of leeches. 'You are lucky your squire is still alive.'

'My lord Abbot,' Sir William shouted, wagging his finger in the direction of Edgar. 'That young pup over there, I sent him to announce my arrival and he did not have the courtesy to come back and tell me what was happening. I trust you will not allow such behaviour to go unpunished.'

A tall, thin man, who was standing beside Sir William, nodded, but his eyes lacked conviction. So this was the lord Abbot. He looked bored by the whole business.

'Sir William,' he said, in a whining nasal voice, 'on behalf of my sons in Christ, who have been most remiss in the observance of due form, may I offer my most humble and sincere apologies. May I also suggest that Father Edwin the infirmarer, you and I meet in my chamber to discuss further the matter of your squire.'

'There is little enough to discuss,' Sir William growled. 'But yes, I will join you there straight away. However, first I will have a few words with my squire. On his own, if you don't mind,' he added threateningly. The room cleared as quickly as it had filled.

As Edwin and Edgar left I felt so alone and deserted I could have wept.

Sir William had a square face with small, harsh features. He was dark, with thick, jet-black hair and eyebrows, and a pointed black beard. His was a face made for scowling and threatening, and these had scored their lines deep into it. So when he tried to look friendly and benign the effect was grotesque, like a smile painted on a war helmet.

As the silence settled on the room, he took my hand and smiled at me.

'Duscath, my boy,' he said, 'forgive my rough entrance, but the insolence of these monks! They've been trying to keep me away from you for days now, and I have been too busy at court to challenge them until today. You are well enough to travel, are you not?' His voice was gruff but gentle. Sir William gentle terrified me more than Sir William angry.

'You're coming back to my household,' he went on. He did not notice that I had not replied. 'Once you're there you'll soon be fit and well, out of this dungeon of a place, and away from these black crows. They've been filling your head with all sorts of nonsense, I've no doubt. I travel to Aberdour today. I have a litter ready to take you with me.'

A litter? For me? I could scarcely believe my ears.

'I — I — could spare you all that trouble, my lord, if I stayed here until I could ride. That should be quite soon. Father Edwin —'

'Let me have a look at you,' he said more harshly. He pulled off my blanket and started poking and pinching my limbs, as if he was judging the quality of a horse.

'They're starving you here as well,' he exclaimed. 'You're as scrawny as a scarecrow. Vegetables and beans! Pah! What kind of food is that for a man? What you need is good red meat and strong wine.'

'We will leave at once,' he went on, 'as soon as I've spoken with the Abbot.'

'But, my lord, it is late in the day. Surely you will not be setting off...?'

'We will be setting off when I say we will be setting off. The insolence of these monks, I see, is catching. A servant will fetch you when we are ready to leave.'

With that he strode out of the room, crashing the door behind him. I lay back and groaned. What was real? Sir William's visit and his command? Or the peaceful sounds of the summer's evening? One must be a vision, sent either from Heaven or Hell, for both could not exist fully in this world. I was young and foolish then, Martin. I did not know.

I was aroused from my trance by Edgar, who put his head round the door.

'He's taking me away,' I whispered, unable to look at him.

'I know. Duscath, I have come to say goodbye. Your time here has been precious to me. I pray God that we will meet again on this earth. But it will not be here in Jedburgh, because I am soon to be moved to the Priory of Inchcolm. I have been told that it is not far away from de Mortimer's chief castle. So perhaps God will grant my prayer. I hope it is your prayer, too.' He bent down and kissed my lips.

In a kiss, Martin, two breaths are mingled and united. It causes a sweetness of mind which rouses and binds together the affection of those who embrace. There are three kinds of kisses: physical, spiritual and intellectual. The first kind is made by the impression of lips upon lips, the second by the union of spirits, and the third through the Spirit of God, by the infusion of grace. In that farewell kiss, which was also a kiss of greeting, soul to soul, all three kisses mingled. My body and my soul were inflamed with such joy and longing that all realities — Sir William and my imminent departure, the whispering of God's voice in the peace of the evening — all fused in that one lingering kiss, filling me with the strength to bear the future.

Then the chaos of my leaving descended. Finally I was bundled into a litter and carried off into the summer's night."

TOTAL ECLIPSE

"It seemed that an age had passed since my Lord and I were last together in Forfar that spring. I returned to Aberdour with the firm intention of leaving his service at the first opportunity, but it was not long before I was dragged down again into the mire. My soul became torpid, and my plans for escape dissolved like a vain dream. But the Lord had not forgotten me.

The Lord saved me, for the waters had risen up to my neck. I sank in muddy depths and had no foothold; I was swept into deep water, and the flood carried me away. I was wearied with crying out, my throat was sore, my eyes grew dim as I waited for God to help me.

The summer lingered that year far into the autumn. We were still in Aberdour long after the harvest had been gathered. Late one evening a group of noisy knights and squires rode through the castle gate. It was my Lord's friend and companion-in-arms, Sir William de Hay. Together they planned a great boar-hunt the next day.

My Lord kicked me off my pallet at first cockcrow and ordered me to get his hunting gear ready. Within the hour a great troop of men, horses and hounds were making their way towards the forest between Dalgety and Cockairnie.

All morning hounds and humans thrashed through the under-growth of the forest. I could not let my Lord out of my sight, for I was to blow the horn, one blast to signal our position to the other hunters, three long blasts if we made the kill.

Finally the quarry was caught and the kill was made beneath the little hill just west of Aberdour. I was ordered to climb to the the top and sound the killing call to bring our scattered party together.

I was happy to escape from the noise and the smell of blood, up on the Dunan, perched high above the treetops, free of shadows. I hated the forest with its lurking shadows and its hidden rustlings. I would have faced ten storms at sea rather than one journey through a forest.

On the top of the Dunan the air was clear and the view was wide and beautiful. Out there in the firth lay Inchcolm, the Island of St Columba, like a great green sea monster.

I gave a loud blast on the horn, and wondered if it could be heard by the brothers out there on the monster's back and if my dear friend Edgar was already there amongst them. For a moment my spirit was there beside the horn's cry, knocking at the salt-stained windows, begging entry. I blew a second time, and wondered why I had done nothing about crossing that narrow strip of sea since my return from Jedburgh. I was sure I would never find the courage or the strength to break away from the blood-thirsty mob down below me. So it was with a heavy heart that I blew the horn for the third and final time.

At first I thought I had blown too hard, for a darkness seemed to be creeping over the world. I knew even then that breath carries the light in some strange fashion to our soul, for often when I practised the horn and blew all my breath away, patches of darkness would appear in front of my eyes. So I took a deep breath and tried to rub away the darkness with my knuckles, but to no avail for the darkness was thickening.

The sun was behind a small cloud, which was not as bright as it had been a moment before. I fell to my knees in terror and prayed for the light to return. A strange silence had fallen. No birds were singing.

It is the end of the world, I thought and what have I done with my life but skulk and dream and long to be what I am not and where I am not? I have been shown the road out of my sinful and useless life and I have not taken it. I have neglected my soul, I have neglected God, and now God is taking away my light.

The cloud had passed away from the face of the sun but it was not the sun any more that hung there but a black hole rimmed with light. I looked over to the island, which was now a black shadow on the dark water, and then it was that I made my vow to God and St Columba.

To you I will give the rest of my days on earth, if any remain; to you, your love, your praise. If the sun comes back to set and rise, tonight will be the last I spend in the household of Sir William de Mortimer.

A shiver of blinding light shone out from the black hole. I threw myself on the ground and thanked God and all his saints, because the sun was returning.

As we rode back to the castle all the talk was not on the hunt but of the sudden darkness. Some of the older men had seen the like before, and old Ralph the chief huntsman proudly spoke the word 'eclipse', and said he had seen hundreds when he was a boy in Huntingdon. You always got them near monasteries. It was all the prayers the monks send up, such a swarm of them that sometimes they would block out Heaven's own light.

There was much laughter at this, although some faces were still pale. It was clear that I had not been the only one to have had the soul terrified out of me by a flash of night at noon.

I have seen several eclipses in my day, Martin. Sometimes the sun completely disappears, sometimes only part of it is covered in darkness. I have seen the moon wax and wane within the night. I have no doubt that some wise person knows a cause for these sudden darknesses, but there can be many reasons behind one cause and all reasons lie with God. I thank God for that first eclipse, for in its shadow the seed planted by Father Edwin and Brother Edgar put forth its first shoot.

My newly made vow was waiting for me when I finally lay down for my afternoon rest. I clutched it to me full of joy and fear. More than anything else I was relieved that at last my life was moving again towards God, and my thoughts were no longer of whether or not I should leave de Mortimer, or when I should leave him, but only of how.

That night there was a special feast in honour of de Hay and his men. I was to pour the wine at the top table. I hated this duty for it seemed to have no end. Stomachs fill with food quickly enough, but soak up wine interminably.

Lady Anicea sat beside her husband, although she had scarcely looked at him all evening. In front of the top table stood Raoul, the young minstrel, making no secret of the fact that all the love songs which he sang so sweetly and sincerely were addressed to her. Sir William clapped and cheered at the young man's performance as loudly as the rest of them.

I was almost asleep on my feet when de Mortimer finally

slumped forward, wine dribbling out of his mouth. His hand, which had been fondling my leg as I stood behind him, now hung loosely by his side.

Lady Anicea spoke quietly to the two guards behind his chair. One of them barked at a servant who was dozing on the floor to fetch a candle. As they lifted Sir William up, all the hall rose, at least all who were still capable of standing, and bade good night to the drunken wreck that was their liege-lord. The guards then dragged him away through the doorway.

I thanked God and St Columba that my last night in de Mortimer's household would not be stained by his attentions. I was supposed to sleep in the passage leading from the top of the stairway to the two chambers where Sir William and Lady Anicea slept separately. Usually it would have been too dangerous for me to sleep elsewhere, but tonight was different.

The hall was stuffy and noisy, and I could not be sure of finding a corner which was not full of piss or vomit. So I decided to sleep outside in the bailey.

It was a still night, and a rising mist carried up from the burn the smell of the dying year. I gulped down the sweet air, then, wrapping myself in my cloak against the chill, I tumbled down behind some barrels out of sight of the murmuring guards.

Although I was by now almost dead with exhaustion I could not sleep. The vow which I had made that day now had a life of its own and urgently drew me on. My body was still within the pale of de Mortimer's household, but already my spirit had left it behind. I could easily have slipped out past the guards there and then, had it not been for my fear of the forest at night.

Excited thoughts raced through my brain. How was I going to reach the Priory? What if there was no boat? And if I ever did reach it, would they allow me to stay, or would they send me back?

When finally sleep came it brought no rest. I was galloping through the forest with a pack of boar-hounds, then suddenly I was being pursued by them, feeling their hot, sticky breath on the back of my neck. I came to a cliff edge, where the sea thundered on the rocks far below. Then I heard Edgar's voice, soft and soothing, telling me not to be afraid, urging me to turn and face the hounds. But it was already too late. I was falling down towards the jagged rocks and the sea.

I awoke with a terrible start, my heart thumping, the sweat of fear all over my body. It was still dark. All I could hear was the whispering of the burn below the castle and the calling of a curlew from the shore. I closed my eyes and prayed that I had not called out in my fright. The whirling in my head began again.

Slowly, anxiously, the dawn came. A cock crowed nearby, then another and another, until all the village rang. The castle was stirring. It was time for me to leave.

I walked through the gate as the first rays of sun were striking the Cullalo heights. The guards gave a cursory nod. They were used to seeing me come and go at all times of the day.

'There goes Sir William's bum-boy,' I heard one of them say, and they both gave a loud guffaw. I was used to such remarks, yet they never failed to leave me as though I had been kicked in the stomach. My legs suddenly became separate beings, reluctant to obey me, but somehow I kept walking. I felt as filthy as their laughter and I said to myself, "What place on earth will take me in?"

The cottages were beginning to spew out their inhabitants, who staggered yawning, stretching and shivering into the cool morning. I did not want to meet anyone, so I decided to go by the coast. I hurried past the small fishing boats drawn up on the harbour beach, and was soon on the path that winds between the rocks and the forest.

The tide was low and still ebbing, revealing the glossy, kelp-covered rocks and skerries. Seals, disturbed by my passing, shuffled clumsily into the calm waters and, more secure in their element, glided close to the shore to investigate what was breaking the peace of the morning.

Beyond the Bellhouse Rock I left the path and walked over the wide sands which stretched to Barnhill Point. There I hoped to find a boat to take me to the island. I could have rung the bell to summon one, but it would also have brought de Mortimer's guards, always eager to find out who was crossing to the Priory, hurrying along the coast.

I struck out across the sands to the water's edge to be as close as I could be to my goal. The solid stone church seemed to be within wading distance from where I was, and I was sure that if my ears had not been filled with the cries of terns and oystercatchers I could have heard the chanting of the canons in their choir.

I waded into the shallows up to my knees. The water was shockingly cold at first, but soon became pleasant. Although the summer was dying the sea still held its warmth. Before I knew it the water was up to my waist, and the shore was far away. Like a fish on a line I was being pulled towards the island.

Suddenly terrified I ploughed back towards the sand. There is an ancient legend hereabouts that between the island and Forthrif the sea is bottomless. By now I was stepping on sand that had never before been uncovered, so far out was the tide, and so far out from the water's edge had I waded. Perhaps the awful chasm started right here, and my next step would find nothing to support it. My clothes were heavy and clinging, and would prevent me from swimming one stroke. I would sink like a waterlogged treetrunk.

Back on the sands I breathed a sigh of relief and hurried on to Barnhill Point as fast as my wet clothes would allow. I would have dearly loved to throw them off there and then, so heavy and restricting had they become, as if the world was trying to stop me from leaving it.

On reaching Barnhill Point I scrambled over the rocks to the little inlet where the Priory boats put in, below the storehouses and the grange-servants' huts. It was all deserted. Not a boat or a person in sight.

I gazed in disbelief and panic rose in me. I climbed the hillside to the bell. It hung there for the same purpose as the one on Bellhouse Rock. I rang and rang for all I was worth. I did not care who heard me this time.

I could see boats on the Island's beaches. Again and again the bell's harsh voice flew like a bird across the still waters to dash against the Priory walls. Still no one stirred, either on this side of the narrows or on the other.

I looked along the coast, and what I saw made my blood freeze in horror. Four men on horse-back were galloping over the sands from Aberdour. There was no hiding, no running. There was only the sea.

I ran down the steep path towards it, over the dark shingle, into the deep black mud. Here I stopped and dragged off my boots and clothes. At once I felt lighter, more agile. My body drew power and hope from its nakedness in the warm air. I felt filled with boundless strength. There was nothing I could not do.

I ran on, my feet disappearing into the mud, which spurted up around me like a black fountain. Stones tore at my feet, but I did not feel any pain. And then I hit the water.

This time there was no fear of the deep. My fear was all behind me, in the dark shape of the horsemen. In front of me was hope, a new life, Edgar, Christ. With my strong young body freed now of its worldly fetters I would conquer that deep and brave its monsters gladly.

I swam away from my fear. I looked back, treading water. The horsemen had reached the rocks at Barnhill Point. One of them had dismounted and was running over the rocks towards the inlet, shouting and waving his arms.

I turned and kept swimming. Over the rush of water I could hear my name, 'Duscath! Duscath!' But it was no longer my name. I had left it in the mud along with my clothes. He might as well have been shouting at a corpse. I was spirit, I was the pale sunshine, I was the bright sea, I had no name. And if I never reached the other shore, my soul would live forever in this new found joy.

On and on I swam. The tide was so low that Meadulse Skerry lay large and exposed like a giant black stepping stone between me and the island. I thanked St Columba for this resting place as I crawled out of the water and lay sprawled face down on the soft shining kelp. I was exhausted. My elation and boundless-seeming strength had both left me. My body was wrapped in a blanket of cold which the warmth of the air could not penetrate. Its only heat came from the burning of jellyfish stings. I felt sick. I crawled on my belly to the low ridge of the skerry, staining the seaweed with blood from the cuts on my feet and legs.

I was well over half way to my goal. Only a short channel separated me from it. I closed my eyes and, humbled now by my weakness, I prayed to St Columba for the strength to carry me over this final stretch.

Then I remembered St Michael. Had he not come to my aid once before when I had been in grave danger? And had I not made a vow to him that I would make some special sacrifice in recognition of his help? I now knew what that would be. I had sloughed off my old name. My new name would be his. If he brought me safely to Inchcolm, and if the Priory took me in, I would become Brother Michael.

My sickness passed and in its place came hunger, a gnawing beast, and I was becoming colder and colder. It was the cold that finally drove me off the rock. If I had been warm I would probably have lain there until the tide floated me off. I slithered carefully down to the water's edge and once again launched myself into the calm sea.

The only sea monsters I had so far encountered were the seals. They seemed to mock my slowness, gliding effortless under and around, popping their heads up near me to snort disdainfully at this ungainly creature of the land.

Often I had to rest, lying on my back, motionless in the arms of the sea. I thought of the great chasm below. If it was bottomless then I was now suspended over infinity.

My imagination dived down and down and, finding no sea bed, returned in a panic. If I drowned now, once my body had risen three times to the surface it would plunge for eternity, never coming to rest, tumbling naked through an infinity of water until the flesh slowly dropped away. Then the bones would keep on falling, at different speeds according to their weights, like the sticks and feathers I would drop over the cliffs at Ha' Craig when I was a boy. And when the last trumpet blew to summon the living and the dead to judgement, who would find my bones in such a place? Not even St Michael himself. These and other wild thoughts whirled around in my head. I was beginning to lose my senses.

I swam on, my determination to reach the island slipping from me as my strength waned. I was very near. I could see figures on the shore, and they could see me, for they were waving and pointing in my direction. I wondered if they thought I was a seal. I turned over on my back to rest.

When at last I forced my aching limbs to swim again I saw a boat coming towards me. Suddenly darkness fell over the earth. Another eclipse, I thought to myself calmly as the water roared in my ears.

If the boat had not reached me at that moment it would have been my last thought on earth. The next thing I was aware of was a large foot in sandals a few inches away from my half-opened eyes. I tried moving but my body was shaken by violent retching. I heard a voice say in French, 'Thank God he's still alive and getting rid of the sea from his guts. He's got half the Forth inside him.'

I rose to my knees wanting to speak, to give thanks for my deliverance from the jaws of death, but all I could do was to retch up salty bile. The cloak that had been thrown over me fell away. I heard a shocked French voice say, 'Dugal, cover up the lad's nakedness at once. He'll have us all damned Away with him to the infirmary.' Sturdy arms lifted me up and swung me over giant shoulders. Like a sack of corn I was carried up the sandy banking and into the infirmary. You might say it was there that I was born into the religious life, and it is there that I will pass out of it and into the arms of my Maker. That time is not now far away."

Michael and Martin, two small figures beside the vast sea, sat for a while in silence listening to the gentle lapping of the waves and the chanting of the gulls above the island cliffs. A bell rang out, calling the brothers to Terce. Slowly, carefully, Martin led the old man to the gatehouse and left him with Malcolm, who took him back to his cell in the infirmary.

PART TWO
A NEW SONG

*I waited, waited for the Lord, and He bent down to me
     and heard my prayers,
He led me out of the pit of wretchedness, out of the mire
     and the dregs.
He put my feet upon a rock and guided my steps,
     and into my mouth He put a new song.*

Novi auxilii petitio psalm 39

FIRST DAYS

"**B**y the next day I had completely recovered from my ordeal by water, and was bursting with curiosity to explore my new world. Would it welcome me or cast me out? But it simply lay quiet and did nothing. Had they all died, I wondered, or were they going to keep me prisoner until de Mortimer came for me? Perhaps they had forgotten me, or perhaps they just didn't care.

My schooling began that day, and my first lesson was in the virtue of patience. I was locked in one of the infirmary cellars and the only person I saw was the servant Dugal who brought me food. At first he refused to speak to me, but I finally got out of him that the election of the new Prior was still in progress, and until it was over I would have to wait.

By the morning of the next day I was desperate for ways to escape. Had they rescued me just to torture me like this? It would have been kinder to have let me drown. All I could think of was getting back into the water again and swimming, this time for the open sea.

The door of my prison crashed open.

'Faither Brice wants tae see ye,' Dugal said gruffly.

At last, I thought, as I followed him out into the cold wind, through the Priory gate and into the cloister. My heart was beating fast with excitement. The scent of herbs and flowers sweetened the air. It came from the well-tended garden in the cloister garth. Dugal opened the door of the chapter house and pushed me inside. There in the centre of the room, his arms folded, stood a wiry little man in his middle years, extraordinarily thin, with dark piercing eyes. He greeted me without smiling, and immediately began to interrogate me. Who was I? Was I a freeman? What was my status and my family? Why had I arrived on the island in such an unusual and barbaric manner? What was I fleeing from? What did I want from the convent: sanctuary, or something more?

I answered his questions as fully and honestly as I could, up to a certain point. I made no mention of Edgar. Something told me that here was not a man of Edwin's stamp, and such ground must be trodden upon with care.

'So you want to become a brother here, do you?' he sneered. 'Out of one life and into another, just like jumping into the water. You have committed a serious crime, Duscath mac Flathbertaich. The hue and cry has already been raised. The fight is about to begin. There is only one question I need an answer to. Are you worth fighting for? Are you worth the struggle that lies ahead?'

So he knew all along who I was. They lock me away for days, I thought to myself, then they ask me questions they already know the answers to, and finally they ask me if I'm worth the trouble. I was angry at having been treated so shabbily and at finding myself at the mercy of this unpleasant little man.

It was nothing but pride, Martin. In the sea, pushing myself through the cold water, I had felt completely in control of my destiny. I was beholden to no one and nothing but the strength of my limbs and the depth of my breath. I had taken a vow, devised a plan of escape and succeeded. Out there on the deep I had tasted freedom, and with it pride. Now my soul smarted for it. Had I done all that I had done to be once more trapped in my own powerlessness? Surely I deserved better than this?

All this must have clearly rung in my voice when I answered, 'Reverend Father, that is the one question which it is impossible for me to answer.'

'Who said I was asking you?' he snapped. 'I will answer it, with God's guidance.' He put his face close to mine. I could smell his breath fetid from too much fasting. I took it into my lungs without flinching. 'On your knees, young man, and pray God for humility. Pride gains no entry here.' Then he strode out of the room, leaving me alone with my thoughts.

I was indeed humbled. Moreover, I was frightened and nothing humbles more than fear. I begged God not for humility, but simply to be allowed to stay. Everything had gone wrong. If the Priory rejected me, I had nowhere to turn. I would be thrown into prison by de Mortimer. I would be finished. My mouth filled with wild and wilful prayers, and my chest heaved with self-pitying sobs. So that when I became aware of a figure standing over me, I flung myself at it, clasped its knees and begged not to be sent back.

'My son, my son, calm yourself. No one is sending you back. You are to stay here for as long as God wills. And God is merciful.' It was a kindly voice, full of reassurance, not the voice of Subprior Brice. I looked up and saw a man in early middle age. His hair was black, but his beard was grizzled, as if old age was creeping up on him from below. He was tall and broad-shouldered, and looked very strong. His eyes, however, assured me that here was not a violent man. They were large, dark, deep-set eyes which reminded me of the eyes of a large, gentle dog, an impression reinforced by his heavy jowls. It was Walter, the newly elected Prior of Inchcolm.

I was the first crisis that Walter had to face in his new office. From that first undignified meeting he became my support, my shield, my advocate. I don't know why. The only thing I brought with me into my new world was trouble, and he must have known that even before meeting me.

He handed me over to Father William the guest and novice-master, saying, 'You will be treated as a guest until tomorrow. Listen carefully to what he has to say, my son, and may God and St Columba hear our prayers.'

He had already explained to me that the following day the community would decide whether or not to accept me as a novice. He had warned me that I would be called before Chapter to answer questions about myself, so that all the brothers might see and hear me, the better to decide my future. I was terrified at the thought. First my ordeal by water, then my ordeal by waiting, and now my ordeal by Chapter. If I could have chosen one, I would have chosen the water.

Father William the guestmaster was very tall and thin with enormous ears. He was very talkative, and when he had nothing else to say, would return to his favourite subject, his intense dislike of St Columba's Island.

'Why they ever had to send me here in the first place I don't know. They knew I couldn't stand water. Just looking at the water in the lavabo makes me seasick. And here I am, surrounded by it. They say Hell is full of fire. Well, I imagine it full of water. And they say you swam here! My dear boy, if the Devil himself was chasing me I wouldn't put even my big toe in the water, unless I was quite sure I'd be able to get it out again. They have to blindfold me every time I cross the firth, treat me like a poor frightened horse.'

William found time amid all this chatter to ask me the questions they have to ask someone wanting to become a novice: what country was I from, who were my parents, how much scripture did I know, how many languages, how many foreign countries; could I write, sing, execute any mechanical art; what obligations did I have, was I in a relationship with a woman, did I have any children, was I in debt?

I did not have to undergo being stripped and examined to see if my body was whole, as there had been ample opportunity to verify that on my arrival. My general state of health must also have been obvious, though he did ask me if I was prone to fits.

I told him about the strange sickness that had befallen me at Jedburgh, but he seemed more interested in whether I had met his old friend Father Richard the cellarer there. Then he told me what I had to do the next day at Chapter, and what to expect. It did nothing to calm me.

I slept a deep, dreamless sleep, and woke feeling refreshed and clear-headed. I waited expectantly for my breakfast, but instead Father William put his head round the door and told me to follow him immediately.

We sped along the cloister into the chapter house and my ordeal by Chapter began.

I had prepared myself to meet a room full of eyes turned on me. I would walk through their staring, up to the Prior, and throwing myself on the ground before him, beg forgiveness for all my sins. These were my instructions, tossed out to me casually by Father William the night before. What he had not told me, or I had not remembered, was that to begin with only Prior Walter and Subprior Brice would be there, the two of them, sitting in their high chairs of office, opposite the door. I stopped in surprised relief, unsure what to do next.

William pushed me forward. 'Go on, prostrate yourself,' he whispered crossly.

I lunged forward, tripped over my feet, and landed in a heap in front of them. I was glad to lay my face on the cold stone floor to hide my confusion.

'Get up, Duscath.' It was Prior Walter's voice. 'When you are led before Chapter after morning Mass, come in more slowly, not as if the Devil is after you. Now, I want you to listen carefully to what Father Brice has to say.'

The memory of my first meeting with Father Brice froze my blood. He was a good man, Martin, some say a saint, and God forbid that I should slander his name. But he spared neither himself nor others in his search for righteousness. He certainly did not spare me.

'Duscath mac Flathbertaich, we are informed that you have been Sir William de Mortimer's catamite for several years now. Is this true?'

I wanted to crawl back onto the floor. His eyes burned into me. I told him the truth. Was it not written all over me?

'Is that what drove you here?'

'I suppose so. One of the things.'

'There is a wise saying, young man, that whatever you run away from will be waiting for you in the cloister. Do you understand what it means?'

I did not understand. My head was spinning. I was very frightened. He went on speaking, but I could make no sense of his words.

'Brice,' Walter cut in, 'the boy is terrified out of his wits.'

At this note of kindness something broke inside me and I started to cry. Someone took my hand. I looked up and saw it was Walter. Brice and William had disappeared.

'Duscath, you must not be afraid. We all have our demon to overcome. The Devil is strong and his demons legion, but our weapons are sharp and good. They are prayer, self-discipline, constant vigilance. You also are strong, although just now you do not feel it, and with God's help and the love and support of our community in Christ you will overcome your demon.'

What is my demon? I thought to myself. Will I know it when I see it? I have a guardian angel, too. When I see a shadow in the night, or hear a voice whispering to me in the silence, how will I know which one it is? I lowered my head in confusion.

'Father William tells me you can read and write and know some Latin,' Prior Walter went on quietly.

'Father Abraham was a good teacher. But there was not much time.'

'I think also that you were a good pupil. The Priory has great need of such skills. Until now we have been more a community of builders than of priests and teachers. Buildings are important, but if they house nothing but ignorance and the unlettered, I do not think God is best served.'

He paused, then asked gently, 'Is there anything else you want to know?'

'I no longer want to be called Duscath,' I replied. 'I made a vow that if by God's mercy I became a brother here, I would take the name of Michael, in memory of the great saint whose power and glory touched me at his Abbey in Normandy.'

'Michael,' Walter said, smiling, 'yes, a good name, and we do not have a Michael amongst us. Also I think it will please many of our brothers, who find Scottish names difficult for the tongue.

'Now, Michael, Chapter is about to begin. At it there will be those who will want to know more about your relations with Sir William. Each must answer to God and his own soul why they want to know, but it is not for you to tell them. I will make that clear from the start. Subprior Brice is concerned not just for your soul, but for those of his brothers. He seems harsh because he is afraid, both of God and of the Devil. And what else is there to fear?'

A bell rang out loudly. He shouted above it, 'That is the bell for Chapter. Let your strength shine, Michael, God's strength will come to meet it. Go now, Father William is waiting for you outside. And remember, not so fast this time.'

When I entered the chapter house for the second time that morning I was completely calm. It was a calmness rooted not just in the reassuring words of Prior Walter, but also in exhaustion. What else is there to fear but God and the Devil? Both seemed to have deserted me, so what indeed was there to fear? I felt as indifferent to my fate as a piece of flotsam, to be pulled out of the water or thrown back in on the whim of the finder.

'I don't care anymore,' I thought to myself, as I obediently lay prone on the floor at Walter's feet and begged his permission to become a novice. Not caring, that is where I got my strength from in that hour, but now I realise also how much Walter was a staff and comfort to me, and that God had not deserted me after all.

We got through the formalities of reception quickly enough, the lecture on the strictness of the Order, its essentials of perpetual chastity, poverty and obedience, which are directly opposed to the flesh, the world and the Devil.

'For many years now,' I said, 'I have wanted to join a religious community, ever since I made a pilgrimage to Mount St Michael when I was in Normandy with my lord. My recent sojourn in the infirmary at Jedburgh, and long conversations with various brothers there, have only strengthened my resolve.'

'He has come from a household which is not renowned for its obedience to God's laws. How can we be sure he does not bring the contagion of the sinful with him?' These words were spoken by a tall young canon with a thin arrogant face. It was Brother Nicholas, an ambitious and unpleasant man, who later became Abbot of Cambuskenneth. I wanted to reply that I had fled at the first possible opportunity, but before I could open my mouth, another brother was on his feet.

'God alone knows that, but what we do know is that he brings with him the wrath of the sinful and of the powerful.'

Then a small, plump, figure stood up. He threw back his cowl to reveal a smooth-skinned ageless face. It was Brother Peter the sacrist. In a strange, high pitched, rhythmic voice he intoned,

'They surround me like bees at the honey, they attack me, as fire attacks brushwood, but in the Lord's name I will drive them away. The Lord is my refuge and my defence.'

He sat down as suddenly as he had stood up, and threw his cowl back over his head. All the brothers murmured 'Amen'.

Then Brother Nicholas spoke again.

'Look how beautiful he is. The Devil is beautiful. He comes to tempt and destroy. He has lured Sir William to perdition, now he comes to lure us. We are fools to take the risk. Send him to live among the demoniacs at Cambuskenneth, or back to Sir William, who has not stopped clamouring for him since the boy arrived here.'

'Only the Devil could have swum over the deep!' someone shouted.

'With God's help, or the Devil chasing, anything is possible!' another cried.

'Send him back!' several cried at once.

'In the name of Christ's charity, let him stay,' another shouted, and some said 'Amen'.

'My sons in Christ,' shouted Prior Walter, stemming the tide of voices that was rising all around, 'this young man has come to us seeking sanctuary, which we are bound to grant him, no matter who he is or who is pursuing him.

'He has also come seeking to be a novice. I have spoken to him at length, I have prayed, and I am certain that he is worthy to be accepted as such. The novitiate is a testing time, and it will answer all our questions and our doubts. Also he has skills which our Priory needs. Father William will report on that shortly. As for de Mortimer, as Brother Peter so rightly says, 'The Lord is my defence.'

Brother Peter was on his feet again intoning, 'They may curse, but Thou dost bless: may my opponents be put to shame, but may Thy servants rejoice!'

'Amen,' everyone muttered.

Walter frowned. 'Thank you, Brother Peter. If I may continue. My decision is that we will accept this youth as a novice. If he proves unworthy, he must return to the world. Duscath mac Flathbertaich,' he said, turning to me, placing his hand on my head, 'Do you, having heard all that the rule entails, and knowing the severe test which lies before you, still want to submit to its harshness, for the sake of your soul and its everlasting salvation?'

'I do.'

Then he offered me the scroll and the bread, which two brothers handed him.

'We grant you part and fellowship in our brotherhood, so that henceforth you may share with us spiritual things as well as bodily things, like a brother.

'Henceforth also, in earnest of your will to become reborn in Christ, you will take the name of Michael. May the strength of St Michael the Archangel and slayer of demons be with you always.' He then kissed me, and ordered all the other brothers to do the same. Several did so with closed eyes.

So I am not being thrown back into the sea I thought, at least not yet."

NOVICE

"I was a model novice, obedient, deferential, eager to learn. This was my chosen life, and I gave myself to it zealously and completely. Everything about it excited me: the rhythm of the day, the chanting of the Psalter, the ritual, even the simple food, which tasted better to me than the finest delicacies on Sir William's table. Also I slept so well in the times allotted for sleep that I scarcely felt tired at all.

My greatest joy was learning, both Latin and writing. I had been given the rudiments by Father Abraham, but there had been no text books, scarcely any time, even less parchment. Now I was able to study the queen of all languages through the great masters Priscius and Donatus. I could practise different hands by copying from the ones in our library, using properly nibbed quills and scraps of well prepared parchment.

No, I was not only able to do this, I was expected to do this. It was my duty, and my head swam with the pleasure of it.

Father William the guestmaster was also the novice master. I got on well with him because he loved teaching, and which teacher does not love the eager, adept pupil? Like most teachers, he also had his stern, impatient side, but it was mostly reserved for my fellow novice Isaac.

Isaac became a good and faithful friend, although he had every reason to hate and envy me during that time. He was slow to learn those things that Father William wanted to teach us. He was not interested, and was often beaten for not understanding or not paying attention.

I tried to help him. Several times I got a beating for it, for nothing could protect us from William's eagle eye. I would pray to St Jerome to give some of my love of learning to Isaac, not too much, for I enjoyed being best pupil, but enough to save him from the flailing rod.

Isaac had been placed in the Priory by his family. His mother was related to Sir Philip de Moubray, from whom they held lands at Cockairnie. His brothers were all fighting men. Isaac, with his broad shoulders and massive hands, would have been far happier wielding the sword than the quill, but the family had too many sword-arms and too few praying hands, so it fell to Isaac, the youngest, to make good this deficiency. The Priory had welcomed him because he had brought with him a good portion of land and a regular annual income. But even if he had brought with him all of Fothrif, Father William would have shown no mercy.

After a few weeks we were joined by another novice, Andrew, a kinsman of Subprior Brice, whose family were burgesses of the royal burgh of Inverkeithing. He was younger than Isaac and myself, a small, scrawny youth with a thickly freckled face, a long, pointed nose, and thin, tense lips. He bore an uncanny resemblance to a rat, and this outward appearance seemed to leave its imprint on his soul.

He, like Isaac, hated learning, but he was too quick-witted to let Father William see this. He always did just enough to get by. He did love learning the weak spots of his fellows, however, and once he had mastered them he would delight in probing them and turning them to his advantage. He liked nothing better than following the Rule which says that we should bring a brother's fault not just to his own attention but to that of others. In this way he secured several beatings for Isaac. But his tale-telling was done with such a show of false humility that the brothers, especially Father William, did not seem to see through it.

With me Andrew's poison took another form.

Every Friday the three of us, with Father William, would walk over to the goose-pens. They are away at the west end of the island, well out of ear-shot of the Priory, so that their infernal cackling does not disturb our peace. There we would collect the best feathers to sharpen into quills for our own use, and for Father Geoffrey the precentor.

One day William was unwell, so the three of us were allowed to go over to the geese alone.

We were climbing the brae when Andrew said to me innocently, 'Aren't you frightened to go wandering about unprotected so far from the Priory, Michael?'

I was completely taken aback by this, but before I could ask him what he meant, Isaac cut in, 'Oh, shut up, you wee wretch, you're the one that ought to be afraid. There are a lot of cliffs around here, and it would be such a shame if your foot happened to slip.'

'Are you threatening me, you little toad? Just wait till Father William hears about this. You heard that, didn't you, Michael, and it was your safety I was worried about.'

'It's two against one, Andrew,' I said. 'Just shut up, as Isaac suggests. I can do without your concern, thank you very much.'

'Oh, listen to him,' Andrew retorted, 'the peasant's son telling me what to do. Sounds like lordly ways rub off in bed.'

'What do you mean by that?' I asked, knowing exactly what he meant but wanting to cheat him a little longer of my anger. Besides we could still be seen from the Priory.

'What do you mean by that?' Andrew said in a simpering voice, mocking my accent. 'As if you didn't know. You might be a Scot, but you're not that stupid. Just watch he doesn't come and take you back again, that's all, though God knows why anyone would want you back. Good riddance, that's what I say. We can well do without whores here.'

I saw red and lunged at him, but he was ready for it, and ran shrieking towards the Priory. Isaac held me back from giving chase. I stopped feeling angry, and just felt embarassed and humiliated. I turned my face away from Isaac and hurried towards the goose-pens.

Both Isaac and I got a beating when we got back that day. Of course we couldn't tell Father William of the provocation, and anyway good Christian brothers are not supposed to let themselves be provoked.

I could have forgotten the wicked things Andrew taunted me with, and that was not the only time he did so, far from it, but I knew he was not alone in the Priory in thinking as he did. This gave barbs to his foolish jibes, so that they stuck in my soul and festered.

The only thing Andrew did not taunt me with was my good

looks. It stuck in his throat to make any mention of them. But sometimes I would catch him gawking at me, and as soon as he caught my eye he would make a great show of crossing himself, as though warding off some evil.

All this nonsense was kept firmly in check by Prior Walter and the more sensible and charitable brothers, including Father William. This was indeed a gift from God, for at that time I was prone to absorb any poison that was spread about me.

The only way I felt that I could prove to others, and to myself, that I was sincere in my vocation, and stood no nearer to the Devil than any other mortal, was by being the perfect novice. And this was where Andrew most sorely tried me.

For a time, however, all these worries were forgotten, when one day in Chapter, shortly after my first Epiphany on the island, it was announced that a new canon was joining our community. He had recently been accepted into the Order at the Abbey of St Mary Jedburgh, and his name was Edgar.

Can you imagine my joy? No one knew of my previous encounter with Edgar, no one that is except Father William, who was also my confessor. I had told him how I had felt drawn towards Edgar in pure friendship, which I hoped could now grow and blossom. I did not tell him that my body and blood had been drawn to him in a darker way. Given what was being said about me in the convent, this was too dangerous a subject to broach, even with William. If only there had not been the talk, the rumours, the suspicion, then perhaps I might have felt free and brave enough, and perhaps, later, the infatuation might not have been so great.

From the time that I learnt of Edgar's arrival my dreams of a friendship with him flared up like fire amongst dry bracken. My heart ached for a friendship that was neither carnal nor spiritual but total. It was through the ache of these dreams that I suddenly became aware of how lonely I was.

The day before Edgar was due to arrive I was sent to the infirmary with a fever. I lay there for three days while strange dreams swirled around me. On the third day Brother Maurice brought visitors in to see me. I watched with pounding heart as first Edgar, then Isaac, then Andrew, filed into the room. Edgar embraced me and gave me the kiss of peace.

'So, my dear brother, we meet again in the house of weakness. I hear you have been anything but weak since we last met. I congratulate you.'

I was blushing, and thanked God it was dark enough to go unnoticed. I felt extremely uncomfortable with Andrew there, who was watching me closely. I longed to be on my own with Edgar, but the thought also terrified me, and set my heart pounding even more fiercely. I thanked him for his kind words.

He had addressed me in faltering French. I replied in his own tongue, Inglis. 'I drew my strength from St Mary's Jedburgh.

Father Edwin was a most inspiring physician, and so was my nurse.'

Here Andrew butted in.

'Michael, you are forbidden to speak Inglis, on Father Brice's orders. Sorry, Brother Edgar.'

He gave Edgar an ingratiating smile and sat back.

It's only because Andrew cannot understand what we're saying, I thought, furious at this interference. Imagine coming from Inverkeithing and not speaking Inglis. It shows what a stuck-up family he comes from. I almost gave voice to my thoughts, but I checked myself, not wanting to quarrel in front of Edgar.

We exchanged a few commonplaces, and the visit was at an end, with Andrew reminding us that the bell for Vespers would soon be ringing.

In the following weeks I saw hardly anything of Edgar, and why should I? He was a brother, I was a novice, he was not the novice-master, nor was he my confessor. But I thought of nothing else. Even my lessons seemed dull. The effort of keeping my recalcitrant mind on them left me exhausted and dispirited. I did not want anyone to know what was going on inside me. In confession I talked a lot about Demon Sloth, little about Demon Lust.

Perhaps that was how I saw it myself at that time. Our ability to deceive others is surpassed only by our ability to deceive ourselves. Father William was taken in, as was Isaac. Even I might have been taken in. From Andrew there were no snide remarks or vicious comments, and so I thought that he too had been taken in.

He had not been taken in, but held his tongue because he knew that there was something far worse in store for me than his taunting.

It must have been quite unnerving for Edgar. As soon as he arrived in his new home he was afflicted by an infatuated novice making eyes at him wherever he turned. His reaction was naturally to avoid me as much as possible, which only made me worse.

One day about a month after Edgar had arrived on the island, I was sitting in the cloister after Nones, supposedly doing Latin grammar, but instead I was staring into the cloister garth and thinking of Edgar.

Suddenly a touch on my arm made me jump. It was Andrew. Putting his finger to his lips. He whispered that he had an important message from Edgar. I was to meet him at the east end of the island as soon as possible. He was already there waiting for me. I could not believe my ears. I wanted to jump for joy right there and then, but I restrained myself.

Instead I whispered, 'But how am I to get there without being seen?'

'It's all right,' Andrew replied, 'everybody's asleep as usual, and if you're stopped say you're away to gather gulls' eggs for the kitchen.'

I was off like an arrow from a bow. Thrusting my Donatus into Andrew's hands I sped out the gate towards the isthmus.

As I was in a hurry I decided to go over the top of the east island rather than round the track by the shore. There was scarcely a track going over the hill, but I knew the ground well and I knew that it was the quickest way to the east end.

It was the gulls that gave me the first warning. They seemed to be very disturbed, so many of them wheeling and crying out in their harsh voices that something was amiss. One person waiting quietly at the east end could hardly cause such commotion amongst them. I slowed my pace as I descended, treading more cautiously.

I began to feel as uneasy as the gulls. Why would Edgar have used Andrew of all people as a go-between? Why use a go-between at all? And why choose such an out-of-the-way spot? Suddenly it didn't make sense.

There was a low clump of bushes nearby, where the land fell away steeply to the sea. I crept over and, hiding behind them, peered towards the east end. What I saw sent my heart into my mouth: a man on the rocks by the sea holding a rope attached to a small boat wedged in amongst the skerries. While beside the track nearby stood three other men. They were obviously waiting for someone coming along the track by the shore. They were waiting for me. If I had been coming along the track I would not have seen them till the very last moment, too late to run away. From the cover of the bush I could see their faces clearly. I recognised them, de Mortimer's men, every one of them.

I was frozen to the spot, sure that I would be seen as soon as I left my hiding-place. But even then I had a head start, and they could only pursue me so far. How far? With a sickening fear I realised that the enemy was not just out there in front of me. Andrew was involved in this, nor would he be acting alone. My mind flashed back to all those who wanted rid of me. Head of the list was Brice, though I found it hard to believe he would stoop to such an underhand business. They could take me at the Priory gate. They might even go further. Who would lift a hand to help me? Precious few, what with Walter away in Rome and — "

"What?" exclaimed Martin. "Walter was in Rome?"

"Of course he was in Rome," Michael replied irritated. "At the Great Lateran Council. He had left just after Christmas and didn't get back till midsummer. What was more he had Father Nigel with him, who also liked me and wanted me to stay. Surely I told you that."

Martin was sure he had not, but the old man's voice was

querulous, so he replied meekly, "Yes, I think you did. Sorry. Please go on."

"Well, I knew I had to keep out of sight. Crouching as low as I could I started making my way back up the hill. The three men on the track were not the problem, for I could easily keep out of their sight. The problem was the man by the boat. He had been crouching down attending to the boat when I first saw him. Now he was standing up and looking around.

I had gained the summit of the hill when he must have spotted me, and up went the cry. I sped down the other side like a stag before the hounds, and was half way across the isthmus by the time my pursuers came thundering into view along the shore track. I did not shout for help. I decided to save my breath for the run.

I got to the gate, only to find it was barred from the inside. Now was the time for shouting. My pursuers had already crossed the isthmus. There was no other way into the Priory except by going back onto the shore and round by the infirmary. By now I had lost my momentum, and my head-start. I had to get through the gate. There was no other way.

I could hear voices on the other side of the gate, as if there was an argument going on. What a time to choose to have an argument, I thought. For God's sake, please let me in! Then I heard the bar being drawn back and the gate swung outwards. I threw myself in through the gap and slammed the gate behind me, pulling the bar across. I fell back exhausted against the thick wooden planks as my pursuers thudded into the other side. I closed my eyes and offered a prayer of thanksgiving to St Michael.

When I opened my eyes again in front of me stood Edgar and Andrew, both staring at me as if they had seen a ghost. For one terrible moment I thought Edgar was involved in the plot too.

As if from a great distance I heard Edgar shouting at me, 'Go to the church, get into sanctuary, at once.' He grabbed my arm, pushing me in the direction of the choir. 'I'll stay here and make sure no one lets them in.'

I heard Andrew shouting half-heartedly, 'Ring the alarm bell, we're under attack!' as I hurried down the cloister into the dark, quiet choir.

In fact de Mortimer's men did not try to force their way in. As soon as I had disappeared through the gate they turned tail and ran back to their boat. From the church I could hear the alarm notes of the bell change to the slower call for Vespers.

Pale and trembling I waited at the south door for my brothers to file in, taking my place with the other novices beside Father William at the back of the choirstalls.

By collation everyone knew that de Mortimer had tried to abduct me. With tightly pursed lips Subprior Brice offered up a prayer of thanksgiving for my deliverance, and Amen was muttered with varying degrees of conviction.

I was still trembling inside but now more with rage than with fear. Several of the brothers offered me the kiss of peace and shook my hands. Andrew was one of them. As his face drew near to mine he whispered, 'You tell them I sent you, I'll tell them what you were going for.'

'Judas,' I hissed, and he squeezed my hand and smiled. Wait till Prior Walter gets back, I thought. Oh God, if only he were here now, this would never have happened. They would never have dared.

At Chapter the next day Edgar broached the subject of my abduction, accusing Andrew of complicity, not because of anything I had said, but because he had been so tardy in opening the gate when I was pleading to get in. Andrew squirmed and reddened. He started to speak, very softly, so that everyone had to lean forward to catch his words.

'I was so afraid that I was unable to draw the bar back, because I saw something more terrible than anything on this earth. Michael was running away from a great horned beast, black, with an awful red mouth and huge teeth. I swear it was the Devil himself. I was terrified. I did not want to let the Devil into the Priory.'

'Preposterous!' Edgar shouted. 'I saw three men from the dormitory window. That's why I came down to the gate, to find Andrew barring it.'

'I saw the Beast!' Andrew screamed. 'I saw the Beast coming after Michael! You're trying to protect him because he's cast a spell on you. You'd better watch out that the Beast doesn't come and get you.'

'Did anyone else witness these events?' Brice snapped.

'I saw three men running away from the Priory,' said Serlo.

'I smelt sulphur in the cloister!' Henry shouted.

'Your farts, Brother Henry,' retorted Edgar.

'Brother Edgar, this is not a matter for levity.'

'Father Brice, I apologise. But really! It might have been the noontide devil that appeared to Andrew, but there are enough witnesses to testify that three corporeal men were on the island yesterday, and got as far as the Priory gate, and those men intended harm to novice Michael.'

'The Devil appears in many forms, my sons,' Brice said solemnly. 'I fear we may never know the truth. But Brother Edgar, you show scant understanding for the plight of novice Andrew. The youth was only doing what he thought best, and all you did was to abuse him. Brother Edgar, apologise to novice Andrew. Now.'

Edgar looked round, an expression of astonished outrage on his face, looking for support from his brothers. None was forthcoming, least of all from me, who could have said most.

He mumbled an apology and sat down. I felt I had betrayed him.

In the days that followed, I longed to explain things to him, but no opportunity presented itself. I had considered requesting an interview with him in the parlour, and asking Father William to listen in, but decided it was too risky. I might say too much. Once I started, God knows what might come tumbling out. So I prayed to St Columba and to St Valentine, because Valentine understands and looks with sympathy upon the pangs of love. They heard my prayer.

You don't know what a joy this is, Martin, to talk without restrictions or eavesdroppers. It is a privilege rarely accorded those who follow the Rule of St Augustine, and quite right too, I may add. Imagine if we were all allowed to chatter idly on as I am doing now, God's work would never be done, and His praises never sung.

It was hard, though, not being able to exchange any words with Edgar. Then one warm, still afternoon, we found ourselves on our own, hoeing and weeding in the vegetable garden by the old hermit's hut. As we worked we were able to talk, quietly, never looking up. First of all I told him what had happened that terrible afternoon.

'I knew that boy was trying to keep you out, may God punish his wickedness. But I am sorely vexed that he used me as the bait.'

'It was cruel,' I said, suddenly overwhelmed with self-pity, and holding back the tears. 'I so wanted to see you, and speak to you. Edgar, I love you.' I blurted it out, unable to stop myself.

'Michael, keep your voice down.' His harsh tone hurt, but brought me to my senses, and saved me from further indiscretions.

'Edgar, I want to be close to you all the time, to share the secrets of my soul with you, in the way old Father Edwin told us about. We shared something special that time in Jedburgh. I know it wasn't one-sided. Why can't it go on and grow?'

'Michael, listen carefully. Whatever we feel does not matter. If we were Cistercian monks under Abbot Ailred in Rievaulx forty years ago, it might be different. But we are not, we are Augustinians, it is the year of our Lord 1179, and Mother Church now frowns upon such things. You must put these thoughts out of your head. Father Edwin was foolish to talk like that to you in the first place.'

'I can perhaps put such thoughts out of my head,' I replied. 'I cannot put such feelings out of my breast. Nor can you, if you were honest.'

There was silence. We both hoed more vigorously, angrily, but in unison. After a while I spoke again, calmer now.

'Edgar, if we go about this sensibly, we can work something out. I'll speak to Prior Walter when he gets back. He allows Serlo and Geoffrey to work together and sit together in choir. He will do the same for us.'

Edgar stopped hoeing and looked at me.

'Michael, don't you know the reputation you've got? Some brothers look at you as though you were the Whore of Babylon. Any closeness between us would be completely misconstrued. Even Prior Walter couldn't alter that.'

'So that's it!' I rounded on him angrily. 'You don't care about me at all. You're just worried about your reputation. You probably believe the wicked stories they spread about me, but you're too cowardly to admit it. If that's what you really feel, I wouldn't want your friendship anyway.'

'That's not true, Michael, and you know it,' he said in an aggrieved voice.

'It is so true,' I growled, giving a furious thrust with my hoe and cutting down a row of young lettuce. 'The Devil take it,' I swore. 'Now see what you've made me do! Father William will kill me. And I don't care.'

'Michael, I'm sorry,' Edgar said. He stopped hoeing and bent to repair the damage. The sun shone on his hair, making it bright yellow. I can still see it, like stubble in a cornfield on his tonsured crown, and a profusion of curls around his ears. My anger drained away and I was filled with love for him. 'It's all right,' he was saying, 'you cut deep. We'll put what's left of the roots back in the ground and hope for the best.'

I bent down beside him. He went on.

'Michael, it's a dangerous game you want us to play. Your enemies are everywhere, waiting for another chance to pounce. Don't make it easy for them. We can wait. One thing we have plenty of here is time. Let's wait till you have finished your novitiate, and have been accepted as a canon here. Then perhaps we can each have a word in Prior Walter's ear. Till then let's be prudent, and pray for times such as today. There now, you'd never know those lettuces had been cut down in their prime. With a bit of care they might live to see a ripe old age. And Michael, one other thing. Please don't keep staring at me. How else do you think Andrew and his accomplices knew what bait to use?'

I was about to lift my hoe to him in jest when Father William came strolling into the garden to inspect our work.

St Columba, even with St Valentine interceding, did not grant another such afternoon to Edgar and me for a long time, but he had already granted enough. My spirit was lightened once more and free to devote itself to the joys of learning and worship. I had explained myself to Edgar. He had not rebuffed me. We had a plan, we had a future, and he was on my side.

Since the attempt on my person Brice had forbidden me to leave the Priory precincts. He also gave me a bell to ring if I was ever in danger.

'It won't do you much good, of course, if you go gallivanting around the island, but then you've no business to be outside the precincts, have you, Michael? Not for gulls' eggs, not for anything.'

'No, Father Brice.'

'And I've told Father William you're no longer to go to the goose-pens with the other novices. You can help prepare parchment in the cloister.'

'Thank you, Father.'

'One other thing. Prior Walter will be back soon. He'll want a full report of what happened, so that he can lodge an official complaint with Earl David. This is the kind of thing that happens when we have no Bishop to watch over us. I have already written down the details as you recounted them in Chapter. They are official. You will not be changing anything once our Prior returns, will you?'

'Changing anything, Father?' I asked innocently, my heart beating fast. So, he did know about the plot. He is trying to protect Andrew and himself. I've got him, I thought triumphantly.

'Father, what has happened has happened. I believe in forgiving and forgetting, as is my duty as a Christian.'

'Very good, my son, very good.'

There was almost a smile on his sour face. I soon put a stop to that.

'But, Father, if anything similar should happen again, or if there should be any undue or undeserving talk about getting rid of me, then I am afraid that Prior Walter will have to know all the circumstances.'

I stressed the word 'all', looking him straight in the eye. He held my stare for a moment with his bright, piercing gaze, then turned away. It was the first time I had outstared him.

'Go in peace, novice Michael,' he snapped, 'and go carefully.'

I knelt to receive his blessing, then hurried away. The moment of triumph had passed, but I felt more secure in the Priory than I ever had. Yet I knew that I must always be on my guard, especially while Prior Walter was still away. I prayed fervently for his safe and speedy return.

Prior Walter did return, safe and sound, shortly after the Feast of St John the Baptist, thinner and paler than when he had left six months before.

No one rejoiced more than I did that Walter had returned safely, but my rejoicing was short lived, for he brought stern words with him from Rome and the Holy Father.

After years of struggle with Emperor Frederick, Pope Alexander had seen him prostrate himself at his feet to beg for mercy and the papal blessing. He had crushed those who had set themselves up as Pope against him and had seen the Papal Court return in triumph to Rome.

As the jewel in his crown, he had called a Great Council in his Lateran palace. Churchmen and women came from every corner of Christendom to celebrate the victories of the Holy Mother Church over the forces of darkness, and to expound her law loudly and clearly for all to hear and to obey.

For days after his return Prior Walter went through these pronouncements in Chapter, taking them one by one, explaining them, pointing out how they would affect the life of the convent, the managing of our estates, the care of the souls entrusted to us.

It was at one of these Chapters that he read out the Great Council's dictate on sodomy.

'Whoever shall be found to have committed that incontinence which is against nature, on account of which the wrath of God befell the sons of perdition and destroyed five cities by fire, shall, if a cleric, be deposed from office or confined to a monastery to do penance, if a layman, shall suffer excommunication and be cast out from the company of the faithful.'

I have it word for word, written in my memory in letters of fire.

There was silence as Walter's words sank in. He carefully scanned our faces. I was blushing, not daring to look around to see who else might be, but I could hear much fidgeting and clearing of throats.

Suddenly Brice broke the tension, clapping his hands and praising God.

'Happy is the man who does not take the wicked for his guide, nor walk the road that sinners tread, nor take his seat among the scornful; the law of the Lord is his delight, the law his meditation night and day.'

Others joined in, until all of us were on our feet, singing. It was certainly better than sitting in an uneasy silence, with burning cheeks.

When we had finished, Walter went on.

'I thank God this does not apply to anyone here, but we must be ever vigilant. We must be prepared in case any of our brothers fall into this terrible pit. Our penances must be burnished and sharp, like swords ready to smite the foe.'

Brice was on his feet again.

'My lord Prior, we already have a noble guide, divinely inspired, hallowed by the ages, and given blessed approval by the saintly Peter Damian. It is written that any cleric caught in an impure situation which might lead to this sin is to be publicly flogged and lose his tonsure. When his hair has been shorn, his face is to be besmeared with spit and he is to be bound in iron chains. Six months he is to spend in prison, fasting on barley bread, then another six months in a segregated cell, giving himself to manual labour, prayer and vigil. Only then might he mix again freely with the faithful, but never again is he to associate with young men in private conversation or in counselling them. What more do we need to discuss? The Holy Spirit itself has spoken!'

Some of the canons applauded. Others looked glum. But Brice had not finished.

'The blessed Peter Damian, whose words burn with a pure, heavenly flame, goes further. He says clerics guilty of this most heinous crime are to be cast out to pray among those possessed by demons, for they themselves are possessed, and are never again to hold the body of Christ in their polluted hands.'

Prior Walter interrupted him.

'You will also recall, Father Brice, that Pope Leo chastised Peter for being overzealous and lacking in humanity.'

Brice retorted, 'But you will agree, Father, that it is false humanity to spare the sick man the sharp blade if the cut might save his life.'

At this point Edgar asked permission to speak.

'My brothers in Christ, I condemn this sin as much as any of you, but no one should be given up as lost. God will judge us all on the Last Day. It is our part to show charity and mercy, not to abrogate the power of God.

'By all means punish those caught in this sin. Flog, confine, impose the harshest of penances, but do not abandon the sinner to those possessed with devils, who do not know what they do or where they are, or even who they are. Do not abandon them to despair.'

Many nodded approval, but nobody had the courage to clap. I certainly did not.

'One other thing I must say,' Edgar added. 'As the consequences of being caught in this sin must be dire, as a deterrent to all those tempted, we must not condemn without good evidence. It must not be based on gossip, nor accusations by the malicious or envious, but be soundly corroborated.'

Now came the applause and many shouted 'Amen'. Walter thanked him warmly. Brice scowled at him. Walter said, 'There are many other important matters still to discuss today. Let us pray that if it so pleases God to try us in this way, we may be severe and strong, without becoming sinners ourselves in overzealous punishment. Amen.'

'Amen,' we all repeated.

So that was the story of the Great Lateran Council's pronouncement on sodomy. It brought one immediate change with it, one that I observed with great sadness and foreboding. Father Geoffrey and Father Serlo were no longer permitted to work together, and in choir they sat apart."

HOLYROOD

Michael sat at his window listening to the small waves breaking sluggishly onto the beach. Usually the sound soothed him, but not today.

Outside his cubicle he heard the jangling of keys, and Brother Peter thrust his head into the room. "That young man is here again, wanting to speak to you. I told him you had a restless night and weren't feeling well. Shall I send him away?"

"No, don't do that," Michael said in a tired voice, then muttered, half to Peter, half to the sea, "Now it's begun, it will have to be finished."

"What was that, Brother Michael? You don't want to see him?"

"No, tell him to wait outside for a few moments. I'll call him when I'm ready. Thank you."

Michael had had enough of young Martin's prying. His head ached and his spirit was troubled with too much remembering. Even in his sleep he could find no respite, for strange dreams crowded in on him. Last night he had dreamed of Edgar for the first time in many years.

He was aware of someone standing nearby. He called out Martin's name sharply, and Martin answered.

"Come in, come in," Michael said impatiently.

Martin stepped into the cubicle, taken aback by the old man's tone. When they were both settled on either side of the window Michael sighed and said, "Well, what do you want to know about today?"

"I'd like you to go on from where we left off last time, leading up to the time when you first met Prior Simon," Martin said gently.

"Prior Simon is a long way off yet, so you had better be patient," Michael snapped.

The previous evening the King's representative had finally arrived, and the hearings proper were about to begin. With a pang of worry Martin thought how they would not last for ever, and the Archdeacon had said he expected Martin to leave the island with him. He sent up a short prayer to St Columba, crossed himself, and asked Michael to continue with his tale.

"What more can I tell you about the rest of my time as a novice? It went smoothly enough. Even Andrew taunted me less, or perhaps I had simply become inured to it.

I had one other narrow escape, however. Archdeacon Jocelin of Dunkeld, one of the most powerful men in our diocese while we were without a Bishop, came to our Priory on a routine visitation.

He had heard of my case, and I was summoned to appear before him. He asked me many questions. He had a bland, almost fawning manner, and his words were soft and soothing, but his hard eyes put me on my guard.

I learned later that he had wanted to hand me back to de Mortimer, and it was only a payment of silver, corresponding to my blood-money, out of the Prior Walter's own purse, that stopped me from travelling to Aberdour in his baggage boat there and then.

When our year's novitiate was over, Isaac, Andrew and I were accepted as brothers, took our vows, and looked to the next stage on the path to becoming a Black Canon, the priesthood.

Subprior Brice no longer cast up my past to me in front of my brothers. Instead he took to railing against de Mortimer as if he was the very Devil. I was now a lamb to be protected from the ravening wolf. At first this was reassuring, till he turned his next weapon against me. This was a book, written by Peter Damian, a priest of our Order who had lived a hundred years before my birth. It was called *Book of Gomorrah*.

Brice had already quoted from it at the Chapter at which the Lateran Council's pronouncement against sodomy had been expounded, and I had been appalled by its savagery. A short time later it was gifted to us by Prior Osbert of St Machur, Lesmahagow, and it soon became popular reading amongst a section of the brothers. I am sure you know it, for I have heard that there is now not a religious house in the kingdom which does not have its copy, and in some they even read from it at Chapter.

Damian's words are tongues of flame to scar such souls as mine. For he writes without mercy that those who have fallen into the sin of Sodom can never rise to the priestly order, and the purest and most religious life cannot wipe away that sin.

For Brice and his zealous friends it was clear. I would never be allowed to become a priest, to hold the body of our Lord in my hands. I was not even on trial for I had already been condemned. And, sadly, I never did become a priest, because of this book and the power invested in it by the Church.

Also I was left in no doubt. If I put one foot wrong I would be thrown off the island, vows or no vows.

My love for Brother Edgar had therefore to be consigned to hidden glances and secret signs. Only rarely did we have the chance to speak together unobserved, and Edgar was reluctant to risk such a meeting. His caution was justified, because Brother Andrew was always watching us, like a predator stalking its prey.

The few times we were able to exchange words were always fraught. Our eyes had to carry all our love, while we held our tongues and kept our distance. It was a difficult time. I was often unhappy. The dream of love that I had brought with me across the water seemed to have turned to dust.

While all the time the world outside grew darker as the storm gathered around the bishopric of St Andrew's: Bishop John, who had been elected by the Cathedral Chapter, was not to be allowed to enjoy his office. King William was still insisting that his chaplain Hugh was the rightful Bishop and the Cathedral Chapter had had no right to elect anyone without first consulting him. So he refused to recognise John as the true Bishop.

Because of this calamitous state of affairs Prior Walter, with other leading churchmen and women, was summoned to the Abbey of the Holy Rood, where Alexis the Papal Legate was to hear the case and make, God willing, final decision.

I could not believe my good fortune when I was informed that Brother Edgar and I would accompany Prior Walter. Walter made no secret of the fact that he was uneasy about my going, still fearing for my safety. He told me that it was Subprior Brice who had persuaded him I should go. He said it would show the world that I now belonged to God, not man.

'But, Michael,' he said, taking my hand, 'if you are afraid, and your soul trembles at the thought of this journey, then beg premission to stay and it will be granted to you.'

Afraid of the thought of escaping from this tiny island I had not left for a summer and two winters? Afraid of the thought of a journey into the world with my beloved Edgar? I stared at Prior Walter in disbelief. Yes, my soul was trembling, not with fear but with joy and excitement.

That Subprior Brice was my advocate in this should have been like a bell rung at the approach of the enemy, but joy made me deaf to its sounds.

On St Barnabas Day, a fine June day just after Whitsun, we were out on the sea going south to the Lothian shore. My soul was singing with the terns and the oars were beating time. Quicksilver droplets and tiny whirlpools danced in our wake. Words from Prime still rang in my ears:

'The Lord rules, let the earth rejoice, let coasts and islands rejoice.'

It was a great joy to be going into the world again after so long. The summer and the two winters had seemed like eternity, and now they fell away as though they were nothing, and all time was here on the sparkling waves.

I had an oar. Edgar sat opposite me. We had permission to put back our hoods so that the glory of the morning shone upon our bare heads. When was the last time we were able to look at each other for so long, with such ease, so undisturbed?

Prior Walter was in the stern, deep in conversation with Father Serlo. Brother Andrew was in the bow with Dugal the servant.

Edgar, my beloved friend, every time I lean forward with the oar my hand touches your knee. Why can this voyage not last for ever? But all too soon our bow crunched on the sands at Cramond. We disembarked and filed up the hill into the little church to say Sext.

'Have mercy on me, God, have mercy on me,

for my soul seeks refuge in you,
and in the shadow of your wings I take refuge until the
calamity has passed.'

Afterwards the priest gave us bread and ale, then it was onto
our horses and away to Edinburgh, dipping and winding beneath huge trees, past bents and fields and golden gorse. The
heavens were filled with larksong. I too was singing, a song I
had often heard sung in Normandy by the troubadours. It was
not a song of God. And yet.

'When I see the lark
spread its wings for joy and fly towards the sun,
forget itself and fall
in the bliss that rushes to its heart
Alas! how I then envy
all creatures that I see happy.
I am amazed that my heart
does not melt away there and then with longing.'

A melancholy song, but also of such sweet joy, a foolish song,
shameful, yet I did not cross myself against it, because at my
side rode Edgar.

It was just as we were approaching the brow of the Abbey
Hill that we saw the men-at-arms, blocking our way like a solid
wall.

'Halt and dismount!' shouted a fully armed serjeant on
horseback. 'If it please your Reverend Father,' he added stiffly
on seeing Prior Walter, who had been bringing up the rear.

'We thank you for breaking our journey,' Prior Walter said,
drawing himself up to his full height, 'but we are almost at our
destination. We would rather rest there than on the road,
despite your company. Now stand aside, there's a good fellow.'

He smiled benignly as he moved his horse forward. The
serjeant's horse whinnied and threw back its head. Almost losing
ground the serjeant said, 'Reverend Father, Sir Richard de
Moreville, Lord High Constable of Scotland, the Lothians and
Strathclyde, wishes to speak with you. You are requested to
dismount and await his arrival.'

A breathtaking announcement indeed, although Walter was
not deterred. 'But my dear chap, we'll be late for Vespers. Sir
Richard, I know, is a pious man. He would not want to keep a
few harmless canons from their one purpose in life, praising
God, maker of all things, visible and invisible, and His only
begotten son, who died upon the cross so dreadfully for our
sakes and who rose again on the third day, and the Holy Spirit,
who moved across the face of the waters...'

The serjeant's face relaxed, allowing itself a thin, mocking
smile. As he turned to say something to one of his companions,
Walter immediately moved his horse forward again, edging his
way through the men-at-arms. They fell back in confusion and

looked to the serjeant, who was just as confused. I spurred my horse on to follow him. The others did the same.

We were brought to a halt again by the arrival of a large body of knights accompanying the tall, splendid figure of Sir Richard. There was no mistaking the gaunt face, the hooked nose, the shock of white hair, even if the arms of the Lord High Constable had not been blazened all over him, his horse, his knights and his squires.

'Reverend Prior, greetings! I have a matter of importance to discuss with you. I will not delay you long.' He had the grace of a cat stalking a mouse. He leapt off his horse, agile as a young man. Walter had no choice now but to comply. Slowly, almost as if in pain, he dismounted, beckoning us to do the same.

'Sir Richard, you will permit my dear sons to be privy to our conversation.' It was a statement rather than a question. Sir Richard studied us through half closed eyes.

'What I have to say, Reverend Prior,' he said haughtily, 'is for your ears only. The King speaks through my mouth. Now, if it please you.'

We were left standing on the dusty road surrounded by the snorting horses, the quiet curses of the men-at-arms, and the laughter of Sir Richard's knights, loud and braying. While beyond them, as if from another world, was the clear, sweet song of the larks.

'When I see the lark
Spread its wings for joy and fly towards the sun.....
Deliver me from my enemies, O my God, be my tower of
strength against all who assail me.
Rescue me from these evil-doers, deliver me from men of
blood.'

At last Walter came back to us. He looked grim. 'On your horses, my sons, and to the Abbey without delay. They will let us pass.' Then under his breath, so only we could hear him, he added, 'We must tread carefully, and may the Lord have mercy on us.'

At a shout from the serjeant the men-at-arms fell back and at last our road lay clear before us. They bowed their heads, and the serjeant asked for Walter's blessing. Turning he made the sign of the cross high in the air. His eyes cursed them while his mouth spoke the proper words.

Soon we were riding through the Abbey pend into the great courtyard. Everything was in an uproar: servants scurrying around like rabbits; huddles of newly arrived churchmen deep in the exchange of news; horses heavy with baggage being unloaded and led to the stables.

We had already dismounted when a plump, red-faced young canon broke away from a group of Augustinians and came smiling towards us. He was Prior Robert of the Abbey of the Holy Trinity at Scone.

'Prior Robert,' Walter shouted joyfully, 'how good to see you. I had not expected you here. Was your Father Abbot not able to come?'

'Abbot Robert is indisposed,' Robert replied and pulled down the skin below his left eye, as if to say, 'Don't believe a word of it.' Walter nodded sagely.

Old Abbot Robert is keeping his head low until the storm passes, I thought to myself. How wise. This was his nephew, as well as his Prior, and his namesake. He looked remarkably like his uncle, with the same kindly face and twinkle in his eyes. I had seen Abbot Robert when he visited our Priory as Head of our Order in Scotland. He had not wanted to hand me back to de Mortimer, unlike Archdeacon Jocelin.

'Did you have a good journey?' Prior Robert was asking.

'The King thoughtfully sent out his Constable to greet us,' Walter replied.

'To greet you?' Robert repeated, surprised.

'He also took the opportunity to remind me of the virtues and rights of Father Hugh.'

'Ah, yes, he would,' Prior Robert said, less surprised.

I was puzzled by this conversation. I could still see Walter's tense face as he turned away from his conversation with de Moreville. He's lying, I thought. Perhaps Prior Robert is not so trustworthy after all.

Then Walter turned round and said, 'Edgar, Michael, please find the guestmaster and tell him we have arrived.'

Walter and Robert remained in conversation, but their words were soon swallowed up in the general hubbub as we wove our way towards the guesthouse.

The Abbey guesthouse at Holyrood is the biggest in the kingdom, but that night there was room only for Walter and Serlo. Our servants slept with the horses, while Andrew, Edgar and I were sent to an outbuilding near the main drain.

My heart leapt when I saw where we were to sleep. There were no cubicles, no partitions, not even pallets, just a thick covering of bent-grass and straw on the uneven floor. One side was already dark with the sleeping forms of monks, their arms and legs uncovered, because the air was stifling hot. The rules of the dormitory did not seem to apply in this warm, dark place.

So Edgar and I are to sleep here together like calves in a byre! I was filled with both joy and panic at the thought. My next thought was, what if Andrew sleeps between us? I was dismayed that he might but terrified that he might not.

'That corner over there,' the guestmaster's servant was saying, 'and put the candle out when you've bedded down. The latrine is through the back. Follow your nose. Good night and God be with you.'

He handed me the light and disappeared. Stepping carefully over arms and legs we made our way to our corner. Brother

Andrew was behind me. When we were about to lie down, Andrew whispered, 'Give me the candle, I need to go to the latrine.'

'Be careful, Brother Andrew,' Edgar replied, 'it attracts toads.'

A laughter demon spluttered out of my mouth almost dousing the candle.

'Shoosh, the pair of you,' Andrew hissed, adding angrily: 'You should know all about latrines, seeing that you crawled out of one.'

'Shut up,' a gruff voice said out of the darkness near by.

'Good advice, Brother Andrew,' Edgar said. 'Away and do what you must, but don't expect us to go looking for you if you don't come back.'

Andrew growled and disappeared with the candle. By the time he came back Edgar and I were lying next to one another.

Andrew whispered, 'I should be between you two.' We did not reply, pretending to be asleep. Andrew did not press his point, because the gruff voice reinforced its request for silence with a blow to Andrew's head.

The only window in the room was above the door. It was hung with old sacking, which let in a little light from the June evening, enough for me to make out Edgar's face inches from my own. His eyes were open, looking at me. Slowly, quietly, like a mouse moving through the straw, my hand crawled towards him under my outstretched cope. Somewhere between us our hands met and clasped.

We lay like this without stirring or moving even a muscle, drifting in and out of the sweetest sleep, not wanting to drift too far from the sweetest of all, the looking and the touching.

It was not true, however, that all the rules of the dorter were suspended. The circitator still did his rounds with his lantern, but when he came past us we did not have to draw back guiltily, for what else were we but sleeping brothers beneath tousled copes on a hot June night?

The next morning after Prime we all packed into Good King David's fine, long nave. He would never have allowed such a crisis to arise in his kingdom, and I prayed that his spirit might guide his stubborn grandson.

Benches two deep lined the sides and a dais with six chairs upon it stood at the east end against the rood screen.

The benches were for the senior clerics. Young brothers like myself and Edgar had to stand. I took my place behind Prior Walter. My head was clear and my spirit light, although I had hardly slept a wink. My only discomfort was fleabites. The straw had been alive with fleas. I longed to scratch, but deemed it improper amongst such a noble gathering of clerics.

All the Augustinians sat together. There was Jedburgh, Cambuskenneth, Scone, Holyrood, and at the front near the platform

Walter, Prior of St Andrews. At his back stood a crowd of his canons, most of whom had taken part in the election of Bishop John.

As if by some unspoken agreement the supporters of the two contending Bishops had taken their places facing each other across the narrow nave. Opposite us were the Benedictines from Dunfermline clustered around the large, dark figure of Abbot Archibald, who glared fiercely across from under his black, bushy eyebrows, and looked as formidable as his reputation. Then there were the Cluniacs from the Priory of St Mirren Paisley, and, next to them, right up beside the platform, the Tironensians from Kelso and Arbroath, led by their Abbots, Osbert and Henry.

So that was Abbot Osbert, I thought to myself. He had only recently been elected Abbot of the great Abbey of St Mary Kelso, but already his was a name that sent a shiver of fear through me. Had he not sent Damian's *Book of Gomorrah* to our community, a weapon in the hands of my enemies? He was much younger than I had imagined him, with a smooth, thin face, a towering brow, and strange bulging eyes. His tonsure was marked with a few whisps of hair, because he was almost completely bald. He sat with his head back and his eyes turned upwards, as if silently imploring heaven for a miracle.

The Cistercians — beholden to no Bishop but that of Rome — perhaps considering it beneath their dignity to take sides, had taken their places on both sides of the nave. Along from us were Melrose and Newbattle, while opposite us, near the west door, sat Coupar and Dundrennan.

The bray of a trumpet made me jump. The babble faded and all eyes turned towards the west end where the Papal Herald now stood. He was young and handsome, dressed in a magnificent uniform of yellow and purple, and from his trumpet hung a cloth richly embroidered with the Papal arms. I stared at his beauty quite shamelessly. It was as if I had become emboldened by the bliss of the previous night and the old rules had been, in the words of St. Paul, superseded by the new law of love.

A dig in my side made me gasp. I swung round. 'Your eyes betray you,' Edgar whispered. 'Be careful.'

Then through the west processional door stepped Alexis, Archdeacon of the Roman Church, invested by Pope Alexander with full legatine powers. I fell to my knees with all the rest of the congregation, for it was as if the Holy Father himself was amongst us.

As soon as I set eyes on Alexis I feared for the future. I saw a haughty, proud and uncompromising man. He looked down his great beaked nose at us and his lips seemed to curl in a disdainful smile.

He was followed by the Scottish Bishops. Directly behind him lumbered the great bulk of Jocelin of Glasgow. His heavy jowls trembled as he walked. Next came Matthew of Aberdeen, who

101

was Bishop John's uncle and chief supporter. He was followed by Simon of Dunblane and Christian of Galloway, sent by York to take up the cudgel for John.

Before they had even reached the dais the great west door swung open and in marched the King's Bishops, Hugh and Andrew. Only two of them! This was a surprise, for we had expected more.

Hugh had the effrontery to be decked out in all the badges of his disputed office. He wore the episcopal ring and hood and in his hand he firmly held the staff. He reminded me of a terrier, small, stocky, broad-shouldered. A permanent scowl on his face, he always held his head back at an angle so that his sharp chin and little black beard jutted out angrily.

If Hugh reminded me of a terrier, Andrew of Caithness made me think of a weasel, small and sleek, with beady eyes glinting maliciously. With much of his flock a ravening pack of Norsemen, he never strayed far from his bolt-hole, which was the King.

'Where's Simon of Moray?' Father Serlo asked Prior Walter.

'Ill,' Walter replied. 'I suspect he has the same illness that afflicts Abbot Robert of Scone.'

'And Gregory of Ross?' Serlo asked.

'We won't be seeing him. It would take the Pope himself to bring him south of Inverness,' Walter said, then turning round to us with a smile he added, 'You shouldn't be listening to all this, my sons. Keep your minds on higher things than your superiors.'

Just behind Hugh stalked the tall, striking figure of Archdeacon Jocelin of Dunkeld, the man who had wanted to send me back to de Mortimer. I shuddered at the sight of him. He towered over everybody, especially Hugh. He was a close friend of Hugh's and had been doing very well out of it. Hugh had already given him benefices and lands from the bishopric of St Andrews which he had absolutely no right to give.

The Legate and the Bishops slowly took their seats on the dais, surrounded by their entourage of Archdeacons, Deacons, clerks and canons. Only Hugh was not among them. He was ordered by the Legate to stand to the right of the dais. All that could be heard was the subdued buzz of voices, as from a scriptorium. The question that was being whispered on all sides was, 'Where is John Scot?'

Even in his absence John commanded attention. All eyes searched for him, none knew where to look. Suddenly the buzz increased and clapping broke out. Edgar nudged me and pointed towards the rood screen. There, to the left of the dais, stood a tall, slightly stooping figure in a simple white tunic, with jet black hair and a long, flowing beard. It was John Scot, Bishop elect of St Andrews. I scarcely recognised him, for when I had seen him at court he had been clean shaven.

Brother Andrew was clapping furiously. He leant towards me

and said, proud of his knowledge, 'Bishop John has vowed not to cut his hair or beard until he has been consecrated to the bishopric God has chosen for him. The man's a saint!' He clapped even louder, as if by clapping he could share in John's heroism and sanctity. Prior Walter turned round and gestured to him to be still.

With John in his place the proceedings could begin. Everything hinged on how John had been elected, if his election had been in accordance with Canon Law or not. It had taken place over a year before, but memories were knife-sharp, whetted on the hard stone of dispute.

Alexis led the questioning with Archdeacon Jocelin presenting the evidence on Hugh's behalf.

Jocelin began by challenging the right of the canons of the Priory of St Andrew's to elect the Bishop. 'From time immemorial,' he was saying, in his deep, booming voice, 'the Bishop has been elected in consultation with the Culdees of St Mary's of the Rock. I call Gillander Mac Fertath, Abbot of this ancient and holy foundation, to testify that he and his sons in Christ were totally excluded from this travesty of an election.'

Before Abbot Gillander could even take his place on the floor of the nave in front of the Legate, Prior Walter of St Andrew's was on his feet waving a piece of parchment in the air.

'My lord Legate,' he shouted, 'I have here a copy of the Bull of Pope Eugene, recognising the right of the canons regular of St Augustine of the Priory of St Andrew's to elect the Bishop of St Andrew's.' He strode over to the platform and placed the parchment into the hand of one of Alexis' clerks. The clerk began reading it, his mouth quietly forming the words.

Prior Walter went on. 'Where in this Bull, my lord Legate, do you read of the participation of the Culdees in the episcopal election? Nowhere is it written in this the most recent, most consummate confirmation of our privileges that any but the canons of my Priory enjoy electoral rights.'

The legate's clerk had by this time read through the Bull and nodded his head vigorously in agreement with Walter's words.

Hugh jumped to his feet, claiming that the Bull was a forgery, for he had never heard of any such thing.

Alexis rounded on him angrily, saying that the seal was indeed Pope Eugene's, and how dare Hugh slander such worthy churchmen.

Next the argument shifted to the conduct of the election itself. This took up the rest of the first day. By Vespers I had heard so many details that I felt I had myself been present at that fateful Chapter.

It was a complex matter. The election itself was *per scrutinium* and each of the three *scrutatores* had to give their own account of it and present their lists of votes. Though these votes were originally taken in secret, we would by the end of the hearings know exactly how each had cast their vote.

The first scrutator to appear was Ajulf Dean of Lothian. I could understand him without effort because his Latin was poor and stumbling, his native Inglis showing through like flesh through a tattered garment. He explained exactly how the election had been organised, how the scrutatores themselves had been chosen, the manner in which the votes had been collected, and where and for how long the scrutatores had met. His account seemed to have no end. My watch-night was beginning to tell on me, for a slumber demon sat heavy on my eye-lids, and I kept slipping down a long, dark tunnel strewn with hay, where the air was warm and choking.

At last Alexis dismissed Ajulf and the second scrutator was summoned, Walter Prior of St Andrews. He spoke rapidly and fluently and his words were just a jumble to me. Edgar whispered that he was mainly repeating what Dean Ajulf had said. 'Then why is he taking twice as long about it?' I whispered back. Edgar shrugged his shoulders and smiled.

Finally the third scrutator, Peter the precentor, strode out to stand in front of the legate and give his account. He spoke as if his body was on fire, twisting his torso from side to side and waving his arms around wildly. This time I did not even ask Edgar what he was saying. All I wanted to do was to lie down on the floor and give myself up to the slumber demon and the long dark tunnel.

Then the Holy Spirit moved Alexis to adjourn the hearings. We said Vespers hurriedly. I found the familiar chanting comforting and reviving. My head spun with the effort of understanding the hearings and staying awake, the strangeness and tumult of the wide world, the nearness of Edgar.

After supper in the crowded refectory the Legate blessed us, commanding us to put up our hoods and keep silence until we reconvened the following day after Prime.

We thronged the cloisters and chapter house until Collation, even spilling into the nave. There were no books to read, and a heavy shower of rain stopped us going into the gardens and the Abbey precincts. So each of us sat wrapped in our habits and our thoughts.

The strangeness was deep and I began to feel as if I was drowning in it. There were so many hooded figures, sitting, standing, leaning, kneeling, everywhere I turned, yet the only sounds were quiet breathing, rustling tunics, muffled coughing. Among them all I had lost Edgar. I felt painfully alone. With God and my brothers in Christ all around me I knew it was sinful to feel thus, but I knew with equal certainty that only the sight and touch of Edgar could take away the pain.

I walked out into the garden behind the dorter wing. I did not care that the rain was falling heavily, for it was also sweet and warm, and eased my aching spirit. I stretched out my hands to grasp it. Over the great hill and crags beside the Abbey a rainbow had arched itself. It was God's promise that all would be well. But when, O Lord, when?

Then the strangest thing happened. I am no longer in the garden but up there on the high hill, with Edgar beside me. We are naked and the rain pours over us like a torrent. Our drenched skin is all the colours of the rainbow — purple, red, yellow, gold, changing and glowing. Suddenly a great surge of warmth sweeps over me and with a loud roar the world falls apart into a thousand pieces, yet each piece holds in itself the beauty of the whole, so that the beauty is a thousand times greater than it was.

I staggered back weak from the weight of this wonderful vision and would probably have fallen had a hand not caught my arm and supported me. Before I even looked beneath the hood I knew it was Edgar. I wanted to sink towards him, giving myself to his proffered support, but he pushed me away and I stood swaying beside him. I turned round and saw the garden slowly filling up with my hooded brothers who had come out into the rain to admire the beauty of my rainbow. I stood alone, trembling, empty.

When finally after Collation we crawled into our straw to sleep, I was too tired even to care that Brother Andrew had lain down between Edgar and me. On top of my own exhaustion the Collation ale had been strong and laced with sleeping herbs. I do not even remember the candle being blown out.

When we were wakened for Prime, and the dawn light was already streaming through the open door, the only dream I remembered was getting up in the middle of the night for Matins and Lauds."

DEBATE

"On Friday, the fifth day after Pentecost, the second of the hearing at the Abbey of Holyrood, twenty of the original twenty three members of the Chapter which elected John were present. They were not only the canons of the Priory, no more than twelve of course, but also officials of the Bishop's administration and household. Each one had to be questioned.

All day long the canons and officials of St Andrews appeared before Alexis, who railed against those who had opposed John.

But those who supported John did not escape without a mauling, not at the hands of the Legate but of Archdeacon Jocelin, Hugh's advocate. For his cause to make any headway he had to prove that those who voted for John — although the majority — had not been the sounder part of the electoral body. For Canon Law decrees that he is declared elected who has obtained the votes of either the greater or the sounder part of the Chapter.

No one was spared. Jocelin recited every fault, misdemeanor and crime, of John's supporters who stood to give evidence. He seemed to know every detail of each one's past. Probably Walter de Roxburgh, Archdeacon of St Andrews, a supporter of Hugh, had supplied him with these details, for they were the sort of things an Archdeacon would know, personal, scandalous, damaging. Archdeacon Jocelin threw them at John's supporters like stones.

Soon it was the turn of a small, fair-haired canon to stand before the Legate. He had a snub nose, a strong chin and pale, unsteady eyes. His sight was so poor that he had to be led into the centre of the nave. Abraham was his name, and he had voted for John.

Archdeacon Jocelin accused him of fathering several children in the town of St Andrews, and said he could supply the mothers' names.

Brother Abraham replied sharply, keeping his head always turned in the direction of the Legate, 'Cupid, they say, is also blind but I can assure my lord Legate that there the resemblance ceases between myself and that lascivious imp.'

Laughter erupted amongst John's supporters at this reply. I looked at John, who remained completely impassive, his eyes closed as usual. Brother Abraham had not finished. He went on in his flat, toneless voice, speaking this time in French, 'My lord Legate, why should I defend myself against the venom of this whore's son? We all know that if his arse were as fertile as his imagination, he would have born Hugh several brats by now.'

A gasp of astonishment went up from all sides. Before someone could translate this insult into Latin for Alexis, Hugh was on his feet, shouting and threatening. He looked as if he was about to make a lunge at Brother Abraham, but was restrained by Abbot Henry and two of his clerks. Insults started flying across the nave, base and malicious, framed in the nearest language to hand. Someone from Hugh's side ran up to Abraham and knocked him to the ground, while from John's side several came to Abraham's rescue. A fight broke out in front of the dais.

Legate Alexis leant back and passed his hand across his face in a gesture of despair. I stood behind Walter and looked on at the chaos in total disbelief. In de Mortimer's household, late at night after much drinking, such brawls had been commonplace, and even at the royal court they were not unknown, but to see churchmen behave thus, and while completely sober!

Archdeacon Jocelin took control of the situation. He leapt up onto the platform with a great roar which cut like a knife through the brawling and shouting. Then in a deep, sonorous voice which echoed down the dark nave he began to intone Psalm 37.

'Do not strive to outdo the evildoers or emulate those who do wrong. For like grass they soon wither, and fade like the green spring.'

Others took up the chant and soon the whole assembly was singing. It is a long psalm, and by the time it was over passions had cooled, and all had returned shame-faced to their places, except Brother Abraham, who was on his feet again, standing before the dais.

Legate Alexis, trembling with rage, again in control, threatened to excommunicate the whole Scottish Church if any such thing happened again. He ordered Brother Abraham to go down on his knees and beg forgiveness from those whom he had slandered. He ordered the rest of us to give our neighbour the kiss of peace, a greater penance for some than for others, for on that day also I was standing next to Brother Edgar.

It was almost time for Sext. Alexis told us to sing the Hour, then to go to dinner. He also commanded us all to keep silence until we reconvened. This was the greatest penance of all, because everyone was bursting to talk about the morning's events, with those slandered wanting to speak in their defence and seek sympathy from their friends and supporters.

Dinner was not followed by the usual rest, but there was not a sleepy eye in the assembly when we reconvened.

'This morning's fiasco,' Alexis said sternly, 'was a deep disgrace and insult to the dignity of Holy Mother Church. I consider the question of the soundness of the electors closed. I have more than enough evidence on which to base my judgment, which you will hear in the fullness of time. We will proceed to the next point, namely, what happened after John was elected.'

It had been a terrible time. The King swept down on St Andrews like a wolf on the fold, bringing with him all the leading churchmen of the realm, at least all those who he knew would support him, including Bishop Andrew of Caithness and Bishop Simon of Moray. He also brought with him his chaplain Hugh, who stood high in his favour. The King immediately pronounced John's election invalid on the sole ground that royal permission had not been sought. He called another election. As Hugh was the only candidate, the King said it was not necessary to cast any votes: he simply declared him elected by the inspiration of the Holy Spirit.

At this point John, who had been hiding in a house in the town in fear of his life, fled St Andrews disguised as an Augustinian canon. He spent the night in our Priory before continuing his journey south to England and beyond, to lodge an appeal against Hugh's election with Pope Alexander.

Meanwhile the King wasted no time in having Hugh consecrated Bishop of St Andrews in the Cathedral church. Just before the ceremony began, Ajulf Dean of Lothian, John's cousin, announced to the crowd that John was at that moment on his way to the Pope to appeal against Hugh's election. Therefore the consecration must wait until the appeal had been heard.

It was Ajulf himself who in his stumbling Latin was telling this part of the story. Alexis interrupted him and turned to Bishop Andrew of Caithness. 'Andrew, my brother in Christ, did you hear and understand what Ajulf was telling you on the morning you consecrated Hugh?'

'There were many noisome flies buzzing around the church that morning, your grace,' Andrew piped defiantly. 'We asked him for proof but he could give none. A large part of the kingdom's nobility was gathered for the ceremony. You surely would not expect us to have called it off simply on the basis of partisan tittle-tattle?'

Alexis said nothing, only frowned and shook his head. Ajulf finished his account, telling how he was thrown out of the church by the King's men-at-arms, how the consecration went ahead despite his protests, how the very heavens had darkened and thunder roared out at the flaunting of the Church's laws.

Things now looked very bleak for Hugh's cause. Alexis stood up and shouted that he could bear to hear no more of this sorry tale. A deep hush fell upon the assembly. It was then that my own Prior, Walter, got to his feet and asked permission to speak.

'My lord Legate,' he said, his voice quavering a little. I had never heard him sound so unsure of himself. 'My lord Legate, my lords Bishops, fathers, brothers in Christ. God's power and glory fill the world. His is the power and glory, He is power and glory. Power flows in Him and from Him, and through the meekness and humility of His only begotten son it flows to us. All power that we wield on this earth we have but borrowed, so to speak, from God, and in the end we must return it to him with interest. That interest is the good that we have performed in the wielding of that power. God's power in the world manifests itself in many different ways, in the priestly and monastic Orders, in the Bishops, and in the Holy Father, the direct successor to the Apostle St Peter, keeper of the keys of Heaven.'

I could feel restlessness ripple through the church like a wave. I scarcely dared look round me at the yawns and fidgeting, the raised eyebrows and the sly, mocking smiles. I blushed for my father in Christ. Prior Walter went on undeterred.

'Power also manifests itself in the monarch. God created the power of the monarch, and God sanctions this power through the holy rite of the coronation. The monarch is Christ's anointed, and we must not be seduced into the simple view that when King and Church clash, the King must always be in the wrong, and the Church always in the right.'

Walter paused to let his words sink in. Suddenly all yawning and fidgeting stopped. Everybody's attention was on Walter. I heard Abbot Richard of Jedburgh hiss from nearby, 'Walter, has the Devil come between you and your senses?' Walter bowed his head and ignored him. Meanwhile applause had broken out from those sitting near Hugh. Alexis glared over at us and rose to his feet, but Walter had not finished.

'My Lord Alexis, you are here as the vicar of the Holy Father. Your thoughts and judgments are therefore guided by the Holy Spirit. I have no doubt that you will avoid this easy error. But let me remind everyone here,' — he was shouting now, as murmurings rose all around us — 'the King's power surrounds us. My lord Legate, you will soon be leaving this power behind you. We must live with it, and in it.'

I could not believe what I was hearing. Here was our Prior, an Augustinian, a relative of John, a man who had always spoken for Church control of Church affairs, speaking as though he was one of Hugh's men. Hugh was on his feet now, shouting, 'A Solomon has come from the Forth! This man is wise, my lord Legate. Listen well to what he says — '

A strange voice cut across Hugh's words, loud until it had silenced him, then quiet, so quiet we had to bend forward to catch the words. It was John Scot. It was the first time he had spoken.

'I thank my son Walter for his words. They are indeed wise. Far be it from me to urge on our Holy Mother Church anything that might be described as simple.' He threw back Walter's own word with a sneer. 'But I was chosen by the Church and deposed by a monarch. These are two separate areas of competence.'

Now it was John's turn to be interrupted, drowned out by the deep booming voice of Abbot Archibald. 'The Church entered the realm of the King when she became an owner of land and serfs. First give these up, then we can talk about separate areas of competence.'

'My son,' Alexis shouted, 'this is not the place to start that debate. If you had seen, as I did, the great Emperor Frederick prostrate himself, in all his worldly glory, at the feet of our Holy Father Alexander, and give his kingdoms into the Holy Father's sacred hands, to receive them back as God's vassal, and vassal of the servant of the servants of God; if you had wept for joy at this miracle, as I did, then you would never again question that ultimate power on earth rests with the Church, and that whosoever gainsays the Church gainsays the Holy Trinity itself. I should not need to say these things. We have before us Canon Law as broken as St Catherine's own body, and you stand up and praise the power of the King, you, the head of an Augustinian house, who ought to know better.'

'With all due respect, my lord Legate,' Walter replied, 'our

King has not been worn down by endless wars in Italy. He remains powerful. We ignore this fact at our peril.'

'Prior Walter of Inchcolm,' Alexis thundered, 'enough of this. I will hear no more. Dean Ajulf, please go on with your account.'

Walter turned round to me. He was flushed. He said in a strange, hoarse voice, 'Michael, I am unwell. Take me outside. I need some air.'

We slipped along the side aisle towards the west processional door. Walter was leaning on me and holding his head. But as soon as we reached the cloister he shook me off and stood upright.

'Right,' he said, his voice firm and normal, 'we've not a moment to lose. Follow me.' He hurried along the cloister, with me close on his heels wondering what was happening.

When he got to the south west corner, he flung open a door, behind which a narrow, winding stair disappeared into the darkness. Up we went at full pelt till another door blocked our way. Walter gave three sharp knocks. After a moment Father Maurice the guestmaster appeared and ushered us into a dimly lit chamber.

Before he had even entered the room Walter snapped, 'Maurice, get the clothes.' Then grabbing my arm he said, 'Michael, listen carefully. You have to get away from here at once. De Mortimer is after you, and he has the King on his side. I can tell you now what happened out there on the road when de Moreville stopped us. He said that if the council's decision went against Hugh, then one of my sons would find himself back where he belonged. Make no mistake, Michael, he meant you. I warned him that he was putting his mortal soul in danger by threatening an Augustinian brother. He laughed and said that was nothing compared to threatening a consecrated Bishop, which was what the Papal Legate was doing.

'He also said there were enough irregularities about your joining the Priory to keep a Bishop's court busy for some time, and there were enough Bishops to preside over it. "If the Pope wants to play God," he said, "the King will play the Holy Ghost, and the Holy Ghost knows how to move people." The impudent blasphemy of the man!

'It's clear now that only a miracle will stop the decision from going against Hugh, King or no King. I knew in my bones I should not have brought you. Why did I do it? What a fool I've been!'

I listened with growing fear. Walter's words were like waves crashing over me, crushing me with their weight. I felt helpless.

'Michael,' Walter was saying, 'at least thanks to de Moreville, God rot him, we're not totally unprepared. Put these clothes on. They're the livery of the Abbot's messengers. This means you should have unimpeded passage. Ride to the Abbey's village of Inverleith on the north side of the river mouth. If you're stopped and challenged, say you have an important message for Father Alwin the priest. That is no lie, for here is a letter for him, telling him to get you a boat which will take you straight to Inchcolm.'

While Walter was talking I struggled into my new clothes. It felt strange to be in the clothes of the world again, boots and hose, short tunic and leather jerkin with the arms of the Abbot of Holyrood emblazoned upon the back. My heart was racing now. I no longer felt helpless and dismayed.

Walter and I said a quick prayer together. He embraced me, then Father Maurice led me down another stairway, even darker and narrower than the first, and out into the courtyard, where a horse stood ready for me.

Angry clouds were banked up in the western sky as I left the safety of the Abbey precincts. The gates slammed loudly behind me. Outside there was a group of royal guards. One of them held on to my bridle and questioned me carefully. My answers must have satisfied him, for he let me go. With soaring spirit I spurred my horse up over the Abbey Hill and galloped to Inverleith as though all the devils in Hell were chasing me.

Father Alwin did not delay in carrying out the instructions in the letter, and before sunset I was back on Inchcolm with another tale of escape to tell my amazed brothers.

A few days after my flight from Holyrood, Prior Walter returned to the island bearing grim tidings.

Shortly after I had left, Alexis had brought the hearings to an end, but by late that evening he had still told no one of his decision.

A huge mob had gathered outside the Abbey gates and an early curfew bell was rung in an attempt to disperse it, with only limited success. The King refused to send any help. Alexis met the King's representatives at the Abbot of Arbroath's town house, a way having been forced through the crowds for his litter. The King was to be the first to hear the judgment, a piece of diplomacy which many had thought Alexis incapable of.

When he returned he summoned everyone to the church yet again and announced that John would be consecrated Bishop of St Andrews on the following day. Not only that, but the King would be present at the consecration. This news filled John's supporters with foreboding.

The next morning the Abbey church was packed. The screens had been removed so that part of the nave could be used as the choir and everyone could see what was going on at the High Altar. The western end of the nave had been given over to the common people of the two burghs, who spilled over into the courtyard beyond.

Next came the lesser court officials and retainers while the chief nobles were with the King in the south transept. The King himself sat at the front, grim-faced and silent, nearest to the High Altar.

Surrounding the altar stood the Bishops although Hugh was nowhere to be seen. John, beardless now and with short hair, knelt in front of Alexis, who stood on the altar steps.

Alexis began by saying that King William in his wisdom as a dutiful son of the Holy Mother Church had promised to bring the insignia of the Bishop of St Andrews, in particular the hood, staff and ring, to the consecration. The King bowed his head and said he would produce them at the appropriate time in the ceremony. Alexis bowed graciously, and the long ceremony began.

At last the point was reached when John was to be invested with the hood, staff and ring. Alexis sent a priest over to the King to ask him for them. A row of royal guards stepped aside to reveal Hugh decked out in all the insignia of the Bishop of St Andrews.

Alexis demanded that Hugh hand them over. Hugh refused. Alexis appealed to the King for support. The King replied that this was a Church matter and so, as a dutiful son of the Holy Mother Church, it was not his place to interfere. Alexis replied that if Hugh did not hand over the insignia at once he would be bound with the chains of excommunication.

'I will never hand them over!' shouted Hugh. The King smiled.

'I hereby declare you excommunicate and cut off from the eternal benefits of our Holy Mother Church,' Alexis shouted back.

The King jumped to his feet, sending his chair crashing.

'But the Church is merciful,' Alexis added hastily. 'You have fifteen days in which to come to your senses and make amends.'

'Never,' Hugh shouted again.

'Then you must suffer the consequences,' Alexis bellowed.

'Excommunicate our chaplain, our friend, our counsellor!' the King roared. 'You insult our royal person, my lord Legate. You offend the royal dignity. It is as if you would excommunicate us.'

Everyone held their breath, because it looked for a moment as though Alexis was going to do just that, but he restrained himself.

'Furthermore let it be known,' the King shouted, 'that never as long as we live will our kingdoms of Scotland, Lothian and Strathclyde contain both ourself and John Scot. And it will not be we who will be departing, we can assure you. Now take your consecrations and your excommunications and your pishinations back to Rome where they belong.'

By this stage some of the nobles had their swords half out of their scabbards. De Moreville had drawn his fully and was waving it threateningly at the Legate. The crowd in the nave surged forward to see what was happening. There were screams and shouts of murder as people were crushed. The cry went up to clear the church, and the King's guard started fighting their way out towards the west end. Several people were killed and many were injured.

The King stormed out, taking with him Hugh and all his court as well as many churchmen. Then all the doors were barred, and Alexis commanded the remaining Bishops to complete John's consecration. These were Glasgow, Dunblane, Aberdeen and Galloway.

Outside a riot had broken out, and the smell of burning filled the air. It was later discovered that some of the King's men had set fire to the house of Bishop Matthew of Aberdeen, John's uncle.

That same night John, consecrated in blood and fire, and without the insignia of his new office, fled the country. Alexis left with him, as did many of John's relatives including Bishop Matthew and Ajulf. Everyone else scurried home for safety.

Before he left, Alexis laid the whole bishopric of St Andrews under an interdict, for the King had seized it in Hugh's name. Hugh himself left for Rome, taking the hood, staff and ring with him.

'In short, my sons,' Prior Walter concluded, 'all is chaos and darkness, and I believe that far worse is to come.'

Martin, my son, I don't think any of us, even Prior Walter, could have imagined how bad things were still to become."

Old Brother Michael sighed deeply and fell silent. Martin stared out of the window. While Michael had been speaking Martin had watched the sea darken and grow light again, as the clouds thickened or thinned. Everything was now a uniform grey and rain was falling heavily.

"I don't want you to come to me tomorrow, Martin," the old man said with sudden firmness. "In fact, I don't want you to come to me until I send for you."

Martin could only nod agreement. He wanted to demand a reason, but he knew he might as well ask the rain to stop falling.

"I am very tired," Michael muttered, almost to himself. "Go in peace, and pray for my soul."

Before Martin could reply Michael took Martin's hand in his and kissed it. Martin, moved by this simple gesture, did not pull his hand away.

"God be with you, Father," Martin said. "I look forward to seeing you again. Please do not forget to send for me."

In reply Michael let his hand go and gave a weak smile. His head had fallen forward before Martin had even left the room.

INTRUSION

A s Martin stepped into the warm, stifling air of the infirmary, his heart was beating high and fast. The old man
had asked for him. He was overjoyed. His spirits had been
very low the past few days, since the time Michael had sent him
away saying that he did not want to talk to him for a while. Had
he been too greedy for his memories? Would the old man ever
want to see him again? These questions would not leave him in
peace. Now the old man had asked for him, and all his doubts
and questions disappeared.

"Martin, my dear boy, you have come. I am so pleased."
Brother Michael's voice was more cracked and hoarse than
usual, and his bony fingers dug into Martin's arm. "Listen, I have
much to say. You must listen and try to understand. On no
account must you go to the mainland. De Mortimer is there and
will attack you and imprison you, and worse. Promise me you
will not go. I could not stand to lose you, like I lost him."

Martin was taken aback by these wild words. His joy faded.
He had not expected this.

"Brother Michael," Martin said, trying to sound reassuring,
"de Mortimer has been dead many a long year. He will not harm
me, or you. We are quite safe."

"Dead? Many years dead?" The old man sighed. His hand
loosened its grip on Martin's arm, but did not let go. "I will
never be safe from him. But yes, you are right, he is dead. Not
buried, but dead. But he tried to kill my friend, and kill our
friendship."

"Brother Michael," Martin went on, soothingly, "you must
explain a little more what you mean. I am young and ignorant.
I was not even alive at the time of which you speak."

"The more blessed you are for that. I will tell you the terrible
story, one thing after another. Where had we got to when I last
saw you?"

"You had just returned from the Abbey of the Holy Rood.
Alexis had consecrated John rightful Bishop of St Andrews in
defiance of the King, then left the realm, taking John with him."

"Not only John," the old man said shaking his head. "With
him went John's uncle Matthew Bishop of Aberdeen, as well as
many other relatives and friends, for the anger of a King sweeps
wide.

Alexis left the bishopric of St Andrews under an interdict, like
a body whose spirit had departed. The King seized the corpse,
but already it was starting to decay. The night sky was lit up by
flames and during the day smoke rose against the sun. On both
sides of the Forth villages and granges and sometimes even
churches belonging to St Andrews were burning. Some said it

was the Devil, roaming unchecked now that the grace of God had been removed, others that it was supporters of Bishop John, pledged to the destruction of the bishopric's wealth since the rightful Bishop had been exiled and his cause routed.

The King and his barons sent their men-at-arms throughout the stricken country. Terror stalked the land, and Brother Peter the sacrist had a vision of the end of the world. Frightened refugees from the worst areas fled to the nearest parish in neighbouring bishoprics. Our churches of Rosyth, Dalgety, Aberdour and Auchtertool were overrun. They were like Bethesdas in the desert. But they soon became Gehennas, for these refugees brought their own curse with them, like smoke clinging to a cloak.

A brawl broke out in the churchyard at Aberdour between some local peasants and some of the refugees. A villager claimed they had stolen one of his sheep. Father Abraham tried to break up the fight and got a spit between his ribs for his pains. He died before Maurice the infirmarer could reach him.

Prior Walter immediately went to de Mortimer, who was in Aberdour at the time, to demand justice. He was told that all those concerned had been subjected to ordeal by fire and found guilty: six villagers and refugees already hung from the gallows tree beside the east high road.

Worse was to come. Walter was told by de Mortimer that Abraham's successor at Aberdour had already been chosen, in flagrant breach of the rights of our Priory. That church was our benefice. The Priory alone had the right to present the priest. For as long as anyone could remember it had been served by one of our canons.

Moreover the man chosen to succeed Abraham was Robert de Alconbury, a clerk in Earl David's household. Earl David had been de Mortimer's liege-lord since Countess Ada's death, and was the King's brother. The court was on the attack, while we were at our weakest, with the Bishop of St Andrews in full flight, half the kingdom under an interdict, and no Bishop at Dunkeld. Abraham's death had come at exactly the right time for our enemies, and those who could have contradicted de Mortimer's version of it were already rotting on Gallows Knowe.

When Prior Walter returned with this news, there was much discussion as to the best course for us to take. Some said that we should bide our time and let de Mortimer and Earl David do whatever they wanted with the church at Aberdour until the storm over St Andrews had passed, for the cause of the righteous would prevail in the end. Others said we could not let the honour of St Columba be so insulted. The storm over St Andrews showed no signs of abating. The cause of the righteous might prevail in the end, but in the meantime precious revenue which belonged to us was going into the coffers and the granges of de Mortimer and his lord. Also, if we let one church go like that, then would not all our churches, all our lands even, be in danger? No, we had to make a stand; we had to act.

Edgar was the most vocal advocate of the course of action. In the end it was this course that Prior Walter decided to steer. Father Serlo was appointed Abraham's successor. I liked Father Serlo and trusted him. He was solid and reliable. He did not smile much and his face was usually set in an expression of stern disapproval, but he was neither stern nor disapproving. When he did smile it came from the heart, not like some other brothers whose smiling covered a sour soul. He had been kind to me. Ever since my arrival on the island I had known he was on my side. Prior Walter in his wisdom had assigned him to me as my confessor, for he understood my soul and its temptations only too well. But in the fear which Walter had brought back with him from Rome I was given a new confessor, Nicholas, whose arrogance and harshness seemed in themselves a penance for sins which I had not committed.

So I was sorry Father Serlo was leaving the island, although I knew he would make a good parish priest. Also I was afraid for him, for he would be going into the lion's den.

Prior Walter gave me three letters to write out in my best cursive. The first was to Bishop Jocelin of Glasgow, asking him to support our candidate for the church at Aberdour. He was one of our nearest Bishops, and certainly the most important in the kingdom, with Dunkeld vacant and St Andrews in chaos. It was difficult to know on whose side Jocelin really was, but who else powerful in the Church could we have turned to? In his letter Walter tactfully let him know that if his support was not forthcoming we might feel constrained to write to Archbishop Roger of York. He would be only too pleased to help, for we knew that there was nothing Jocelin wanted less than York's interference in the Scottish Church.

The second letter was to King William himself. In it we complained bitterly about Robert's intended intrusion, pretending the King would share our outrage. This was really a waste of precious parchment and ink, but it was a necessary formality. The sentence which would have the greatest effect on the King was the one slipped in casually at the end, informing him of the third letter that we had written.

This was addressed to King Henry of England. Remember that at this time King William was still paying off his ransom after his capture at Alnwick six years before. The main coin of this ransom was subservience. Henry's soldiers still garrisoned William's four chief castles, and Henry acted in many ways as his sovereign lord. King William hated to be reminded of this. But we could not fall much lower in our King's favour, so we had little to lose and much to gain from this third letter.

Time was running out. We could not sit back and let bishops and kings solve our problems for us. Robert de Alconbury's induction into the church at Aberdour was to take place in three weeks' time.

It was decided after a long and heated Chapter that the whole convent would be there at Aberdour church on the day of Robert's induction and by all peaceful means would prevent the ceremony from taking place. We would have with us the holy relics of St Columba and St Fillan. Who would dare to defy us with such powerful companions?

Prior Walter said I should stay in the Priory. After my narrow escape from Holyrood it would, he said, be the height of foolishness to walk into the shadow of de Mortimer's castle, even under the protection of such holy relics.

Subprior Brice argued against it, as did Father Nicholas, saying that the spiritual power of the convent would be diminished if the whole of it was not present. I mistrusted their sudden desire to regard me as a vital part of the convent, they who had for so long wanted to cast me out. But many voices were raised against them, and I was allowed to stay.

Now, Martin, I regret it. If I had been there perhaps I could have protected him, perhaps he would not have acted so rashly, perhaps the blow would have fallen on me.

The day chosen for the induction, or rather the intrusion, of Robert de Alconbury added insult to our injury, for it was the feast day of the blessed founder of our Order, St Augustine himself. Although summer, it was drab, grey and blustery. After Prime Prior Walter gave us his blessing, and we all begged St Columba for his special protection.

'Remember, my sons,' he said, 'we are not going to the mainland to fight, to accuse, or to heckle. We are going as the children of God, the representatives of St Columba, holy witnesses to a vile crime. By our meekness let their violence be shown, by our prayers let their wickedness be known, by our silence let their sins cry out. Be strong in the Lord and in the power of His might. Put on the whole armour of God, that you stand against the wiles of the Devil, for we wrestle not against flesh and blood, but against principalities, against powers, against rulers of darkness of this world, and against spiritual wickedness in high places.'

Strengthened by his words, I could have taken on de Mortimer single-handed, and was bitterly sorry that I was not going with my brothers. In such a crisis, I did not want to let Edgar out of my sight.

Then in procession we sang the psalm *Miserere mei*, we walked out of the church to the main gate and down the path to the waiting boats.

'Have mercy on me, God, for man tramples me underfoot.
All day long he fights against me and is my tribulation.
My enemies trample me all day long, for many make war
against me.'

And our voices soared and rose above the wind as we sung the sublime words,

> *'My hope is in God; I will not be afraid of what man may*
> > *do to me.*
> *For you have snatched my soul away from death,*
> *and my feet away from stumbling,*
> *so that I might be pleasing to God in the light of the*
> *living.'*

Edgar was just in front of me. As we reached the beach I pretended to stumble and pushed him in the back. He turned round.

'God be with you,' I murmured.

He smiled and went on singing.

In the general confusion as the brothers, the lay-brothers and the servants were getting into five boats to convey upwards of twenty men, I was able to whisper to Edgar, 'Please, be careful. You are very precious to me.' He frowned, and shook his head, as if he were disagreeing with me. In another place, at another time, his frowning would have hurt me, but not today, when all I wanted was to keep him with me and protect him from the danger waiting on the mainland.

The sharp voice of Subprior Brice cut between us like a sword.

'Brother Michael, you are in the way. Stand back at once and let your brothers get into the boats.'

I stood back, and watched as my whole world sailed away. I could hear them singing,

> *'Lord, when will you turn your eyes back to me?*
> *Rescue my soul from their wickedness,*
> *rescue my precious life from the lions.'*

Their voices were lost amid the wind and waves. I walked slowly up the path to the Priory, saying with them the words of the psalm to the end.

I had never known the island so empty. It was as if a terrible plague had struck, leaving only a handful of survivors. I stood beside the church wall. I watched the boats hurrying across the water. I watched the gulls, and envied them. They could be here and there, with the boats and on the island, with Edgar and with me, without effort. Could I not become a gull, just for a day, so that I could follow unnoticed, be near, watch over?

All day my spirit was in turmoil. I wandered the deserted Priory like a ghost, unable to rest or settle to anything. Even copying could not hold my distraught mind. I kept the Hours, sitting alone in the choir, but they did not bring the usual comfort, for my spirit turned and wheeled around my brothers.

In the middle of Nones, hurrying through it so that I could rush for the hundredth time to look out towards Aberdour, I heard a voice from the nave calling my name. It was Duff, one of the watch servants. He told me that boats were approaching the island from the Fothrif coast We ran outside and strained our eyes towards them.

My brothers were returning, slowly, laboriously, in the teeth of a rising west wind. I sped to the kitchen and worked for a while helping to prepare a hot meal. Then I went down to the beach to wait.

Eventually the first boat crawled round Swallow Craig into the lee of the island. As it glided towards the beach I could see strained, pale faces staring back at me without greeting. In the stern sat Brother Isaac, his face bruised and bloodied, beside him, gripping his side and gasping for breath, Subprior Brice. Before the boat even touched the sand two servants leapt out and ran up the slope towards the Priory.

'What happened?' I asked fearfully as soon as the boat beached.

'We were beaten up in the churchyard,' replied Brother Maurice, who was the first to climb out of the boat. 'Some of us have been badly hurt. Help get everyone out of the boats and up to the Priory. I've already sent for biers to be brought down.'

Biers! It felt as though a great worm turned inside me. Were they for the injured or for the dead? I did not dare ask.

As I helped my brothers out of the boat, I noticed that some of them had torn habits, and that Isaac was not the only one with a bruised face. Brice had to be carried onto the beach, screaming with pain. My eyes sought everywhere for Edgar. He was not in the first boat, nor the second, which followed close behind, carrying the same bruised and battered cargo. Even Prior Walter had a gash on his forehead. With mounting panic I watched the third and the fourth boat arrive. Still no sign of Edgar.

Father Serlo was in the fourth boat. I rushed up and asked where Brother Edgar was. He looked at me sadly and shook his head. Blood trickled from the corner of his mouth. When he spoke I saw he had lost a tooth.

'I do not know, my son,' he said. 'They have kept him on the mainland.' Who have kept him? Why? Is he injured? All these questions I wanted to ask, but before I could, Serlo said. 'I am in great pain. Please, help me out of the boat.'

My unasked questions were answered soon enough. I went straight to the infirmary, where all the injured were brought, and helped tend their hurts and bring them food. The whole place buzzed with stories of the day, and soon I had put together a clear picture of what had happened in the churchyard of Aberdour. I have heard the stories so often I sometimes forget that I was not with them that day. Perhaps my distraught spirit did inhabit a gull and sat screaming and useless on the roof of the church.

The convent arrived before the induction ceremony had begun, and tried to enter the church. It was securely barred against them from within, so they stood outside the church door, singing psalms. Soon Robert arrived in procession from the castle, in the company of clerks and chaplains not just from the households of de Mortimer and Earl David, but from the royal household itself.

Edgar had been given the altar cross to carry because of his strength and height. He stood beside Prior Walter and Father Serlo, and the three of them faced the oncoming procession. It was not cleric facing cleric, but cleric facing man-at-arms, because de Mortimer and Earl David had surrounded Robert the clerk with their soldiers.

First they shouted at us to clear out of the way. Our reply was to sing more loudly. Then they laid hands on Prior Walter and pushed him violently aside. He fell headlong onto the grass. Edgar struck at them with the cross, felling two of them at one blow. A great roar went up and the men-at-arms lunged forward, punching, pushing, kicking. No swords or daggers were used, as they had probably been given orders not to kill. The brothers were thrown to the ground or fled down the path towards the boats.

Edgar was one of the first to be struck down, the cross wrenched out of his hands. Several of my brothers saw a great bear of a man sling Edgar over his shoulder and disappear with him in the direction of the castle. Nobody had seen the man before. He was probably one of Earl David's.

Soon the way to the church door was clear enough for the procession of the wicked to pass. Even our precious relics had been scattered in the fray, and were trampled under foot. Imagine the blasphemy of it, Martin. On his way to be wrongfully intruded into one of St Columba's own churches Robert de Alconbury stepped on the bones of the saint himself. Is it any wonder that years later his feet rotted and he died the lingering death of a leper?

After the procession had entered the church, my brothers gathered together their scattered treasures and helped the injured to the boats. Some started to sing psalms again, but their presence was a reproach to the wicked, and they were driven away by the jeering, violent men-at-arms. Prior Walter insisted on speaking with de Mortimer about the taking of Edgar, but he too was driven roughly away, and had no choice but to go down to the boats with the rest of the convent and embark for the Priory."

INTERDICT

"The convent lay and licked its wounds for many days. I spent all my time in the infirmary, helping Brother Maurice and the infirmary servant, but my thoughts were always on Brother Edgar, and my only prayers were for his safe delivery from the hands of our foes.

Some of my brothers blamed Edgar for the fight, saying that he had turned a dignified protest into a foul brawl, and had desecrated the altar cross by using it as an instrument of violence.

Prior Walter had hurt his arm when he had been pushed to the ground. It swelled up at the wrist and he could not move his hand. He often came to the infirmary to allow Brother Maurice to examine his injury and change his poultice. Every time he appeared I would ask him about Edgar, and he would tell me that there was no news. He was always very short with me, and finally he rounded on me.

'Why this great concern with Brother Edgar? Do you think we will forget him if you do not bleat his name in my ear every time we meet? We have not forgotten him, Brother Michael, and he is often in our thoughts and prayers. Let him be a little less in yours.'

Father Serlo was nearby when Prior Walter spoke to me thus and caught my look of desperate hurt. Later he took me aside and told me Prior Walter had already sent a messenger demanding Edgar's release, and that as soon as he was able to travel, he was going to de Mortimer. If he still refused to hand Edgar over, he would go to the King and seek justice there. Unlike Prior Walter Serlo did not counsel me to forget, but he did urge me to be patient and trust in God and St Columba. Edgar was taken into captivity while protecting the relics and the honour of St Columba. That good, powerful saint would not forsake him, or forget to reward him. I clung to Serlo's kind words of comfort, and I no longer sought out news of Edgar, but waited for news to come to me.

So the days passed in sadness, but always there was the hope that Edgar would return. Then came the day of the Exaltation of the Holy Cross. I had been on the island exactly two years. It should for me have been a day of celebration and thanksgiving. Instead it brought only grief.

Prior Walter had just returned from the mainland, where he had met with Sir William de Mortimer. He was to announce to us in Chapter the outcome of this meeting. My first disappointment was that Prior Walter had not brought Edgar back with him when his boat had landed on the island just after Prime;

but it was nothing to the disappointment that awaited me in Chapter.

Prior Walter hurried in looking grim. He told us the news was bad. De Mortimer still refused to make any concessions regarding the church at Aberdour. He had laughed in Walter's face when it was suggested he make amends for the vicious attack on our convent and the bodily harm he had caused. When Walter had threatened to go to the King, de Mortimer had laughed even louder.

However, there was one thing de Mortimer had given us, a thing dear to us, but worthless to him. Brother Edgar. My hope soared at the news, only to be dashed as Prior Walter continued, 'They brought him to me, tortured and starved, looking more dead than alive. He begged my forgiveness for having lost himself to his anger in the churchyard, and for desecrating the Holy Cross. I forgave him with all my heart, but he begged for one further penance. He said he had wounded the honour of the blessed St Columba, and felt that he was no longer worthy to serve his church. He begged to be allowed to serve God at another house than this. I granted his request.'

At Prior Walter's words there was a great hubbub amongst my brothers. I sat in silence, stunned, wrestling with my grief. Out of the many voices around me I could hear one, louder than the rest, coming as if from a long way off. It was Father Serlo.

'My Lord Prior, brothers, sons, Brother Edgar is half crazed with pain and want of food. Let him come back to us, regain his strength of body and soul, then decide. Do not allow him to exile himself from his brothers in Christ in a moment of despair. Let him come back to us, if only to say farewell. And let him see that we all forgive him, and that through our forgiveness, he will come to forgive himself.'

Prior Walter replied, 'These are wise words, Father Serlo, but it is too late. He is already on the road to the Abbey of Scone with a letter of recommendation from me to the Lord Abbot and the convent. It is the will of God. So be it.'

'Amen,' many muttered. The arguments went on, with people speaking on both sides, but I could no longer understand what was being said. It was as if part of my soul had died. What did it matter what was said now? It was as clear as daylight that Prior Walter had made up his mind and Brother Edgar would not be returning to the Priory.

The winter which followed [1180-81] was long, hard and full of grief. I missed Edgar terribly. After the infirmary emptied, and the life of the Priory returned to its usual order, I was allowed to go back to my copying.

In January, when all the world was frozen white and most of humanity was huddled around fires and looking inwards, at this dead time, at this safe time, I was given permission to make a journey to the Abbey of St Mary Melrose to collect manuscripts which Prior Walter had persuaded Abbot Arnold to lend us for copying.

Walter had hardly spoken to me since the events of the autumn, and when we passed each other in the cloister, he would nod to me and hurry on, where previously he would have stopped and asked after the state of my soul. When he summoned me to tell me I was to go to Melrose, he did it with few words, but I knew he was saying to me, 'Brother Michael, I have not forgotten that you have suffered a great loss, and that I am partly to blame. Take this journey and these manuscripts as balm for your aching spirit.' This I did with all my heart.

One of the manuscripts that I brought back was called Spiritual Friendship. It had been written about forty years previously by the blessed Aelred of Rievaulx, Father Edwin's teacher. It was a most precious book, and throughout it I could hear the echo of Edwin's voice. I wept many tears while copying it. Ask Brother Roger for it, Martin. It must be somewhere in the Priory, though it has long been out of fashion.

While the blessed Aelred was writing it he lost a close friend, a friend as dear to him as Edgar was to me. And so he breaks off to lament him. My tears mingled with his words. His friend's name was Simon, but several times I started to write the name of Edgar instead, and had to subpunct. You had to tell Father Geoffrey when you made a mistake, and usually he gave you a cuff round the ears or a penance, or both. He must have taken pity on me, for he would simply grunt and shake his head when I told him. I must have been a pitiful sight, sniffling and peering up at him with red eyes. Sometimes he would come over to me and lay his hand on my shoulder. This simple act of kindness would make my tears flow even more, and he would say, 'Be careful not to smudge the ink, Brother Michael.'

Please read it, my son, it is a very fine book, and it can speak so much more clearly than I can. If you read it, and you find one of those foolish mistakes, say a prayer for me and Edgar, and for Geoffrey, too. Perhaps one day you will bring it to me and read out of it. You will not need to read me the lament, for it is engraved on my heart.

'But my grief prevents me from going on any further and the recent loss of my Edgar violently drives me to weeping. I am full of sadness, and I cannot even find relief in sleep, for my beloved friend has been snatched suddenly away. Who is there that does not marvel at the fact that Michael can live without Edgar? Only the person who does not know how sweet it was to be alive at the same time as he was, or how sweet it will be to return to our homeland together.....

'Oh, it is wretched and oh, it is grievous to live without Edgar. The holy David wept for his dearest Jonathan, and so I weep for you. Where have you gone, paragon of my life? Why have you been snatched away from my embraces, taken away from my kisses, removed from my eyes? I know, some may judge by my tears that my love was too carnal. Let them think what they wish. You, Lord, see my tears and you respect them. Others see what is done outwardly. They cannot perceive what I suffer within. But your eyes are there, Lord. No one knows what goes on inside a person, no one except the person's spirit within them. But your eyes, Lord, penetrate even the point where mind and spirit divide. Oh Lord, receive my tears as a sacrifice for my dear friend, and if in it there is anything faulty, either overlook it or lay it to my account only, and let nothing stand in the way of my dear friend going straight to your embrace.'

Oh, Martin, tears are a balm for the hurt soul. Father Geoffrey and Prior Walter understood this, but Subprior Brice did not, and grudged me even my tears.

'What are you snivelling for, Brother Michael?' he would snap, if I had been unlucky or foolish enough to show him my tears. And before I could reply he would say, 'I know, it's for Brother Edgar. Do you deny it?' I would shake my head. 'And Father Abraham, where are your tears for him? Both are no longer with us, the one an innocent victim of violence, the other the victim of his own stupidity. We are enjoined, Brother Michael, as I have pointed out many times, to love all our brothers in Christ with equal charity and with equal spiritual fervour. Until one eye weeps for Abraham and the other for Edgar, you sin. It is this special friendship nonsense. I knew it would all end badly, for God's hand is against it.'

God help me but I hated Brice then, with a hate as pure and great as my grief. But my hatred fortified my soul against his words, where, had they gained entry, they would have worked as poison. Even hatred can be from God, Martin, and it melted when I no longer needed it, for it did not outlast my grief. It might even have helped contain it.

Always, like the crashing of waves in a storm, unceasingly the question beat against me, why had Edgar done it? Why had he gone away so suddenly, completely, without even bidding me farewell?

The affairs of the world offered only dark distraction. Soon after Prior Walter had been so insultingly rebuffed by de Mortimer, we wrote more letters to the powerful: Bishop Jocelin, King Henry of England, and our Holy Father Pope Alexander. We did not write to King William again.

Our letters told of the terrible events at Aberdour. The replies said, 'Wait! Wait until John is rightfully restored to his own, then all will be well, and all wrongs done to the Holy Mother Church will be righted.'

If the violent intrusion at Aberdour had happened at any other time, an outcry would have reached the ears of the Holy Father before he had read about it in our letter. Now it was lost amongst the chaos, the interdicts, the attacks on our Holy Mother Church throughout the realm. As the days grew shorter and the world dragged itself into darkness, there were many, including myself, who wondered if the light would ever return.

We were wrong. Spring did finally come, bringing with it light, though little warmth. But the darkness of the interdict, now confirmed by the Holy Father, still lay over the bishopric of St Andrews, and the air was thick with the stench of rotting corpses piled high awaiting Christian burial.

As life and light returned to the world the first of the powerful to make a move was King Henry. He was in Normandy over Easter and ordered King William to attend him there. All winter his ears had been filled with complaints against King William and his Bishop Hugh. For Bishop John, Bishop Matthew and their friends and relatives had gone to Normandy after being chased out of Scotland the previous summer, and around them gathered other exiles from the persecuted Scottish Church.

So off the proud King William had to go, his only consolation being that in Normandy there would be good jousting. Earl David, de Mortimer and some of the other barons went with him, leaving Sir Richard de Moreville in charge of the kingdom.

When we heard this news we all breathed a sigh of relief, and it felt as though summer had moved a step nearer.

There were great royal comings and goings in Normandy all that spring and summer. Most of the Scottish court found its way there. Four kings, they say, met peacefully together and departed in peace, a rare event indeed in this world of strife. There was old King Henry, his son King Henry the Younger, our own King William, and King Phillip of the French.

At this peaceful gathering of worldly rulers, peace for our suffering Church seemed also within reach. Old King Henry knew where such a quarrel could lead. Only ten years before, his men had killed his own Archbishop, the saintly martyr Thomas, and his life would not be long enough for the penance Heaven demanded. Henry must have seen the ghost of his own crime in what was happening in Scotland, so that his advice came from the heart: 'Be reconciled'.

Under his auspices King William met with Bishops John and Matthew, and came to a fine arrangement. Matthew would return to his own see of Aberdeen under a safe-conduct, and would take up his episcopal duties there without let or hindrance. John agreed that he would give up his claim to St Andrews if he could get another bishopric of his own choosing, no doubt our own see of Dunkeld, next in importance after St Andrews and still vacant. The end to our suffering seemed near. Soon the see of St Andrews would be able to bury its dead, and justice for the wrongs committed in this dark time was at hand. The only thing that was needed was the agreement of the Holy Father.

Pope Alexander was an old, sick man. All his life he had fought to set the Kingdom of Christ over the kingdoms of men. The Pope is Christ's viceroy on earth before whom all secular rulers must bow down in homage. Above all they should not interfere in affairs which do not concern them, affairs of the Church.

When the news of the Normandy settlement reached him he was furious and denounced it as the tinkering of seculars, who should keep their lame compromises for their own secular doings. The Church of Christ would never compromise, bartering bishoprics as if they were sheep skins or sacks of grain. It would be an insult to the Holy Trinity itself.

I never saw Pope Alexander, but I always imagined him to look like Subprior Brice.

Martin, God's Kingdom on earth is not established easily. Christ Himself says, 'You must not think that I have come to bring peace to the earth; I have not come to bring peace, but a sword.' We are weak and sinful creatures, and sometimes we confuse true peace with a quiet, easy life.

Pope Alexander, in his wisdom inspired, I am sure, by the Holy Spirit, cut through this confusion. He declared that unless King William yielded totally to the will of the Pope, he would excommunicate the whole kingdom.

That summer, while rumour and counter-rumour swept the land, a terrible portent appeared in the heavens. It was what they call a hairy star, or comet, and it presages the death of princes. We stood outside the church after Lauds on the night it appeared and prayed that the disaster which it foretold might be averted. May God forgive me, but I strangled my prayer in my breast.

Not long after this, death and destruction threatened from the north. A great army had gathered to attack the kingdom of the Scots, and overthrow King William. Its leader was Donald, eldest son of William, eldest son of King Duncan II, himself the eldest son of the great King Malcolm Canmore. King Duncan was the older half-brother of good King David, our own King's grandfather. Donald claimed that the kingdom of Scotland was rightfully his. Many agreed, secretly in the south, openly in the north. Wherever there were complaints and grievances against the Norman friends of King William and resentment at his infinite generosity towards them, Scots would whisper in their own tongue, 'If Donald were King, things would be very different.'

I had always believed that, for all the evils the Normans brought with them, they also brought order and fruitfulness to the land, as well as safety and prosperity to the Church. The Church would flourish more under them than under a northern King with a pack of heathens at his heels. But now I was no longer sure of anything, and it seemed as if we were being crushed between two great querns.

All the coast was put on the alert. There was talk of evacuating the island. Then we heard that Earl David was mustering the host and that the King himself was on his way home from Normandy.

Almost a year had passed since the fight in the churchyard and the disappearance of my dear brother Edgar. We were preparing to gather in the harvest Then without warning the men-at-arms arrived in their long-boats.

It was the feast of St Bartholemew, and Subprior Brice was preaching a sermon on the saint's dreadful death, comparing the pain of being flayed alive to the pain the Church of Christ was suffering at the hands of the haughty. Suddenly a servant burst in and ran up to Prior Walter. He whispered something in his ear. Walter stood up and quickly followed the servant out of the church.

Nobody was listening to Brice any more, and his voice became more hesitant. Before long Walter was back again, shouting that we were under attack. I was immediately bundled off and hidden in the sacristy, as it was feared that they had come for me. I wondered as I lay trembling in the darkness whether the thick walls and the great iron-bolted door would protect me from the treachery of some of my brothers.

Later that day Brother Peter came to tell me that I was to go to the refectory for my meal. He said that twenty men-at-arms with their scullions and harlots had ensconced themselves on the East Island. They had forbidden anyone to leave the Priory, but so far had shown no intention of carrying off any of the servants of the Lord. 'Not even you, Brother Michael,' he said, fixing me with his bulging eyes. 'Like bees at the honey, Brother Michael, like bees at the honey, but in the Lord's name we will drive them away.' As I followed him warily out of the safety of the sacristy, I could not find it in my soul to share his confidence.

They had indeed come to stay. They were under the command of a serjeant, Robert Giffard by name. There was no bigger or uglier man in the kingdom. He was built like a keep, one-eyed, with a puckered scar across his mouth and chin.

Not only had he ordered no one to leave the Priory, he had forbidden us to receive anyone from the mainland, including any of our brothers who happened to be away on Priory business. As far as provisions went, his men would see to it that we did not starve. All this was, Giffard assured us, to protect us from the marauding army of Donald mac William. When asked how long this state of affairs was to last, he would only say, 'As long as necessary.'

Four weeks later they were still with us, loud, obscene, and oppressive, and not a word of what was happening beyond the water had reached us. Several times we saw them in their big, black boats turn back would-be visitors from the Lothian shore. No one coming from Fothrif got as far as the water. One of the boats forced back flew a magnificent flag. We could not make out whose it was, but its gold thread gleamed in the sun.

They sat upon our necks and breathed their stinking breath in our faces. We brought in our corn from the scant island acres, and feared for our main harvest from our estates scattered throughout Fothrif, Fife and Lothian. It was a blessing that Brother Henry the cellarer had been on the mainland when we were cut off, but our granger had been at the Priory that day, so he had become a prisoner with the rest of us. What with dishonest, unsupervised grange servants, as well as armies on the march, there would be little of the harvest left over for us, and the prospect of a famished winter loomed large, no matter who won the struggle in the north.

One morning, we were woken for Prime by the ringing of the small hand-bell, instead of the great church bell. Then, once we had taken our places in choir, Geoffrey announced that we were not to sing the Hour, but say it under our breath, even the morning hymn. The older brothers crossed themselves, and I heard a word whispered which sent a cold shiver down my spine: 'interdict'.

A strange silence had fallen upon the Priory. Usually, after the bells had stopped, a group of the men-at-arms came clattering into the nave to chatter and cough throughout Prime and morning Mass. Today in the nave there was complete silence, until suddenly we heard shouts from outside and loud hammering on the doors. Subprior Brice hurried out of the choir towards the noise.

'You are all excommunicate,' he shouted, his shrill voice echoing in the empty nave, 'by command of the Lord Pope himself. You cannot worship with us. All sacraments are forbidden to you, your lord, your lord's lord, and the lord King.'

The hammering and shouting stopped, our praying stopped. All heads turned to Brice as he came back through the roodscreen, triumph in his eyes. Geoffrey thumped his fist on his stall to bring us back to our prayers.

When Prime was over we were told to go straight into Chapter, as there were to be no morning or private Masses said that day. Prior Walter, who had been absent from Prime, was already seated in his high seat. He greeted us with a weak smile as, full of trepidation, we filed in and sat down. Then he leant forward and spoke, so quietly that we also had to lean forward. From outside came the shouts of angry men.

'My sons,' he said, 'last night a messenger came and went. May St Columba guide him safely back. His message was that since the feast of St Gregory the Great, the King and his whole realm have lain under an interdict.

'The Archbishop of York, now legate in Scotland, and the Bishop of Durham sent messengers to the Bishops, Abbots and Priors throughout the land telling them to come to John Scot at Roxburgh and offer him the obedience due to the Bishop of St Andrews.

'The ones whom the messengers reached and who dared to set out on the journey, the King exiled along with their convents, and even their kinsfolk. He has seized their lands, their serfs, their granges. Jedburgh, Dunblane, Dryburgh and St Andrews have all been persecuted. For this wickedness York excommunicated the lord King and all that he rules over, and the interdict lies upon every convent and Bishop that has ignored the summons to Roxburgh. But we at the Priory of St Columba are prisoners. We are exempt.'

He said this firmly, turning towards Subprior Brice, who sat scowling.

'So, my sons,' he went on, 'we can exercise our privilege of holding our services behind closed doors in an undertone, without the ringing of bells, but no outsider may worship with us. I have ordered Brother Peter to bar all the outer doors to the church and veil the cross and the statues as though it were Lent. Let me make one thing quite clear. As soon as our guardian demons allow me to cross to the mainland, I too must try to make the journey to Roxburgh, and beyond, if God so wills.'

When Prior Walter had finished speaking all due form was ignored. Some of my brothers sobbed, some begged Walter not to leave them, some urged him to go, or asked to accompany him. In the confusion you could already hear the bells of discord which were to clash so jarringly in the coming weeks.

That morning at Terce the Devil himself appeared. First we heard shouts outside the church, a voice desperately begging for mercy, then a blood-curdling scream.

The north east window shattered. Pressed against the leaded frame and still dripping blood, danced the head of a man on a pole. It was a guard who had been on watch that night. This was the punishment for having let the news of the interdict reach us.

The guardian demons never came near the church after that, but their vigilance increased. The gales around the feast of St Matthew were severe that year. By the time they had blown themselves out, supplies for warders and prisoners were uncomfortably low. Three of our sheep disappeared, and we had to kill another three for ourselves. Usually our warders brought us supplies from our own stocks at Barnhill, helping themselves liberally in the process. Their main supplies were brought over from Aberdour.

As the storms raged up and down the Forth, strife tore through the convent. No one had left the island for over a month. We were like a flock of sheep surrounded by marauding wolves. Wherever we looked we saw land which lay under the interdict. Some amongst us believed that we also deserved no better. Subprior Brice and Father Nicholas were the most outspoken of these. Nicholas argued that we should bow our heads and accept the interdict, suspend all services and pray only for the return of Scotland to the fold. Brice went further, arguing that Prior Walter should take our holy relics and try to reach the mainland. 'It is only then,' he would say, his dark eyes narrowed to slits, his finger stabbing the air or the nearest chest, 'that we can rightfully enjoy our privilege of continuing our services, and it is only thus that we can wash ourselves clean of the sin of disobedience.'

Prior Walter would reply angrily, 'So that you can! So that your conscience can be clean, I have to lie at the bottom of the Forth clutching the holy relics, or get my brains splattered against the church wall. These men are ruthless. We are prisoners. Besides, I have not even received an official summons to go to Roxburgh. The night messenger brought news only.'

"If you were blind' said Jesus, 'you would not be guilty," Brice would retort haughtily.

'We are neither blind nor guilty, Brother Brice.'

So it went on. Brice even offered to go in Walter's place, but Walter would not allow it. Finally Walter forbade any further discussion on the matter, and had Isaac and Andrew flogged in Chapter for arguing about it. Rancour fed on the enforced silence, and with the Prior and Subprior, our father and mother, at loggerheads the Priory was split to its bedrock.

I agreed with Walter, but I still had doubts, as most of us had. These made our times in church even more joyless and fraught. I longed to sing, to be free of the dull mutterings and dark fears. I would hear the wind tearing at the church roof and beating at the windows and my heart would swell not with the love of God but with hatred for Brice and Nicholas and the others who would not submit.

The curse which lay on the land could not be kept out simply by barring the doors, but like the wind that was shaking the world outside, it found its way through every crevice into our very hearts."

PERTH

It was the feast of St Luke. We were in Chapter when we heard loud footsteps in the cloister. The door burst open, revealing the hulking figure of Robert Giffard, fully armed. He stood there like a cyclops, his one eye sweeping the room. His gaze settled on me for a moment and he smiled. Although we had met when I was in de Mortimer's household, it was no smile of greeting.

'Father Prior,' he boomed, 'the King commands that you attend him in Perth. He has important business to discuss with you. You are to bring with you one who used to go by the name of Duscath mac Flathbertaich. I and my men will accompany you. We leave before the tide turns. Finish your Chapter, make yourself ready and meet me at the boats. Him I will take with me now.' He swung round and pointed straight at me, at the same time barking a command. Two armed men stepped forward.

'Come with me, Duscath mac Flathbertaich,' he roared, 'and say farewell to your brothers.'

I stood frozen to the spot. My brothers were all around me, protesting and pleading; Giffard and his men stood at the door, glowering; while I watched it all from somewhere far away, unable to believe it was happening.

Because I did not move I was seized and bundled out of the chapter house. It had been so easy. As I was dragged out the main gate, my only thought was, 'How could this happen?' Night and day servants were posted to warn of our warders' approach; if the warning was given, I was to go immediately to my hiding place in the sacristy. Yet that morning our enemies had walked into the heart of the Priory and not a murmur of warning had been raised. I was sure I had been betrayed.

Dejected and shivering I stood on the shore and watched the men-at-arms carrying tents and baggage down the steep slope of the East Island and loading them into the boats. It seemed they were leaving the island altogether.

They laughed and sang, happy as children that their long confinement on this windy rock was over. They wanted to leave as much as I wanted to stay.

I looked up and saw the half rotted head grinning at me from its pole above the beach, the reward for a duty ill-done, or a command ill-obeyed. I prayed for the salvation of his soul, as well as for the safety of my body, and my pity embraced us both.

Wrapped in the thick winter cowl that Walter brought me, tucked into the bow of the largest of the four long-ships, I left

Inchcolm. We sailed eastwards, heading for the open sea. Waves smashed against us, sending great silver showers high into the air. The boat pitched and lurched, the planks groaned, the movement comforted.

Some of the men sprang around, tending to the sail-ropes, bailing out, avoiding the spray, losing their balance. Others sat ready at the oars. From inside my hood I watched intently. It had been a long time since I had watched men, ordinary men, so closely. I had almost forgotten the shape of their bodies, the angle of their heads, the quickness of their limbs. Their bodies pulled my eyes to them as much as their souls repelled me. I tried to close my eyes and pray, but still I stared, and my prayer was left half said. It was as if my fear had quickened my baser senses.

All day long our ship battered its way through the waves. Some of the crew were seasick. So was Prior Walter. I could see him at the stern, hanging over the side, retching violently. Giffard himself was standing beside him, holding him by the scruff of his habit. He was determined not to lose at least one of his prisoners. This was reassuring.

I had been secured by having my feet bound together. If anything happened to the boat, I would sink like a stone. The wind was fierce, and showed no signs of abating. We were on a long voyage round the stormy ness of Fife, and the crew seemed inexperienced, so the fear of shipwreck and drowning soon became greater than all my other fears. I decided I had to catch the eye of one of the crew, so that if the worst happened I would not be left to drown like a hamstrung dog .

I pulled back my hood. My looks had been my curse in de Mortimer's household, and later they had almost got me thrown out of the Priory, but now, I thought, they could be a blessing. Beauty can harden hearts or it can soften hearts, but it rarely leaves them unmoved.

I saw some faces turn towards me, and I looked for a sympathetic one which was not a sickly green. Yes, one of them was showing interest, staring and looking away, then his eyes creeping back again. He had a good-natured face, blue eyes and long brown hair swept back and tied by a leather thong. I risked a slight smile and he smiled back. I looked away, feeling safer. Often after that during the long, cold voyage I warmed myself at his smile.

The sky was darkening when we finally reached land. It had been some time since we had left the open sea. I had watched the high wooded hills glide above us and knew we were approaching Perth.

Walter had to be half carried out of the boat. He knelt on the wooden quay more in exhaustion than in prayer. He was hauled to his feet and we were marched hurriedly up to the castle, where the royal standard was flying. There we were pushed into a small guardroom at the courtyard gate. Walter was too exhausted even to protest. An age passed before the bolt shot back and we were led out into the windy night. It was clear that a feast was being prepared. Delicious smells wafted on the night air.

We were taken into the great hall itself, ablaze with light and full of people, but that was not our destination. We were led along the side wall and into a small chamber. A brazier glowed in the centre, and beside it stood a huge figure swathed in black, Jocelin Bishop of Glasgow. His fat, shapeless face broke into a grimace of welcome. Walter and I both fell to our knees. Jocelin pulled Walter up as he was about to kiss his ring.

'No, no, let me embrace you,' he said unctuously. 'We must all cling together when God averts His face from the land.'

I was also hauled to my feet and for a moment was lost in a sea of fine cloth.

'You are very wet, both of you. Robert, go and fetch some dry clothes for our friends. And tell a servant to bring some food and wine.'

It was then that I noticed two figures in the shadows behind Jocelin. One was Robert de Ayr, Jocelin's chaplain. The other was introduced as William, a chaplain of the King. I did not trust any of them.

Bishop Jocelin lowered himself down into a finely carved chair.

'Now, Walter my son, let us get straight to the point,' he said, rubbing his chins with his hand. 'I know you have suffered much. We all have. But an end to our sufferings is in sight, God be praised for His mercy. You have heard the news that our Holy Father Pope Alexander is now with his Maker?'

We both gasped, for we had heard no such thing. We crossed ourselves and prayed together, '*Tibi, Domine, commendamus.*'

'And the interdict?' Walter asked.

'The interdict had been confirmed before he was taken to the Lord,' Jocelin replied gravely. 'York had the letters of confirmation with him when he met with the King at Redden. It would have taken a miracle to have stopped him using them. As you know, there was no miracle.'

'York pronounced the interdict at Redden?' Walter asked.

Jocelin nodded.

'Who is our new Pope?'

'Hubald, Cardinal Bishop of Ostia, that blessed old man who smoothed so many ruffled feathers at the last Lateran Council.'

'Yes, I remember him,' Walter said, 'truly a man of peace, but very old. What name has he taken?'

'Lucius, third of that name.'

'God guide and protect Pope Lucius,' Walter said.

'Amen,' we all muttered.

'Walter,' Jocelin said, leaning forward, lowering his voice, taking his hand. 'God has been angry with the King. God's anger is always deserved, but the King is truly penitent. All things on earth must change. I have heard that York too is close to death. The King wants peace. He longs to lead himself and his people back into God's light. He has walked in the ways of darkness too long. Now, my son, let me be frank with you.'

He sat back, his heavy jowls trembling slightly.

He was interrupted by a red-faced servant, who staggered into the room draped in black cloth and carrying a tray laden with wine and food. I took the tray from him as it was about to pitch its contents onto the floor. The servant shook himself, shedding the clothing he had brought for us, then helped us out of our sodden habits, poured wine into silver goblets and served us all with slices of pigeon pie. Walter and I fell onto the food like starving wolves.

As soon as Walter had finished eating he looked up, 'You were saying, my lord?'

Jocelin turned his already empty goblet nervously in his hands.

'Yes, well, you see, the King wants to send a delegation of Scottish churchmen to the new Pope to sue for peace and forgiveness. I will be leading the delegation. He wants you, Prior Walter, to grace it with your presence.'

Walter did nothing to hide his surprise. I almost dropped my goblet. Jocelin went on quickly, 'I know, I know. He has looked the other way while his kinsmen and lieges have done you great wrong. Now he wants to make amends, heal the wounds, right the wrongs.'

The wine was caressing the inside of my body with its warm tongue. Jocelin's words were almost as sweet.

'Your neighbour, Sir William de Mortimer, might be prevailed upon to give you back the church of Aberdour,' the Bishop went on. He leant forward and added in a whisper, 'It is of course rightfully yours.'

Then raising his voice again he said, 'There is also talk of half a plough-gate of good arable into the bargain. And this young fellow here,' he nodded his head towards me and all his chins rippled, 'I understand that Sir William has some claims on him. He could be persuaded to renounce all such claims. In gratitude for these kindnesses, the King asks only one favour, that you go to Rome and help plead with our Holy Father to lift the bitter sentence of excommunication which lies so heavily on our land.' He paused, wiping the remains of the pigeon pie from his mouth. 'And to prevail upon our Holy Father to implement the Normandy agreement.'

'You mean that Hugh stay at St Andrews and John become our Bishop at Dunkeld?'

Jocelin nodded vigorously.

Walter was silent for a moment. Then he said slowly, 'Just

because Pope Alexander is dead surely does not mean that John's rights are, too.'

Jocelin scowled, 'John Scot himself has conceded these rights, as you call them, which have caused so many wrongs and brought such suffering...'

'You yourself, my lord Bishop,' Walter interrupted, 'were present when the Pope's own Legate upheld those very rights, and you were one of the Bishops who consecrated him.'

'Prior Walter,' Jocelin boomed, 'you are being awkward. We have a new Holy Father and a new spirit of reconciliation and peace is abroad. This is no time for obstinacy.'

Walter was silent again. Then he asked, 'Who else would be going, apart from yourself?'

'Apart from ourselves,' Jocelin replied pointedly, 'the delegation will consist of Abbot Arnold of Melrose and Abbot Osbert of Kelso.'

I wondered what bribes the King had offered them.

'No other Augustinians?' Walter asked.

'A noble representative of a noble Order, my son,' Jocelin replied.

'I must have time to think and pray about it,' Walter said slowly. 'I would also have to discuss it with the head of our Order in Scotland, Abbot Robert of Scone.'

At the mention of Scone my heart leapt in my breast.

'Or is Abbot Robert also a fugitive in England?' Walter asked grimly.

'No, he is not,' Jocelin said, scowling. 'Ill health prevented him from obeying John's summons. His Prior went in his stead. Yes, by all means, take counsel with Abbot Robert in this matter. Only be quick.' I noticed William the King's chaplain bend forward towards us, like a tree swaying in a breeze.

'We shall be back here by Nones tomorrow, if that is not too late for his Majesty,' Walter said.

Jocelin looked at William, who gave a curt nod. Then he whispered something into Jocelin's ear. Jocelin nodded.

'At very latest. One other thing,' Jocelin added, shifting uncomfortably in his seat, 'your son in Christ here will not be accompanying you. Do not protest, Prior Walter,' he said, holding up his hand, as Walter rose angrily to his feet.

'This is outrageous, my lord,' Walter cried.

'It is the King's will, my son. He will be under royal protection.'

Jocelin too had struggled to his feet and the two men stood glaring at each other.

I sat rooted to the spot. My heart was racing. I was listening so intently to their conversation that I could hardly understand them, each word burst in my head, almost obliterating the next. Then I remembered I was sitting in the presence of my lord Prior and the Bishop of Glasgow. I too got to my feet. The room began to heave, and for a moment it was as if I was back on board the longship. Somewhere in the distance I could hear Walter's voice saying, 'I will be back here before Nones, my lord, and I expect to be reunited with my Brother Michael.'

'And I expect a sensible and mature decision from you regarding the delegation,' Jocelin said. 'Now, Prior Walter, you may go. Good night.' He held out a fat hand adorned with his ring of office. Walter knelt and kissed it, then looked at me. His eyes gleamed full of anger in the torchlight. My heart froze, because it seemed as if his anger was for me. I knelt to receive his blessing. He brushed my head and muttered something. Then he hurried out of the room, followed by William.

I got slowly to my feet. Jocelin eased himself down into his chair again and with an impatient flick of his hand bade me be seated. Then he motioned to the servant to pour him another goblet of wine. There ensued an uneasy silence which was broken by the return of the royal chaplain followed by two guards.

'William, my son, I commend this man Michael, also known as Duscath mac something or other, to the royal protection. Take him and guard him well, and may God be with you.'

He did not hold out his hand for me to kiss and I was bundled out of the dark, warm room into the blazing lights and din of the great hall. The meal was about to start. Not many heads turned to see a young churchman in ill-fitting clothes being marched out into the courtyard escorted by two royal guards.

The night was cold and windy. I was taken to the little room near the gate, where Walter and I had been thrust on our arrival. Well, at least now I was dry and fed. I was also alone. The door shut behind me and I heard the bolts slide into their sockets. I felt frightened, lonely and abandoned, and the darkness lay like a weight upon my eyes. I threw myself down on the rough floor. Sleep came to me quickly, but despite my exhaustion I did not sleep deeply. I woke often, unable to shake off the vivid, unpleasant dreams that oppressed me.

Somewhere a single bell tolled the Hours, one for Prime, three for Terce, six for Sext, Hours which, because of the interdict, would remain unsung. Terce had been rung when the door to my prison swung open and a servant came in with a pitcher of ale and a chunk of coarse bread. No pigeon pie today, but I was so hungry I did not care. From outside came the usual sounds of horses and men, the harsh, warlike sounds that accompanied the King wherever he went. William the Lion was well-named. My ears strained to catch anything that might pertain to me, but there was nothing.

As time crept on, I became certain that Walter had abandoned me. He had taken counsel with his brothers and with Edgar, who had told him of our love. They had decided to abandon me to my fate and stand firm for the sanctity of our Holy Mother

Church. Walter had sacrificed much for me already. Now it was my turn to be sacrificed for a far greater principle.

It was only right and just, and nothing less than I deserved. I remembered his eyes of anger that he had turned on me as he left me the night before. Yes, Walter had abandoned me. And if Walter had abandoned me, then so had God, somehow I could not separate the two in my half-crazed mind. I fell on my knees and prayed. 'Thy will be done, Lord.' But, oh, Martin, they were the hardest words I had ever said.

The bell tolled nine times. Nones. Prior Walter had not returned, would never come. Wait! Someone was at the door. Hope leapt in my heart. The door flew open and a tall, familiar figure strode in carrying a blazing torch. In its flickering light I recognised the face of Sir William de Mortimer.

I shrank back in horror into a corner. He fixed the torch to a bracket on the wall and its unsteady light filled the room, leaving no hidingplace. I pulled my hood up over my head. He grinned at me.

'Well, my little monk, here we are after all this time. Why so shy? Do not be so mean with your looks.'

I said nothing. I could not speak. My breath came in short, sharp gasps. I knew he was going to kill me. He swaggered over to me. One hand tore back my hood, the other found its way under the folds of my tunic.

'This is sacrilege, my lord,' I managed to gasp. 'I am a man of God.'

He laughed, threw back his head and showed a mouthful of black teeth.

'There's no such thing just now, my little man of nothing. We're all godless, haven't you heard? He's not even looking.' He pressed his whole body against mine, and with his mouth over my ear he hissed, 'You have been mine, you are mine now, and you will be mine again, for all time.'

By this time he had pulled my tunic up to my thighs, so that when I brought my knee up sharply there was nothing to cushion the blow to his crotch but his own breeches. He reeled back, doubled up, groaning.

I flew to the door but it was bolted from the outside. He roared like a wounded boar and charged me. I leapt to the side, grabbed the torch from the wall, and jabbed it in his face. He fell back and drew his sword.

I lowered the torch to the floor, which was strewn with dried bent grass. It flared up between us. Then I swung the torch above my head to the dry thatch roof. Soon it was blazing and crackling.

Sir William swiped at me with his sword, cutting into my right arm. I did not feel the pain at first, but I dropped the torch, which continued to blaze where it lay.

I saw him draw back his arm ready to strike another blow. I threw myself onto the floor as far away from him as I could. I have no doubt he would have run me through there and then, had not a large piece of burning thatch fallen on his head. He had to beat it off with both hands. I could hardly see him now for the thick smoke.

Dimly I saw the door open. Guards in war-helmets rushed in and dragged my attacker out of the burning hut. Shouts of 'Fire!' filled my ears. My eyes were smarting. Flames were leaping up all around me. I could scarcely breathe. Fire has succeeded where the sea has failed, I thought. 'Into Thy hands, O Lord.' I felt myself being lifted roughly into the air. There was a searing pain in my right arm, then everything went black.

When I returned to my senses I was still lying on the ground, but further away from the burning hut. The fire had won, and servants and soldiers were simply standing round watching the flames consume what was left of my prison. Part of the pallisading had been removed so that the fire could not spread. Everything seemed strangely quiet. Sparks flew on the breeze and were extinguished where they landed. From where I lay I could even see servants perched like huge crows on the roof of the great hall, ready to pounce on any spark that dared to land there.

I became aware of a face leaning over me and peering into mine. It was the face of a young man, kind, anxious, familiar, with soot staining the cheeks and brow. Where had I seen him before? Of course, it was the oarsman whom my eye had caught on the boat, who had made me feel safe in the storm. I smiled at him weakly, and he smiled back.

Behind him there was another face, thin and stern. This face I did not recognise, nor did it comfort me. It belonged to a man of religion. He was dressed in the black habit of a Benedictine. He pushed the young oarsman gently out of the way and knelt down beside me, touching my arm. The dull ache in it flared up into a sheet of pain. With a knife he cut away my sleeve, then taking out a flask from his scrip he poured a thick black ointment onto the wound. The fire from which I had just been rescued could not have burnt more fiercely than this ointment. My vision clouded. I wanted to throw up. Then with deft hands he tightly bound up my wounded arm, and the pain gradually ebbed away again to a dull ache.

As the monk tended my wound, he spoke softly to me in French. His voice was kinder than his face, and reassuring. 'The Lord sent an angel to save the three youths from Nebuchadnezzar's furnace. Likewise He has sent one to you in the guise of this young man. You owe him your life, you know: he risked the flames to pull you to safety. He did so just in time. Seconds later the roof collapsed.'

The oarsman's face appeared again, looking over the monk's shoulder. He smiled and winked at me. 'Thank you,' I murmured.

'You cannot lie here,' the monk was saying. Then turning to the oarsman he said loudly, in simple French,

'Take to east chamber, east chamber, careful, right arm hurt, understand?'

'Aye, Faither,' the oarsman replied solemnly. Then half walking, half supported, I was led towards the great hall.

'Whaur's de Mortimer?' I muttered out of the corner of my mouth, once my head had stopped spinning.

'I the jyle, by word o the King,' he replied.

'An Walter, ma Prior?'

'He's here i the castle, jaist arrivit. Noo haud yer wheesht, an save yer breith.' He gave me a broad smile.

'Thank ye,' I said again weakly. My heart sang with thanks to God and St Michael for this news, and for this young man, who out of the host of my enemies had become my friend.

The east chamber was filled with light which streamed through a tall, narrow window. In the centre of the room stood a brazier. Walter sat on one side, the huge bulk of Bishop Jocelin on the other. Walter rose and gave me the kiss of peace. The anger in his eyes was gone and in its place were joy and kindness. He had not abandoned me and because of that I felt strong enough to bear even the pain in my arm. Yet one thing still troubled me.

'They tell me de Mortimer is in prison,' I whispered.

'He is to be confined at his Majesty's pleasure,' Walter replied. 'He will be punished for breaking the King's peace. I have the King's own word for it. We need fear nothing more from that quarter.'

'Thank God for that,' I sighed. Then I felt my knees buckle under me and, gently guided by Walter and the young guard, down I went. I lay on the floor feeling very foolish. I heard Jocelin's voice, deep and smooth and insincere, 'I'm truly sorry about the state of Brother Michael, but all's well that ends well and Brother Simon the physician says that the damage to his arm is not serious.

'As I was saying, Walter, the King is delighted with your decision, and so am I. He wants to see you before you set off, and of course you can take Brother Michael back with you. You can take him to Rome, too, if you want. Considering what's just happened, it might not be a bad thing if he were out of the kingdom for a time. He's yours now, safe in the bosom of Holy Mother Church.'

Their conversation flowed on and over me. My heart swelled with joy, for one thing above all else was clear, I was safe. Walter had accepted the King's offer. He had chosen the path of reconciliation, had decided not to sacrifice me, not to abandon me to my enemies. All my terror and despair melted away as if they had never been.

A doubt came into my soul, like a cloud before the sun. By obeying the King, taking the King's bribes, were we not sullying the principle for which the Scottish Church had suffered so much for so long? Were we not confusing the easy way with the right way? Then the doubt passed and the sun shone again.

Nothing is fixed and certain in this life, Martin, and nothing lasts for ever. You are too young to understand that now, but if God spares you, you will come to know it as well as I. It is both a blessing and a curse. Only the Word of God remains the same, but we are whirled around it like water in an eddy, and so our vision and our understanding even of the Word is ever-changing.

Nevertheless, there is a still point that we can win to, where we can hear a voice whisper to us what is right and what is not right. It is the voice of our angel of truth, a compelling voice that can never be ignored. There are those who fear it because they say they cannot distinguish between it and the voice of the Devil. Perhaps they are right, and it is I who am deceived and eternally betrayed. I will know that only when I stand before my Maker and my Judge on the Day of Doom.

Yet as I lay on the floor of that warm, bright room in the King's castle at Perth, with my Prior and my guard beside me, I knew it had been granted to me to reach for a moment that blessed still point, and the voice of the angel told me that nothing of importance had been sullied. I closed my eyes and gave thanks to God.

Later that day I was taken in a litter to the Abbey of Scone, and lodged in the infirmary. As soon as I arrived I asked the infirmarer for permission to speak with Brother Edgar. He told me that there was no brother of that name in the convent, and besides he had been given strict instructions that I was to see nobody except my Prior. I was puzzled and disappointed, but it did not keep me from sleep. I slept soundly the whole night, so soundly and deeply that no demons or nightmares were able to bring bad dreams to my soul.

The following morning I felt well and strong, but my arm was still throbbing and raw. Prior Walter came to me and said we were travelling south that very day. Abbot Robert had lent us two good mounts and the King had given us two strong guards.

Before we left Scone I prayed to the blessed Aelred to grant me a glimpse of my beloved Edgar. My eyes searched eagerly amongst the group of brothers waiting at the gate-house with Abbot Robert to bid us farewell, but I left heavy-hearted, my prayer ungranted.

On such a morning it was difficult to remain sad for long. The golden brown leaves were bright and burnished in the strong autumn sunlight. The briars were hung with sweet, black fruit. The rich odour of fruitfulness and decay filled the air. It was not just from the beauty of Creation that my soul took joy. There was a strange, new feeling within my breast, so strange that I could not at first name it. Then it burst on me like a warm ray of sunshine striking my face. It was the absence of fear.

'That young man who pulled you from the flames, Brother Michael,' Prior Walter said to me as we looked back over Perth from Craigend, 'he was one of our enemies, yet he risked his life to save you. God changed him from a guardian demon to a guardian angel. We must give thanks to God for all his works, must we not?'

'God works in mysterious ways, Father Prior,' I replied with a smile.

Then for the last time turning our backs on the town of St John, we rode gently over the hills towards Fothrif and home."

PART THREE
THE . HOLY . CITY

I was glad when it was said to me, we shall go to the
house of the Lord,
Our feet stood in your halls Jerusalem,
to where the tribes go up, the tribes of the Lord,
to celebrate the name of the Lord;
because the thrones of judgement are set there, the
thrones of the house of David.
Pray for the peace of Jerusalem, and for the prosperity of
those who love you,
May there be peace within your walls, and prosperity
within your palaces,
For the sake of my brothers and my friends, I said peace
be upon you.
For the sake of the house of the Lord our God, I have
prayed for your good.

Salutatio Jerusalem, urbis sanctae Psalm 121

THE JOURNEY

Martin sniffed the damp, salty air. The sun was a pale golden disc in a haar that had been rolling in from the open sea all morning. He could not see the coast, or the other end of the island. Sometimes he could not even see the top of the Priory tower. Quiet white shifting walls surrounded him.

The air in the infirmary was hot and stuffy, as always. After greeting Brother Michael, whom he found sitting in his usual place by the window, Martin remarked on the heat.

"My old bones have been starved of warmth all my life," Michael replied. "Do not grudge me some now. Cold is everywhere, cold from the sea, cold from the air, cold from the stone, with the cold of death waiting, just beyond the warmth."

"In that place there is neither cold nor hot," Martin said, trying to console the old man.

"I will feel heat and cold at the same time, and both will be unbearable," Michael muttered, half to himself. He was obviously in bad humour. "And you, young man, have you been sent by God as the start of my Purgatory? You make me remember, when all I want to do is to forget. Why do you plague me in this way? Will Simon never leave me be? He has sent you, hasn't he? He'll haunt me to the grave, and beyond."

At the mention of Simon's name Martin's heart beat faster. Was the old man ready to talk of him? He would have to tread carefully. "Father, why would he want to do such a thing?" he asked gently. "Was he not a good man?"

"A good man!" Michael snapped, his voice full of scorn. "Simon, a good man! When his whole life was a crime against everything sacred! I do not want to burden your young soul with the life of Simon de Quincy."

"Father," Martin said firmly, "the young are made for burdens, and the old must shed them, lest they take them into eternity with them. I am not a priest, so I cannot absolve you, but I know that it is no sin to have known a wicked man."

"It is a sin to have loved him, though," Michael said sadly, all scorn and anger now gone from his voice. "Please, my son, go and get me my drink. Then I will tell you how I met Simon de Quincy. Perhaps then you will understand."

Soon Michael was looking in better humour, sitting comfortably with both his wizened hands around the warm beaker.

"What was I telling you about last?" he asked.

"You were about to set off on a journey to Rome with your Prior and other important churchmen. You were going to beg the Pope to lift the ban on Scotland and the King. But you had been wounded in the arm..."

Martin's voice trailed off. Was this the road that would lead quickly to Simon? "And the last thing you said was that you were about to meet Simon de Quincy," he lied.

"Well, many a tale I could tell you about that time and journey. I was sent down from Scone straight to Newburgh Priory near York to recover from my wound, a safe distance from the man who had inflicted it, and from the court which had allowed him to inflict it. There I waited for Prior Walter and the others on their way south.

I left Newburgh with all the company, about eighty of us in total. Not that all eighty were going to Rome. It was only the four envoys with their chaplains and clerks and servants who were going to cross the Channel, about forty in all. The others were going no further than King Henry's Christmas court at Winchester.

This was the first destination for everyone. Since the war every Scottish delegation to the continent had to tell King Henry their business and seek his approval and permission. This galled many, but there was no choice in the matter, as it was from King Henry's ports in England that we sailed and at his ports in Normandy that we landed.

We arrived several days before the great Christmas feast. All the world seemed to be there. The town was filled with jugglers, minstrels, acrobats, men dressed as women, women dressed as men, performing animals, dwarfs, giants and other freaks of nature. Beauty and ugliness tumbled all around us. I remember it as a time of much laughter and much temptation.

As soon as the twelve days were over we went to Southampton and boarded a ship for Barfleur — with King Henry's permission, of course. He approved thoroughly of our mission, for there was no profit for him in a quarrel between King William and the Pope.

It was a smooth crossing. Just as well, as we were a day and a night on the water. It was bitterly cold, and by the time we reached Paris the snow was falling thickly. We moved south through Burgundy, where it felt even colder, although there was less snow. Perhaps that was because we were becoming very tired.

But you do not even know who I was travelling with, do you? I'll tell you about some of them. Prior Walter had brought with him Brother Isaac, my friend, and Brother Andrew.

Prior Walter was the lowest ranking of the four envoys. The delegation was led by Bishop Jocelin. Every time I saw him I shuddered at the memory of how he had used me to try to force Prior Walter to join the delegation. He had pretended to be sorry, to be the tool of a higher power, but I could not forget the ruthless gleam in his little, pig-like eyes. I had known even then that he cared about my fate as much as he would have cared about a worm under his foot.

Next in rank came Abbot Osbert of Kelso. The highest ranking of all the Scottish abbots, he claimed the dignity of a bishop and never tired of quoting papal privilege to support this claim. It was lucky that Bishop Jocelin was clearly his senior, which avoided disputes about precedence. But whenever Osbert had to yield to him in procession or at formal introductions, he always managed to make some comment such as, 'In deference to my lord bishop's length of service' or, 'In respect of Glasgow's seniority'.

It galled him greatly that the King had made Jocelin head of the delegation, but the proud are skilled at turning everything to the advantage of their pride. Osbert considered himself to be a close friend and confidant of the King. He would often begin a story with the words, 'So I said to the King... So I said to the King, 'My Lord, let me give you some advice: appoint Jocelin head of the envoys. This will please the Holy Father, as he too has risen from the ranks of the Cistercians, just like Jocelin, and you know how clannish the Cistercians are.' And the King said to me, 'Osbert, you are right, that is sound advice'.'

Osbert's obsession with rank and status was eclipsed by only one other thing, his obsession with sodomy. For him no sin was more heinous or a greater threat to humanity.

I remember once we were passing through a little town in northern France. A crowd had gathered in the market place to hear a travelling gleeman sing the latest songs about the great men and women of the land. He looked like the devil himself, with a twisted body and a face raddled with strong drink and vicious living. Nevertheless he looked up clearly and shamelessly. His expression seemed to say, 'there is no one who is superior to me, whatever their earthly rank and wealth.'

The crowd that had gathered was so dense we could hardly make our way through it, and often we came to a complete halt.

People turned and hissed, showing little respect, angry at us for disturbing their entertainment.

The gleeman stood on the roof of the town well, where the market place narrowed to a dark street. When we were almost level with him he turned on us with a most impertinent expression. Osbert as usual was riding up ahead and the gleeman took him to be the leader of our party.

'My lord Abbot,' he shouted, nimbly bending over so that his rear end was thrust towards Osbert and his head appeared through his open legs upside down, 'I can tell, my lord, from your face that you are from Orleans, the Sodom of France, where the knights must wear their shields at the rear. I beg of you, bless my arse.'

The crowd roared with laughter. Osbert went purple in the face. He became so agitated, I thought he was going to fall off his palfrey.

'You insolent dog,' he shouted, 'we are not from Orléans. We are from Scotland, where the detestable sin to which you so impiously allude has been beaten back to hell whence it came.'

'Beaten back to Orléans!' someone shouted from the crowd.

'That comes to the same thing,' the gleeman shouted. There was another roar of laughter.

'My sons and daughters, do not jest about such things,' Osbert yelled. 'The devil enters a mouth open in laughter, and will stir you to the very sin you mock.'

Then before even the quick-witted gleeman could say anything in reply Osbert had started to preach his favourite sermon.

'No, my children,' he shouted, standing up in his stirrups, 'do not jest about a sin which condemns you to the lowest pit of hell, a sin worse even than murder. For does not St Peter Damian tell us that it is the death of the body, the destruction of the soul; that it pollutes the flesh, extinguishes the light of the mind, casts out the holy spirit from the temple of the holy breast and replaces it with the devil?'

The crowd shifted restlessly and many looked expectantly at the gleeman. They had come here to listen to scurrilous songs and jokes, not a sermon. There was enough of that in their lives as it was. But the gleeman, no longer in his obscene position, looked seriously at Osbert, nodding as if agreeing with every word and quietly tuning his lute.

Suddenly he burst forth in a loud, clear voice, into a song which drowned out Osbert's words. I was to hear it again often, as it was one of Simon's favourites. I will whisper the words to you, Martin for if they heard me singing it here, they would throw me off the island, old and infirm as I am. Listen.

'Many a man, as you will find,
who denounces Sodom's kind,
preaches thus on sin with boys
when it's what he most enjoys.

He who talks the most of sin
all the while is dipping in:
the sinner, to deny it,
loud preaches, to keep it quiet.

Venus kindles many fires
but the hottest of desires
comes when males ignite a flame
— try yourself, you'll find the same!'

Osbert went bright red and started shouting at the top of his voice, threatening immediate excommunication. His armed servants, not understanding a word of what was going on, but alarmed by their master's violent tone and gestures, held their weapons ready for an attack. This caused great anxiety amongst the crowd, who closed ranks and started jeering abuse. Bishop Jocelin was shouting too, entreating Osbert to shut up and move on. Osbert however was beside himself, unable to do either.

It was the gleeman who saved the situation from violence. Suddenly he was on his knees, begging Osbert for mercy, apologising profusely for his insolence and innuendoes, and declaring that the Scots were indeed a pious and God-fearing nation untainted by such unspeakable sins.

Osbert stopped shouting and stared at him in disbelief. He had little choice but to give the gleeman his forgiveness and a curt, ungracious blessing. He told his servants to put up their weapons and we all rode on. The crowd fell back and our progress was no longer impeded. As soon as we had left the market place the jeers and laughter began again and Osbert was scarcely out of earshot than the gleeman was singing the next verse of his shameless song.

The fourth member of the delegation was an Abbot second only to Osbert in importance in the Scottish church, Abbot Arnold of Melrose, a Cistercian of the old school, who saw the Devil in all luxury. Luxury for him was anything not absolutely needed for keeping body and soul together.

He was constantly at loggerheads with his fellow-Cistercian, Bishop Jocelin, for whom comfort and good food were more important than prayer. He kept icily aloof from Abbot Osbert, whom he regarded as hopelessly worldly. Whenever Osbert began preaching on his favourite topic, sodomy, Arnold would roll his eyes and say that there were many other sins in the world, such as what Osbert was going to have for dinner.

'All of the flesh, that is the enemy,' he would say, 'not just one part of it.' Arnold, of course, had grown up in St Aelred's Abbey of Rievaulx, under the guidance of the blessed man himself.

Arnold had brought with him four monks and five lay-brothers. Following the lead of their Abbot they would often pull faces and laugh at Osbert and his entourage behind their backs. If Arnold caught them he would scold them, but not as harshly as he might. He never laughed.

It was only Prior Walter, the most amiable and tolerant of the four, who moved easily from one envoy to another, and had the task of smoothing the often ruffled feathers of these powerful, difficult men.

In Burgundy we stayed at the great Abbey of Cluny. Arnold and his party had wanted to stay at the Abbey of Citeaux, the mother-house of his order, but he was overruled by both the Bishop and Abbot Osbert. They knew that the food at Cluny would be much more palatable, and there would be more of it. Also the beds would be softer.

It was at Cluny that we decided to cross the great barrier of the Alps. At that time of year it would have been usual to continue south to Provence and from there to sail to Rome. We were strongly advised against this, as the Mediterranean was infested with pirates, Christian and Saracen, and few ships made the journey to Italy unscathed.

The Alps in winter, with their blizzards and avalanches and yawning chasms, seemed in comparison more inviting and held out a better chance of survival. Brigands lurked there also, but as with other vermin the winter usually cleared them away.

After several days of comfort and rest at Cluny we reluctantly set off, leaving Burgundy behind us, with its gently rolling countryside studded with rich villages and sturdy churches. Gradually the land rose up higher and higher, until before us towered the Alps, like some great rood-screen stretched across the horizon with travellers crucified upon it.

Through the great chasm of St Bernard we began our ascent, with local guides and ox-carts. I thought often of that brave monk as we stumbled up the winding mule-tracks amidst mountains that seemed to touch Heaven itself. Fervent were my prayers to the same spirit that had kept him from tumbling headlong down the sickening drops that yawned now on one side, now on the other.

I was on foot, thank God. The four envoys were given the dubious privilege of riding in the ox-carts. Sometimes their wheels were only inches from a terrible precipice, and I was sure that my dear Prior would be cast down into the abyss. And from the strained look on his face, I could see that he was as sure as I was.

Behind us, led by our servants, came the horses, their eyes bound to shield them from sights which filled us poor humans with such terror. I was almost grateful when a blizzard struck, because at least we could not see the great drop at our feet.

It took us four days to cross. Two days to reach the top of

the pass, two to make the equally terrifying descent. At night we stayed in the little guest-houses which St Bernard had founded and were served by lay-brothers of our Order.

Finally the mountains around us were less high, the gullies less deep. The plains of Lombardy opened up before us like the Elysian Fields and we could feel on our faces the milder air.

Our journey was far from over, however, and we still had the barrier of the Appennines to cross. Exhausted, we crept along beside them for many days, passing through the rich towns of Piacenza, Parma, Modena and, most splendid of all, Bologna, with its famous university and its host of churches. Finally, gathering whatever strength still remained to us, we turned south and once more found ourselves in a desert of snow and rugged mountains.

We emerged from the mountains at the town of Florence and at last it felt as though our journey was drawing to an end. We left Florence shortly after the feast of St Mathias, and three days later, in sunshine that on our island might have graced the midsummer feast of St John, we got our first glimpse of the Holy City. The whole party, united for once in thanksgiving and joy, threw itself down on its knees and sang a psalm of praise."

SIMON . DE . QUINCY

"Our journey was not yet over. Two nights and a day we had to wait in a tumble-down inn within sight of our goal, its myriad churches glittering in the sun or etched against the night sky under an almost full moon.

Already in Florence we had heard wild rumours of strife between the Pope and the people of Rome. Some said that the Pope had fled, others that he was still in the city but that like a volcano it could erupt and spew him out at any moment. Thus we did not even know if Rome was in fact our destination. Perhaps the Curia was already installed in another town, and we would be savaged by the Roman mob if we came too close to their city.

For these reasons Jocelin sent one of his clerks, with two armed servants, ahead of us to find out exactly what was happening in the Eternal City, while in deep frustration and impatience the rest of us had to sit and await their return.

After Terce on the second day the sound of horses and excited shouts of men roused me from dark thoughts. The three scouts had returned. The news they brought was not good. The Pope and the Curia were still in Rome, but for how much longer none could say. Only the previous night a papal official had been attacked by a mob and had barely escaped with his life.

Nonetheless the decision had to be to press forward to Rome. The Holy Father was still there, and it was he whom we had come to see. Jocelin's clerk had already made arrangements for a representative from the Curia to meet us outside the city walls and take us to our lodgings.

The roads were thronged with travellers from every corner of Christendom. A hundred different languages rose into the air around us, but the groundswell was always the musical and excited language of the Campagna.

We could see the city walls clearly now, lifting up their massive heads, but I began to despair of ever reaching them, so great was the crush of people blocking our way.

From afar I could see a huge church, its bricks glowing red in the sun, its towers capped with little golden domes. As we drew slowly closer to it I asked Prior Walter what it was called.

'That's St Laurence-without-the Walls,' he shouted above the din. 'In it rests the body of the blessed martyr Laurence himself, the gridiron on which he was roasted and the chains that bound him to it.'

I was deeply moved by this. As I looked at the church which housed the bones of the blessed martyr it was as if I was transported back to that terrible day in the churchyard of St Laurence in Warkworth when I had been forced to dip my hands in the blood of the innocent.

Yes, I had done penance for my part in that slaughter, and on every feast day of St Laurence I fasted and wore sackcloth and ashes. Yes, St Michael had wrought his miracle of healing when I had visited his shrine all those years ago. But still sometimes, when my memory was stirred, I would find myself standing again in Warkworth amidst the carnage, and the protection of the years and saints fell away.

Such a moment was now, when I found myself passing the church of St Laurence-without-the-Walls.

Let us pray, Martin."

The old man eased himself painfully onto his knees, gesturing to his young companion to do the same. Together they said St Laurence's prayer.

"Laurence did good works; by the sign of the cross he gave sight to the blind.
My soul adheres to you, o Lord, for my flesh has been burnt in the fire for your sake.
The Lord has sent his angel and he has saved me from amidst the flames,
And I did not perish in the fire."

The old man fell silent, his lips moving without a sound. Martin watched him with sinking heart. He added his own prayer to that of the old man's. "Sweet Christ and blessed St Laurence, please, let him reveal something of Simon de Quincy soon."

"Where was St Laurence on that day at Warkworth?" the old man was speaking again as he slowly got back onto his seat. "And Christ, where were you? Was it a day when Christ and all his saints were asleep? And the soldiers who bound Laurence to the gridiron and lit the fire: who thinks of them, who prays for them now? Perhaps there was one who was young and terrified out of his wits as I was that day. Laurence is indeed blessed, the victim is indeed blessed.

The horses at the head of our procession swung off the road onto the open court in front of the church. Some of the Bishop's clerks and servants were already dismounting, and Jocelin himself beckoned to the rest of us to follow suit. The court was as crowded as the road, with vendors of food and rough-hewn relics of St Laurence — gridirons, tongs, crude models of the saint enveloped in brightly coloured flames.

'We are to meet the papal messenger here,' Walter announced to those around him. 'That must be him there,' he said, pointing to a figure in the shadow of the west door talking to the Bishop's clerks. 'The blessed saints preserve us,' Walter gasped as the figure stepped towards us into the light. 'Simon de Quincy!'

I gasped too, although I had never seen him before or heard his name. He was dressed in a simple white habit and around his neck he wore a stole emblazoned with the livery of the papal court. He was of medium height, slim, with gleaming black hair and a trim little beard which was much fairer than his hair. His skin was unusually pale, and he had large, solemn dark eyes. His features were as if finely chiselled, each one perfect in itself, as well as in proportion to all the rest.

I had never before seen such perfection of looks, either in man or woman. God could not have created a face more beautiful, and still, when I think of beauty, despite everything, I think of the face of Simon de Quincy.

He greeted Bishop Jocelin with a dignity and poise much beyond his years — he was scarcely older than I was. Then he swept us all with a dazzling smile. I had completely forgotten St Laurence and the churchyard at Warkworth, and strained to catch what he was saying. Although he was formally addressing only Jocelin and the other envoys, he obviously intended his words to be heard by all those who eagerly crowded round.

He spoke confidently, in good, clear Latin, with a Norman-French accent. He introduced himself as a deacon, of the Scottish nation, related to the great de Quincy family. After welcoming the envoys to Rome in the name of the Holy Father he apologised without undue show of humility for the fact that they were being greeted by one as humble as himself, a mere secretary to the Cardinal Bishop of Palestrina. He raised his voice slightly as he said the name of his master and paused to let its significance sink in. Although I had never heard of the Cardinal Bishop of Palestrina, I knew from this that he was a very important man. I knew it also from the way in which Bishop Jocelin inclined his head respectfully.

'Today being Sunday, the Cardinals should of course be in their churches, but because of the recent events they are worshipping with his holiness at the Lateran. With each day the city becomes more unsafe for the Fathers of the Church.'

I was ready to forgive the absence of every Cardinal in Christendom as long as this young man would go on speaking. However he was almost finished. He explained where our lodgings were, and what arrangements had been made for the next day, when he hoped the business of the Curia would be continuing as usual. He then requested us to follow him and to stay as close together as possible.

'Danger,' he said, 'lurks round every corner.'

With these ominous words in our ears we started on the last leg of our journey. We turned off to the left and skirted the city walls.

Brother Isaac rode beside me. 'It doesn't look as though we are going into the city at all,' he said in a low, anxious voice. 'Do you think the Pope's already left?'

'That secretary said we were staying near the Lateran. The Lateran's in the city, isn't it?'

'God and His saints only know,' sighed Isaac. 'I just wish this journey was over. Perhaps the Lateran is wherever the Pope is,' he added with a frown. 'Perhaps he's breaking the news quietly to our masters right now. He's a smarmy character anyway. I wouldn't trust him.'

'Smarmy? Who?' I asked in surprise.

'That secretary fellow,' Isaac said, screwing up his face in Simon's direction. 'He's scarcely older than us, and look at him, welcoming Bishops to Rome. I ask you!'

'You're just envious,' I replied, shocked that anyone should have taken a dislike to such a perfect-looking creature.

'You're right I am!' Isaac exclaimed. 'And with those looks as well. I bet he's got half the women in Rome falling at his feet. Lucky devil!'

'Isaac, you're terrible,' I said. 'He's a deacon. He has taken vows.'

'Vows or no vows, if I had looks like that I'd use them. Anyone in their right mind would. God forgive me for my honesty!'

'God forgive you for your lechery,' I retorted self-righteously.

'It's all right for you,' Isaac said. 'You don't have to worry about things like that, do you? You have it easy, you know.'

'I don't see how you come to that conclusion,' I rejoined,

blushing.

Our conversation was broken off by another halt.

'What's happening now?' Isaac groaned. 'Will this journey never end?'

'It looks like we're going in that gate. Yes, Isaac, look, we're going into Rome! Look at all those towers and domes over there behind the walls. I bet that's the Lateran!'

It was. We had skirted the walls to the Lateran Gate, the Gate of the Asses. An argument had broken out ahead, at the very gates of Rome. We edged forward to find out what was going on. Abbot Osbert was in the middle of it as usual.

Everyone entering the holy city has to pay a toll, St Peter's levy. Despite its name, it goes straight into the coffers of the Senate. For a time during Pope Alexander's pontificate visiting churchmen and women were exempt. With the renewed trouble between the city and Pope Lucius the toll was being levied again, double what it had formerly been. For a company the size of ours this was a hefty sum.

For all Osbert's protestations, backed this time by all his colleagues, we had to pay. During the argument Simon stood quietly by, shrugging his shoulders at all the appeals made to him.

As we finally rode through the Gate of the Asses the gate-keeper shouted at us in the debased Latin they speak in Rome that we could have saved ourselves the expense as it would not be long before the Pope would be outside the city walls. 'Then all you'll have to pay is the levy to every other saint in Rome!' he jeered, his jaw thrust forward mockingly. He was obviously saying something insulting, but neither Isaac nor I knew what. He was too proud of his words to let us pass without us understanding them.

'Do you know what I mean, young clerks?' he shouted as we slowed down our horses to go in single-file through the half-open gate. I shook my head without looking at him.

'I mean,' he said, suddenly bringing my horse to a halt by grasping the bridle and leering up into my face, 'that if you want anything from the Holy Father you must pay a bribe to every Cardinal and Cardinal's clerk. Bribe, yes, understand?' He went on relentlessly. 'Gold, goods, or whatever treasure you have.' He roared with laughter and slapped my rump, at the same time releasing the bridle.

Once through the gate we all dismounted and kissed the earth of the Holy City. As I bent down I could hear the jeering voice of the gate-keeper echoing in my ears and feel his hand upon my body, debasing a moment that should have been sublime.

We did not remount. We were almost at our goal. Nothing now separated us from the Lateran except a small cobbled square. In front of us to our left stood one of the greatest churches in Christendom, the basilica of St John Lateran. A narrow passage squeezed its way between the church and the palace, which lay to our right, and it was down this passage that we plunged, to emerge into a much larger square.

Here was the main entrance to the Lateran Palace. A magnificent marble staircase swept up to enormous wooden doors studded with gold. On either side of this staircase stood two marble columns. On one was balanced a massive bronze head with finely carved features, while on the other was an equally massive hand holding a sphere of bronze, the remains of a colossal statue which the pagan Romans had erected to Phoebus their sun-god. It had been destroyed by Saint Sylvester, the great Pope, chosen as God's instrument to lead the Empire of the Romans from the darkness of paganism to the light of the true faith. They had placed its remains in front of the palace of the Popes as a sign that the old religion was broken and dead, much as they stick the heads of criminals or traitors upon poles at city gates. But it was a fine face, the hair so delicately carved it looked as if the breeze could stir it, and the mouth half open as if it was about to speak.

There was no time to linger and stare at the wonders that surrounded us. We crossed the second square and down a wide road. Our way was soon blocked by a strong, squat building with a square tower. It looked like a castle but was in fact the monastery of the Four Crowned Martyrs where we were to stay.

After all the tales of attacks on clergy I was reassured that we would be lodged behind thick and formidable walls. The monastery stood on a small hill, so that it looked down on the houses and gardens surrounding it, giving it even more the appearance of a castle.

I was put in the guests' dormitory, along with the other younger members of our company, including Isaac and Andrew. Bishop Jocelin had a chamber to himself, while Walter, Osbert and Arnold were put together in a large, airy chamber overlooking the city. Arnold however refused such 'luxury', as he called it, and insisted on sleeping in the dormitory with the rest of us.

Although now, having reached our destination, we should have attended the night services, we were given special dispensation to sleep through our first night in Rome, all that is except Arnold's Cistercians. I slept the sleep of the exhausted and was only dimly aware of Arnold and his sons dragging themselves to Matins. God forgive me, but it made my sleep the more delicious."

POPE LUCIUS

"We saw the Holy Father the next day, about twelve of us. Simon de Quincy appeared, spruce and trim, as we were filing out of church after Prime, to lead us up the wide street, across the large cobbled square, past the broken god, up the marble staircase and into the Lateran Palace.

Because we came from a country which lay under an interdict, we had to approach his holiness by way of the Sacred Stairs. These are the stairs of Pilate's palace in Jerusalem, which our Lord went up to face his trial, and came down to face torture and death. Since they were brought to Rome centuries ago no one has ever walked up these stairs, only crawled up on their knees.

This was a real torture for Bishop Jocelin. Supported on both sides by his clerks he heaved his great bulk painfully from one step to the next, groaning with every movement he made. The rest of us had to keep behind him, for it was unthinkable we reach the top before the leader of our delegation.

It was indeed a humiliating penance. Crowds of people milled around at the top of the stairs. Some scrutinised us with interest, some were deep in conversation and cast only an occasional, indifferent glance at us.

Simon was up there too, having left us at the foot of the Sacred Stairs and climbed up some back way. He was half turned in our direction, half turned towards another official, with whom he was talking, very quietly, scarcely opening his mouth. I could see his eyes on us as we struggled up towards him. From the expression on his face he could have been watching insects crawling in the dust.

At last Jocelin pulled himself onto the marble floor at the top of the stairs. As he lay like a stranded whale, gasping for breath, the crowds parted and the whole length of the upper room was revealed. It was in fact a chapel, the chapel of St Sylvester.

At the far end in front of the altar on a huge wooden throne sat a tiny figure dressed in the habit of a Cistercian monk. It was the Holy Father. A group of Cardinals surrounded him, dressed in flaming red robes. Two of them helped him to his feet and down the altar steps. Then motioning them to leave him he tottered alone through the length of the chapel towards the prostrate Scottish delegation. He was ancient. I could hardly believe that such a dried up husk could contain any life at all, let alone the life of Christ's vicar on earth. They say he was almost eighty years old. Even now I am still a young man in comparison — a wizened old thing like me!

Yet when he spoke his voice was clear and strong, the voice

of a man half his age. He had a beautiful voice, with the gentle, flowing accent of a native of one of the Italian states.

'Jocelin, my brother, and you, my sons,' he said, 'blessings upon you. You are more welcome to me than a thousand sacks of gold.'

Jocelin stretched out his hands, begged for mercy for the whole kingdom of Scotland and pleaded for the lifting of the ban.

'We have much to discuss,' the Pope replied, 'but get up, all of you, up on your feet. Come, embrace me.'

He embraced all of us in turn, bestowing the kiss of peace. I wept. It had seemed as if our journey would never end, it had been so hard, so fraught. The Sacred Stairs had also seemed endless. But now, truly, we had reached our goal, the embrace of the Holy Father.

Then Pope Lucius said, 'Come, it is the hour of Terce. Let us celebrate it together. After that we meet in consistory, and then, later today, or it might be tomorrow — you see how the whole world waits upon our judgment,' he added apologetically, making a sweeping gesture at the crowds surrounding us. 'But we will hear your case,' he said, stamping his foot to give added emphasis to his words, 'every detail of it, and Christ's infinite mercy will inform our judgment.'

With that he tottered back towards his chair. The crowds closed in behind him, and he was lost to view.

The whole company then said Terce together. It was thrilling to be intoning the psalms with so many great men of the Church, mingling my voice with the voices of Cardinals, Archbishops and the Holy Father himself.

On the walls of the chapel, behind marble columns, were paintings from the life of St Sylvester, exquisitely drawn and gloriously coloured. There was the Emperor Constantine struck down by leprosy and on the verge of death; there St Sylvester stretching out his healing hand towards him; there the baptism of the Emperor, when the greatest ruler on earth had received the breath of Christ. It had happened not a hundred steps from where I was standing. That was the great beginning, when Pope and Emperor were entwined in harmony like voices in the choir.

What had gone wrong? For as long as I could remember the whole world had buzzed with stories of Pope and Emperor inflicting dreadful wounds on one another, savaging, banning, raiding, warring. And like a poison spreading from the head into the limbs, as did Pope and Emperor, so did Archbishop and King, Bishop and King, prelate and prince. Indeed a leprosy had smitten the souls of the powerful, and where now were the saints to heal it?

My heart swelled with the hope that in the tiny, shrivelled body in the Cistercian habit there inhabited a new St Sylvester.

When Terce was over the Holy Father disappeared through

a door near the altar, followed by the Cardinals, some even frailer and more stooped than himself. The rest of us filed out through another door beside the top of the Sacred Stairs, along a corridor hung with rich, brightly coloured tapestries, and into a large and sumptuous chamber with cushioned benches around the walls. This was the antechamber where, along with scores of others, we were to await the summons to the Consistory.

We spent the rest of the day between antechamber and chapel. Every so often the usher would appear, knock his stick on the floor and shout out a name into the sudden quiet. Then he would disappear as quickly as he had come, followed by an excited group of clerics.

It was the minor clerks and chaplains such as myself who kept the Hours in the chapel: their superiors remained in the antechamber discussing or negotiating, amongst themselves or with curial officials.

Our four envoys were no exception. Simon de Quincy was with them the whole time, introducing to them this Cardinal-deacon's clerk or that Cardinal-bishop's chaplain. Sometimes a Cardinal himself would appear to exchange a greeting and a platitude, or to ask some relevant question about the state of the Scottish Church.

Jocelin, Osbert and Walter stood in a close group beside Simon. Arnold was more interested in talking with his fellow Cistercians. This was probably for the best, because I do not think he would have approved of what was going on around Simon. What Simon was doing was discreetly preparing the way for approaching the Cardinals with gifts, not gifts freely given in the spirit of love, but base gifts. 'Turning gold into mercy,' Simon called it, 'a holy transformation indeed.' I was watching him carefully as he said this and there was mockery in his eyes.

Yes, I thought, perhaps it is turned into mercy this time, but what might it be next time? An interdict? A war? A false demotion or advancement? We had brought large quantities of treasure in gold, jewels, coin. I knew this, but I had not given much thought as to why. Had I thought it was all for paying inn-keepers?

Simon on the other hand was an expert in this, and as I learned later, this was only one of the many unsavoury duties which gave him a living at the papal court.

Although shocked at what I heard, I pressed close in behind Walter so as not to miss anything. Simon fascinated me as a weasel fascinates a rabbit. He was saying that not all the Cardinals were open to such gifts; Cardinal Hyacinth for example and the Holy Father himself. How my heart rejoiced to hear that! It would be a very bad move, he said, to offer them anything worldly.

He named others it was not worth offering anything to, either because they would not be present at the hearing, or because they had so little weight in Consistory that their opinion was of no importance.

In return for such gifts, we would expect the ban to be lifted: from the King; from the individuals named by John at Redden; from the whole kingdom. However there was something more — the urgent need to settle the St Andrews dispute once and for all. For without the healing of this root malady the abscesses and boils would erupt again and again in interdicts, exile, persecution and untold suffering. Both King William and King Henry had charged us to press for a settlement according to the Normandy agreement — that Hugh remain Bishop of St Andrews, while John became Bishop of Dunkeld.

It was this Normandy agreement that Simon felt would be the real stumbling block, because one of the last acts of Pope Alexander had been to oppose it. He had cursed it with his dying breath, and so great was the respect for this lion of the Church that few would lightly brush that aside, no matter how many treasure chests we dragged to the Lateran.

All day we waited in vain. In fact it was not until after Sext the following day that the usher called out the names of the four Scottish envoys.

We all quickly gathered and hurried out behind him. We were led into a long, narrow room, smaller than the antechamber but much more sumptuous. Murals depicting the life of Christ adorned the walls, their colours glowing and warm.

The Holy Father sat on a high-backed chair at the far end opposite the door. He was in a kind of alcove or apse. On its rounded ceiling directly above his head was a brilliantly coloured mosaic of St Peter receiving the keys to the kingdom of Heaven. It glittered and danced in the light of two enormous candles that burned behind the papal throne.

On chairs round the walls on either side of the Pope sat the Cardinals. I counted thirteen. I was amazed at how old so many of them were. Each in turn introduced himself by standing up and bowing. Some had to be helped to their feet, others excused themselves because of age or infirmity and simply nodded their heads. From the conversations of the previous day I was already familiar not only with their names, but also with their characters and opinions as they would affect our case.

Each Cardinal had his clerk, who perched behind him on the narrow stone ledge that ran round the walls. There was Simon behind his Cardinal-bishop of Palestrina, Paolo Scolari, a sickly looking man with a pasty face and puffy cheeks.

Servants placed four chairs for the envoys across the middle of the room, at the base of the semi-circle of Cardinals. The rest of us stood behind them. I stood behind Walter's chair. There was a total silence, which lasted longer than I found comfortable. The Holy Father sat with his head bowed and his eyes closed.

He could have been asleep, except that every so often his lips would move, and he would wring his hands.

Then, without at first opening his eyes, he spoke. His voice sounded weaker that it had done the previous morning in the chapel of St Sylvester, and we all had to strain to catch the words.

'My brother Jocelin, my sons, representatives of a kingdom in travail, of a King who wanders in darkness. King William — I knew his grandfather, a saintly man, truly a saintly man. And your country, Scotland, a land on the edge of the world, yet a land to which all Christendom owes a great debt — Columbanus, Gallen, Columba — Bobbio, Montecassino, Echternach — the strong light of the north when the light of the south was almost extinguished. Yes, the Scots have always had a special place in my heart.'

There was another embarassed silence. This was a good start, but not one any of the envoys wanted to pursue, as Lucius was obviously confusing Scotland with Ireland. Besides none of the four envoys were of the Scottish race.

'And I am deeply grieved,' he continued, 'that this kingdom, enduring as it must the cold and the darkness which assail the body, should also be plunged into the cold and darkness which assail the spirit.

'My brother Jocelin, my sons Arnold and ..' here he faltered, and his clerk whispered in his ear. He went on, unsteadily: 'and Osbert and Walter, open your hearts to us, tell us truthfully what has been happening in your dear, cold, suffering land.'

He sank back into his chair and closed his eyes once more. Jocelin stood up and carefully unfolded before the Consistory the events of the past two years relating to the bishopric of St Andrews. He did it so carefully, so delicately, that I hardly recognised it as the same sordid, cruel and bloody struggle I had known it for. He was particularly delicate about his own less than praiseworthy role in events.

He drew his speech to a close thus: 'So your holiness, we beg you to bring a repentant King, a repentant court, and a repentant realm back from darkness into the light of God's mercy and forgiveness.

'Furthermore we humbly and respectfully crave the thing that both contenders for the bishopric of St Andrews desire with all their hearts: that Hugh keep St Andrews in full canonical right and John be appointed to Dunkeld. May you give your blessing to this settlement, so that the wounds of our bleeding Church may be healed once and for all.'

Jocelin had finished. There was a lot of fidgeting amongst the Cardinals, and many frowning glances and anxious whispers were exchanged.

Then all of us except Jocelin and his two clerks were led out of the Consistory. Each of the envoys were to be questioned separately.

When it finally came to Walter's turn Isaac and I went with him. Many questions were asked, about Walter himself, about his monastery, about how it had fared during the interdict. Walter answered frankly, for he had nothing to hide, unlike Jocelin. Lucius was outraged when Walter told him of the attack on our convent in the churchyard of Aberdour.

'You have suffered much at the hands of King William and his barons,' he sighed when Walter had finished.

'We have, your Holiness,' Walter replied, 'but we are prepared to forgive.'

I clenched my fist, trying in vain to think forgiving thoughts. Hearing Walter unfold before the Curia all the indignities and injustices we had been subjected to over the past two years filled me with rage. I wanted to beg the Curia to damn the whole of the Scottish nobility to hell, with de Mortimer at their head. It was a blessing that no one asked me my opinion, and that I had no power.

'Have any promises been made by the King or his barons to make amends for the wrongs that they have done to you?' Lucius asked.

'In promises there is none who is not rich,' Cardinal Hyacinth shouted.

'Yes, your Holiness,' Walter replied. 'I have it here in writing that land and multures from a neighbouring village will be made over to our convent. But only,' he added, raising his voice above the sounds of approval being uttered around us, 'in gratitude for the success of our mission.'

A tall sprightly old man jumped to his feet unaided. His hair gleamed pure white against the dark skin of his face and tonsured crown. It was Umberto, Cardinal-bishop of St Laurence.

'My Lord,' he shouted, turning in the direction of Lucius, who seemed to shrink back into his chair, 'I say you grant a bull of confirmation of this promise, whatever we decide. It is not for excommunicated Kings and nobles to strike bargains with the Holy Mother Church.'

As if rallying his strength Lucius sat forward, looking annoyed. 'Yes, yes, St Laurence, we have much to discuss. Now, Prior Walter -'

But Umberto was not to be put off so easily. 'Your Holiness, if I may, I have a question to put to the Prior.' It sounded more like a command than a request.

Lucius gave a deep sigh and slumped back again in his chair. 'Go on, Cardinal Umberto, go on,' he said, waving his hand in a gesture of resignation.

'Prior,' the Cardinal said, turning his glittering eyes on Walter, 'in your own opinion, as a man who is not ignorant of the laws of God and the Church, tell me, was John canonically elected Bishop of St Andrews?'

Walter was silent for a moment. My heart was in my mouth. Of course he had been canonically elected. Everybody knew that, including Cardinal Umberto. So why was he asking? Had his gift not been large enough? I exchanged a glum look with Isaac.

'Come along, Prior,' Umberto was saying, 'have you lost your tongue?'

'Father,' Walter replied quietly, 'that question is for this Consistory court to decide.'

'I asked for your opinion,' the Cardinal snapped, 'not your decision. Come now, Prior, you said you were present at his election and consecration in the church of the Abbey of the Holy Rood.'

It was at this point that it suddenly became clear to me what was happening. Cardinal Umberto must know that Walter had spoken up in Hugh's favour at that fateful gathering. He knew it, and he was punishing him for it.

Walter replied: 'Subdeacon Alexis the papal legate, who presided at the election, was of the opinion that the election was canonical. He would not have consecrated him had he thought otherwise. The legates that the Apostolic See send out are experts in canon law, you do not need me to tell you that.'

'You are still avoiding the question, Prior Walter,' the cardinal went on relentlessly. 'I asked you for your opinion.'

'My Lord, I had no reason to disagree with Alexis on this matter. Nevertheless,' he said loudly, as Umberto opened his mouth to speak again, 'at the time I argued for a compromise, for a solution which would not completely alienate the secular power. But my argument fell on deaf ears, and the last two years have been filled with untold suffering, both spiritual and physical.

'We are here now because this suffering has become intolerable. We are men of the spiritual world who are pleading for men and women of the secular world: our very purpose here is a compromise. We have travelled from the other side of the world to beg for a compromise, and for the fruit of compromise, which is peace.'

There was a great stir amongst the Cardinals at these words, and much angry muttering. It was the spirit of Pope Alexander that swept the chamber like a menacing wind.

Prior Walter could restrain himself no longer. I had never seen him as he was that day. Red in the face, he roared like a wounded bull: 'Fathers of the Church, it is peace we crave. In Christ's name give us peace!'

Pope Lucius struggled to his feet, shouting above the rising noise: 'And peace you shall have, my sons, our peace we shall give to you. Now you may go, go, at once.'

We did not wait to be told twice. The three of us, Prior Walter, Brother Isaac, and myself, all bowed and fled the chamber. As we hurried down the long corridor we could hear a tide of angry voices rising behind us.''

THE . PAINTED
CHAMBER

"I t was good to get back to the quiet darkness of our lodgings after such a day. However the day does not always end with the setting sun, especially in Rome. As I was finishing my bread a servant came up to me and whispered that Bishop Jocelin wished to see me in his chamber. With foreboding I went slowly up the spiral stairs and stood for a moment outside the heavy wooden door of the Bishop's chamber. I was about to knock when, as if anticipating my action, the door swung open to reveal the massive figure of the Bishop sitting behind a small table. The servant who had opened the door for me bowed and disappeared, closing the door behind him. A fire blazed at Jocelin's back, and the room was stifling hot.

'Brother Michael, my son, come in and stand by the fire. You are well, I take it?' Jocelin's voice was smooth and ingratiating. I looked at his face. His lips were smiling, but his eyes were not. I saw him as I had seen him for the first time on that stormy night in Perth. I had not trusted him then. I did not trust him now. But, then as now, whether I trusted him or not, I was in his power.

'Tomorrow I have an errand for you, my son,' he was saying, stroking his chins. 'If it is carried out successfully, it will bind you to me in a deep debt of gratitude. It is a matter of the utmost delicacy, which you must mention to nobody — nobody, you understand? I should add,' he went on, reading the anxious question in my eyes, 'that your Prior knows about it, or at least he knows all he needs to know, and is content to know no more. He trusts me.'

Here he cleared his throat, as if something was sticking in it. 'And you must trust me, too,' he said softly. 'There are great things at stake. Tomorrow you will go to a merchant's house in the city and give him these letters.' He tapped his finger on some sealed documents on the table. 'And this bag.' He drew out from a fold in his gown a leather pouch and handed it to me. It had the heaviness of gold. Reluctantly I took it.

'But you will not be alone,' Jocelin continued. 'After Prime you will go to the gatehouse where you will meet with Simon de Quincy, the secretary to Cardinal Bishop Palestrina. You know who I mean?'

I nodded, wondering if I was really awake, or if this was some devilish dream that had been sent to weigh down my soul. I looked into the fire. It was real enough, as it spluttered and spat and reeked, as real as the fires of Hell. Jocelin's voice purred on.

'He will be your guide through the city, and you are to obey him in everything — everything, you understand? You keep hold of the letters until you can give them into the hands of the merchant. The bag of gold you will give to Simon. He knows what to do with it.

'You will both be dressed as laymen. It is too dangerous for clerics to be wandering around the back streets of Rome at the moment. Simon will have a set of clothes for you and you will change before you leave the Four Crowned Martyrs. Kneel now, and I will say the prayer to release you to wear profane clothes.'

I knelt like someone in a trance. Jocelin finished his prayer and told me to get up. 'There is one other thing, my son. Should anything happen tomorrow that might lead you to sin in any way, I want you to know that I am prepared to confess you. I have told your Prior this, and he is in complete agreement. So remember, Brother Michael, it is to me you must come to unburden your soul. Is that clear?'

'Perfectly clear,' I replied, even more puzzled.

'So, if there are no other questions, you may go,' Jocelin said waving his hand in the direction of the door, then presenting his ring for me to kiss.

Questions screamed in my head, but I could not bring them over my lips. Why has he chosen me? Out of all his servants, clerks, contacts at the Curia, why does he want me, a stranger in a strange city, to do this errand for him? It doesn't make sense. There must be something more to it. What?

As I opened the door to go, I heard Jocelin call my name. 'Brother Michael, haven't you forgotten something?

I turned round and saw him holding the sealed letters in his outstretched hand.

That night I could not sleep. My mind worried ceaselessly at the questions I had not dared to ask. The darkness held no answers, but the darkness held a face, the face of Simon de Quincy. I could not escape the thought that it was Simon and not Jocelin who held the key to the riddle that was plaguing me.

When I finally fell into a fitful sleep Simon was beside me, half in my dreams, half outside them. I wanted to push him away, into oblivion, into a place where he could not touch my life, while part of me, that part where demons enter and make their homes, knew that I would never be able to do it.

The next morning at Prime I was unnaturally awake after such a night. The words of the psalm touched my heart with sadness, for already part of me must have known that I was bidding farewell to my innocence.

> *'Put me to the test, O Lord, burn my loins and my heart*
> *Since your mercy is before my eyes, and I rejoice in your*
> *truth.*
> *I have not sat with vain people, nor will I enter with*
> *those who do evil.*
> *I have hated the society of the wicked, I will not sit down*
> *with the impious.*
> *Do not let my soul be lost with the impious, God, nor my*
> *life with men of blood,*
> *Whose hands are stained with iniquities and whose right*
> *hand is heavy with bribes.'*

Yes, I knew I was going to be put to the test, and I knew I was going to be found wanting.

I slipped out of the church as soon as Prime was over, and ran straight into Brother Andrew.

'Where are you off to in such a hurry, Brother Michael?' he asked. 'Another appointment with the Holy Father?' He did nothing to disguise the sneer in his voice. He was angry that Prior Walter had not taken him with us to the Consistory court the previous day. This gave an added edge to his usual insolence. Over the years I had learnt how to deal with Andrew, and normally I could parry his sneering. That morning, however, I was off my guard.

'I — I have important business to do for — for —.' I hesitated. I did not know what to say. Should I even mention Jocelin's name?

'For?' Andrew echoed, with a supercilious smile.

'For Bishop Jocelin,' I said firmly. It was no good. I could not show any uncertainty or doubt in Andrew's presence. It made me too vulnerable.

'Bishop Jocelin?' Andrew said in mock surprise. 'Yesterday the Pope, today the Bishop. You're coming down in the world, Brother Michael. I hope you don't fall any further.'

'If you don't mind, I must go,' I said brusquely. 'Good day, Brother Andrew.'

'I understand, Brother Michael,' he said insultingly. 'You don't want to waste your time on a mere brother.'

Annoyed and confused I hurried off towards the gate-house, and all the time I could feel Andrew's eyes boring into my back.

Simon was waiting for me in the lobby of the gate-house. His head and shoulders were lit up by the light which poured through the roundel above the door. He looked very different from the last time I saw him, for he was wearing a green velvet cap and cloak. In clerk's robes he had looked handsome. In these clothes he looked magnificent.

Clothes are but a vain shell, we all know that, and we must

believe it. Yet they can somehow imprint themselves on the spirit. Simon was never meant for the Church. He loved the things of this world too much. Even now, when I think of Simon, and God knows I do that often enough, it is in worldly clothes that he appears to my mind's eye.

'Greetings, my little brother,' he said jauntily, throwing me a bundle of clothes. 'We have a lot to do today, you and I, so change into these quickly and let's get moving.'

I started pulling off my tunic. He made a harsh sound. 'Not here, you wicked boy. You're not in one of those monasteries where the monks go round with half-naked buttocks. Old Aelred of Rievaulx almost had an apoplexy when he saw that, so they say. You don't want to do the same to some poor old monk here, do you?'

I blushed and looked at him sheepishly.

'In there,' he said, pushing me through the open door of a small guard chamber. 'I'll wait here,' he added. 'But do hurry up, old chap. We haven't got all day.'

When I emerged I too was finely dressed, in blue and black, a dagger in my belt and at my side a sword. It felt very strange to be in worldly clothes again. They clung to you in a way that made you feel your body and aroused bodily sensations. Truly they were clothes of the world, forcing the spirit down to earthly things.

We stepped out into the sunshine that was already warm. We shone like two gorgeous dragonflies upon a summer's day, and like dragonflies we would shine for one day only.

'Have you got the gold?' Simon asked when we were out of sight of the monastery, stepping carefully around pools of ordure in the narrow streets.

'Yes,' I replied eagerly, taking it out of a deep pocket inside my doublet. 'And I have the letters, too.'

'Put it away, for Christ's sake,' Simon growled, anxiously looking around. 'Weapons or no, we won't get out of here alive if they know we've got that amount of gold on us. Give it me later when no one can see us.'

We walked for about a mile, twisting and turning along narrow lanes, and crossing broad squares packed with markets which sold everything from slaves to swords. We passed hills crowded with towering ruins, where broken columns grew like weeds, and at their feet people lived in tiny shacks, like vermin that had invaded a corpse. The sight saddened me, for I knew that this was once the splendid heart of the Roman Empire, and I prayed to Christ to keep our shrines and glories from the fate that had befallen the pagan Romans. It was hard not to believe that the world had become a more squalid place since the days of ancient Rome.

At last we came to a small street where the houses were large and fine. It was obvious that wealth dwelt there. There was less dirt in the street and the smell was less overpowering, or perhaps I was simply more used to it by this time.

Simon pulled me into a doorway. 'We're almost there,' he said. 'Give me the money now.'

I handed over the pouch and felt my spirit lighten.

'You have the letters from Bishop Jocelin?' he asked me.

I nodded, touching my side.

'Come on then,' he said.

'Do you know what this is all about?' I asked, risking a rebuff.

'It's none of my business,' he replied curtly, 'and it's certainly none of yours. Just do as you're told, and no more questions.'

I shrugged my shoulders, feeling hurt.

We left the doorway and quickly found our way to the merchant's house. We handed the gold and the letters over to a servant who answered our knocking. Simon muttered something to him which I could not make out and the door was slammed in our faces.

Simon now took me a different way from that which we had come. The lanes got narrower and more stinking, the houses smaller and meaner, until we were amongst mere shacks scarcely taller than the height of a man. Out of the low, dark doorways hands stretched towards us, many mutilated and covered with open sores. Swarms of half-starved naked children crowded round us tugging at our tunics, half-mocking, half begging.

'Well, my little brother,' Simon said, giving me a cheerful smile, 'what do you think of the glories of Rome? Is she not beautiful?'

With his smile he seemed to be mocking both me and the squalour. I felt angry and disgusted with him, both for bringing me here, and for smiling upon it. I did not reply, but he read my eyes.

'Why the reproachful look? I have brought you here to show you something other than ugly poverty. Poverty you will find everywhere in the world: our own country is not without its share, you must admit. This, however, you will find only here, in the Mother City, where beauty grows in squalour like a flower on a dung-hill. Look!'

As he was speaking we rounded a corner and there before us towered a group of enormous marble statues: two naked men, straining with every muscle in their bodies to restrain two stampeding horses, and in front of them a naked woman sitting with a great open shell in her outstretched hands and surrounded by serpents. They were perfect, beautiful giants that had been trapped in stone by some pagan magic.

These pagans knew no shame, but how was it that the shame of our first mother and father did not touch them? They must then have been utterly savage and close to the beasts. Yet if that was so how could they have created such perfection? Whoever had created these statues knew no shame, but neither surely had they known poverty, ugliness, squalour.

'They must have been created before the Fall,' I blurted out. Simon snorted. 'Then so must I!' he replied, mocking me.

'Who are they? Why were they made?' I went on in my amazement.

'Why were any of us made?' he said, suddenly serious. Then, once more in his sneering tone, he said: 'Our art conceals. Theirs revealed. I will be like them, and I will reveal everything to you, all their secrets. But not yet. Come on.'

Before I knew it Simon had disappeared amongst the maze of huts, and I ran after him, disappointed that I could no longer gaze at the statue, scared that I would be left alone in this hostile place.

Rome is built on many hills, and now we were climbing yet another. Up ahead was a huge church with a massive palace rising beside it, and my heart leapt for joy because I thought it was St John Lateran, and we were almost home.

Then another strange thing happened. Simon, who had up until then been as cold as ice suddenly became the warm sun. He shone on me, and I melted.

'Michael, my dear, I am sorry if I have been short-tempered with you today. Do you forgive me?'

'Of course,' I muttered, confused, delighted, ready to forgive him anything.

'You're a good, kind soul,' he went on. 'I am neither, I warn you.'

'Your honesty will purge you of your demons,' I said, naively.

'You think so?' he replied, the sneer again in his voice.

'Is that the Lateran up there?' I asked, quickly changing the subject.

'No,' he replied, 'the church is Mary Major, for the snow fell there one May many years ago to mark the site where Pope and Prefect were to build a great church in honour of Our Lady. In pagan times the temple of Cybele stood there, goddess of the earth and mother of the gods.'

'And the palace?' I asked. I did not want to hear any more about pagan times. This was the mother city of our faith, and yet sometimes it seemed to be more pagan than Christian. This troubled me deeply.

'It is my master's house,' Simon replied, 'Paulo Scolari, Cardinal-bishop of Palestrina. We will change and refresh ourselves there. It is not far from the Lateran. Pull your hat over your forehead, keep close to me, and speak to no one.'

We passed through huge heavily guarded wooden doors alive with carvings of angels and devils, pagan goddesses and gods. We crossed the bustling courtyard which lay beyond and stopped in front of a small door in the corner. It had no handle, but on the door jamb a brass animal head stuck out, a weasel with a piece of rope hanging out of its mouth.

Simon pulled the rope smartly three times. A moment later the door swung open. There was no one behind it. I stared at Simon in amazement.

'Don't worry,' he whispered, 'there's no witchcraft in it, it's all pulleys and levers. My master loves weights and counter-weights.'

He disappeared into the darkness behind the door. I hesitated, suddenly afraid. I wanted to be back with my father and brothers in Christ at the Abbey of the Four Crowned Martyrs, familiar faces, speaking a familiar tongue. As I stood on that threshold I felt as if two worlds were tugging my soul in opposite directions.

Then dimly in the darkness I could make out the face of Simon de Quincy, smiling, reassuring, enticing. I no longer felt torn, and I was happy to follow him.

Down a dark, narrow passage we went, then up a winding staircase, lit only by slits which the breeze blew through, sharpened to coldness by their narrowness.

It occurred to me then that I had left my habit at the Abbey. So how was I supposed to change into it here? I asked this question of Simon's heels, as we were going up the twisting steps.

'I gave orders for both our habits to be brought here. Trust me.'

We came to an abrupt halt halfway down another passage-way, wider and much lighter than the first, it was hung with rich tapestries of hunting scenes. Simon moved one aside and went behind it. On it there was woven the picture of a huge eagle carrying a naked youth upwards into the sky, where the clouds were parted as if to receive them. I was shocked that the sweet, corrupting smell of paganism had penetrated even the house of a Cardinal-bishop.

'Come on, little brother, or are you going to stand there staring all day?' Simon was already completely hidden by the tapestry. I pushed it aside to find him holding open a little door.

'Is nothing straightforward in this house?' I asked.

'Just you, brother,' he replied with a grin. 'Now in you go.'

The small, windowless room he led me into was bright and warm, as the walls were lined with sconces, each one holding a burning candle: there were so many that it resembled the high altar at Eastertide. The walls were painted with scenes which I am ashamed even to remember, let alone describe. Yet I do remember them, vividly, for in the heat of my shame they burnt themselves onto my memory, and they have enmeshed my body in their baseness ever since.

If I am ashamed to describe them to you, then how much more ashamed should I be to tell you what happened there in front of them?

My story with Simon, it seems to me now, started in that warm, bright room, surrounded by obscenities. It was a long, dark, sorry story. Yet that room shines for me as bright as the brightest star, in a world of its own, high above shame and sin. What happened in that room was wonderful, despite all the evil that flowed around and from it.

Even when I stand before God on Domesday I will not retract that, I could not retract that, without blackening my soul with perjury. Martin, you are young, and they say that such things are not for the young to hear, but I think it is the young who understand them better than any.

I was not seduced, I will make no such paltry excuses. As soon as I stepped into that room I knew what was going to happen; in some dark, secret part of me I knew even before I stepped into the house. Yet I stayed. I could have refused to enter, I could have demanded to be taken back to Walter. I could have said: 'Go to the Devil that sent you!' But I did none of those things because I had already said yes. So that when we stood there naked and Simon pointed to a wall-cupboard and said that I would find my habit in there, I said 'Let it stay there' and took him in my arms. For his lips were like lilies, his cheeks beds of spices, his belly ivory overlaid with sapphires and his thighs were columns of marble set in sockets of gold.

His smile was not empty, but warm and soft and meant for me. As I explored his body with every part of me I knew that it was what I had been wanting to do ever since I had set eyes on him; even before I had set eyes on him; for as long as I could remember. All that I had denied myself with Edgar was suddenly crying out that its time had come. The fire in the flesh raged like fire through dry gorse, and as the flames leapt for joy it was not just Simon whom I lay with, but Edgar, too. My heart ached and opened to both of them, gave itself up to something more, much more, than Simon's fleshly beauty.

I know that many would condemn me for heresy when I speak these words, but it was pure and good, Martin, and if it was not from God then nothing in this life is from God. Neither Church nor King nor Devil will take that from me.

As we spent our passion on each other my love grew and blossomed like an erect palm. We lay with one another until the candles were but stubs, and darkness crept out from every corner. 'You are beautiful, my darling, beautiful without flaw.'

We were almost asleep, lips pressed on lips, breathing into one another, drinking each other's sweetness, his left arm under my head, his right arm embracing me.

I was startled out of my sweet trance by a nearby scuffling, followed by a sad, wistful sound like a sigh. I sat up with a start. It was as nothing, yet it had jolted me out of my dream and I was consumed by shame and worry. Here I lay naked in the arms of a naked stranger, in a secret chamber in a mysterious palace. What if we were discovered like this? I had done something for which I could be thrown out of the Church. I had broken my vow to God, and my pledge to Walter. I had committed the sin which many condemned as being worse than murder.

I knew that the star which shone in the heavens was good, but we were no longer there, we were on earth, where all pure things are soiled.

'What was that noise?' I whispered.

'My little brother,' Simon said tenderly, running his hand down my back, which had never been touched so gently, 'you are such a worrier. Relax, we are quite safe. It's just a rat in the wainscoting.'

He knew he lied, and yet it was the truth.

When we were dressed we stood looking at each other, and it was as if our habits formed a wall between us, high and insurmountable. We held hands briefly, and as the candles flickered out one by one, he asked me if I felt I had sinned.

I said yes, if I thought about it, I would say I had, but I did not want to think about it. 'When we held each other, there was no sin. Now, as I stand here, apart from you and in my habit, the shadow of sin falls over us.'

'Are you saying it is a sin to be apart?' Simon asked jokingly.

I laughed and shook my head. Before I could answer properly, Simon went on, serious again, 'If you should feel the need to confess what we have done today, choose your confessor carefully, I suggest you go to your Bishop Jocelin, or to my master. There you will find an easy absolution, for they will understand.'

I was puzzled, but with a kiss he took away the question that was forming on my lips.

'Better still,' he said, 'we will confess to each other, and I will give you such a penance as will make you want to confess again and again.'

We hurriedly left the palace under a sky that was already darkening, through the courtyard that was now quiet and empty. We arrived at the Four Crowned Martyrs just as Vespers were ending.

And if I'm not very much mistaken, Martin, that's the bell for Vespers ringing right now. I don't want you to miss them, as I did. Go, and pray for my soul. I had almost forgotten how much in need of prayer I am.''

THE . ROSE . OF . GOLD

"The next days passed as in a dream. Simon was my whole thought, my whole doing. Every moment I spent not thinking about him was a moment wasted and incomplete. Except, of course, when I was in church, when my love and longing for him carried my soul upwards towards God, singing at the gate of Heaven itself. From that vantage-point I could see my star shining bright and serene.

What was happening at the Curia I followed with interest only in as far as Simon was involved, for by following it I felt closer to him. In itself the fate of kingdoms or bishoprics seemed of little importance to me, even as it affected my brothers and my Priory. I had left my self so far behind that this strange shift of affection and interest scarcely troubled me. It was as if the centre of my being and my loving had moved. I had never known such longing. In my dreams I held him with all the sweetness with which I had held him in the painted chamber. In my waking I wanted nothing else.

The following Sunday was Laetare Sunday, Rejoice Jerusalem. My own joy rose to Heaven with the joy of all Christendom. On that day the Holy Father, when he is in Rome, goes in procession from the Lateran to the church of the Holy Cross of Jerusalem. In that church the most wonderful of relics are kept, which one day, Martin, I hope you will see for yourself, for they take many years off your time in Purgatory. There is a piece of the True Cross; there is the cord which bound Christ to it, the sponge which the soldier soaked in vinegar and offered Him as He was dying, and one of the nails that transfixed Him. Also, hanging from the roof-beams, is the complete cross of St Dismas.

The church of the Holy Cross is not far from the Lateran, and it was considered safe for the procession to go ahead, despite the city's mounting hostility towards the Curia. Even the Roman mob, they said, would not dare attack a holy procession, not unless there was open war.

Pope Lucius was determined to go ahead, not in any spirit of defiance, but in order to extend the olive branch of peace to the Prefect and the Senate of Rome. For Laetare Sunday is the day on which the bond between Pope and city is celebrated and renewed in the ceremony of the Rose of Gold. This is a rose made of pure gold, scented with musk and balsam. The Pope carries this exquisite treasure as he rides in procession to and from the church of the Holy Cross; he holds it while he celebrates High Mass there, and while he preaches his sermon on the theme of the rose. Then, as the procession approaches the Lateran on its way back the Pope presents the Rose to the Prefect of the city, as a special sign of favour and harmony.

Lucius had sent letters to the Prefect and the Senate, urgent, pleading, appeasing letters, requesting their presence at the ceremony of the Rose of Gold. Simon was involved in this because his master was one of the Roman nobility, cursed folk, and he stood higher in the people's warped esteem than the simpler, holier men of the Lateran.

Rumour even whispered that Lucius was offering money. Some were relieved at this, others outraged. But in truth Lucius had offered nothing but entreaties and peace. It had been left to Scolari and the other less scrupulous Cardinals to offer gold. The Romans, however, wanted more: they wanted the Pope to bind himself and his successors to this shameful bribe. They wanted a papal charter. This even Scolari's gold and influence could not buy, for it meant Lucius himself giving his consent, and this he refused to do.

So when we followed Pope Lucius on the procession that Laetare Sunday, all of us wearing the rose coloured stoles and robes special to that day of joy, it was through a joyless and deserted city that we passed. All the windows overlooking the road had sacking over them. They looked like the eyes of the dead. Only some beggars huddled near the entrance to the church, and shuffled into the nave behind us, eager for alms.

I turned my eyes away, searching for Simon amongst the Cardinals' clerks. There he was, his eyes turned heavenward, a picture of piety. So help me, I even felt jealous of God, which was so absurd it made me smile.

Rejoice, Jerusalem, and exult in her, all those who love her,
Be glad, you who were sad, so that with soaring heart you might be sated at the breasts of her consolation.

After the Mass we started back in procession to the Lateran. Pope Lucius was too old to ride, so he was carried in an open litter. He was still clutching the Rose of Gold. His eyes were closed and his lips moved in silent prayer. He had commanded Jocelin to walk beside him on his right, where the Prefect of Rome usually walked just before being presented with the Rose. This filled our hearts with hope, and we were not disappointed. For on the road between the church of the Holy Cross and the church of St John Lateran Pope Lucius, third of that name, gave to Bishop Jocelin of Glasgow the Rose of Gold to present to our King as a symbol of special favour and indulgence. Now all must be well, we thought. Now, after such a favour everything King William sought would be granted.

Already by that evening, however, the sweet fragrance of the Rose was turning foul. The Prefect and the Senate of Rome had been given every opportunity to take part in the ceremony of the Rose, and they had stubbornly and wickedly refused. They were not interested in the Rose of Gold, only in stirring up the Roman mob against the Holy Father and the Curia.

Most of the young folk of Rome scarcely knew what the Rose of Gold was, for the Pope had been in Rome over Lent only once or twice in the previous twenty years. The City Fathers, however, made sure that the Rose became the most desirable object on earth for the people of Rome, young and old. Also the fact that it had been given away to a barbarian King on the edge of the world became the mightiest of affronts to their dignity.

The rioting began that evening. The uproar even penetrated the thick walls of the Four Crowned Martyrs, disturbing us at Compline.

The next morning our host Prior informed us that a rioting mob had attacked the houses of several Cardinals in the city, and had even attempted to reach the Lateran Palace itself. However the Sicilian Guard had beaten them back, though not without difficulty and some loss of life. It was not the common people who had been primarily involved, he informed us, but the paid thugs of a few of the city's rich families. Threats and bribes and the promise of loot were now bringing more and more of the mob into the fray.

'I will not hide from you,' the Prior went on gravely, 'that our Holy Father and his Curia are in direst danger. Their wish is to weather the storm of the impious here, where they belong, but apart from the strength of prayer they need the strength of arms. This morning an appeal went out from the Lateran for all able-bodied churchmen, especially those who have had some training in the use of arms when they lived in the world, to proceed directly to the Palace and report to the head of the Guard. Appropriate clothing and arms will be issued there. The Holy Father bids me remind you that you remain men of God, so you will wield your weapons only in defence. Though God knows,' he added, his voice trembling, 'any blow struck against this evil mob would have my blessing.'

So it came about that for a few days of my life I served as a member of the Lateran Palace Guard. For a second time within days the prayer of release was spoken over me and I was thrown into the company of Simon de Quincy.

I strode to the Lateran elated that at last I had the chance to do more than simply cower while the impious devoured us like bread.

The first person I met inside the main gate of the Palace was Simon. He did not smile, but grasped my arm in greeting. He was wearing the uniform of the Palace Guard. He looked as though he had not slept: his face was pale and drawn and he had shadows under his eyes, which made him look even more delicate. I wanted to cradle him in my arms, lull him to sleep, protect him from harm.

In a flat voice he said, 'As soon as you have collected your weapons come and see me. I'll be over at the chancellery. You will be in our contingent, under my command, at my master's palace at Mary Major. Just give your name to the sergeant. By the way your name is Duscath. Don't forget.' A smile flickered across his tired face, then he walked away and was swallowed up in the general confusion of the Palace yard.

Here I was once again in the clothes of the world. More than that I was in the clothes of war. All was chaos without, all was chaos within. Nothing seemed firm or secure: my clothes, my name, my broken vows, my broken bonds. The only fixed point was Simon de Quincy, and my longing for him, around which all else swirled. I felt certain that this would be the end, that I was going to die in the imminent fight, at Simon's side, perhaps in Simon's arms. There would not be time to do the penance necessary to heal the wounds he had inflicted on my soul. So be it. Purgatory would be long and hard, but I would take his image with me, implanted in my immortal soul, and I would be the stronger and the more able to bear the torments.

It was with such mad thoughts whirling in my head that I strode out to find Simon at the chancellery.

'You look very dashing, my young blade,' Simon said without looking up from the parchment he was scribbling on, 'but I doubt you'll be needing your sword and cudgel at my master's palace. The good Cardinal-bishop of Palestrina is on excellent terms with the Senate, no matter how much Pope and Prefect bash each other's brains out. So if I am not very much mistaken, we can look forward to a few quiet nights.'

'Then why on earth does he need a guard?' I asked in amazement, my heroic dream fading before my eyes.

'He's got to keep up appearances,' Simon replied. Then, looking up, he said. 'You look disappointed. Cheer up, we'll find some other action to console you with.' He gave me a lewd wink, and I despised him, and I despised myself, for I could not pretend that in my heart I was not glad.

'But, Simon, we must not, we dare not. I have given it much thought since the last time, and no matter which way I turn it, it remains a sin.' Our first night on guard at the Scolari Palace of Mary Major had passed, as Simon had predicted, very quietly. Now Simon was trying to persuade me to come again with him to the painted chamber.

I was thrilled. But my protestations were no false show: I had been beset by doubts from which I could not escape. If I turned one way Abbot Osbert was there, eyes ablaze, accusing me of the most atrocious sin known to humankind. If I turned the other way, there was Prior Walter, looking sad, and chiding me gently for having broken my vow. So I was not going to let myself be persuaded easily, although in the depths of my heart I knew that if Simon tried hard enough, I would not have the strength to resist.

'Duscath, listen to me,' he said, putting his hand on my arm, 'Burchard, who wrote the Great Penitential, said that if a married man lay with a man, it was as nothing: a few weeks penance and all is well. And that is for married men. He does not even mention as a sin the union of unmarried men.'

'But I am a married man, married to the Church,' I replied vehemently, feeling his fingers burning into my arm. 'Besides, Burchard does condemn clergy who sin as the Sodomites. Walter told me.'

'Not the Burchard I know,' Simon said scornfully.

'Anyway,' I went on, 'you should hear Abbot Osbert on the subject of Penetentials: they are thorns and thistles in the noble grove of the Church, honeyed poison for the soul, and those who wrote them —'

'Abbot Osbert this, Abbot Osbert that,' Simon cut in in his most mocking voice. He took his hand from my arm, and it cried out for his fingers to return. 'The man's a pompous ass, with nothing better to fill his empty soul than fear of Sodomy. He's the sort that would grope a pretty novice with one hand, while with the other he's bringing down brimstone and fire upon the heads of every Ganymede this side of Creation. And you are just as much of an ass to listen to him. You know, there's a song about people like him.'

Then in a quiet, mocking voice he began to sing the song which I had heard the French gleeman sing to Osbert. I burst out laughing, and in that laughter I moved a few steps nearer to the painted chamber.

'No more,' I gasped. 'I know it already. But it is not only Osbert,' I went on, serious again. 'What about the Great Council that was held at the Lateran just a few years ago? Did it not decree that clerics caught at the sin against nature are to be deposed from office or sent to a monastery to do penance, and that laymen are to be excommunicated? That is clear enough to me. Prior Walter was at that Council, and he explained it all very carefully to us on his return. Up until then he had not been afraid of brothers showing affection to one another, nor of allowing special friendships to develop: holding hands, sitting next to each other in Chapter and choir, that sort of thing. When he got back from the Great Council, however, it was as if a new wind blew, and all such tendernesses were swept away. That was a hard and bitter wind.'

Simon replied with his usual sneer. 'The Lateran Council!' he said contemptuously. 'The pronouncements of old men guilty about their own licentious youth, and envious of the youth of others.

'They say it is against nature, but by saying so they dishonour something more sublime than nature: they dishonour reason, God's special gift to humankind, the only thing that places us above the animals.

'Nature is the sum total of God's creation, you would agree? It includes everything from the blind worm under our feet to the eagle that soars into the eye of the sun. There is no universal law which we can point to and say: This is nature.

'It is the wolf's nature to prey on sheep, therefore it is against nature to prevent it, therefore shepherds are against nature. It is the hare's nature to enjoy Sodomy, as it grows a new anus every year, as the old one wears out. And the hyena has a hole specially for pleasure, as well as having one for generation and for defecation. Therefore for these animals it is against nature not to perform Sodomy. Just as each animal has its own nature, so each of us has our own nature, which we must follow.

'How do I know this? I can hear you ask yourself. I know this by using that God-given faculty, reason.

'So what is my nature? My nature is many things, but part of it is to be drawn to men in the same way that many men are drawn only to women. It is good that not all men are drawn to men, otherwise the human race would cease to exist. Unless, of course, you ascribe to that delicious heresy which says that the flesh of human beings is totally evil, and that all procreation is of the Devil because it traps souls in sinful matter.

'This heresy is not new, I know: it caused St Augustine to have bad dreams. Amongst its adherents any sexual conjunction which does not lead to procreation is especially prized. This includes, of course, men with men and women with women. It is absurd, of course, but it does seem to be growing fast in the fertile soil of Provence, and our Holy Mother Church is becoming very concerned about it.

'But it is dangerous to talk about such things, is it not, my little brother?' Simon said, laying his finger on his lips, and giving me a sly wink. I did not reply. His words held me in their spell, as a weasel holds a rabbit.

'For good or evil,' he went on, 'the fact remains that most men feel lust for women, and most women, I assume, feel it for men. Not all, however, and this is my point: there are men who feel it for men, and women who feel it for women, for that is their nature. There are even some, like myself, who feel it for both.

'Through God-given reason each human being is different from the next, each is, as it were, a species in his or her own right, and each has choice. In respect of their nature men like you, and, partly, like me, have three choices: they can subdue it with fasting, mortification and prayer, beating it into submission until it is a small and crippled thing. That is against nature, yet the Church tells us that it is good.

'The second choice is to follow the nature of the greater part of humanity and to force their members where they, by their own nature, will find little joy. This, too, is against nature, yet the Church tells us that it is good.

'The third choice is to go the way their nature beckons them. That is not against nature; on the contrary it is with nature. Yet the Church tells us that it is evil.

'Listen, Duscath called Michael, and listen carefully. The Church now rails against earthly love as the greatest corruption in the world, and love between men as the greatest of all sins. However, my reason tells me something different. My reason tells me that it is greed that is the greater sin. Yet the Church is greedy; the Cardinals, the very hinges of the Church, are proud, greedy hypocrites. Their college is a table of money changers and a den of robbers. The Pope is not the successor of Apostles as a shepherd of souls, rather he is a tyrant who grows fat on the property of others.

'Those are not my words. I would never dare criticise my masters thus. They are the words of one who is far greater than you or I will ever be — the words of St Bernard of Clairvaux.

'Greed is the very ground on which our Mother Church has built her house, the tree in which she has made her nest. Therefore to shout against greed is to shake her very foundations and to destroy herself. That is against her nature, no matter what reason and virtue demand.

'Against earthly love, however, she screams, loud and shrill, in the hope that no one will notice the true corruption in which she sits and stinks. The ultimate aim of this greed is power, and beneath the mantle of power many things can hide, even painted chambers, as you yourself have seen.'

Simon fell silent at last. I stood amazed, at his eloquence, at his reasoning, but most of all at his audacity. Here he was, arguing against the unarguable, against the very canons of the Church, and making them sound foolish. I was at once appalled and excited.

Lamely I said, 'The Church has spoken, Simon; to speak in favour of that sin could be considered heresy.'

'Then you are so much more the heretic for having done it!' he exclaimed with a laugh.

'But if I repent and do not repeat,' I replied, blushing and confused.

He looked at me, his head slightly to one side, a comical smile on his face. 'Yes,' he said, 'what a good idea.' Then his tone changed from sarcasm to tenderness, and he added softly, 'But not yet, my dear brother.'

Then, more cheerily, he said, 'Now, how does that Lateran decree go? Whosoever shall be found to have committed that incontinence which is against nature, on account of which the wrath of God came upon the sons of perdition and consumed five cities with fire, shall, if a cleric, be deposed from office or confined to a monastery to do penance; if a layman, shall suffer excommunication and be cast out from the company of the faithful.

'Now you, Duscath called Michael, are a cleric, and you will soon be back in your monastery, where you can do enough penance to bring you five times through Purgatory unscathed. There cannot be much else to do on that little island of yours, anyway.

'Of course, to repent you must confess. I have already told you what to do: confess to Bishop Jocelin, or better still, to my master, the Cardinal himself, one of the most powerful men in the Catholic and Apostolic Church. I promise you, they will lean much more to Burchard than to Peter Damian and his brood. Your Prior Walter, well, I do not think he has the necessary imagination to see you gently through the thorns of this delicate matter.

'My master hears confession every second day before High Mass in St Mary Major. Just say the word and your soul shall be healed.'

On hearing Bishop Jocelin's name I frowned. Simon, misreading this, immediately said, 'And now you are worried about your vow of chastity, is that it?'

I had been so disturbed by his reasoning and his casuistry, so dazzled by his eloquence and his audacity, and so ready to yield to him, that I had forgotten about this, perhaps the greatest of all objections. Now, suddenly, because he had spoken it, it loomed large between us. Not that it mattered, for Simon had his answer ready even for this.

'However lightly you hold the sin of Gannymede,' he said, 'what we have done, you will say, has broken your vow of chastity, and to do it again will break it into even smaller shards, like stepping on an already broken pot.

'But look at yourself, Duscath, dressed like a courtier one day, like a soldier the next, you stand outside yourself. The prayer of temporary release from your Order has been spoken by your Bishop. You have given your name back to him to hold in his safe-keeping until you return to claim it on the appointed day. He also holds your vows, Duscath.' As he spoke my name he leant forward and brushed my ear with his tongue, thus giving irrefutable force to this otherwise absurd argument.

'You are free,' Simon whispered. 'For a few days in your life you are free. You have the rest of your life to repent. It would be a sin now to do nothing. So come with me.'

'You are the Devil incarnate,' I said to him, half laughing, half serious, knowing that the time had come for me to yield.''

THE.EYES
OF.THE.EAGLE

"I have heard tell of a stone which, under water, is pure gold, but in the air, changes into a dull, lustreless and base metal. The hours I spent with Simon de Quincy in the painted chamber were like that stone. Within the warm darkness they were precious gold, outside they became dulled and debased by the language of sin. In my memory, however, the painted chamber still exists, and because of that so, too, does the gold.

We had three days together. At night we would watch the Scolari Palace, then at dawn we would go to the Lateran to report to the captain of the guard and to hear the latest news of the riots. Afterwards we would attend High Mass, then Simon and I would return to the palace. We would spend the afternoon there in the painted chamber, where we would lie together, sleeping and waking.

Food was always available in the huge, well-stocked kitchens, but I ate very little, my ordinary hunger having deserted me. Hunger usually sits in the stomach, and is good, for without hunger we would not eat, and if we did not eat we would die. During that strange time a hunger grew in every part of me, not for food, but for the body, the breath, the being of Simon de Quincy. I do not think that this hunger was as good as the hunger for food, for it could not be stilled; nor was it a hunger which was a bridge between two states, emptiness and fullness. Rather it was a state in itself which never changed, no matter how much I devoured his body with my own, and consumed his sweet breath with my mouth.

Sometimes I think it was rather a sickness of the soul, making me forget my brothers and my duties to God and Christ. Yet also it was an ecstasy which brought me to the very gates of Heaven, the like of which I had never experienced before, nor would I ever experience again. At that time I thought that if those few days could have stretched out into eternity, then I would have my Heaven.

What selfishness, Martin! Brimstone and fire were falling all around, the very head of our Mother Church was hedged about by stalking violence, and I thought that I could taste Heaven there in the midst of it all. It was not only selfishness, it was also blasphemy upon the name of Heaven, and Heaven's revenge was swift and terrible.

I had almost forgotten the haughty, scheming curial official that I had met only a short time previously. In his place was an ardent, caring lover. Only occasionally, like skerries glimpsed beneath a heaving sea, was I reminded that that other Simon de Quincy was still there, menacing and dangerous.

Our third watch together was drawing to an end. Upon us lay the cold, dark hour before the sky starts to lighten. The wound de Mortimer had made on my arm was aching badly. It had healed well, but recently, with the bearing of weapons and the unaccustomed embraces, it had started to hurt again.

Simon crept up beside me, making me jump.

'Don't do that!' I shouted, startled and annoyed. 'I could have brought my cudgel down on you, you gave me such a fright.'

'No more than I deserve,' he replied cheerily. Then he went on, quietly, seriously, almost as if he were talking to himself, 'Remember the other day you called me the Devil incarnate? Well, sometimes I think you might be right.'

'Delusions of grandeur,' I said, trying to make light of it, although it frightened me to hear him talk this way.

'And what do you know about it,' he said contemptuously. 'You wouldn't recognise the Devil even if you tripped over him. Though for once I agree with you: I'm not the Devil. I'm not even a minor demon. But I do find the Devil so much easier to believe in than God, don't you? No, you wouldn't, you're too foolish. Look around you! Open your eyes! Use your reason! Whose work do you see most of in this miserable world?'

'Simon,' I exclaimed, horrified, 'you must not say such things. You are a cleric, and you work for a Cardinal-bishop of the Apostolic Church.'

'All the more reason for me to say such things. Be careful of me, Duscath. That's not a threat, it's a heartfelt warning, a token of my affection for you. You do not know the half of what is going on around you. Even if it was explained to you, you would not understand, because you are too innocent, too naive, too 'good'.' He spat out the last word as if it had a bitter taste.

Then he gave a cold, dry laugh, and changing his tone completely, he said in a low, passionate voice, 'Duscath, I love you, I want you always near me. You love with such zeal, such conviction. You were never made for the hard and lonely cloister bed, you were made for warm embraces.

'Why don't you leave your Order, stay here with me? My master's family is rich and powerful. We could easily find employment for you. A cousin of my master owns some brothels, catering for all tastes. With your looks, and your rare colouring, you could be rich within the year. And I could see you often. My master's business keeps me near Rome, no matter where the Curia is.'

I was utterly dumbfounded. The proposal was so disgusting, so absurd, he could only mean it as a cruel jest. Yet his voice was plausible, serious, enthusiastic. I felt as though I had been violated, as though it was no longer Simon de Quincy standing next to me, but William de Mortimer. Finally I shouted at him to stop. 'In the name of God, tell me you're joking, but stop, I beg you, I cannot hear another word.'

'Duscath, my dear brother,' he said contemptuously, 'if your little soul wants me to be joking, then I am joking. If not, then I am not. Really, it is up to you.' With that he walked away into the cold dawn.

I stared after him, unable or unwilling to call his name. When I am lying in his arms this afternoon, all this will dissolve like a bad dream, I told myself, and desperately I tried to believe it in order to bear the desolation which the dawn wind breathed.

It was time to go back to the Lateran. We walked along the now familiar vennels, running the gauntlet of the night slops. We did not speak.

Then, just as the side-gate to the Lateran came into sight we heard behind us, far away, the sound of screaming. Cautiously we made our way towards the noise. As we got nearer we could hear another sound behind the screams, mingled with them, but separate. It was a dreadful sound, like a muted, agonising groan. We turned a final corner and there, stumbling towards us, one behind the other, came a line of men who had no faces. The man at the front had eyes, which stared out wildly above a ghastly mess of bloody flesh. The others did not even have eyes. Their clothes were drenched in their blood, but I could still make out the papal livery. They were, or rather they had been, Lateran guards.

The screams which had first led us to them were coming from those who looked on them. They had come out to taunt, but they soon shrank back in horror, screaming, when they saw what was shuffling past.

They had been on guard at the church of St Mary in Cosmedin, old Cardinal Hyacinth's church. They had been surrounded by hooded men, who had bound them and carefully mutilated them one by one. Eyes, noses, lips, all were gone. They had spared the eyes of one only, so that he might take their handiwork back to the Pope.

This was the final, horrible insult to the Pope from the detested people of Rome. Lucius and his Curia could bear it no longer. They decided to leave the city immediately and go to Velletri, a town one day's journey away in the hills to the south. All those who still had business to do at the Curia had to follow them. This of course included the Scottish delegation.

However, despite the horror of the mutilated guards, despite the chaos as the whole of the Lateran household and the papal Chancery were dismantled about their ears, the Holy Father and the Cardinals sat in Consistory. There was such a weight of business to deal with that they could not afford to miss more than one day. If they could have found a litter big enough, they would have held Consistory during the journey as well. A miller is no more thralled to his mill than the Curia is to the business of Christendom.

The Scottish King was to receive their judgment that day, and receive judgment he would, even if half the Lateran guard had been murdered and Rome was burning. I was present at that judgment.

That morning, after giving the alarm and alerting the physicians and surgeons, Simon and I went our separate ways. He went to inform the Holy Father and his master of the outrage, I rushed off to the Four Crowned Martyrs to find comfort with my brothers. So later, shortly after Terce, I was with them in the chapel of St Sylvester to hear Pope Lucius lift the ban from King William and all his kingdom. But I could not shake from me the horror of the morning in order to rejoice with everyone else. Besides, only part of the request made by our Delegation had been granted: the weeds had been cut back only, leaving behind the roots of dissension to put forth new shoots.

When the Pope and his Curia cannot reach a decision, for whatever reason, they set up a Commission of Inquiry. After the announcement had been made that the ban had been lifted, and the cheers and the applause had died away, we were informed that the complexities of the dispute between Hugh and John were so great that Roland, Archbishop Elect of Dol in Brittany, and Silvan, Abbot of Rievaulx, would come to Scotland to hear the controversies in detail. They would then send a written report to the Holy Father, following which a final decision would be made.

This was a bitter blow to us all, or should have been. So I was puzzled by Jocelin, who seemed satisfied with the outcome. As leader of the Delegation he should have been dismayed that half our purpose had been given over into the dangerous jaws of time and an official investigation. I put it down to the fact that he had just received several papal privileges for his Glasgow See.

Abbot Osbert seemed indifferent, but this was more understandable. He was well favoured at King William's court, safe against the storms that blew from St Andrews to buffet other parts of the Scottish Church. Also he had managed to obtain for his Abbey an exemption from interdict.

Abbot Arnold accepted the decision with Christian patience, saying that our sins had been many, and so God's rod of chastisement must fall heavily. However, just the day before, his Abbey had received exemption from papal teinds, which must have helped a little to ease the blow.

We from Inchcolm were afraid. We had suffered more than any of the others from the struggle for the See of St Andrews. Thus we had most to gain from a clean, complete peace, which was being denied us.

By the time we left the Lateran it was almost Nones. Horse-drawn carts piled high with books, furniture and chests were already making their way towards the Gate of the Asses and the road to Velletri. All that remained for us to do was to return to our lodgings at the Four Crowned Martyrs and get ready to move at first light the next day.

We all dispersed in our own little groups. It was as if the Scottish Delegation no longer existed, as if the Curia's decision had broken it up into its constituent parts, divided yet again.

I walked behind my brothers in utter dejection. In the last few days a deep gulf had opened up between me and them, between me and my Prior, between me and St Columba. Without Simon beside me I stood on the far side of that gulf completely alone.

Then suddenly Simon was there, sweeping down on us as we crossed the square, all charm and poise and perfect manners. He did not give me a glance, all his attention was fixed on Walter.

'Worthy father,' he said suavely, 'I have come to take my leave of you. Sadly I will not be going with you to Velletri. My duties to my master keep me in this den of iniquity. I wish you a safe journey, and that you find our country happier on your return than when you left it. My master, Cardinal-bishop Paulo of Palestrina, sends his apologies for not being present himself to bid you farewell, but his health does not permit it. The recent terrible events have taken their toll on his fragile body, and his physicians have ordered him to keep to his bed. However, he asks me to give you this,' — with a flourish of his arm he handed over to Prior Walter a small box — 'in token of his love and respect. And he craves one final boon: that you allow your son Michael to come to him. He wants to thank him personally for guarding his home during the riots.'

All eyes turned towards me and I felt my face, already blushing at the nearness of Simon, turn crimson. In particular I felt the eyes of Brother Andrew on me, narrow and unsmiling. I heard Walter give reluctant consent, urging me to be back as soon as possible. Then once again I was alone with Simon, hurrying along the vennels towards the Esquiline Hill and the palace of Paulo Scolari.

'Does the Cardinal really want to see me?' I asked in disbelief as soon as we were out of sight of my brothers.

'Oh, Duscath, what would he want to see a dolt like you for?' and he gave a scornful laugh.

'So where are we going?' I persisted.

'God's blood, you are stupid sometimes,' he replied impatiently. 'Where do you think we are going? Don't you want to say farewell to me?'

'If you're thinking of going to the painted chamber,' I replied angrily, 'you can think again. I am in my habit. I am no longer Duscath. There can be no excuse.'

'There can be no excuse,' he mimicked cruelly. 'My God, you're tiresome. Why in the name of all the saints should you need an excuse? I thought we had been through all that.'

I bit my tongue. I did not want to spend our last hours together arguing. But I was determined not to be lured to that chamber. It was not only for the reasons which I had given. The horror of what I had seen that morning still clung to me like a bad odour. And there was something to do with respect for the suffering of those poor wretches. But how could I explain all that to Simon, who was angry and scornful at being thwarted, and who would have torn my explanations to pieces.

'Please, Simon,' I pleaded, 'I want to be with you, but not like that, not now. Let us walk a little —'

'With you in your habit!' he exclaimed. 'They wouldn't even bury us on consecrated ground, they would be so sure it was suicide.'

'Then let us go and eat something at Scolari's, then you can accompany me back to the Four Crowned Martyrs.'

Simon did not respond. He was silent for a moment, then abruptly he asked, 'Have you given any more thought to the proposal I made to you this morning?'

Oh no, I thought, not that again. I had come to the conclusion that he had been teasing me then, and for all I knew he still was.

'I-I did not think you were serious,' I stammered.

He stopped in his tracks and gave me a cold, impassive stare. I had never seen him look more beautiful, or more terrifying. I shuddered.

'You didn't think I was serious,' he repeated my words slowly, stressing every word, making them sound ominous. Then he walked on, quicker than before, so that I had to run to keep up. We were almost at St Mary Major now. He made his way unswervingly towards a side door near the choir and disappeared through it. I followed breathless.

Inside it was cold and dark, and the white marble column shone like smoke. I saw him exchange a few words with the sacristan, who pointed to a small, empty side chapel. He strode over to it and knelt down as if in prayer, but he did not bend his head. I knelt down beside him, not saying a word, waiting.

Without looking at me he started to speak, quietly, but with terrible clarity of words and purpose.

'So your conscience is too nice to consider working in a brothel, is it? Well, what do you think of this? I told you this morning that you did not know the half of what was going on around you. You realise that by not coming to the painted chamber with me today it is not only me whom you have disappointed. You have disappointed my master. My master, you see, is pleased when I am pleased, finds pleasure when I find pleasure, joy when I find joy. And I have found both pleasure and joy in you, Duscath called Michael.

'Every moment we spent in each other's arms he has shared, for he was there, quietly watching and enjoying. His body is weak for his heart is not well, and so he uses my body and my heart.

'He noticed you the first day you came to the Lateran. He wanted to see us together. My master usually gets what he wants, because he has so much that other people want: he has power. So people are prepared to give him whatever he asks.

'He had something your Bishop Jocelin wanted. You think that Jocelin is here to settle the St Andrews' dispute in Hugh's favour, do you not? Well, you are mistaken. Jocelin is here to keep the quarrel going for as long as he can, so that when the combatants drop from exhaustion, he can step in and take the prize for himself: the bishopric of St Andrews.

'Pope Lucius was all for settling the bishopric on Hugh, anybody with half a mind could see that, even you. He had some powerful Cardinals behind him too. Umberto of St Laurence, of course, was totally opposed to such a settlement, but Umberto alone, for all his blustering, could not have carried the day. So Jocelin needed my master, whose power and influence in Consistory, as elsewhere, cannot be ignored.

'My master had already been approached by Jocelin, but there was nothing in particular Jocelin could offer him which he did not already have. So he informed Jocelin that he would keep an open mind.

'Then he saw you. Jocelin obliged, not without some scruples, I should add, but when Paulo Scolari makes a request, nobody can afford to treat it lightly, not even a Bishop with scruples. So you were sent on some trifling errand in my company to end up in my arms in my master's painted chamber. You should have looked more closely at the eyes of the eagle.'

I felt sick and cold. My arm hurt. My heart felt as though it had been pierced by a dagger.

'You should feel honoured, Duscath called Michael. Not many people can say they have been a Cardinal's gift. And don't go crying and confessing to Walter. There is nothing much he can do, anyway, and anything he did do would involve a full inquiry. Nobody would want that, now, would they, least of all you?

'I think Walter's patience with you must be wearing just a little thin. You have been nothing but trouble to him and his Priory from the outset, so I hear. This would probably be the final straw.

'Take the advice which has already been given to you several times: if you must run and cry to someone, run to Jocelin. He will understand.

'Goodbye, Duscath called Michael called fool.'

Simon's parting words had taken away from me everything: his love, my dignity, even, it seemed then, my memories. My soul was left exposed to all the demons that hover about us waiting for an opportunity to destroy us. He had taken away from me the strength to fight them.

I wanted to confess, to do penance. For what I was not sure. I could not even look at Jocelin, let alone confess to him, and I did not dare confess to anyone else in our Delegation. So I imposed on myself my own penance. How dangerous it is to minister to one's own soul when the demons are attacking. It simply becomes a tool in their hands."

VELLETRI

"Velletri was a miserable little town, tumbling squint and squalid down a hillside into a valley. Nothing was flat, not even the floors of the houses. We were assigned cramped, dirty lodgings in an inn near the city walls. As in most towns in the Campagna the city walls were its finest feature.

The Curia ensconced itself in the ramshackle palace perched on the tip of a rock which dominated the town. It was one of many such eyries the Popes maintained near Rome for such emergencies. They were more used than the Lateran itself.

Poor Pope Lucius, when he left Rome that cold March day, was never again to set eyes on the Mother City, although there were several more years of life left in his ancient body.

We stayed in Velletri until after Easter. I tried to get my life back into its accustomed routine. I said every Hour, either in the cathedral church or in the small chapel built into the town gate near our inn.

I immediately launched into my penance. I ate only once a day, rough bread and water in the evening. My full daily allowance of food I gave to the beggars who were always lounging around the side door of the inn. I heard Mass five times a day, and every morning I asked one of the sacristans to scourge me, one blow for every time I had lain with Simon.

My guilt sat on my shoulder like a great raven. Every word of the Mass, every word of the Psalms, fed it so that it became fatter, heavier, and fiercer as it reached over to tear at my heart with its sharp, black beak.

Holy Week was almost upon us, and the demon raven whispered in my ear that it would be sweet and fitting to die at that most blessed time. My soul, half-crazed by starvation and the pain of guilt and loss, took up the whisper. Here was release indeed, and the ultimate expiation for my sins. As Good Friday approached I felt myself drawn ever closer to the tortured Christ. By some devilish trick I became Christ, suffering with him, feeling all his grief and humiliation, watching the chalice come nearer and nearer. The spirit was willing, and so was my hated flesh. And every one of Christ's tormentors had the face of Simon de Quincy.

At first nobody noticed my strange behaviour. All was upheaval amongst our Delegation, what with the flight from Rome and the pressure to conclude all the Scottish business at the Curia before Easter. Also Walter and my brothers had got used to my absence, and I was not required to attend Consistory.

Prior Walter was in fact particularly preoccupied during that first week at Velletri. Jocelin had advised him to obtain a confirmation of a grant of land in Aberdour from de Mortimer. The charter had been written out, but was being kept by King William against a successful outcome of the Roman mission. The mission had not been a complete success, and the King might use that as an excuse to withhold the grant. If this happened a papal confirmation would be very useful.

By Palm Sunday all the business of the Delegation, and of individuals in the Delegation, was complete. Prior Walter had his charter of confirmation, and all that remained was to celebrate the greatest festival with the Holy Father, then to set off on the long road home. But what had all of that to do with me, I thought. I was preparing myself for my own long and lonely journey.

By the time Prior Walter noticed that something was amiss it was almost too late to turn back. It was my dreams that first gave the alarm. I was sleeping very badly. Sometimes I would stay in church most of the night, not going back after Lauds to the inn with my brothers. When I did sleep, I was troubled by the most awful nightmares, which still haunt me, even today. In one, which plagued me almost every night, I lay with Simon and we were kissing and caressing and my heart rose in joy like the lark. Then all of a sudden my lips were on a face that was no face, but a mutilated, bloody mask, but the arms still held me tight so that I could not get away, and the monster that held me made a low, gurgling sound, as if drowning in its own blood. It had no eyes, and yet it had the eyes of an eagle. My screams would waken the whole inn.

After several nights of such disturbance Walter called me into his little attic room. He soon got from me that I was practically starving myself to death. He asked me what burden it was that I was carrying. I lied to him. I said that I had committed a sin in Rome which I had confessed to a priest there. I was now doing the penance which he had given me.

'It must have been a grievous sin, my son,' he said sternly, 'for you to be behaving like this. When we return I will expect a public confession in Chapter.'

I did not care. I would not be going back.

'What is more,' he went on, 'you will stop fasting at once. Fasting can engender many demons, Brother Michael. It is very dangerous. It must be done in the right spirit, and under supervision. You are obviously fulfilling neither of these conditions. It was wrong of you not to have consulted me first.'

Then he added, almost muttering to himself, 'I wish I had never brought you to this accursed place. But then you seem to carry your own curse around with you. Now go away and get a proper meal down you.'

Simon had been right. Walter's patience with me was wearing thin. Well, I thought, he will not have to put up with me much longer.

'Then he'll be sorry he said those things to you,' my demon raven whispered.

Prior Walter had ordered Brother Isaac to keep an eye on me and to make sure that I ate regularly with the rest of them, and that I did not spend too long at prayer.

Isaac was as cheerful as ever. He seemed to inhabit a different world. He told me how broken-hearted he was because he would no longer see the beautiful Roman women. One in particular had caught his eye. Every morning he had watched her drawing water from the cistern near the Four Crowned Martyrs. He had considered pining for her, but all this walking up and down hill, and the fresh country air, had given him too much of an appetite, so he had decided to pray for her instead.

A day or so after my talk with Walter Isaac said to me, 'Michael, what is it that's on your mind? Come on, spit it out. You're going around with a face down to the ground, and every time I see you you're thinner. Are you pining for someone? You can trust me.'

'Brother,' I replied, 'I can trust nobody, but I thank you for your concern. I have important business to conclude. You must leave me to get on with it. I am going to die.'

'Brother Michael, ' Isaac said calmly, 'we are all going to die.'

'No, no,' I protested, 'I mean I am going to die soon. I will be taking the low road back to Inchcolm.'

'Oh, as soon as that,' Isaac said, nodding sagely. 'Well, if that is the case, had you not better make a full confession before you do?'

Then like a flash of lightning it came to me what I was to do. It would make my suffering complete, it would purge my soul entirely before death, it would bring me even closer to my dear Lord Jesus.

I spoke my thought. 'I am going to confess to Abbot Osbert.'

Isaac looked horrified. 'Listen, Michael,' he said, 'I have a shrewd idea what it is that is troubling you, and who it is you are pining for. I'm not blind, you know, and neither is Brother Andrew. I am only amazed that Walter has not seen, though I suppose he has a lot on his mind right now. I am also amazed that dear Andrew has not chosen to open his eyes, though there's time enough for that.

'If you confess to Osbert he'll have you flogged from here to Scotland. He'll hang a sign around your neck to tell the world how you have sinned, and he'll make you walk behind us unprotected. He'll   no, Michael, this is pure madness. A demon has put this into your mind.'

From far away I could feel his consternation and his concern, like feeling the sun weakly through a clearing haar. It touched me. Perhaps that was going too far, after all. I said, uncertainly, 'Who do you think I should confess to, then?'

'There's Father Peter, Jocelin's confessor. They say -'

'No!' I shouted. 'It cannot be anyone connected with — No, I would rather take my confession with me to Purgatory.'

'There's an old chaplain in the entourage of John Cummin,' Isaac went on quietly, 'the man of King Henry they have just consecrated Archbishop of Dublin. I forget his name, but they say he has a special gift of confession. People make long journeys to confess to him when he is at home in England. Hilary, that's his name. He's a Cistercian.'

In some strange way the name pleased me. 'Hilary: happy. Are you sure he doesn't know Bishop Jocelin?'

'Of course I'm sure,' Isaac sighed. 'Shall I ask him to see you?'

'It's just another trap, isn't it?' I said, my fear mounting. 'Wherever I turn I'm trapped.'

'My brother, you must trust me. It's Isaac, your old friend. I do not wish you any harm. You are safe with me.'

'Safe with you?' I replied. 'I thought I was safe with him, but the eagle was watching.' My head started to spin violently and I put both hands to my face. 'Isaac, I am sorry,' I muttered. 'Yes, I think you had better ask Hilary if he will see me after all.'

'He must be somewhere,' Isaac said, peering into the gloom of the great church. 'He said he would be here after Mass.'

It was the Tuesday of Holy Week. We had just heard High Mass, so every detail of our Lord's terrible sufferings burned in my mind. Why should the bitter chalice pass me by, and not Him? Miserable sinner that I am, why do I deserve any better? My grief had become entangled in my bones and the very sinews of my soul. I could not bear the thought of unravelling it, pulling it out to lay before another person. I wanted to die. It seemed the easier way.

The night before I had had my first proper meal, under the watchful eye of Brother Isaac. Later, when I was alone in the latrine, I had made myself vomit it up.

'Brother Isaac,' I pleaded, as we stood there in the church, 'please, let us go. He's not here. It is not God's will.'

'Let's have one last look, Brother Michael,' Isaac replied. 'Father Hilary said he would be in the chapel of St Bartholemew. That's Bartholemew, isn't it?' he said, pointing to a mural above the side altar which depicted St Jerome. Isaac had never been very good on saints.

I said nothing, but started for the door. Isaac held on to me. I was so weak I could not pull myself away. Suddenly he shouted at the top of his voice. 'Father Hilary the Englishman! Is Father Hilary the Englishman in the church?'

The vast building echoed with his voice. Silently praying priests and monks turned and scowled. A sacristan came rushing towards us waving his hands angrily in the air. Behind the sacristan, and, peeping up over his shoulder, I could see a small figure in a Cistercian habit.

'Did somebody call out my name?' he said, slightly out of breath. 'Or am I a second Samuel?' Then, recognising Isaac, he said, 'Ah, it's you Scots. I might have known. Always causing some disturbance or other.'

Father Hilary was not at all how I had imagined a famous confessor would look. He was small and round, with a jolly smile and rosy cheeks. He was not young, but somehow he exuded youthfulness. His eyes twinkled, as if he was always about to burst out laughing.

'So this will be the young man you were telling me about,' Hilary said, addressing Isaac. 'I've already forgotten his name, and yours. I've a terrible memory for names. I never forget a face, but names, no, I'm hopeless with them. Which is perhaps no bad thing for a confessor, would you not agree?' He giggled.

Then, turning to me, he said, 'So you want to make a full confession, your friend tells me. All right. Follow me.' And he trotted back towards the choir, to the chapel of St Bartholemew.

In the cool darkness I knelt beside Father Hilary. Together we said Psalm 39:

> I have put my hope in the Lord, and he has leant towards
>   me and heard my cry.
> And he has pulled me out of the pit of destruction and
>   out of the filthy mire,
> and has set my feet upon rock and has made my steps
>   firm.
> And he has put into my mouth a new song, a hymn to our
>   God.

Then in a matter-of-fact voice Hilary asked me to make my confession.

'Forgive me, Father, for I have sinned. It is two weeks since my last confession. Here are my sins.'

I had to wring every word from my soul. Often I had to stop and rest, for it exhausted me. Each time that I stopped I did not want to start again. Each time Hilary was there, softly questioning, quietly repeating, firmly urging.

Without mentioning any names, without having to, for it concealed nothing, I told him everything: about the painted chamber, the joy, the doubts, the deceit, the bribe.

'And how did you know all this was going on behind the scenes, so to speak?' Hilary asked.

Silently I pleaded with him not to ask me that, silently I prayed to God not to have to answer it.

'I was told,' I replied.

'Who told you?' Hilary persisted.

I said nothing.

'You must tell me. It is sticking in your throat and it will choke you if you do not spit it out. Who told you?'

I took a deep breath, and closing my eyes and clenching my fists I said, 'It was the man I loved, the man I thought loved me, the man I shared so much joy with, in that room.'

'Speak his name,' Hilary said firmly. 'You don't have to speak it out loud, but speak it. Move your lips around it, take it in your mouth. Speak!'

'Sìm,' I said in my own tongue. 'Sìm mac Cuinsi.'

As the name passed my lips I started to tremble in every part of me, as if a great dog was shaking my heart like a rat. I was enraged, and in my rage I cried out and I cursed his name, and the name of his master. I cursed and fell on the floor and tore my clothes and cursed again until my curses filled the great church.

When I had no curses left, the tears started to flow. I wept for Simon, I wept for myself, I wept for what I had lost and what might have been and what had never been.

I was dimly aware of Hilary kneeling beside me, making soothing noises. I thought my tears would never stop, that like a river they would flow forever, drawing on hidden, unknown sources, the bottomless pool beneath the earth. But at last they did abate, and the weight on my shoulder was no longer the great demon raven, but the comforting hand of Father Hilary.

When I was able to speak again Hilary asked me more questions, this time about my past life and my past sins. My words were flowing now as easily as had my tears, and I would probably have talked all day had not Hilary finally said, 'Michael, my son, it is almost Sext, and I must go and attend on our new Archbishop. Ireland, I think, is more blessed than Scotland, at least in the matter of Bishops, although I must admit I've never been to either place myself.'

'What about my penance?' I asked meekly.

'You have committed several sins, my son,' Hilary replied, his eyes twinkling. 'One sin in particular cries out, you do not need me to tell you which one. You could not have brought to me a more difficult confession. Do you have any idea of the arguments that have raged around this sin? I have never known the like.

'Some would say you have forfeited your right ever to become a priest or even to remain a cleric, and to enter Heaven you must spend the rest of your life on earth torturing your flesh. Nowadays churchmen sit around exchanging penitentials about sodomy like other people exchange jokes. But it is no laughing matter. Some of them are terrible, including being publicly flogged, spat upon and bound with chains, months of imprisonment and fasting on barley bread.'

He glanced over his shoulder and lowered his voice even further. 'However, I see it slightly differently. I think much of it is just foam. They say that the contracting of the genitals changes blood into semen in the same way that the agitation of the wind changes seawater into foam. Well, I believe that all the fuss about spilling a little semen here and there is so much foam from too much wind, and from too many contracting genitals, as well.'

He gave a mischievous little laugh. I stared at him in astonishment.

'Listen, my son,' he went on, 'from what you have told me you have already done more penance that I would ever have imposed on you, and in a quarter of the time. Your penance now is to eat, and not just barley bread. Look at you, just skin and bone. There will soon be nothing left of you to do penance with.

'Breaking your vow of chastity, well, that is a lot more serious, and you must tell your superiors now, and make a public confession in Chapter when you get home. You will not have to go into details. You will probably get flogged and put on bread and water for a few weeks, which is no less than you deserve. But by then you will be fat from my penance so it will be no great hardship.

'However, you must learn not to throw yourself into the arms of every passing stranger who gives you that special look. You are a good-looking young man, so you will certainly be tempted again.

'That Brother Edgar you told me about, I have some other things I still want to say to you on that subject. But not just now. You are tired and hungry, and I am late. Come back here tomorrow at the same time, just after High Mass. And, please, not so much noise next time. Those poor priests, they must have thought that the Roman mob had arrived, and instead it was the Scottish one.'

The next day was the Wednesday of Holy Week. If we had been in Rome the Pope would have said High Mass at the church of St Mary Major. But we were not in Rome, and the Pope was ill. A few Cardinals had come in procession down the hill to the big church, where Cardinal Umberto said Mass. I attended with my brothers.

As soon as Mass was over I went to the chapel of St Bartholomew. The demons that had left me there the day before, as I lay screaming on the floor, had not returned. I had eaten two large meals since, with relish, and had kept them down.

Eagerly I sought out Father Hilary in the gloom. I found him kneeling before the altar of the flayed saint. I knelt beside him and together we sang the *Nunc, Sancte, nobis, Spiritus*. He took up the conversation from the previous day almost as though there had been no interruption.

'It is not a war between us and our carnal lusts,' Hilary said, wagging his finger at me, 'although nowadays that is how most people like to see it. Our carnal lusts are part of us, and so are part of God's Creation. Our task as clerics, men of God, is to transmute or transcend them, not to beat and strangle them.

'Since your little adventure in Rome you have been trying to strangle them. However, if you strangle something, you kill it, and so in strangling your lusts you kill part of yourself, and you are the smaller and the poorer for that. Also if you kill something, you create a nothingness, which can be transmuted only into nothing.'

'So how do you transmute them?' I asked, intrigued.

'Each person must find their own way. That young brother whom you told me about yesterday, the one with the English name —'

'Brother Edgar?' I said.

'Yes, Brother Edgar. From what you were saying it sounded to me that you were on the right road, both of you, but you were trying to do too much too soon.

'Sometimes in order to transmute carnal lusts you must yield to them, for how can you transmute something if you do not know what it is?

'At other times you must resist, as this can give them shape and form.

'There is one way, however, that you cannot go, and that is the way of guilt. Yet that is the way that our Holy Mother Church seems bent on going. A seed cannot grow into a flower just anywhere, at any time, and our soil for such a delicate seed is becoming more and more bitter, and the winds are blowing more and more keenly.

'So perhaps after all, and it saddens me to say this, the work is now to beat and strangle, to pull out any young shoot, rather than nurture it, for it will surely die in the approaching winter.

'How best you do this I do not know. You must ask someone else, ask your Abbot Osbert and his friends. I thank God that I am no longer young, and death is near, but I pity you your youth in such a time.

'Nevertheless, if the way of transmutation is still open to you, and you choose to take it, let me warn you: it is essential that the person to whom your lust draws you is striving to follow the same path. Otherwise you will always fall back into the mire of your lusts, into the painted chambers of the world.

'From what you have told me about this young man you met in Rome, he has no such noble intentions. Look always for the morally attractive, even when physical beauty is shining right into your eyes, blinding you to everything else. Shade your eyes, look for the moral beauty in the heart of the light, and if you see none, turn away, no matter how much it grieves your soul.

'For physical beauty which is not tempered by moral beauty, which is not joined to it in holy matrimony, is indeed an instrument for the Devil, and will scorch you and destroy you. Your young man has already burnt you, but God took you away before you were destroyed. Give thanks to God for your salvation, and let that be a warning to you never again to turn towards such false light and deadly heat.'

I wept again as I listened to his words, but they were quiet, gentle tears. In their soft flood it was as if all the sweetness and tenderness that I had felt with Simon de Quincy were being washed clean of their loss and betrayal, while they remained behind like true gold in a sieve.

My soul was quiet now, and empty, and I knew that within me new life was stirring.

'If it is still possible,' Hilary whispered, 'and with the permission of your father in Christ, find someone who is worthier of your love, young man, and in the end you will find God."

PART FOUR
THE AGE OF
MIRACLES

Lord, what is man, that Thou hast noticed him?
Or the son of man, that Thou shouldst give him a second
thought?
Man is as nothing; his days pass like a shadow.
Lord, tilt the heavens and come down;
touch the mountains and they smoke.
Shoot forth Thy flashes of lightning, and scatter them.
Stretch out Thy hand from on high, snatch me away,
and save me from the great waters.

Pro obtinenda victoria et prosperitate preces Psalm 143

THE RETURN

"After the Easter celebrations we set off on the long road home. The hand of winter had lain heavy on our journey south, making it bitter and hard, but now spring had come into the land, lining our way with flowers and shading us from the warm sun with new green leaves. Winter still lurked like a wolf in the high lands. Icy winds threw hail into our faces as we trudged through the mountains north of Lucca; and we shivered for three days in the monastery of Saint Michael perched high above the plain of Turin until a terrible storm had blown itself out and allowed us to climb over the top of the world on a fresh blanket of snow. But spring was waiting for us again in Savoy and Burgundy.

By the time we reached the Normandy coast it was summer and the heat hung in the dusty air, making my spirit heavy and dull. The fresh breezes revived us all, and seeing the sea made me forget, just for a while, that almost a month of travelling still lay ahead.

It was just before we boarded an English merchant ship at Barfleur that we were joined by Hugh, who did not leave us until we reached the Scottish border. He had been in attendance on King Henry. In those days the King of England's power stretched even into Scotland. It has pleased God to make his offspring weaker.

Hugh had gone to King Henry certain that his claim to St Andrews was secure at last. The news from Rome that the whole affair had been referred to a commission came as a bitter blow, but it seemed only to strengthen his determination. I can see him still, sitting on horseback, a small, squat, immensely powerful figure, his head tilted back, his little black beard jutting aggressively forward. He rode with the purpose of an arrow, and his mark was always St Andrews.

It was not until after the feast of St John that I saw my dear home again. Our last day's journey from Melrose to Cramond had been through a countryside which lay quiet and slumbering under a baking sun. It seemed at times that we were the only life in the kingdom awake and on the move.

The stillness was deepened because suddenly we had become a tiny group, no more than the members of our convent and our servants. At Melrose the delegation had broken up, with Arnold already at home, Osbert heading east to Kelso, and Jocelin north-west to Glasgow. Hugh and his retinue had already left us at the border to hurry back to St Andrews, to reassure himself that it was still in his control. St Andrews drew him even more than the King, who was hunting in Ettrick Forest and had sent a messenger to Melrose commanding Jocelin, Osbert, Arnold and Walter to attend him in Jedburgh in seven days' time. There they would report on their embassy, give him the letters from the Pope, and present him with the Rose of Gold.

The bell of the little chapel at Cramond was already chiming out Vespers as we trudged weary and sweat-stained down the hill towards the sea. The air now was cool and pleasant, and there before us lay our Priory. The evening sun had changed its stones to gold and its grassy islands to emerald. It was the end of half a year of travel and travail. We all burst into the chant of that day's first Vespers psalm.

How sweet and good it is for brothers to live together.
It is like unguent on the head, which runs down onto the
beard, the beard of Aaron,
which runs down as far as the edge of his cloak.
It is like the dew of Hermon, which comes down upon
Mount Sion.
For there God has given us blessing and life everlasting.

We had left our island in the grip of winter storms and interdict. Now we returned to light and serenity and the grace of God shining upon it once again. Tears of joy rolled down my face, and I was not alone in my weeping.

Walter had sent a servant on ahead the previous day, so two boats were waiting for us on the shore. As we sped across the smooth sea towards the sunset and home we could hear amidst the gulls' cries the bells of our Priory ringing out a welcome for us.

I did not go with Walter when he left the Priory again six days later to travel south to Jedburgh. The shadow that had fallen on me in Rome still darkened my life, for I was condemned to three weeks confinement in the Priory's cell.

On the homeward journey I had told Walter a little more of

what had happened. Not everything, of course, but I did not hide that something carnal had taken place between me and Simon. He had been very upset. Unlike my brothers Walter had not noticed what was going on. He had had enough on his mind, what with the business of the delegation and the upheavals in the city. Even Brother Andrew, who, as Isaac told me later, had been following my movements with great interest, and could hardly contain his glee when things went so badly for me, had not been able to approach Walter with his tales. This meant that Walter had known nothing about it until I told him.

We were in Burgundy, where the wine is good. Walter loved his wine. If he had any weakness, it was that. He was beginning to shed the burden of care that had been piled so high in Rome and Velletri, and the good Burgundy wine was playing its part.

I chose my moment carefully, and I think I chose it well. At first he was horrified, but he listened with growing charity as I told him of my suffering and repentance. My talk was all of the suffering, nothing of the pleasure. I told him that I had made a full confession, that I had done my allotted penance, and that I had been absolved.

'I knew it was right, separating you and Edgar,' he had said, and I said nothing. Then he said that I had suffered enough, I had looked like a soul in Purgatory for most of the time we were in Velletri. He would exempt me from having to make a public confession when we got back to the Priory.

Neither of us, however, had reckoned with the poisonous tongue of Brother Andrew, who at confession and accusation time at Chapter the day after our return laid before the whole convent everything he had managed to piece together about me from observation and rumour. I could not deny the fundamental accusation. There was a terrible uproar, with Brice shrieking for me to be thrown off the island and out of the Church.

'Our miserable brother,' he cried, jabbing his finger wildly towards me, 'has been cursed with physical beauty, and this has been an invitation to all the demons in hell that grow fat on lust like flies upon a corpse. When male with male commits impurity, it is not the natural impulse of the flesh but the goad of diabolical impulse. He must be sent to the colony of demoniacs at Cambuskenneth, where they will scourge the demons out of him. Here we will pray for his soul.'

I trembled with fear. The colony of demoniacs was as good as a death sentence. Some of my brothers muttered against the harshness of Brice's reaction, but he quickly silenced them by reminding us all that demons will support demons. The voices supporting Brice grew louder and louder.

It was left to Walter to step in. He pleaded for moderation and clemency. He did not doubt that Brice was correct in his assumption that demoniacal possession played an important part in such unnatural crimes; but he swore by the blessed Saint

Columba himself that any such demon had been driven out by heartfelt repentance and harsh mortification. These had brought me to the verge of physical death. This he, Walter, had witnessed with his own eyes.

Only Walter could have come between the terrible righteousness of Brice and my poor, sinful self. He gave my friends and supporters the courage to speak in my defense, and finally a compromise was reached.

I was flogged there and then, in front of all my brothers, but Walter chose Isaac to wield the whip, as he knew he would not be brutal, and he did not allow it to go beyond ten lashes.

Then I was condemned to be shut away for three weeks in the Priory's cell, not allowed to see or speak to a living soul, and to be fed only on bread and water. During this time I had to contemplate my great sin and learn true repentance once again.

'A twice tempered blade is all the stronger, Brother,' Andrew assured me as I was led away.

Thank you, Brother Andrew, may your soul be thoroughly tempered in purgatorial fire, and many times over.

They had deprived me of light, of company, of sustenance, but they could not deprive me of sound. I lay in the dark of my prison cell and listened eagerly to the chanting of the gulls, you can hear it now, listen, like a throbbing pulse. It is the voice of the island. It was here long before it became mingled with the voices of monks, and it will still be here when all our voices have fallen silent. It comforted me then, it comforts me now.

For all the harshness of my confinement I was glad to be quiet and on my own. I had been through my Purgatory in Velletri, I would not be tempered again. I smiled to myself when I remembered Hilary's words, for it was just as he had said it would be on my return. And my thoughts often went back to Rome and to Simon, and it was in the darkness of that cell that the bright star of the painted chamber began to shine again. It was as if my Purgatory had burnt away all the guilt, the loss, the betrayal, leaving a bright, hard, jewel whose rays warmed me in my darkness.

During the time I lay in my cell, Walter and Isaac had journeyed to Jedburgh, lived through the turmoil and confusion of the meeting with the King, and returned to the island: all this before I was allowed to stagger out into the blinding summer sun.

It was not long, however, before I had the whole story from my good friend Brother Isaac, who was not afraid of conversing with a demoniac.

The two Papal commissioners, Roland and Silvan, had arrived in Scotland a fortnight previously, ensconcing themselves in Jedburgh Abbey, which soon became a hive of activity as they settled down to their business. They had already written from England to those they wanted to question, summoning them in the name of the Holy Father to appear before them at Jedburgh. John Scot had accompanied them through Northumberland, but had not come any further north than Roxburgh, at that time still held by the English. John trusted King William about as much as a rabbit trusts a fox, so he felt safer surrounded by English soldiers. He had not been idle over the winter, and his labours were about to bear fruit.

The council in Jedburgh had begun well. King William was in high spirits, and delighted with the Rose of Gold. He personally handed Prior Walter Sir William de Mortimer's charter for the land and mill-rent in Aberdour. Sir William himself was not present, as he was still in disgrace after his breach of the King's peace at Perth Castle.

Of course the King knew the whole business between John and Hugh was still not settled, but what did that matter? Surely what remained to be done was a mere formality? 'The mills of the gods grind slow,' he joked to Prior Walter, 'and the mills of the Pope and his Cardinals even slower, but we are sure the flour will be all the finer, as fine as the flour from your new mill, eh, Prior Walter?'

Isaac was very proud that he had laughed at a joke made by the King, and he never tired of telling it to his brothers, although we all soon tired of hearing it. Fortunately there were not many more royal jokes told in Isaac's presence, for all laughter and good humour ceased when Roland produced the fateful letter.

It was as if the sun had disappeared behind black storm clouds. The letter astonished everyone, not just the King and his counsellors. It was not even an original letter, it was a copy of one addressed to Bishop Hugh from the Holy Father.

It praised Hugh's abilities and said how suitable he was to be a Bishop. But it also admonished him for acting so defiantly towards the Papal Legate Alexis at Holyrood the previous year. Because of this, the letter said, Hugh had forfeited his right to St Andrews. It also made it clear that the Apostolic See had restored to John his right to accept another bishopric from that to which he had been consecrated, if such would be more acceptable to the lord King. This meant he had the Papal permission to accept Dunkeld, if it was offered him.

'How on earth did he manage it, Michael?' Isaac asked incredulously. 'Pope Lucius never let on he would agree to anything like that, did he? He never said he would cut Hugh off from St Andrews?'

I was surprised, too, at first. The letter was dated after the departure of our delegation from Velletri, at the beginning of April.

Isaac said that the King was furious. His face had gone redder than his hair, but he did not shout and storm and threaten, as he might have done on another occasion. Six months of interdict had tamed the lion, or perhaps it was the sweet scent of the Rose of Gold that had softened him.

He said he was prepared to negotiate with Bishop John. Both John and Hugh would renounce all claims to St Andrews. John would then receive Dunkeld, his relatives and friends still in exile would be allowed to return to Scotland, and the King would restore all the property which he had seized when they fled.

The King had also been very worried about the documents from Pope Alexander of blessed memory, which John still had in his possession. These supported John's claim to St Andrews, and cursed the King and any mortal who might stop him from enjoying what was his by divine right. The written word is powerful, even Kings fear it. The King wanted John to burn all these documents as part of the agreement.

As for Hugh, subject to papal approval he was to be given Glasgow. When Isaac told me this, suddenly all my dark, half formed suspicions became light and clear. Yes, Glasgow was to be vacated by Jocelin, who would move to St Andrews as first Bishop of the realm.

It was Roland who then pointed out that there might be canonical problems with the exchange of Bishops between Glasgow and St Andrews. If this was so, Roland had said, and if Hugh had to give up St Andrews without obtaining another bishopric, would the King still give his blessing to John as Bishop of Dunkeld?

The King had grimaced, saying that such canonical problems were the Church's affair; all he could say was that yes, John would still get his blessing. But, he added menacingly, he would not love him quite so much.

After three gruelling days the council broke up, and the King sent Silvan and Roland to John at Roxburgh with this offer. But while they were away Hugh arrived from St Andrews, claiming loudly that Pope Lucius' letter was a forgery, and that he would prove it in the presence of the Holy Father himself.

This threw the court once more into uproar. By the time Silvan and Roland returned with John's agreement to the offer, the King had changed his mind. His only reply to Master John Scot now was that Hugh, after all, was to remain at St Andrews. He then asked Silvan and Roland to go back to John and inform him that this was now final, and that if he could not accept Hugh at St Andrews then he could stay in Roxburgh and rot. As for the bishopric of Dunkeld, there were plenty of other able churchmen who could fill that post.

By now the two commissioners were very tired. Silvan, who was old and troubled with the ague, took to his bed. Roland quite simply, but politely, refused, saying that there was no point in returning to John, for he had made it plain that he would never agree to Hugh's remaining at St Andrews.

The King, however, was as persistent as the rest of them. He seemed determined to get the matter settled once and for all. But to do that, he said, he needed John there with him, to negotiate face to face. As Roland would not go back to Roxburgh the King sent two of his clerks to bring John to Jedburgh into his presence. But John refused to take one step towards the King without a safe conduct. Everyone was sure that the King's patience was now at an end, and he would do something terrible.

Yet to everyone's amazement the King sent again to John. This time it was a royal delegation that went, and it included Bishop Jocelin, Earl Duncan of Fife, Sir Richard de Moreville the Constable, and our own Prior Walter, which meant that Isaac went along as well. They had with them the royal safe conduct which John had demanded. The King's patience seemed suddenly boundless. Many said it was a miracle wrought by the Rose of Gold.

Isaac was with Walter the whole time the delegation was at Roxburgh. He said that from the way John talked you would have thought he was the Pope himself. He said he was most flattered that so many great men had come to bring him to the King, and he would be delighted to come with them. But there was one condition, and without this condition, he said, it would be a waste of the King's time and effort.

The condition was that they swear that the King would offer no less than he had offered through Roland and Silvan, and this included Hugh's removal from St Andrews. This was of course the one thing that the delegation could not do. Why else did the King wish to see John, if not to discuss this very matter?

The nobles in the party saw this as a great insult to the King. De Moreville drew his sword. John fell back, threatening excommunication on the next man that moved.

'Is not the blood of an Archbishop and Saint enough of a stain on any family?' he cried.

The English soldiers who were lining the wall behind him stepped forward. Bishop Jocelin restrained de Moreville, and got him to put up his sword. De Moreville said that he had wanted only to trim his hair and see who he was speaking to; for all he knew it might be the Devil himself behind all that fur. For John had once more allowed his hair and beard to grow unchecked, in accordance with his vow.

With that the delegation returned to Jedburgh. The King rode north in a fury, his patience finally exhausted. Roland and Silvan were left with no option but to pass the case back to the Curia, and they fixed a date in three months' time when Hugh and John were to appear together before the Holy Father. The King had ridden away in such haste that he had left behind the Rose of Gold — so Bishop Jocelin took it with him to Glasgow.

John and Hugh did in fact arrive in Velletri for the appointed date, the feast of St Remigius, but it was not until the following Easter that the Holy Father gave them judgment.

At last the prize seemed to be secure for Hugh and King William. Hugh was to remain at St Andrews, and John was to accept Dunkeld and everything else the King had offered. Nothing more was heard of the letters John had obtained against Hugh, and so we all knew they had been forged. Forgery was one of the curses of the age, Martin. I thank God it seems to have abated, and we are not now so foolish as to believe everything that is written down.

It was never revealed who had been responsible. John always asserted that he had been as duped by them as everyone else had been. John had his faults, as we all do, but he was not a liar, and so those who did not hate him believed him.

The news was brought to us by Father Serlo, who had heard it from a clerk who had been in Velletri on other business that Easter. Soon an official letter arrived from our new Bishop. Our Priory held a special Mass of thanksgiving. It was a double joy for us for it meant that now, after four years, we had our own Bishop. The dues owing to him had of course been snatched up by the Crown during this time, and the Crown's officers always took more than they were owed. Half sacks would always become full sacks, twelve hens would become thirteen, six cheeses seven. There had been nothing we could do about it.

John was quite different. As our Bishop he took not a grain of corn more, or less, than was his due. Everything had to be done exactly according to law or custom, and wherever there was any doubt or dispute he would immediately hold an inquiry and summon witnesses.

I have known many Bishops whom God in His wisdom has placed over us, and I can say that none was more conscientious or more just than John. Yet he was also unbending and stern. There was no mirth in him, no softness, no compromise, and at times I think he could have shown a little more charity. But who am I to judge? I thank God I have never had to carry the burden which a Bishop has to carry, especially that Bishop, and that burden.

If John had given his blessing to Hugh remaining at St Andrews when the Pope's commissioners were here, if then he had yielded, the King would indeed have loved him more and the wound would perhaps have healed completely. Instead, trusting in false parchments, he had defied the King and made him look a fool. For that the King would never forgive him.

John was back in Scotland by the autumn. He went straight to Dunkeld, and started getting ready to visit his new diocese. He had been ordered to yield by the only authority on earth he would acknowledge, the Holy Father himself. The King grudgingly accepted him into his peace.

This peace did not extend to other members of John's family, and here the King's vengeance blazed forth. John's whole clan lived in and around St Andrews. From the time of Bishop Robert, John's uncle, they had run the Bishop's household, managed the Bishop's lands, and become rich. Some even muttered that John saw the bishopric of St Andrews not just as his canonical right but as his inheritance. Now the worst had happened, he had lost St Andrews, and his rival Hugh was firmly planted there and was growing with the blessing not only of the King but also of the Pope.

During the terrible time of the interdict all of John's family and friends had fled the country, so afraid were they of the King and Bishop Hugh. Those that had not fled were chased out.

Now that the interdict was over and the quarrel had been settled by the Chief Pontiff, the King promised them safe return to their country and their homes. But when they returned they had found their goods despoiled, their offices at the Bishop's palace filled by Hugh's friends and royal servants, their lands taken over by Hugh's tenants.

They appealed for justice to the King. He was much occupied with the wars in Galloway, he said, and would deal with the matter when the crisis there was over. Peace came to Galloway, but still no justice was given to John's people. Roger of Fedinch, a cousin of John's, and one of the loudest in the cry for justice, was way-laid one dark night and beaten up. Then his house was set on fire and his cattle, sheep and goats slaughtered. He swore it was Hugh's servants who had done it.

Then there was Odo, John's uncle. He had been steward of the Bishop's household for many years. He was allowed to keep the title but all his authority was taken away by Hugh's appointees.

So it went on. Louder and louder were their appeals for justice. Deafer and deafer grew the King. Harsher and harsher grew Hugh. The wound of strife in the body of the kingdom, which should with time have healed, festered and erupted yet again.''

H U G H

''It was the year of our Lord 1185. All that year the news had been that Pope Lucius was failing. It was well known that as the old Pope grew weaker, Cardinal Umberto, now Archbishop of Milan, grew stronger. He was the Cardinal who had questioned Prior Walter so roughly in Consistory. Lucius had seemed afraid of him even then. Umberto was not afraid of anyone, especially not of the princes of this world, nor was he afraid of strife. He was a man after John's own heart. So John set off to bring his complaints against Hugh and the King before the Curia and the sympathetic ear of Cardinal Umberto.

The Curia at that time was in the city of Verona. This was a great boon for the Church in the north, for it shortened the journey to the Pope by more than a week.

It must have grieved the old Pope's heart to know that the Rose of Gold he had planted in our kingdom had not brought the sweet fragrance of peace, that St Andrews was still the bone of bitter contention it had been eight years before. With the din of squabbling Bishops ringing in his ears, old Pope Lucius turned his face to the wall and died.

Two days later Umberto was elected Pope, and called himself Urban, third of that name. The balance had finally shifted in John's favour.

Then Hugh arrived, for the King's agents in Verona had told him that unless he came quickly all might be lost. After much delay, for as always there was much other business pressing, Pope Urban decided to re-open the case and fixed a date for a full hearing in Consistory.

Both Bishops were to be present, and the judgment given was to be final. Hugh begged permission to return to Scotland to prepare his case. Permission was given, along with a stern warning that if he did not appear on the appointed day he would be suspended from office and excommunicated.

John did not need to prepare anything. He was secure in the justice of his cause. Besides, it was much safer to be in Verona with a Pope who supported him than in Scotland with a King who hated him. He feared for the very lives of his relatives, so he wrote to various houses asking them to give his family asylum and succour if they should need it. We were one of the houses he wrote to. The letter arrived with the first refugees.

Hugh was also given a letter with the papal seal for King William. He arrived from Normandy at the time of the King's wedding. Already with a brood of bastards to his name, and a grandfather several times over, King William was finally seeking the sacrament of holy matrimony to give the kingdom a legitimate heir. The wedding took place in the south of England, under the watchful eye of old King Henry. Sometimes it was as if he cared more for the weal of our kingdom than did our own King.

It was a bitter wedding gift Hugh brought to his King. The Pope's letter was stern, ordering King William to stop persecuting John's people, and above all to stop Hugh from persecuting them; and it ordered Bishop Jocelin, Abbot Arnold of Melrose, Abbot Hugh of Newbattle and Abbot Archibald of Dunfermline to take John's people under their protection and to safeguard

John's interests in the diocese of St Andrews. It told of the hearing to be held at the Curia, and it gave to Bishop Jocelin and his colleagues the unenviable task of suspending Hugh from office and excommunicating him if he did not obey the summons to appear on time.

The date set for the hearing in Verona was Whitsun the following year, 1187, and so it was agreed that if Hugh had not set off on his journey within the Octave of Easter Sunday then the papal doom would fall.

This was black news not only for the King and his barons, but also for the whole of the Scottish Church. Time seemed pinned to a great mill wheel that turned always on the same spot, grinding and crushing all in its turning.

The following Lent was a very tense time. The rumour was that the King had forbidden Hugh to go to the hearing in Verona. The shadow of excommunication hung over Hugh. If it fell we knew it would darken everything. Pope Urban was of the same stamp as Pope Alexander. If the King did not yield immediately, he too would be excommunicated, along with all his kingdom, just as had happened seven years before. Every day we offered prayers for the turning away of the storm. Our Lenten fast was more severe than in other years.

The gathering clouds grew even blacker. The King was in defiant mood: defiance breeds defiance in the hearts of the proud. A King's messenger arrived on the island just before *Laetare* Sunday, summoning Walter to St Andrews to attend the consecration of the new Bishop of Moray. A Bishop had been elected in the royal chapel at Crail the week before.

Who was he?

Richard of Lincoln, one of the royal chaplains, the messenger replied.

What kind of election had it been?

The messenger blinked his bright blue eyes in astonishment.

The kind of election that you have when the King is present; very regular, very proper.

And who will be consecrating this royally and properly elected Bishop Richard?

You ask the strangest questions, said the bright, mocking eyes of the King's messenger, but he replied civilly enough he would be consecrated at St Andrews by the Bishop of that place, the chief Bishop of Scotland, Bishop Hugh. He will be assisted by the other Bishops of the realm who are in Scotland and in health.'

The King was cunning. He was gathering around him all the heads of the Scottish Church, including of course those who had been given the mandate by the Pope to suspend and excommunicate Bishop Hugh. He would keep them with him until after the Octave of Easter, and defy them to excommunicate his Bishop while they were at his court enjoying his hospitality.

At the same time what was more right and fitting than that the King should want the fathers of his Church around him at this most holy of times, and for this most solemn of occasions, the consecration of a new Bishop.

Yet in the end it was all to no avail. God's justice can only be delayed, it cannot be thwarted, and in his heart the King himself must have known this. It did not stop him from trying, or perhaps he was merely playing.

They say he even promised Bishop Jocelin St Andrews if he survived Hugh. If this was so Jocelin must have been sorely tempted, but what could he do? He and his colleagues had been given a clear command by their spiritual lord. There could be no equivocating with Pope Urban. Any undue delays and excuses would simply bring down the curse that hung over Hugh upon them all. They say also that the King was in the best of humours, the discomfort of his churchmen was as a spice to his festive meat.

This festive meat was eaten not at St Andrews but at Kinghorn, for there the court went after Richard's consecration. Bishop Hugh had been there too for the whole week, but had left the court on the Saturday after Easter, one day before the Octave. He had ridden off north along the road to St Andrews, refusing to answer any questions about the summons, saying only that it was not yet the Octave, and besides, Verona is less than five weeks' journey away for one who is determined to get there.

It was quite obvious that Hugh was not one who was determined to get there, not in five weeks, not in five years. The King kept his Easter court together for another eight days, allowing none to leave, not even servants and messengers, except his own, and those of his closest barons.

Prior Walter said it was the strangest of feasts, when most of the guests were prisoners twice over: prisoners of the King and prisoners of the flesh, commanded to sit and eat and be merry. Walter would often joke about it in later years, but at the time it was no laughing matter.

When the King finally allowed his guests to disperse, he rode off to Dunfermline, taking Abbot Archibald, one of the Papal delegates, with him. This left Bishop Jocelin and Abbot Hugh of Newbattle to carry out the Pope's orders. They needed to act immediately, and they needed a secure place. Prior Walter invited them to our Priory. They accepted.

Thrice they sent a messenger to Bishop Hugh. The first time he was told the Bishop was away on important business and the messenger was to come back the following day. The next day he was told the Bishop had been unavoidably delayed, but the business would definitely be finished by the morrow. The third time he was told the Bishop's business was finished. Then from an upstairs window a pot of slops was thrown over him.

So on the Feast of St Leo, Pope and Confessor in our Priory church here on Inchcolm, Hugh was first declared suspended from his episcopal office, and then the solemn curse of excommunication was pronounced upon him by Bishop Jocelin and Abbot Hugh of Newbattle.

I was given the bell to ring. Bishop Jocelin was the officiating priest. He pronounced the curse.

'We exclude Hugh, one time Bishop of St Andrews, from the bosom of Holy Mother Church in Heaven and on earth, and we judge him condemned to eternal fire with Satan and his angels and all the wicked, so long as he will not burst the fetters of the demon, do penance and satisfy the Church.'

Then he slammed the Bible shut, and the twelve priests standing on either side of the altar blew out their candles and threw them to the ground, plunging us all into the darkness where now Hugh's soul would dwell forever. Then it was that I had to ring the bell, as if I was ringing the bell for the dead. It was much more terrifying than the death-knell, for it was proclaiming the death not of a body, but of a soul. Somehow it brought us all nearer to the pit of the damned. As I watched the snuffed out candle wicks glowing weaker and weaker, I prayed with all my heart that Hugh would repent, prayed as though my own salvation depended on it.

Jocelin's presence on the island repelled me, wafting like rotten air the memory of his sin, and mine. Yet there was also satisfaction, almost pride, for I knew that I had gained much more than he had from that time in Rome, six years before. I had cleansed my soul of the sin and the pain, and the star still shone brightly. He had gained nothing but false hope.

As I stood beside him at the altar and he pronounced the solemn curse on Hugh, I could see his face clearly in the flickering candle light, smooth and round. His mouth seemed to have to work hard against the heavy flesh which pressed it in, and the heavy words which weighed down the tongue. I knew his hope of ever achieving his ambition was gone forever, and he knew it too. The small, hard eyes were sad and cross. Only the grimness of the occasion prevented me from exulting in his discomfiture.

Yet it was reassuring to be on the same side as he was. When he left with his retinue of twenty clerks, chaplains, messengers, servants, and the island seemed lighter and more spacious for their absence, there was a feeling that we were now less protected from the wrath of the King and his barons which our actions were sure to bring down upon us.

So it was with many different feelings that I watched the large covered barge, deep in the water, pull away from the beach, followed by a shoal of smaller boats piled high with luggage and servants, head west towards the Queensferry Passage. Then looking out over the bright sea towards Aberdour it was as if I could see de Mortimer sitting in his castle, watching and waiting.

William de Mortimer had been lying low over the past few years. During the interdict the King had nodded and de Mortimer had raged against us like a wolf. The King had nodded again, when Walter came back from the delegation which brought with it the Rose of Gold, and the raging had stopped.

Now what? From our Priory the King's beloved Bishop Hugh had been suspended and excommunicated. Would the King nod again, again unleashing the wolf? If he did, the wolf would be fiercer than before, having nursed great anger and resentment for so long.

Sir William had had to pay dearly for his attack on me in Perth. Through him a guard-house had been burnt down, putting the whole of the castle at risk, the King's peace had been broken, and a cleric in the King's custody had been wounded. The King had been furious, more on account of the first than the last, and had banished de Mortimer from his court for a year. Also he had had to pay a large fine to the King, as well as to Inchcolm for the wound he had inflicted on me. Then there had been the charter which the King had extracted from him in our favour concerning the mill-dues and the lands of Aberdour. And he had been forced by the King to remove Robert his priest from St Fillan's church and give the right of patronage back to us.

The list was long, the resentment deep. I prayed to God and to St Columba to deliver us from our enemies, from the wolves whose hot breath I could almost feel on my neck.

Sometimes our prayers are answered in strange and terrible ways. Already salvation was on its way, in the form of a brutal enemy.

For as long as I can remember, and in my mother's time, and in my grandmother's time, my people in the north had been angry at their Kings in the south. According to my grandmother, ever since old King Donald the Fair had been so cruelly put away, blinded by his own nephews and thrown into prison to die like a dog, the Kings of Scotland had been in love with the Normans, Norman laws, Norman ways, Norman language, Norman barons. As the years passed, more and more land and wealth was taken from the native Scots and given to these foreigners.

I can vouch for this myself. To be at the court of King William, you might as well have been at the court of the King of England or the King of France. For all spoke French, and listened to French songs and stories, and played French music, and laughed at French gleemen. The only Scottish you heard was when they spoke to their servants or shouted at their dogs.

This was seen by my people in the north as a great insult and a great wrong to the race of Kenneth MacAlpine and the great

MacBeth. They said that there would never be peace until the Kings of Scotland looked to the north as well as the south, and favoured native Scots as well as they favoured Normans.

Already by the time I was a young man I could remember three or four rebellions. There was the clan of Aedh demanding restitution of Ross, their ancient inheritance. Then there were the MacWilliams, who demanded not only Moray but the throne of Scotland itself, for they were of the blood of Malcolm Canmore.

Each rebellion was fiercer than the last, committed more atrocities, pushed nearer to the heart of King William's power, and was put down with more violence and more cruelty. After each rebellion the north groaned louder under the burden of castles and iron-clad men and horses. Many were the outlaws who lived among the rugged mountains, and every year their numbers were swelled by men, women and children fleeing from the incomers installed by the King in their rich lands. And many were the raids from the high lands into the low.

It was one such raid that had gone wrong in the early winter of 1186. Led by Aedh, Earl of Ross, it had run into a war-band led by Malcolm, Earl of Atholl. He had chased them across the great strath and cut them off from their mountains. The Abbey of Coupar lay nearby, and there they took refuge. Abbot Ralph had tried to stop the slaughter. He had no love for the outlaws, for his lands had suffered many losses at their hands, but sanctuary was sanctuary and had to be respected.

Earl Malcolm and his men were like a pack of dogs mad with the scent of a wounded stag. The altar smoked with blood as in the time of the idols, while outside the monks prayed and chanted the psalms and wept. When it was all over they washed the broken bodies, sixty of them, and buried them beside the church.

When my people began visiting the graves, and claiming cures and visions were taking place, the King ordered the bodies to be dug up, every last bit of them. He had them burnt and the ashes thrown into the river.

When the winter was over, the whole of the north rose against the King. It was more than vengeance that they sought, it was the throne of Scotland itself, for they were led by Donald son of William son of King Duncan eldest son of King Malcolm Canmore.

News of the uprising must have reached the King at Dunfermline almost at the same time as the news of Hugh's excommunication. So the King's serjeants rode through our lands not to take vengeance on us but to summon the host to protect us.

That year, the year of our Lord 1187, was a year of strife not just here in Scotland, but also in the true homeland of all Christians, the land where our Lord Jesus Christ became flesh. The news from the Holy Land grew worse and worse, and all Christendom watched with horror and despair as the wave of infidels swept towards Jerusalem, snatching back the holy places from our men.

The Curia could think of nothing else, and Bishop John had to kick his heels and wait and wait for his final hearing.

He was waiting when the greatest disaster of all struck. Jerusalem fell to the Saracens.

He was still waiting when the news of it killed Pope Urban. They say he never spoke another word, and God was merciful and took him away quickly from his grief to the eternal Jerusalem.

He was still waiting when they elected the Papal chancellor Alberto, who took the name of Gregory the eighth, and who was even older than Pope Lucius had been, almost ninety years old.

He was still waiting when Pope Gregory called a new Crusade, then died before that terrible year was out, the year Jerusalem fell, the year of three Popes.

And he was still waiting when the choice of Gregory's successor finally fell on the Cardinal Bishop of Palestrina, Archpriest of St Mary Major, Simon's master, Paulo Scolari, who called himself Clement, third of that name. I was filled with dread when I heard this news, for was it not written that when Jerusalem fell the Anti-Christ would appear?

Within a month of his election Pope Clement had written letters to King William and to the Scottish Church. They were brought back to Scotland by a triumphant Bishop John. A copy of one of these letters arrived on Inchcolm at the start of Lent.

Hearing its long, rolling phrases being read out in Chapter was like hearing distant thunder; I wondered if Simon had had a hand in composing it. I had heard that he was now his master's chief secretary, and was always with him. I knew he would enjoy creating thunder.

Not only did the letter confirm Hugh's suspension and excommunication, but it also strongly recommended Bishop John as his successor at St Andrews, and even asked Bishop Jocelin, Abbot Arnold and Prior Bertram of Coldingham to ensure that the Chapter at St Andrews elect him.

The rising in the north was over by the end of the summer, before Jerusalem fell. Donald MacWilliam had been captured, and his head had been brought to the King at Inverness. The King and many of his barons had stayed on in the north until All Saints, for many were the embers of rebellion still to stamp out.

When Bishop John arrived back from the Curia carrying these bold and uncompromising letters from Pope Clement, the King was only just beginning to turn his mind again to St Andrews and its disgraced Bishop.

Then came the news that we could scarcely believe. First it was whispered around the cloister and the dorter, and then days later it was confirmed in Chapter by our Prior himself: Bishop John had been received in peace by the King, who had embraced him in front of the whole court.

Perhaps this new access of love had struck John like a blow on the head and turned his brain, perhaps God had wrought a miracle of reconciliation, but whatever the cause, the result was that John humbly renounced his claim to St Andrews forever, and gratefully accepted Dunkeld.

The King promised to put a stop to the persecution of John's people and to safeguard all John's hereditary rights in St Andrews. John went even further: he promised he would not complain even if Hugh was reinstated at St Andrews, although at that time it seemed unlikely that he ever would be.

It was not yet all over, for Hugh still sat in his palace at St Andrews, fulfilling all the duties of its Bishop, enjoying all its revenues, suspended and excommunicated by the Holy See. It was of course an intolerable situation, one that even King William could not allow to continue for much longer.

Old King Henry sent an embassy to our King, suggesting that if the St Andrews dispute was finally brought to a peaceable conclusion, then he, King Henry, would be more disposed to withdrawing his soldiers from the three Scottish castles they still occupied.

This was tempting meat indeed for King William, and by May Hugh was on the road to the Curia to beg for absolution and reinstatement.

The Curia was once again in Rome. Clement was a Roman, and was ready to give his godless people anything they wanted so as he could live once again in Rome, where most of his wealth was.

So it was to Rome that Hugh went. And it was in Rome that he was given absolution and was restored to his bishopric of St Andrews.

Oh, by the blessed heart of Jesus, how vain and transitory are the glories of this world. We are like the grass, fresh and green in the morning, cut and withered in the evening. Hugh had finally achieved what he had been trying to achieve for the last ten years, undisputed possession of St Andrews, and all parties were reconciled and at peace. A week later he lay dead amidst the corpses of his retinue, struck down by the lethal summer fever that is the scourge of Rome.

Then came more letters from Pope Clement. The thunder was rolling nearer, and how much more fearful and downcast we were when we heard it, for peace had been within our reach, and now it was snatched from us once again.

Pope Clement ordered the Chapter at St Andrews to elect John Scot as their new Bishop, otherwise the whole See would be placed under an interdict. The chief Bishops and Abbots of the realm were to go to St Andrews Cathedral and purify the church vessels which Hugh had polluted while excommunicated.

Furthermore they were to go to the King and tell him that if he did not allow John to move to St Andrews then he and his kingdom would be placed under an interdict. Time indeed seemed crucified to the great mill wheel.

Yet time had moved forward after all, quietly, stealthily. All of Christendom was gathering together its forces to fight the Infidel. The Pope could not afford to cut off a whole kingdom, however small, at this crucial time. When the thunder is at its worst the storm is already dying.

Jocelin, along with his brother Bishops and Abbots, had indeed gone to St Andrews as commanded, and purified the church. The King's constable Sir Richard de Moreville was already installed at the palace, and John's people were being restored to their own, reduced, lands and property. Compensation was even paid to those who had suffered most.

Then all the Church in Scotland received a licence from the King to preach the Crusade throughout the land. John sent us word that he was our Bishop and would remain our Bishop. Nothing more was heard about the interdict, or of John's election to St Andrews, which the Pope had so recently insisted on.

It slowly dawned on us, as slowly as a midsummer sunrise, that the quarrel over the bishopric of St Andrews was finally at an end."

SCONE

"During Lent the following year a King's messenger arrived on the island, summoning Prior Walter to attend the King's Easter court at Perth, where, amongst other business, a new Bishop of St Andrews was to be elected. Walter immediately sent to Bishop John to find out what was behind this, and received the curt reply that he was to obey his sovereign and go to Perth, just as he, John, and every other important Church official would be doing. So Prior Walter made ready for the journey north.

Since my return from Rome seven years earlier I had scarcely been to the mainland, let alone the court. I knew why, of course, but my stubborn soul had never really accepted it. I always envied those Walter did take with him, even when the business of the journey was difficult or dangerous. When they returned my pride would pretend I was not interested in hearing what had happened, although in truth I was hungry to hear everything.

What I did not learn from my brothers about events in the world, I would learn from the letters I had to read and write for Walter, for Walter had made me his secretary in the Priory. You see, despite the scandal sticking to my name, my talents, in writing and learning, were not wholly unrecognised.

I had also been made Precentor Geoffrey's assistant, with special responsibility for the books and parchments, lending out, getting back, copying, and keeping the mice and worms at bay. It was a task that gave me much delight and satisfaction. Walter, whenever he went away, would usually bring back a codex or two for us to copy or to keep. So the sting was taken out of my envy and my hurt at not going with him, and I did not become completely bitter. God takes with one hand, and gives with the other, and so my foolish heart was kept light.

When Walter told me I was to go with him to Perth to attend King William's Easter court, and the election of the new Bishop, I cried out for joy and clapped my hands.

Walter gave me a stern look, and said it was a very serious business, and not a cause for such foolish outbursts.

'And we have no idea how it will turn out,' he went on, shaking his head. 'I want you with me because you can be very sensible, when you put your mind to it, and you have a good grasp of affairs. We might need to make some difficult decisions.'

Instead of feeling rebuked by this, I felt flattered and proud and even happier, but I kept a solemn face, apologised, and asked when we would be leaving, and how much writing material he wanted me to get ready.

'One other thing, Brother Michael, there will be three of us. Brother Andrew is coming, too.'

At this my soaring heart crashed to earth. Over the years I had not grown to like or trust Andrew any more than I had done when we had been novices together, and he had certainly not grown any closer to me.

The winter had been hard and bitter cold, but it was short, and by the time we set off for Perth, spring had crept up upon the world and when the sun shone its warmth went into your bones.

The whole world seemed to be converging on Perth. At Dunfermline we fell in with the large retinue of Abbot Archibald, and were obliged to travel the rest of the way with them. So stupid, those Black Monks. We had to thole their silly jokes such as when were we going to make one of our brother seals Prior Phocus, or what was it like singing with a thousand gulls, and would it not be more practical if we were White Canons.

I let Andrew banter with them, he was much better at it than I. I often thought he should have joined the Abbey of Dunfermline, he would have fitted in there more than here on Inchcolm, but rich as his family was, it was obviously not well enough connected. You have to be very well connected to join the royal foundation of Dunfermline.

Andrew, knowing I had no pleasure in such foolish talk, tried to draw me into the conversation. I did not mind, for behind their empty chatter I could hear sweet birdsong, while the sides of the road were bright with yellow flowers, the branches of the trees were swollen with buds, and the sun was warm on the face and hands.

It was not the beauty of spring alone that filled my soul: there was also the hope that at the Abbey of Scone, where we were to lodge, I might once more see Edgar.

Despite myself I could not keep at bay snatches of a worldly, pagan song that Simon had taught me in Rome:

Iam liquescit	Melting, clearing
et decrescit	disappearing
grando, nix et cetera;	rain and hail and snow and sleet
bruma fugit	fog is going,
et iam sugit	spring is growing
ver estatis ubera	sucking hard at summer's teat.
illi mens est misera	It's a miserable soul
qui nec vivit	who does not thrust
nec lascivit	and bust with lust
sub estatis dextera	now that summer's in control.

By the time we were nearing Perth it was sunset, and the roads were so jammed that it was easier to dismount and lead our horses through the crowd. It might be a serious matter that brought us to Perth, but some were going to amuse themselves, for amongst the crowds were players, gleemen and women, jugglers, minstrels, and all the other riffraff that swarm after the court like a plague of flies.

Dark memories awaited me when I stood in front of the castle at Perth, but I hardly recognised it. The whole outer defences had been strengthened, and where my prison had stood was a tall tower.

We trudged on over the wide ford to the Scone Abbey. Some empty beds in the canons' dorter were assigned to us, as the guesthouse was already full.

We arrived just in time for Collation, which we shared with

our brother canons. My eyes were everywhere, searching for Edgar, but in vain. I dared not ask about him; but as I stood at Matins, sleepy and cold in the darkness of the large choir, I imagined him somewhere nearby in the shadows, and the thought warmed my soul.

It was not until Prime, in the grey light of dawn, that I saw him, in the choir stall opposite me. He looked thinner, and his head was almost completely shaved. If he had seen me he did not let on.

Then, after Chapter, I was sitting in the cloister, waiting for Prior Walter and Brother Andrew, and watching the bright sunlight creeping towards me over the garden and the stone. Suddenly I felt a hand on my shoulder. I thought it was Andrew. I turned slowly. Edgar stood there smiling and tense. My heart leapt for joy. We embraced and gave each other the kiss of peace. Now I was close to him I could see that time had drawn many lines on his face, making his kind smile a sad smile also.

'Michael,' he whispered, looking round nervously, 'my prayers have been answered. Every day I have prayed that I would see you once more on this earth.'

'Edgar, it is wonderful to see you. How are you?'

'Yesterday I was well enough,' he replied. 'Today I am glorious. I don't need to ask what brings you here. I knew that Prior Walter and some brothers were coming to the Abbey, but I didn't dare hope you would be one of them. Every time I have seen Walter you are never with him. I asked about you once, and got short shrift.

'Michael, we may not have much time together. I must tell you, it took me a long time for the wound of our separation to heal. I — I did not think it would be like that. If I had known, I do not think I would have.....' He stumbled in his speech and looked miserable. 'I do not think I would have asked to be moved away from you.'

'What!' I exclaimed. He put his fingers to his lips.

'Come with me to the parlour, we are disturbing the peace of the cloister here.' As I followed him I let the understanding of his words sink in. So Walter had lied to us, saying that Edgar had asked to be moved because he had wounded the honour of St Columba. I felt angry and betrayed.

'You never knew that, did you?' he said once we were inside the cramped little room, and he had pushed back the grid in the wall to make sure that there was no-one in the listening box.

'No, I never knew that. I had thought... Well, you know what I thought. Damn Prior Walter!' I exclaimed.

'No, Michael, you must not blame Prior Walter. As a final boon I asked him not to tell anyone the real reason. I have paid for my deceit many times over. You know you were dearer to me than my own soul, but I did not know how to push your body away from me and hold your soul close, and so I had to push both away. I did not know how, I was not strong enough.'

'But, Edgar, you were always the one who was strong and virtuous. I would have fallen into sin with you, had it not been for your virtue and your strength.'

'Virtue and strength!' he sneered. 'It was all a pretence. And when I could not keep up the pretence any longer, I ran away.'

'Edgar, we were trying to do too much, too quickly,' I said firmly, remembering the wise words of Father Hilary.

'Michael, you must know I am no longer called Edgar. When I came here I asked to take another name. They gave me permission, and so I took the name of Michael. It was the closest I could get to you.'

Tears were in his eyes. I moved towards him to embrace him.

The click of the latch on the door to the cloister made me jump back as if a sword had come between us. An old canon shuffled in, bowed to us in greeting, and went into the listening box. Edgar shrugged his shoulders.

'I must get back to the cloister,' I said. 'Prior Walter and Brother Andrew will be looking for me.'

As we left the parlour he whispered, 'Perhaps we could go for a ride together. I am subcellarer now, and am always out visiting our granges. Tomorrow I am riding to Invergowrie. If you could get permission from Walter.....'

'I'll try,' I said. 'Goodbye, Edgar, we'd better not be seen together.'

'I see you're the cautious one now. How time brings its changes.' We laughed and parted, just before Walter and Andrew came hurrying round the corner.

Walter was in a bad mood. Abbot Robert had just told him who the King was proposing for St Andrews. It was his cousin and his chancellor, Roger, son of the Earl of Leicester, one of the richest of the English barons. There was no other candidate, the King had made sure about that by sending Richard, his clerk of the Provender, with a band of armed guards to St Andrews to remind the canons not to be foolhardy enough to elect their own candidate again.

John was remaining Bishop of Dunkeld, and was remaining quiet, satisfied at last with what he had, which was the King's peace for himself and his kin, and the bulk of his income from St Andrews. Or perhaps even he was now tiring of the struggle. Amidst all the speculation of the previous week no one had really believed that John would get St Andrews.

Jocelin's name had been mentioned a lot, only to be dismissed, for everyone knew that the King had never forgiven him for excommunicating and suspending Hugh. But that it should be someone so close to the King, a royal servant, a member of such a noble family: this was no compromise, this was a complete victory for the King.

'Well,' grumbled Walter, 'just wait till this Crusade is over and the Holy Land is ours again, then he'll regret it. The Pope will never allow it. Then we're back to where we started ten years ago. Oh, my God, how You try Your people!'

I made sympathetic noises, while my thoughts turned on only one thing, obtaining permission to accompany Edgar the following day. Then goaded by the demons of impatience and selfishness, I finally blurted out, 'Father, I have a request to make.'

He scowled at me, 'Can it not wait?' No, it could not wait, my demons saw to that. 'I was just wondering, Father, if tomorrow between Nones and Vespers, if you do not need me, I might have permission to accompany the subcellarer of the Abbey of the Holy Trinity when he rides out to Invergowrie.' No, that was wrong. It was as if I was ashamed of mentioning Edgar's name. It was as if I was hiding something.

What a fool I was, thinking I could hide anything from Walter.

'And who, pray, is the subcellarer that he should deserve such an honour?' My heart sank further. When Walter spoke like that it was a sure sign he was angry.

'He is an old friend, his name is Michael.' Oh, my God, first the sin of omission, now the sin of commission, deliberate deceit. St Columba, come to my aid!

'He must be a very old friend.' Walter was saying. 'Someone you knew from your days with de Mortimer, is he?'

'No, father.' I paused and took a deep breath. 'He was one of your sons on Inchcolm. When he was with us he was called Edgar.'

'Ah' said Walter, his face brightening, 'Brother Edgar, now why didn't you say that in the first place? So you've seen him. How is he?' For a moment it seemed that my prayer had been answered.

'Yes, Father, I bumped into him in the cloister this morning. He is well, although he looks much older, but then, so do we all. He sends you his blessing,' I added, confident now of success.

'Good, good, I must make a point of seeing him while I'm here. He was a good brother. And he's subcellarer now, you say. Good, good.' And before I could say anything else he had dropped behind and was calling on Andrew to attend him. So I was left with my request unanswered and sticking like a fish bone in my throat.

Later that day, in the huge hall of the royal castle at Perth, the King presented to the leaders of the Scottish Church his candidate for the bishopric of St Andrews. Roger was a tall, thin, fair-haired man with a large nose, hardly any chin, and pale watery blue eyes. He had the reputation of being, for a nobleman of such high birth, mild and unassuming, although some said that this was only pretence, and that really he was ambitious and very greedy. Everybody agreed that he was totally loyal to the King his cousin.

The proposed Bishop-elect of St Andrews was a mere shadow cast by the King. Thus all eyes were fixed not on him but on the man who had fought so long and hard to be in Roger's place, Bishop John of Dunkeld. Surely he would not stand there for long, head bowed, hands clasped before him as though in prayer?

He stood surrounded by those churchmen who had remained steadfastly against a royal puppet at St Andrews. But all held their tongues. They were all worn out. It was not the King who had won, but time.

Time seemed even to have taken away the triumph from those churchmen who had so vigorously supported Hugh from the beginning. Abbot Archibald of Dunfermline was scowling, but then, he was always scowling, there was nothing unusual in that. Abbot Henry of Arbroath looked bored; while Archdeacon Jocelin of Dunkeld looked sad, for not only had he lost his friend, Hugh, but for years now he had had to work for a hostile master.

In none of these eyes was there triumph.

It was very different when I looked over at the King and his chief men. They were radiant with triumph, full of smiles and jests. Most of them were there, the one more murderous than the next. There was Earl Duncan of Fife, who had led the terrible slaughter in Warkworth church, and beside him tall and broad Sir William de Hay, de Mortimer's old friend.

Where was de Mortimer? He was nowhere to be seen, thank God. He probably dared not show his face in Perth, the scene of his disgrace.

Earl Robert de Quincy was there. I looked at him long and hard, for he was a kinsman of Simon, and I had to cross myself and look away, for I could see a resemblance in the regular features and the dark eyes.

There was plenty to take my mind off such thoughts. The King had ordered one of his clerks to read out the Pope's latest letter. This he was doing in a grating voice, stumbling over many words, and getting lost in the long, twisting phrases, but the meaning of the letter was clear enough. It praised the King as a good and obedient son of the Church and one of its chief defenders at this time of need. It stressed the importance of filling the vacancy at St Andrews as quickly as possible. It described it as a bleeding wound in the body of our Holy Mother Church that had to be stopped. And it left this urgent business to the wisdom of the King. There was no mention of John, or of interdicts, or of God's wrath.

Then the King asked if anyone objected to Roger as his candidate for the post, or if anyone would care to propose another candidate.

The great hall echoed with much shuffling and rustling and coughing, but no one spoke.

So the King set a date three days hence for Roger's formal election. Then there was a royal grant to witness, to the King's own foundation of Arbroath, just to show what a dutiful son of the Church King William was.

Before we were dismissed, the royal command was that all were to attend a banquet in the great hall that very evening after Vespers. The King would take no excuses, the world would not go to hell any faster if a few less monks were at Matins that night. And so we dispersed, many of the churchmen scarcely daring to look at each other for fear their eyes spoke too loudly.

Outside it had begun to rain. Walter signalled to me and Andrew to follow him, and we sheltered under a nearby awning.

'My sons,' he said with a sigh, 'this banquet is not for you. It's not really for me either, but I have no choice but to attend. So I want the pair of you to go straight back to the Abbey, and tell the guestmaster that I won't be back till tomorrow. I hope I'll be there for Chapter. All right?'

No, it was not all right, I still had not received an answer to my request.

'Father,' I said, wishing Andrew were a hundred miles away, which was, God forgive me, nothing unusual, 'May I have a word with you alone?'

Walter frowned.

'It's about that request I made, about tomorrow, about riding out.'

Walter shook his head vigorously.

'Brother Michael', he said crossly, 'do you remember the last time I took you away with me on a journey?'

I groaned inwardly. 'You mean to Rome, father,' I said meekly.

'I mean to Rome. That is correct. And do you remember what happened in Rome when you went gallivanting off on someone else's business?'

Andrew had turned his back on us and put his cowl up, but I knew he could hear every word. He was probably sniggering quietly to himself.

To stop any further humiliation I quickly added, 'Father, I withdraw the request.'

'Very wise, very wise. But, Michael, as you have already been discussing outings with Brother Edgar, I have to order you not to exchange any more words with him while you are staying under the same roof. It is hard, I know, but it is for the good of your soul — both your souls. And I'm sure Brother Andrew will make things easier by keeping an eye on you. Won't you, Brother Andrew?'

Andrew spun round, throwing back his cowl.

'Of course, Father,' he said with an ingratiating smile.

'Now go, the pair of you, I want you to be back at the Abbey by Compline. And pray for the soul of your poor Prior, exposed to so many deadly sins at this cursed banquet.' Then he gave us both his blessing and hurried back into the great hall.

We found our mounts and rode slowly through the rain back towards the Abbey.

'Not getting to go off for a ride with your old friend, then?' said Andrew, as soon as we were over the Tay. 'My heart bleeds for you.'

I said nothing. I wanted to push him into the river. 'Not to worry,' he went on remorselessly, 'Brother Andrew will keep you right, because there's not much that Brother Andrew doesn't see.'

He chuckled, and I kicked the sides of my mount and rode on ahead. Andrew kept behind, but I could feel his eyes upon my back the whole way. I consoled myself by imagining the many torments that awaited him in Hell.

It was all the fault of the old woodcutter. He came along the road towards us with his axe dangling around his neck and a huge bundle of sticks and logs on his bent shoulders. It was the day after the banquet. Andrew and I were riding down the road to the river to see if we could see Prior Walter. It was already after Sext and he still had not appeared. I had wanted to walk, but Andrew insisted we take the horses. He would not go anywhere unless he was on horse back.

As the old woodcutter drew nearer he looked up at us, twisting his neck, defying his burden. He scowled and spat upon the ground in our direction. Often young peasants would look at you with anger or malice, but you rarely saw that look in the eyes of the old, for their spirits had long ago been broken, along with their bodies, by the toil that ended only in death.

'Did you see that?' Andrew screeched indignantly, reining in his horse and blocking my way. 'He shouldn't be allowed to get away with that, that's not just disrespectful, that's blasphemous.'

I too was shocked, but I was certainly not going to show Andrew. I said nothing.

Andrew then turned his anger onto me. 'Of course, you're probably related to the evil old oaf. Pagan peasants, the lot of you.'

'You stuck-up little Norman prig,' I spat, my anger flaring. 'My people were Christian when yours were still slaughtering goats to Thor.'

This elevated conversation was cut short by the sudden appearance of three horsemen, who came thundering along the road behind us. They were all black canons, and with a start I realised that one of them was Edgar.

He gave me a curt nod and would have ridden on at once. However the road was narrow and all six of us, the three canons, the old woodcutter, Andrew and myself, were level and blocking each other's way. Andrew was beside the woodcutter, and so as he pulled over to let Edgar and his brothers pass, he pushed the old man off the road and into a ditch.

The next thing I knew Andrew's horse had reared up violently, flinging him to the ground. He landed with a shriek at the feet of the woodcutter, who stepped over him and hurried on, muttering. The rest of us jumped off our horses and rushed to the ditch.

Andrew lay motionless, his eyes closed, blood trickling down one side of his face from a gash on his forehead. His left arm poked out from under his body at a grotesque angle. For one terrible moment I thought he was dead and my wicked prayers had been answered in order to punish me. Then he started to groan.

Edgar immediately ordered his two companions, one of whom was a lay brother, to pick up the injured man carefully, lay him over the back of his horse and take him straight to the Abbey infirmary.

Andrew screamed as he was lifted up, and my heart swelled with pity for the poor creature. It is strange how hatred can be turned to pity when the hated one becomes powerless. From the strength of his screams he was obviously nowhere near death. I thanked God for this, and prayed to St Columba to stand by him in his pain.

'I'll go with them,' I said, still following my pity.

'He's in good hands,' Edgar said. 'You might as well continue on your way.'

I stood and watched the horses walk slowly back towards the Abbey with their miserable load. I turned to Edgar, suddenly realising that we were alone.

'No, I'd better go,' I said, all pity forgotten, panic rising as I saw disobedience loom.

Edgar was saying, 'Why didn't you tell me you wouldn't be coming with me this afternoon?' He sounded hurt.

'I have been forbidden to talk to you. Walter is in a bad humour just now. He was angry that I even asked. He says he is afraid for our souls.'

'Then you have already disobeyed. Michael, there is nothing now that can happen between us that could endanger our souls. It is not in vain that I have fought against my passion for you these past seven years.

'My love for you is just as great, but my passion, well, that has gone. God's love has swallowed it. I did not have to follow the example of St Benedict, throwing myself into nettles and brambles whenever I felt the sweet lure of the flesh, but I did not shrink from opening my heart and my passions to God. He made them, so why should I feel shame in offering them back to Him? They were wise, our Fathers in Christ who gave us our

Rule and our Customs, they made it hard for us, and they made it easy. Have you not found this too?'

I was confused, and I did not know what to reply. Demons and angels contended in my soul. There was sadness at his words, sadness that his passion for me was gone. I felt I had lost something precious, that I was somehow diminished. I felt disappointed.

It suddenly became clear to me that I had been hoping for something more than conversation with him. In that secret chamber of my heart a terrible wanting had grown, had always been there, perhaps, but now the door was open I could not look away, could not pretend any longer that it was not there.

Also I felt envy that he had learnt to do something that I had never learnt to do, to overcome the ache of body for body, flesh for flesh. Partly I wanted to draw back, accept his words, close the door on that secret chamber and join him in his virtue. Partly I wanted to lead him into the wood, envelop him in my bodily love, hold him tight, and put him to the test.

We stood there, neither of us knowing what to say or do. A thrush was singing nearby. Suddenly I was back in the garden at Jedburgh Abbey all those years before, when Edgar had led me out of the darkness of the infirmary into the sunlight and the bird-song. A strange fate had brought us together then, and that same fate seemed to be at work again, for here we were, alone and together, far away from prying eyes, in spite of all my good intentions and Prior Walter's safeguards.

Now this fate had slipped away into the woods, leaving my blood to do the rest. I could feel it singing in every limb, and the song it sang was wild and dangerous and soon drowned out the song of the birds. It was my blood that finally spoke, breaking the word-silence between us.

'Edgar, God has given us this time, let us not waste it.' I put my arms around him and kissed his lips. They were rough and dry.

His body stiffened and he recoiled.

'Michael, this is not the work of God, it is the Devil's. Lead us not into temptation, but deliver us from evil. Amen.'

He shut his eyes and his lips moved in prayer, lips that were softer now, moistened by my kiss.

My blood was singing louder and louder, and in my soul I knew that it had nothing to do with either the Devil or God. This sounds like blasphemy now, but it was no blasphemy then, it was the truth.

I took the horses and tethered them in a small clearing near the road. Then I took Edgar by the hand and led him into the thick wood beyond. He resisted at first, but only for a moment, for his blood too had started to sing the same song.

In that wood, filled with the song of birds and with the sound of the river, there was an outpouring of love and passion that had built up for ten years, like water bursting through the wall of a mill pond. Through our skins our souls sweetly touched each other. Whatever base things happened there were ennobled and elevated by the love which burst around us and flowed between us.

In Rome Simon and I had been animals, drunk on animal pleasure; but pure and perfect love now transformed Edgar and me into angels, and those brief moments into eternity. Yet without my time with Simon, that precious time with Edgar would have never been.

We were brought back to our imperfect human selves by the distant thunder of horses' hooves.

Edgar's face, which had become young again through the joy of love, darkened and grew older.

'My brothers will be looking for me. We must be on our way. We have already been too long delayed. My God, Michael, what have we done?'

'We have done nothing that we need be ashamed of, nothing. It was good, Edgar. Was it not good?'

Edgar buried his face in his hands. There was so much else to say, but our time together was over. I had to leave my joy, Edgar his guilt.

He said, 'My dearest Michael, you must get back to the Abbey, and pray that Andrew has not yet realised you're not there.'

At the mention of Andrew's name I groaned, for behind his weasel eyes I saw the pained and angry face of Prior Walter. Then suddenly I was filled with a new, grim strength. It did not seem reckless, although when I look back now I am not so sure. I did not care what Andrew thought; I did not care what Walter was told; I did not even care if I was thrown out of the Priory. All of that seemed unimportant compared with Edgar and the need that Edgar had for my love and reassurance, here and now.

'Edgar,' I said urgently, 'Remember old Father Edwin, remember what he told us, about there being three kinds of love, carnal, worldly and spiritual, and how one can lead into the other, strengthen the other, as long as the spiritual love is greatest, as long as...'

Edgar cut in, 'I know, I know, but Edwin is long dead, and where is there another to take his place? Besides, he was in error, Michael, our Holy Mother Church teaches that, he was in error.'

'No, Edgar,' I replied, 'Our love proves that he was not in error. Our love will become pure by passing through the flame of our bodies, not by avoiding it, extinguishing it. There are still holy men and women who believe this, no matter what our Holy...'

Edgar kissed my lips, saving them from blasphemy.

'Enough of this, you've become a devil for argument. We must go because soon the servants will be out looking for us. Tell them at the Abbey that I've ridden on to Invergowrie on my own and...'

It was my turn to stop his words with a kiss. Then we jumped up and ran to our horses. Luckily whoever had ridden past had not seen them.

Before Edgar rode off he said, 'Michael, you have changed. I cannot curse the fate that brought us together today, no matter how severe my penance will be. I pray that it is God's will that we will meet again on this earth but it cannot be now at Scone. In the name of all the saints, get back and show yourself to Andrew. And wipe that lovely smile off your face. You look too happy. He'll know at once what's happened. And you're making it even harder for me to leave you.'

I made a grotesque face at him, slapped his horse's rump and told him to be on his way. Then I trotted back towards the Abbey, my heart soaring heavenward like the lark.

When I got back I went straight to the infirmary, only to be told that Brother Andrew was in a deep sleep and was on no account to be disturbed. I considered going into the church to pray, but the sun was shining now so beautifully, I did not want to leave it. So when I heard that Prior Walter still had not arrived back from Perth, I decided to walk back down the road to meet him, past the sweet memories of Edgar."

A   N E W   B R O T H E R

"Neither Andrew nor Walter ever found out what happened between Edgar and me that spring afternoon in the woods near Scone. I did not feel the need to confess, as I did not feel that we had sinned, and I still do not feel that we sinned, nor do I see the terrible things that later befell us as in any way a punishment from God.

Do you hear that, Martin? I want you to hear that and remember it. Do not ask me how I know this, for no words could ever explain, but it is a rock of certainty, and I could build a church upon it."

At this Martin could not contain himself.

"Reverend Father," he blurted out, "you stand on the threshold of eternal life. Do you not think you are putting at risk for all time the well-being of your soul by maintaining such a.." he paused, and his lips trembled as they formed the awful word, "heterodox opinion, about a matter on which the Holy Mother Church is very clear."

"The well-being of my soul is my business," the old man snapped, "and the business of my Maker's. It is not yours."

Michael was shaking with rage. Martin had never seen him so angry. He was shocked, both by his opinions and by his anger. He murmured an apology and quickly changed the subject, pushing aside the troubled thought that perhaps he had a duty to report the old man to the Archdeacon.

"You said you were going to tell me something more about Prior Simon," Martin said flatly.

"Did I?" he sighed, the anger draining from his voice. Then he bent his head, muttered something, crossed himself and looked up with a smile. "You're a persistent young devil," he said. "You know, sometimes I wonder if my Purgatory didn't begin when you landed on this island.

Well, we returned safely from Bishop Richard's election in Perth, and life settled back into its usual rhythm. Yet my heart ached for Edgar in a way that it had not ached for a long time, and all my undirected and idle thoughts made straight for his image, which sat at the very centre of my soul. In church during the Mass and the Hours I could feel God's love and light like sunshine on the back of my neck and I realised how dull and cold my soul had become over the past years. It was as if I had come alive again, with all the joy and pain which that brings with it

The sun shone also on the land, and it was peaceful. Many of the barons were preparing for the Crusade, to fight at last for God and not against Him. Oh, what a happy and harmonic convergence, the love of God and the love of war. The King and those barons who remained behind stayed mainly in the north, for fear that the broken rebels who still lurked in the mountains might strike again while so many fighting men were overseas.

But the Crusade had brought with it problems as well as blessings, for the Crusade needed gold. Today our Priory has goods and chattels enough to ensure its future, and there is even talk, I have heard, of petitioning the Pope to become an Abbey; but in those days we were weighed down with debts, and struggling to pay our creditors.

How simple and beautiful is our Lord's injunction, consider the lilies of the fields, how hard it is to follow, even for men of God. To pay for the building of the great tower and the extension to the church, as well as improvements to our living quarters, we had borrowed large sums from various Jews in Edinburgh. Unhappily we had not reckoned with a series of poor harvests and a disease of our sheep which had carried off more than a third of our flock.

Nor had we reckoned with the King's new tax. This was to buy back the chief castles of Scotland from the English, who had occupied them since the war. Old King Henry had died that same summer of '89, and now his son Richard was ruler of England, Normandy, Anjou and half the world — King Richard the fair with the heart of a lion.

King Richard had only one ambition, to recapture Jerusalem from the Infidel. For this he needed money. So at a price he offered King William back his castles. The price was high. Our King accepted the offer gladly, then turned to his subjects for the gold, and as usual the houses of God had to find the biggest share. The mighty of the earth, pah! they give with one hand and take away with the other.

It was around the Feast of St John, midsummer, although it was as dull as the dullest November day. I had been appointed succentor, with all the manuscripts to look after, and the copying to oversee, so I had to keep the writing materials in good order.

In fact in all but name, and duties in choir, I was precentor, and Father Geoffrey worked mainly with the novices. We had never got a proper replacement for Father William, whose prayer, to be delivered from the clutches of his detested sea, had been answered at last, and who was now priest in charge of Auchtertool.

I would sometimes help Geoffrey with the novices, much to Subprior Brice's disapproval. He had not wanted me to have anything to do with them for fear I corrupt them, but both Walter and Geoffrey had spoken strongly in my favour and Brice had been overruled.

That day I was taking the novices to the goose-pen for quills. It was when we were up by the pagan stones, Novice Hugh shouted out and pointed towards the Lothian shore. The dark shape of a boat was making its way steadily towards the island. I could tell by its size that it was not one of ours.

My heart sank. I was sure it was one of our creditors coming to take away more church silver, or even one of our precious manuscripts. Instead of reproving Hugh for shouting out like that, most unbecoming for an Augustinian, I ordered the novices to go back to the scriptorium. Then with great foreboding I hurried away to warn Prior Walter.

The rain was falling heavily by the time the strange vessel swung into the south bay. Even before its snout had struck the beach we were all on our knees, because the tall, thin figure standing alone near the bow was none other than our Bishop, John Scot.

This was most irregular, a visit from the Bishop without any intimation. It must be something serious.

My eyes quickly ran over the others in the boat. If I had been standing upright, I would have leapt back as if I had touched fire. If I had been sitting I would have jumped up as if I had sat on a thorn. But I was kneeling, so I swayed violently like a tree in a storm, and had to put out my hand to stop myself from falling: because there in the boat behind our Bishop, his head tilted back as though gazing at something on top of the Priory tower, stood Simon de Quincy.

My brothers and our servants were already crowding round the boat, pulling its bow onto the sand and helping the Bishop and his retinue to disembark. I remained kneeling for I could not rise, and Simon was lost to view. I decided that it must have been a trick of the light, or some demon. It would not have been the first time since my return from Rome that the image of Simon de Quincy had deceived my senses. I crossed myself and got to my feet, only to have to go down on my knees again almost immediately to kiss the Bishop's ring.

It was as I got to my feet the second time that I found myself face to face with Simon. This was no impish trick, this was the Devil himself. He flashed me his most charming smile and bowed. The years had not diminished his beauty one jot. In fact it was uncanny how little he had changed. My head spun. Perhaps the last ten years had been a dream and I was still in Rome and it was only yesterday that we had parted. Then he was gone again, and I was left standing in the rain on the south beach of Inchcolm, greeting John's clerks and his chaplains.

Bishop John had been with the King in Haddington, and was visiting Inchcolm on his way north to Dunkeld to bring us the tidings that Pope Clement was dead and that old Hyacinth Bobo had been elected in his stead, taking the name of Celestine.

Yes, the world had survived Paulo Scolari as Christ's vicar on earth. It was not the first time an evil man had sat on the throne of St Peter, nor I am sure will it be the last. As St Brigid herself says, even though there are many Popes who are now in Hell, their just and reasoned decisions while they were in the world are enduring and acceptable to God. I had no doubt that Clement was in Hell, beyond the reach of our prayers, although scant prayers would he get from me.

John was also bringing to us a precious servant of the Lord, the bearer of these sad tidings from Rome, who had decided to withdraw from the hurlyburly of the Curia, who had turned his back on high office to seek out Christ in a quiet place. Yes, he was bringing to Inchcolm Simon de Quincy.

So Simon had come not as part of Bishop John's retinue, to depart again within a few days. He had come to beg permission to join our community. He had come to stay. If he had arrived alone, simply another poor petitioner in clerk's robes on the run from some secret crime, and God knows there were enough of those, we would probably have turned him away. But he had not arrived alone. He had arrived with our own Bishop. Our own Bishop was commending him to us. Simon had even brought with him a letter from Pope Clement himself, urging us to accept him without him even having to undergo a novitiate. The letter set out his many virtues and skills which would make him a great asset to our community, and concluded by saying that Simon had made a full confession of all his sins to the Holy Father himself, for which complete absolution had been granted.

Nor was this letter all that he had brought with him. Simon, it appeared, was a rich man: in his scrip he had credit notes from the Knights Templar which amounted to more than the whole annual income of the Priory. You do not work for many years as an official of the Curia without amassing large amounts of gold and silver. Of course all this gold and silver would belong to the Priory as soon as Simon became one of our brothers.

It is written by St Paul that the love of money is the root of all evil, and there are some who in reaching for it have spiked themselves on many thorny griefs. Evil has, however, another root, and that is the need for money, real or imagined, and what is greed but imagined need? At that time our need was anything but imagined, and the very existence of our Priory was threatened.

Not that Simon had it all his own way, for even with such weighty references and recommendations he still had to answer questions in Chapter. Brother Andrew's malicious tongue had not been slow in letting everybody know that this was the man with whom I had fallen into such great sin in Rome all those years before.

Brice was of course outraged, but did not Simon have written absolution of all past sins from the Holy Father himself? This did not deter Brice from raising the matter in Chapter. Walter groaned and covered his face with his hand. Bishop John glowered, but Brice was determined.

Simon handled it well. He did not wave the Papal pardon in the air, or run and hide in Bishop John's robes, he meekly and contritely made a full confession , there in Chapter before the whole convent. He did not name any names. He did not have to, for pointed looks and my blushing did that for him. But he repented so convincingly, so movingly, so delicately, that even I was taken in.

Then, taking the lead from Brice, Henry the cellarer asked why Simon had given up such an apparently successful career at the heart of Christendom to become a brother in a small, poor and insignificant Priory on the edge of the world.

With touching humility and the sweetest of smiles Simon replied that it had taken him many years to discover what the wise already know, and have been telling us from time immemorial: that God's peace is not to be found where power and wealth abound, and that his soul, like most mortal souls, was too weak to resist the terrible temptations that such a life offered.

Therefore he had decided it was time to return to his own people, and to search for God among the humble of spirit. Our Priory had been recommended to him as a veritable haven of peace and virtue, and so he had come to beg the privilege of joining us.

A thrill went through the room. It was a thrill of pride, of awe, of admiration. Here was a remarkable man, who had known the mightiest of the earth, who had been trusted by them, who had advised them, here was a man who looked like a prince, who had known the secrets of Christendom, who had been a staff to the Holy Father himself, and yet he was choosing to live amongst us, proclaiming by his actions the wonderful fact that all men are brothers in Christ, from the highest to the lowest. In the bowels of us all, even in mine, who had the greatest reason for distrusting this man, his flattery was turned into adulation and our hearts went out to him.

Prior Walter had welcomed Simon with a suspicious frown, yet he never said a word against him. He accepted his arrival, backed as it was by Pope, Bishop, and gold, as one would accept some upheaval in nature. Simon was received as a full brother of the convent.

Before Bishop John left he had secured the acceptance into our convent not only of Simon de Quincy but also of Simon's servant, a young Roman called Orsino. Orsino had not arrived with Simon and the Bishop, he had fallen ill at Haddington and was not expected for about a month. As he was requesting only to become a lay-brother, and as both Bishop John and the Papal letters recommended him to us, he was accepted in absentia.

Orsino did not in fact arrive until the eve of the feast of St Laurence, in a boat full of pilgrims who wanted to celebrate St Laurence's Mass at our altar. I first set eyes on him when he was brought before Chapter the next day, the day of my strict fast, in atonement for the sacrilege I had committed in my youth at St Laurence's church in Warkworth.

Orsino means 'little bear', and it was a most fitting name. Although he was scarcely more than a boy, he was a hulking creature with massive, broad shoulders. Yet his features were delicate, just as the bear, despite its huge bulk, has a face as appealing as a dog's. But in the dark eyes, which squinted slightly, there was malice.

It was then, as he was standing before us, that Simon informed the convent that although Orsino understood Latin, if spoken slowly and clearly, he could not reply except by nods and signs, for he had been born without a tongue.

'He is like the dumb beasts,' Subprior Brice boomed, glaring at him as if he was the very Devil, 'and he bears the name of a beast. I suggest, Father Prior, that he take the name Laurence, for today is that saint's day, and today is the first day of his new life. And let us pray that this blessed name will subdue whatever of the beast remains in him.'

Prior Walter nodded his head gravely and welcomed Laurence as a lay-brother of the convent of Saint Columba.

For some time Simon never made any attempt to speak to me, but he would greet me with an exaggerated show of reverence when our paths happened to cross. I would simply give him a curt nod, before hurrying on.

Then one day I found myself standing next to him in the queue for the wash-basin. He started to whisper loudly in my ear, to my utter confusion.

'God has forgiven me, Brother Michael,' he said. 'Have you?'

'I don't know what you're talking about,' I hissed back at him, 'But whatever it is, this is not the place.'

Others were looking at us disapprovingly. If it had been anyone else but Simon, he would have probably gained a sharp rebuke, but everyone stood slightly in awe of him. Besides, this sounded interesting.

I prayed that he would now shut up, but his voice went on, wheedling. 'Please, I must know, I'll kneel and beg forgiveness if you want.'

'Brother Simon, I refuse to talk with you just now, we're not allowed. You must first ask Prior Walter's permission.'

Simon looked crest-fallen, sad. With amazement I noticed that some of the other brothers were looking at him with sympathy.

But he had not finished with me. As I bent over to wash my face I felt his hand on my body. He pinched me hard, so that I almost let out a cry. All through dinner my flesh where he had hurt me cried out and would not be still.

For many months after that Simon never tried to speak with me again, which simply added to my confusion. Part of me thanked God that this was so, and part of me cried out in pain.

In fact Simon scarcely spoke to anyone except his confessor, Subprior Brice. It had not taken long for Simon to realise who might be his greatest enemy in the convent, and it was to this man that he turned, winning him over to his side before you could say ten 'Hail Mary's'.

He chose him as his confessor, announcing in Chapter that he expected from his saintly righteousness the most stinging of penances. He had come to us to purge his soul of all the sins of his past, and to begin a new life of simple holiness. What better guide into this new life could he have than Subprior Brice?

Since Father Nicholas had left to become Prior of Cambus-kenneth, Brice had remained aloof from everyone, sourer than ever. Now God had sent Simon, weighed down with all the sins he had to confess, to Brice, weighed down with all the penances he had to give.

Throughout that summer and autumn they would spend many hours together before the altar of St Mary Magdalene, and many were the fasts Simon had to endure and long the hours of prayer.

It was around the Feast of All Saints, just after Chapter. I was on my way to air the manuscripts, when I heard my name being called.

'Brother Michael, to the parlour please, immediately.' It was Brice.

What had I done now? I thought guiltily. Brice only had to look at me to make me feel guilty. Now he wanted to speak to me. It could only be to chastise me for something.

I followed him meekly into the dark little room, where I was surprised to find Simon. My heart beat to another tune. He gave me the kiss of peace, then, as Brice climbed into the listening box, he kissed me again, stealthily, on the lips.

'Brother Michael,' Simon said in a loud voice, 'My brother in Christ, my brother in sin, we have much to purge our souls of. We sinned greatly together in Rome, did we not?'

He nodded encouragingly.

I nodded too, slowly, cautiously, confused.

'I have spoken much about it to my inspired confessor, who tells me that we were both possessed by devils. I am not sure that I am free of mine. Are you free of yours?'

He shook his head vigorously and gave me a sly wink. He was up to something. But what?

'I...I did full penance many years ago. I have not been troubled since.' I added in a whisper, 'Well, hardly.' I thought of my last trip to Scone. There were no devils there, I knew that, but Brice would not see it that way, and Brice was listening to every word.

'Well, Brother Michael,' Simon went on, 'I have never done penance for that sin, and every day it weighs heavier on my soul. I know there are the demoniacs at Cambuskenneth, I could exile myself there for a time, a fine cure for possession by unclean devils, according to my holy confessor. But in his mercy he has admitted another way out of my morass of sin. We may scourge each other naked before the altar. We would do it after Lauds, at the dead of night, with only Father Brice present.'

Then suddenly his lips were close to my ear, and he whispered, 'But not too hard, sweet Duscath.'

I gaped at him in disbelief.

He went on in a louder voice, 'What could be more fitting? Two bodies, once goaded by devilish impulses to find base pleasure in each other, now drive out their devils from each other by pain. It is the perfect penance, Brother Michael.'

I said nothing. I was appalled. Already I could see his body stretched out naked and pale at my feet, lit by a candle, or perhaps only by cold moonlight. Already my flesh was stirring. This was a penance more sinful than the sin. Simon knew it, and his eyes were laughing at Brice's foolishness.

Still he went on, 'I beg of you, say yes, and save me from Cambuskenneth. Be merciful.' And he fell to his knees and gripped my legs.

I stuttered, 'I...I scourge you, and you...?'

'We scourge each other, yes, for the penance to be complete. I know you have done hard penance for your sins with me, but for such a heinous sin no penance can be too great.'

Then he pulled my head down close to his lips and whispered again, 'But not too hard.'

Then louder, 'And so it is agreed? Tonight?'

I wanted to shout out, I wanted to run away. But I was trapped, as trapped as I had been in the painted chamber, trapped by Simon, trapped by Brice, trapped by my own desire.

I shrugged my shoulders. Brice came out of the listening box. I knelt down beside Simon. Brice placed his bony hands on our heads.

'So that is settled then,' he said in a hushed voice. 'I will inform Prior Walter and Brother Peter. The wisdom of this is deep, my sons, deep and holy. You will not regret it, neither in this life nor the next. Both of you, after lunch you must eat nothing except bread and water. Wait for me at the east door after Lauds tonight. Brother Michael, you have work to do. Brother Simon, you and I must go to the church, it is time for your confession.'

Off he went, as quick and nimble as a robin. As we rose to our feet Simon thrust his hand at me and pinched me in farewell, leaving my flesh sore and burning.

When the bell rang for Matins and Lauds it did not wake me for I had not been asleep. How could I sleep, when my body was on fire with fear and longing? Simon had not changed, after all, that one thing was certain. He was spinning a new web, and I felt hopelessly and helplessly drawn into it.

No, I would not go through with it, I would rather see him sent to Cambuskenneth, amongst those possessed by demons. That's where he belonged, after all, and if I got sent there with him, well, perhaps it's where I belonged too. There we could stew in our lusts, commit the sins of the flesh together as much as we liked, because there no one cared, for there they were all lost souls anyway, abandoned by God and the world, thrown together like pigs in a sty, living in filthy hovels, fed on the slops from the town, no heat but the heat of scabby, stinking bodies. My God, no, we would not survive one winter, hardly any of the poor wretches did.

And so we rose at midnight and filed into the church to praise God.

May there be nothing filthy or
dangerous in the conduct of our body,
because of whose fires the fires of
Hell burn with a fiercer heat.
With Your help. O Lord, it will be all pain, and it will be
good penance, but only with Your help.

The church was empty now and quiet, except for Brice, Simon and myself. It must have been cold, for our breaths made little white clouds around our mouths. But I was hot, burning with a strange fire. The altar candles still cast their flickering light.

Brice broke the silence. 'The time has come to scourge the flesh that once the Devil tempted you to desire. Remember, my sons, we are but a dung-hill, encased in skin. Think of the butchering of an ox, out gush the stinking entrails, the heart, the liver, slimy with blood and bile. Think always when you see fair flesh that it is but a bag for these repulsive things, a sack for gore and stench, a crust upon a cesspit.'

Brice's harsh voice was trembling and his eyes, which moved constantly between Simon and myself, gleamed triumphantly. In his hand he held the scourge.

'Now you will see how thin that crust is, how threadbare that sack, how fragile that bag, for with this scourge you will break it open, and in the blood of your body you will let the devil out that led you into that unnatural sin, you will let the devil out and the Lord will enter in.'

As Brice was speaking, Simon was already taking off his clothes. I watched spell-bound as he carefully folded each piece of clothing and placed it on his choir stall. His choir cope he laid on the floor. Soon he was standing there, naked and shameless, half in shadow, half in light, and I could not take my eyes from him.

Brice thrust the scourge into my hands. 'You see how the proud flesh is fooled into thinking that it is being stripped for pleasure,' Brice said, his voice rising almost to a shriek. 'But it is written, Lo, pride comes before a fall!'

Simon was already on the ground, lying face down on his choir cope, his arms stretched out as if he was about to be crucified. It did not seem as if his body had changed at all in the last ten years, still slim and firm and with a beauty that tortured. A flame of wanting swept over me, I wanted to throw myself upon him, be one with that beauty in the flame of ecstasy.

There, in front of the High Altar, I would have done those things! Oh, the blasphemy of it. Because of those fires the fires of Hell burn with a fiercer heat. But I pulled back from the brink because Brice was there, pressing the scourge into my hands, urging me to give that body not pleasure but pain.

'Strike, my son,' he was whispering, 'Strike the hateful flesh, and liberate the spirit. We will sing 'How good God is to the upright', and we will sing it together, the three of us, and the scourge will fall upon the back of the sinful until we have finished it.'

He then started to intone in his high, cracked voice,

'How good is God to the upright. But my feet had almost slipped, my foothold all but given way.'

As Simon and I started to intone with him, I struck the pale, thin body prostrate before me. Again I struck, and again; struck the back, struck the buttocks. My arm seemed to have a life of its own, it and the scourge forming one strange and violent beast.

Simon cried out in pain, and I heard him hiss, 'Saftly, ma hairt, saftly!' He spoke in Scottish so that Brice would not understand.

I recalled my arm to myself and checked my blows, swinging as hard as before, but jerking back my hand just before the scourge struck. Simon sighed and fell silent.

'Keep chanting, my son, keep chanting,' Brice urged. 'Do not falter, lest the Devil gain power over you.'

'And they say, 'How does God know? Up in Heaven he knows nothing.'
Behold it is sinners, and those who own much in the world who amass riches.
And I said, 'And so there was no reason for me to have kept my heart pure'.

Simon started to writhe and jerk, and his hands moved to his sides. I tried to shut my eyes, not wanting to see the red marks staining his white flesh. Awful torn sounds came from his throat. I chanted louder, trying to drown them, for I recognised those sounds. I had heard them before. They were not the sounds of pain, they were the sounds of passion; and his body was moving in an obscene way.

I glanced at Brice. His eyes were fixed on the altar, his hands clasped in prayer, his voice trembling and hoarse.

On and on I struck. It was easy for me not to strike him with all my strength, though God knows he deserved it. But I have always found it difficult to strike another being. Old Father Abraham used to say it was my guardian angel holding back my arm from doing harm. Was my guardian angel here now, looking on at this? I blushed to think it.

Suddenly as the psalm was almost finished Simon's body gave a terrible lunge, and an awful cry broke from his lips, a sigh, a moan, that made my flesh stand on end.

'It is the Devil,' cried Brice. 'The Devil is leaving him. That is no human sound. Oh, it is a miracle!

Lo those who are far from Thee will perish;
Thou destroyest all who fornicate out of Thy sight.'

Now the psalm was finished, the scourging at an end, and Simon's body lay as still as death.

'Get up, my son, and put on your clothes.' Brice's voice was soft now, almost tender. 'There is more of God's work to do before daybreak. Brother Michael, prepare your flesh for its just deserts.'

I was beside myself. Now I was longing for Simon's scourge on my body, as I felt it was the only thing that would quench the lust that was raging in me. I was trembling, almost sobbing, as it wracked my body.

'Do not be afraid,' Brice said, grasping my bare arm with a grip like iron. He thought it was fear that made me tremble so. 'Be strong. God is with those who suffer the pains of this transitory body for the sake of their eternal soul.'

I did as Simon had done, except that I did not spread out my choir cope on the stone floor, in the hope that the cold would quench my lust. I cried out as I touched it with my chest and belly, for it was like immersing myself in icy water.

The chanting of the psalm began again.

I heard the scourge hiss through the air and felt its stinging thongs upon my back. Yes, it was good, the pain was taking away my desire. The cold and the pain and the chanting of the psalm, yes, they were good, my lust was being conquered.

Oh, God, please wipe out from my heart for all eternity that vision of Simon's naked body lest it return to enflame me when I have no scourge to check it. Please let my lust be conquered for ever.

Simon was true to his whispered promise, he did not strike hard, but still my back and buttocks were tender for days after. And that was good, too, for God had not granted my final prayer, he had not wiped out from my heart the memory of Simon's body, and my lust had ebbed only to flow again. So every time the memory forced its way into my soul I would rub my back or move in my seat and the pain would take it away, along with the lust it brought with it.

Yet something else was happening, something terrible, something that sent me running to the church to pray. For if by chance I would knock my back against something and the pain made me cry out, suddenly Simon was there lying before me, and the flame of lust would leap through my body despite the pain, because of the pain.

Whenever we met, Simon would ask me how my body was, his face serious, his eyes bright with laughter. And if no one was looking he would prod me in my back and I would have to bite back a cry.

Once he came asking for a manuscript, and we had to go together to the book-cupboard; and as I was searching for the one he wanted, it was St Augustine's City of God, he bent over beside me and whispered, 'Michael, have you forgiven me what

I did to you in Rome? No, not the loving. I mean the parting. I deserve a thousand scourgings for that.'

I turned and looked at him, and if I had not forgiven him long ago, I would have forgiven him then, for he looked so humble and contrite. I wanted to enfold him and to keep him in my arms for ever. I told him I had forgiven him, and loved him as a true brother.

'Only as a brother, eh?' he whispered, and squeezed my arm. 'Michael, you're mine again, aren't you? Just as you were mine in the palace of my master all those years ago. Just as you were mine before God's altar, and will be mine again.'

In the darkness of the book-cupboard I closed my eyes and saw in the darkness behind my lids his body as it had been in the painted chamber, and as it had been just a few days before on the floor of the church, and I knew what my flesh had already known for weeks, perhaps even for years, that, yes, I was his now and would probably be his for the rest of my days on earth.''

The old man sat back and gave a deep sigh.

Martin stared at him as if in a trance. The bell for Vespers had long since rung, but he had ignored it, and the old man had not even heard it, otherwise he would have chased Martin away. But he had been too engrossed in his story. Soon Brother Peter would be back, and would chase both of them away, Michael to bed, Martin to Compline.

"Still troubling the poor old man?" he would say, poking his red face round the door.

And Martin would reply, "No, Brother Peter, it is the other way round. If you only knew. Now go away and leave us alone."

But that was in thought only. If Brother Peter appeared, Martin would bow stiffly, take leave of the old man, and follow Peter meekly out.

He decided not to wait for the indignity of being thus ejected, so he took his leave before Peter appeared. Deep in thought he crossed the narrow bridge over the latrine, where the black waters of a flood tide heaved and slapped below.

Malcolm the gate-keeper had left the side door open, knowing that Martin was still in the infirmary. Thankfully Malcolm was engrossed in a conversation with the boatman, so Martin did not have to exchange pleasantries with him.

He went straight to the church to say a prayer for the soul of Brother Michael, for his own soul, and for the soul of Simon de Quincy.

OBSEQUIES

"The next morning was bright and warm. Immediately after Prime Martin hurried over to the infirmary. His step was as light as his heart, for was not old Brother Michael talking and talking about Simon de Quincy? And the tales he was telling were strange and stranger. He only hoped the old man was in a good humour today, and would not send him away, complaining and sad, as he had done the other morning.

"God and his saints alone know what it was that Simon was confessing to Subprior Brice," Michael was saying, "but it certainly can't have been all his sins. If it had been, Brice would have had him thrown into our dungeon, Papal letters or no Papal letters, and he would never again have seen the light of day."

Michael sighed. "The light of day. There is a lot of light today, is there not? Is it warm outside?"

"It is glorious," Martin replied.

"I would like to go outside then. I want to sit in the sun. Please, Martin, take me outside."

Martin was delighted, for he too longed to sit outside. Such a morning was truly a gift of God, and it seemed almost a sin to sit skulking in the dark. So at a shuffling pace they walked out of the infirmary, away from the Priory, down the path towards the harbour, and there they sat on a pile of stones, overlooking the beach, the sea, and the coast of Fothrif, all the way to Kinghorn. Michael sat in the sun, as if his old bones could not get enough of the warmth, while Martin sat in the shade of a bush.

"Brother Simon, yes, he knew how to get round people. He could read people like books. He knew how to turn their pages, and when he had finished reading, and gathered all he wanted from them, he knew how to snap them shut and put them away, where they would lie patiently until he might need them again.

He had completely won over Subprior Brice. It is a strange thing, Martin. Those who most fervently believe, or love, or hate, they are more easily fooled than those who live without fervour. Prior Walter was such a man, without fervour, a man of the middle way, an exemplary Augustinian. Yet he, too, was taken in by Simon. Walter wanted life to run as calmly as possible. Not that he wanted an easy life: if he had wanted that, he would never have become the head of a convent, and remained its head for thirty years. But he wanted all unnecessary roughnesses smoothed away. In this he could have found no better ally than Brother Simon.

In a haphazard way I had been an amanuensis to Prior Walter, writing letters for him, keeping his parchments in a kind of order. Simon soon replaced me in this, and I was glad, because it meant that I had more time to copy manuscripts and build up our library. At that time there were so few of us with any skill at writing, or any interest in writing. Copying was a favourite penance given out by Father Geoffrey, but often the penitent would make such a botch of it that it would have to be re-done, and usually I was the one who had to re-do it.

At first Walter had been very suspicious of Simon, but Simon's advice in practical matters was always so sound, his skill at letter writing so great, and Brice's reports on the state of his soul so glowing. Besides, there were serious practical matters to be dealt with.

Although Brother Simon's money had saved us from our main creditors, it could not solve the underlying problem: our income was not enough to support us.

Furthermore we had had another bad harvest, and although this pushed the price of grain up, we were not able to produce a surplus to take advantage of it. It also brought a river of beggars to our stores at Barnhill. As if these were not troubles enough, God saw fit to try us even further."

The old man hesitated, then with a deep sigh he said, "For more than thirty years I have kept silent. I am old and on the threshold of death. There are things I have told you I never thought I would share with another mortal, so why should I not tell you this too? The story needs telling, so many foolish tales have grown up around it, like weeds around dirt. I am talking about the burial of Sir William de Mortimer.

Yes, Martin, not even de Mortimer was eternal, though he strutted around most of his life pretending he was, and in my most dejected moments I believed him. But let me tell you the story from the beginning."

He paused again, his mouth twisting as though he were in pain. For a moment all that could be heard was the lapping of the sea and the harsh, rhythmic calling of the gulls. Then he spoke again.

"It was around Lady Day, the first after Simon's arrival. We had just been wakened for Matins when we heard a shout from the sea. I looked out from my cell and by the light of the moon, which was full that night, I could see a coracle approaching the harbour. My heart beat faster, for a boat arriving in the middle of the night must mean something of grave importance. We filed into church, our breath whitening the cold, black air.

You know, Martin, if you are a brother here, you must make friends with the cold. Cold sits in every chamber, in every corner, you must welcome him like a friend, for you cannot drive him away like an enemy.

That night the cold was searing. In the weak light thrown out by the altar candles I saw that Prior Walter's place was empty. He must have been detained by whatever it was the coracle had brought. What could it be? I exchanged glances with some of my brothers, and I could see my question in their eyes.

We hurried through the service. It was so cold that our haste did not even draw disapproving looks from Father Geoffrey. We were soon back in bed, but cold and curiosity kept sleep from me far into the night.

The next morning after Prime we crowded into the chapter house, eager for news. Prior Walter and Subprior Brice were already in their places. They both sat there stony-faced, not looking at one another. We all knew this meant that they had been arguing. It was a familiar enough sight.

We did not have to wait long to discover what it was the night coracle had brought. When the death notices were read out, all was clear. Sir William de Mortimer, lord of Aberdour, had died the day before of wounds received at a tournament on Bucklyvie Moor.

When it came to the business of the day there was only one matter to discuss. Prior Walter was the first to speak.

'As you all know, Sir William, God rest his newly departed soul, was eager to be buried amongst us here in our church, and to this end he made generous gifts to us for the honour of God and St Columba. I want now to discuss the preparations we must make for fetching his body and for his funeral.'

Old Brother Robert asked permission to speak.

'My lord Prior, my brothers, you have all heard how this nobleman met his death. Are you not all aware that the last Great Council, which you yourself, Father Prior, attended, forbade all those killed in tournaments to be given Christian burial? I think this matter requires careful thought and prayer.'

Brice squirmed in his seat and gnawed his lips. He was obviously longing to speak, but Walter must have ordered him to keep silent, at least for a time.

It was Brother Andrew who spoke next.

'My lord Prior, my brothers, surely our course is clear. There can be no funeral for him here. We give back all his gifts and refuse to accept his body. In that way we cannot be accused of making false promises, and we remain obedient sons of the Church, and a shining example to all.'

'You show a true nobility of soul, Brother,' Simon said, 'and it grieves me to have to raise a very worldly objection. Against the lands Sir William gave us we have already borrowed a great deal of money to make our Priory a worthy temple to the Lord. How can we repay our debts within the allotted span unless we keep every scrap of land and every mark of revenue which we now hold? These are difficult enough days for us as it is.'

Many nodded agreement at this. Brother David went further and said that it would threaten our very existence if we refused to accept the body of such a powerful baron, no matter how he had lived, or died. 'The King himself fights in tournaments. Would we refuse his body if he had been killed on Bucklyvie Moor in similar circumstances, and his relatives were seeking to bury him here?'

David loved arguing, and the taste of words in his mouth was like blood to a hound.

He went on, 'Our Priory is an infant. The wealthy men and women of this kingdom are its mother. If an infant has a mother who cares for it, yet who is otherwise sinful, should that infant turn away from her breast to die, or must it not stay with her to live?'

Andrew rounded on David angrily, 'Our Priory may be an infant, but we are men, and we know good from evil. Therefore we must risk earthly wrath and even earthly ruin for the sake of heavenly righteousness. Surely that is the very foundation of our faith. As our Lord said.....'

'Brother Andrew,' David cut in, 'We need no reminder from you of what our Lord said. You are not the only one here who is familiar with the teaching of Jesus Christ.'

Faces were becoming flushed and tempers were rising, varying opinions were being thrown around the room, but Subprior Brice still said nothing, although a little trickle of blood stained his chin, so violently had he bitten off his words.

Prior Walter commanded silence from everyone. 'My sons, my sons, I pray you, let not your ardour for what you believe to be right blind you to that most Christian of virtues, brotherly love.' Then, taking pity on Brice, he said, with a sigh, 'I believe your Subprior has something he wants to say to you. Father Brice?'

Brice nodded grimly to Walter and stood up. His small, wiry frame was trembling all over.

'Tournaments!' he spat. 'Why do we waste our breath on tournaments? There is something far more important to talk about than the organised killing of the body, and that is the wanton killing of the soul.'

I braced myself, for I knew what was coming.

'This Sir William was a sodomite, brazen and unrepentant. How often did we not urge him to turn away from this most evil of sins? How often did he not laugh in our faces? And how often did I not say we should do our duty as Christians and excommunicate him? But my words fell on deaf ears, and because of this God is angry with us and tries us sorely.

'Yet we can still turn away his wrath if we now treat the deceased as excommunicate. It is too late for him to repent, and I know he is in Hell, beyond the reach of our prayers. Why taint our holy places with the corpses of the wicked and the damned? If we were not strong enough to stand up to his sins in life, let us at least pray to God for the strength to resist him in death. God will reward us for this. He will not desert those who abide by His law.'

Brice had raised his arms heavenward. His head was thrown back and his eyes were closed. He looked liked a drawing I had once seen of the prophet Elijah.

'I say unto you,' he went on, almost shrieking, 'Bring de Mortimer to our Priory for burial, and you bring with him God's curse.'

He had finished. He sat down as abruptly as he had stood up. The blood on his chin was now mixed with saliva. He made no attempt to wipe them away.

A shudder went through the room. Even Brother David was lost for words. How do you argue against God's curse? It was Brother Peter the sacristan who broke the silence. Flinging back his cowl in his usual way he intoned,

'Save me, O Lord, for the waters have risen up to my soul.
I am stuck in deep mud, and there is nowhere for me to
*   put my feet.*
I have come to the depth of the sea, and storms pour over
*   me.'*

Brice muttered, 'Amen.'

Prior Walter spoke again, quietly but firmly, 'Sir William was a man, and so his sins were many. We prayed for his repentance when he was alive, and we will pray for his eternal salvation now that he is dead. Benefactors of a house of God such as ours are entitled to privileges. Why else would they be our benefactors? How else could we live?

'If we reject the gifts of all who are stained with sin, then we will soon be beggars, wandering across the face of the land in rags. I know there are many of you here who have no reason to love Sir William. There have been times when I myself have cursed him. Did he not set armed men on us when we went to assert our rights over the church of Aberdour? But Christ taught us not just to forgive our enemies but to love them. This is the cross we must bear not for the sake of our possessions, but for the sake of our Lord Jesus Christ.

'Have no fear, my sons, God's curse will not fall on those who are merciful. Sir William de Mortimer will be buried in our church, even if I have to send to our Holy Father himself for special dispensation.'

I sat through all this, my mind in a turmoil. My soul was torn between the wise words of Prior Walter, and the fiery vengeance of Subprior Brice. I had no wish to see the corpse of that accursed man laid in our church. Somehow his presence here, even in death, would taint the place for me, just as he had tainted my life when I was part of his household.

Yet this was selfish and vengeful and lacking in charity. My soul ached to agree with Prior Walter, but my spirit was swollen with the words of Brice, and for the first time during my days in the Priory, I wanted his will to prevail. It was as if Prior Walter had read my mind, for I heard him mentioning my name.

'Brother Michael, I entrust to you the task of fetching the body of your former lord. I cannot think of a more able companion in this delicate and difficult task than Brother Simon. Leave at once, both of you, for there is a strong wind blowing up.

'I myself will remain here and personally supervise the preparations.' He looked sharply at Subprior Brice. 'We will have all ready by the time you return, as soon as the elements and Sir William's household permit.'

I bowed my head and accepted this command as I would have accepted a penance for my hatred. I had a foreboding that our task was going to be difficult and dangerous; the thought of Simon accompanying me made me even more uneasy.

Walter quickly brought Chapter to a close, carefully avoiding further argument, and soon we were all singing the Verba mea.

Within the hour the best and largest of our boats was toiling over the choppy grey waters towards Aberdour in the teeth of a bitter east wind. In it were Simon and myself along with Donald the boatman and his son Gillebrigte. Also Malcolm, the priest's servant who had brought the tidings, had slung his coracle into the stern and was sailing back with us.

We crept along the coast, trying to avoid the worst of the wind, and after an hour's hard rowing we finally reached the shelter of Aberdour Bay. We were greeted at the harbour beach by a small group of peasants who had left the ploughing and digging in the nearby acres. Many of them I had known as a boy. They were so familiar to me, as familiar as my own hands, and yet their world had become as a foreign land to me.

This was the first time I had set foot in Aberdour since I had fled from de Mortimer's castle all those years before, when I had slunk along the coast at dawn to swim across to Inchcolm. Now here I was, come back to collect the body of my former master.

As we were exchanging greetings, and giving blessings to those who sought them, we saw two horsemen careering down the road from the castle to the beach. As they drew near I recognised one of them as my own earthly brother, Gillecolm.

He was older than I, and had taken over as Sir William's reeve on the death of my father shortly after I had left the world. We were very different, in looks and in spirit, and I am ashamed to think that we came from the same womb.

If Sir William had been unloved by his tenants and serfs, Gillecolm was loathed. Not only was he Sir William's hand around their throats, squeezing out every ounce of tribute and rent due to him, he was also the hand of the King, exacting cain and tribute for the royal household whenever it passed by. It is true that he was only doing his duty, but he did it with such ruthlessness and greed that he was nicknamed The Wolf.

The man who rode beside him was Kenneth, Gillecolm's faithful servant and constant companion. He never hesitated in carrying out even the cruellest of his master's commands, and therefore he enjoyed his special favour, and received special protection for his crimes, which were many. Tall and skinny, he was nicknamed The Heron. 'Cross the Wolf and feel the Heron's bill' was a common saying of the people in these parts.

'Greetings on this saddest of days, good brothers', Gillecolm shouted when he had ridden up to us, scattering the peasants, who were kept at bay by his two great snarling wolfhounds. He looked me straight in the eye and gave a disdainful smile. He had always despised me, even before I entered a monastery. However, he enjoyed the prestige of having a man of God in the family, even if it was his contemptible little brother.

He addressed us in French, his mouth distorted with the effort. He had learnt it, as I had, in Sir William's household, and he thought it made him sound more lordly.

I replied in our native Scottish.

He flushed with anger and continued in French.

'Lady Anicea and the funeral guests await you in the church. You are to take my lord's body for burial tonight. Follow me.'

Then he turned his horse and sped off in the direction he had come, spraying us with sand. Kenneth waited to escort us.

Simon and I looked at each other, crossed ourselves, and started up the path in the tracks of Gillecolm's horse.

When we reached the church Gillecolm was standing waiting for us at the south door of the nave. Kenneth, who had followed slowly behind us all the way, tethered his horse to a nearby post and went to stand beside his master. Suddenly I saw them as they must have been all those years before, when on this very spot they had attacked my brothers, including my beloved Edgar. I grew even more afraid. Then they turned away brusquely, pulled off their hats, and strode through the low door, Kenneth bending his neck to avoid knocking his head against the lintel.

The nave was full of people, sobbing, wailing, praying, and generally behaving in a way which Sir William would have strongly disapproved of. Tapers blazed along the walls, and a brazier glowed in the centre. The warmth was overpowering, and made my head spin. All Sir William's household seemed to be there, as well as his wealthier tenants.

A high trestle table stood in front of the rood, and on it lay the bier bearing the body of my former lord. He was dressed in his hauberk, with his sword lying on top of him, extending down from his hands which were stiffly folded in prayer. In the crook of his left arm lay his helmet. He still clung to his weapons, even in death. The pallor of his face, usually so ruddy, made him look more like a man of wax than of flesh. Whatever the injury that had brought his death, it was concealed beneath his hauberk.

Two figures knelt before the bier, their backs to the nave. One was Lady Anicea, her head thrown back, keening in the ancient manner of our people, a sound that sent shivers down my spine. The other figure was as still as the corpse itself, and in similar battle apparel. He had massive shoulders and a neck as thick as a bull. It was Sir Robert de London, King William's eldest bastard.

The vultures are gathering already, I thought to myself, but I knew it was not the body of the dead that Sir Robert was after.

We approached the bier, bowed low, and muttered prayers. We could hear amidst the din of the nave muted chanting coming from the chancel, while outside the wind howled.

'You are to join Father Serlo in the masses for the dead,' Gillecolm whispered in my ear. 'When the funeral procession is ready to leave for the harbour you will be summoned.'

It was cooler and quieter in the chancel, and I at once felt more at home. It gladdened my heart to see Father Serlo. I still missed his friendship and good sense although he had been on the mainland now for many years. We embraced and gave each other the kiss of peace.

He at once resumed his prayers, and we joined in. All day we celebrated the offices for the dead, masses, psalms, prayers. At noon Malcolm, Serlo's servant, brought food to the sacristy, where we ate and rested in turns, so that our stream of prayers should not dry up.

It was almost Vespers when a great noise of many horses and people filled our ears. Everyone was gathering for the last farewell. Many of the most powerful of the kingdom were present, for the tournament at which Sir William had been killed had attracted many nobles and their ladies, despite the sinfulness of such useless and dangerous games of war.

Finally the time came to stop our prayers, put on our rain copes and step out into a blustery twilight. The churchyard was full of people scurrying to and fro, slipping and slithering on horse-dung, dodging the blows of the men-at-arms as they tried to beat the crowd into an orderly procession. We were led through the confusion, our habits clearing a way for us as effectively as any staff.

At the boundary of the churchyard things were much calmer. A proper procession had formed behind the bier, which was being borne by six of the most noble men present, including de Mortimer's own liege-lord Earl David. This was indeed an honour.

Simon and I were placed at the very head of the procession, and told to start walking slowly down the track towards the harbour beach. Father Serlo and his mass-boy, bearing holy water, incense and spergill, took up their places one on either side of the bier.

We moved off, the hollow roar of the wind in the trees drowning out our chanting. Sometimes a gust of wind would catch a sprinkling of holy water and fling it against my back. The incense was immediately whirled up into the dark clouds, and only rarely did I catch a whiff of its heavenly and comforting smell. The wind bearing off the incense into the night, I thought, was like death bearing off a soul and scattering its precious perfume throughout the world. Perhaps this was the worst that could happen to a soul, perhaps the best. I crossed myself against the pagan darkness of such a thought.

Although the pace was slow, the way to the harbour was not long, and we were soon there. Already on the grass behind the harbour beach lay a large open coffin made of wood and lined with lead. The six bearers laid the body in it, then solemnly nailed on the lid with hammer and nails provided by the servants.

Lady Anicea, who had been quiet on the road from the church, started to keen once more, and her ladies-in-waiting joined in. She flung herself onto the closed coffin and howled. Sir Robert gently led her aside, while Sir William's servants performed their last service for their dead lord, the lifting of the coffin into the boat. Planks had been laid across the stern so that the coffin lay level with the gunwales. It was made fast by thick rope.

All knelt as Father Serlo said the final prayer. Then a way was cleared through the crowd and the nobles, headed by Earl David, strode to their horses, which had been led down behind the procession, to ride up to the castle and the warmth of the funeral feast.

Soon the only people from the funeral party who were left on the beach with us were Sir Robert, Lady Anicea and Gillecolm. Father Serlo had been told to return to the castle with the other guests. Gillecolm mounted his horse and ordered the already dwindling crowd of peasants to go back to their homes. If they came to the castle the next day, he announced magnanimously, they would receive the broken meats and a drink of beer, or perhaps even wine, in memory of Sir William.

Aye, depending on how much the great pour down their gullets tonight, I thought.

Twilight had thickened almost to night by now, but the fat yellow moon, which was climbing up from behind the Craig, flooded us with light, despite the clouds constantly tumbling across its face. By its light I could see that some men-at-arms had now stationed themselves on the approaches to the harbour beach from both east and west, while others were patrolling the road to the castle and the village, clearing it of stragglers.

Gillecolm remained on horseback. 'Goodbye, brither,' he said. He spoke in Scottish this time, and seemed very subdued.

'Gillecolm,' I replied, suddenly afraid, 'shairly ye're no sendin us oot in thone wind.'

'Dinnae speir at me,' he said, nodding to Lady Anicea and Sir Robert.

I turned towards them. 'Ma Lady,' I said, speaking in Scottish, because I knew she had never laid any great store by the French, 'We cannae pit tae sea the nicht, no in thone wind, wi anely the muin tae licht oor wey, an the muckle wecht o the deid-kist tae rug us doon. Gaird the boat till the furst tide the morn's morn, syne we'll cross safe. We can bide wi Faither Serlo at his hoose.'

She stared at me. Her face was in shadow, so I could not see the look in her eyes. The wind tore at her cloak and her tightly bound hair, which gleamed dark red in the moonlight.

Then she spoke, softly, so softly I had to bend towards her to catch her words before the wind carried them away.

'Brither Duscath,' she said, oh, I can still hear that voice, soft and sweet it was, nor was it cracked by crying, 'Brither Duscath, whit's better nor twaa monks prayin fur the sowl o ma deid laird? Wud ye no say it's twaa monks tae gang wi him ayont the grave?'

'Ma Lady,' I gasped, crossing myself, 'ye cannae dae this, it's no Christian, it's...it's the auld, deivilish weys.'

'It's the wey A want it, Brither Duscath, an twaa sic bonnie men an aa. Wull that no please ma laird? An ye'll yet ken weel hoo tae ser him, wull ye no, Duscath? Ye'll no hae forgotten. Monks dinnae forget sic things, A hear. Noo, awaa wi ye, A wish ye a guid gate.'

Before I could say anything more she had turned on her heel and was walking quickly to her horse. She swung herself up onto the saddle before her servant could help her, and rode off. Sir Robert immediately went to his horse, without even a side-glance at us. I saw him cross himself before he galloped off behind her.

I shouted to Simon, who was standing beside the boat with Donald and his son.

'This is madness, they want us to sail tonight!'

Simon looked at me calmly, not saying a word. He made me feel foolish in my anxiety. Donald reacted more humanly.

'Whit did ye sey, Brither? They want us tae sail the nicht? Ye're jestin. A thocht aa yon geggie wis jaist fur the lairds an ladies. Kenneth, ma fere, whit's aa this stite aboot sailin the nicht? Come awaa, you an me, tae ma brither's hoose fur a drink an a bittie warm beild.'

Kenneth ignored him. He bent down and whispered in my ear, motioning to the men-at-arms.

'Aa the men ye can see hae nae muckle love fur monks nor their servants. They've been telt tae send ye doon the same gate as Sir William gin ye dinnae sail. Noo,' he added sharply, and put his hand on his hilt. The men-at-arms near us on the beach stiffened and did the same. Donald and Gillebrigte stood gawping in disbelief. Simon still stood beside the boat.

Then he spoke, quietly, calmly.

'Michael, get in the boat. Don't you understand? We can expect more mercy from the sea than from these men.'

Slowly we prepared to set sail. Kenneth and some of the men-at-arms pushed our boat over the rasping sands to meet the incoming tide.

'An mind,' Kenneth said, as the sea took us, 'ye'll no be thinkin o snuvin ashore alang the coast, the forest is fu o wolves the nicht.' "

MORTIMER'S.DEEP

"As soon as we left the lee of the Craig the full force of the wind hit us. We dared not hoist the sail, and the oars were of little use amidst the troughs and peaks of the waves. Donald clung to the helm, keeping the wind behind us always. With wind and waves pushing us eastwards with such force we might have made good progress, but because of our heavy load we were too low in the water. The waves threw freezing spray over us, while the sea crept quietly over the sides. Simon, Gillebrigte and I were all bailing out frantically.

'We're owr laigh i the water,' Donald shouted. 'Ye'll hae tae bail fester.'

Without interrupting his bailing, without looking at me, Simon said, 'Well, Michael, it looks like Sir William wants to drag us down to Hell with him. I say he has to go, now.' I stopped bailing and looked at him in astonishment.

'What did you say?'

'Don't stop bailing, my brother. I said ...'

'I know what you said. Are you mad?' I shouted, resuming my bailing with increased vigour.

Donald shouted again. 'Gille, there are mair bailin-coggies forrit, ilkane o ye will hae tae tak twaa. And gie me ane. A've a toom haun.'

'Do you hear that, Michael, the sea is winning. De Mortimer's determined to take us. Are you going to let him?'

'We can't arrive without the body,' I shouted back at him. 'Can you imagine the scandal?' Then in the howling of the wind

I thought I heard Sir William's laughter, loud and deep. I looked at Simon in dismay.

'Come on,' he said. Then he shouted: 'Donald, Gille, gin ye dinnae want tae droon, gie's a haun wi heavin this deid-kist intae the sea.'

He started untying the ropes that held the coffin fast. For one moment we all stared at him, unable to move. A huge wave crashed over us, soaking us to the skin, and sending foaming water swirling around our feet.

Then I, too, started to untie the ropes, while Donald took out his knife and began hacking at them. Only Gillebrigte did not join in. We told him to help us, but he fled to the bow. His father swore and shouted at him, but all to no avail.

Once all the ropes were untied we bent every muscle in our bodies to pushing the coffin towards the stern, at the same time trying to prevent it from going over the port or starboard side. If it did, it would probably capsize the boat.

We began to edge it out over the stern. Suddenly I had a last, desperate idea.

I shouted, 'Let's get the body out before the coffin goes. As long as we get the body out.'

'It's too late,' Simon shouted.

Just then another huge wave hit us. The coffin lurched to the side, almost crushing me. There was no holding it. It caught my habit and I felt it pull me with it. Gillebrigte started to scream. With all my strength I pulled myself back. Almost as if it were a living thing, the coffin leapt into the dark waters, taking the sleeve of my habit with it.

The boat lunged forward and righted itself, as if glad to be free of its lethal burden. Donald threw the planks which had been supporting the coffin into the bottom of the boat and tied the helm back in its proper place at the stern. Simon and I returned to our bailing with renenewed effort. We were no longer fighting a losing battle with the sea.

Donald, cursing his son, who still cowered in the bow, unfurled the small hide sail, and steered a confident course towards the island. The wind and the waves were no longer our enemies, but sped us homewards.

No one spoke at first. Then Simon bent his head towards me and shouted against the roaring wind, 'You do realise what this will mean, don't you, my dear brother?'

I shook my head, not wanting to think ahead, not wanting to think at all.

'It could be the ruin of the Priory,' he went on relentlessly. 'Who's going to pay good land and good money for burial with us now, once they hear that our chief benefactor has ended up at the bottom of the sea?'

I groaned. 'Listen, can't we talk about this tomorrow? Let's just get home and dry and get to bed.'

'No, Michael, it can't wait till tomorrow; it can't even wait until we touch land. Listen carefully, it was a miracle, do you hear. It was a miracle. St Columba himself threw the coffin overboard.'

I stared at him. Has he gone mad, I thought.

'Come on,' he went on, 'we must talk to Donald. You sit one side, I'll sit the other. Listen carefully and don't interrupt. You got us into this mess, let me get us out.'

'I what?' I shouted, outraged.

But he was already beside Donald, shouting into his ear. I quickly jumped to the other side of him, so that I could hear what he was saying.

'Donald, ma mannie, whit dae ye want maist in life fur yersel an yer faimily?'

Donald gave us both an odd look, thought about it for a moment, then replied, 'Tae get hame sauf. A'll gie an offerin at Colum Cillie's altar gin he brings us sauf tae land, so A will.'

'Aye, Colum Cillie'll bring us sauf hame, efter the meericle he's warked for us. Him it wis whaa coost the deid-kist intae the sea. Shairly ye maun hae seen him. Noo, answer ma speir, whit dae ye want maist?'

Donald gave him an even odder look, then he smiled.

'Gille, ye wee scunner,' he shouted at his son. 'Tak doon the sail. The sea'll cairry us hame aaricht fae here. Dae it noo, ma mannie, or A'll skelp yer erse till ye cannae sit doon for a seiven-dey.'

Gillebrigte, moving as if in a trance, slowly obeyed.

Donald tugged at the tiller, then turning to Simon again said, 'Ma freedom, fur masel and ma faimily, ma near faimily. A dinnae mean the hale jing-bang o ma kin, but ma bairns, and ma bairns' bairns, till the end o the warld, like. An a wee pickle land tae fairm, as a husbandman, no as a serf. Oh, an ye're richt, it wis a meericle. It wis the blessit Colum Cillie hissel heistit the deid-kist owr the side like it wis a dod a sharn. By the sea, an aa, Faither, ma wee pickle land. A widnae want tae bide awaa fae the sea.'

'Noo dinnae get grabbie, Donald. Whit aboot Gille?'

'Dinnae ye fash yersel aboot him, Faither. A'll see tae him.'

'Noo listen weel, ye tae Michael,' Simon said, laying his hand on my arm. 'We wur aa prayin tae Colum Cillie tae redd us fae the waves. The boat wis gaun doon. Syne a figur o a man kythit itsel on the port side. The port side, mind. Tall it wis an cled in a white cope, an its heid wis bauldy at the front, no at the back, like the brithers, ye unnerstan?'

We both nodded.

Simon went on, 'An a lang white beard, wi a cord aroon his middle. He comes owr tae us, walkin on the water he wis, an raxes owr an taks the deid-kist wi ane hand, an aa the rapes brak, an he coosts it owr the side, jaist like Donald said, like it wis a dod o sharn. An syne he jaist saintit like sea-bree.'

'Oh, A can see it noo, Faither,' Donald was saying enthusiastically. 'Jaist like ye said it wis: on the port side, as in white, he raxes owr, dod o sharn, aye. A'd sweir on ma mither's sowl it wis the blessit Colum Cillie hissel. Aboot hoo mony acres were ye seyin, Faither?'

'Ye auld deil,' Simon laughed, slapping him on the back. Then, suddenly becoming deadly serious, he added, 'Gin ye sweir tae onythin else, ye'll no jaist tyne yer acres. A'll ban ye an yer faimily fur aa eterneety, an A'll mak shair they bide oor serfs till Doomsdey. Dae ye unnerstan, Donald?'

'Aye, A unnerstan fine, Faither. Oh, it wis a meericle, a meericle!'

'Noo, awaa an hae a wurd wi yer laddie,' Simon said. 'Brither Michael'll hud the tillie, he kens the waters roon here.'

Donald obeyed immediately.

'Simon,' I shouted, hardly believing my ears, 'have you gone gyte, making up miracles, promising freedom and pieces of land you don't even possess? You've no right.'

'I've every right to want to save the Priory. Prior Walter will understand, even if you're too stupid to. Now shut up and steer, or you'll get us into even more trouble.'

His words stung me more than the spray which the wind was flinging into my face. Unable to speak I turned my face out of the wind and clung on to the tiller.

We were almost home. Donald and Gillebrigte rowed us into the harbour. As we dragged the boat and ourselves onto the beach, Simon said a prayer of thanksgiving to God and St Columba for our miraculous delivery. It was indeed a miracle, even without Simon's story.

We all lay quietly on the sand. I could hear Gillebrigte sobbing quietly to himself. My heart went out to him.

Then suddenly Simon sprang to his feet, brushing away the sand that caked like clay to his wet cope. 'Come on, look lively. I'm off to speak to Prior Walter, and tell him about our miracle.'

We sat up. He gave Gillebrigte a light kick in the side. 'Hey, ma laddie, whit side did Colum Cillie kythe hissel on oot there?' Gillebrigte looke up at him in terror.

'A ... A cannae mind, Faither,' he stammered.

'The port side, ye tink, the side the bris is on!' and he gave the lad a vicious kick on the left side.

Gillebrigte screamed and leapt to his feet, holding his side.

'Aye, he'll mind better noo,' his father said grimly, getting slowly to his feet. 'Let's redd up this boat and get awaa hame tae oor beds. It's been a sair nicht.'

'Come on, Michael,' Simon said, 'on your feet. You come with me. But let me do the talking.'

We struggled up the path, the wind tearing at our robes. I

had never seen the Priory looking so beautiful. It stood out clearly in the pewter moonlight. The newly finished tower, the dark east gable of the church, even the old wooden chapter house seemed transformed in the unearthly light. It looked as though it would stand forever, yet what we had done tonight had put it all in danger.

We went and awakened Walter, and soon the three of us were sitting by a roaring fire in the warming house, deep in secret conversation.

'My sons, you were the last people I expected to see tonight. Whatever possessed you to make the crossing in such weather? You've brought the body I take it?'

'No, father,' Simon said. 'It was afraid of getting sea-sick.'

Walter gave a weak laugh, then, impatiently, said: 'Come now, you didn't get me out of my bed in the middle of the night to tell me jokes. What's happened? Have you got the body or have you not?'

'Father,' I burst out, unable to contain myself any longer, 'Sir William de Mortimer lies at the bottom of the Forth, and had it not been for the grace of God ...'

'And the blessed Saint Columba,' Simon cut in.

'And the blessed Saint Columba,' I added blushing, 'we would now be lying there beside him.'

'Blessed Mary and all the saints preserve us,' cried Walter, 'you're not telling me you've lost the body?'

We both nodded.

'Oh my God, this is a disaster. This could be the ruin of us. But how on earth did it happen? Tell me the whole story.'

So Simon told him everything, from the threats of Lady Anicea and Kenneth, to the final jettisoning of the coffin. He made no mention of the miracle.

When he had finished, Walter said, 'We'll pretend this never happened. We'll go through with the burial. Nobody must know. Who else was in the boat?'

'Donald and Gillebrigte mac Donald,' Simon replied.

'Well, go and tell them they've not to breathe a word of it. We can make it worth their while. The only other person who needs to know is Brother Peter, who'll be digging the grave. If only we had a spare coffin! Then Brother Maurice, he'll have to lay out the corpse. No, we can say it had already been prepared before it was given to you. And ...'

Walter was speaking more and more quickly now, the ideas tumbling from him like water. Simon sat in silence, his face without expression. I got caught up in Walter's plan. It involved deceit, too, but at least it did not involve blasphemy. Also deceit from Prior Walter seemed to me less wicked than deceit from Simon.

Finally, when Walter had talked himself dry, Simon spoke.

'Father Prior, they sent us to our death, which would have

been certain had we not thrown the coffin overboard. Also I think we were probably seen from the shore, for there were men posted all the way along, according to Kenneth, and the moon was bright. If there is even a hint of suspicion, then they will come and check. That is not difficult. No, if you will permit me, my lord Prior, I have a better idea ...'

Now at last it was the turn of the miracle. Walter listened intently as Simon carefully told him his story. While Simon was speaking I gazed at the flames as they consumed the wood. Every so often the fire would sink together with a sigh and become smaller. Not like the fires of Purgatory, I thought, which burn forever, unabated.

Then I heard Simon saying, 'It's all quite reasonable, Columba did not want such a wicked man on his island, not even in death. He lived in sin, and he died in sin, unshriven. He has caused much harm to Columba's Priory. Did he not once cause the Saint's own relics to be violated? No wonder Columba would not tolerate him on his soil, in his church.'

No, I thought to myself, but he tolerates you, you who are no less evil. Then I remembered how keen Simon had been to get rid of the coffin, and I began to wonder if it had indeed been necessary.

Suddenly I became ashamed, and begged God's forgiveness for my suspicious and churlish thoughts. Had I not done my share of evil in my time? Had it not been me who had first drawn Sir William's wrath upon the Priory? And had I not drawn Lady Anicea's revenge upon myself? If I had not been the one to fetch the body, reminding her of past hurts, perhaps she would never have thought of forcing us to put out to sea in the storm.

Had I, too, not put my shoulder to the coffin and felt a pang of joy at the thought that Sir William would never reach my home, that he would be condemned forever to lie in the outer darkness of the deep? And here was Simon doing his best to save us from yet another storm, and all I did was impute wickedness to him. I was a miserable wretch, I thought, and deserved all the pain that this world brought me.

So I gave myself completely to Simon's plan. For it was indeed a terrible thing we had done. I saw that as clearly now as I saw the flames licking up around the wood. So much of what the Priory owned we owned because of our duties to the dead. Yet here was a great noble, one of Earl David's chief men, who had given us rich gifts to be buried in one of the holiest spots in the land, and he had been cheated of that burial. You can cheat the peasants of their grain, or the Jews of their gold, or the nobles of their tribute, that was acceptable and everybody did that, but to cheat a man of his place in Heaven, adding on countless years in Purgatory, that was unacceptable, that was unforgivable.

My head started to spin, and I felt sick. 'I must excuse myself,' I blurted out. 'If I don't get to bed, I'm going to fall down.'

'Of course, my dear boy,' said Walter, getting to his feet. 'What you must have been through. All right, Simon. You seem to have thought this through very carefully. I will pray about this, and tell you my final decision tomorrow at Chapter. I'll also speak to Donald and his boy. You're both excused from attending Matins and Prime. And not a word to anybody.'

I quickly took my leave of Prior Walter. As I was hurrying out of the room, I heard Simon saying, 'One other thing, Father Prior. I took the liberty of making certain promises to Donald on behalf ...'

I did not wait to hear what Prior Walter's reaction to this was. In five minutes I was in bed.

I slept fitfully that night, for all my exhaustion. The wind howled mournfully around the dorter, penetrating every crevice, swirling around my head, blowing through my dreams.

When I finally awoke it was bright daylight outside. I leapt up, afraid that I had missed Chapter. I looked along to Simon's pallet. It was empty. Before I had taken two steps I knew I was unwell. My limbs felt like lead, my body trembled, and my head ached. But I forced myself down the cloister steps. The convent was just filing in to Chapter.

Simon was waiting for me at the door, and we went in together behind the novices. He whispered, 'It was a miracle, that's official. Try looking as though you've just seen a saint. You look more like you've seen a ghost.'

I nodded in reply, and my head swelled with pain.

Chapter seemed interminable. We had to give a full report of what had happened the previous day. I left that to Simon, who did it masterfully. When he came to the part of the story when St Columba himself appeared on the waves, Superior Brice and Brother Andrew fell on their knees, praising God. They were, of course, delighted by what had happened, and felt thoroughly justified in the objections they had raised the day before.

When Simon had finished, Prior Walter added that he had spoken with all concerned, even the boatmen, and he was convinced of the miraculous intervention of our beloved Saint.

He went on to say that he was going to dedicate to the memory of Sir William that place in the church where his body was to have been buried, and that we were to direct our prayers for the welfare of his soul. Perhaps after regular Masses for his soul, and after he had been purged in the Purgatorial Fires, the blessed Saint Columba might perform another miracle, and bring the coffin to our shore. We would always keep that place free of other burials in case that second miracle occurred. As soon as Chapter was over, he said, we were to go to the church and say a Mass for for the dead man's soul, and at the same time we were to pray for such a miracle.

As Chapter dragged on I was feeling worse and worse. I wanted to lie down; if I didn't lie down soon, I knew I would fall down. But it was unthinkable that I miss the Mass for Sir William. Was it not the least I could do? Had it not been my hands, my strength, that had helped consign him to the dark, unconsecrated waters?

So when the time came I staggered into the church. The only miracle I prayed for was that I stay upright until the Mass was over.

Before we started to chant the Placebo, Prior Walter marked out with his staff the place dedicated to Sir William, the place that would always be kept for him, and where his name would be carved. It was the very place where Simon and I had scourged each other, the place which held for me more than any other place the image of Simon which my flesh desired too much.

Suddenly I saw the full horror of what Brice had wanted me to see that night when Simon had stood there naked and beautiful before me. I saw the putrefaction and the stinking flesh. I saw worse than that, for I saw bones with their tatters of half-eaten flesh crawling with sea-creatures, twisted round with black, slimy seaweed. The cold and the horror of it seemed to pierce me to the very heart, and I started to shiver violently. Each movement, from kneeling to standing, from standing to bowing low, required a supreme effort of the will.

Then I froze in horror. I felt as though my soul was leaving my body, as though I was waking up out of a dream-like sleep, but I knew I was awake already, so what was I waking up to? I was terrified, and shouted out. I ran out of the church and down the path towards the harbour.

It was there by the shore that I saw it. At first I thought it was a seal, a sleek, black shape amongst the waves beyond the harbour skerry. Then it started rising out of the water, higher than any seal, growing taller as it glided towards the shore. It was making straight for me, coming nearer and nearer, the figure of a man wrapped in a white shroud, festooned with seaweed, streams of water pouring from him. And before I could make out the half-decomposed face and the naked eyeballs, I knew what it was and why it had come.

The next thing I remember was feeling a cool cloth on my forehead and hearing the soothing voice of Brother Maurice, the infirmarer. I cried out, still gripped by the fear of my hideous visions. I lay ill for many days. No one was allowed to visit me.''

Brother Michael's head had fallen forward and he seemed to be asleep. One of the Archdeacon's servants came hurrying along the path and said that the Archdeacon wanted to see Martin.

"Brother Michael, I must go," Martin said gently. "Shall I take you back to the infirmary?"

"What?" Michael said, as if he was speaking from a long way off.

Martin repeated the question.

"No, no, just leave me here, beside the sea. They call it Mortimer's Deep now, you know," he said, gesturing towards the mainland. "Mortimer's Deep. Imagine. That man has left behind him more than an evil memory, he's left behind him his name, left it in the sea. I doubt they'll ever name anything after me, eh?" he chuckled. Then he added, serious again. "But of course he paid a high price for it, you know, a high price, the price of a Christian burial." He fell silent again.

"I'll see you later on, Father. Goodbye."

"If de Mortimer doesn't come and get me before you do." The old man heaved a great sigh and stretched his hands towards the sun.

Martin hurried off through the warm June morning, but he did not feel the sun or see the brightness. He called in at the infirmary on the way to tell Brother Peter where he had left the old man. He walked away with Peter's complaints ringing in his ears.

BROTHER ISAAC

"There was indeed a terrible storm over the unceremonious burial of de Mortimer, and for a time we were all in danger of being blown away.

The first thing we did was write letters to John our Bishop, to Earl David, and to the King. In them we complained about the way we had been treated, how our lives had been threatened, and how only the miraculous intervention of St Columba had saved us from certain death.

We also had a proclamation made at the mercat cross in Inverkeithing. The burghs are always a hot-bed of rumour. Scandalous stories were already being spread abroad that some pagans had paid us a large sum of gold for the body. The pagans had come disguised as monks and taken the body away to sacrifice to the silkies.

Bishop John hurried to our side, for the honour both of the Church and of St Columba was at stake. He ordered a full inquiry, which was held at his palace at Cramond. John himself presided. Lady Anicea and Sir Robert de London were summoned to attend. Neither appeared, but they did send representatives. Bishop John knew it was useless to summons them again, because the King would not back him, and without the backing of the King, he was powerless. Simon and I gave our evidence. Lady Anicea's representatives denied it, and brought eye-witnesses to testify against us.

One of these was Kenneth. He stood in the middle of the hall, as quiet and as menacing as he had been that night on the harbour beach. He spoke slowly, while one of the Bishop's clerks translated into Latin.

Yes, he had been on the shore that evening, near Barnhill. He was there because he had been ordered to be there, to keep an eye on the boat with his lord's body in it. Besides, was it not seemly that a faithful servant should watch his lord on his last journey? Yes, there had been a wind that night, but nothing to speak of, nothing to endanger a good-sized boat with a coffin as ballast. There had also been a full moon, and only a few clouds, so the light had been good. Yes, he had seen the coffin go overboard. Yes, he had seen figures in the boat struggling with it. No, he had seen no sign of a figure walking on the waves, he had not seen anything that smacked of a miracle; everything he had seen smacked of treachery.

Then Donald was brought before the Bishop. He trod very carefully at first. He denied all knowledge of any force or threats being used before we sailed. This was wise, he had many relatives in the village, and they would pay dearly if he spoke too much truth. He said he had been busy with the boat and did not hear everything that was being said.

However, he had much to say about the miracle. He declared that it was no wonder that Kenneth had not seen St Columba pushing the coffin overboard because he had appeared on the port side, the side away from the shore. Also the moon had been behind a large black cloud at the time of the Saint's appearance, and so the view from the shore, which would have been poor at the best of times, would have been even poorer.

Also he swore to God that the wind was strong and the boat was in peril, and that the high waves, too, would have obscured the view of anyone standing on the shore.

He invited the Bishop to hear the evidence of his son, only a lad, but honest and without guile. He then dragged a terrified Gillebrigte over beside him. He stammered out his story and gingerly felt his left side as he told of the Saint's appearance.

In the end Bishop John declared that a miracle had indeed occurred, to the eternal glory of the blessed St Columba. And because it was a miracle, all who had acted that night, however they had acted, must be seen as having acted under the guidance of God, for without their actions there would have been no miracle. This was a different John from the one who had fought against the King and his nobles so bitterly and single-mindedly for ten long years. This was a John who was tired of fighting, and who enjoyed being Bishop of Dunkeld.

Miracle or no miracle, people's faith in the Priory of St Columba had been shaken. Walter, Lord of Lundin and Christiana his wife had already become members of our spiritual community through their gift of silver a few years before, and so it was understood of course that they would be buried in our church. But at the following Whitsuntide they sent us an impertinent messenger, who said that they did not want to risk offending the blessed St Columba by being buried on his island, as he seemed to be very choosy about whom he allowed to come there. So they were making arrangements to join the spiritual community of the Abbey of St Thomas Arbroath, and there they would be buried when their time came. Also, because they felt it was immoderate to be members of two communities, they were withdrawing from ours, and stopping their annual payment.

So we had to start a long and expensive law-suit against them, for we had their charter sealed with their seal and valid for all time coming.

The Lord and Lady of Lundin were not the only ones to turn their backs on us. Where we had a charter, we could challenge them. This was expensive, but usually successful in the long run. If we had no charter, there was nothing we could do except pray to St Columba for another miracle. Every month saw a reduction in our lands and our income, and every month the chorus of our creditors grew louder.

The feast of St John came round again. Simon had been with us for a year now. Many were muttering against him, saying that he must be accursed. At the blood-letting there was much guessing as to why he had come to us in the first place, and what terrible crimes he must have committed in his past to have fallen so far from Papal favour. The more our difficulties grew, the greater grew the resentment against him.

Simon himself kept very quiet, secure in the support both of his Prior and his Superior, so he had nothing to fear from the calumny of his brothers. He sailed through it all like a sturdy ship through a rough sea.

Then one day in Chapter he spoke, long, and carefully. He said that our convent was like a sick man, getting weaker every day. If no remedy was found soon, the man would die. The cause of the disease was foul slander, 'and slander breeds slander, at home as well as abroad'. As he said this he looked around the room, and many blushed.

'Slander is like a serpent,' he went on, 'choking on us, cutting us off from the abundance of gifts and alms that are rightfully ours. We must kill the serpent before it kills us.

'Where does the serpent have its lair? In the hearts and

tongues of the people, that is where it lives. So it is there, in the hearts and tongues of the people, that we must root it out.

'We know that St Columba intervened on our behalf, out there in the storm, saving four of his servants from certain death. Yet it is sinful to sit skulking at home, fearful and slothful, and expect miracle upon miracle. St Columba will come to our aid again, but only if we go out into the world to grapple with the foe and scotch the serpent ourselves.

'St Columba did not sit at home in times of crisis, he went out into the world and drove out demons and dragons and monsters. And this is what we must do. We must proclaim the miracle of St Columba, and at the same time explain it, for it is not an easy miracle to understand.

'We must tell the world the reason for the Saint's anger: we all know the wrongs he suffered at de Mortimer's hands, we all know that de Mortimer had even caused the very relics of the saints to be trampled under foot, but the world has forgotten this, and the world must be reminded, for it is not enough for us to be justified in the eyes of God, we must also be justified in the eyes of the mortals.'

Brother David stood up and asked him what it was exactly that he was proposing to do.

Simon replied, 'There are various paths that lead to the hearts and the understanding of the people. One of these is the spoken word. I will, with the permission of my lord Prior, and of the convent, go out into the highways and the by-ways and teach the people about the miracle which I experienced at first hand. I will speak in the market-place, I will speak in the hall. I will speak at the church porch.

'I will start in those places where we have lands or a mill or other tributes due, especially those which have recently refused us our rights.

'Another path is by the quill and the parchment. We must write an account of the death and burial of Sir William de Mortimer, and of the miraculous doings of our patron Saint, and we must copy it out and send it to all our brother canons throughout Scotland, as well as to the houses of the Benedictines, the Tironensians, the Premonstratensians, the Cistercians. Let us but proclaim the truth, and God and St Columba will magnify our voice a thousandfold.'

Simon finished speaking and sat down. Prior Walter applauded, and the rest of the convent followed suit, most with enthusiasm, though some remained doubting. Brother Isaac, that good and simple soul, stood up and begged for permission to go with Simon. I said that if it was my brother's will, I would write an account, which could be copied out. This too was applauded.

Within the week, after obtaining a licence to preach throughout the diocese from Bishop John, Simon and Isaac, along with Laurence the dumb lay-brother, set out towards the Fothrif coast to scotch the serpent.

That they were going into danger was clear to us all. There were many on the mainland who felt that de Mortimer's fate cried out for vengeance. Every day we sang for them.

I have lifted up my eyes to the mountains, whence my
help will come.
The Lord guards you from all evil. May the Lord guard
your soul.
May the Lord guard your going in and your going out.

To die young, Martin, is to be guarded from much evil. It is only our fallen state that makes us feel it as a great sadness. Yet it still hurts my heart when I think of it, after all these years.

My friend Isaac, quiet, brave, loyal, he had never turned his back on me through all my trials and tribulations. He had never shunned me or spoken evil of me, and now he was dead. I had to rejoice, knowing he was with God. I wept and felt great loss because he was no longer in this world, and this world was the poorer, and I was the poorer.

This is how it happened. Simon and Isaac had been away from the Priory for several weeks. They had been all over Fothrif and Fife, even as far as St Andrews, where they had obtained their preaching licence for that diocese from the Archdeacon. They were on their way to our most distant holding, a toft which lies in Tibbermuir near Perth, beside our Bishop's estate there. We knew their mission had not been in vain, for already our granger was reporting that dues and tributes were beginning to flow again. Soon their work would be done, and they would come home to rest.

They were near Perth. It was evening, and the summer sun was low in the sky. They were aiming to reach the town before sunset, and then make Tibbermuir the following day. They were traversing the great wood that lies south of the town, when suddenly an arrow came flying out from among the trees and pierced Isaac in the chest. He died almost immediately.

Laurence gave chase, while Simon tended the dying man. But the coward who had shot the arrow had disappeared, and by the time Laurence returned, Isaac was dead. They put the body on the one horse which they had with them and directed their steps towards Scone Abbey.

Father Gilbert, a canon of Scone on his way south to Jedburgh, first brought the news to us. A fussy little man with bright, beady eyes, he told us the whole story in vivid detail. He had been at the gate when the sad group arrived, well after Compline, and he had helped lay out the body.

'A fine figure of a man the dead canon had been, tall and strong. The arrow had pierced his lungs, and blood and air frothed from the wound. His companion, your Brother Simon, seemed very upset. He said that Brother Isaac had been a most saintly man, without equal in virtue and charity. He told me he had seen something truly miraculous at the moment of his death, but he would not say what, for he wants you to hear of it first. Is it true that Brother Isaac had been such a good man?'

His listeners, clustering around him in the cloister, murmured agreement, not wanting to detract from the memory of the dead, but puzzled at the excessive praise.

Dear Isaac, he had been a man, as full of sin as the next man. He had been tortured by lust. Once I found him weeping with the longing for a woman's embraces. Some men, whether they feel lust for women or for men, are made for the life of the cloister, its stillness, its privations, its opportunities for learning and study. Isaac was never such a man. He should have been married, with a brood of children, active in the world as a soldier or a farmer. It was a cruel fate that had led him to the cloister.

We all knew he had lain with women, for Brother Andrew had denounced him for it in Chapter several times, and he had received beatings and imprisonment. He had received his most severe punishment after he had attacked Andrew in the cloister, knocking him to the ground.

A few days after Father Gilbert had left us with his strange and gruesome tale, Laurence the lay-brother arrived with a letter from Simon addressed to the whole convent.

I was reader in Chapter that week, and so it was I who read it out to my brothers. Beautifully written, of course, it retold the story we had all already heard, but there were many new revelations in it, revelations so momentous that the Priory was never the same again. Simon wrote that he was in no doubt that Isaac was with God, for just as Isaac gave up his spirit, his head in Simon's arms, Simon had seen in the eastern sky a great shaft of light, like a burst of sunlight, but how could it have been the sun, for the clouds were thick and the sun was setting at the opposite end of the firmament?

He praised Isaac's virtues, which had shone forth with especial brightness throughout their journey together. He had died on God's work, and that very morning he had been filled with a fervent desire to confess his sins, which he had done in the little church of Kinross.

This was not all. There had already been a miracle attested by independent witnesses, so it could not be attributed merely to the excessive and partial love which Simon bore the dear departed. It had happened in the church of Scone Abbey. One of the Abbey's serfs had come into the nave to pray for his sick wife, while the canons were singing Nones. To his horror he saw one of the canons come through the rood screen towards him with an arrow sticking out of his chest.

The peasant was about to rush to his help when he noticed that the canon was still chanting the psalms along with his brothers in a strong, firm voice, and was walking quite normally, not staggering like a man who had just been pierced by an arrow. He came up to the peasant and told him to go home and he would find his prayer answered. Then the canon turned and walked back through the rood-screen.

The serf hurried back home to find his wife sitting up, her health greatly improved. Simon had spoken with the man later that day, when he had returned to the Abbey to give thanks to God, and to proclaim the miracle. The man had said that he had not recognised the canon, he was sure he did not belong to Scone. From his description Simon recognised Isaac.

Simon then informed us that he was having Isaac's body embalmed at Scone, but not buried there. He was sure Isaac would want to find his last resting place amongst his brethren on Inchcolm. Also he was sure that this would not be the last miracle of the blessed martyr Isaac — yes, those were his very words — and that such a holy and efficacious corpse would be a great asset to our Priory.

He ended the letter by urging the convent to make all haste to bring Isaac home. There should be a solemn funeral procession from Scone to Inchcolm. If Father Prior and his brothers were in agreement, he would accompany the cortège the whole way, proclaiming to the people as he went the merits of the dead man, and the miracles already performed.

Imagine, Martin, the great stir this letter caused among us. Brice fell to his knees, praising the Lord for his mercy and greatness, and saying that there are arrows of God and arrows of the Devil, and he was sure that the arrow that pierced the breast of our brother Isaac was from God. Others, too, fell to their knees in prayer.

Yet I could not suddenly leap into rapture out of the deep pit of grief that Isaac's death had cast me into. No matter how hard I tried I could not see Isaac as a saint and martyr. I prayed to God to soften the hardness of my heart against Simon's smooth words and well-framed miracles.

I was not the only one whom Simon's letter had left cold and untouched. As we were filing out of Chapter I heard Brother Henry mutter to Brother Luke, 'This man breeds miracles like meat breeds flies.'

Luke replied, 'He also breeds trouble. We are only at the beginning, you mark my words.'

Isaac's body was brought down from Scone in solemn procession, just as Simon had urged. Superior Brice himself went with the contingent to bring him back. By the time the cortège had reached Barnhill there were other miracles of healing for Simon to proclaim, and the whole world buzzed with the news of the new saint.

We have always had a trickle of pilgrims to the island to pray at the altar of St Columba, which contains the Saint's precious relics that Bishop Gregory gave us, long before my time; also to visit the little chapel where St Columa himself prayed when he was preaching the Word of God to my people. Mostly the pilgrims would come just for the day, some spending the night in our hostel at Barnhill. If they were nobility or clergy, they would be lodged in our guest hall attached to the Priory. Our guest hall was so little used that we had never had a full-time guestmaster.

However, after Isaac's body was laid to rest in the chapel of St Sebastian in the Priory church, many things changed. Soon a stream of men, women and children, broken in body or mind, was making its way to Barnhill and our boats. Some even returned healed, which never ceased to amaze me. I would often watch the faithful arrive by the boat-load in the little bay beneath the church, to limp or shuffle or crawl up the steep brae into the nave and over to the tomb.

I would have to tell myself over and over again that it was the tomb of Isaac that they had come to pray at, and I would recall him as he was, slow, lumbering, good-natured, pining after some woman or other.

Sometimes I would see him standing beside his tomb, scratching his head, looking puzzled at the crowds trying to press close to him. Then he would grin from ear to ear at the strangeness of it, and I would grin with him. Tears would then start to my eyes, as I felt that he was double dead, for there were very few who now remembered Isaac as he had really been. There were even fewer who wanted to.

Often when the nave was full of pilgrims, Simon would preach to them, recounting miracles already performed, not just through the intercession of Isaac, but of the saints, and of Christ himself. He would urge them to live a life free from sin and filled with charitable love. Then he would preach the virtue of giving to God and the community in which the blessed Isaac had lived.

He had set up a large box for offerings, fixed to the wall with a wooden bar, beside the main door to the nave. He would say to the pilgrims that the person who gives most gladly and generously will be the person who will receive the most, either in this world, or the next. Giving opened the soul to the grace of miracles.

Simon himself supervised the emptying of the box every evening. Some of it of course went to pay our debts, and some went on the maintenance and enrichment of the tomb. But some, Simon argued, should be put aside to pay for a mission to the Pope to press Isaac's canonization. This would be a very expensive undertaking, not so much the journey but the gifts that would have to be offered to the Holy Father and his Cardinals to persuade them to the candidate's saintliness. Nobody doubted that Simon knew what he was talking about on that score.

Not everybody was happy with the changes that Isaac's fame had brought us. Some of the older brothers, such as Robert and Geoffrey, would mutter that the crowds that filled the nave might bring revenue, but peace and quiet was more valuable than gold. Poor old Brother Robert, one morning he was knocked down and almost trampled underfoot when opening the doors.

For us younger ones, though, it was exciting to see some bustle and life around the place. We were allowed to chat to the pilgrims: no idle gossip, mind you. It had to be about religion and virtue and the turning away from sin. But much news was exchanged as the pilgrims waited patiently for their turn to approach the tomb, and we could not help but overhear. And when our opinion was sought about the rights and wrongs of some action or other, then we had no choice but to join in the conversations.

After the death of de Mortimer it seemed that the days of our Priory had been numbered. Now, a year afterwards (Spring 1193), our affairs were in remarkably good order. Teinds and tributes and other dues were being paid on time. We were regularly receiving new grants, and old grants were being augmented, while the steady flow of pilgrims to our church was like a river of silver into our coffers."

PART FIVE
SCHEMES

Lord, why hast Thou withdrawn far from me? Dost
Thou look away from me, in both favourable times and
times of tribulation?
While the impious man behaves proudly, the poor man is
ruined,
They are caught in the schemes of their own devising.
For the sinner glories in the desires of his soul,
and the wicked man is blessed.
The sinner has angered the Lord,
He does not have God before his eyes.
His paths are defiled for all time.
Thy judgements are beyond his ken.

Contra oppressores iniquos Psalm 98

BEASTS

"One day around harvest time [1193], I was sitting at my copying desk, watching the dust dance in the sunbeams that streamed through the window beside me. With me were Father Geoffrey, who was dictating my text, and Brother Hugh, who was botching his way through copying a Psalter as penance for falling asleep in church.

I was trying to keep my mind on my work. The whole convent was out in the fields bringing in the harvest, brothers, lay brothers, servants, and I longed to be out there with them. But Walter had forbidden it. He wanted the manuscript, a Book of Beasts, finished as soon as possible. We had had it too long already, and he had just received a sharp reminder from Prior Walter of St Andrews. It belonged to his Priory, and he wanted it back by the Nativity of the Virgin [8 Sept.].

The door opened and Simon walked into the room. My heart leapt towards him like a dog. *Now none is more sagacious than the dog, for he has more perception than other animals and he alone recognises his own name.* A dog was certainly more sagacious than my heart.

'Brother Michael, our lord Prior requests that you come to him at once.' Then turning graciously to Father Geoffrey, he said apologetically, 'It's very urgent, Father Geoffrey.'

'No matter, no matter. I think we could all do with a rest. Will he be coming back, do you know, or should I clear away his pens?'

'He'll be coming back, I think. But only for today.'

Simon was already at the door. He was obviously in a hurry. Intrigued I followed him out into the cloister. He turned and gave me his most charming smile. It had been many a long week since I had seen that smile. It had been many a long week since he had even acknowledged me. We had not scourged each other since Easter.

I tried to suppress my excitement. I told myself that the time had come for me to be used again, to be taken down off the shelf, dusted, and opened. For Simon it was as calculated as that. Yet still my heart raced with the thrill of it. As we got to the door of Prior Walter's room, he squeezed my arm.

Up until that year Walter had used the parlour for any work he needed to do, interviews, conversations, admonitions — the parlour, and sometimes the chapter house. If he needed any documents someone would be sent to fetch them from the chest in the sacristy.

Once Simon had taken over as Walter's amanuensis, however, Simon had persuaded him to have his own room, or scriptoriolum, as Simon called it. Here he could conduct private business at any time, and here all the important parchments which he might need to refer to could be kept.

There had been a little chapel dedicated to St Brigit, between the chapter house and the south wall of the choir. Amidst much protest from the older brothers an altar was dedicated to her in the chancel, and Walter's scriptoriolum was set up where her altar had been. It was to this room that Simon led me that sleepy harvest afternoon.

Walter was sitting peering at one of the parchments that covered his desk. I saw at once that many of them had numbers written on them, mostly those strange digits that have recently come from the east, from the Infidel. Some say they were invented by the Devil, for they make reckoning too easy, and reckoning should not be easy. Access to material amounts should be difficult and laborious, so that a decent distance is kept between us and the material world. This is especially true for the clergy. Simon used only the new digits.

'So you found him,' Walter said, looking up. 'Good. Shut the door, Michael, and come and stand over here beside me. Now I want you to understand that what I am going to say is for you only. I know you are discreet. We have a very difficult situation on our hands. As you know Simon and our dear departed Isaac travelled widely over the land, visiting most of our estates, until the flight of an arrow put a stop to that particular journey. But Brother Simon is most observant, I'm sure I don't need to tell you that.

'While preaching and proclaiming the miracle of St Columba, he was also making a careful note of the extent of our arable and our pasture. Brother Isaac was helping him in this. I have here a detailed report of what he found. He is convinced that we are not receiving everything from our lands that we should be. And I am afraid he's right.'

'Now, what Brother Simon has requested is permission to

travel once again throughout our estates, especially to those which he and Isaac did not manage to visit. He wants to confirm his estimates, and see if he can find the cause of the shortfall. I am granting that permission.

'Of course he cannot go alone. He is taking with him Lay-brother Laurence, a stout staff in times of danger. He also asks to be accompanied by you. Reluctantly I am granting this request as well. You are discreet and sharp-witted. You tell me the Book of Beasts is almost complete. Go back to it now, work until today's light fails. You are excused Vespers and Compline. Brother Matthew has a good hand and eye, and he can finish it.

'At Chapter tomorrow I will tell the convent that I am sending you around the estates because Bishop John wants a new rent assessment. And while you are away you will take orders from Brother Simon in all matters. All matters which do not offend God's law, or nature's,' he added sharply.

'One other thing, you will have with you one of our lay-brothers, Brother Ethernan. He is base-born, but he is honest and trustworthy and has a sharp eye. He can assist you with the survey, as long as it does not interfere with his main task.'

I stole a glance at Simon. His face was expressionless. I started to blush, because I knew what Walter was about to say. 'And Lay-brother Ethernan's main task is this,' Walter was saying. 'To make sure that your bodies do not ensnare your souls in the sin to which I know you are both prone. If I do not send Ethernan along with you, then I will share in any guilt you might incur. Am I making myself clear?'

We both nodded.

'I might add, ' Walter went on, 'that Ethernan will know no more about the real purpose of your journey than will the rest of the convent. But he will know why I have sent him along.'

Lay-brother Ethernan? Which one was he? I did not have much to do with the lay-brothers. They mainly worked with the cellerar and in the fields, and most of them lived at Barnhill for much of the year. Well, I would soon find out. Whoever he was, I was glad he would be with us. Yet why was I already feeling such resentment towards him?

As we prepared for our journey I could not get Isaac out of my thoughts. He too had gone out into the world with Simon, travelling from estate to estate, secretly gathering information about our land and its produce, and he had died at the hand of an unknown murderer. Was there someone who did not want that information gathered? Was Isaac's death meant as a warning to us all? Would I share his fate?

I am not ashamed to admit that I was a coward, Martin. I was not afraid of death, no Augustinian, no religious, should be afraid of death. But I was afraid of dying, dying suddenly and unprepared, by the arrow that flies by day, or by the terror that stalks by night.

All that autumn our little band travelled throughout the land, to Lothian, Fothrif, Fife and as far north as Fortriu, where we had a toft in Tibbermuir, that fateful destination which Isaac never reached. For the first few days we travelled in hot, dry weather, and the whole world seemed to be out in the fields, bringing in the harvest.

Then the rains came, lashed by a wild west wind, and the corn that had not been brought in soon lay rotting in the wet. It was not long before it felt as though we, too, were rotting in the wet. Our rain copes could not keep the lashing rain out for more than an hour, and we spent most of the day wet to the skin, our feet black with mud.

Every few days Brother Simon would send copies of our estimates back to the Priory by means of a local carrier. He always paid him well. He seemed to have an endless supply of silver in his pouch.

Lay-brother Laurence shambled beside us, his dark eyes always searching for danger, his right hand always on the hilt of the sword concealed under his habit. I felt safe in his shadow. As the Book of Beasts has it, a bear's head is feeble, his greatest strength is in the arms and loins.

And always at our backs shuffled Lay-brother Ethernan. In the Book of Beasts there are many strange creatures described. One of the strangest is the monkey. Simia is a Greek word meaning 'with squashed nostrils'. This is why we call monkeys Simia, because they have turned-up noses and a hideous wrinkled countenance, and lewdly puff out their cheeks like bellows.

Every time I looked at Ethernan this description of the monkey came into my head. He had been born in the Priory of St Ethernan on the Isle of May, during the time when darkness had descended on that place, and all discipline had broken down. His father had been one of the brothers, his mother the laundry servant. I was sure he had been conceived in the scriptorium, and a Book of Beasts had lain open at the page with the drawing of the monkeys. His mother had looked at it as his father lay on her. This was the only way I could explain the uncanny resemblance.

His eyes were quick and cunning, as they say monkeys' eyes are, but he hardly ever spoke. When he did his words were slow and slurred and it was an effort to understand him. He never once let me out of his sight for more than a few minutes.

Simon had been disturbed by what he had seen the first time he had travelled through our estates. This second time he was outraged. Until then I had not known that he was capable of such an emotion, I had not known that he was capable of caring for something so much.

When we arrived at one of our estates he became like a man possessed with the demon of boundless energy. Exhausted by the journey and often soaked to the skin, all I wanted to do was to change my wet clothes for damp ones, say the Hours that remained to be said, and rest. But Simon would scarcely have thrown down his satchel than he was out looking for the steward and walking the marches. Finally when the light failed and drove him back to our quarters, his work was still not done, for Simon would have ordered the steward to attend us at supper, and would ply him with questions and strong beer. No eating in silence for us.

Simon would keep the steward talking late into the night, until his senses were reeling and he did not know what he was saying. In this way Simon hoped that things would be told to us that were supposed to remain a secret. And several late nights and flagons of strong beer later, his hope was justified.

It was on our estate of Ecclesmaline. We have fifty-two acres of good arable there. The steward, Murdoch was his name, after the fifth jug of beer blurted out that the whole estate lived in fear and dread of our cellarer Brother Henry.

He told how Brother Henry had thrown the old widow Brigit out of her cottage to make more land for ploughing. It had broken the old woman's heart, she had not lasted the winter. Then there was the young widow Katriona and her bairns, her man had died of the wasting disease. She was not thrown out of her house, but she had to thole a visit from Brother Henry at least once a month, and her last bairn had been born a good year after the death of her man. It was the speak of the whole village. And Brother John the granger, when he comes by everybody complains to him about Henry, for everybody has something to complain about, and Brother John listens sympathetically, and promises that he will bring their grievances to the attention of the convent, but God knows if he does, but nothing ever changes. And it's the same when Brother Luke the almoner comes. More than anybody else he sees the misery the people are suffering, but all they get from him are a few extra handfuls of grain. And now the people believe that the convent must be deaf, either that or they're all as bad as Brother Henry.

'But whan A see the likes o ye, Faither, A ken ye're no aa like him' he added ingratiatingly. And then, leaning forward, almost whispering, 'Oh, dae somethin, Faither. But dinnae sey A telt ye. Please.'

'Dinnae fash yersel, Murdoch,' Simon said, grasping his arm. 'We'll dae somethin. Whit dae ye think we're here fur? We'll help ye, but aiblins ye can help us. It's aboot thone shortfaa, thir acres can gie a bonnie wheen mair nor we're ever seein at the Priory. Somethin's gettin tint, or reivit. Or is it jaist that ye cannae fairm them richt?'

'Cannae fairm them richt!' Murdoch exclaimed indignantly. 'Faither, ye'll nae see better fairmed land this side o the Ochils.'

'Weel, whaur's it aa gaun tae?' Simon said, his voice taking on a menacing edge.

'It aa gans intae the girnel, Faither, A sweir tae it, it aa gans intae the girnel.' Murdoch sounded almost desperate.

Simon went on relentlessly. He had his prey cornered now, and he was not going to let it go.

He turned to me and said, 'Brother Michael, A jalouse oor baillie here kens mair nor he's lettin on. A'm thinkin oor Faither Prior wud be gey interestit in speirin at him a thing or twaa. An the Priory dungeon is mirk an cauld.'

To my astonishment Murdoch's face crumpled and he started to cry like a child.

'Greetin'll no save ye fae it,' Simon said sharply.

'Aa the corn gans tae the girnel,' he gasped. 'A've.. A've naethin tae dae wi the horses that come i the nicht. But dinnae sey A said, Faither, it's mair nor ma life's worth, an the lives o ma faimily.' And his words were lost in a flood of tears.

Simon sat back with a sigh. He had got what he wanted.

'Hoo aften dae they come?' he asked, adding, 'A'll mak shair nae hairm comes tae ye, or yer faimily, as lang as ye tell me the truth. The truth'll beild ye, an lees'll damn ye, in this wurld, an the neist.'

Murdoch looked up. His little eyes had almost disappeared behind puffed eyelids and his face looked swollen and grotesque.

'It's aye aboot three deys efter a fraucht has been brocht in, or efter teinds hae been gaitherit. But we're aye telt no tae stir, onybody fund ootside on ane o thae nichts will tyne their tongue.'

'Whaa seys?' Simon asked.

Murdoch looked down at the candle again and fell silent.

'Whaa seys?' Simon repeated firmly, adding, 'An mind whit A said, the truth beilds, but lees — '

'Brother Henry!' Murdoch blurted out. 'But dinnae tell A...,'

'Caum yersel, Murdoch,' Simon said soothingly. 'Weel dune, guid an leal servan. Whan dae ye think the horses'll be back?'

'The morn's nicht. We brocht in a muckle fraucht o aits yesterdey.'

Simon had finished with him at last, and so he told Murdoch he could go home, and that he was not to breathe a word about the conversation to anybody. 'An that includes yer woman, mind, Murdoch.'

'Dinnae fash yersel, Faither,' Murdoch said as he staggered out into the night, 'ma woman cannae clype, She hasnae got a tongue.'

'Well, my brother, what do you make of all that?' Simon said, turning to me, his beautiful eyes shining triumphantly in the candle light. I blew out the flame so that he became a dark shape in the glow of the fire.

'What a beast!' I said.

'Who?' Simon asked. 'That old fool of a bailie, or our dear

cellarer?'

'Our cellarer, of course,' I replied crossly, realising too late that Simon was teasing me.

'Quite a clever beast, though,' he said, 'to have got away with it all this time. Those are the sort of beasts I admire.'

'He deserves to be hanged,' I said.

'Anyone who lets themselves be caught deserves to be hanged,' he said. 'Who do you think takes the grain?'

'I've no idea,' I replied. 'Friends of Brother Henry I suppose. 'Where's he from?'

'Lochore, it's about five miles from here, over the hills, going towards Perth.'

'Handy, that place, for a lot of our estates, wouldn't you say?'

'Do you think it's his relatives?' I asked.

'I think that at least we should go and visit it,' he replied.

My heart sank. I had come on this journey to do an assessment of our estates, I had not come to visit thieves in their lair. I said so. Simon chuckled.

'Life is full of surprises, my dear Michael, especially when you are with me. You should know that by now.' And before I could reply — but what could I have replied? — he kissed my lips. His lips were soft and warm. My hands of themselves went round his neck, but he pulled away.

In the corner, where our two Lay-brothers slept, Ethernan stirred. He had snored roughly through all the time that Murdoch had been with us. Now it was as if the touch of our lips had been like a clap of thunder in his mind which had only one thought and one task.

'Whaa's there?' he muttered. I could hear the straw of the pallets rustling as he felt to see if we were beside him, one on either side.

'It's aaricht, Brither Ethernan,' Simon said reassuringly, 'it's anely us. We're jaist comin tae oor beds.' Ethernan gave a grunt. 'Come on, Michael, let's get some sleep, because I don't think we'll be getting much tomorrow night.'

'Why not?' I asked, my head still spinning from the kiss.

'Because we're going to watch the granary,' he replied softly. 'Laurence will be there, too, so there's no need to be afraid,' he added mockingly. 'But not a word more. We're keeping Brother Ethernan from his sleep, he'll not go back to his disgusting dreams until we're safely on either side of him.'

It was true. Ethernan's snores did not start up again until we were both on our pallets. But sleep would not come to me, despite my aching tiredness. My mind turned to thoughts of Brother Henry and Murdoch and Murdoch's wife. And on my lips I could still taste Simon."

THE GRANARY

'Just think what we could do with all this land, if only it was properly husbanded,' Simon was saying excitedly. It was the day after our conversation with Murdoch. Dull, warm, and windless, it threatened a storm. Once again we were walking the marches of our estate at Ecclesmaline. I was tired, and my spirit felt as leaden as my feet.

'By St Melin,' he went on, 'but land is more precious than gold or silver.' It was as if he was remembering something he had once known long ago, but had forgotten. It was something I had always known. Had not my father farmed his own acres, as well as supervising the whole of the demesne? I knew where the roots of wealth ran, and it was not into the coffers of cardinals, even if that is where much of the fruit was bound.

'And look at that hillside! All that gorse and rough grass, there should be an assart there, and there, too, where that copse is. I'm thinking Murdoch's not quite the great bailie he makes himself out to be.'

'What's the point, when half of it is being stolen?' I said dully.

'But not for much longer, my boy,' he said, slapping me on the back. 'And when I'm cellarer, and you're granger, we'll make these acres thrive, will we not?'

'And who says you're going to be cellarer, or I'm going to be granger, for that matter?' I replied.

'Brother Simon says. And what Brother Simon says today, Prior Walter will be saying tomorrow. Haven't you noticed?'

'Sometimes you're insufferable,' I muttered, shocked by his arrogance.

'Then when I'm cellarer and you're granger,' he went on undaunted, 'we don't always have to be running away from each other like we do in that gloomy cloister. We can meet out in the fields and the woods, away from prying eyes.' He turned round and shouted back at Brother Ethernan, who was ambling along behind us. 'Can't we, Brother Ethernan?' Ethernan, understanding only his name, as he spoke no French, smiled and grunted.

'There are prying eyes at all times, and in all places,' I replied warily. 'And a good thing too,' I added, remembering his kiss. 'It is not becoming for an Augustinian to cherish such dreams, and you know it.'

'Will you scourge me again for them?' Simon asked eagerly. 'I'll confess to Brice as soon as we get back.'

He laughed and grabbed my shoulder. I shook him off, hissing, 'Brice is watching us right now. Stop it.'

Simon let his arm fall from my body, while his words burned inside me like fire in dry brushwood.

That evening we said Compline in the little chapel of St Melin. We were staying in the small stone hut just to the south of the nave, where the priest from Kinghorn stayed when he came this way, which was not very often, by the looks of the place, and the people. A more sour and godless lot it would have been hard to find in all the kingdom.

As neither Simon nor I were priests, no Mass was said while we were there. It was partly to this that I attributed the terrible dryness of the body where the fire of my lust burned. Mass purges the soul of such basenesses, and that is why you should attend Mass at least once a day, if possible. This is why I was always more prone to lust when I was outside the cloister, because often I could not hear Mass often enough.

You don't grow old during Mass, either, and it protects you from sudden death for the rest of that day. So I have read at any rate, although it did not protect poor Isaac.

At Compline there were only the three of us, Brother Simon, Lay-brother Ethernan and myself. Lay-brother Laurence was nowhere to be seen, as was usual whenever we went to pray. The peasants, who had come at first to gawp, had not been near the chapel all day. And besides, now that it was dusk, who in their right minds would be out and about on an evening in harvest time, knowing that it was three days after a load of grain had been brought to the granary.

After Compline Laurence appeared again, already dressed for his night's work in doublet and hose. We all went into the priest's hut for Collation. Earlier that day I had asked Simon what he intended doing with Lay-brother Ethernan while we were out keeping watch at the granary. Surely we could not take him along. But equally surely he would not allow the two of us to disappear into the night together, even if Laurence was with us, no matter what excuses we gave him.

'You just leave Brother Ethernan to me,' Simon had said with a wink.

Shortly after our Collation drink I understood what Simon had meant. Ethernan started to stagger, as though drunk. He lurched over to the privy, set into the thickness of the wall, almost falling into it as he relieved himself noisily. Then staggering back across the room, muttering and scowling, he collapsed onto his pallet and started to snore loudly.

'Well,' said Simon with a satisfied air, 'that's Brother Ethernan out of the way. It will be Prime before he comes to his senses. He won't even be able to get up for a piss. Or a kiss,' he added, coming over and kissing me again on the lips.

I pushed him away, looking anxiously, not at Ethernan, who did not stir, but at Laurence, who sat in the shadows beside the door whittling away at a stick with his dirk.

'Don't worry about him,' Simon said. 'When I tell him to see nothing, he sees nothing.'

'We have dangerous work ahead of us,' I said, finding it difficult to catch my breath. 'We need God's blessing on it. Let us not jeopardise that blessing, or our souls, at such a time.' Yet if I am quite honest, Martin, I would have jeopardised everything had not Lay-brother Laurence been sitting in the shadows.

'I was simply showing you how deeply Brother Ethernan sleeps,' Simon replied, laughingly. 'My mother had two great skills. She knew how to mix potions which could affect the soul as well as the body, and she knew how to love men, so that once they had tasted her body, they could never forget her. I am my mother's son, Michael.'

Then suddenly serious he added, 'But we must be about our business. Here, put these on. Habits were not made for creeping around in the dark, or for climbing trees. Brother Laurence is setting the fashion for tonight.' Out of the pannier in the corner he took a pile of clothes, and threw them at me. There was a hose, a short doublet, and a light tunic, all of coarse woollen thread, and all black. Simon had come more prepared than I had thought possible. Yet, as he himself had said, with him life was always full of surprises.

We already knew where we were going to place ourselves. We had spent time that day looking carefully at the granary. The granary yard was surrounded by oak trees. They were old and gnarled, with many hollows and deep clefts in their trunks. Two of these trees were to be our place of vantage.

As I changed out of my habit into the clothes of the world, time swung back like the beam of a quintain, striking me on the skull so that for a moment I was not in the dark, smoky priest's hut in Ecclesmaline but in the guardhouse of the monastery of the Four Crowned Martyrs in Rome, and Simon stood before me, dressed all in green, dazzlingly handsome in the sunlight that fell upon his head. Before my senses had returned to me I was in his arms, and nothing stood between the shining of our bodies.

Suddenly there was a noise at the door and Laurence sprang up. In my confusion I thought at first he was going to attack us for our shameless behaviour. Still naked Simon leapt across the room and tried to open the door. But it was no good. The door was firmly bolted from without. Simon stood shaking the door and cursing quietly.

'Too slow, Orsino, too slow,' he muttered angrily. 'Somebody's beaten us to it', he said, turning round.

'Was it Murdoch?' I asked my heart pounding, struggling into my new clothes. Simon was doing the same.

'Perhaps,' he said. 'But why should Murdoch want to keep us locked up? If he had wanted that, he would never have told us what he did in the first place.'

'He did not tell us. The beer, and whatever you put in the beer, did.'

'I didn't put anything in the beer. No, I don't think that was Murdoch. Anyway, what does it matter who it was? We've got to get out of this damn hole, and quick.'

'I don't see how,' I said, trying to sound despondent. There was only one opening in the walls, a tiny window high up above the door. Even a child could not have squeezed through it.

'As usual, you're only looking one way,' Simon said. 'Look up. I'm going out the same way as the smoke.'

I looked up. Of course, the smokehole. It was just large enough for a slender adult to get through, but it was very high up. 'How on earth are you going to reach it?' I asked.

'I'm going to use the table, and that great oaf of a servant of mine. Eh, Orsino?' He ordered Laurence to stand on the table, and lift him up so that he could grab hold of the roof. Luckily the fire that Brother Ethernan had lit that evening was almost out. We placed the table over it and Simon and Laurence crawled up onto it. Laurence took Simon in his great embrace, and for one awful moment I thought I saw them kiss. I looked away, telling myself it was the shadow-demons playing tricks on me.

The smokehole was just a different shade of black with a scattering of stars above our heads. Simon and Laurence became one shadow, then Simon was propelled towards the stars. They swayed violently, and I ran forward to steady them. Just as I thought they were both going to tumble headlong onto the floor, Simon caught the rooftree at the edge of the smokehole, becoming a fixed point against which Laurence could steady himself. Then he wormed his way upwards out of Laurence's grasp. Laurence had scarcely climbed down off the table when we heard the bar being drawn back, and Simon swung the door open.

At the granary I climbed one of the great oaks, ensconcing myself into its deep cleft. The greatest problem was the cold. The night at first felt mild, but the cold crept stealthily upon me. I prayed that the night visitors would not wait too long.

Simon and Laurence had hidden themselves in the tree opposite. Yet stare as I might, I could see no trace of them, despite the light of a half grown moon. This was of course as it should be, but I longed to catch just a glimpse of them, so that I would not feel so alone.

After about an hour my limbs were numb with the cold and my body ached fiercely. I kept thinking I was falling into the arms of sleep, softly and painlessly, and sleep had the face of Simon. But I was fighting this demon with all my strength,

277

because if I fell those arms would not support me, and it was a long way to the ground.

Suddenly I heard footsteps coming across the yard. All thoughts of sleep vanished. There below me walked a hooded figure in a long black cape. I was sure he was one of our Order. But who could he be?

Looking neither to the right nor the left he went up to the door of the granary. In the quiet night I heard the sound of a key turning in the lock. But instead of going inside the figure walked back across the courtyard and disappeared into the night.

There is something very exciting about watching without being seen, especially watching things that are forbidden. There is a feeling of great power, and great vulnerability. It is like being the eye of God, with all the danger of being poised on the crumbling brink of Hell.

Suddenly other noises filled the night, and soon the whole courtyard was alive with men and horses. No one spoke. Everybody seemed to know what they had to do. The barn door was swung open. Sacks were carried out, two being loaded onto each horse, which had great panniers slung on either side. I counted eight horses in all.

The men were dressed in black cloaks, but they were not of any religious Order. Their business did not delay them long, and soon the courtyard was empty again, the muffled sound of horses' hooves growing fainter towards the north west.

I wanted to jump down from the tree, run over to where Simon was hiding, and talk about what we should do next. But I decided to wait until he made the first move. This was very wise, because it was not long before our hooded brother came treading softly over to the granary door, and with a grind and a click the lock sprang shut. He turned and paused, as if listening, then walked hurriedly back the way he had come.

Suddenly a black shape dropped as if from the sky, knocking him to the ground. Laurence had jumped on him from his hiding place in the tree. I scrambled down and ran over to where the two figures lay struggling. Laurence stood up, grinning from ear to ear, while at his feet, writhing and gasping, lay his prey, his hands already tied behind his back with his cord.

A shout from behind made us jump. My first thought was that the raiders had returned. Simon came hobbling towards us, cursing. 'I've twisted my ankle,' he spat, 'coming down out of that damned tree. Now what have we got here?'

The figure was still gasping like a stranded fish, as if he could not get his breath. 'Is he all right?' I asked.

'He's just winded. Wouldn't you be if this little bear had just landed on you? It's me you should be worrying about. You've done well, Laurence,' he added, patting him on his massive shoulder.

'That was some height he jumped from,' I said, impressed.

'Athletes of God must be prepared for anything,' Simon said with a sneer. 'But at least he had a soft landing.' And he kicked the figure at his feet. This seemed to hurt Simon more than his victim. 'This damned leg,' he cursed. 'Come on, let's get out of here, before his friends come back. Laurence, bring him.'

Effortlessly Laurence heaved our prisoner onto his shoulder and carried him off towards the hut. Simon and I followed on behind, Simon leaning heavily on me because of his injured foot.

Once inside the hut, Laurence slung his burden down onto the floor. The prisoner was breathing more normally now, and his gasps were turning into whimpers.

Simon barred the door from the inside. Before I had even lit the candle from the dying embers of the fire, the prisoner began to speak. And so before the light told us who he was, we recognised the voice of our own brother. It was Brother John the granger.

Before the night was out he had told us everything. Was he not, as Simon later put it, swollen with guilt and ready for plucking, like an overripe plum? 'He just fell from the tree into our hands,' he would later joke callously.

That night, however, was no joking matter. Brother John was beside himself with terror and contrition. He begged our forgiveness and the forgiveness of God. Then he broke down weeping, unable to say any more.

I could not help but put my arm round him to comfort him.

'He doesn't deserve that, you know,' Simon said contemptuously. He was still rubbing his ankle, which had swollen up to twice its size.

'Can we not undo his hands,' I said, ignoring Simon's comment.

'Laurence, search him for weapons,' Simon snapped. 'If he's unarmed, untie him. But listen, Brother granger,' he snarled, 'if you so much as move an inch in any direction, our friend here will tear you limb from limb. Will you not, Brother Laurence?' Laurence nodded, and made a movement with his hands as if he were wringing the neck of a chicken.

As Laurence searched him, then untied him, Brother John wept even louder.

Ever since we had got back to the hut, Simon kept asking him who the men were who were stealing the Priory's grain. Finally John's sobbing subsided enough to allow him to answer.

'I cannot tell,' he whined piteously. 'For the sake of my family, I cannot tell.'

'What's your family got to do with it?' Simon asked. His voice was crisp and firm.

'I have to save my family. I cannot tell.'

'Listen carefully, Brother John,' Simon growled. 'What do you think will become of the honour of your family when one of them is branded with the mark of a thief and thrown out of the cloister? But if you tell us everything you know, you will be spared this punishment, and your family's honour will remain untarnished. If you don't.....'

'I don't care what you do to me. Rather their honour tarnished than they're killed or enslaved. I would do anything to save them, anything.' John's voice was clear now, almost defiant, and as he spoke he raised his head and for the first time looked both of us in the eye. Simon was silent for a moment.

'Is there no way they can be protected?' I asked.

'No, there is no way,' John replied emphatically.

'How can we know that when we don't know what it is that threatens them,' Simon said. 'But it must be a terrible threat, from a powerful man,' he added.

'Oh, it is, it is,' John said, his voice trembling.

'Where does your family live?' Simon asked. John opened his mouth, then shut it again quickly. Simon looked at me. 'Where does Brother John come from? Or is it a secret of the confessional?'

'He comes from Lochore,' I said quietly. 'His father is overseer there for Sir Philip's demesne lands.'

I felt as though I had betrayed him. What a soft-hearted fool I was, Martin.

'Is it Sir Philip who is threatening your family?' Simon asked. John shook his head vigorously.

'Simon,' I said, 'you know who Brother Henry is, don't you?'

He rounded on me angrily, 'Is this some kind of a sport? Do you want me to tie you up and interrogate you, as well? Yes, I know who Brother Henry is. He's our cellarer. Anything else?'

'Brother Henry,' I said, biting back my anger, 'is a younger son of Sir Philip de Lochore.'

John gave a little whimper. Simon's face lit up.

'Aha!' he exclaimed. 'Now, why did nobody tell me that before? So it's Brother Henry who's threatening you, with the power of his father?'

John shook his head even more vigorously.

'Listen, Brother John,' Simon said, bending forward, putting his arm on his shoulder, 'there are men more powerful in this realm than Sir Philip de Lochore.'

'Not where my family is concerned,' John blurted out. 'He's got the right of pit and gallows — .' He stopped in mid-sentence. 'But it's not Sir Philip,' he said defiantly. 'And it's not Brother Henry, either.'

Simon sat back with a sigh. 'We're not getting very far, are we? Now let us assume for a moment that it is Sir Philip,' he continued, holding up his hand to stop further protestations from Brother John. 'Just let us assume, so that we can look at ways of protecting your family. Brother Michael, you should know this as your father was overseer for de Mortimer, was he not? How could your family have been protected if de Mortimer had wanted to harm them?'

I thought carefully. It was a difficult question. It's almost impossible, I thought, for a lord can do what he likes with his peasants and his officials. Only if they are knights themselves could they have any recourse to a higher court of justice. 'Change lords,' I said at last. 'Move to another estate, to another master, under the protection of that new master. But who's going to.....'

'Change lords?' Simon cut in. 'Brother John, what would you say if your family could be moved to the estate of another lord, in the way that Brother Michael has just described? Would that make their life, and the truth, any easier?'

'It's impossible,' Brother John said flatly. Silently I agreed with him.

'It's not impossible,' Simon said. 'Brother John, do you know who my family is?'

'You're connected with the de Quincys, aren't you?' Brother John said slowly.

'I am indeed, and although I was born on the wrong side of wedlock, I am not without some influence on my cousins conceived in the matrimonial bed. Did you know that I am a nephew of Earl Robert?'

Both Brother John and I looked at Simon in astonishment. I had known he was related to the great Earl, but I had not known just how closely. He had never boasted about his relatives like this before.

'Brother John,' Simon went on, 'because you are my brother in Christ, and because my first duty, after my duty to God and to St Columba, is my duty to my brothers, I will do something I have not done for a long time. I will ask a boon of my uncle the Earl. I will ask him to put your family under his protection and move them to one of his estates far from Lochore.

'I will ask even more, I will ask him to give your father the work and the status that he once enjoyed under Sir Philip. I will write to him tonight, as we have parchment with us. My uncle has never refused my petitions in the past.

'In return, of course, I will expect a full confession of your sins in Chapter, and a full accusation of all the others involved in this shameful theft of the Priory's goods.

'God is merciful to those who bring their sins, and the sins of others, out into the open, and help put an end to injustice and oppression. What do you say, Brother John? Is it that, or branding, imprisonment, dishonour and exile?'

Brother John's face was contorted, torn between hope and fear. He cried out like a man being tortured. 'Yes, do it! Petition Earl Robert. Get my family away from Sir Philip, away from Lochore. And I will tell everything.'

'So it is Sir Philip, then?' Simon said softly.

'Yes, it is, egged on by Brother Henry. It's Brother Henry. He's behind it all. Will you write the petition tonight?'

'Brother Michael,' Simon said, turning to me, 'please get parchment and a quill ready. I will write it while you sleep. Tomorrow morning, before I seal it and send it, you can read it. Then we will all return to the Priory. Our work is far from over.'

Then, hobbling over to Brother John, he gave him a kiss which I thought was the kiss of peace, but I know now to have been the kiss of Judas.

I slept fitfully that night. Brother John kept shouting out in his sleep, as if a nightmare was crushing his chest. I prayed for his soul, and thanked God that for him the nightmare would soon be over. And always, like the never-ending splashing of a millwheel, Ethernan's snores tore the silence of the night. How I envied his deep and innocent sleep.

I opened my eyes the next morning to see Simon and John sitting at the table poring over the letter. Ethernan was preparing breakfast. He was still a bit unsteady on his feet, and he kept rubbing his head and casting suspicious glances at Simon and me. Laurence was sitting at the open door, whittling at his stick.

When I had got up and splashed my face with water from the bucket, Simon showed me the letter. Beneath its flowery phrases its burden was clear. John's family, and each of them was named, was to be moved immediately under armed protection into the safe-keeping of Earl Robert de Quincy. No time was to be wasted, as it was a matter of life or death. None of the promises made by Simon the night before had been broken. Simon then sealed it with his ring, 'a secret de Quincy mark,' he explained, 'and a mark the Earl cannot ignore.'

The letter was entrusted to Laurence to deliver into the hands of Earl Robert himself in Leuchars. Before he left, Simon spoke to him at length in his own language, giving him his exact instructions. When he spoke quickly, it was impossible for any of us to understand a single word.

'But how do you know the Earl is there?' John asked miserably. 'I had not heard that he was back from the Crusade.'

'He's there all right,' Simon replied confidently. 'I was speaking to some pilgrims yesterday who were returning from St Andrews. They said they had seen the Earl on the road to Leuchars.'

As we were preparing to leave Ecclesmaline, Murdoch the bailie came up to us. He stood staring at us, scratching his head, saying nothing, waiting for us to speak.

'Hae ye tint yer tongue an aa?' Simon snarled at him. Murdoch's brown face went dark red. He shook his head. I blushed, too, at Simon's cruelty. 'An gin ye're speirin yersel whit fur A'm hirplin, A fell owr a sack o aits lest nicht. Noo gie us a hand up ontae this cuddy.'

If I had been Murdoch I would have given him a hand over the horse and onto the ground at the other side. But it would have been more than Murdoch's life was worth. Sullenly he obeyed. Once Simon was on the horse, he looked down at Murdoch and said, 'A dinnae think ye'll be hearin muckle mair fae the men fae Lochore. But gin ye dae, Brother Simon wants tae hear aboot it. Dae ye understan?'

Murdoch nodded slowly, casting a frightened glance at Brother John.

We set off along the road which led south west, towards the coast to Barnhill and the Priory. We went slowly. Simon rode on our one horse as it was impossible now for him to walk more than a few feet. We often stopped to dip his bandages in cold water, for cold water is very good for bringing down bad swellings. I had learnt that from Brother Maurice.

We had just stopped by a spring near Auchtertool. Brother John was sitting on a stone beside the road, staring glumly into space. Simon and I were down beside the spring. I was unwrapping the bandages to dip them into the cool water.

'Do you think the Earl will act quickly enough?' I asked voicing the worry that had been besetting me all morning.

'Eh?' Simon said crossly. 'What are you talking about? God, but this ankle hurts!'

'Do you think Earl Robert will get John's family out quickly enough, before Sir Philip.....'

Simon sighed. 'Michael, are you really so stupid, or do you just do it to plague me? Do you think my proud uncle would do anything to please one of his younger brother's bastards? My God, if I had his ear to that extent, I wouldn't be stuck out on that accursed island.' Then fixing me with his dark eyes he said quietly, 'If I ever approach my uncle, it will be to crave a favour for me, not for the relations of some poxy thief.'

I jumped up as though I had been stung by a wasp. 'Calm down,' he said, 'and keep that to yourself. Pick up those bandages, they're going to float down the burn.'

I quickly walked over to Brother John and laid my hand on his shoulder. I could hear Simon calling me back, but I ignored him. John looked up at me as he had just wakened up out of a deep sleep. I opened my mouth to speak, but no words came. What was there to say? There was no turning back his accusation. If he did not accuse, Simon would accuse for him, and I could not deny that I had heard him speak the accusing words. Should I tell him to run away now and warn his family? But what could his family do? If they tried to run away without the protection of a lord, they would be caught and sent back to Sir Philip within the day. They would not even make it to the mountains, the only place beyond the reach of the barons. So all I could do was to shatter Brother John's only hope.

'What is it, Brother Michael?' he asked meekly. 'Is there

something troubling you?' I shook my head and walked back to Simon. He was scowling at me. I rescued the bandages from the burn and tied them round his ankle, jerking them tight so that he cried out in pain.

Do you now see, Martin, the kind of man Brother Simon was? See it clearly, hold it in your mind, never forget it. Do not be like me, who could never hold it in my mind, always blinded by what I then thought was love, but I know now to be lust.

I will spare you the terrible details of what happened next. Brother John in full Chapter accused not only Brother Henry of theft and fraud, but also Brother Luke the almoner, who it turned out had been Henry's accomplice from the beginning. Much of what we thought we had been giving in charity to the poor had in fact been ending up with the other stolen grain at Lochore.

Brother Henry sat through the accusations grinding his teeth with rage. But he did not deny them. He was flogged, defrocked and thrown out of our Order. We could not brand him, his blood was too noble for that, his kin too powerful. But we wrote letters to all the convents of our Order throughout the kingdom, warning them not to accept him as a postulant.

Brother Luke, too, was flogged, defrocked and thrown out, but we did not have to go to the trouble of writing warnings about him. His flesh was base enough to brand, and he left us with the sign of the thief forever on his forehead.

As for Brother John, he was stripped of his office and ordered to fast for forty days. He was not branded, nor was he expelled, to this extent Simon's promises held good. But the Devil had much worse in store for Brother John. A week after Brother Henry had been thrown off the island, news came that John's whole family was dead. A band of armed men had swept down on them one night and burnt them alive in their house, mother, father, brothers, sisters, nephews, nieces. The grief was too much for Brother John, whose wits were already weakened by fasting. At dawn the day after the news had reached the Priory, Brother Peter the sacristan found his broken body at the foot of the tower."

CHANGING. OFFICES

"The exposing of Brother Henry's crimes against the convent was a triumph for Simon, and a small part of the glory was reflected onto me. It might have made me proud, had I not felt the death of Brother John and his family weigh heavily upon my soul.

Now we needed not only a new cellarer, but also a new kitchener-almoner and a granger. Simon was appointed cellarer, which surprised no one, and pleased most. Brother David was made granger to replace Brother John, and I was made kitchener-almoner to replace Brother Luke.

Simon threw himself into his new office with great enthusiasm. Throughout that first winter [1193-1194] we ate better than we had ever done before. An abundance of all sorts of food was delivered to my kitchen every day.

Then around the Epiphany Subprior Brice resigned office. He had been unhappy at the changes in the Priory over recent years: the introduction of meat into our diet three times a week, the shorter Hours in church, the increase in the number of our servants. He had also been very shaken by Brother Henry's terrible crimes, for they had been kinsmen and had known each other since childhood. The company of his fellow-men had become unbearable: he requested permission to withdraw from the convent and live as a hermit in our cell in the wood of Kilrie.

Prior Walter gladly granted him this, with food and fuel, as well as a servant to look after him until he died. None of us thought that Subprior Brice would be in this world much longer.

But who was going to take his place? Two names more than any others were being whispered: Father Geoffrey the precentor and Brother Andrew the subsacrist. Prior Walter was believed to favour Brother Andrew. He already relied heavily on him for knowledge of what was going on in the hearts and minds of his sons. For Walter, you see, Andrew's tale-telling was a useful virtue. Andrew knew the Rule better than anyone except Brice, and rejoiced to see it obeyed. This alone made him a suitable candidate for Subprior.

If anyone had asked my opinion, I would have said that he rejoiced more in seeing the Rule broken, but no one did ask, and so I kept silent. This was always the safest course of action at times like this, because you could be sure that whatever you said would come to the winning candidate's ears, and then there were a myriad ways in which he could make you regret your words.

Brother Andrew had another quality which made him even more suitable for the office. He was not afraid of being unpopular. In a Subprior this quality is the key to all the rest. I was not alone in fearing Andrew as Subprior, and many were the prayers that begged God and St Columba to change Walter's heart.

The other candidate, Father Geoffrey, was very different. He was a bad-tempered old soul, but good-hearted and no lover of tittle-tattle. He was no lover of Brother Andrew either.

There were those who supported Andrew because they knew it would please Walter, the flatterers and the toadies like young Brother Matthew, or those who were ploughing their own furrow like Brother Simon. Others, like old Brother Robert and Brother Peter, said we had no right even to have an opinion about it, let alone talk about it. Our part was merely to accept whatever God gave us through the Prior. God's will be done, amen.

The rest of us, especially Brother Maurice and Brother David, as well as Father William and Father Serlo, the two priests nearby on the mainland, believed that we should appoint Geoffrey, as he was mature, literate, eloquent, skilled in the cure of souls, not in their disease. Furthermore he had had the experience of keeping good discipline in the choir for the past twenty-five years. 'Trust the experienced master', as the divinely inspired Virgil says.

The others grumbled against us, saying that Geoffrey was bad-tempered, impatient, quarrelsome, a disturber of the peace, and they made snide remarks such as, 'You recognise a man's wisdom from his patience.' Also they said that he would not be hard enough on special friendships, which Brice had always been very good at rooting out. Andrew, they said, would be even better.

We countered by saying that Andrew was practically illiterate, and it would be a great set-back for the Priory if it became known that we were promoting such an ignoramus as Andrew over the head of such a learned man as Geoffrey. This would mean that in future literate clerks with an interest in learning would shun us.

We also argued that whoever became our Subprior would be our Prior whenever Walter was away, which was happening more and more frequently. Andrew, we said, was too young and too inexperienced for this weighty office. He had only just become old enough to be a priest.

So the secret debates went on, whispered in the cloister, spoken in the garden, shouted in the fields, but chiefly debated at the blood-letting, when we are most able to exchange opinions and secret thoughts. In our hearts, however, we all knew that Walter's will would prevail.

At last the day came for the matter to be discussed in Chapter. It was Candlemas [Feb.1194], and the church was full of light, although outside it was grey and dark, even at Terce. Walter commanded that each of us bring from the church a candle into Chapter, so that the blessed light might illuminate our minds and help us see the right way ahead. We stood our candles on the window-sills. I had never seen the chapter house look so bright, not even at the height of summer.

Walter was the first to open the discussion. He spoke at length about the qualities which he was looking for in a Subprior. Then Brother David stood up and said in a loud voice that Geoffrey was a worthy and suitable person, possessing all the most fitting qualities to the greatest degree.

Brother Matthew jumped up shouting, 'No! A man of peace! Give us a man of peace!'

All the candles flickered in the wind he made.

I spoke up, saying that Geoffrey was a good choice, because he was older, more mature, and more experienced in the cure of souls. Did not our Customs say that, just as the Prior is our father, the Subprior is our mother. We must have a mother whom we can all respect.

Walter commanded silence. 'I am vexed,' he said gravely, 'to see that feelings are running high on this matter, and that opinions are so divided, even before I have proposed anyone. After Chapter I will take counsel from all of you individually, and on the basis of what I hear, and with the guidance of the Holy Spirit, I will announce my final decision tomorrow. Then perhaps there will be more light and less heat.'

This was a clever move on Walter's part, for he must have already known that the majority of brothers would support him in his choice of Andrew. But by doing it this way it would not seem such a personal affront to Geoffrey.

The next day in Chapter Walter seemed very upset. He had been unable to sleep that night, he said, so anxious and afraid had he been lest he appoint someone who would be unpleasing to God. Therefore he had decided that he would nominate four of us, who in his opinion would be useful and suitable. First of all he named Peter the Sacrist. This surprised us greatly, not least of all Peter himself, who jumped up and swore by all things holy that he was not suited for the post. No one gainsaid him.

Then he named Brother Maurice the infirmarer, Brother Andrew, and myself. Now this was cruel, because it would simply give people the chance to cast my past sins in my face. Walter spoke at great length on the merits and virtues of Brother Maurice, but said that he did not think we could afford to lose such a skilled medical man from the infirmary. Then why did you nominate him in the first place? I thought to myself.

I was dreading the discussion which would ensue when it

came to my name, when Simon jumped to his feet and shouted, 'My lord Prior, you have first voice. Name Brother Andrew.'

'Yes!' shouted Matthew, like an echo, 'name Brother Andrew!'

Walter turned to Simon and said, 'I will gladly accept Andrew if that is what you want.'

At this many shouted, 'He is a suitable man for the post, and worthy of our love and respect.' The rest of us sat in silence. It felt like a wave was sweeping over us and there was nothing we could do to stop it.

Then Brother Simon walked over to Andrew and led him to the centre of the room. At first he humbly excused himself, saying that he was unequal to such a great dignity. This was standard form. Then he said that his learning was not sufficient to allow him to preach the sermons in Chapter that were expected of a Subprior. This humility is beginning to smack of honesty, I thought to myself with surprise.

Walter was already dismissing this objection, however, saying that Andrew could always memorise the sermons of others. Besides, who needs perfect Latin in a sermon? In some monasteries they were preaching in French nowadays. He had even heard of one where they preach in Scottish. After all, sermons are there for the edification of morals, and not for the display of literary learning.

I thought I could hear another voice in what Prior Walter was saying, for I had never heard him express himself like this before. The voice I could hear was Simon's.

Then Andrew walked over and threw himself at the Prior's feet, saying that unworthy as he was he would accept the burden of the office.

Walter beamed and said, 'May the Lord preserve your going out and your coming in.'

We all replied, 'From this time forth for ever and ever'. Then raising him up Walter placed him in the Subprior's seat at his right hand.

It was difficult for me to accept in my soul that Andrew was my Subprior, but I knew that now I had no choice. So I prayed to God to help me. I had felt hatred and contempt for him for so long that they had etched themselves into my very soul like acid on metal. Whenever I wanted to I could trace their form as fresh as on the first day, remembering how he had tried to betray me into the hands of de Mortimer; how he had brought down on my head double punishment for my sins in Rome; how he had taunted me with my love for Edgar in Scone. The list was long, each remembered hurt making the flame of my hatred burn stronger. But now these flames must be doused, or they would scorch my soul. Now at last I must learn to forgive the wretch, for he had become my Subprior.

'God, Your ways are hard. But it was Your own son who said, "Forgive us our trespasses, as we forgive those that trespass against us." Up until now it has been easy to live with my hate. Now You have made it impossible. Thank you, God.'

So I tried to stand back from myself, my old grudges, my old prejudices, and look at Andrew as if I was meeting him for the first time. As a youth he had looked like a rat, and behaved like one too. No, I had to stop thinking that way, as it just led down the old path. Yes, he had looked like a rat, but over the years his face had filled out. The beard suited him, and in certain lights he could look almost handsome.

He had a good, strong singing voice. He was healthy and young and full of zeal. But he was malicious, petty, full of envy. He was a menace, and he hated me with as much passion as I hated him, with his whispered jibes, his wicked accusations, his beady eyes, always watching, always waiting for that slip of the foot, that slip of the soul, which he could then broadcast like seed before our brothers. I became afraid, and the days ahead looked dark and forbidding, for who would protect me against his wickedness?

Then I had to start from the beginning once more, for all my good thoughts had been burnt out of me again by the flame of my hate.

Then another pang came to my breast, not hate this time, but envy, for was he not ages with me? Had we not been novices together? Had I not in fact been in the Priory longer than he had? So what made him so special, apart from his tale-telling? Why could I not have been nominated, seriously nominated that is, not thrown in as part of some kind of trick.

Subprior Michael! Don't be absurd, I thought. You don't care enough about the faults of your brothers. You say too often that it is between themselves and their Maker. If I don't care about their faults, perhaps it means that I don't care about them, don't love them enough. For does not the Rule say, 'If your brother has a wound in his body which he wishes to keep concealed because he is afraid of an operation, would not your silence be cruel, and your speech merciful? How much more then should you not give information, to prevent the rottenness in his heart becoming worse?'

Perhaps I hope that if I remain silent about the faults of others, others will care less about my own. Well, whatever the reason, I would not make a good Subprior. Besides, I want too much to be liked, despite my sins.

Suddenly there before me was Andrew, on his knees, begging my forgiveness for all the wrongs he had done me, weeping, apologising. 'Honours change characters,' he said between sobs. 'This honour will surely change mine. I will be a good Subprior to you, and to all my brothers, because I now no longer envy you.'

I smiled a smile full of compassion and understanding, and raising him up gave him the kiss of peace and said that I forgave him and would love and respect him as my new mother in Christ. And then I opened my eyes and the choir was empty, and the voices of the pilgrims in the nave were a distant murmur.

No, I said to myself, I will wait before I judge our new Subprior. Wait and pray.

What Andrew's ghost had said to me in church was true, when I was wrestling with my hate: honours change characters. But he should have completed it: but rarely for the better. He no longer whispered hateful things to me, nor taunted me with my desires. He now had more important things to do, such as torment the whole convent.

The first year of Andrew's subpriorship was very difficult. As he became less petty, he became more dangerous, more stern and strict, both with others and with himself, subjecting his flesh to fasts and mortifications, urging or compelling others to do the same. His eyes lost their small-minded maliciousness and smouldered with the righteousness kindled in visions of Purgatory, that bright staring which had shone in the eyes of his predecessor, and which still sometimes haunts my dreams.

We had not realised how much Brice had withdrawn from the cloister in the months before his resignation. Suddenly Andrew seemed to be everywhere, creeping around the dormitory at nights lest anyone stir, stalking along the choir stalls with his lantern at Matins lest anyone sleep, prowling the cloister and the garden by day lest anyone let fall idle words from their lips.

My office kept me in the monastery almost constantly. Days would go by and I would not put a foot outside. I would not even know what the weather was like. Once a week, however, I would make a journey to the mainland to distribute the broken meats and excess food and drink amongst the poor.

Whether I was exercising my office as kitchener or almoner, I would see Brother Simon almost every day. Usually he was in a hurry, and preoccupied. But he would contrive to accompany me on my weekly journey to or from the mainland, and we would sit together in the boat, and if chance would have it that no other brother was with us, we would talk and laugh and feel as though the world could not touch us.

My office was beset with difficulties. These were rooted in the squabbling between Brother Simon and Brother David. Brother David was not a stupid man but he was very stubborn, and he was easily roused. Moreover he did not trust anybody, least of all Brother Simon, who took particular delight in thwarting and angering him.

Our Customs are wise, for they say that if the cellarer and the granger do not get on, the goods of the monastery will not be multiplied, the brethren will serve God and the Church with less devotion, and murmurings will be rife.

How true this was! Sometimes in Chapter recriminations between the two of them would be sparked off by a complaint about, say, the quality of the bread or a shortage of beer. And soon bitterness was on every tongue, and the taste was much worse than the worst beer.

It was I who bore the brunt of their dissension, because it was my office that had to cope with the shortages and the uneven flow of stores. One day I put this to Simon when we were crossing to the mainland.

'Be patient, my dear brother,' he said. 'Did I not tell you that one day I would be cellarer and you would be my granger? Nothing comes to us in this life without our sweating for it. But just you wait, within a year we will be working together. Then we will show them how to run a monastery, eh?'

Then under the cover of our copes he squeezed my leg, and I began to understand the game he was playing.

By the following Lent [1195] Simon had got his way. Brother David was moved to the kitchen and I was appointed granger. David was furious, for he was now completely subordinate to Simon. But the kitchen is a good place if one has pain or anger, for in its heat and its busyness they dissolve. I know this because I took with me into that office the pain and the anger, at myself and at Simon, about the death of Brother John and the slaughter of his family. I came out with a dark but distant memory.

What did I want at this time? I certainly wanted out of the kitchen, but I was afraid of leaving the cloister. The world seemed a very big and dangerous place, both for the body and for the soul. I knew that Simon had more at heart than the good of our lands when he had imagined us working together, him as cellarer, me as granger. This knowledge was always there, like the sigh of the sea or the chant of the gulls.

'Lead us not into temptation', I would pray, often and fervently, but I did not dare approach Prior Walter with my concern. If I had done, he would certainly have granted my prayer and kept me in the cloister. Sometimes our desires are deeper even than our prayers. That is one of the many ways in which the Devil mocks us.

For the next two summers I was more on the mainland than I was in the Priory, moving from estate to estate; hearing Mass and saying the Hours whenever I could, in whatever church or chapel lay at hand; sleeping in cottages and granges; eating with the stewards or the tenants of our lands, whose duty it was to feed me. Only once every few weeks I would return to the Priory to report on the state of our lands and to confess the sins that I had gathered like mud along the way. Often Simon would ride out to meet me on one of our estates to discuss planting or breaking new ground or stock-breeding or harvesting.

My life has never run smoothly or easily. Whatever road I have gone down it has always seemed that a demon was spinning some invisible thread across my path which would catch at my feet and hold me back. And so it was during my time as granger. It might have been a fine time, with the security and comfort of my Priory at my back, and in front of me the world of spring and summer, when the world should be kind and beautiful.

However, shortly after I had become granger, clouds darkened the sun and rains began to fall. It was the start of the worst weather that I have ever known, evil weather that lasted for years and brought with it dearth and famine. The price of grain soared in the market place, and with the extra silver we obtained from selling our small surplus we were able to feu new land, and this, too, had to be stocked and supervised.

As always, it was the poor who suffered most. If Simon and David quarrelled about everything else, there was one thing they agreed upon, that the allotment to the poor should be reduced. During those years there must have been many in Fothrif who died the terrible death of starvation cursing our Priory.

I was told to harden my heart, for too much charity abroad would mean hardship for our brothers. Besides, we needed extra silver because, without consulting even Prior Walter, Brother Peter the sacristan had taken out a large new loan to refurbish the church. Pilgrims were still flocking to the shrine of Isaac, but their offerings were paltry, for with every year they had less to give.

Our whole Priory started to stink of greed. In order to cleanse myself of the stink, sometimes as I was taking grain to market I would allow a sack to fall off the back of the cart beside a cottage with a swarm of half-naked, half-starved children at its door, and I would forbid the servants to look back.

No one could remember anything like it before, not even old Brother Robert. There had been floods and droughts and shortages aplenty, but God had always sent a gentle, fruitful time to follow. Now God was piling one bad year upon the next, and there seemed to be no end to the suffering.

It was not just Scotland that was suffering. Travellers returning from all parts of Christendom brought with them the same dreadful stories. In France, it was said, the poor roamed the land in great armies, looting and pillaging. Even the houses of God were not safe.

It is at such times that men and women should look to the state of their souls and repent of their sins, for nothing is sent from God without a reason, either the good or the bad. But times of hardship, want, and fear of want, breed more sin, and the rain that beat down month after month, summer after summer, caused strange humours to rise in the world and in those who lived in it.

When I first became granger no one could have suspected that such fearful days lay ahead, and the first spring was glorious. It gave me the strength to resist the snares that Simon placed in my path, for he was trying to tempt me to the sin that we had fallen into in Rome, which, like a cat, had been stalking us ever since his arrival on the island.

However, when the rains started everything began to slip and slide. Even my faith seemed less sure. They were dark days indeed, when I became as a lost sheep on the moors.

Like a lost sheep I took shelter wherever I could find it. And it was on the moors, high above our estate at Bothedlach, that Simon once again opened his arms to me and offered me the shelter that my soul thirsted after. You shelter in a cave from a raging storm. Later you might find that in the cave lives a poisonous snake, but it does not lessen the first sweetness of that shelter.

We had climbed the high hill to look down upon our new land at Clune. It had been feued to us by Sir Philip of Lochore as part of the settlement we had extracted from him after the Brother Henry affair. It was good land, although it flooded easily, and it adjoined our own land of Bothedlach. It was the land where the family of Brother John had lived. It was land that had drunk blood.

The clouds hung low, almost touching the crest of Benarty, and rain streamed steadily down. There was not a breath of wind. Nothing stirred. It was as if we were standing on the bed of a loch, looking up to the grey surface above our heads, and all the trees were giant water-weeds. The only sound was the gurgling of a thousand burns.

'We're going to have to deepen the drainage ditches over there,' Simon said, pointing to the land nearest the side of Loch Ore. 'Otherwise we're going to lose it.'

'We're going to lose everything anyway,' I replied glumly. 'The old people are saying the rain is going to last at least till the harvest.'

'It's nothing that a bit of sun won't give us back next year,' Simon said cheerfully. 'Have you no faith in our prayers?'

'Sometimes I wonder if I have any faith at all,' I said, and my words echoed in the emptiness that was in me.

'Is it as bad as that, Brother Michael?' Simon said, taking my arm. 'Is this your dark night of the soul? Well, it comes to us all at some time or other.'

He spoke gently, without mocking. Suddenly tears welled up from deep inside me, and I could not hold them back. They were tears for my loneliness, my emptiness, for the suffering of the land and the suffering of my heart.

'Come, come,' Simon said, 'tears will just make the rain worse.'

I clung to his arm. I felt I could not go another step alone.

A small sheiling stood nearby and Simon led me towards it.

Inside it was dry and cool and the air was thick with the smell of mouldy hay. I sat down on a log by the door. Simon sat beside me. I leant against him and he put his arms round me. My sadness became a longing that swept through me like a storm wind, and I had to cling to Simon so as not to be blown away. The same wind seemed to sweep through him, and we clung together in the storm, seeking comfort from each other. So it began, like shelter in the storm, warmth in the cold, food in the famine.

When it was all over we lay quietly, still holding each other, and the smell of rotting hay was like a sweet perfume. I felt that there was nothing else in the world, Heaven, or Hell, but this humble hut and the water that drip-dripped from the roof, and the mice that rustled and scuttled in the corners. A peace enveloped my soul, a peace so deep and thick that nothing could penetrate it, no guilt, or shame, or terror. And when we finally stepped outside the rain had stopped and a pale sun was struggling to be seen behind the thinning clouds.

This peace, like all earthly peace, did not last, and soon I was plagued by a swarm of doubts and fears. And so the next time Simon sought me out I declared I would not go with him. No, I would not go. And I told him that as soon as I returned to the Priory I was going to confess our sin to Prior Walter.

Yet Simon had a tongue of silver. He had all his arguments ready, like sharpened quills, and I could not argue back, because all these arguments he had written on my soul in Rome. They were still there, deeply scratched, time and guilt had not been able to erase them, and my fingers could read them, even if my eyes could not. It was like following the beads of a rosary in the dark. Had they not led me to Edgar, and to the wood, and to the heights of love, both carnal and spiritual?

In case I wavered from Simon's certainty he made me swear by St Columba that I would not confess, and he told me that a perjured oath was a far greater sin than two bodies finding pleasure in one another. Why, it was like taking an extra dish at meal time. There were greater sins to worry about, like neglecting the well-being of the Priory, or perjuring one's self.

Subprior Andrew was very worried about the spiritual well-being of his brothers. He was particularly worried about the demons of lust that lurk in lonely places.

He had obtained Prior Walter's permission to forbid two brothers to be alone together at any time, except in church. If it ever happened, they were to confess it in Chapter. If it was clear that it had not been their fault, and that nothing untoward had taken place, then no punishment would be meted out. But changes would then be made in the structure of their day and their duties, so that it would not happen again. If it did, and the same two brothers were involved, the punishment was flogging and forty days fasting. However, this punishment was considerably reduced if one of the brothers involved had previously brought to justice one of his fellows for the same fault. Otherwise no mercy was shown.

With Prior Walter away on Church business more and more often, there was no one who could effectively moderate Andrew's zeal. Needless to say neither Simon nor I ever told our brothers about the times we were alone together. It always happened a long way from the Priory, and we were very careful that there were no zealous or jealous eyes anywhere near.

In those days I felt closer to Simon than I had ever done before, and never again would I feel as close. It was as if we had created a world which belonged only to us, a world within a world, which would shatter into a thousand pieces if it ever touched the larger world outside it.

On the few occasions when I would attend Chapter, Subprior Andrew would be preaching a sermon on carnal knowledge, naming all the demons of lust that haunted him. It was then that the secret world that I shared with Simon would be sweetest, matched only by the sweetness of lying in his arms.

When I look back on those days, it is as if the clouds that covered the land had sealed off our deeds from the eye of God, just as our own cunning sealed us off from the prying eyes of our brothers.

How could I have trusted such a man, I can hear you ask yourself. How could I have risked my eternal soul for him, knowing even then what I knew?

I answer you that I do not know. There were clouds in my soul as well as over the earth. And rain, day after day, grey sunlessness which seemed to last for ever, these things trailed strange humours after them like mist. But whatever the reason, trust him I did. Besides, after our bodies had known each other again, who else was there I could trust?

Nevertheless, during the winter, when the rains abated, and I had to live again amongst my brothers, things seemed very different. It was as if in the cloister my conscience, that precious child of our Holy Mother Church, was waiting for me. And all that winter we wrestled, my conscience and I, and I swore that the next summer I would move my friendship with Simon from the carnal to the spiritual.

We had shared the secrets of our bodies. Now we must share the secrets of our souls. Now our love must move onwards and upwards. Many an hour I spent in church, praying and singing to the Lord, reaching out again to touch that love that is greater than all human loves.

Once, and only once, that winter I found myself alone with him for a short while, despite the vigilance of our Subprior. I whispered to him then what my hope was for the following summer, that we would bare our souls to each other more than our bodies. He gave me his most withering smile, as one would smile at a foolish child.

'We'll see about that', he replied, and bent towards me.

I thought he was going to kiss me, but instead he bit my ear so hard that I gave a little cry, and I feared for our friendship, and our souls."

HARVESTS

"In the spring the rains returned, and I was again out in the world, and trying not to see the fear in the eyes of the people as they gazed at the sky and contemplated another year like the last.

As I moved from estate to estate I would see the woods and hills and secret places where Simon and I had lain with each other, and soon I was aching for him, body and soul, and my eyes were searching the highways in the hope that they would bring him to me.

When he finally came, he did not come alone. With him was Lay-brother Laurence, sporting a trim black beard, and looking very handsome.

Why had Simon brought him? He never used to bring a servant along with him to our trysts the previous year. It had meant one fewer pair of eyes we had to avoid.

Simon left me in no doubt. This summer, he told me, Laurence would always be by his side. He stressed the word always. This summer we would talk only of crops and land and animals. As he spoke these words, casually, with a slight smile, it felt as though he was twisting a knife in my heart.

Yes, he had done it again. I had trusted him, and he had betrayed me. I had leant towards him, and he had walked away. It was as if my spirit had touched fire and shrunk to a hard and brittle lump. But it still glowed darkly with the heat of jealousy, every time I looked at Simon and Laurence together.

Jealousy is a demon who takes our sentiments, skins them, then rubs salt into their gaping wounds. It is a tongue of fire from Hell itself. But demons do not come alone, and there was another that would prick my tortured soul every time I looked at Laurence, and that was the demon of envy. Yes, I was jealous of Laurence, but I was also envious of Simon.

Then one night when we lay at Leny, I was sleeping alone in the hut built on to our great barn there, I was woken by a loud rustling in the straw. Still half asleep, I imagined some monstrous creature about to leap on me, and I stiffened with terror. Then I heard my name being whispered. I recognised the voice immediately. It was Simon.

He had come to talk to me, but it was not to share the secrets of his life and his soul, it was to pour obscenities into my ear. I lay there as one without the power to move, without the will to move. I was like the rabbit which comes face to face with the weasel. I could not even tell him to go away.

He told me what he and Laurence were doing together, what happened when their bodies came close. He told me everything, every detail. And I am ashamed to tell you that he set my flesh on fire, and I lay there groaning with the pain of it all, of jealousy and envy, of lust and loss.

All I could stammer was, 'Why are you doing this to me? Why are you torturing me like this?'

He would not answer me, but the stream of his filth flowed on. I reached out to touch him, to discover if he was really flesh and blood, for perhaps it was an incubus. He grasped my hand and squeezed it until it hurt. In my despair I wanted to cling to him. There was no one else, Martin, and I was so alone in my burning, so alone that I would have clung even to my torturer, but he would not let me.

Then suddenly I was filled with rage. I found my strength again, I found my will to move. I sprang up and shouted at him, told him to get out and leave me in peace. I let my fist fly into the darkness towards his voice. It smacked against flesh. He made a strange sound that was both a laugh and a cry of pain, and he was gone.

It was as if I had made the sign of the cross in the presence of a demon. I could hear voices outside and one of the grange servants appeared in the door carrying a lantern. I told him it was all right, I had just been visited by the nightmare, but that she was gone and I was at peace.

Yet as I settled down again to sleep I was very far from peace. My flesh still burned with the words that Simon had poured into my ear like drops of molten lead. At last I found peace in sleep, but only after that most shameful of acts. It had begun in shame, and it ended in shame, for he had already pushed me too far along that path. If I could have got to the chapel to pray it might have been different, but it would have meant going through the barn, and I was afraid that Simon and Laurence lay there.

The next morning at Prime Simon greeted me with the kiss of peace as though nothing had happened. If he had not been bruised and swollen around his left eye, I would have said that I had indeed been visited by an incubus with the voice of Simon.

I could not now look at either Simon or Laurence without remembering the obscenities whispered in the night, and without feeling again the tumult that they had brought, both to my soul and to my body. I never wanted to see either of them again, and yet I could not take my eyes off them when they were with me, nor my thoughts off them when they were not.

Yet I was still granger, and Simon was still cellarer, and we still had to work closely together, for if the cellarer and the granger do not work together in harmony, then many ills will befall the whole community. And with the prospect of the famine's tooth biting ever deeper, the last thing we needed was strife amongst the offices of the provender.

All that summer, cold and wet as it was, purgatorial fire consumed me, and I longed for release in oblivion. My love and friendship with Simon lay in ruins, my hopes shattered. But I could not stop and weep, I had to go on, for a thousand tasks cried out for my attention. And when the harvest failed for a second time, and the grain rotted on the stalk, and the cattle were dying with strange diseases, I asked myself again and again whether the whole world was being punished for my sins.

It is a strange thing, Martin, when we are deeply troubled and unhappy we are sure that neither the angels nor the world care about us, and yet at the same time we believe that the well-being of creation hinges upon us. What foolish worms we are.

Then winter finally came, cruel and harsh, and my tasks became fewer, and I was living amongst my brothers again. But instead of bringing greater peace, it brought greater pain, as I had less to distract me from my grief.

One day in Chapter Simon asked permission to confess his sins to Subprior Andrew. Every day during Advent he wanted to bare his soul 'to the healing balm of God's mercy and forgiveness as dispensed by holy Father Andrew.'

All day my thoughts raged around this request, and that night in the dorter sleep would not come to me. I was tortured by double jealousy. In summer Simon had forsaken me to share his body with Laurence, and now in winter he had chosen to share his soul with Andrew, whom we had both considered our enemy.

Yet even stronger than jealousy was rage, at Simon, and at myself. Then, as I tossed and turned on my pallet, a voice spoke, loudly and clearly. It was my angel of truth. We all have our own angel of truth that speaks to us often, but it is rarely granted to us to heed their words.

The voice said, 'You wanted a friend who would replace your brother Edgar, a friend bound to you body and soul by never-ending bonds of love. 'Deep in your heart you knew that Simon could never be that friend. You wanted a spiritual friendship with Simon so that you could cloak your lust in a fine and spotless-seeming garment.

'You remember what old Brother Edwin said about the three forms of love. Well, your friendship with Simon could never have been anything more than a carnal love, a love founded on the shifting sands of the body's desires. But you pretended it was something more so that you would not have to see it as sin.

'That was your sin, Michael, and that alone, not what you did with your body, but what you did with your soul, pretending there was something higher, nobler, greater than there really was. This is why you are suffering now.'

I cried out and put my hands over my ears to try to stop the voice, but it cut through into my soul like a knife. I started to weep — deep, heart-rending sobs for the love that I suddenly saw had never existed, for a love that was nothing more than my body's deception of my soul.

For the first time I felt the need to confess, because for the first time I saw clearly the sin I had to confess, not what Simon and I had done together, but what I had done to myself through Simon.

Who could I confess to? Who would understand? There was no one in the Priory, except perhaps Father Geoffrey, but confessing to him was like confessing in Chapter, as he was so deaf you had to shout to make him hear.

No, there was no hurry, I would bide my time, and in the meantime I would confess to God, and He would give me fitting penance.

Suddenly a light loomed up out of the darkness and a harsh voice whispered, 'What on earth is the matter with you, Brother Michael? You'll wake the whole convent.'

It was Brother David, who was circitator for that week. I thought I had been stifling my tears, but they would not be stifled. For too long they had wanted to flow, and now there was no stopping them. I stuffed the rough blanket into my mouth and pulled my hood over my head. I did not want to speak to anybody. But Brother David was insistent.

'What is it? Are you all right?'

'It was just a dream,' I managed to gasp between sobs, 'such a sad dream, but it's all right, it's over now.' And I started sobbing even more violently.

'Well, if you can't stop that noise,' the voice behind the light said, 'you're going to have to go to the church. The Holy Spirit wakes there always and will dry your tears. This is a place of sleep. Come on, I'll light your way.'

So it was that I spent most of that night in the church. I did not seek out the High Altar, or the altar of St Columba, but I knelt beside the tomb of my friend Isaac, and I poured out to him my troubled soul.

His presence comforted me, as it had done so often when he had been alive, and I heard his laugh in the waves that washed the island beyond the church wall, and I saw his kind, sensible eyes shining in the candles.

My brother Isaac was no saint, but there was some kind of miracle wrought at his tomb that night, for the next morning when I saw Brother Simon at Prime, I felt as cold to him as he had come to be towards me, and I could look on the beauty of his face without a terrible pinching in my heart. And the tongue of flame called jealousy had returned to Hell.

I filled my winter with fasting and penance. Fasting was easy because every time I took a piece of food in my hand I saw the eyes of the starving staring reproaches at me from the shadows. I began to feel less stained with sin, but as my soul grew stronger, my body grew weaker, until finally I fell ill and had to be carried to the infirmary with a raging fever.

While I lay ill I begged Prior Walter to remove me from my office of granger. I used the excuse of my poor health. I did not mention Simon's name at all. Walter was reluctant at first, but finally agreed that for the following summer at least I would be allowed to stay in the Priory. I asked if I might return to my copying. He said he would pray about it, but let me hope that it would be so. He must have heard the desperation in my voice.

Young Brother Hugh was made granger in my stead, and once again I felt safe within the refuge and the strength of the Lord. I hardly left the Priory, and was allowed to spend much of my time in the scriptorium.

Also, although Subprior Andrew prowled ceaselessly in search of sin, bringing no peace to himself or others, I was safe in my own righteousness, for I kept my eyes cast down and my thoughts to myself. And if incubi came to me in the night with the eyes of Simon or the form of Laurence, and made my body do shameful things, how could I be to blame for that?

At last the sun returned, after three summers of rain and three winters of famine, to dry the land and bring forth crops for the starving. It was the year of our Lord 1198. Every day that summer we prayed for the good weather to stay with us, and whenever black clouds gathered and rain fell, the whole convent would hurry to the church.

Harvest time drew nearer and nearer. The corn was standing high and full. But fear filled every heart until the first scythes cut into the ripe swathes, and the carts started taking the stooks towards the barns. Yet even with the best of harvests, it would take several years for the fear of the Third Horseman to fade from the hearts of the people.

The harvest was over by the feast of St Giles. The whole convent was to be present at a thanksgiving service and feast on our acres at Barnhill when the last standing corn of the harvest would be cut, what we call in Fothrif cutting the neck.

Pagan things were done at such times, especially when the people were afraid. Once at harvest-time when I was a boy I had seen a hare being sacrificed and its blood scattered on the fields. When I told my father he had frowned and said that little boys who told such tales would end up like the hare.

Whatever the Priory and the local priests did, such things would happen. But at least after our service the spirit of Christ would be strong and the demons that some of the people put their trust in would be kept at bay. And after the feast, most of the people would fall asleep, because Brother Simon had ordered several casks of strong ale to be broached.

The service was to be after Sext. Subprior Andrew had gone over to the mainland after Chapter to make sure everything was in readiness. Brother Simon was already there, as during harvest he often slept at Barnhill.

There are several granaries and storehouses at Barnhill, as it is where all the provisions for the Priory are stored. They are, of course, all kept carefully locked. There are two bunches of keys. The cellarer has one, while the Prior keeps the other in his scriptoriolum.

All that morning our servants, tenants and lay-brothers had been working in the fields around Barnhill, gathering the last of the corn, so that by the time the convent arrived, only the neck would remain.

It was a hot day, with hardly a cloud in the sky, and only the faintest breath of wind. The whole convent crossed the Deep together, using all our boats. We landed in Barnhill Bay, where the tide was low so we had to wade ashore onto the flat sand. The cold water around our feet was refreshing. We could see on the hillside overlooking the bay the crowd that had gathered for the service and the feast. They formed a large half circle around the neck, which stood up like a tuft of hair on a bald pate; while down by the shore we could see the barrels of ale and the piles of food, which two servants were zealously guarding from the attentions of dogs and children.

Brother Simon had been waiting by the shore to greet us. He informed Prior Walter that everything was ready, and that when Subprior Andrew arrived, the service could begin. Prior Walter said that we should form ourselves into a procession at once, and move off as soon as the Subprior appeared. We stood on the cool, damp sand, in the hot sun, waiting.

As I was one of the more senior members of the convent I had taken my place near the rear of the procession, not far from Prior Walter. Although Brother Simon should have been further forward, Prior Walter had asked him to be beside him at the very back. I heard him mutter to Simon, 'Where on earth is our Subprior? Was he not with you, Brother Simon?'

'I have not seen him since he arrived this morning,' I heard Simon reply. 'We talked about the arrangements for this afternoon, then I had to go and supervise the transport of the ale and the food. He said he had business to do in Dalgety. He said he would be back in good time for the service.'

'What business would he have in Dalgety?' Walter exclaimed.

'My lord Prior,' Simon replied, 'you know that wherever there is moral laxness there is business for our Subprior. I believe he had heard of some fornication in Dalgety, and he wanted to talk with the vicar there about ways of rooting it out.'

Prior Walter sighed. 'Very well. Let us sing Psalm 17. If he has not appeared by the finish we will start the service without him. But it really is most annoying. There will always be fornication in Dalgety. There will not always be a service such as this.'

He summoned three of the servants who were waiting by the boats just behind us and sent them along the coast towards Dalgety. One of them he sent up to the granges at Barnhill Point, in case Subprior Andrew had been delayed there. Everyone was restless. The sun was getting hotter. The tide was coming in quickly, so we had to keep shuffling forward.

This is typical of our Subprior, I thought to myself crossly. Not content with mortifying his own flesh, he has to mortify the flesh and the spirits of us all.

'Precentor Geoffrey!' Walter's voice rang out harshly. 'Diligam te, Domine, fortitudo mea. To the end.' We struck up the psalm, and slowly, as measured as the waves, we swept through it. The crowd on the hill-side fell on their knees. They thought the service had begun.

We had almost finished the long psalm and Subprior Andrew had still not appeared. Suddenly out of the corner of my eye I caught sight of Duff, one of the servants whom Walter had sent to search for him. He was running silently over the rocks beneath Barnhill Point. As soon as he reached the flat sand he started shouting and waving his arms.

The word he was shouting was, 'Murder!'

The procession wavered and broke, and soon the whole convent was streaming towards Barnhill Point, the youngest and most agile to the fore.

I was one of the first to arrive. Duff led the way to the smallest of the storehouses, where our most costly goods were kept. The door was ajar. Inside on the floor lay a brother, face down, the back of his head and neck broken and bleeding. We turned him over. It was Subprior Andrew. He was dead. He had been dead for some time, because he was already stiff and cold. Beside him on the floor lay a sickle, covered in blood.

Duff told us that the door of the storehouse had been shut but not locked. He would never have thought of looking inside if a dog had not been whining and scratching outside. It could smell the blood. Clasped in the hand of the dead man was the

Prior's bunch of keys. Later Brother Simon informed us that a side of bacon had been stolen, nothing else.

By the following day it was clear to us who had killed our Subprior. Lay-brother Laurence, Simon's servant, had disappeared. No one could remember seeing him since the morning of Andrew's death.

When after a week he still had not appeared, he was solemnly declared the perpetrator of the dreadful crime and cursed and excommunicated. Then the King's Sheriff proclaimed him an outlaw

The convent talked of nothing else for weeks.

'I've always been afraid of that great bear.'

'The Subprior must have caught him stealing red-handed.'

'But how did he get in there in the first place? He didn't have the key. No, he must have taken the bacon some other time, and when he saw Subprior Andrew go into the storeroom he knew his crime was about to be discovered, so he followed him in and...'

'But Andrew wouldn't have known if there was a side of bacon missing. He didn't know what was in the store.'

'Ah, yes, but Laurence didn't know that. You know how the lay-brothers think we know everything.'

'Poor fools!'

'Well, that's what comes of allowing pagan rites to be practised on the lands of St Columba.'

'Perhaps it was a pagan rite, and Laurence had been hired by some baron or other to make a blood-sacrifice. You know what some of the barons are like.'

'Lady de Mortimer, for example. I wouldn't put it past her. She's probably hiding him in her bed-chamber.'

So it went on, day after day, yet few could completely hide their relief at the absence of Andrew from the daily life of the convent.

Brother Simon had his own ideas about what had happened. He said to me at the blood-letting one day, 'You know, Brother Michael, I think our holy Subprior tried to seduce young Laurence, and Laurence wasn't having any of it. Then Andrew started threatening all sorts of terrible things, and Laurence lost his head and hit him with the first thing that came to hand.'

I looked at him in disbelief, and he winked at me.

'I've always had my suspicions about Andrew,' he went on, 'all that talk of demons of lust waiting to leap out in lonely places. I think there was a demon of lust lurking in that storehouse. The trouble was, it had a sickle in its hand.'

'You're disgusting,' I said. 'Have you no respect for the memory of the dead? And he was your confessor, too.'

'Of course I have respect for him. I think he was showing extremely good taste. But it's a pity Laurence is not around any more. I miss him.'

'I don't want to hear any more of this,' I said. I suddenly felt sick, and it was not just on account of the bleeding.

So once again we were without a Subprior, and once again the discussions started, the opinions, the arguments. Some eyes turned again to Father Geoffrey, but they saw only an old man with trembling hands and sight which was failing as fast as the light on a winter's day. Most eyes turned towards Brother Simon, the trusted cellarer, who had carried out his duties so well, who was such a support to Prior Walter in all practical and financial matters.

'But what about his discipline?' some said. 'He's a bit slack. Should he not be receiving discipline, rather than dispensing it? Are we not putting our feet on the slippery slope by appointing such a man our Subprior?'

'God preserve us from would-be saints!' another said. 'We've had more than enough of them recently.'

Prior Walter made his choice clear to everyone by sending Simon to represent us at Bishop Roger's consecration. And when on Simon's return Walter announced in Chapter that our new Subprior would be Simon, and did anyone have anything in their heart that spoke against him, we all said 'Amen' and shrugged our shoulders, for we knew it was inevitable.

I had many things in my heart that spoke against him, but they were between myself and my Maker. Perhaps if I had spoken out I could have averted much evil. But what words could I have used to express my misgivings, without condemning myself at the same time?

I was not the only one who felt doubt but kept silent. A few days later at the blood-letting I overheard Brother Hugh asking Brother David what he thought of our new Subprior.

'I think,' David had replied, 'that like the frogs in the fable we would have been better appointing a log of wood to rule over us rather than a serpent that hisses so finely, but will devour us all in the end. He's devoured some of us already.'

The death of Subprior Andrew brought many changes in the Priory. One of them was that I was removed from the scriptorium and pushed into the office of cellarer. It was very difficult. I already knew its duties well, from the outside, but it is one thing to understand a job from the outside, it is quite another thing to be doing it oneself.

Simon had made it seem all so effortless. I found that it took every ounce of my effort and my skills, and still it demanded more. I had little time to think of anything else but keeping the supplies of victual and drink flowing to the kitchen, and of the fuel to the fires and the ovens. Sacks of grain, barrels of beer, and cartloads of firewood were even invading my dreams, and as I sang the Hours and heard Mass, my thoughts were chiefly on cheeses, chickens and salt-fish.

It was not only duties and offices that changed. Simon had changed too. As with every part he was given to play, he played it skillfully and to the full. In his eyes having a lover or two might be all right for a cellarer, as long as his duties were being done well. But a Subprior, now that was something very different.

In the two years since I had returned to the scriptorium Simon had often greeted me with a sweet smile and a mocking twinkle in his eye, as if to say 'You think you're strong, well, just you wait!' And there had been times when I must confess, despite my new-found strength, I might have weakened. But God was merciful and did not provide the opportunity, and Simon's duties kept him away from me most of the time.

Now that Simon was Subprior, however, there were no more smiles. He spoke with me only on Priory business. He kept his distance from us all, except Prior Walter. He did not even join us for the blood-letting. Nor did he acquire any handsome young servant to replace Laurence.

Sometimes he even reprimanded me for not attending the Hours often enough, and using my duties as cellarer as an excuse. I would stare at him in disbelief and look for the twinkle in his eyes. It must be a joke, I thought at first. When Simon was cellarer he used to boast to me about how rarely he attended the Hours. But there was no twinkle, no smile.

I remembered the other times, in Rome, and here in Scotland, when he had suddenly turned away from me when I had wanted him most. And I thanked God that my angel of truth had spoken its warning, and that Isaac had comforted me that long, cold night in the church, and I had found the strength to break free.

For I saw that yet again I could have been deeply hurt as yet again Simon slammed shut the manuscript which bore my name and shoved it aside.

Amongst the cheeses and the salt-fish, it came to me like a vision that Simon was merciless and cared for no one and nothing but himself.

Yet really only half this vision was true, for Brother Simon did care about something other than himself, he cared about the glory and the reputation of the Priory. In fact it was not the Priory of St Columba which had adopted Simon de Quincy when he arrived from Rome, mysteriously ousted from the heart of the Curia. No, it was Simon de Quincy who had adopted the Priory of St Columba.''

DUNFERMLINE

"By the end of that year [1198] we had a new Pope. The last of the old men had died, and now it was the turn of the young. He was a brilliant canon lawyer, who took the name of Innocent and whose power and glory were felt like rays of sun in every corner of Christendom.

Then in the following year, around Easter, good King Richard of England died. I always regret never having met him. They say that he was the most handsome of men, that he loved men more than he loved women, and that he did not care who knew.

Besides, who but the mean-minded would dare speak out against such a brave and generous King, who had spilt his blood in his efforts to regain Jerusalem for Christendom? Who, except his evil brother John, nicknamed Lackland, who had been trying to wrest the throne from him ever since Richard first went to the Holy Land on Christ's business.

Now finally John got his way, because no children had sprung from Richard's loins; though some said that if Richard had sown his seed where it would have grown then John might have stayed Lackland. But others said that it was a blessing that Richard never sired any children, for the children's sake, for pity the child who had John for an uncle, because look what happened to poor Prince Arthur.

Immediately after Richard's death, John sent to King William asking for his support. The King sent a delegation, consisting of Prior Walter and Sir William de Hay, to tell John that he was prepared to give him his support in return for Northumberland and Cumberland, which he regarded as his hereditary right. John prevaricated and William flew into a fury, declaring that if John did not hand the lands over, he would take them by force. John haughtily ignored this threat and King William began summoning the host.

So in the summer of 1199 we were teetering on the brink of war with England, and every day our prayers for peace rose to Heaven.

War is a terrible thing, Martin. It is the Second Horseman, the greatest of the curses that we brought down upon ourselves when we lost Eden. It is the men and women of God who see the worst of it. We are the ones who have to look after those maimed and mutilated by war. They say it is for honour and justice and all the virtues that our masters fight. Yet when you look at it carefully and thoughtfully it is always greed that you see behind it all, like the form of the skull behind a beautiful face.

I was afraid for my Priory, for look at where it lies, out here in the middle of the firth. The sea protects us, yes, if the enemy comes on foot and horse, but what if the enemy should come by ship, as they did in the dark days of the Vikings? Then our protection becomes our bane, our shield becomes a sword in the hand of the foe.

May God forever preserve the peace with England, for England is rich and strong and could strike at our very heart.

That summer we were gripped by the fear of war. Yet I could see in the eyes of some of my brothers something else, I could see the excitement of war, for in war's train comes chaos, and in chaos anything can happen. In chaos not just nightmares, but dreams too can be fulfilled, dark dreams that demons whisper to us at the dead of night or noon-time.

Subprior Simon was most concerned about our property, especially in Lothian. Brother Hugh, our granger, was sent to visit our Lothian estates. He was ordered to prepare for everything movable to be brought to our grange in Cramond, but nothing was to be moved until the word came that the Scottish host was on the march.

The King was in Dunfermline, where all the host north of the Forth was to assemble by St Alban's day [20 June]. The Lothian host was to assemble at Caddonlee and to await the northern host there.

It was when our fear and excitement were at their height that the two monks arrived from Dunfermline. With the morning boat of pilgrims they came. Yes, the pilgrims were still coming, war or no war. The hurts of soul and body that drove them to seek miracles did not suddenly stop because the King of Scots was about to lead an army against the King of the English. All the more reason, in fact, to make a pilgrimage and cleanse the soul, to pray for the loved ones who were going to fight, and to beg the Saint's protection in the approaching storm. The Black Monks, however, had not come to pray to the blessed St Columba or even to the blessed Isaac. They had come on quite a different errand.

I was on my way over to the mainland on cellarer's business when they arrived. I almost collided with them at the bottom of the steep path at Church Beach. I was very surprised to see them. Black Monks do not often visit Black Canons, especially these Black Canons stuck out on an island. Black Monks know well the way to the King, and that is all.

One of the visitors was small and thick-set, the other tall and gangling. It was the small one who addressed me. Dark eyes looked at me disdainfully from above pale, puffy cheeks and a thin, upturned nose.

'Brother Geoffrey, Order of St Benedict, serving God at the Abbey of the Holy Trinity Dunfermline,' he said in that clipped way which the Normans have of speaking French. 'And this', he said, moving only his eyes in the direction of his companion, 'is Brother Solomon. We require to speak with your Subprior, Brother Simon. Would you be so kind?'

'Yes,' I said, wanting to get on my way as quickly as possible. The boatman was waiting for me. 'If you just go up to the church and ask one of my brothers there, he'll fetch him for you. I'm sorry, I have to be on my way. I'm the cellarer, Brother Michael,' I added, feeling that no other explanation for my haste was necessary. 'May God be with you.'

'Brother Michael the cellarer?' he said in a bored voice. His eyes kept slipping off me, looking past me, as if I was getting in his way. 'Well,' he announced, 'we have to speak with you too. So you might as well come up to the church with us.'

Cursing under my breath I hurried over the sand to the waiting boatman and told him to give a message to my subcellarer, who was already at Barnhill. Then I quickly climbed the path, catching up with the two monks before they had reached the top.

The monks had brought an urgent request from Robert their Abbot for Subprior Simon to attend him as soon as possible.

'Why?' Prior Walter growled. We were gathered in the Prior's scriptoriolum, Walter, Simon and myself, along with our two visitors.

'I do not know all the details, but it concerns the King, and the approaching war. And something else,' he added, making the sign of secrecy with his finger. 'Not a word must you breathe about it to anyone.' He pulled his gaze away from nothingness and looked each of us in the eye. I noticed then just how piercing his eyes were.

'Not to anyone,' came a thin, reedy voice, like a distorted echo. It was the first time Brother Solomon had spoken.

'So Abbot Robert is going to deprive me of my Subprior, without any notice, and for an indefinite period of time?' Walter said angrily.

'My lord Prior, we have also come to take away your cellarer.'

'You want Brother Michael to go with you!' Walter thumped his desk with his fist. His face was flushed with rage and he was shouting. 'You want to take away my cellarer, and at a time like this, with a war about to begin. This is unheard of. I'm sorry, Brother Geoffrey, but you must tell the lord Abbot that.....'

Brother Geoffrey held up his hand in a gesture of peace.

'My lord Prior, I pray you, calm yourself. I know it is hard, but you must look upon this as a summons from a far higher authority than our lord Abbot.'

'Oh must I?' said Walter. 'That is easily said. Words do not bear the royal seal, even when they come from the lips of a monk of the Order of St Benedict.'

Brother Geoffrey nodded curtly to his companion. As if he had been ready for this moment for a long time, Brother Solomon took out from his scrip a roll of parchment with a large seal attached and thrust it towards Prior Walter. Prior Walter took it and looked at the seal in astonishment. It was massive, almost as big as the Papal seal.

'Open it, my lord Prior,' Brother Geoffrey snapped, 'read it, and say nothing of its contents, not even to your Subprior. But do not say again that my words are empty.'

Walter did as Geoffrey said, turning his back on us as he broke the seal and read. When he turned towards us again, he was pale and subdued.

'There is nothing more to say,' he said gravely. 'Subprior Simon, Brother Michael, prepare for your departure at once. Brother Geoffrey, I owe you an apology. Will you take a little refreshment after your journey, and before you start for home?'

The Black Monks were insistent we leave after Sext. They had fast horses waiting at Barnhill, and we could easily reach Dunfermline by Vespers. However I would be allowed to make a brief visit to our grange and stores at Barnhill to give instructions to my subcellarer.

It was only as we were rowing over the Deep to the mainland that I had time to collect my thoughts. Here I was once more being thrown out into the world with Simon. Here he was, beside me, smiling, chatting, acting as though the time of ice between us had never been. All hope of tenderness, all breath of friendship, had died in that coldness. Once more I was whole, once more I was able to look at Simon and not feel a knife twist in my belly, or a sadness crack my heart.

Now, suddenly, everything seemed at risk again. Just to hear his laughter sent a thousand longings tumbling through me, longings which should long since have ceased to trouble a Black Canon of mature years and important office, many would say should never have troubled a Black Canon of any age. Then his arm was on my shoulder and he was smiling in my face, and anger swelled up in me as fierce as any love. No, I thought, I will not let my peace be shattered by the caprices of this man, by his weasel arguments and his sweet breath. I will show our new Subprior what virtue and self-restraint really mean, and if he goes one step beyond what is proper, so help me God I'll accuse him in Chapter in front of all my brothers, and then everyone will see what a hypocrite he is.

Far away behind my rage I could see his face, still smiling, but no longer at me, and I felt his arm move from my shoulder. My anger left me as suddenly as it had come, leaving me sad and lonely, and I raised my hand, wanting to touch his face and call him back. Instead I leaned out over the side of the boat and let my fingers trail in the cold water.

Our journey to Dunfermline was difficult, despite the good mounts. The highway was packed with men who were answering the call to arms. So it was not surprising that we were often stopped and asked to give our blessing. Finally Brother Geoffrey, who was in a great hurry, started to push people rudely aside. This brought jeers and taunts from the men. At one point we came to a complete stop, much to Brother Geoffrey's anger.

'Hurry back to the cloister now, before the English catch you!' somebody shouted.

'They are English!' another shouted.

'Well, hurry up before we catch you!' shouted the first, and a roar of laughter went up. By this time Brother Geoffrey and Brother Solomon had forced their way through. I felt that what Geoffrey was doing was ungodly, refusing blessings to those who were going to war, perhaps to die, and treating them like cattle. So I dismounted and laid my hands upon the heads of those that knelt down. Simon, who had ridden on ahead, turned back and came up to me.

'Listen, Michael, we must hurry. We have more important business to do than to bless peasants.'

'There can be nothing more important,' I replied airily.

'You'll be surprised,' he said gently. 'As your Subprior I allow you to bless five more men. On the condition that the first one is me.' As he spoke, he jumped off his horse and knelt down before me.

'Brother Michael,' he said, 'forgive me for all the hurt that I have caused you.'

At this extraordinary sight, of one Black Canon kneeling at the feet of another, a hush had fallen on the crowd surrounding us. I stared down in disbelief. My spirit was paralysed by surprise. Of themselves my hands went out and touched his head, and my voice spoke the blessing.

A great cheer went up from the crowd. The spell was broken and in confusion I mounted my horse. Simon, waving and smiling and making the sign of the cross in the air above the cheering heads, did the same.

The Abbey of Dunfermline is one of the finest in the land. It stands upon its hill like the city of God. On the west the land plunges down into a deep glen, and where it rises on the other side there stands the King's tower, the heart of the Kingdom of the Scots in the time of King Malcolm Canmore and good Queen Margaret. So human and divine power seem to face each other across the gorge and the rushing river, but they do not stand opposed as you might think, although elsewhere so often those two powers clash. No, they do not stand opposed, for only the

King's most favoured servants become Abbots of the Abbey of Dunfermline.

Abbot Robert was waiting for us in his chamber. A huge fire roared in the grate, taking the chill out of the evening air. Its light flickered on the finely carved heads on the chimney hood, making them look alive.

He was tiny and fine-boned, reminding me more of a sparrow than a man. He was light on his feet and quick in his movements, with a snub nose and eyes set wide apart in a face unusually broad for such a small, thin body.

He and Simon embraced warmly. They had known each other for a long time, having met at the Curia. I knew that Simon thought highly of him, because he had done nothing to hide his delight at the news that old Abbot Archibald was dead and Robert de Berwick had been appointed in his place.

It was only after I had been introduced to him that I became aware of another person in the room. A shadow moved out of the darkness between the fire and the window. As the light fell on him we both knelt, for it was the King's chief clerk and close adviser, Richard of the Provender.

By sight I knew him well, although I had never spoken to him. He was a small, sinister man with a round face and a round belly to match. If Abbot Robert was a sparrow, Richard was an owl, and like an owl he sought out dark places.

He and the Augustinians had never got on well, ever since the struggle over St Andrews. He was implacably opposed to a Church which was not thralled to the throne, and he had been one of those named in the interdict that old Pope Alexander had laid upon the land when Hugh had seized St Andrews and John had been driven from the Kingdom. But times had changed, old enmities were being forgotten, and we were being drawn more and more into the affairs of the realm.

The time had come for us to hear why we had been brought here. It was Abbot Robert who explained to us, while Richard returned to his shadows.

'Subprior Simon,' Abbot Robert said, taking his hand, 'and Brother Michael.' He took my hand, too, and pulled me towards him. 'I thank you both with all my heart for coming so promptly. Now I won't beat about the bush. I'm sure Brother Geoffrey will have told you how delicate the matter is. May your lips be sealed with seven seals, even to your Prior. You can tell me later how old Walter is getting on. Do you promise, eh?'

'Good. Now, you know what our King is like. He's never really grown up, but then Kings rarely do grow up, do they? They don't have to. They let others do that for them.' He cast a glance towards the shadows where Richard sat.

'Our King, bless him, has committed himself and his Kingdom to this dreadful war that nobody wants and nobody can afford. Imagine the stupidity! A war with England! Half the nobility in

Scotland own estates down there, to say nothing of the monasteries. Do you have any English lands? No? Well, the big ones do, we certainly do, and Holyrood, Lindores of course, and Arbroath, and, well, need I say more? Even the King is regretting his rashness, but a King's word is a King's word, so they say, and a King's honour is a delicate thing.

'News has just come from Bishop Roger, who's down in England right now. He says that King John won't even speak to him, so it looks as though he's going to let the forty days' truce run out without a reply. John's also given Northumberland and Cumberland into the keeping of William de Estuteville, a fierce war-horse if ever there was one.

'Now, Simon, I know you of old. You've got the most cunning mind this side of the Alps. Am I not right? Now don't put on that innocent look as if butter wouldn't melt in your mouth.'

He gave a little cry of delight and shook Simon's hand vigorously.

'You know,' he went on, 'I'll never understand why you exiled yourself to that Ultima Thule. No offence meant, Brother Michael. A house of God is a house of God, whether it's among the gulls or the crows. But this man, your Subprior, he could be a King's counsellor. You know he was a close counsellor to Pope Clement of blessed memory, don't you?'

Suddenly a sharp, dry cough rang out from the shadows behind me. I jumped, for I had forgotten that the royal clerk Richard was still there.

'Yes,' Abbot Robert said hurriedly, 'we've got a lot to talk about later, we three. As I was saying, we've brought you here quite simply because we need your advice. How do we get the King out of this predicament in such a way that the people are to lose no blood, the great are to lose no land, and the King is to lose no face? There's our problem.

'Now, we want you to pretend that you're back at the Curia, and we want you to solve it. Think about it, pray about it, talk about it with your colleague Brother Michael. You two have put your heads together very successfully in the past, so I've heard. And solve it. We do not have much time to lose. The army is to march within three days. Richard and I will be here till Compline. Have you any questions?'

Simon was looking thoughtful.

'Only a miracle could get the King out of this one,' he said slowly.

'Exactly,' said Robert. 'We're praying for one night and day. Go to the church and look for yourself. You're the other string to our bow.'

'Perhaps we're one and the same string,' Simon mused.

Suddenly a voice spoke, low and soft like the voice of an owl. It was Richard of the Provender.

'Whatever he does will be a miracle if it solves this problem.

Quite frankly I think we're wasting our time. My advice all along has been for the King to fall ill. God often intervenes in human affairs in the form of illnesses.'

Abbot Robert kept his back to Richard. He rolled his eyes heavenward, as if to say, 'You see what I've got to put up with!'

'The problem with that,' Simon said quietly, 'is that it looks as though King John is under some kind of special divine protection. No, we need something — how shall I put it? — something more positive. What feasts have we got coming up? Let's see, today is the octave of St.Peter and St.Paul [6 July], then tomorrow is the feast of St Boisil.'

'What about Queen Margaret?' I muttered, almost to myself. I had been thinking of her a lot since we had arrived in Dunfermline, where she had lived much of her life, and where she now lies buried. I had even tried to imagine what she would have advised in this predicament. But I could not remember in what season the day of her death fell.

'What did you say?' asked Simon.

'I was just wondering when the feast of Queen Margaret might be,' I replied, suddenly feeling very foolish.

'It's not until November,' Richard said quietly, 'and besides, she's not a saint.'

'She should be,' Abbot Robert said vehemently.

'Queen Margaret,' Simon repeated slowly. 'Brother Michael, you are inspired,' he said, beaming at me. 'She might not be a saint yet in the eyes of the Church, but she's certainly a saint in the eyes of the people. She's the forbear of both of them, both the Kings, William and John, so she wouldn't want her own flesh and blood to be tearing itself to pieces. The people often look to her for protection, so she doesn't want to see Scottish blood flow, either, and here's the King, at Dunfermline, where she is buried.' He rubbed his hands gleefully. 'It is indeed a miracle, my brothers,' Simon went on. 'God has prepared the parchment and drawn out the lines. All we have to do is to add the colour.'

'Is that all?' said the voice from the shadows, softly mocking.

'Yes, that is all, sir Richard,' Simon mocked back. 'The King will keep vigil at her tomb the night before the army is due to march. He will seek her help and protection for the coming campaign. What is more fitting than that the King should pay such respect to Scotland's saintly protector, and his own grand-mother.'

'Great-grandmother,' Richard put in.

'And what a great grandmother she was,' Simon retorted insolently. 'Five times great, greater than all grandmothers, the patron saint of grandmothers.'

'Simon,' Abbot Robert whispered, tugging at his sleeve, 'you are being disrespectful, both to the blessed Margaret and to the King's counsellor.'

'Forgive me, father,' Simon replied humbly. 'During the vigil at her tomb Queen Margaret herself will appear to the King, warning him not to make war upon his cousin, or rather his second cousin once removed.'

'Third', said Richard, almost in a whisper. Simon gave an exaggerated bow towards the shadows. He went on, 'She also tells him not to spill Scottish blood when peaceful talking will achieve much more. Many will witness this miracle, for the King will not watch alone that night, and so the news will spread like wild fire.'

'Of course, it's one thing to think up a miracle,' the voice from the shadows said. 'It's quite another matter setting it up and making it work.'

'That's where Subprior Simon here will really show his worth,' Abbot Robert said proudly. 'We haven't gone to all the trouble of fetching him here just for an idea. The work has only begun.'

'Well', Simon said in a businesslike voice, 'the first thing we need is a woman who will be Queen Margaret. I can't see any of us playing that part succesfully. Sir Richard, you have the advantage over us here, you are lucky enough to live in a world where there are women. You must be able to think of a woman who would be suitable, one whom the King does not know well, of course. A young woman, and handsome, would probably make the most impression on our sovereign lord.'

'That might be a problem,' Richard said dryly, stepping out from the shadows. 'The King knows most such women of the court too well.'

'Not at his age, surely,' I blurted out.

Richard raised his eyebrows disdainfully.

'What would you know about it, Sir Canon?' he snapped. Then, addressing us all, he added, 'Admittedly the lord King's interest in women has abated somewhat since his illness, but mostly his officials and barons keep their young womenfolk away from the court, unless they have come to beg a special favour. The Queen, however, has many young ladies about her, whom she keeps well away from the King.'

'Are you often in the presence of the Queen?' Simon asked.

Richard again raised his eyebrows.

'Sir Richard is the Queen's confessor,' Abbot Robert explained.

'Then is there not one of her ladies who might be persuaded?' Simon went on.

'You decide to have a miracle,' Richard said, 'and you want others to do all the work for you. I will introduce you to the Queen, and you can ask her yourself.'

'Is it wise to take the Queen into our confidence?' Simon asked cautiously.

'Queen Ermengard,' Richard replied icily, 'expects to be told everything, and what she is not told, she finds out.'

'The Queen will be delighted to know that something is being done to stop this mad war,' Abbot Robert put in, 'and I'm sure she will be only too pleased to help.'

'When can we see her Majesty?' Simon asked.

'Tomorrow, after Prime,' Richard drawled. 'She will know why you have come, and, if she approves of the idea, will probably already have chosen a suitable lady.'

'I hope it will not be too much trouble for you to speak to her Majesty,' Simon said sarcastically.

Richard took this remark in the spirit in which it was made and snarled back, 'Be careful, sir Canon. If you use that tone in front of the Queen you will leave her presence much quicker than you entered it. I will send a servant to fetch you from the Abbey west gate immediately after Prime tomorrow.' With that he swept out of the chamber, giving Abbot Robert a curt nod. I knelt. Simon remained standing.

'Presumptuous little toad,' he muttered, as the footsteps died away.

Abbot Robert chuckled. 'You haven't changed, my son. Tell me, why is it that you're not confessor to the Queen? You've got twice the wits, and the looks. I'm sure Queen Ermengard would rather have a pretty man like you to confess to. It would make her confession the sweeter.'

Simon was not smiling. 'I was aiming higher than this mouldy, rustling court, but like Icarus, you know.....'

'Yes, I know, my son,' the Abbot said, 'but let us hope things are about to change.'

'Let us hope so,' Simon replied. Then quickly changing the subject, he added. 'But we have much work to do. As clerk Richard said, no-one else will do it for us. Let us see exactly where this miracle is to take place.'

'Of course, of course,' Abbot Robert said, and led us down the wide steps, through the splendid cloister and into the vast church.

As Abbot Robert was taking his leave of us outside the guest dorter, he requested my presence in his chamber after Compline. So as soon as Compline was over I hurried up the great stairway and proudly gave my name to the monk who was standing outside the door to the Abbot's chamber. With a disdainful look, he opened the door for me and ushered me in.

Abbot Robert was sitting in front of a roaring log fire. He held out his hand for me to kiss, then, after dismissing my usher, he made me sit on a stool by the fire opposite him.

'You're probably wondering why I've asked you here, Brother Michael,' he said gravely. 'Well, it's a very serious matter, and I expect your full cooperation. I am going to ask you some questions about your Subprior, Simon de Quincy.'

As he spoke he lifted a gold chain from around his neck. I had not seen it before, as it had been hidden beneath his habit. Attached to the chain was a large and beautifully wrought pendant. I took it and gazed at it in wonder. The pendant was a frame of filigree gold around clear glass, and set within the glass was a thorn.

'Do you know what that is, Brother Michael?' Abbot Robert asked gently.

I crossed myself and spoke my thought, that it was a piece of the Crown of Thorns.

'That is correct, my son,' he said. 'You will hold it in your hand while you answer my questions, and it will help you remain upon the path of truth.

'I cannot say why I am asking these questions, nor should it matter to you. However, I can say that Subprior Simon himself will never know what passes your lips this evening. Never,' he repeated firmly.

I grew very afraid for I thought that he would ask about our carnal friendship. How could I perjure myself while holding in my hand such a precious relic? Yet how could I condemn both of us to I knew not what terrible punishments?

I cannot now remember every question Abbot Robert put to me that summer's evening, by a blazing fire, between Compline and Collation. He asked how Simon had carried out the duties imposed on him by the various offices he had held; how he was regarded by his brothers; how he treated his brothers?

Abbot Robert was kind and encouraging, and my fear began to recede. In all my replies I was charitable and generous towards Simon. Although I was still deeply distrustful of him, I could not help but be touched by the kind words he had spoken to me that day, the first kind words he had spoken to me for years.

The Abbot asked also whether there had been any scandal attached to Simon's name since he joined the convent of St Columba. I could honestly reply that there had been none.

However, I was not to escape so easily, for, almost in a whisper, he then asked whether I had ever heard Simon express any opinion which could in any way be construed as heterodox?

Suddenly the heat of the fire became unbearable, and like a red-hot coal the precious relic seemed to scald my hand. I sat on the brink of eternal damnation. Yet in my hand I held a token of the ultimate sacrifice of self, for the sake of love, love even for one's enemy. If I perjured myself for Simon's sake, would that not be an even greater sacrifice, the sacrifice of the soul's eternal salvation, a sacrifice that even God would turn his face from?

As I wrestled with such thoughts, my silence and obvious confusion had already answered the Abbot's question. I felt his eyes boring into me.

'What kind of heterodox opinions?' he asked quietly, adding, 'Do not be afraid, my son, you will come to no harm if you tell me the truth.'

'Father Abbot,' I muttered, 'his opinions about nature and lust and...and sodomy cannot be considered orthodox.'

There, I had said it. I shut my eyes and waited for the thunder.

'Oh, that,' Abbot Robert said dismissively. 'I know all about that. Oh yes, Simon made no bones about his thoughts on those subjects when he was in Rome. They're very quaint and amusing. No, my son, what I mean is anything seriously heterodox.'

'No,no,' I said, shaking my head vigorously, feeling a great weight roll from my shoulders, 'nothing seriously heterodox.'

'Good, very good,' Abbot Robert said decisively, getting to his feet. 'You have done well, my son. You may go.'

Trembling with relief I kissed the holy relic and returned it to him. Then I kissed his hand and hurried back down the wide stairway, through the cloister and into the church, where I gave thanks to Christ for my deliverance, unsure exactly what it was that I had been delivered from.''

THE . LADY . AFFRICA

"The following day, after Prime, a servant fetched us from the west gate of the Abbey as arranged. Richard was waiting for us outside the Queen's solar in the old tower. We were out of breath. The climb up from the deep glen had been bad enough. Then there were the steep, narrow steps which seemed to go on forever. No wonder the King did not stay in Dunfermline as often as he used to. Richard scarcely greeted us and immediately ushered us into the solar.

I had never met Queen Ermengard before. As we entered she was standing at the window with her back to the room. A minstrel was singing in the far corner, a young man with a fine, soft voice. My heart melted as we stood and listened.

'Iseult she holds him in her arms.
She joys to see her lover's face,
to hold him close in her embrace
till she cannot contain her joy.
Lest he at night should go his way,
she says his lodging shall be fair,

his bedding soft and made with care.
Tristan's whole felicity
is with the Queen, where she may be.
Tristan sees his joys excel,
knowing he is sheltered well.'

The Queen held up her hand. The minstrel stopped singing, but the beauty of his song seemed to hover in the room. We could hear the river far below the tower, and the call of birds. Only a Queen had the right to disturb such a silence. Finally she turned round and asked who we were. She spoke French without a trace of a Norman accent, although she had lived in Scotland for almost fifteen years. It sounded strange and very charming. Then she moved away from the window to greet us.

Queen Ermengard was not a beautiful woman, despite the poems you might have heard praising her beauty. She was a Queen, and a Queen is always beautiful in the eyes of a poet who wants good payment for his work. She was small-featured, with a pinched look about her mouth. Her eyes I remember most clearly, for they were large and round and very blue. Her fair hair was plaited high on her head.

'We will go into my privy chamber,' she said with a little smile, 'where there are fewer ears. I am always surrounded by so many ears. Affrica!' she called, 'come with me and bring my braid. The rest of you, stay here till we return, especially you, my dear Bernard,' she said, addressing the minstrel. 'I want to hear the rest of that lai. It is so beautiful. We shall all hear it together.'

Richard frowned. She laughed and gave him a playful slap on the face.

'Why am I surrounded by such unchivalrous men, who do not care for love? Now you, sir Canon,' she said, addressing Simon, 'you would not be so ungallant as to deny a lady's request. I can tell you have a chivalrous heart, even if your spirit is devoted to God.'

Simon bowed low. Yes, I thought, I could see him in some chivalrous romance. But in what role? The love-sick knight? The cold, disdainful lady? Or the felon?

The room was full of ladies-in-waiting, servants, dogs. As we moved towards the door of the privy chamber, a tall, graceful lady and a large fluffy dog detached themselves from the crowd and followed us.

The little chamber, which also served as the Queen's private oratory, was quiet and dim, lit only by a narrow slit of a window filled with stained glass. It had been Queen Margaret's oratory too, and I prayed to her for the successful outcome of our plan.

Once the door was closed the Queen presented the tall young lady to us as Affrica de Mertoun. 'She is beautiful, is she not?' she added, and putting out her hand she gently stroked the young lady's cheek.

Affrica smiled. She was indeed very beautiful, tall and slim, with long fair hair which fell unbound to her waist, as she was still a maiden. She had eyes which were the colour of violets, and her smile revealed teeth which were perfect, even and white.

The Queen sat down on a stool, and for the rest of the meeting Affrica worked gold braid into the Queen's hair.

'Now, gentlemen,' the Queen said, 'I know why you are here, and I wish you every success in what you propose. This foolish war must be stopped. If wars are to be fought, they must be fought in the Holy Land to save the sacred places from the Infidel. Besides, my lord King is too old to be gallivanting off at the head of an army. My son, God be praised, is too young.

'Now I hear, sir Clerks,' she went on, lowering her voice, 'that you need a woman.' With a high-pitched peal of laughter she threw her head back, causing Affrica to drop the braid. 'Well, what do you think of Affrica?'

Affrica stood up with the braid in her hand. Her cheeks were flushed from bending, and she looked even more beautiful.

'Your Majesty,' Simon said, 'she is most fair, and she is tall, but there are two things I must ask. Firstly how well does the King know this young lady? She will of course be veiled, but, as I'm sure you understand, it is important that he does not recognise the person —' he hesitated, 'the person through whom the blessed Queen Margaret will choose to speak.'

Queen Ermengard laughed again, but this time she kept her head still. 'Sir Clerk, I have many ladies-in-waiting who are less beautiful than Affrica. These accompany me when I am with the King. If he had noticed her, I blush to say that she would probably not be with me now, and she would no longer be a maiden. Although I am a mere woman, I do have some sense, I know how to keep the best for myself, away from the greedy eyes of men. You, of course,' she said with mock seriousness, 'I do not regard as men, for you have become eunuchs for Christ. Is that not so?'

I blushed and nodded, and her laughter came again, like the tinkling of bells.

'But you had another question for me, handsome eunuch, did you not?' she said to Simon.

I looked at Simon and was amazed to see that he, too, was blushing and seemed quite confused. This was a rare sight indeed.

'Madame, your Majesty, yes, there was something else.' Surely he had not forgotten what the second thing was? 'Your Majesty,' he said again, 'the great beauty of your lady is outshone only by your own.'

Yes, I thought, he has forgotten. The Queen rolled up her eyes pretending to be annoyed.

'You disappoint me, sir Clerk. You are a flatterer like all the rest. I am a middle aged woman and I have never been beautiful.

It is not beauty that made me a Queen, but blood. I have the blood of Kings in my veins, and fairly ugly Kings at that. Come, sir Clerk, your other question.'

Simon had regained his composure. 'Yes, your Majesty, I wanted to ask about Lady Affrica's voice and manner of speaking. Queen Margaret will of course speak French when she appears to the King, for it is given to all the inhabitants of Heaven to speak all languages, but she should speak with a tongue more used to speaking English, or Inglis at least, for that was her native language.'

The Queen beamed. 'Sir Clerk, they say that you are very clever. You men, whether you are eunuchs or not, always believe that you are the only ones who can think. Lady Affrica, please tell these clerks something about your family.'

From Lady Affrica's own lips we learnt that her family had been lowly tenants on de Moreville's land in southern Lothian, near Dryburgh. They were of native stock, and so Inglis was her first language.

Both her parents had died when she was scarcely more than a child, leaving her and her younger brother Gervase to fend for themselves. As there were no near relatives to look after them, she had seen to it that Gervase was taken into the school run by the white canons of Dryburgh, while she threw herself on the charity of the nuns of Eccles.

Gervase was an outstanding pupil, and it was not long before he was brought to the attention of Bishop Jocelin of Glasgow, who made him a clerk in his chancery. Because of his great skill at writing, and the quickness of his mind, Jocelin had recommended him to the King's chapel, where he rose to be one of the chief royal scribes. Soon after he had arrived at court he heard that the Queen was looking for a lady-in-waiting, and he immediately summoned his sister and presented her to her Majesty.

She told us all this clearly, in good Norman French, but it was obvious that her mouth and tongue had been shaped by Inglis.

'She has left out one most important thing,' the Queen said mischievously. 'Gervase had heard that I was looking not just for a lady-in-waiting, but for a beautiful lady-in-waiting!'

Affrica blushed. Simon, addressing her, said, 'Your brother knew what he was doing, my lady. But may I ask you one final thing? What do you think about becoming the mouthpiece of the blessed Queen Margaret?'

'I am deeply honoured,' she replied, bowing her head.

So it was settled. That afternoon, between None and Vespers we would bring Lady Affrica to the Abbey church, and with the special dispensation of Abbot Robert we would take her into the choir and show her how she was to appear, and tell her the words she was to say. Then I was to write out these words and bring them to her the following morning. She would have a whole day to read them over and over and so engrave them on her memory for that same night, which would be the night of the King's vigil.

She could read a little, and the Queen said that she would help her.

'Write out all the letters, sir Clerk,' the Queen said sternly. 'I don't want any of your dots and scratches just because you're too lazy to write out the whole word.'

I had never written French before, and had rarely seen it written, and so I wondered if they would be able to read it even with all the letters put in, but I kept my mouth shut, and put my trust in God, the blessed Margaret, and the sharpness of the Queen's mind.

'Affrica, have you finished braiding my hair?' the Queen asked.

'Yes, ma'am.'

'Then let us go back into the solar. Together we will all hear the rest of that beautiful lai. Oh, don't scowl at me like that, sir Richard, it does no harm.'

'Not to you, ma'am, who are so wise and pious,' Richard replied, 'but it is not for young ladies to hear, because it heats the blood, and can be dangerous.'

'Oh, I keep a good eye on my ladies,' Queen Ermengard said, taking Affrica's hand. 'Don't I, my dear?'

'Yes, ma'am,' Affrica said bashfully.

The Queen went on, 'Because I don't want them to come to harm any more than you do, sir Richard. I'll look after their bodies, you look after their souls, is that not the way of it?'

Richard bowed low again, but I could see from the sour look on his face that he was not pleased.

We had to obey the Queen's command and hear the minstrel's lai to the end. It was a pleasant duty, for it was indeed beautiful, as was the man who sang it, a young Norman, tall and well-built, with hair so blond it was almost white. His voice was clear and sweet and true, and when he sang words of love he would look at the Queen, as was proper, but his eyes would often stray to the corner of the room where Lady Affrica sat, as if they were iron being drawn by a lode-stone.

Simon's eyes, too, often strayed to that same corner. Affrica herself sat as though entranced, gazing towards the window. She was motionless except for her hand, which gently stroked the big dog that had accompanied her into the privy chamber, and which now sat with its head on her lap.

The lai he sang was a strange mixture of many love stories. I was quite taken aback by it, because it was about a clerk who was trying to win the love of a lady by telling her the stories of famous lovers. The Queen was mocking us more than I had realised when she called us eunuchs for Christ. He sang of Amadas and Ydoine, Dido and Aeneas, Paris and Helen, but most of all he sang of Tristan and Isolde, and of the many disguises love-crazed Tristan assumes in order to be with his beloved.

Reflected in the madness of Tristan I could see my own madness for Simon, as clearly as if I was gazing into the still waters of a loch. I felt tears well up from deep below my surface, tears of pity for myself, and for the love that I had had to kill.

In the end, despite all the pleading of the clerk, the lady refuses his advances, although it often seemed as though she would yield.

'There,' said the Queen, offering us her hand to kiss, as the signal that we were dismissed, 'it has a holy end, has it not, sir Richard? So there was nothing to worry about, was there?'

'It is not the end that people listen to, your Majesty,' Richard said reproachfully. 'It is easy to put a good end onto a bad song.'

'Away with you,' Queen Ermengard said, feigning anger. 'But you, sir canons,' she said, more softly, addressing Simon and me, 'can come again, for I can see that you are moved by earthly as well as heavenly love.'

As we left the solar we could hear the sounds of laughter behind us.

In the choir of the Abbey of Dunfermline there is an arcade that runs above the main arches. Nowadays in the great churches they are putting two arcades up there, one above the other. However Dunfermline was already old at the time of my story, and so it was built when churches stayed closer to the earth. It was in this arcade that the vision of Queen Margaret was to appear. There was a doorway to the arcade from the Prior's chamber at the north end of the monk's dorter. Through this door Affrica was to step, between Lauds and Prime on the night of the King's vigil.

The next two days were very busy, with much coming and going between the Abbot's lodgings, the church and the royal tower. Fortunately for us the world was plunged into the chaos that precedes war, and so nobody paid much attention to our scurryings to and fro.

It took me many hours to write out Affrica's words. I can still remember how they began.

'Oh, son of the son of my son David, why do you torment my spirit so.'

She begged him not to attack his cousin, who was of her blood too, and warned him that if he did she would send not her benison but her curse with the Scottish army.

'The saints in Heaven will be ranged against you, and your defeat and dishonour will be as certain as the rising of the sun at dawn.'

We had tried to imagine the questions King William might ask her, for he would certainly not keep silent, even in the presence of a vision.

Would he get back Northumberland and Cumberland?

'You will get what you deserve, my son, I can say no more.'

Could he trust King John?

'He is a King. Trust him as much as you would trust your own word.'

It was Queen Ermengard who suggested that reply. The Queen also told her that she was not to let herself be questioned too much by the King.

'Always remember, my dear, that you are a dead Queen, and dead Queens are allowed to put up with a lot less nonsense than live ones.'

She was to say, 'I am not a spey-wife, I am a Queen. I have come to tell you one thing, and one thing only. Do not attack England.'

As soon as she was sure she had made her message clear, she was to withdraw into the shadows of the arcade and wrap her black cloak round her so that her white dress could no longer be seen. She was then to go back through the doorway into the Prior's chamber. There was in that chamber a secret doorway which led into a closet within the thickness of the wall. She was to go straight into this closet and shut the door. There was air and food in there, but no light. On no account was she to come out by herself. When it was safe someone would come and fetch her.

The night of the King's vigil was upon us. The whole church was packed, for when the King watched, who in the court or the monastery would have the affrontery to sleep? The nave was full of court officials and lesser barons, as well as the royal serjeants who had been marshalling the host. Into the choir, apart from the convent, crowded the King and the greater barons, all in full armour, as well as the Queen and her retinue.

Simon and I sat with the monks. Before Collation we had installed Affrica in the secret closet in the Prior's chamber. She was to wait until the three Nocturns of Lauds were over, then she was to count to one thousand. After that she was to say to herself silently what she was going to say to the King, everything from beginning to end, and only then was she to come out, go through the door to the arcade and make her appearance.

The only light in the church came from the tomb of Queen Margaret, which was radiant with candles, and from the High Altar, where two large candles burnt. The rest of the church was in darkness. The only part of the upper arcade that you could see was just above the Queen's tomb, where Affrica was to appear.

Matins and Lauds seemed to go on for ever. There was no need to hurry them, as is usual with the night Hours, because no one was being kept from their sleep. At last the final antiphon died away, and a restless silence settled on the vast church. Like deafening hammer blows the pounding of my heart filled my ears, and I prayed that no one else would hear it, because it seemed to drown out the shuffling and the coughing and the clinking of chain mail. I too counted one thousand, then I started going through Affrica's words.

I was so caught up in this that the clear voice that rang out into the darkness made me start with surprise. Yes, there she was, a tall, pale figure, hovering, or so it seemed, above the tomb. The effect was magnificent. A great gasp went up from the choir, and suddenly the darkness was full of hurtling shapes as everyone jostled for a better view. The voice from above was lost amidst the uproar.

Then came the voice of the King, like the roar of a lion, ordering everyone to keep still and keep quiet. Stillness again, but this time total stillness, no shuffling or coughing or clinking, the whole choir seemed to hold its breath.

Then the voice came back, clear and firm, speaking all the words that we had put together so carefully. There was no trembling in the voice, no stumbling. I thanked God and the blessed Margaret for the strength and the courage of that maid.

'Put up your sword, my son, my Guillum' — Guillum was the name his mother had used for him when he was a boy — 'and earn the blessing of your ancestress, who is with the saints in Heaven.' That was the end of her speech. Silence again. She had spoken so well, and with such authority, that even the King was speechless. By the time he had gathered his wits to address her she was gone.

'Praise the Lord for a miracle!' a voice shouted. It was Abbot Robert, and all his monks sang back amen.

Then came the King's voice again, roaring, 'Search the monastery, we'll see if it's a miracle, or a trick!'

'It is a sin to doubt the miracles of the Lord,' Abbot Robert shouted, but his words were drowned in the general uproar.

Suddenly, as if from nowhere, men with lanterns loomed out from the darkness around the walls, and some of the King's bodyguard began the search. Everyone else had been ordered to stay in the church and continue the vigil, for dawn had still not come.

At last the blackness of the windows began to lighten, and we began Prime, which marked the end of the vigil. Then the King announced to the whole church that after a thorough search he and his chief counsellors were convinced that his blessed ancestress had indeed miraculously appeared that night, and that he would out of respect for her memory and her saintliness order the Scottish host to disband and negotiations with his cousin John to be resumed.

A cry went up from the congregation. People embraced and wept openly, chain-mail clashed against chain-mail, not in war, but in peace and joy. Queen Ermengard embraced the King and wept on his shoulder. I too wept, and in a rapture of joy and relief I embraced my brother Simon.''

Martin stared at the old man in astonishment, not because he had revealed the secret of the miracle, but because he had, without knowing it, been telling of Martin's own mother. Trying to suppress the excitement in his voice he asked Brother Michael if he knew what had become of Lady Affrica. The old man shook his head and said that he had never seen her, or heard of her, again.

THE . QUEEN'S CONFESSOR

"A fter the night of the miracle Simon told me to go back to the Priory at once, saying that he would be staying a while to see the business through to its conclusion. I longed to stay too, not wanting to leave at the height of excitement and success. But I could not argue against the command of my Subprior, and certainly not for such selfish reasons.

As I took my leave of Abbot Robert, he did not let me kiss his hand, but gave me the kiss of peace, and thanked me warmly for my help. 'You have done more than you know,' he said. 'Take this as a gift for your Prior and your Brothers, as a token of my gratitude.' So saying he took from his neck the pendant containing a thorn from our Saviour's Crown of Suffering. 'You have earned it well, my son,' he said, as I stared at it in disbelief. I had never received such a precious gift in all my life. I stammered out my thanks.

'Tell your Prior that I want you to wear it next to your heart until the day you die,' he went on, and with his own hands he hung it round my neck and tucked it under my habit, pressing it against my chest.

I felt such joy and pride I thought my heart was going to burst. Instead of being humbled, as I should have been, I was swollen with pride, and perhaps this is why God saw fit, years later, to take this emblem of His son's suffering away from me. Or perhaps for other reasons I had become unworthy of it. You can judge for yourself, later, when I tell you the whole tale. The emblem He took, the suffering He left.

The news of the miracle and of the dispersal of the host had preceded me to the Priory for such news flies swifter than the flight of gulls. I was so besieged with questions by my Brothers that Prior Walter gave me permission to speak about it in Chapter. I carefully avoided, of course, any reference to the part Simon and I had played, and I pretended not to recall everything Queen Margaret had said to the King, although I knew every single word.

Then I took from under my habit the gift I had received for the convent from Abbot Robert. All my brothers at once fell to their knees. Prior Walter, who already knew of it, said that in accordance with Abbot Robert's wish, he was appointing me the steward of this relic for the rest of my days. Many were the looks of awe and envy my brothers turned upon me, and some eye-brows were raised in suspicion, wondering how I had come to deserve such a great honour. I did not care. Our purpose had been well served, and the war had been averted. There were many worse suspicions they could harbour.

Several months passed, and still we had heard nothing from our Subprior. Because of Prior Walter's many absences on Church business, it was necessary to appoint someone in loco Subprioris. So Brother David the kitchener and almoner was made acting Subprior. He was heart-sick of the kitchen, so he was delighted with the change of office. He was delighted also to have more authority. David was an ambitious man, and would have moved from the kitchen long before, had not Walter, on the advice of Simon, kept him there. He was a splenetic man, very argumentative, with a temper that could flare up like burnt fat. I liked him well enough, as long as I was not in his company too often.

As our acting Subprior, and thus often as our acting Prior, he sorely tried our patience, and sometimes terrible arguments erupted in Chapter. He was, however, as quick to forgive as to blame, and usually the arguments passed like summer storms, leaving everything clear and bright.

When Simon was acting Prior, it was very different. He would always smooth things over, never allowing such arguments in Chapter. This meant that grudges and resentments would build up in the silence like silt on the bed of a quiet-flowing river.

But where was Subprior Simon? Around All Saints of the year of the miracle of Queen Margaret, Prior Walter, newly returned to the Priory from one of his journeys, addressed us in Chapter.

'As you know, my sons, I have just come from the court where it was lodged at Stirling. There I spoke at length with the Queen and with our Subprior. Queen Ermengard asks the convent of Inchcolm a great boon. She wants Subprior Simon as her own private confessor.'

I had suspected that the taste of the court would be too tempting for him, but I had not expected this, confessor to the

Queen. I wondered darkly how Richard of the Provender would take being thus supplanted.

Voices now began to be raised in opposition. Prior Walter silenced them. 'I have not finished speaking, my sons. Have patience. I see you have been teaching your brothers some bad habits, Brother David,' he added with a grim smile.

'My sons,' he went on, 'our gracious Queen recognises what a great loss Subprior Simon's absence must be to the Priory.'

Some of my brothers nodded in hearty agreement with this, while others remained silent, their eyes downcast, trying not to show their satisfaction at the prospect of losing Simon. I, too, remained silent, but not from any satisfaction.

'Therefore Queen Ermengard,' Walter said, 'is prepared to make us a generous grant of a tenement in her burgh of Haddington.'

At this applause broke out from all sides.

'There is one other condition attached to this offer,' Walter said, raising his voice to command silence. 'It is this: that the office of Subprior remains de jure his, to be resumed by him whenever he or the Queen might wish.'

This is typical of Simon, I thought to myself, to leave himself a bolt-hole should anything go wrong.

Already protesting voices were again rising all around me, the prelude to a long and heated debate.

'How can he become a confessor,' someone asked, 'when he's not even a priest?'

'He has already been ordained,' Prior Walter announced.

David remained unusually silent. When he was asked by Prior Walter if he was prepared to remain our acting Subprior, and to move to another office if Simon ever came back, it was clear that an anger-demon was squeezing his spleen. However, he overcame it. He stood up, face bright red, eyes bulging; he nodded his head violently; then without saying a word, but with a loud exhalation of breath, he sat down again.

For he knew, as I did too, that Simon would get his way. The offer of a fat tenement in Haddington was impossible to refuse. As usual we were tottering along the thin line between credit and debt. This was Subprior Simon's doing. Although our income was so much greater than it had been when he had joined the convent ten years before, he never allowed gold and silver to accumulate. He was always ploughing them back into some scheme or other: a new refectory, a new guest-house, a new hostel for pilgrims at Barnhill. And if there was not enough, he did not scruple to go to the money-lenders in Edinburgh. 'Why lay up treasures for rust to gnaw at?' he would say. Why indeed? But it meant we were at the mercy of bad harvests or sudden rises in masons' wages, or war. It also meant that we could not afford to turn down such offers as that made by Queen Ermengard, no matter what conditions were attached to it.

Apart from arguments in Chapter, life in the Priory became quieter. Gradually the sounds of mallets and chisels and the shouts of the masons died away as the building schemes slowed down and stopped. Fewer pilgrims were coming to the island: St Columba was falling out of fashion, except amongst the very poor, and new, and more accessible, saints and martyrs were pushing the memory of the blessed Isaac out of the hearts of the people; and no one seemed minded to push him back.

Then at the start of the third summer after the departure of Subprior Simon, without warning and to the great surprise of everyone, he was back amongst us, our Subprior again *de facto* as well as *de jure*.

He was no longer a priest. At the great Council of Perth the Papal Legate, Cardinal John de Salerno, had declared that all those ordained on a Sunday were to be removed from the office of the altar. This included Simon. The Papal legate had spoken, and there was no gainsaying a Papal legate, especially Cardinal John de Salerno.

However, when he wanted to be, Cardinal John could be very decisive. From Melrose he went to the Abbey of Dunfermline, and soon the news was flying from one monastery to the next that Abbot Robert had been deposed. But why? At first no one was sure, although rumours were rife. It was Simon, finally, who gave us the official reason, for he had been at Dunfermline with the Queen when Cardinal John had descended upon the Abbey, and it was not many weeks after this that Simon returned to the island.

Moral laxity and lenience was the reason given by the legate. He had not been strict enough with his monks. Various complaints about broken vows of chastity had already reached the legate's ears when he was in Melrose. Abbot Robert had even allowed an unmarried woman to give birth to her bastard in the Abbey infirmary, and the rumour was that one of his monks was the father.

Simon was more than willing to give us all the scandalous detail of Abbot Robert's removal from office. He was much more reticent about the reasons for his own sudden departure from court and appearance at the Priory. He told us simply that he had grown tired of the court and its intrigues, and longed to return to the quiet, simple, pious life of the Priory. He said that he had taken Cardinal John's decision about his Sunday consecration as a sign from the Lord that he had been away too long from his brothers and from his spiritual home. This is why he did not seek reconsecration.

A sigh of approval went up from those brothers who were glad to see him their Subprior once again. From the others there was narrow-eyed disbelief. To those who remembered his first arrival on the island, these words sounded strangely familiar.

Simon's return meant, of course, that Brother David ceased

to be acting Subprior. He stepped down with as good grace as he was capable of, which was little enough. He pleaded in Chapter not to be sent back to the kitchen, where Brother Hugh had been doing a passable job in David's stead. Prior Walter asked him which office he craved. Turning to me he said loudly that he wanted to be cellarer.

I shrugged my shoulders. I had been cellarer now for many years, and was growing tired of it, although, as with most tasks in this life, I had not found it such a burden as I had done when I had started it.

All eyes were on me. 'I demit office gladly, with the permission of our lord Prior,' I said, 'and request permission to return to the scriptorium.'

Before Prior Walter could speak, old Father Geoffrey, who had been craning forward to catch the words with his failing hearing, waved his hand and got slowly to his feet.

'I have been precentor now for more years than most of you here can remember,' he said in a quaking voice, 'longer even than Walter has been our Father Prior. I am half-blind, half-deaf, although not so deaf that I cannot hear some of you whisper "half-dead" as well.'

There was laughter at this, and strong denials.

'Thank you, my brothers,' he went on. 'You are right: I am not half-dead. I am still very much alive, and intend to be in this world to plague you for some time to come. However, I want to leave my office before my office leaves me. I do not want to go to the infirmary, not yet, while I can still dress myself and see enough to find my way to the church.'

We all applauded. I wiped away a tear. He held up his hand again for silence. 'My brothers, my father in Christ,' he went on, 'let Brother Michael be my successor. I know, Brother Peter,' he said, raising his voice above the murmurings, 'you have been my succentor, and you have carried out your duties with great dedication. But you cannot copy. It is not your fault. A demon sits on your hand whenever you take up a quill. And a precentor who cannot copy is like a cellarer who cannot count.'

Brother Peter looked crest-fallen. He hung his head and was lost for words, which was unusual for Brother Peter. By his silence he was agreeing with Geoffrey's judgment.

I was delighted. There was no office which I had craved more than that of the precentor, and so it was the office I had expected least. Yet here was Geoffrey urging it upon me. I looked expectantly at Prior Walter, who said, 'Geoffrey, more of a brother than a son in Christ, how can I refuse your request? If Brother Michael is in agreement, then so be it.'

Thus it came about that in the year of our Lord 1202 I became precentor of the the Priory of Inchcolm. I looked forward to a time of peace amongst the manuscripts. But my time of peace had not yet come."

PART SIX
AMBUSHES

For the sinner has said in his heart, 'I shall remain
unshaken from generation to generation, free from harm.'
His mouth is full of curses, bitterness and guile;
beneath his tongue are trouble and affliction,
He lies in ambush near the villages
in order to kill the innocent man...
He lurks in his hiding-place like a lion in his cave...
He has said in his heart, 'God has forgotten, He turns
away His face and sees nothing.'

Contra oppressores iniquos   Psalm 98

LEVERITH

"At the beginning of the following winter, as the frosts were starting and the first snowflakes swirled in the wind, we received an unexpected visit from our Bishop John Scot. Stooped with age, he had to be helped out of his barge and up the path to the Priory guest hall.

He had come to bid us farewell, for he was laying down his staff of office and was on his way to the Abbey of Newbattle to die in the habit of a Cistercian. Also he had come to warn us that the King had chosen as his successor at Dunkeld Richard of the Provender, chief clerk of the royal chancellery and manager of the royal household, whom John himself had excommunicated during the struggle for St Andrews, and whom Subprior Simon had ousted from the Queen's favour.

This was bad news indeed. John had been a good Bishop, despite the bad beginning. Always scrupulously just, and trusting more in the Church and her holy Orders than in the King and his less holy ones, he had never sought to interfere in our affairs more than was right and proper for a Bishop to do. Nor had we given him cause to, for we had always kept the parishes in our possession well provided with priests.

The prospect of Richard as our Bishop was alarming. He was a servant of the King, and would remain so, whether he bore the title clerk of the Provender or Bishop of Dunkeld. Furthermore he had always disliked the Augustinians.

I remembered vividly how much he had resented our being called upon for help and advice when the host was assembling to attack England. How much more must he have resented it when Simon took his place as confessor to the Queen.

Before leaving us finally, Bishop John reconsecrated Simon, despite Simon's initial reluctance, along with the other priests who had been consecrated on a Sunday. Then in a solemn procession we accompanied him to the shore and said farewell. Filled with grief and fear we watched his barge pull out of the south bay: grief for the Bishop that was passing away, fear of the Bishop that was to come.

Yet as we stood on the sand, some of us with tears in our eyes, Subprior Simon rubbed his hands vigorously and said in a loud, cheerful voice, 'Well, let us gird our loins, for a time of strife lies ahead.'

Prior Walter rebuked him openly, saying, 'You may well be right, Subprior Simon, but it is unbecoming for someone in your position, and with the sacred oil scarcely dry upon your forehead, to sound so delighted about the prospect of strife.'

'With all due respect, Father,' Simon replied, 'I am not delighted. It is simply that I am prepared, and I want my brothers to be prepared likewise.'

The Bishop's barge was by now only a dark shape against the Lothian shore. With the words of our Subprior ringing ominously in our ears we made our way slowly back to the Priory.

Shortly after Christmastide a royal messenger came to the island to summon Prior Walter to the King's presence in Kinghorn for the election of a new Bishop of Dunkeld. A week later Walter returned to confirm our worst fears: our Bishop-elect was indeed Richard of the Provender. There was of course no election, simply a royal appointment, with the relevant clergy looking on.

His consecration was held at Easter, in the Cathedral church of St Andrews. A week later Bishop Richard visited the Priory of Inchcolm. This was quite regular, that a new Bishop should visit his chief monastery. What was not regular, was the size of his retinue, and the length of time he stayed. Not only did he grossly exceed all acceptable limits, but also, without consulting us, he had invited the clergy from the Dunkeld peculiars in Fothrif and Lothian to come to him while he was here.

It was like a plague of locusts, and soon our storerooms and granges, already seriously depleted by the winter, were almost empty, and we had to start buying grain and ale at the market in Inverkeithing.

I was present when Walter, at Simon's prompting, asked Bishop Richard for silver to buy extra supplies.

'But we brought supplies with us, Prior Walter,' Richard said, 'huge amounts of supplies. Are you trying to tell me they have all been used up, along with your own?' His tone was one of outraged indignation, but there was menace in it, too.

'My lord Bishop,' Walter replied, 'the supplies you brought did not last more than two days. You have been here eight days now.' Out of respect he did not add that a Bishop should be supported on a visitation no longer than three days, and that he should have with him a retinue a third of the size of Bishop Richard's.

'The supplies I brought should have lasted at least a week,' Bishop Richard said, adding insultingly, 'if they had been well managed, that is. It is the fault neither of myself nor my household, if you and your cellarer are incompetent.'

At this point Simon, who had been standing listening to this exchange, said quietly, 'My lord Bishop, with all due respect, it is a matter not of our incompetence, but of your greed.'

The Bishop's face flushed. 'You insolent wretch,' he said, his voice rising in anger, 'I could have you excommunicated for that remark.'

'If that is what you think,' Simon replied, still in his quiet, even voice, 'then you have a lot to learn about being a Bishop.'

At this I thought Bishop Richard was going to strike him.

Hurriedly Prior Walter intervened. 'Subprior Simon,' he said, 'your concern for the situation makes you forget the respect due to your Bishop. Not another word, Subprior,' he added angrily, as Simon opened his mouth to speak again, 'unless it be to ask our Lord Bishop's forgiveness.'

There was a moment's terrible silence, all eyes on Simon. I held my breath. If he chose to continue this quarrel, the consequences could be dire. Slowly he got to his knees and bowed his head. 'Forgive me, my Lord Bishop,' he said, in a loud, almost sing-song voice, 'for having implied you were greedy and ignorant.'

Bishop Richard mumbled something that could be construed as an acceptance of this strange apology.

'My apology, and your gracious forgiveness, my lord,' Simon drawled, getting to his feet, 'do not solve the problem of the supplies.'

'Do you think I am still Clerk of the Provender?' Richard asked, his voice rising again. 'I have my own Clerk of the Provender now: Master Abraham. If you have incurred any extra expense on our account, list the items in question and give a copy to him. He will discuss it with you. If he is satisfied that your claims are justified, he will pass it on to me. Then and only then will I give it my attention. Do I make myself clear?'

Without waiting for an answer, he stormed out of the room, and his clerks scurried out behind him. I was heartily relieved that he went so quickly, because Simon had opened his mouth again to speak.

It was another four days before Bishop Richard and his retinue departed. All the last day Subprior Simon and Brother David the cellarer sat with Master Abraham over the Bishop's reckoning, arguing over every grain of oatmeal and drop of ale. Finally a price was agreed. The Bishop left saying he would give it due consideration in due time.

Due time was many months, and several messengers, later. Finally Prior Walter spoke to the Bishop personally, when they met on Church business. The Bishop was still reluctant to pay his debt to us in silver or in kind. Instead he proposed a complicated deal which involved our island of Leverith, the tidal island which lies just off the coast at Cramond. It had in fact been one of our earliest grants, given to us by Bishop Gregory of Dunkeld soon after our foundation. It was known jokingly as the forgotten island, because it had been inadvertently omitted from the great charter of confirmation of Pope Alexander. Walter, who had himself brought this charter back from Rome, had quite simply forgotten to include it. This was rectified later by Pope Lucius, when he had confirmed de Mortimer's grant of our half ploughgate of land in Aberdour.

Bishop Richard wanted to graze his cattle on this island, and was offering us a rent for this privilege far higher than it was worth. He said he was prepared to do this for as long as he lived, the agreement terminating only with his death. At the rate Richard was offering he would have completely repaid his debt to us within two years. So Prior Walter accepted what appeared to be a generous offer.

The rent would be paid, Bishop Richard had promised, at Michaelmas each year. The first payment would be accompanied by a charter setting out the terms.

Michaelmas was almost on us, and there were many different opinions amongst my brothers as to what would happen. In fact Richard paid promptly, but there was no mention of the promised charter. When Walter saw him at St Andrews the following summer, he broached the subject, and the Bishop promised sincerely that it would accompany the next payment. This payment did not arrive until the Epiphany, and there was still no charter.

The next Michaelmas [1206] came and went with neither payment nor charter. Every time Prior Walter spoke to Bishop Richard he was fobbed off with some excuse or other. Subprior Simon asked permission to go and speak with the Bishop. Walter refused. Simon then said that they must appeal to Rome. Walter said that he would write first to Bishop William Malveisin of St Andrews, who was no great friend of monasteries, but was strict and upright. Besides, he had dreams of making St Andrews into the Scottish Archbishopric, so he welcomed any opportunity to interfere in the affairs of the smaller Bishoprics.

However, before Bishop Malveisin could reply, the matter had taken a much more serious turn.

It was the following Whitsun. We were just coming out of

church when we heard shouts echoing along the cloister from the gatehouse. A figure came running towards us and threw himself down at Prior Walter's feet. It was Donald, our former servant, now a freeman on our land at Nether Cramond. In a trembling voice he announced that that very morning all the Bishop's cattle and goats on Leverith had been found with their throats cut. The shepherd boy, who lived on the island had not heard a sound all night, and already people were muttering that it was a sign of St Columba's wrath at the Bishop.

We all crossed ourselves. St Columba's wrath it might have been, but Bishop Richard would certainly look for more earthly causes, and the first place he would look would be here.

The whole convent swarmed down to the boats to see whether any were missing or showed signs of having been used in the night. All were there, carefully drawn up into the noosts, and completely dry.

Later that morning Subprior Simon and Brother Matthew the sacristan accompanied Donald back to Cramond. When they returned they confirmed the whole story, and had been unable to add anything to the mystery, despite having questioned the shepherd boy and several of our and the Bishop's tenants on the neighbouring shore. Some of the Bishop's servants had arrived while Simon and Matthew were on our land in Cramond, and had driven them away with threats of violence.

Each day we prayed that God and St Columba would avert the wrath of Bishop Richard. But our prayers were to no avail, for within the week our grange at Cramond was burnt to the ground, and our former servant Donald, his wife and daughter were found dead on the shore, their throats cut.

The Bishop was with the King at Forfar. Prior Walter immediately sent Brother Matthew and Brother Roger, the young succentor, to him with a letter urgently requesting a meeting. When they returned several weeks later they were not alone, bringing with them two boats crowded with clerics. One of the boats was flying the pennant of the Bishop of Dunkeld.

The whole convent was waiting anxiously on the beach to greet them, and all eyes were on the Bishop's boat. To everyone's relief it brought not Bishop Richard but the Bishop's Archdeacon, Henry, a bright, mild-mannered man. He was a friend of the Augustinians, and honey to the sourness of Bishop Richard.

With him was John de Leicester, the Archdeacon of Lothian for St Andrews, tall, suave, impeccably groomed as usual. Two Archdeacons at the Priory at once: this showed how serious the situation had become.

My eyes moved to the other boat: Matthew and Roger were waving eagerly from the prow. Behind them stood two more Augustinians whom I did not know; one white-haired, tall, stooping; the other younger, smaller, darker.

The boats hit the sand and there was much scraping and splashing and shouting as the servants pulled them onto the shore. Suddenly with a great leap of my heart I recognised one of the Augustinians: it was Edgar! I heard Matthew introduce him and his companion as Father Michael and Brother Mark of the Abbey of Scone.

Our eyes met. We bowed to each other. I went over to him and gave him the kiss of peace. Although neither of us smiled — the situation was too serious for smiling — I was filled with joy to see my friend again, and I thanked God and St Michael that even such a dark time as this brought with it its own consolation.

Apart from during the Hours I did not see Edgar — or rather Michael — until the next morning in Chapter, when the whole convent, as well as all the visiting clergy, were present. We had to give up our seats to the visitors and sit on the floor. I gave my seat to Michael.

It was more a hearing than a Chapter. Subprior Simon set out the events as they had happened, emphasising the lack of evidence for both of the crimes: on Leverith, the chief witness, the little herd boy, had been asleep. At Cramond the chief witnesses, Donald and his family, were dead. No one living near to either place had heard any untoward sounds of men or horses. However, several peasants at Cramond, woken by the burning grange, claimed to have seen a boat slipping along the coast towards the Queen's Ferry.

'The whole convent, my lords,' Simon said in his most sincere voice, 'will swear before you on the relics of Saint Columba, not only that none of our boats was on the sea the night of the slaughter on Leverith, but also that none of us, canons, lay brothers, servants, had any part in the deed.

'There is much to suggest that the slaughter of the Bishop's cattle on Leverith was the wrath of St Columba against a bad tenant,' he concluded. 'The slaughter of Donald mac Gillebrigte and his family, and the burning of the grange, however, would appear to be a vicious act of revenge by someone all too earthly.'

Archdeacon Henry, looking very uncomfortable, got to his feet. 'My sons, just as you will swear on St Columba's holy relics, so shall I and all my clerks, that we are as ignorant and innocent of the second crime as you claim to be of the first.'

'But will your Bishop?' Simon said almost to himself, his head back and his eyes fixed on the ceiling.

We all gasped at his boldness. Prior Walter told him he had no right to make such remarks, insulting the Archdeacon, who was our guest, by impugning the honour of his master, who was our Bishop. Despite Walter's rebuke, however, many of my brothers nodded approvingly at Simon.

Prior Walter then invited Matthew to give an account of his journey to the court to deliver his letter to Bishop Richard. The

Bishop, Matthew said, had refused to see them, and the rumour was that he had thrown Prior Walter's letter onto the fire unopened.

From the court they had gone to Dunkeld itself to speak with Archdeacon Henry, knowing that there at least they would not be turned away. He had agreed to come with them to the Priory.

On the road south from Dunkeld they had visited Scone Abbey. There they were joined by Father Michael and Brother Mark, both brothers of that Abbey.

'Why they are here with us,' Matthew said humbly, 'they will be able to say far better than I can.'

I could feel the rush of air around my head as Michael stood up. His voice was strong and young, and if I did not look up at him, I could believe that time had gone backwards, and the day of the fight in Aberdour churchyard, which had taken him away from me, was still to come.

'My lords, my brothers, my sons in Christ,' he said, 'my brother and I have come to you not only to offer you moral support in your time of need, but also practical help. We have come to put ourselves at your disposal, if it is your wish to use us.

'May I say, with all due respect to Subprior Simon and Archdeacon Henry, that what is needed now are not oaths, but actions, actions which will bring this sorry and dangerous state of affairs to a happy conclusion, and ensure that no more blood is shed.

'Brother Mark and I are on our way to the Holy Father. As you know we have just elected a new Abbot, William, to rule over us. We wish to secure the Holy Father's blessing on him, as well as a confirmation of our rights and possessions.'

Bishop Malveisin, he explained, had been harrying the Abbot and convent of Scone over various matters connected with their rights and possessions. As Father Michael was speaking, all eyes went to John de Leicester, one of Bishop Malveisin's two Archdeacons. He sat there completely impassive. He did not care what his Bishop was doing. It was said that he did not care about anything except John de Leicester. He had come to the Priory only because his master had told him to, and besides, he was on his way to Lothian anyway. He put a well manicured hand up to his face to stifle a yawn.

Michael went on, 'What I and Brother Mark propose is that we take the case of the renting of Leverith before the Holy Father and urge him to make a final decision. We have full details of this case from both Prior Walter and Archdeacon Henry, representing both sides in the dispute. For this is the root of the evil that we have seen so recently, and more evil will grow unless this root is pulled. It is my opinion, and the opinion of Brother Mark, that the only authority which can pull the root is that of the Holy See.'

There were cries of 'God bless you!' and 'Praise be to the blessed St Columba!' from several of my brothers. Amidst all the jubilation my eye caught Subprior Simon's face. Usually so expressionless, it was tense, almost scowling. It was clear that something was displeasing him greatly.

Both Prior Walter and Archdeacon Henry accepted Michael and Mark's offer, and applause broke out on all sides. Subprior Simon clapped, too, but it was as if his hands were hurting.

After Chapter I had to go to the Prior's scriptoriolum with Simon and there write a letter for our two brothers from Scone to take with them to the Holy Father. Simon dictated it to me, using his most flowery language. 'This will certainly impress his Holines,' I said, as I copied out the long, rhythmical phrases.

'Well, something has to impress him,' Simon snapped. 'Those two shabby clerks from Scone certainly won't.'

'You are being unfair, Subprior,' I said, quietly hurt that he should refer to Michael in that way. 'What is it? Is it because they thought of something you didn't?'

'Fool,' Simon growled. 'Of course I'd thought of it. If you must know, I had thought of sending you.'

'Me!' I exclaimed, completely taken aback. 'And who were you thinking of sending with me?'

'Me,' he said, staring at me. I laid down my quill and stared back at him. 'Close your mouth, Brother Michael,' he said with a sneer. 'That's the way devils enter, you should know that.' Then he added quietly, all sneering gone, 'Wouldn't you like to go to Rome? Do you remember Rome? We were happy then, were we not? Just for a moment in this accursed life we were happy. You're still as handsome as you ever were, Duscath.'

My head reeled at his words. 'My lord Subprior,' I said, 'Simon de Quincy, you have not spoken that way to me for many years. In fact for many years you have scarcely spoken to me at all, no more or no less than a Subprior should. Why, suddenly, now?' I shook my head, not wanting to continue the conversation. I wanted to forget he had ever spoken. I wanted to finish the letter and go to the church to pray. I wanted something else, too. I wanted to seek out Michael and talk to him. I did not want to talk to Simon. I did not want to spend any more time in his company than was absolutely necessary, no matter whether he was talking to me as a Subprior or as a lover. It was too painful, reminding me of all the things we had said to each other.

'Who is that Father Michael from Scone,' Simon asked, ignoring my question. 'You know him, don't you?'

'Yes, I know him,' I repeated, slowly, suspiciously. 'So what?'

'I saw you give him the kiss of peace. It was more than the kiss of peace. And I saw you looking at him in Chapter, lying at his feet and gazing up at him. You have known that man just as we have known each other. Am I right?'

'Simon,' I exclaimed, rising to my feet, 'you are jealous. Simon de Quincy with the heart of stone is jealous! I don't believe it!' And I threw back my head and laughed.

'What in the name of all the saints is going on here?' It was Prior Walter. He was standing at the door, his face flushed with anger. 'I thought I had walked into the wash-house instead of my scriptorium. Have you finished the letter?'

'Almost, my lord Prior,' I mumbled, sitting down abruptly and taking up my quill.

'Well, finish it. I want to show it to the Archdeacons. Bring it to the warming room as soon as it is ready.' With that he disappeared as suddenly as he had appeared. When he had gone, Simon muttered to me under his breath, with icy menace, 'Don't you ever laugh at me like that again.'

'I'm sorry,' I said, confused. 'I didn't mean to hurt you. Although God knows, you've hurt me often enough. Too often. Look, let's get this letter finished, before we get into any more trouble.'

I read out the last sentence I had written. Simon took it up again smoothly, flawlessly. The only way I knew he was still angry was that he pronounced the r longer and sharper than he normally did.

Father Michael and Brother Mark left the following day to take our case to the Holy Father. A kiss of peace when he arrived, a kiss of peace when he left, a smile and a blessing for the journey, that was all I had been able to exchange with my old friend. There was no desire in the touching or the looking — Good Lord, we were old men of over forty by this time! — but there was a deep warmth, a flowering of the knowledge, which had been growing quietly for years, that here was my true spiritual friend.

It was a bitterly sad moment when, alive with this knowledge, I had to part from him, watch his boat move slowly away from the shore, watch him grow smaller as the long and dangerous journey swallowed him up. I longed to go with him with a longing as sharp as any I had ever known.

In the weeks which followed we braced ourselves for another attack. We armed all our servants, both on the island and the mainland, and ordered night-watches throughout our estates. We even allowed Brother Stephen the granger to carry a sword, and we gave him an escort of three armed servants. We said special prayers, for the safe and speedy return of the canons from Scone, and for reconciliation between ourselves and our Bishop.

There was no other attack on any of our properties, nor did the Bishop suffer another on his. Meanwhile both Bishop and King maintained a stony silence."

SUSPICION

"Father Michael and Brother Mark set off for Italy shortly before the midsummer feast of St John. They returned at Christmastide, the bearers of bad news. The Holy Father had listened with sympathy to our case, and had carefully read the letters from Prior Walter and Archdeacon Henry. He would probably have made a final decision in our favour, had he not consulted Bishop Malveisin, who was also at the Curia at that time. Bishop Malveisin was there to strengthen his own position in his conflicts with the monasteries in his diocese, just as our brothers from Scone were there to strengthen their position in their conflicts with Bishop Malveisin.

Always on the watch for an opportunity to support a fellow Bishop against a monastery, he persuaded Pope Innocent that our case was more complex than it seemed, and that he should appoint judges-delegate to call a hearing in Scotland. This meant delay, and any delay was against us.

The judges-delegate whom the Holy Father appointed were John Prior of the Isle of May, Guy Abbot of Lindores, and Rannulph Archdeacon of St Andrews. We could be sure of support only from Prior John. He was one of our closest neighbours, and understood well the problems of an island monastery. The other two were uncomfortably close to the court and to Bishop Malveisin for us to be sure of anything.

Michael stayed several days with us on his return. This time we were able to exchange more than the kiss of peace and a smile. He asked Prior Walter for permission to speak with me. In recognition of all that he had done for the Priory, Walter not only gladly granted this, but also allowed us to use his scriptoriolum.

We stood in silence, listening to the wind howling around the building. We had till Vespers together, and we had just finished Nones. Silence when it is imposed against our will can be a torture; yet when freely chosen between friends it can be as sweet as honey. Michael was the first to break it. 'I have prayed so often for this moment: now it has come I do not know what to say.'

I took his hand and said, foolishly, 'We don't have to say anything.'

'Do you remember when we met at Scone?' he asked.

I nodded.

'The memory is still as fresh for me as on the first day,' he said. 'Perhaps that is because I never confessed it,' he added wistfully.

'Nor did I,' I said, 'for there was nothing to confess. It was good, Michael.'

'Yes, that's what you said then, too. I have held on to your words like a prayer. But it has not always been easy. The things that are said about what we did are many and terrible, and those who say them are spreading like lice. But why are we talking about the last time? That was long ago, and so much has changed. I can look at you and feel pure love, untainted by the stirrings of the flesh.'

'That's what you said the last time,' I replied, teasing him.

'Yes, yes, but then I was trying to hide my lust from myself. Now I have no lust to hide. At least no lust for you, as St Valentine is my witness!' he added with a smile.

I believed him, and I was content. Nor did I feel any lust for him. Yet there was a great longing in me, whose roots went deeper than the roots of lust, which entwine themselves in the flesh, and with the flesh pass away. It was a longing whose roots entwined themselves in my very soul. It was a longing for friendship.

'Edgar,' I said, using his old name, which came as naturally to my lips as the name of my own parents, 'our love has been tested by time and distance, tested and tempered. What was it Father Edwin said when we first met in Jedburgh all those years ago? Love purified through prayer and through time of its baser elements will shine forth like gold and be pleasing to the Lord.'

'Father Edwin said many things,' Michael replied frowning. Then he added bitterly, 'I sometimes wish that Father Edwin had not said anything at all.'

'Edgar — Michael!' I exclaimed, 'What do you mean?'

'If he had never spoken of friendship the way he did, if he had never planted the seed, then..' He hesitated.

'Then what?' I asked gently. Michael shook his head and said nothing. I knew what he was thinking. I had thought it, too, but only to reject it.

'Michael, my dear friend,' I said firmly. 'A seed cannot grow unless there is soil.'

'I know, I know,' he said impatiently, 'but a seed also needs sun and rain in right measure. Mine has been almost drowned by rain.'

'The sun is shining now,' I said. 'Why complain about the rain when the sun is shining?'

'Because it's become a habit, I suppose,' he sighed. Then, changing the subject, he went on. 'My dear friend, are we destined to see each other only every twenty years? If that is so, then this will probably be the last time we meet on this earth.'

'Michael,' I said, 'why don't you come back to the Priory here?' I surprised myself with my words. I had never thought them before, and in my dreams, when Michael and I were together, it was never here. However, my words did not surprise Michael.

'Yes,' he said quietly, 'I have thought of that often. Scone is not in a good state. It has not been since the King foisted that man Reimbold upon us as our Abbot. He is dead now, and I do not want to speak ill of the dead, but he cared as much about the Abbey as a wolf cares about sheep. It was simply a means of fattening himself and his family. And now our new Abbot, William: he's from Cambuskenneth and a close friend of Abbot Nicholas, and we both know what sort of a man Abbot Nicholas is.'

We both shuddered at the memory of Nicholas, as haughty and ambitious as a baron, with a tongue as venomous as a serpent's.

'Abbot William is from the same mould,' he added bitterly. 'We have a scourge, also, in Bishop Malveisin. Each year he finds new ways to harass us. His weapon is Canon Law, and it is a sharp sword in his hands. It was useful at times in checking the worst excesses of Abbot Reimbold, but he will not be satisfied until he has subjected us entirely to his power and taken all our rights for himself. I would rather have to fight ten of your Bishop Richards than one Bishop Malveisin. Tell me,' he added, 'what are things like here, apart from this feud with your Bishop?'

'Tolerable,' I said. 'Prior Walter is away more and more. He seems tired of life on the island and wants to return to the mainland for good. He is often at the Abbey of the Holy Rood. Our Subprior has ruled him and us now for many years, except for the time he was away at court.'

'I do not like that man,' Michael interrupted. 'I never have done, not since the first time I met him at the consecration of Bishop Roger. I don't trust him. It would not surprise me if he was involved in the slaughter of the Bishop's cattle.'

'How could he have been?' I protested. 'He had not been anywhere near Cramond or the Lothian shore for months. And we all saw with our own eyes that none of our boats had been out that night.'

'People like Subprior Simon have long arms, I'm thinking,' Michael said. 'There's more to him than meets the eye. But I see he's got you under his thumb, too.'

'That's unfair,' I said, stung by his remark, and feeling a strange loyalty towards Simon. 'He's been a good Subprior, although he did abandon us for a time. And he was a good cellarer before that, although he did say some hurtful things to me, but then, it was because I allowed him to − I have no one to blame for that but myself. And before that he was a good Brother, although there was that terrible affair with Brother John−'

'There are too many although's for my liking,' Michael cut in. Then he asked, his face darkening, 'What sort of hurtful things did he say to you?'

'Oh, I've almost forgotten them,' I lied.

'No, my dear friend, I want to know. How did he hurt you?' There was no way round the question. I longed to touch truth with him, and yet I was afraid. But if he was my special friend, then must I not be able to share with him the innermost secrets of my soul?

'How he hurt me is really not important,' I said. 'But what you must know is that for many years I loved him, and we shared a carnal, lustful friendship. For a time I was blind and foolish enough to think it could be something more, but he finally opened my eyes to my foolishness. He did it roughly, cruelly I thought at the time, but now I see that he could not have done it any other way. I should be grateful to him, I suppose.'

'You're too good for your own good,' Michael said.

'A man of Christ can never be too good,' I replied.

'Yes, even a man of Christ can be, if he is dealing with a demon,' Michael said grimly.

'Come, now!' I exclaimed, finally exasperated.

'Listen, dear friend,' Michael said, lowering his voice, 'I heard a terrible thing when I was at the Curia. It must not go beyond these four walls, do you understand? It must not. There is no proof. I was not going to tell anyone, not even you, but I had not realised you had been so involved with the man, and so —' His voice trailed off.

'Please,' I said. 'What is it? You are frightening me.'

Taking a deep breath, Michael went on. 'We were at the Pope's palace in Viterbo when we finally found the opportunity to discuss with Pope Innocent the strife between yourselves and Bishop Richard. The Holy Father was furious when he heard what had happened, both about the rent and the reprisals. Then he asked me again the name of the Priory. I told him. He was silent for a moment, then he asked who the officials were. I told him that, too, and he gave a great sigh and dismissed me, saying simply that he would pray about the matter. It was then he must have taken counsel with Malveisin, and appointed the judges-delegate.

'I was puzzled at this. What was it that had stopped the fury of the Holy Father and caused him to give such a sigh? I had mentioned only three names, Prior Walter, Subprior Simon and yourself. It was then I remembered that Simon had worked at the Curia many years ago. So I started mentioning his name in conversation and asking a few questions.

'A few days later one of the Papal notaries came up to me and asked me why I was interested in Simon de Quincy. I lied, saying that I had never seen him before, but that my monastery was in dispute with his over a common boundary. He said that he was a dangerous man, and that we should be on our guard. I asked him what he meant by dangerous. He would not tell me at first, but finally he told me, after making me swear never to breathe a word to another soul. I am only telling you, my friend, because we are one soul.'

Then, lowering his voice almost to a whisper, and taking both my hands firmly in his, he said, 'Do you remember how Bishop Hugh of St Andrews and all his retinue perished on their way home from Rome, in the time of Pope Clement?'

'Yes,' I said, feeling slightly sick. 'They said it was the marsh fever.'

'The notary told me that it was no marsh fever. It was poison, administered by the hand of Simon de Quincy, who was then in the service of Pope Clement himself.'

I closed my eyes and tried to pray, but behind my eyelids there was nothing but a bottomless black pit. I opened them to be rid of it, but still I felt myself on the brink of the abyss. I grabbed Michael's arm lest it claim me. 'We have no proof,' was all I could gasp. 'Without proof there is nothing — '

'My dear soul,' Michael said, urgently, 'has there been anything else, anything similar, any sudden, mysterious deaths here in the Priory since he came? Anything?'

I closed my eyes again and again there was the awful abyss. Deep in the heart of the abyss a face was beginning to form, indistinct at first, just eyes and the vague shape of the head. It came floating up like a jellyfish floats up out of the depths of the sea. It was the face of Brother Andrew.

I could hear Michael calling my name, but his voice was coming from far away.

'I should never have mentioned this,' he was saying. 'I was a fool. Oh, my heart, forgive me. The first time we speak together in years, and I spoil it.'

'No, no, don't say that,' I said. 'I'm all right. It's not you who have spoilt it,' I added grimly. Then, making the sign of the cross, I said, 'Yes, there has been a sudden death here since his arrival. Don't you remember Andrew, our Brother? He later became Subprior. You must have heard how he died.'

'Yes, of course,' Michael said. 'The story was that he was attacked by a thief he had caught red-handed. Though I would imagine there were plenty of people wanting to kill Brother Andrew. I was one of them once, if you remember.'

'Laurence,' I said, 'it was supposed to be Laurence, one of the lay-brothers, the servant Simon brought with him from Rome. They never caught him.'

At that moment the bell for Vespers rang out, signalling the end of our conversation.

'Michael,' I exclaimed, all the dark thoughts about Simon suddenly vanishing, 'there was so much else to say. And you still haven't answered my question about returning to Inchcolm.'

'If Walter goes to the mainland,' he said dolefully, 'that man will become Prior. I don't think I could serve under him, not even for your sake.'

'Perhaps we should both ask to go somewhere else,' I said with a sigh. 'What about Jedburgh, where we met?'

'If only Father Edwin were Abbot there, but he has been with God now for many long years.'

'I can see one very particular problem between you and Simon, if you were to come here,' I said, remembering the strange conversation I had had with him recently. 'He's jealous of you!'

Again I could not help laughing at this absurdity, and Michael, too, started to laugh. At this moment Prior Walter walked in.

'The whole convent is waiting in choir for their precentor,' he said with a scowl, 'and I find him convulsed with laughter yet again. This is getting to be a habit. Though I suppose it's better than crying. Oh dear, Father Michael, I can hear you thinking what a crotchety old man Prior Walter's become.'

'My lord Prior,' Michael said with a charming smile, 'I wish all superiors were like you.'

'Thank you, my son, thank you. But come now, or it will soon be time for Compline.'

With that we all hurried along the cloister and into the choir.

Father Michael left the island the following day, on the last stage of his journey from Rome to Scone. A bitter easterly wind was blowing hail into our faces as we stood and watched his boat battle its way across Mortimer's Deep. The hail stung my face, but I did not care, for it took away the stinging in my soul, the sting of parting from my friend, and the sting of dark suspicions about my Subprior.

For weeks afterwards I could think of little else. Had Simon really killed Bishop Hugh? What did Pope Innocent know about him? Is that why he had been sent away from the Curia? Had he killed Andrew? If so, why did Laurence run away? Who? Where? Why? What? They became demons that would not leave me in peace, in church at my praying and singing, in the scriptorium at my copying; and in my bed for long hours they would keep sleep from me till finally exhausted I fell into fantastic dreams: Simon as Pope Culpability, hitting Andrew with his staff, while Bishop Hugh looked on and gave his blessing; and it was no longer a staff in Pope Culpability's hands, it was a naked man whom he held by the foot, it was Laurence, and he was smashing him down upon the skull of Andrew. And when his victim lay as still as death Pope Culpability, who had become Pope Clement, threw the broken body of Laurence on top of the broken body of Andrew, but it wasn't Andrew any more, it was my beloved friend Michael. I would awake from such dreams drenched in the cold sweat of fear, not daring to move.

Slowly, with the rhythm of the Hours and with fervent prayer, calmness began to return to my agitated spirit. And when after Easter [1208] Prior Walter asked me to accompany him to the Abbey of the Holy Rood, where the judges-delegate appointed by the Pope were to hear the case between the Priory and Bishop Richard, I saw it as an answer to my prayer. Besides, it was quite possible that Father Michael would be there."

BROTHER.WILLIAM DE.COLCHESTER

"The date of the hearing had been fixed for Whitsun [1208]. We were due to leave after Chapter on the Thursday. At Prime that morning there was no sign of our Prior, and at Chapter his seat was empty. Subprior Simon announced that our father Prior was ill with a bad fever and would therefore be unable to travel to the hearing at the Abbey of the Holy Rood. Simon himself would be going in his place.

We set off later that morning. Subprior Simon and myself were accompanied by young Brother Thomas, and three servants armed with swords, daggers and cudgels. We were armed, too, our weapons being charters and Papal Bulls. I had made careful copies of them all, which we left in the Priory. The originals of course had to accompany us to the hearing, as it was the seals which proved their authenticity.

In Chapter on the morning of our departure these originals were all shown to the convent. Each brother in turn touched and examined each one, in case, God forbid, they were stolen or destroyed before we reached the Abbey of the Holy Rood. Then the whole convent could swear on oath that they had existed.

The documents were divided into three lots, wrapped in linen, and each of us sewed one lot inside our innermost garment next to our skin. Simon carried the most important one, the confirmation of our possession of Leverith granted by Pope Lucius.

St Columba sped us on our journey and by Vespers we were riding into the forecourt of the Abbey of the Holy Rood, overshadowed by the massive crags. The judges delegate had already arrived, and the guest-house was full of monks from the Isle of May and Lindores, as well as clerks and canons from the Cathedral Chapters of Dunkeld and St Andrews.

There was, however, no one from Scone, nor, I was disappointed to hear, was anyone expected. The three judges-delegate were given lodgings with the Abbot, while we were asked to go to our own house in the Canongate, as it was improper for us to be sharing a table with our judges. Nor was Bishop Richard staying within the Abbey precincts. He was with the King in the Castle of the Maidens.

The hearing itself, held in the Abbey's great chapter house, went more smoothly than we had expected. Simon spoke well and at length about our rights. Bishop Richard himself never appeared, but he was ably represented by his Official, Master Abraham. In the end a compromise was reached. The Bishop was ordered to pay all the outstanding rent immediately. However, from the following Michaelmas the rent would be reduced to a more reasonable level, as it was agreed that by then he would have paid off the debt he had incurred.

It is not the hearing that looms large in my memory when I think of that visit to the Abbey of the Holy Rood. Rather it is my first meeting with Brother William de Colchester, a canon of that house. You know him better as Prior William of Inchcolm. If it had not been for his irregular behaviour, you would not have come here, and we would not have met. God chooses the strangest of intruments to show His mercy.

It was after Nones on the first day of the hearing. It had gone well, and Simon was in excellent humour. He had asked Abbot William of Holy Rood to show us the decoration in the new church, and to introduce us to the famous master of works, Brother William of Colchester.

Every Augustinian in Scotland had heard of the new church at Holy Rood, and likewise of Brother William. The Abbot had brought him from England for the sole purpose of supervising its design and decoration.

Abbot William, a vain and garrulous man, was delighted to grant Simon his request. There was nothing he liked better than to show off his new church.

It was indeed a magnificent work, light and graceful. The colours danced and leapt like flames up to the intricately vaulted roof, which was a calmer blue. Although the building was in the latest style, many of the capitals were more traditional, reminding me of ones I had seen in the great churches of Burgundy. Each capital was different from the next. Some had figures carved on them and told stories from the Holy Scriptures, others told moral tales from the pagans, while others still told pagan tales which seemed to me to have no moral at all. On the arcading along the walls each capital sprouted exquisitely carved leaves and flowers.

347

In the north transept scaffolding still covered the walls. Three figures were at work at varying heights above the ground. I have never liked heights, and my head span just looking at them. They were all drawing or painting the freshly plastered walls. Two of them were lay brothers, while the third was a canon. He was small and squat and his tunic was tucked up to reveal thick, swollen knees and powerful thighs.

'Brother William,' the Abbot called, 'I would like to introduce to you fellow canons from the Priory of Inchcolm.'

Brother William, who was engrossed in painting the figures from the Last Supper, did not show any sign that he had heard. The Abbot launched into a long description of the scenes around us, his words flowing without pause. Brother William suddenly broke away from the painting and clambered down the scaffolding with amazing agility. He bowed low to us, then his eyes went straight to the face of Abbot William, who continued his discription unabated. There was a cool mockery in those eyes, which reminded me unpleasantly of the eyes of Subprior Simon. Yet in appearance Brother William could not have been more different. He reminded me more of a brute than a man, with his broken nose and his great jaw thrusting out to the side of his face. He was as displeasing to the eye as Simon was pleasing.

I touched the holy relic at my breast as though to ward off evil.

Simon spoke to him. 'Brother William, these are good, very good.'

'That is praise indeed, Brother,' Abbot William butted in. 'This man has lived in Rome, so he knows good work when he sees it, is that not the case, Subprior Simon?'

Simon gave him a scornful look, but before he could reply, Brother William spoke. 'You will thee nothing ath fine ath thith in Rome,' he said proudly, in that thick slurred way of his. It makes him sound stupid, but it is the greatest mistake you can make to think William de Colchester stupid. He has a mind as sharp and calculating as any I have encountered. He knew exactly what he wanted: power. And he knew exactly why he wanted it, so that he could feed his appetites — which are as brutish and grotesque as his appearance — and so that he could paint not what pleased God, but what pleased himself and the Devil. This is what he has achieved. It is the fault of Simon de Quincy that he has achieved it here, in our Priory.

Just because I am old and blind and have been shut up in this cell for years does not mean that I do not know what has been going on since he became Prior. If I had been present when he was elected, things might have been different. But by that time I was powerless.

The Abbot kept talking. Brother William did not wait for him to finish, but went back to his work on the scaffolding.

'Father Abbot,' Simon said softly, 'you have perhaps heard

that we at the Priory of St Columba are proposing to build a new chapter house?'

'Yes, yes,' the Abbot nodded vigorously, 'my good friend Prior Walter told me that you have some such plan, although he's not sure where the money is to come from. He was saying —'

'St. Columba will provide for his work, my lord Abbot,' Simon cut in. 'He has provided in the past. He will provide in the future. In the name of that great Saint, and of fraternal charity, I would like to ask you a special boon. I would like to transfer Brother William to our Priory to supervise the work — when he has completed the work here, of course.'

'Subprior Simon,' the Abbot said, stroking his grey, bushy beard, 'this is a most unusual request. But it is not unreasonable,' he added, almost as if he were arguing with himself. 'However, you understand that I would have to discuss it with the convent, and with the head of our Order in Scotland, and of course with Brother William himself. He has many skills and virtues, but obedience to his superiors is not one of them. His God-given talent makes him sometimes proud and head-strong.'

We do not have room for another Brother in the Priory, I thought to myself, especially such a one as William. But I said nothing. What was the point, if Simon had made up his mind?

'I really must leave you now,' the Abbot said. 'We will talk again of this matter before you leave. May God be with you.'

'And also with you, my lord Abbot,' we both said, as he waddled off in the direction of the cloister.

When he had gone, Simon fell to looking at the murals again. 'Quite extraordinary,' he muttered, more to himself than to me. 'What we could do with such a talent.' Then, turning to me he dismissed me summarily, saying that I should be writing the report of the day's proceedings. As I left the church I could hear him softly calling Brother William's name. I looked around and already Brother William had clambered down from the scaffolding and was standing beside him.

At Vespers that evening my eye was drawn not to the murals and carvings which surrounded me, but to a tall, slightly stooped figure of a canon standing in the shadows of the south transept. He had not been there when Vespers had begun. There was something familiar about him, yet I was sure he was not one of the canons of Holy Rood.

My eyesight was not as sharp as it had once been, so I decided I would have to wait until after the Hour before satisfying my curiosity. I turned my thoughts back to the Psalms.

'I look to my right, I find no friend by my side.
There is no way of escape. No one cares about my soul.'

Then, as if a voice had whispered it in my ear, I knew it was Father Michael, whom my heart still called Edgar. My prayer had been answered.

349

It was not until the next day after Nones that Michael and I were able to exchange conversation. We were in the small walled garden to the east of the dorter. Above us loomed the great mountain of Arthur's Seat, which the canons jokingly called Mount Gloom, because often in winter it looked so bleak and dark, and obscured the sun. However, on that day it was resplendent, its slopes ablaze with the yellow-blooming gorse.

'My soul,' Michael said, 'I have thought and prayed much on what we spoke about when we last met, and now I can say with all my heart, yes, I want to come back to Inchcolm. Yes, I want us to spend our last years together. But I am also determined not to serve under Simon de Quincy. I saw Prior Walter on my way here. I had hoped to accompany you, but I arrived too late. I spoke to him a little about Simon, and the future of the priorship. I was very discreet, of course. Walter seems to be completely taken in by Simon, and thinks the sun shines out of his tonsure. Walter sees it as inevitable that Simon will succeed him as Prior, and Simon will have his blessing. But I will stop it, my dearest friend, I swear by the relics of St Columba that I will stop it: not just for our sakes, and not just for my own ambition, although I would dearly love to be Prior of Inchcolm, your Prior. I want to stop it because Simon de Quincy is a man of evil. For the sake of the Holy Mother Church and God's justice he must not be allowed to become Prior of Inchcolm.'

Michael's eyes were bright and hard with their new-found purpose. They made me slightly afraid.

'Michael,' I said softly, 'do you not think that God can look after His justice without your intervention?'

He shook his head violently. 'No. You know as well as I do that God sometimes uses us, mere mortals, as tools to carry out His design. Have we not countless testimonies of this in Holy Scripture? He has entrusted me with this mission, dear heart, and He has used our friendship as my spur. And because we are one soul, He has entrusted this mission to both of us.'

It was my turn to shake my head. I did not want to hear any more, but he went on. 'When I was at your Priory yesterday I talked also to some of the other Brothers there — it was easy for me to find out those who have seen through their Subprior's disguise. Brother David, for example. He is the most ambitious of them. So is young Brother Henry, although his time is yet to come. But even David admits that it would be impossible for someone from the Priory to become Prior over Simon's head. He agrees with me that it would have to be someone from outside. He told me he would support me if I put myself forward.'

'Edgar, Michael,' I said, trying to keep my head clear from the growing fear and unease, 'if Walter nominates Simon as his successor —'

'Because I trust you as I would my own soul,' Michael said,

stopping for a moment and lowering his voice, 'I will tell you what else I have done. You must tell no one, however. I have gone to someone higher than Prior Walter. I have gone to your Bishop.'

'What!' I exclaimed horrified. 'You're not going to involve Bishop Richard in this, are you?'

'Sometimes one must fight evil with evil, my soul. Without his support and permission, I could never move into his diocese, even if Simon himself elected me Prior. Bishop Richard will support any act that curbs Simon's power. But he warned me that Simon enjoyed the protection of one much higher than a Bishop, otherwise Richard would have removed him from office long ago. He would not or could not say anything more.'

'Did you tell him what you had been told in Viterbo?' I asked.

'Of course I did not,' Michael replied, offended. 'I told you I was sworn to silence. I broke that silence to you only because — you know why.'

'Yes, I'm sorry,' I said meekly. I was glad, although I was still unsure to what lengths his zeal as an instrument of God's justice might drive him.

'What I want you to do,' he went on, 'is to keep me in the minds of those of your brothers who are no friends of Simon. Remind them that my constant wish and effort is to become their Prior. Remind them, too, that I am not afraid of Simon de Quincy..'

'Michael,' I said, 'you must be careful. Simon could be a dangerous man to cross.'

'We stand in God's hand,' he replied in his most sonorous voice. 'He will not fail us.'

Two days later we were riding away from the Abbey of the Holy Rood, well-pleased with the outcome of the hearing. It was a bright day, with a cool breeze from the sea: a perfect day to be out riding in the world. The spring had come late that year, so it was only now, the end of May, in its first flush of glory. We rode over Wardie Moor under a canopy of lark song. Worldly songs tumbled in my spirit in spite of myself, and I was not alone, for Subprior Simon, too, was whistling melodies which I knew were not religious. Even Brother Thomas, such a quiet, shy young man, was humming to himself, his eyes glittering with excitement, emboldened by his Subprior's behaviour.

'Brother Michael,' Simon called out, interrupting his whistling, 'A word, please.'

The track on that part of the moor was wide enough for us to ride two abreast. I rode up beside him, our legs touching.

'We have done well, have we not?' he said, smiling. 'I managed to talk to a few of the Brothers at the Abbey,' he added.

'About Brother William de Colchester?' I asked.

'More about Prior Walter than Brother William, actually,' he said with an enigmatic smile.

'What is there to say about Prior Walter?' I asked, my curiosity alert.

'Well, we cannot expect to take Brother William away without giving anything in return, can we? I made a few inquiries as to whether they would like Prior Walter as their Abbot.'

'What!' I exclaimed.

'Well, you know,' he went on calmly, 'he's well-liked there, for the same reasons that he's well-liked in the Priory. He's fair, moderate, firm, clever.'

'Indeed,' I said, 'and that is why he is so precious to us.' Under other circumstances I would have been outraged at Simon's effrontery; that he was prepared to barter even our father in Christ. But the conversation with Michael was still troubling my soul, and I was afraid. Simon was bringing the day of reckoning nearer.

'Yes, very precious to us,' Simon repeated. 'But can you not see that we are losing him anyway? Losing him to old age, to the mainland, to the greater business of the Church. He wants to go, but he is too loyal to his sons in Christ. It is our duty to look after him now, just as much as he has looked after us all these years.'

'But what about Abbot William?' I asked, trying to muster my confused thoughts.

'Abbot William has no stomach for remaining in his office for much longer,' Simon replied.

'Have you spoken with Abbot William about this — this exchange?' I asked.

'Oh yes, I mentioned it to him. Apparently he has even raised the subject with Walter — not about Brother William, of course, but about Walter succeeding him. But Walter cannot bring himself to desert his Priory. So you see, brother Michael, we must simply push a little from the back, while the Abbey of the Holy Rood pulls from the front.'

'We!' I exclaimed. 'Who said I wanted anything to do with this?' There was too much scheming here, and I was being drawn into it from both sides. Besides, not even for my friend Michael's sake was I eager to see Prior Walter depart. That at least must be left entirely in God's hands.

The day I had fled to Inchcolm, forty years before, away from de Mortimer and his world, was the day when Walter had been elected Prior. If it had not been for him I would certainly have been sent back. I had known no other Father in Christ, and I loved him more dearly than I had my earthly father. I could not, I did not want to, imagine life without him, and the thought of helping him to leave was repulsive to me.

'Think about it, Brother Michael,' Simon said soothingly. 'And pray about it. I think you are being selfish. It is the good of Prior Walter that I have at heart.'

I thought about little else in the weeks that followed. Each time I thought about it, I saw with my mind's eye two riders galloping at night towards each other along a narrow, twisting path. One of these riders was Michael, whom I loved dearly. The other was Simon, to whom I felt, despite myself, a certain loyalty, and whom I could not find it in myself to hate.

Yes, I felt a loyalty to Simon which I did not understand. He had done nothing to deserve it or encourage it. In fact he had done everything to break the ties that once had bound me to him. He had done everything by doing nothing. Only twice since his return from court had he approached me in any other way than befitted a Subprior: once to express an absurd jealousy, and now to involve me in his scheme to acquire Brother William. And the last time we had embraced had been for joy and relief at the miracle of Queen Margaret.

I trusted Simon as much as I would a venomous snake. Yet in the struggle between our Priory and Bishop Richard, he had been as much a lion as a snake.

I wanted to shout out a warning to both of the riders, but I was helpless, for any warning would also have been betrayal.

Finally I decided to talk to Prior Walter, not to tell him of the plots that were being spun around the Priorship, but simply to find out for myself what he really wanted. I was left in no doubt that he wanted to go, but it was as Simon had said: he did not want to leave his flock. He knew that the canons of Holy Rood would be happy to see him as their new Abbot. He knew also that Abbot William wanted him as his sucessor. He even told me that Abbot William of Scone, the head of our Order in Scotland, had given his blessing to the move. 'But somewhere in my soul I have a deep foreboding,' he said with a frown. 'The Priory is still so vulnerable. I have steered it through so many shallows, past so many reefs: I am frightened to hand over the helm to someone else, even to someone as competent as Subprior Simon.'

'My lord Prior,' I said more as one would speak to a friend than to a father, 'is there not pride or vanity in that thought and that fear?'

He was only too ready to agree with me. 'You are right, my son,' he said, shaking his head slowly. 'I am a vain man. I must be more humble and obey the will of God. God does seem to be telling me that it is time for me to leave, does He not?'

'Yes, father,' I said with a sigh, believing it to be true, while at the same time feeling that I was part of a plot against him. But whose plot? I was not sure.''

A NEW PRIOR

"The following Whitsun [1209] Brother William de Colchester arrived on Inchcolm. Before that year was out, Abbot William of Holy Rood had retired, and Prior Walter had been invited to stand for election as the new Abbot. He agreed, with the blessing of his own convent. However, without the permission of Bishop Richard, such an important transfer could not go ahead. When Prior Walter sent to him to request that permission, the reply was that he was to come to the Bishop's presence at Cramond to celebrate Easter with him, and to discuss the matter of the move to Holy Rood.

Walter chose Subprior Simon, Brother David, and myself to accompany him. It was the first time for many years that both the Prior and the Subprior had been away from the Priory at the same time, and was a mark of the importance of the visit.

We arrived at Cramond after Nones on Easter Saturday, to be met with the news that Bishop Richard was gravely ill. The Bishop's palace was in turmoil. We were informed that it would be impossible to see the Bishop while he was so indisposed, and we should go back to our Priory and offer up prayers for his recovery. Walter would have complied with this, had not Simon insisted that we complete the business we had come for. I agreed with Simon, for, although I did not say so, I thought that the Bishop's illness was yet another way of causing us annoyance.

We retired to our house on our Cramond lands. We would spend the night there and decide finally our course of action the following morning. Simon then returned to the palace. By Compline he came to us with the news that Bishop Richard would see us that very night.

A servant came to summon us just before Vespers. As soon as I stepped into the great bed-chamber where Bishop Richard lay I knew he was a dying man. Despite the burning herbs and spices, and the wood-smoke that issued from the crackling fire, I could smell the smell of death in the warm, heavy air. I begged God's forgiveness for having thought evil of the dying.

We approached the bed and each of us kissed the ring on his hand, which lay limply on the coverlet. His face was grey and his cheeks were sunken. His eyes were closed, but his lips moved soundlessly, as if in prayer. Then he spoke, his eyes still closed, his words often interrupted by sharp, wheezy intakes of breath.

'Walter, my son, I know why you have come. St Columba has

sent you just in time — huuh — you have my blessing to leave my diocese to become Abbot of Holy Rood — huuh — I am sorry if I have offended your Priory in the past, and have not treated St Columba with all the respect he is due — huuh — I wish to make amends. I am not far from death — huuh — I want my mortal remains to await the Day of Judgement at his Priory of Inchcolm. I have been unkind to you in my life. I wish to be kinder to you in my death.'

His eyes opened momentarily, as if to see for himself the look of joyful surprise on our faces. He was requesting burial at Inchcolm! There had not been an important burial on the island since the death of Sir William de Mortimer. No one of any rank, either spiritual or secular, had been prepared to risk the wrath of St Columba, or whatever else it was that had consigned Sir William's body to the deep. If Bishop Richard was to be buried in the Priory, then the last scruples would be swept away. I blessed the Bishop for his bravery and goodness, and I gave thanks to God for having turned the Bishop's heart towards us.

Bishop Richard had started to speak again, and we all craned forward to catch his words. His voice was trembling and his breathing was becoming even more difficult.

'There is one boon I crave in return,' he wheezed. 'I wish to appoint Prior Walter's successor.'

No one spoke. All were waiting for the Bishop's next words. He was gasping for breath. It was as if something was trying to smother him.

Finally he spoke again. 'I nominate Father Michael, canon of the Abbey of the Holy Trinity at Scone — huuh — he is a worthy son of your Order, and knows and loves your Priory well.'

I crossed myself. Michael had certainly laid his plans well, and my heart went out to him in love and admiration. Then my eyes went to Simon's face, and my heart shrank in fear. For he was staring at me with undisguised rage, and in his eyes there was a look that I had never seen there before, the look of a man betrayed.

My thoughts were interrupted by a great choking sound. Bishop Richard's chest heaved violently, as though his lungs were bursting. One of the physicians told us to leave, and Prior Walter beckoned us to follow him out into the great hall.

'My sons,' he whispered, 'what shall we do?' He addressed all of us, but he turned to his Subprior. For once Simon seemed lost for words.

It was Brother David who spoke. 'We cannot refuse such an offer. The Bishop's body is worth more to us than ten coffinfuls of gold.' He scowled at Simon as if to say, 'or ten Prior Simon's.'

Prior Walter again looked at Simon, who still remained silent. I then suggested that it was too great a decision to be made without the advice of the whole convent.

Finally Prior Walter asked Simon outright for his opinion.

Frowning he replied, 'My lord Prior, with his dying breath our Bishop has tied my hands, my thoughts and my tongue. I cannot move, I cannot think, I cannot speak in this matter. I will submit my will to whatever decision is taken, but that decision will have to be taken without me.'

Prior Walter stood silent for a moment, his eyes closed as though in prayer. 'Very well,' he said at last, 'we will inform Archdeacon Henry that we will return to the Priory at once. There is enough light left to make the journey tonight. By tomorrow at Prime he will know whether Bishop Richard is to be buried amongst us or not.'

As we were embarking we heard the death-bell tolling from the palace chapel, and we knew that Bishop Richard was dead. We sang the Placebo for his departed soul as our boat glided over the calm, darkening waters towards Inchcolm.

By the time we arrived it was almost night. All was still, for the convent was already asleep. Prior Walter ordered the summonsing bell to be rung. Soon from their beds brothers and lay-brothers came stumbling, rubbing their eyes, their faces full of alarm, for only the most momentous of events could have called them to Chapter from their sleep. Even the servants crowded eagerly around the chapter house door.

When the whole convent was assembled, Prior Walter announced the death of our Bishop. From the very back of the crowd someone cheered. To this day I do not know who it was, but the rumour was that it was Lay-brother Ethernan. It was certainly the sort of insolence he was capable of. It was followed by an awkward silence. Prior Walter then ordered the lay-brothers and servants to go immediately to the church to say prayers for Bishop Richard's soul. They were to stay there until he, Prior Walter himself, gave them permission to disperse and return to bed. Thus they were all to do penance for the soul who had been goaded by a demon to shout out so irreverently. The rest of us, the brothers and the novices, were to follow him into the chapter house.

There was much unhappy muttering at this from amongst the servants and lay-brothers. Subprior Simon shouted that if he heard one more word of complaint he would order them to stay in the church till dawn, and the first one to fall asleep would be whipped to within an inch of his life.

As we took our places in the chapter house, candles were brought in from the church. Then Prior Walter explained exactly why he had summoned us together at such an irregular hour. Everyone crossed themselves. Old Father William was the first to speak.

'My lord Prior,' he said, his gaunt, stooped figure throwing fantastic shadows on the walls, 'I urge that we accept the body of our Bishop. It can only bring an increase in honour for our Priory. An increase in honour will mean an increase in revenue.'

Then looking pointedly at Subprior Simon, he went on, 'Then perhaps we can have our new chapter house and whatever else we are told we need, and fulfil our spiritual duties to those who have been placed within our care. What better memorial to our late Bishop than this.' He sat down. Several of the brothers applauded, notably Brother David, Brother Hugh and Brother Peter the infirmarer.

This whole speech was aimed at Simon, and in a spirit of anger and bitterness. Father William had never forgiven Simon for removing him from his church at Auchtertool. This had happened several years previously. Simon had urged it on the grounds that Father William was too old to carry out his duties properly. However Father William had been replaced by a young vicar in deacon's orders who could scarcely read or write. He received a vicar's stipendium, which was barely enough for him to live on, while the Priory drew the rest of the income. This was, of course, far more than if a priest had been serving the church.

This had infuriated not only Father William, but also Bishop Richard, for he had made it clear that he wanted a fully ordained priest in every parish of his diocese, and one who drew all the teinds and cain that were his due.

Simon had caused all this to be done not merely to infuriate Bishop Richard, but also to bring more revenue to the monastery, which could then be spent on the great buildings he was planning, foremost among them the new chapter house.

When Father William had sat down, and the applause had been cut short by a scowl from Prior Walter, Brother Matthew spoke. He was our sacrist now, as old Brother Peter had finally become too disturbed in spirit to carry out his duties.

Brother Matthew was a quiet, trim man, with a deep, doleful voice, and dark doleful eyes to match. He was also a fawning man, drawn always to the most powerful. 'My brothers,' he said, looking at Prior Walter, 'is it not a deep dishonour that we do to our Subprior if we accept the condition which Bishop Richard attached to his body? Subprior Simon,' he went on, inclining his body towards him, 'has led us with a sure and skilful hand over the last years on the many occasions when important affairs have taken our Father Prior from us. Far be it from me to speak ill of the dead, but I would be a hypocrite if I did not remind you all that in life the hand of Bishop Richard lay heavy upon us. His hand in death now threatens to take from us the man who is best suited to become our Father in Christ. There is no doubt in my mind that there can be only one successor to Prior Walter, and that is Subprior Simon. I say, therefore, we resist the Bishop's hand in death, just as we resisted his hand in life.'

He sat down. There was again applause, this time from Brother William de Colchester, Brother Roger and Brother Thomas. Brother David jumped to his feet and shouted, 'My

brothers, if we accept the Bishop's body, it is not that we are
losing Subprior Simon. He will still be here to guide the steps
of the new Prior. We all know Father Michael from the Abbey
of Scone. He too has shown himself to be a true friend of the
Priory.

'Furthermore, my brothers,' he went on, drawing himself up
to his full height, and looking at Subprior Simon, 'we cannot
afford to pass over this God-given opportunity to heal finally the
wound that was inflicted upon us by the alleged intervention of
St Columba during the obsequies of our patron Sir William de
Mortimer.'

Prior Walter glared at him. 'You had better sit down, Brother
David,' he growled, 'before you insult even further the honour
of our blessed saint, to say nothing of the honour of your
Subprior.' All eyes were on Simon. Everyone expected him to
speak, to defend himself against the slur that David had cast
upon him. However, he sat without moving and without speaking, his face set in an expression of aloof indifference.

So the debate went on, reaching further and further back into
the past, digging deeper and deeper into angers and resentments that had been growing steadily over the years.

All the time I sat as silent as Simon, without lifting my hand
once to applaud either side, without saying a word, not even
when my own honour had been impugned by the reference to
the obsequies of de Mortimer. What could I say? If I spoke for
the Bishop's dying wish, then I would be speaking for the
complete reinstatement of the Priory's worldly fortunes, as well
as for my friend and his dream, which was also my dream. Why
then did I not? As I sat in the dark chapter house, watching the
grotesque shadows flickering and dancing, I knew why I did not
speak. It was not out of loyalty towards Simon, nor out of love
for him, nor out of respect: it was out of fear. I was afraid of
Simon and of what he might do, not so much to me, but to
Michael. I was afraid of this man whom I had once loved, and
who had given me the greatest joy and the greatest pain on this
earth. When will I be free of this man? I thought to myself. Only
when you feel nothing for him, no love, no hate, no fear. I closed
my eyes, prayed to St Michael, and asked permission to speak.

'One moment, Brother Michael,' Prior Walter said to me, 'our
Subprior wishes to speak.' Simon had risen. He looked even
paler than usual, and his face glimmered ghost-like in the
candle-light.

'My Father in Christ,' he said, 'my brothers, Matthew, Thomas,
William, Roger, I thank you for your loyal support, but I must
agree with Brother David.' There was a moment's silence, then
uproar. Prior Walter commanded silence, so that Simon could
continue. 'Yes,' he said, 'I would gladly be your Prior: it is an
office I have long desired; and, owing to the frequent absence
of our dear Prior, it is an office I have been given ample

opportunity to practise. Yet as an Augustinian I fervently believe that personal wishes must be put aside when they clash with the best interests of the convent. I have prayed and thought much about this, and I am convinced that it is in the best interest of the convent to accept the body of our late Bishop for burial, and with an open and loving heart I will embrace my new Father in Christ, Father Michael, from our mother Abbey.'

'I praise God that He has finally loosed your tongue, my son,' Prior Walter said, 'for through it He has taken away from us a most difficult and divisive decision. May God bless and reward you for your wisdom and humility.' 'Amen,' everyone replied.

So it was decided on the eve of Easter in the year of our Lord 1210 that our new Prior would be Father Michael of the Abbey of the Holy Trinity Scone, whom I had known as a young man as my brother Edgar.

Letters were dispatched immediately to Father Michael, inviting him to become our Prior, and to his Abbot, William, asking him to release Michael from his vow of stability. We stressed to them both that we were carrying out not only our own wish, but the dying wish of our late Bishop.

Meanwhile we buried Bishop Richard. The funeral went without mishap. Prior Walter himself accompanied the coffin in the Bishop's state barge, which sailed in the midst of a whole fleet of boats. With him were not only Bishop Malveisin, who was to lead the service, but also young Prince Alexander. How different it was from the funeral of Sir William de Mortimer.

I did not go to Cramond. It was my duty to organise the procession which was to meet the coffin and lead it up to the church. Also as precentor I was to lead the singing in the choir.

A tomb had been prepared in the north wall of the choir. Brother William had worked on it without stopping for two nights and a day. It would require many weeks work to complete, but he had made a fine start. That man, he had the skill of an angel and the energy of a demon: already two angel-heads had appeared out of the stone on either side of the niche, and the back of the niche was smooth enough to receive its first coat of plaster as soon as the coffin was in its place.

The cost of the whole funeral had of course to be borne by us. However, we did not complain, as we knew we would receive many grants from his friends and retainers. This indeed happened: even the King gave us ten shillings a year to pray for the memory of his faithful servant.

After the last funeral guests had departed, and Bishop Richard was safely buried, letters arrived from Scone: Michael had accepted the Priorship, and Abbot William had released him from his vow of stability. Now nothing stood between Michael and his ambition except time and place.

Brother Thomas and myself were sent to Scone to accompany our new Prior-elect to Inchcolm. Prior Walter was due to leave us for Holy Rood at Whitsun. The plan was that he and Prior-elect Michael would work together for a few weeks, before Abbot William of Scone came to consecrate Michael as our new Prior. At the same ceremony Walter would demit office, then assist Abbot William in the consecration.

My heart was joyous as we rode along the highway towards Scone. Not only was I going to be reunited with my friend, I was also riding away from the fear and the dark thoughts that beset my soul when I was near Simon. However, in my wake, like a cloud or a swirl of mist, I was dragging with me some of that darkness. For at my side rode Brother Thomas. He was young, and shy, and could scarcely look anyone in the eye. Yet I could not forget that he had supported Simon against Michael in the Easter eve Chapter. I would have to warn Michael about that. With a shudder of foreboding, I felt part of a Priory which was already divided against itself.

Three days later three of us were riding back south along the same road: Brother Thomas, myself, and our new Prior-elect. Brother Thomas had fallen behind, so that Michael and I had our first opportunity to speak in private.

'Tell me more about what happened when I was elected, dear heart,' Michael said. 'Simon gave his consent, did you say?'

I nodded. I felt none of the triumph that gleamed in Michael's eyes.

'Edgar — Michael — my lord Prior,' I replied, stumbling over how to address him. 'Prior Michael,' I said, as if I was pronouncing some strange, foreign word.

'I'm only your Prior-elect, my heart,' Michael said with a smile. 'Besides, I want you always to call me Edgar, when we are alone, in token of the times we spent together when we were younger, and the sweet friendship we shared — and still share.'

'No, Edgar, Prior Michael, Prior-elect Michael,' I said. He burst out laughing. 'No,' I said again. 'It must be one or the other all the time. You will be my Prior, therefore it must be Prior Michael, or my lord Prior, or Father-in-Christ. I do not want to live a double life in any way.'

'All right, Michael, my son-in-Christ. I would rather be your brother, but it is a small price to pay to be near you. I shall make you my special adviser, and you shall write all my letters.'

'I do that for most of the officials as it is,' I replied, 'except for Simon, who usually writes his own.'

'I have heard rumours that he writes his own charters, too,' Michael said with a sneer.

'I know nothing of that,' I said more sharply than I intended. 'It is beneath the honour of a Prior-elect to believe in rumours,' I added more softly. I did not want to quarrel with my friend, especially not on the subject of Simon.

'Perhaps it is,' Michael said, but without softness. 'However, it was not beneath the honour of a Bishop to believe in worse rumours than that concerning Simon de Quincy. I will say no more, except that it was easy for me to persuade Bishop Richard to support me against Simon. He swore that Simon would become Prior of Inchcolm over his dead body.'

'Over his dead body!' I exclaimed, puzzled at this strange phrase. 'But it is you who have become Prior over his dead body.'

'No,' Michael said with a laugh, 'it is an Inglis expression. If you say that something will happen over your dead body, it means that you will do everything in your power to stop it from happening.'

'What a strange expression,' I muttered. 'I don't like it.'

'Talking about dead bodies,' Michael went on, 'I have been thinking a lot about how our old friend Andrew met his end. As soon as I'm Prior I want to look into it very carefully.'

'What is there to look into?' I asked. 'It happened over ten years ago, and Laurence the murderer has not been seen since.'

'Exactly,' Michael said forcefully. 'It is my intention to find out where he is.'

'And just how do you intend to go about that?' I asked. I could not help smiling, as it seemed such an impossible and fruitless task.

'I see you think I am a fool,' he said good-naturedly. 'But you will soon discover that your new Prior has special powers.'

'I think he had better have,' I said jokingly.

'Not only am I going to I find out where he is,' Michael went on, 'but you are going to help me. You are one of my special powers. No more questions now,' he said, holding up his hand as I was about to speak. 'Your Prior-elect has spoken!' And with that he gave a whoop most unbecoming for a Prior-elect, and urged his horse on at a gallop.

Amidst great sadness Prior Walter left us at Whitsun, but for our consolation he left behind him a worthy successor.

Prior Michael was hard-working and vigorous. He wanted each official to report to him on the exact state of their office. He took over the accounts and records which Subprior Simon had been keeping. Walter had been only too glad to leave this and many other mundane tasks to his Subprior. Prior Michael made it clear from the outset that he would be doing things differently. He enjoyed sums and accounts, and besides, he was determined to curb the power that they had given to Subprior Simon. Simon did not protest. He handed over the accounts promptly, going to great lengths to explain them to his new Prior.

Prior Michael endeared himself to the whole convent. He was never unnecessarily strict, and always had an encouring word to say to everyone: to everyone, that is, except to his Subprior. To him he was cold, even insulting.

Take for example the Prior's scriptoriolum: in Prior Walter's time Simon had one of the two keys to this room, the room which Walter had had built on Simon's advice, and to Simon's specifications. Latterly, during the many absences of Prior Walter, Simon had been using it as his own. Prior Michael took the key away from Simon, saying that there was no need for a Subprior to use the scriptoriolum at all.

Not only did Prior Michael do this, but he did it in a most public fashion. He made Simon hand the key back to him in Chapter. Then, at that same Chapter, he handed it to me, saying that as precentor and Prior's amanuensis, it was more fitting that I should have access to the scriptoriolum.

It was clear to everyone, even to the dimmest lay-brother, that by this gesture the new Prior was giving me more authority in practical affairs than he was giving to his Subprior. It was a humiliation for Simon. He accepted the decision without a murmur of protest. He simply bowed and said, 'As my lord Prior wishes.'

My brothers started treating me with a new deference. For the first time I was seen to be more powerful than Simon de Quincy. I have never lusted after power, as some men do. The new situation made me more afraid than proud.

Only Brother William spoke out in favour of Simon, but nobody took him very seriously, except when he had a paintbrush or a chisel in his hand.

Next Prior Michael informed the convent that there was to be no more talk of building a grand new chapter house. It was vain show, he said; besides we could not afford it. It was true that we had received many extra gifts since Bishop Richard's body had been buried in our church. These were to be used to do necessary repair work to the church and conventual buildings, and to beautify the Bishop's tomb. The present chapter house, he said, was perfectly adequate for a modest Priory like Inchcolm. Brother William, he added, might like to decorate its walls with some suitable scenes from the life of St Augustine. At this, Brother William muttered something incomprehensible, then Brother David asked permission to speak.

'I am very pleased to hear the wise words of our lord Prior. May I humbly suggest that the first new work to be done is done on the dorter. There is a wind that blows around my pallet which could not be stronger if I were sleeping on Carcraig.'

'And when it rains it is like being on Meadulse Skerry,' Brother Roger chirped. 'At high tide,' he added, and there was a roar of laughter.

Prior Michael promised that although we lived on an island, he would ensure that his sons-in-Christ slept as befitted men, not gulls.

In fact I had been the one who had persuaded Prior Michael to abandon the scheme for a new chapter house. I firmly believed that it was extravagant and unnecessary. Brother William's talents could just as well be used on other, more modest schemes. And what Brother David and Brother Roger had said about the dorter was only partly exaggerated. The end near the church, where Simon slept, was snug and warm, but the other end, by the rere-dorter, where the less senior brothers slept, was very draughty, and when the wind was from the south-west it would blow the rain through the ill-fitting door and in under the eaves. Yes, such things were more important to attend to than the building of a new chapter house.

That winter was one of the wildest I have ever lived through. For months we were beleaguered by bitter winds that hardly abated from All Saints until Eastertide. Sometimes it was all we could do to bring supplies across from Barnhill. By Candlemas many of our cattle had taken a terrible cough and were starting to die. Nor were we alone in this affliction, for the disease was striking cattle throughout Fothrif and Fife.

It was during that winter that Simon too began to strike, not like the lion, but like the snake.

Because you come to know your brothers so well, living with them all the time, the slightest look or gesture can say more than a long speech in Chapter. With my beloved Michael, whom I knew as well as my own soul, the tilt of his chin and the furrows on his brow whenever he looked at me told me not only that he was troubled, but that I was the cause of it.

One day in the scriptoriolum Prior Michael was dictating a letter to me, and struggling to find the right words. I suggested a particluar phrase. He replied crossly, 'If I had wanted that kind of pompous nonsense I would have asked Simon de Quincy to write it. Why can't you think for yourself? You sound more like that man every time you open your mouth.'

I was hurt by this outburst of anger, which was so rare between us. Yet I was also relieved, for now at last I had something to grip hold of, instead of frowns and hurt looks.

'Pompous nonsense yourself,' I replied. 'Anyway, what's so terrible about sounding like Subprior Simon?'

He turned his head away and said that he had no time for idle chatter. I persisted, saying that as a true friend he owed me an answer: 'I've known for some time something's been wrong,' I said, 'but you refuse to tell me. We've shared everything in the past. Why should we not continue to do so?'

'I thought we had shared everything,' he replied bitterly.

'And what do you mean by that?' I exclaimed, growing afraid.

'I cannot,' he replied, his shoulders sagging beneath his despair. 'And please, keep your voice down.' His tone was more gentle now, almost pleading. His anger was broken. Guiltily I lowered my voice to a whisper.

'Why can't you say, my heart?' I said, putting my hand on his arm.

'Because —' he hesitated, then with a curse he muttered, 'He uses God's law against me like a dagger.'

I knew he meant Simon. 'What is he doing?' I asked grimly.

'He's confessing to me. He's been confessing to me for the past week.'

I let out a long hiss of air, then I too uttered a curse. I wanted to ask him what Simon had been saying, but of course Michael was bound by the confessional oath of silence.

'Why do you let him?' I said. 'He's only doing it to hurt — both of us.'

'You know the Rule as well as I do,' he replied. 'I cannot refuse anyone confession.'

'But he's done full penance once before,' I said naively.

'You also know,' Michael said icily, 'that a man can confess his sins as often as he likes, until he feels true contrition.'

I was becoming more and more angry. 'Well, I have done true penance, and I have felt true contrition, not once but several times over, and to see the anger at me in your eyes is yet more penance. Do you not think I have suffered enough for having loved that man? God knows what he has been telling you about me. Your eyes accuse me, even though you shake your head: they are not bound by any oath, even though your tongue is. Yet I cannot defend myself, because I am not allowed to know the charges.'

'You're raising your voice again,' Michael said flatly.

'Raise my voice!' I hissed. 'It's a wonder I'm not crying out for all the convent to hear. Listen, if Simon has come to you for penance, give him it. Throw him into the dungeon, put him on bread and water, send him to the demoniacs at Cambuskenneth. Show him what true penance, true suffering is.'

'For any of those things,' Michael said quietly, taking my hand, 'he'd have to make full confession in Chapter. It would harm you as much as him.'

'I do not care — if it rid this place of him,' I replied, beside my self. I was shaking violently now, not with rage, but with the lust for vengeance. It consumed me like a flame and its heat made me mad.

'It might rid this place of you, too,' Michael said grimly.

'It would be a worthy sacrifice,' I replied, fiercely, stubbornly, foolishly. It was a blessing that on that day one of us remained sane.

'A demon has possessed you, dear heart,' he said gently. 'Let us go to the church at once and pray for you to be freed of it.'

I did not want to go, for the demon had my heart so fiercely in its grip that it was easier to leave it there than to prise its claws out. But my Prior and my friend insisted, so sullenly I followed him to the church.

It was empty, but not silent, for the wind sighed loudly around its roof, and the waves could clearly be heard crashing onto the rocks beneath its walls. These sounds, as familiar to me as the sounds of my own body, create their own stillness, their own prayer, their own peace. And in that peace the demon eased its grip.

We returned to the scriptoriolum. I wanted to destroy neither Simon nor myself. I simply wanted to protect my friend and our friendship.

'Prior Michael,' I said, 'let me tell you everything that happened between Simon and myself, from the first day we met, so that nothing will remain hidden. It is the only antidote I can think of to the poison which Simon is giving to you.'

Michael was silent for a moment, his face pale and drawn. Finally he said in a weak voice, 'No, it is not necessary. I lost my trust in you, and I have suffered for it. You have given me that trust back. I cannot, I need not ask you for more. Nothing that Simon has told me, or can ever tell me, will shake my trust in you again. I swear it. And I beg your forgiveness for having trusted him more than you.'

The wind that imprisoned us on the island for almost the whole of that winter, and blew contagion and death upon our cattle, blew likewise upon men. It was a wind that loosened the soul's grip on the body. That winter we buried Father Geoffrey, who, soon after he had become too weak to shuffle to the church, gave up his spirit to God.

The tormented soul of old brother Peter, who had been our sacristan for so many years, found peace at last, and surely went straight to Heaven, having suffered Purgatory long enough on this earth. Towards the end we had made a bed for him in the infirmary chapel, where he spoke for hours with demons and angels, and was assailed by terrible visions of Hell.

Then, as if death was greedy, Father William, too, passed away, still longing for his cottage and his flock in Auchtertool. We buried him there in the churchyard, away from the sound of the sea he loathed so much.

Perhaps it was not the wind that took so many away from us that winter, but Prior Walter's departure. I have heard of similar things happening in other houses when a loved and respected head, who has ruled for many years, leaves or dies, many of the older brothers go with him, not in body, for that cannot be, but in spirit.

That winter, too, we heard that our aged King was near death, while the royal MacWilliams were yet again fomenting rebellion in the north. And to the south the accursed King John and his kingdom lay under interdict.

Caught between the savage heirs of the old kingdom and the godless machinations of King John, with a dying King whose own heir was a mere boy of twelve summers, we wondered how long our world could survive unscathed.

Subprior Simon seemed to thrive on the evil tidings from north and south, adding his own poison for good measure. He said there was an ancient prophecy, which he had heard in Rome, that in the year of our Lord 1211 the Christian world would become smaller. This, he suggested, meant that the spiritual darkness that had fallen on England would fall also on Scotland, King William's dynasty would be overthrown, and pagan chaos would ensue."

THE GHOST

"The spring brought some relief to our dark fears, with the news that the King was well again and was leading an army towards Moray and Ross against the rebels. It also brought other concerns to divert us from our apocalyptic gloom.

Shortly after Easter we received a letter from Abbot William of Scone concerning the election of the new Bishop of Dunkeld. He wanted to propose to the King that we elect John de Leicester, Archdeacon of Lothian. It was obvious that in Abbot William's eyes what made John such a suitable candidate was that he was hated by his Bishop, William Malveisin, whom he wanted to exclude from both his election and his consecration. This was, as Abbot William explained, to teach Malvesin that he might be Bishop of St Andrews, the first Bishop of the realm, but he was nothing more. A limit had to be set to this man who wanted to create an Archbishopric in Scotland, and who wanted to fill that office.

Abbot William had enlisted the support of Bishop Walter of Glasgow and Bishop Ralph of Brechin, both close to the King. With his letter to us he was seeking the support of the chief monastery in the Dunkeld diocese.

He found a ready ally in Prior Michael, who had been involved in several bitter disputes with Bishop Malveisin when at Scone.

There was much discussion on the subject in Chapter. Simon spoke out strongly against such action. Why antagonise Bishop Malveisin so unnecessarily? And what was wrong with having an Archbishpric in Scotland? It was all very well Scotland being a special daughter of the Holy Father, but it was a long way from Scotland to the Curia. An Archbishop in Scotland would save much shoe leather, for Scottish clergy would no longer have to run to Rome at every turn. Also an Archbishop could assert himself more against the King. He, Subprior Simon, could not name one Bishop, apart from Malveisin, who was not in the pocket of the court. An Archbishop would mean a stronger and more independent Church in Scotland.

Prior Michael argued that to create an Archbishop was to create a monster that would devour us all. Look how intolerable Malveisin was as a Bishop. He, Prior Michael, had at Scone experienced his tyranny and ambition at first hand. We, not being in his diocese, had been protected from him. But if he became Archbishop no clergy would be safe from him.

As for Simon's other argument, what guarantee was there that the King would not appoint the next Archbishop? The English clergy had tried to oppose King John's choice of Archbishop of Canterbury, and look at the disasters that had overtaken that country as a result.

I kept silent, for I did not know what to think. My main concern was that there should be peace amongst the Scottish Bishops, for I feared warring Bishops almost as much as I feared warring Kings.

I was troubled also by something else. I had never heard Simon express such opinions before, and I suspected that he was wilfully stirring up dissension.

A compromise was reached. We would write to Abbot William saying that we supported John de Leicester as a candidate, but make no mention of excluding Bishop Malveisin from the proceedings. The Abbot could take from our silence on the matter whatever he wished.

By Whitsun we had received another letter, this time from the royal chancellor, summoning Prior Michael to Dunkeld for the election of a new Bishop on the feast of St Mary Magdalene [22 July]. The letter did not say who the candidates were, but the royal messenger, when questioned, said that one of them was Archdeacon John de Leicester.

Prior Michael chose me as his companion for this journey, the first he had made since becoming our Prior over a year before. Simon was left in charge. However, Prior Michael had instructed Simon to consult with Brother David the cellarer on any matter that arose in his absence, no matter how trivial. I could only imagine that this displeased Simon as much as it delighted David. But whatever Simon was feeling was hidden behind an unctuous smile and a polite, almost subservient bow.

The journey to Dunkeld went smoothly enough. There was in fact only one candidate, John de Leicester, and although there were several Bishops present, Bishop Malveisin was not among them. John was elected unanimously, and his consecration was fixed for the following Yuletide, by which time the approval of the Holy Father would have been obtained. The Bishops who would carry out the consecration were named as Walter of Glasgow and Ralph of Brechin, and the ceremony would take place at Dunkeld itself. Malveisin was not mentioned once during the whole official proceedings. Away from these proceedings his exclusion was the chief topic of conversation.

Within three days the business was over and we were riding south again. Everyone was in excellent spirits. The chancellor had assured us that the King would let no one interfere with the new Bishop-elect of Dunkeld. By no one we all knew he meant Bishop Malveisin. The King himself was in good health, and his army was triumphing against the rebels in Ross. Even I, who had had such misgivings about angering the Bishop of St Andrews, felt confident that we could weather any storms ahead.

It was only a few days after our return from Dunkeld that the whole convent was thrown into confusion by the appearance of the ghost at Barnhill Point.

Malcolm the gateman told Prior Michael about it after Prime. Malcolm's brother, who was a grange-servant at Barnhill, was one of several who had seen the ghost with his own eyes the previous night.

Prior Michael raised the matter at Chapter that morning, asking if any of us had heard of such a thing before. We all crossed ourselves, and Brother David spoke. 'My lord Prior, it saddens me to tell you that this is not the first time we have heard such foolish rumours. The serfs and lay-brothers believe that it is the ghost of our Subprior Andrew, who died so violently at the place where the ghost is frequently seen.'

'No foolish rumours,' Subprior Simon said, 'for I have seen the ghost with my own eyes.'

'And so have I,' said a chorus of other voices.

'Foolish rumours or no,' David went on, 'none of the peasants will live on the Point any more.'

'Old Bishop John of blessed memory even exorcised the place,' I said, 'only a year or two after it first appeared. However, it seemed to be of no avail, for allegedly it has been seen many times since then.'

'Let us have another exorcism,' Brother Matthew suggested.

'We do not have a consecrated Bishop,' Brother Hugh said. 'It is only a consecrated Bishop who could exorcise such a powerful spirit.'

'We are quite aware of that fact,' Matthew replied haughtily. 'But we could invite Bishop Malveisin to do it for us.'

'An excellent idea,' Simon put in.

'The less we have to do with Bishop Malveisin the better,' Prior Michael said with a frown.

'He is the first Bishop of Scotland,' Simon said quietly.

In no time an argument was raging yet again as to the claims and rights of Bishop Malveisin.

'My brothers,' I shouted, 'may I remind you that we are talking about the appearance of the ghost at Barnhill Point. If Bishop John, who had carried out successful exorcisms elsewhere, was not able to lay the ghost, do you really think that another Bishop will have more success, whoever that Bishop might be?'

'I think,' said Brother Peter, 'that we should offer up more prayers for the soul of Subprior Andrew, to help release him from the earth. It is clear to me that we have not prayed long, or sincerely, enough.'

'We will do as Brother Peter suggests,' Prior Michael said. 'Today we will say a special Mass for the repose of his soul, and every week at this time we will do the same, until we hear no more of this apparition at Barnhill Point. And when our new Bishop is consecrated we will ask him to hold a Mass of exorcism. But in order to still the fears of our servants, we will also hold a Mass on the very place where Andrew died. It was in one of the storerooms, was it not?'

'A former storeroom, my lord Prior,' Brother David corrected. 'It was sealed off after the murder. No one has ever been inside since, except at the time of the last exorcism.'

'Then that is where we shall hold our service,' Prior Michael said.

'My lord Prior,' Subprior Simon said gravely, 'I believe that such an action would stir up even more fears. The local peasants believe that there is a curse on that room. That exorcism by Bishop John was one of his last public acts. Shortly afterwards he became too weak to continue as Bishop, and within months he was dead. I know this is foolish, but such beliefs are hard to remove from minds that are stubborn and ignorant.'

'Stubborn and ignorant indeed, Subprior Simon,' Prior Michael said. 'Bishop John was an old man. You do not have to look for curses when old men die.'

'It was also the place where Subprior Andrew, who was not old, met his end,' Simon went on quietly. 'That is when the story of the curse began, not with the death of Bishop John.'

'Nor do you have to look for curses when men die thus,' Prior Michael replied grimly. 'You should look rather for someone who is accursed.'

'I am merely repeating what the local peasants are saying,' Simon said with a sigh of indifference.

'Are we to be dictated to by the fear of ignorant peasants?' Brother David shouted insolently.

'If it is my lord Prior's intention to allay this fear, as I understand it is,' Simon continued, 'then I do not think that holding a Mass inside that place will do so.'

I was watching Simon's face closely. As usual he showed no emotion. But over the past year, when he was angered or humiliated, as he had often been, a slight trembling would appear just below his right eye. It was as if a small insect was trapped inside, beating its wings against the skin. He would try to brush it away, but he could not. It was the wings of the anger-demon. As Simon exchanged words with Brother David, I could see the trembling begin.

'Then let us hold the Mass outside the storeroom,' I said, tiring of the argument.

'But why should we pander to mere peasants?' This was Brother Peter who spoke, echoing the thoughts of Brother David.

'It is mere peasants who do most of the work around here,' Simon sneered. 'You would act swiftly enough if it was upsetting our cattle, or stopping our hens from laying.'

Prior Michael stood up and brought the discussion to a close. 'No, Brother Peter,' he said, 'Subprior Simon is right: our serfs and servants are upset enough without us upsetting them further. Brother Michael, your suggestion is a good one: we will hold the Mass outside the storeroom on Barnhill Point.'

'May I suggest,' said Simon, 'that we hold it on the feast day of the blessed Saint Laurence in ten days' time. He is a most potent saint, in whom the people put great trust.'

'So be it,' Prior Michael said, and started to intone *Verba mea*, thus bringing Chapter to a close.

As we filed out, Prior Michael asked me to come to his scriptoriolum.

'Well, my friend, what did you make of all that?' His face was flushed with excitement.

'What do you mean?' I asked. 'I'm only thankful that I've never seen the thing. I wouldn't go near that place at night, not even if all the demons in Hell were chasing me.'

'Not even if your Father Prior commanded you — or your dearest friend begged you?' Prior Michael said with a smile.

'You would not be so cruel,' I said, trying to laugh.

'My brother,' he replied, 'this is no jest. Listen, I think God has delivered our Subprior into our hands. It came to me like a vision during Chapter, when I heard that the storeroom where Andrew died had been sealed off. Then, when Simon spoke against opening it up, I knew for certain.'

'What?' I cried, beside myself with curiosity.

'That there is still a body in there, the body of the man that everyone thinks is the murderer.'

'You mean Laurence?' I gasped.

'If that was his name, then that is who I mean,' Michael said with grim satisfaction. 'So as soon as the moon has waned a little, we are going to go over to Barnhill Point one night and look for ourselves.'

'And if we do find Laurence's bones? What does that prove?' I asked.

'It proves that, well, it proves that Laurence was not the murderer. It proves that someone else was,' Michael said haltingly.

'That is all it proves,' I replied. 'It does not tell us who that someone else was.'

'Listen,' Michael said, 'who had most to gain from Andrew's death? Who became Subprior in his place?'

'Simon, of course,' I said, 'but we all gained from it. Andrew was the bane of everyone's life.'

'Yes, but who else would have been ruthless enough?' Michael went on.

'All right,' I conceded, 'it may well have been Simon, if Laurence's bones are there. But it is not enough, my lord Prior.'

'We will make Simon swear the oath of innocence on Laurence's bones. It is too late for them to bleed, but God may give us some other sign.'

'He may, but there again He may not. His ways are not our ways. And Simon, if he has committed all the crimes which you suspect him of, will scarcely shrink from the sin of perjury.'

Prior Michael looked dejected. I went up to him and laid my hand on his shoulder. He shook his head silently, then looking up he said.

'I agree, it is not enough to accuse him, just like the old man's story in Viterbo was not enough to accuse him. But I still want to find out if those bones are in the storeroom.'

'Why?' I exclaimed. 'It's only vanity. You just want to prove that you are right.'

'I swear,' Michael said, 'that if we find those bones, I will go to the Curia in person to gather enough evidence to bring Simon to justice.'

'If you cannot do that here, where it seems that he has committed so many crimes, what makes you think you can do it at the Curia?'

'Because at the Curia there may be those who are at last willing to talk,' Michael said.

'Yes,' I said, 'one frightened old man who would only talk to you after you had sworn never to tell anyone else. For all you know, he may be dead.' I did not like doing this to my friend, taking away his hope at every turn. But it had to be done. He had been blinded by his own zeal.

'I have another idea,' he said slowly. I groaned inwardly. 'You will admit that Simon did not want that storeroom opened up?'

'Yes,' I said, 'you certainly could conclude that from his behaviour in Chapter this morning.'

'So, whether it is complete proof of his guilt or not, he would rather that Laurence's bones were not found. The brothers would start asking questions again about Andrew's murder, and their answers would be similar to ours.'

'Yes,' I conceded reluctantly.

'Well,' Michael went on, growing excited again, 'what if we let Simon know that we are planning to open up the storeroom and search it. If only I had thought of this in Chapter this morning, I would have supported Brother David after all.'

'You can't think of everything,' I replied consolingly.

'Simon does,' Michael replied sourly. 'Let me finish, please. We let Simon know that we are going to open up that storeroom. We assume that he will want to go there first and move the bones. We wait for him as he comes out and then we have him.'

I thought about it for a moment. It seemed full of risks and very difficult, but, yes, if we caught him removing Laurence's remains, then there would be no way out for him.

'I suppose we could try,' I said, without enthusiasm. Then I added, thinking aloud, 'If you are right in all this, then it seems to me that Simon must have an accomplice. He surely can't have rowed over to the mainland every night the ghost has appeared. There must be someone else. And it might be that someone else whom we catch.'

'Then we will make sure that someone else talks,' Michael said darkly.

'Well, it will mean one of us being on the mainland already. We cannot simply watch Simon here, then follow him over. He's sure to see us.'

'We will both be on the mainland, dear friend. You and I will hold a special vigil at Barnhill Chapel the night before the Mass. The day before, I will announce in Chapter that the Mass is to be held inside the storeroom after all. That will mean that Simon has only one night to remove the evidence for his crime, and that is the night when we will be keeping vigil not at Barnhill Chapel, but at the sealed storeroom at Barnhill Point, and so —' Michael clapped his hands together violently '— we have him.'

'May St Columba and St Michael stand by us,' I murmured, full of foreboding.

'Amen,' said Prior Michael, 'Amen.'

The days flew by, and the eve of the feast of St Laurence was upon us all too quickly. The foreboding, which I had felt when we had first devised our plan to trap Simon, had haunted me ever since, waking and sleeping, and often I would awake sick with fear from terrible dreams the nightmare brought, and I would hear her chuckling as she scuttled off into the darkness.

Time was measured by the fearful beating of my heart and the tap-tap-tapping of Brother William's chisel, as he hurried to complete the new work in the chapel of St Laurence, ready for the saint's feast day. This chapel had recently been given a generous offering by Earl Malcolm of Fife, a most pious man. One night in a dream Saint Laurence had appeared to him telling him that his father was still in Purgatory for the outrage he had committed in the Saint's church at Warkworth. It was in the hope of easing his father's torments that Earl Malcolm had given an offering to every altar dedicated to Saint Laurence in the land.

Brother William's chisel stopped only during the Hours, and

at night, but even then I could hear it inside my head, as though my ears had absorbed the sound, as a rag absorbs water.

I watched Simon's face closely when Prior Michael announced in Chapter that the Mass at Barnhill Point was to be held inside the storeroom after all. It registered nothing at all. He simply shrugged his shoulders and said that he hoped nothing untoward happened afterwards to confirm the peasants' worst fears. There was not even a trembling behind the skin beneath his right eye.

That evening after Vespers, Prior Michael, myself, and two lay-brothers set off for Barnhill. When we were on the water we told the lay-brothers that instead of keeping vigil at the chapel, we would keep vigil at the storeroom itself. They looked at us with terror, and begged to be allowed to remain at the chapel. Prior Michael graciously allowed it, and they kissed his hand out of sheer relief.

The moon was down and thick cloud blotted out what little light the stars could give. We welcomed the darkness as our ally. I knew Barnhill Point like the back of my hand, for I had spent more time at Barnhill and the storehouses than I had in the cloister during my years as cellarer.

The row of storehouses at the Point are built high up into the hill, almost at the summit, on a broad ledge. The path that links them to each other, and to the steps down to the little harbour, runs in front of them along the lip of the ledge. The sealed storehouse was the last one in the row, furthest away from the steps.

The night was mild enough, but a fine drizzle became heavier as the night wore on, and chilled us. We had taken up our watch behind a huge, overhanging boulder which lay beside the harbour steps. At its foot there was a small, dry patch of flat ground covered in ferns, about the length of a man. Here we laid the rope and the cudgel we had brought with us, and here we took it in turns to rest, while the other watched.

After each watch we lay together for a short while, embracing one another for warmth. In those embraces I felt closer to my friend than I had ever felt before, as if in the darkness and the tension of the summer night our two souls finally and without stain fused into one.

It was so still that we heard across the deep the small bell wakening our brothers for Matins. Silently we stood together and said the Hour with them.

When it was finished Michael went to rest and I remained on watch. The windows of the Priory church blackened as the candles were extinguished, and the silhouette of the Priory was only dimly visible against the dark sky beyond. Suddenly I noticed a light on the water. It shone so briefly that at first I thought it might be a silkie playing a trick. Then I saw it again, a little longer, nearer to the shore. It was no silkie. It was a boat.

I hissed to Prior Michael to come and see. Trembling, hand in hand, we waited. The light shone again. It was practically below us now, at the harbour. We could hear the scrape of the bow on the pebbles as the boat touched land. Then the light started coming slowly up the steep path towards us, passing within feet of where we were hiding.

The light which the lantern gave out was weak, and shone fitfully, as it was often obscured by the figure's cloak. There was no doubting it, however. It was one of our brothers.

On and up the figure went, losing itself in the darkness of the storerooms, and suddenly the light vanished.

'Now we've got him,' Michael whispered excitedly in my ear, making me jump, so tense had I become. 'Let's get closer to the door to catch him as he comes out. Remember, we stand one on either side of the door. I challenge him, you put the rope around him and, if necessary, hit him with the cudgel on the back of the knees. We must catch him alive.'

We moved up to the door of the sealed storeroom. By this time it was raining hard, but I scarcely noticed it. We stood there for what seemed like an eternity, my breath coming in short, sharp gasps.

Then, as loud in the tense stillness as the rumbling of thunder, the door of the sealed storeroom creaked slowly open.

A figure appeared silhouetted against the sea. I raised the rope ready to ensnare him. Prior Michael stepped forward and commanded him to yield, but before I could let the rope fall, the figure lunged forward and with a terrible cry Michael vanished over the edge of the path. I had already taken the cudgel in my hand, so that when the figure turned and made for me I brought it down on his head with all my strength. He staggered back and without a sound plunged over the edge, following Michael down the steep slope to the rocks below.

I shouted Michael's name into the darkness. A weak groaning came in reply from far beneath me. I lit the lamp we had brought, although my hands were trembling so much I could hardly hold the flint. Finally it flared into light. As I hurried towards the steps to descend to the groaning, a voice from behind startled me so much I almost fell over the ledge.

'Who'th there?' the voice shouted angrily. I turned round to see the figure of an Augustinian standing a few feet away from me, holding a lantern in one hand and a sack in the other. I knew from the voice that it was Brother William.

'It's Brother Michael!' I shouted. 'Follow me at once. Something terrible has happened. It's our Prior and..' Not knowing how to finish the sentence I hurried down the steps. For if it was Brother William we had seen coming across from the island, who was it that had come out of the storehouse?

Guided by the groaning I picked my way over the rock-strewn slope and almost fell over Prior Michael. I thanked God that he was still alive.

'It's all right,' I said, 'I'm here. We'll get you back to the Priory. Brother William is here to help me.'

'I cannot move,' he whispered.

'Don't even try to move,' I urged, my head spinning in panic as I saw his body lying at a strange, twisted angle. 'Just lie there and we will carry you.'

'Who was it?' he muttered.

'I will go and see,' I said.

'Brother William,' I shouted, 'please stay with our Prior. He lies here.' The lantern swung towards me and soon William was beside us.

'There is someone else nearby,' I said. 'I must go and see who.'

It did not take me long to find what I was looking for. The body lay only a few feet away, and slightly lower down the slope. It was one of our brothers. He lay face down, silent, his head at a grotesque angle. I turned him over and held the lantern up to his face. What I saw made me cry out in horror. It was more the face of a beast than a man, scrawny and dark, covered in whisps of black hair, which lengthened on its chin to a scraggy beard. Part of it was dark with blood, where my cudgel had struck. It was nobody from the Priory, and yet there behind the dirt and the blood and the hair was a face I knew, the face of the servant whom Simon had brought with him from Rome, the face of Lay-brother Laurence. His eyes stared back at me without recognition, for he was dead.

We tried to lift Prior Michael to take him to the boat, but the slightest movement caused him to cry out in pain. So we decided that Brother William would cross to the island in the coracle he had brought and bring back a bigger boat with Brother Peter the infirmarer and servants to carry Michael on a bier.

William wanted to take the corpse with him, but I told him to leave it where it was. I did not trust him, although when I asked him why he had been creeping around Barnhill Point in the dead of night he answered that he had come to collect some paints that had been brought there the previous day. These he had needed to finish the work on the chapel of St Laurence, which he had longed to finish before the dawn of the Saint's feast day. Then he added insolently, 'Of courth, Brother Michael, I could athk the thame quethtion of you.'

'You could,' I replied, 'but you would not get an answer. Now, go at once, for St Laurence's sake, and for the sake of our dear Prior.'

The uproar at the Priory when the news broke of the night's events swept past me like waves, while I sat cold and chilled on the rock of my grief. For it was soon clear that Prior Michael had received his death-hurt. Not only had his limbs been broken by the fall, but also his attacker had stabbed him in the stomach. There was little that Brother Peter could do except ease the pain. I sat with my dying friend almost constantly, leaving his side only to eat and sleep and hear Mass. Subprior Simon, who was acting Prior, was gracious enough to exempt me from the Hours.

He did not, however, exempt me from a full interrogation in Chapter. The morning after the tragedy I had to appear before my brothers and give an account of what had happened. I told them everything. I said that we had gone to the storehouse at Barnhill Point because we suspected that there was an earthly reason behind the hauntings, and we wanted to watch more closely, while at the same time keeping our vigil. I did not say that it was our suspicion of Simon that had taken us there. That suspicion had turned to dust. Simon's reputation had emerged unscathed.

Brother William, however, earned a sharp rebuke for being abroad at the dead of night without permission. He gave as his excuse a dream. He said that as he slept his first sleep he dreamt that Saint Laurence came to him and told him that if he did not finish the work on his chapel before the dawning of the next day, the Saint's feast day, a terrible disaster would befall the Priory. Brother William knew that the paints which he needed to finish the work had been brought to Barnhill that very day by Brother Stephen. So he had not returned to his bed after Lauds, but had slipped out of the Priory and rowed over to the mainland to fetch them, intending to work through the rest of the night.

'My brotherth,' he concluded, staring at each one of us in turn, his insolent eyes gleaming, 'I beg you to conthider that, had I not been at Barnhill latht night, even worthe might have befallen.'

'And the dream was a true one,' Brother Matthew exclaimed, 'for the chapel was not finished, and are we not overwhelmed by disaster?'

Many nodded grimly at this and crossed themselves.

If you had not been there, Brother, I thought, we would not have moved up to the door of the storeroom, and our beloved Prior would not now be lying close to death. I could not see how anything worse might have befallen. But I said nothing, too sad and exhausted to speak such thoughts.

'If you are ever again visited by such a dream, Brother William,' Simon said sharply, 'you must not act on it before consulting with your Prior or your Subprior. Is that clear?'

Brother William nodded his head meekly.

'Your penance will be to hear five Masses daily for the next week.'

Brother William bowed his head contritely, although his eyes still gleamed as insolently as ever.

I was then led to the church, where a Mass of purification was said over me, for I had spilled the blood of a fellow human. Since he had been an outlaw, an excommunicate and a murderer, and since I had struck in defence of my own life, there was to be neither punishment nor penance for me. Nevertheless I had to be purified, and my habit had to be washed by the priest-in-charge for that week. During that Mass I tried to pray for the soul of the man I had killed, but the prayer stuck in my throat.

Prior Michael slept fitfully most of the time, calling out sometimes my name, sometimes Simon de Quincy's. I stayed with him holding his hand, wiping the sweat from his face, and helping Brother Peter administer analgesic balms.

He clung thus to life for three days. Then, on the feast of St Hippolytus, as we were finishing morning Mass, the bell of the infirmary chapel began to ring, slowly at first, then more and more urgently, until it was ringing the full alarum. This was the bell I had been dreading most, the bell that summons the convent to attend a dying brother.

In a great swarm we hurried down through the cloister, out the main gate and into the infirmary. I was first to arrive. Brother Peter and Fergus his servant had carried him into the chapel on a bier and placed him in front of the altar. He was quite still, but his eyes were open and watching. When he saw me he gave a little smile. I knelt down beside him and took his hand. Blood trickled from the side of his mouth and I wiped it away with the sleeve of my habit.

'He is bleeding inside,' Brother Peter announced. 'I cannot staunch the flow. There is nothing more I can do.'

As precentor I should have led the singing, but I was unable even to speak for weeping. It was not necessary to explain to my brothers what had to be done. We had been through this often enough in the past year.

Three times my brothers chanted the Creed, and then they began to sing the seven penitential psalms:

'Lord, do not condemn me in Thy fury, do not punish me
in Thy anger.
Have pity on me, Lord, for I am weak; heal me, Lord, for
my bones are shaken, and my soul is greatly troubled;
but Thou, Lord, how much longer? Come back, Lord, and
rescue my soul;
save me for Thy mercy's sake. For in death no one
remembers Thee;
who will acknowledge Thee in Hell?'

I felt my friend's hand clasp mine tightly. His eyes were now closed, but his lips had begun to form the words of the psalms.

'Because I kept silent, my bones grew weak, while all day

long I cried out.
For day and night Thy hand lay heavy upon me, I
writhed in my distress, while my spine was pierced
through.
I made known my sin to Thee, and I did not hide my
guilt..'

He opened his eyes and tried to speak. I put my ear to his mouth.
'My dearest soul,' he whispered, 'the psalms are like a mirror,
in which I see reflected my own folly. When the seventh psalm
has finished, bring me Simon. I have to speak to him before I
die.'

Without thinking, I frowned and shook my head.

'Please,' he said, 'I beg of you.'

'Of course, my dearest,' I whispered.

I stood up, went over to Simon, and quietly told him of Prior
Michael's request. He nodded and together we knelt beside the
dying man, one on either side of him.

'For an enemy has hounded my soul, has laid low my life
in the earth;
he has consigned me to darkness, like the dead of ages
past.
And my spirit is deeply afraid; in me my heart is troubled.
I remember days of old; I meditate upon all thy works..
I stretch out my hands to thee; my soul thirsts for thee
like a thirsty land....
For thy name's sake, Lord, restore me to life;
in your justice, lead my soul away from tribulation;
and in thy mercy destroy my enemies, and kill all who
oppress me,
for I am thy servant.'

The seven penitential psalms were at an end. Simon cleared the
chapel, telling my brothers to continue the psalms and the
proper litany outside, and in an undertone.

'Simon de Quincy,' Prior Michael said in a soft, clear voice,
when all was quiet, 'I beg your forgiveness.'

Simon bowed his head graciously. Prior Michael went on, 'I
have treated you badly, and in my heart I have harboured the
worst suspicions of you. You were judged and condemned
without a hearing. I have been punished for it. Let me die with
your forgiveness on my head. For that, I am sure, the Lord will
judge me more favourably.'

'I forgive you, my lord Prior, with all my heart,' Simon said,
laying his hand on the dying man's forehead. Michael smiled
and closed his eyes. Simon stood up, made the sign of the cross,
and left the chapel.

I stared in astonishment. Since that fateful night at Barnhill,
my suspicions of Simon had become as deep and dark as any
my friend and Prior had harboured. My thoughts, when they

were not hovering anxiously around my fast fading friend, were all of revenge, the object of which was Simon de Quincy. Yet here was my friend forgiving him with his dying breath.

Prior Michael lay there gasping, as if the effort of forgiveness had robbed him of all his remaining strength. He was struggling to speak, and at last the words came, in quick, desperate bursts. It was as if he had read my thoughts. 'My dearest brother,' he said, 'do not think of revenge. He is too strong for you, and too full of guile. He will destroy you as he has destroyed me. Leave him, Michael, to the punishment of God. Promise me that you will. Promise me!' He began to cough, a terrible, deep, harsh cough, as if he would rid himself of his lungs. Blood welled up in his mouth and the trickle became a torrent. His head sank back. He gave a terrible gurgling sound, then all was quiet.

I knew he was gone. I closed his eyes, extended his limbs, but I did not cover his face. I wanted to look one last time at his beloved features. I wiped his mouth clean with the sleeve of my habit, and kissed his forehead.

In the silence I could hear the cry of the gulls, the sough of the waves, like the hissing breath of some great monster, and the quiet voices of my brothers, who were chanting for the second time the penitential psalms.

'If Thou wanted a sacrifice, I would give Thee it;
but Thou dost not love whole offerings.
My sacrifice to God is a broken spirit,
Thou wilt not scorn this crushed and broken heart.'

I became dimly aware of someone entering the chapel. A shout went up and soon all the convent was around us. Some were weeping, some were singing the Commendacio. Brother Peter bent over and covered the face.

After Vespers, along with Subprior Simon, Brother David and Brother Matthew, I carried his body to the church. The weight of my dear friend upon my shoulders was almost as unbearable as the weight of my grief. Ahead of the bier walked the whole convent, each brother, lay-brother and servant with a candle in his hand, while at their head was born aloft the great crucifix. Seeing it swaying over the heads of my brothers, I was for a moment pierced by the memory of the day when it had been held high in the strong arms of the man I had loved, and whom I now mourned, when he had confronted de Mortimer and his men in the churchyard at Aberdour, the day when I had lost him for the first time. 'All my life I have lost you and found you, lost you and found you. Today, too, I have lost you to find you again, and when I do we will never be parted.' And my grief was lightened and the bier no longer wanted to crush me into the earth.

I watched beside the body all that night, leading the singing of the whole of the Psalter. There was such sweet comfort in the words of the psalms, as dear and familiar to me as the face of my lost friend.

When my brothers had finished, they went to the dorter, leaving behind them silence. Then welling up out of some deep fissure in my spirit came the words of the blessed Aelred, which he had written when death had torn away from him his dear friend. I had copied them not only onto parchment, but onto my soul. And my tears flowed as I spoke them quietly to the empty church, and to the empty shell that had once been Edgar.

'I am full of sadness, and I cannot even find relief in sleep, for my beloved friend has been snatched away. And who is there that does not marvel that Michael can live without Edgar? Only the person who does not know how sweet it was to be alive at the same time as he was, or how sweet it will be to return to our homeland together...'

I could almost taste both sweetnesses, like honey upon the tongue: the one made me sad, the other made me joyful, for I knew that our returning together to our homeland could not be far away. It was a sweetness that not even the thought of Simon could sour.

We buried our Prior in front of Saint Laurence's new altar. The consecration of this altar should have taken place on the Saint's feast day, the day of the tragedy at Barnhill. It had been postponed until the Octave. I had not wanted the burial there, surrounded by the new work done by Brother William. But how could I voice my misgivings, without also giving voice to suspicions I had promised to bury with my friend?

My suspicions might linger, but my fears were gone. All my life I had lived with fears. Since Edgar called Michael had come back to Inchcolm, my fears had thickened and darkened. But now the worst had happened, and there was nothing left to fear. In their place came grief, but that, I knew, time would dissolve. Edgar, called Michael, was at peace, and every day brought me closer to the day when we would be once more reunited. This was, and still is, all my joy."

BISHOP-ELECT

"Subprior Simon took charge of everything. He had already ordered the storeroom at Barnhill Point to be sealed, not only with a strong lock, but also with a waxen seal. He then sent messengers to our new Bishop-elect, John de Leicester, as well as to Sir Robert de London, lord of Aberdour, begging them to come to the Priory. Only when they had arrived, Simon explained, would he open the storeroom and search it. And in their presence he would conduct a full hearing into the death of our late Prior, as well as into the reappearance of the accursed lay-brother Laurence.

At Chapter on the day following Prior Michael's burial, Brother Matthew the sacrist stood up and said we should present Bishop-elect John with our choice of successor to Prior Michael. No one was surprised when he proposed Subprior Simon for this office. Nothing now stood in his way. Some murmured assent, some remained silent, no one spoke out against it.

'I thank my brothers-in-Christ,' Simon said with a gracious smile. 'And subject to the approval of the King, of our Order, and of our Bishop-elect, I accept the office gladly. As you have broached the matter,' he went on, 'may I presume to suggest to you a suitable candidate for Subprior? I propose our precentor, Brother Michael.'

I was utterly dumbfounded. Had I heard correctly? I had slept so little in the past nights that sometimes a slumber-demon would play tricks on me when I seemed to be awake. But everyone was looking at me, smiling and applauding. Simon's words still echoed in my head. They must have been real, I must be awake. I stumbled to my feet.

'My brothers, please,' I cried out, not sure what I was going to say. 'Please, my grief for our late Prior is still too great. I cannot see the way ahead. Give me time. Let me pray about it.'

I was granted the respite I had requested. After Chapter, my head still reeling, I went to the church to pray. I knelt on the slab which covered the grave of my friend.

How could I work with his enemy? Would that not be a betrayal? Would it not be better to leave the Priory altogether, ask to go Scone, where my memories of Edgar were sweet and unsullied by the dreadful happenings here, and by the presence of Simon? But Simon was no longer Edgar's enemy, I had forgotten that. He had forgiven him on his death-bed, with his dying breath he had forgiven Simon de Quincy. So I must forgive him too, must I not?

In answer to this question I slowly nodded my head, which was heavy and dizzy. It never occurred to me to ask whether Simon de Quincy had forgiven me.

To prove to God, to Edgar, to myself, that I had forgiven Simon, I accepted the office of Subprior.

Bishop-elect John did not arrive on Inchcolm until after the feast of the Holy Cross. With him was a tall, sickly-looking young man in fine clothes who was presented to us as Sir Alexander de Aberdour, the son of Sir Robert de London and Lady Anicea, widow of de Mortimer. He had come to represent his father, who was still up in the north helping Earl Malcolm stamp out the last sparks of rebellion. He was even more bored by the whole affair than was the Bishop-elect, and did even less to hide it.

Before approving any new appointments, the Bishop-elect conducted a full inquiry into the recent tragedy at Barnhill Point. When the sealed storeroom was opened, a hole was found in the back wall which led to another chamber set deep within the hillside. It was obvious from the remains of food scattered over the floor, from the animal skins piled in one corner, and from the terrible stench, that this is where Laurence had made his lair. Here he had lurked all those years, emerging only at night to forage for food, to breathe fresh air, and to frighten the local people.

Bishop-elect John ordered the whole chamber to be filled with stone and earth and to be sealed forever. Then, after saying a Mass of purification, he declared the storeroom itself worthy to be reopened and used for its original purpose.

The hearing was held in the chapter house. Neither Bishop-elect John nor Sir Alexander was very interested in it. In fact, if form had not demanded it, they would not have held one at all. However, there were others, both in the Priory and in the Bishop's retinue, who would be satisfied with nothing less. Chief among these was Subprior Simon and the Bishop's young chaplain Gilbert.

Often while Gilbert was at the Priory I could feel his cold eyes on me, yet he never spoke to me. This made me uneasy, for he spoke with almost everyone else, especially with Simon.

At the hearing I again told my story of the events at Barnhill. I had already told it so often that it was almost like chanting a psalm. Then Brother William told his, about his dream and his wanting to fetch the paints. Bishop John shook his head and stifling a yawn said that it was a tragedy which would leave its scar on the annals of the Priory and of the diocese for ever. Special prayers should be offered to St Laurence, who had played such an active part in the terrible events, and he himself would make a grant to his altar in the Priory church. He then said that, with the permission of Sir Alexander, he would bring the hearing to a close. Alexander nodded with unaccustomed enthusiasm. Father Gilbert inclined his head towards the Bishop and whispered something in his ear. John looked annoyed, then looked over in my direction. With a loud sigh he nodded to Gilbert, who stood up and pointed at me.

'Brother Michael,' he said, 'I have one question I want to ask you. If you and your Prior suspected that there was someone living in the storeroom, why could you not have waited till the following day, when you were intending to break it open to hold the service? Armed servants would have searched the place in broad daylight, and neither you, your father-in-Christ, nor any of your brothers would have been in any danger. I believe that you must answer this question, and answer it satisfactorily, before the hearing can be closed.'

I stood up and stammered, 'I — we did not think. We were not sure what it was. It might have been a spirit.'

'That does not answer my question. You could have waited until after the search, and the service. There was no need —'

'Put him under oath and let's get this over with,' Bishop John interrupted impatiently. 'We've spent long enough on this wretched affair.'

'It will not be necessary, my lord,' Gilbert said confidently. Then rounding on me, he said, 'I suggest, Brother Michael, that you and your Prior went to Barnhill Point for another purpose, quite different from the one you have stated. You went there goaded by the demon of carnal lust. And it was the wrath of God that fell upon you there.'

There was a ghastly silence, then protesting voices started to be raised.

'How dare you smear the memory of our late Prior!' Brother David shouted.

'It is not true!' I cried.

'Then what is true, Brother Michael?' boomed Bishop John.

'I will tell you what is true,' I said, looking at Subprior Simon, who sat there with a quizzical smile on his face. I'll wipe that smile off your face, I thought to myself angrily. 'We were waiting for our Subprior, Simon de Quincy.' And to a shocked and silent Chapter I gave a detailed description of the suspicions that had driven Prior Michael to his death. And all the time I was speaking I watched Simon's face, and still his smile did not fade. I began to stumble over my words.

'And why did you harbour such dark suspicions of your Subprior? What made you think he could have been capable of perpetrating such deeds?' Gilbert went on relentlessly.

'I am bound by oath not to reveal it,' I said, thinking of the solemn promise I had given my friend not to reveal to anyone what had been revealed to him at the Curia. But if you push me any further, I will reveal even that, I thought, knowing that by speaking such a dire accusation I could unleash a whirlwind.

Almost as though he knew I had come to the brink of the pit, Simon stood up and begged permission to speak. 'My lord Bishop, my lord Alexander, my brother Gilbert,' he said solemnly, 'I am cut to the quick by what has been revealed today. But I am not surprised. I know what the roots of Prior Michael's suspicions were, and they lie in the Leverith affair. I hesitate to mention such a painful matter, which once divided us from the late Bishop Richard, may his soul rest in peace. But it must be said that Prior Michael believed, against all the evidence, that I was responsible for the slaughter of the Bishop's cattle. Is that not true, Brother Michael?' I looked at Simon in amazement. It was true, and yet it was not. Simon was saving us both from the whirlwind. I nodded.

'I know this,' Simon went on, 'because he once in anger accused me of it. And I know this because, despite my sworn denial, he never trusted me. And to that fact all the convent is my witness.'

He swept his hand gracefully around the room. Many of my brothers nodded sagely in agreement.

Bishop John stood up and motioned Simon to be silent. 'Father Gilbert,' he said frowning, 'are you satisfied now? You see where your prying has led you, to a matter which causes deep embarassment between myself and my dearest Priory, a matter which must be left to the mercy and the oblivion of God.' Without letting Gilbert reply to this question he went on, 'I declare the matter closed. And let this whole sad case be a lesson to you that suspicion can be a demon which like the will o' the wisp can lead us to our doom while we think that it is leading us to truth.'

'Amen,' everyone muttered.

'One last thing, Father Gilbert,' Bishop John said. 'You will ask the forgiveness of the convent for letting your own suspicion seduce you into smearing so foully the memory of their late Prior, and of Precentor Michael.'

Father Gilbert lowered his head and sullenly did as he had been told.

After the hearing I expected to be summoned to Simon's presence, but no summons came, not that day, nor any day following. As far as Simon was concerned, it was as if I had never spoken.

The next day Bishop John and Sir Alexander assembled the convent one last time in the chapter house. There John declared that he was granting the convent's request and appointing Simon our new Prior. However, he debarred me from the office of Subprior because of my rash and irresponsible conduct, which, he said, had contributed to the death of Prior Michael. I had shown a disastrous lack of judgment in not trying harder to dissuade him from his dangerous plan and to open his eyes to his folly, a lack of judgment ill suited to a Subprior.

I bowed my head and said 'so be it'. I did not care. I would have more time to grieve for my friend and say prayers for the passage of his soul through Purgatory. I had never wanted to be Subprior, anyway.

However, the next words that the Bishop spoke did not leave me so indifferent. He announced that the new Subprior would be Brother William de Colchester. There were no smiles and applause, such as had greeted the prospect of my becoming Subprior, just a shocked silence.

Brother David was first to break this silence. 'But, my lord,' he spoke up boldly, 'did not Brother William act as irresponsibly in this sad affair as Brother Michael. More so, in fact, for if he had not been prowling around Barnhill Point at the dead of night, our late Prior would never have stepped up to the door of the store room, and to his death.'

Bishop John motioned to Father Gilbert, who said, 'Brother William was led by a saintly vision, not by devilish suspicion.'

Brother David opened his mouth to speak again, but Bishop John stopped him. 'Enough!' he shouted impatiently. 'There has been too much argument already. I forbid your new Prior to allow any more talk on the death of Prior Michael or the appointment of your new Subprior. I commend Simon to you as your father in Christ, and as soon as I myself have been consecrated, I will come and consecrate him.'

Then he bade us farewell and summoning his retinue marched out of the chapter house and down to the waiting boats.

At last Simon was Prior. Almost at once he ordered work to start on a new chapter house, silencing all argument about cost by saying that he had obtained a generous grant from Bishop John for that purpose.

Subprior William was given the task of supervising the work. He would act as master-mason, Simon announced, which would of course save us a considerable amount of money. No one objected, not so much because of the money we would save but because anything that diverted Subprior William's attention from the keeping of discipline in the convent was to be welcomed.

We had had a glimpse of the cruelty of the man the week after his summary appointment over us. A complaint was brought in Chapter against Brother Stephen the granger by young Brother Thomas. Thomas claimed that he had seen Brother Stephen talking and laughing with Ela daughter of Ferceth, our grieve at Barnhill. Thomas had admonished Stephen about it, but had been told to mind his own business. Stephen did not deny the charge, but said that Ela had been telling him how a fox had stolen some of her ducks.

'Then why were you laughing?' Subprior William asked. 'Do you think it funny that a fockth should kill our duckth?'

Brother Stephen hung his head. 'It was just the way she was telling the story that made me laugh,' he muttered.

'Would you like to share the wit of a fair maiden with your brotherth?' William persisted. 'And if you can make me laugh, you will ethcape the whipping you detherve.'

Brother Stephen was silent.

'Thpeak up, Brother Thtephen,' William said maliciously, 'I did not catch the joke. Did you, Brother Thomath?'

Thomas gave a nervous smile and shook his head. I hoped that he was regretting ever having opened his mouth.

'I did not say anything,' Brother Stephen said defiantly, 'nor will I. I cannot remember what it was that made me laugh.'

'I will athk the maiden herthelf the next time I thee her,'

385

William said, lifting his sleeve to wipe away a long slaver that hung from the side of his mouth. 'And I will order her father to punish her for leading my thonth into thin.'

'No!' Stephen cried out in alarm. 'Leave her out of this. It's not her fault. It's my fault, give me all the punishment.'

'What touching penitenthe,' William said with a sneer. 'You may not be able to remember what made you laugh, Brother Thtephen, but you will remember what maketh you cry. And you will remember to act with the decorum expected of an Auguthtinian next time you come near a daughter of Eve.' Then he ordered Brother Stephen to bare his back, and from under his habit he drew a whip of knotted leather. It had belonged to Subprior Andrew, but I had not seen it since his death.

Brother Stephen was a large, robust man. This was a blessing for him, for I am sure that a thinner, frailer man would have been cut to the bone by the whip wielded by the great, thick arm of Subprior William.

Soon Stephen's back was stained with blood and he was roaring and screaming like a wounded bull. I shouted for the beating to stop, and others joined me, but William paid no heed. Then Prior Simon said stop. Immediately William strode back over to his seat, and Brother Stephen collapsed groaning to the floor.

As Brother Peter and I helped him to his feet and led him away to the infirmary, I realised that there was something left to fear after all.''

ST. LAURENCE'S EAR

''The inquiry into the conduct of Prior William was getting nowhere. Archdeacon William de Ednam, with the relieved consent of Sir Gervaise Avenel, the King's representative, decided to take the Prior and Brother Henry with him to Dunkeld and consult the Bishop as to the next step. There was certainly no point in staying any longer on this accursed island.

If only the convent was unanimous in their accusations against their Prior. But there were some brothers who spoke in his favour and accused his accusers of being under the spell of

Brother Henry, who secretly coveted the priorship, which would soon, it was rumoured, become an abbacy.

For the first time since his arrival on Inchcolm, the Archdeacon was smiling. He was smiling at the thought of getting back to his beloved Dunkeld and his beloved work. With every day that passed the tasks awaiting him on the mainland were multiplying. Besides, there was always the fear that someone else might have got the Bishop's ear. Old Bishop Hugh was so easily led. He needed someone like Archdeacon William to protect him from unscrupulous clerks looking for some comfortable benefice or prebend.

Martin was not smiling. His business was not yet over, and he would have gladly continued the hearing till the autumn storms came to imprison them on the island even longer. He begged the Archdeacon for permission to stay behind, but the Archdeacon forbade it. Martin's conversations with that decrepit old brother had brought to light nothing new which could condemn Prior William. Not that the Archdeacon had ever expected they would. They had served their purpose in keeping that insolent young man out of the main inquiry. Now he would be needed at Dunkeld. Besides, the Archdeacon found a certain pleasure in seeing the young man so discomfited. He had had things his own way for long enough. It was time for him to be reminded who was in charge.

So Martin was very downcast when he visited old Brother Michael after Nones that bright summer's afternoon. He was to leave with the Archdeacon immediately after Prime the following morning. He had come to say goodbye.

"But I have not finished my story," the old man said, feeling bereft.

"I will return soon," Martin said, trying to sound as if he really believed it. Brother Michael shook his head slowly. "You will want to return, I am sure of that, and you will try to return, but when you do it will be too late. You must remember that I am old and tired and no longer afraid of death."

Martin could feel desperation rising in his breast. "Then, Father," he said, "tell me quickly the end of your tale. I have until Vespers."

"So be it," the old man said, taking a deep breath and crossing himself. "I have told you how Prior Simon and Subprior William began their offices, and as they began, so they continued, for years, how many years? Seven years? Eight years? What does it matter?

Then one day, it was the feast of the blessed Aelred, I stayed in church after Vespers to say prayers for the soul of Prior Michael. I lit a candle, placed it by his grave, and knelt down. Then I looked up at the statue of St Laurence, which stood above us. As so often before I could see in the face of the statue the features of my late friend, but on this night the face seemed almost alive. Perhaps it was the flickering of the candle, perhaps it was the fond memories kindled by thoughts of the blessed Aelred.

It was as if my late friend himself stood before me. Before I knew it, I had stood up and was moving towards the statue. I realised that I wanted to embrace it. I started back guiltily and crossed myself. What demon had entered into me, that I should even have contemplated such blasphemy? Then I looked around the church. There was no one there, I was completely alone. I knelt again in prayer, but still I could not rid myself of the desire to embrace this statue, which had through some devilish trick become my dear, departed friend. But was it a devilish trick? Or was it the saint himself, whispering to my soul to come to him? Had St Laurence finally forgiven me my sins against him?

I could bear it no longer. Deliberately, carefully, I climbed upon the altar of St Laurence. I stood up and reached out to embrace him, putting my cheek against his.

It was then that I heard the voice. I looked at the face of the statue in astonishment, half expecting to see the lips move. It was as still as death. As I withdrew my face the voice ceased. Again I put my face against the statue's cheek, and again I heard the voice. I could not make out the words, but I knew the voice. It was the voice of Prior Simon.

I jumped down from the altar and looked behind it. There was a space between the back of the altar and the wall. It was wide enough for me to squeeze into. In the dusty darkness I could see a small chink of light. I pressed my ear against the cold wall, and again I could hear the voice, but this time it was clear and unmuffled. It was coming from the Prior's scriptoriolum, which abutted the church behind the altar of St Laurence.

From the slow, deliberate way in which he spoke, I could tell that Simon was writing. I cannot remember the exact words, although their sense has scarred my memory as deeply as the flames which were later to scar my face.

'In-the-end-I-agreed-that-Laurence-were-best-released-from-his-miserable-existence-besides-he-had-long-since-ceased-to-please-me-there-was-one-last-deed-that-Laurence-was-to-do-for-us-to-kill-Prior-Michael-William-was-then-to-ensure-that-Laurence-died-'

Martin, how do I tell you what happened next, when I myself do not rightly know? It was as if a flash of lightning seared my brain, and in its awful light I could see everything that until then the darkness had hidden from me, a ghastly, familiar landscape.

Still blinded by the lightning, still reeling from the words I had heard, I rushed out of the church and started hammering on the door of the scriptoriolum. A great crashing echoed like thunder in my ears. I did not know or care what it was, but I learnt later that as I stumbled blindly from behind the altar I sent the statue of St Laurence crashing to the ground, where it broke into several pieces.

The door opened and a figure stood before me. I knew it was Simon, although I could not make out his features: I could make out nothing clearly. Words screamed in my head: you killed him, you killed him, you killed him! Words that made me lose my reason, words that made me nothing more than a flame of hatred and revenge.

My hands went out and clutched him round the throat, and so help me God, a flame of joy engulfed me as I throttled the years of hurt that I had suffered through this man. It purified me like a Purgatorial flame, and my soul leapt heavenward, and for a moment knelt with pride at Prior Michael's feet and sought my thanks for this long, long overdue revenge. I was the vengeance of the world upon this fiend, and for a moment I had all the world's strength.

In my madness it did not at first seem strange to me that flames and smoke were all about us. The body that I held closer and tighter than I had ever held anything before had ceased its struggling, its gurgling, its clawing. My hands loosed their grip and the body slumped back over the desk and rolled face down onto the floor. I was myself again, and I stared in horror at what I had done.

I looked around and flames were leaping up the walls, tearing with their teeth at the dry parchments which lined the shelves. Thick smoke filled the room. 'Simon is dead, and the Priory is burning.' I spoke these words aloud slowly, without at first believing or understanding what I said. 'Simon is dead and the Priory is burning.' I said it over and over again, and still I stood there, unable to move, as weak as a new-born baby, no, weaker, for I could not even cry out.

Not until a wall of burning shelves and parchments came crashing down and half covered the body which lay at my feet did I find the strength to act. I turned to the door, which was bolted from the inside. I must have bolted it, although I cannot remember having done so. I could hear voices coming as if from far off, and then the ringing of the bell.

As clearly as in the clearest of dreams I remember deciding not to open the door, but to perish in the same flames which were even now consuming Simon de Quincy. They would cleanse me of all sin, and I would be rid of this accursed life for ever. Besides, what was the point of living, now that Simon was gone, I thought, so deranged had I become.

But my body had already taken another decision. It had set my hands clawing at the door, searching for the bolt, for life and air. I could see nothing now for smoke, and the heat was becoming unbearable. I felt the bolt slide back and the door open towards me. There was a great shout and a crash and a searing sheet of pain, as though I had been thrown into the fiery pit. Then there was blackness and blessed oblivion."

The old man's voice was trembling and his hands were making strange, jerking movements, as though they were still searching for the bolt. He put them over his face and groaned. "Why did I survive, Martin? Why did God not let me die in that room? My Purgatory was to live. I know the ways of the Lord are wise and terrible. The flames took away my eyes so that I could the better look inwards at my soul, to purge it of the sins that have stuck to it over my long life.

"I have told you more of my life than I have ever told to any soul, living or dead, even to my dearest friend Edgar called Michael. Do you absolve me of my sins, Martin? I ask you that although I know you are not a priest. I ask you that because you are young, and you are the voice of the future. Do you absolve me?"

The old man's whole body was shaking now, as though he was weeping, although the flames had long ago dried up the wells of his tears.

Martin looked at him, horrified by what he had been told. Everyone had known that Prior Simon had perished in a fire. There had never been even a whisper that he had been murdered. Now here Martin sat, beside the man who had murdered him. Yet knowing everything, how could he condemn, how could he rise up and himself take vengeance? His shoulders sagged beneath the terrible burden of too much knowledge.

"I absolve you, Brother Michael," he whispered, "with my parting breath I absolve you."

The old man put out his hands and embraced him, clinging to him like a child. Martin gently extricated himself from the old man's embrace. His mind was still sharp, despite all the feelings that surged around him, like a high rock towering above a seething sea. "I have one further question," he said. "What was it that Prior Simon was writing when − when − ?"

"When I killed him?" Brother Michael finished the question for him in a flat, emotionless voice. "I have thought on this often and long, young man. There was nothing on the desk, I know that for I had time enough to look as I stood there waiting for my strength to return, not looking for anything, simply looking.

"But like everything else in that room on that awful night, it has etched itself into my memory. I see an empty desk, without even a candle on it. Whatever it was he was writing he must have hidden before he opened the door to let me in. And Martin," here the old man bent forward and motioned Martin to do the same, "I think I know where he hid it. If I am right, then it may still be there, undamaged by the flames. Certainly no one else can have found it, otherwise the sound of it would have echoed like thunder through the Priory, through the whole kingdom, and Prior William would long ago have been thrown out of the Church. Unless of course William himself found it. If so, it might as well never have existed, as he would have destroyed it at once."

"If we can find it," Martin said excitedly, "then we will have enough evidence to condemn Prior William to Hell and back."

"But it will condemn everybody. You cannot use it against him. No, no," Michael protested, distressed.

"But with that manuscript, and your testimony." Martin said, not wanting to hear the old man's distress.

"My testimony!" Michael said with a contemptuous snort. "Who will believe the ravings of an old man? I raved for months after the fire. No one listens to me any more. They think the flames took my senses, as well as everything else. No, you must not use that manuscript. I wish I had never mentioned it. Promise me."

"I promise," Martin said, not knowing whether he was lying or not. He would decide later. The most important thing now was to find the manuscript.

"There was a secret aumbry on the east wall of the scriptoriolum. It was scarcely larger than a man's forearm. Here Prior Walter used to keep the foundation charters, before we got the fire-proof charter-chest. Then he cleared it out and sealed the cover-stone with mortar.

"On that last night I told you I saw nothing on the desk, no manuscript, no candle, nothing. But there was a candle in the room. It was on the floor, just below where I know the secret aumbry was. Simon must have put it there when he was hiding the manuscript. It was from there that the fire spread. I have imagined this to myself a thousand times, so often that it as it I saw him with my own eyes, fumbling at the wall as I battered on the door, leaving the candle burning dangerously on the floor beside the shelves of dry parchment, hurrying over to the door to let me in in order to stop the terrible din that I was making. To let death in.

"They tell me that the walls of the scriptoriolum are still standing, although it is now the parlour. Go there, tonight, secretly. Count ten stones from the north wall along the lowest course, then five stones upwards: the sixth stone from the floor covers the aumbry. The cover-stone is roughly triangular. Tell me tomorrow, before you depart, what you find."

Martin lay on his pallet in the guest-house waiting for the night-silence to settle on the Priory. Berenger, a fellow clerk who slept beside him, had already fallen asleep, and his snores reverberated around the chamber. Martin nudged him. He grunted and turned over, and the snores became gentle, regular breathing.

Gradually, one by one, the noises died away, until all was still.

Quietly he got up and threw on his cassock. He had decided not to take a light, for that would make him too conspicuous. He knew the Priory well enough by now to be able to find his way around in the dark. Before he tip-toed out of the chamber he drew from beneath his pallet the knife he had taken from the kitchen while the convent was at Compline. Berenger stirred, muttered something sleepily, and began to snore again.

Carefully he descended the inside stairs, then made his way along the dark cloister, past the chapter house, to the door of the parlour. Here he stopped, thinking that it must have been on this very spot that Michael had stood hammering on the door that cold, black January night. What was that distant hammering he could hear? He crossed himself in fear, then he smiled, realising that it was nothing more than the beating of his heart.

He turned the handle. He knew it would open, for there was no lock on the door, he had checked that before going to bed. The hinges shrieked as he swung the door open, and shrieked again as he closed it behind him.

He stood still for a moment, and the darkness seemed to dance around him, the darkness that was without end. Then he felt his way slowly over to the far wall. A coarse wall-hanging covered it from ceiling to floor. He grasped beneath it and felt for the stones, which stood out proud beneath his fingers. He started at the north wall, which abutted the church. One, two, three, he counted under his breath, until he reached ten; then upwards, one, two, three, four, five. His hand rested for a moment on this stone, which felt as solid as all the others. His fingers explored around it. It was triangular, but so were so many of the stones in this roughly built wall. He counted back to the floor, then along to the north wall. There was a clear sequence of stones. Yes, this must be the one. But would there be anything behind it? Whoever repointed the wall after the fire would have noticed how loose it was, and might well have tried to pull it out. The manuscript would have meant nothing to him, so he would have taken it to Prior William, who would have gratefully destroyed it.

But already his knife was cutting through the doubts, cutting into the mortar, sending a dry trickle of grainy dust down the dark wall. Often he would stop and take the stone firmly between his chafed and bleeding fingers, trying to move it as much with his willpower as with his strength.

At last he felt a tremor of movement which was more than his imagination. He worked away once more with his knife, then tried again. Straining every muscle in his aching hand and arm he slowly eased it out of the wall until he could get a proper grip. As he pulled it free he said a prayer to St Martin, then he laid it carefully on the ground at his feet.

Wiping the dust and grime off his hands, he reached into the hole. He shuddered as he touched the cold parchment. It was like touching a corpse. His expert fingers told him that it was a roll of four or five folios of the best quality vellum.

There was something else as well. He had heard it drop onto the floor. He felt around in the darkness at his feet. His fingers became entangled with a thin chain. Attached to the chain was some kind of a pendant. He put it round his neck beneath his tunic.

Only now did he realise that finding the parchments had taken him by surprise. He had had a vague plan of taking them to Dunkeld, where he would have a chance to read them in secret, and at his leisure. But now that he held them in his hands, close to his chest, he knew that he could not wait until then. How could he sleep with these parchments unread beside him? He could sooner sleep with a firebrand, or, he blushed at the thought, with a beautiful woman at his side.

No, he would have to read them now. Besides, he would want to tell the old man what they had contained, and tomorrow morning was his last chance.

But where could he go? The only place there was light at this time was the church, by the high altar and the altar of St Columba. But you knelt by those candles to pray, not to read, the ever-watchful sacristan would make sure of that.

Then it came to him. Malcolm the gate-man would surely allow him to use his candle, and would not ask for any explanations. Martin had always been friendly and generous towards Malcolm, for he had been Martin's other door to the infirmary, bypassing the whims and bad temper of Brother Peter.

Carefully Martin replaced the stone and swept the darkness at his feet with his hands and the sleeve of his cassock, hoping thus to scatter the dust and mortar that his efforts had left behind. Then he tiptoed out of the parlour and along the dark cloister towards the gatehouse.

Malcolm was playing chequers with himself by the light of a tiny candle when Martin opened the door of the gateman's tiny chamber.

"Ye're no wantin tae gan in tae see the bodach the noo, are ye?" he asked in surprise. Not waiting for a reply he went on: "A cannae help ye, laddie, no at this time o the nicht. Come an hae a game wi me insteid."

"A dinnae want neither the yin nor the ither," Martin replied. "A jaist want to yaise yer caunnel fur a wee. A've foon an auld bit pairchment that A hae to hae a keek at afore the mornin's morn, an A thocht ma auld freen Malcolm wud len me his licht."

"Aye, aye, come awaa ben," Malcolm said, shrugging his shoulders. "It'll be guid tae hae the company, even gin ye hae yer neb in a buik. Aiblins ye'll gie me a game o chequers whan ye're feenishit?" he added hopefully.

"Aye, aiblins," Martin said, settling himself on the pallet

beneath the ledge where the candle stood. Before he had even sat down he had begun to read: it was as if the letters on the parchment had hooked his eyes as a fisherman hooks a fish.

In the tiny, ill-smelling chamber of Malcolm the gateman, by the light of a weak and stinking candle made from the stubs of old altar and kitchen ones, Martin read the manuscript of Simon de Quincy. It was written in a small, tight, even hand, in heavily abbreviated Latin. It was for this moment, Martin thought, that he had been educated.

As if from far away, he would sometimes hear Malcolm's voice making comments such as: "It maun be richt fine tae be sic a learnit cheil an ken whit aa yon scretchins mean." And: "Are ye aa richt? Ye're luikin gey fleggit." But these comments soon died away, for the only reply he would get from Martin was a grunt.

PART SEVEN
THE.TESTAMENT
OF.SIMON
DE QUINCY
SOMETIME SECRETARY
TO.POPE.CLEMENT.III
NOW PRIOR
OF INCHCOLM

The fool has said in his heart, 'There is no God.'
Corrupt they are, and have become abominable in their
iniquities; there is none who may do good.
God looked down from Heaven upon the sons of men, to
see if there was any who understood or sought God.
All have turned away from him, as though they have
become useless; there is none who may do good, not one.
Surely they will repent, they who do evil, who devour my
people like a loaf of bread?
They have not called upon God; they were in fear, where
there was no fear. Since God has scattered the bones of
those who are pleasing to men: they are confounded,
since God has spurned them.
Who will issue from out of Zion to save Israel? When God
has liberated his people, Jacob will exalt and Israel will
be glad.

Corruptio omnium eorumque castigio Psalm 52

THE . MANUSCRIPT

I t is the year of the Lord 1219, and I am growing old faster than the world. I have made my confession many times, to many priests, some of them more foolish than others, and I have laid up a great store of absolution. But absolution for me is as worthless as gold given into the hand of a corpse, for the sin that is mine cannot be forgiven even by the Pope himself. Shall I write it down in black ink? I have enough other sins to keep you, future reader, entertained, without exposing your delicate soul to the fountainhead of my wickedness. However, without the knowledge of that fountainhead, how are you to understand all the deeds that have flowed from it? And I want you to understand, dear future reader, believe me. You are beloved of me, therefore I will allow you to know me. You are beloved of me because I will allow you to know me. No one else is beloved of me. No one else knows me. In return I will not ask you to pray for my soul, for it is not my soul which I want you to protect from the flames in the hereafter, it is this parchment which I want you to protect from the flames here. Yes, read and tremble, dearest one, for what I am about to say could easily condemn this parchment to the flames. You will know the hands which would threaten it, so you will know the hands to keep it from. I trust you, you see how much I trust you.

I do not believe in the Father, the Son or the Holy Spirit, nor do I believe in Heaven or Hell. I do not listen for the roar of thunder that my simple brothers would expect as I write these words, nor must you listen for them, dearest. And what if thunder did roar? A thousand different tongues are giving voice to a hundred different thoughts all around us at this very moment. Who am I to say for whom the thunder roars? Let those who are oppressed with guilt cross themselves and swear to change their ways when the heavens fart.

Sin, guilt, absolution: how I hate these words. They stain the very air I have to breathe. How I long for a new, strong wind to let me, and you, my dear, breathe more freely. The wind blows fiercely enough on this little island, yet in their perversity my brothers cling stubbornly to their guilt as if such a tattered cloak could keep them warm.

The name of my God is Reason, and Reason knows no guilt.

Three wise men have brought their gifts to my God. Master Peter Abelard taught that understanding is more important than believing, knowledge more important than faith. Before him Roscellinus taught that one cannot believe something without first having understood it. And many centuries ago my own countryman, John Scotus Erigena, taught that the human Reason is the habitation of God.

Yes, for as long as Reason allows God to dwell there. Long ago I ousted him from my Reason, by my Reason, and in his place my Reason reigns supreme. I ousted him because he had fouled that habitation.

Master Peter also taught that sin is when one acts against one's conscience, for conscience is the seed of the divine in every breast. But if I reason that there is no divine? Then there can be no conscience, and without conscience there can be no sin. So with one stroke of Reason I have achieved what the Holy Mother Church and all the saints have not been able to achieve: I have cleared the world of sin.

Do not think, my beloved, that it has been easy. I have needed every piece of learning that I could glean, first at the Cathedral School of St Andrews, where I learnt the seven Liberal Arts, and then Theology and a little Philosophy. It was Philosophy that awoke a hunger in me that I knew could be stilled only in one of the great Schools of Paris herself.

Paris! Queen of cities, moon among the stars,
Island of palaces, royal island where
is found Philosophy's most ancient seat.
There alone with her sole companion, Study,
she holds the immortal citadel of undying light,
her foot in triumph set where the flower of ages withers.

Perhaps it was there that I first became fascinated with islands. But then I have always felt my soul to be an island, surrounded by a sea of fools. That was, of course, until I met you.

In many of the Schools in Paris the masters were trying to pretend that Master Peter's star had never shone, but there were still some who would not let that light die. Light? Rather it was a flame, and with it I cauterised my soul, cleansing it of all the foulness Mother Church had charged it with.

Trusting in my Reason revealed other things to me as well. It revealed that Mother Church might be corrupt and hypocritical, but she was also powerful, and a career in the Church was the only means to power for a landless bastard like myself, with only the sharpness of my wits, and the beauty of my body, between me and starvation.

I wanted power in order to be my own master, to be the master of others, and to bring humankind one small step closer to my vision of a world where Reason ruled in the stead of superstition and fear. I would ride the power of the Church as a sailor rides the currents of the seas. I would not openly turn against it. Master Peter had done so and they gelded him and forced him to burn his books. His pupil Arnold de Brescia had done so and they hanged him and burned him and scattered his ashes in the Tiber. No, I was not going to have my body destroyed just because it contained the knowledge of the true nature of the world. With perfect compliance and deceit I would slip into the topmost chamber of the Church, where I would do whatever was necessary to destroy her.

It was not those who had mastered Philosophy, however, who rose in the Church, but those who had mastered Law. So I left the shrine of Philosophy for the shrine of Canon Law, Bologna. I studied under the great Huguccio, and wondered at the great tower of Reason he and the other canonists had constructed on the quagmire of Faith. I climbed it with ease, not caring if it shook and groaned beneath me. I trusted in my God and knew he would not let me fall.

It was in Bologna that I met Lothar. He was a fellow-student, even more brilliant than I. He was from a rich and noble family from near Rome. I was a poor illegitimate scholar from near the edge of the world. Yet we became friends, for we were both giants among midgets, so that wherever we looked, we looked into each other's eyes.

When I left Bologna I made for the very hub of power, Rome. The Pope and the Emperor had finally fallen exhausted into each other's arms after years of warring. Emperor Fredrick was clever enough to allow Pope Alexander to think that the Church had won. The Pope returned in imagined triumph to Rome after his long exile. I was not far behind, carrying in my scrip a letter from Lothar to a friend of his father's, the powerful Leo de Monumento. Although Leo was a man of this world, a Roman senator and a confidant of the Emperor, he also had strong links with the Church, for he too knew that you ignore her at your peril. He had a close friend called Paolo Scolari, a Roman nobleman and the Archpriest of St Mary Major.

Rome at that time was full of bright, ambitious young men clutching degrees from the Schools in Paris and Bologna. Few, however, were as gifted, or as good-looking, as I was. How could Scolari resist me, he who had such a sharp appreciation for wit and such a sharp hunger for beauty? So he took me into his household as a junior secretary. He was quick to recognise that

I had few scruples. Yes, we had a lot in common, my master and I. I rose rapidly in his household until I was his private amanuensis.

Then my master was made Cardinal Bishop of Palestrina. [January 1181] It was part of the deal the Pope had made with the Senate of Rome: if the Curia wanted to remain at the Lateran, more Romans of good family had to be given cardinalships. Although no one was named, it was understood that one of these Romans should be Paolo Scolari.

One of the greatest problems with Cardinals is their longevity. For men who so often proclaim the glories of Heaven and the boon of eternity, they cling to this life with a tenacious grip. However, one of the many skills I had from my mother was the art of loosening even the most tenacious of grips by the use of herbs and unguents. I knew also how to tighten grips that were letting go. My master's health was poor: his heart was lazy and his stomach was delicate. Foxglove helped remind his heart of its duties, while gentian made his stomach more robust. Other plants ensured him a sound sleep and pleasant dreams. Many were the ways in which I served my master.

It did not worry me that my master was so sickly. If he died there were other Cardinals who would be happy to employ me. Some had even secretly approached me and tried to win me from my master's side. However, I knew it was important that I be thought loyal, both by my master and by his fellows. There is a time for loyalty and a time for betrayal.

Before my 25th summer I was chief amanuensis and adviser to one of the most powerful men in Christendom. I saw no limit to the heights of power which I might reach. An Englishman had been Pope only a few decades before. Why should not a Scot also aspire to the Papal crown?

Through my master I became privy to the secrets of the College of Cardinals of the Holy Mother Church. The table around which they met in Consistory was more like a table of money-changers. They cast their net into the waters, not to catch souls, as the first Apostles had done, but to catch gold and silver. At the Curia it was not Reason which had replaced God, it was greed.

How different it will be when I have more power, I would say to myself. Arnold de Brescia had preached a Church and a priesthood debarred from possessing worldly wealth. That would be my first goal. To strike at greed and the worship of Saints Albinus and Rufinus would be to strike at the very heart of the Holy Mother Church.

I would look around at the Cardinals, the Cardinals' clerks, the amanuenses, the chaplains and the whole host of clergy growing fat on the gullibility of the people, and I would ask myself 'Am I the only one here who does not believe, the only one to see that it is not only the members of the bride of Christ that are rotten, it is the heart itself?' I knew that I was not the only one, but even I could not tell who the others were. For to betray such thoughts was to risk not only one's livelihood, it was to risk one's life.

Because I come from this poor land of Scotland I was given the task of liaising between the Cardinals and the two warring Scottish Bishops John and Hugh. How my master and I would laugh at their antics! They were like two dogs fighting over a bone. My master did not care who won, Church or Crown, Pride or Greed, John or Hugh. What he and most of the other Cardinals cared about was what gifts either side could offer. In the end it was neither of them who offered my master the most tempting gift, but Bishop Jocelin of Glasgow, whose bloated spirit ached for the highest bishopric in the realm. My master and Jocelin understood each other well, and just as my master had steered between the Scylla and Charybdis of Pope and Emperor in the recent wars, so too Bishop Jocelin steered his course carefully between Church and Crown.

For a time my master worked to realise Jocelin's ambition, and I worked with him. We had a carefully elaborated plan which, had it worked, would have terminated the dispute there and then. It did not work, and so the dispute dragged on for another seven years.

This was the plan. I wrote a letter to Hugh purporting to be from Pope Lucius. That was easily done. We kept a copy of his seal, and the old man was becoming so forgetful that often he could not remember from one day to the next what he had agreed to do. This letter removed Hugh from St Andrews and suggested he take a lesser Bishopric. Also it gave John permission to accept a Bishopric which was not St Andrews. Thus the way was clear for Jocelin to take St Andrews. I wrote also to King William, informing him of the contents of Hugh's letter. Our agent was none other than Roland Archbishop-elect of Dol, one of the delegates the Pope had sent to Scotland to hear the case again and make the final decision.

Our plan almost succeeded. The King, whose heart had been softened by the gift of the Rose of Gold, was prepared to bow to the instructions of the letter. John agreed to accept Dunkeld. However, at the last moment, we were betrayed to Hugh, who alerted the King. He immediately refused to allow Hugh to change Bishoprics, and the negotiations with John collapsed.

How I delight in the duplicity of humankind, for it knows no bounds, and if all else fails, it alone will bring the Holy Mother Church to its well-deserved destruction. Archbishop-elect Roland had also been in negotiation with Cardinal Laborans, who was in the pay of King William and Bishop Hugh. It was Roland who had betrayed our plan to Hugh.

How did we know? From our spy in the household of Cardinal Laborans. There is honour among thieves, they say, but there is none among Cardinals. Many had a paid servant in the households of their fellows. For a time I was in receipt of an allowance by Cardinal Gratian to spy upon my master. This I did most diligently, asking my master what he would like Cardinal Gratian to know.

Unfortunately we found out about Roland's betrayal too late. Roland was fighting to keep the see of Dol an Archbishopric, against the claims of Tours. From that time on my master became a fervent supporter of Tours. Later, through the labours of Laborans, Roland was made a Cardinal Deacon. My master and I ensured that he did not enjoy his new office for long.

The Curia's triumphant return to Rome under Pope Alexander was short-lived. Within two years we were again in exile, wandering around Italy, from Velletri to Verona, from Verona to Ferrara, from Ferrara to Pisa. Often enough we had to live in cramped, ramshackle towers, and to work in ill-lit, ill-smelling scriptoria. My master hated it, away from his beloved Rome, and his comfortable palace at St Mary Major. I hated it, for adversity always strengthens the hold of the Trinity over men's minds. Besides, I was bored, for the delights and diversions of Rome were not to be found elsewhere. Thus both of us longed for the Curia to return to the great city.

My master was the only Cardinal who had the skill, the standing and the respect of the Romans to negotiate such a return. But there were many who were against it, chief among them Henry de Clairvaux, Cardinal Bishop of Albano. He believed that the Church would never find peace until the Pope and his Curia settled forever far away from Rome and her sacred hunger for gold. The only way for us to overcome such opposition, then, was for my master to become Pope himself. To this end, therefore, I began to bend all my efforts.

When Pope Lucius died, the star of Cardinal Umberto was in the ascendant. He was elected Pope, taking the name Urban. This splenetic old man could see no further than his hatred of the Emperor. Rome would have no truck with such an enemy of the Emperor, and Urban was incapable of making any compromises. He had to go. His person was guarded more closely than his gold. His whole household was made up of fellow Milanese, right down to the meanest kitchen servant. But no household is completely proof against attack, especially when the attacker is Simon de Quincy.

Despite his age Pope Urban was a passionate horseman. He insisted on riding everywhere, and would use litter or barge only when he was unwell, which was rarely, for he had the constitution of an ox.

His kitchen was impregnable, so I turned my attentions to the stables. Gold is unsuitable to use when bribing a lowly servant, as it is difficult to keep, and difficult to spend. Lust, however, is hidden easily enough inside the body, and is spent in a secret place with only a smile and a sweet memory to show for even the most outrageous extravagance.

The Pope's marshal lusted after me. There are so many men like that, especially in the Church. Using my body as bait, it was not difficult to ensnare him.

It is the day before Pope Urban is intending to ride from Verona to Ferrara. My lusty marshal is looking very down-in-the-mouth: the Pope's favourite mount is unwell. The Pope will be furious if he cannot ride him, and the marshal will probably receive a sound beating. It is the moment I have been waiting for. I tell him I will bring him a potion that will make the horse well enough to carry the Pope even to Rome, if that were his will.

The next day, about half way between Verona and Ferrara, the old man, who loved to travel at speed, was spurring on his beast when it collapsed under him, throwing him violently to the ground. Badly injured, he was carried by barge the rest of the way to Ferrara, where he died a few days later.

Let me tell you, dear reader, a most amusing tale about the death of this cantankerous old man. He never swore, of course. How unseemly that would have been. But he did have a kind of oath: 'If such and such happens,' he would say, 'may I never ride my horse again.' The very day of his fall he had been stopped at the gate of his lodgings by a messenger from the Archbishop of Canterbury about some dispute or other with the monks of Christ Church. The Archbishop at the time was Baldwin the meek — Baldwin the feeble, as Urban liked to call him. Impatient to be on his way, and the mere mention of Baldwin's name rousing his anger, he shouted, 'May I never ride a horse again if I don't soon knock that Archbishop from his cathedra.' This was a happy coincidence, for the gullible, by which I mean most of humanity, were only too ready to see the accident as nothing less than God's punishment for Urban's rash and unkind outburst against saintly Baldwin the feeble. I certainly ensured that was what the marshal believed.

Pope Urban's death was a great relief not only to my master but even to many of his own supporters. They had elected a man whom they hoped would stand up to the Emperor more firmly than old Pope Lucius. Urban had outgalloped all their hopes, and seemed bent on leading the Church into another war.

Just before the election of the new Pope, which we hoped would elevate my master to the highest pinnacle in Christendom and smooth our way back to Rome, the news arrived that Jerusalem had fallen to Saladin. Rome was forgotten in the ensuing panic. Those who could bleat the name of Jerusalem the loudest got the best hearing. The man whose bleat was heard above all the rest was my master's enemy, that self-righteous busybody Henry de Clairvaux. Not that he wanted the papal crown for himself, although it was pressed upon him. Oh no, he was too humble for such a great honour, and besides he longed to preach the new Crusade throughout France and the Empire. However, before he left on his holy mission he made sure that my master would not become the next Pope.

There were two candidates after Henry stepped down: my master and the doddery old papal chancellor Cardinal Alberto de Morra. Everything hung on the word of Cardinal Henry. 'Whom shall we elect?' cried the Cardinals. Henry closed his eyes and pretended to pray, a simpering smile on his scrawny face. Then he said in a voice which was not to be contradicted, 'The lord Cardinal of Palestrina is weak and infirm, and is no match for such a burden. So it can only be the Cardinal chancellor. No one amongst us is more suitable, no one knows the customs and rights of the Holy Mother Church better, and no one is more pleasing both to God and to the princes of the earth.'

So within ten days of Urban's death. Cardinal chancellor Alberto was elected Pope Gregory. If what Cardinal Henry had said about him had been the sum total of this man, then he might have been tolerable. However, as with most things, Cardinal Henry was speaking only half the truth. Gregory was an ascetic who was in the pockets of the Cistercians. This meant that he made a great show of being above bribery and corruption. One of the first things he did, after announcing the new Crusade, was to forbid the Cardinals to receive gifts from those pleading their case at the Curia. This was a great blow to my master and to many other Cardinals, for much of their income depended on these gifts. What was the world coming to if one was not allowed to take a little gift here and there as just reward for all the trouble one had taken on the plaintiff's behalf?

Gregory believed also that the riches of the Church should be squandered on the new Crusade. Just like a Cistercian he did not believe in wealth unless it was being put to some seeming-holy purpose. He certainly did not believe that it should be used to pay the sums of money which the Roman Senate was demanding for the Curia's return to Rome.

Now, gentle reader, I can hear you saying to yourself, 'But was not this your secret heart's desire, to strike at the greed and cut the Church off from wealth? Surely Gregory was closer to your true ambition than was your master, who was in love with worldly wealth and luxury?'

You are very perceptive as always, dearest one, but let me make things perfectly clear. The Cistercians and their friends at the Curia, the descendants of St Bernard de Clairvaux, they wanted to curb the luxury and pomp of the Church by reducing its wealth, but they did not want to curb its power over men's and women's minds. On the contrary, by striking at greed and corruption they wanted to increase that power. I, however, wanted to break that power, to free the minds of men and women from the Church's hold. I wanted to break the Church, and I recognised from the outset that worldly men such as my master, greedy and debauched, would break it, whereas the subtleties of the Cistercians would strengthen it.

In short, dear reader, Pope Gregory VIII could not be allowed to carry the papal burden for long. Because he was a friend of the Emperor he did not think that he had anything to fear. Gregory and his kind are without guile, so they are easily destroyed. He was dead within two months.

There was an election immediately. Cardinal Henry was in France, and the only other candidate was Theobald, Cardinal Bishop of Ostia. He had during his long life shown an unchurchmanlike interest in young girls, and he knew that we had found several who were prepared to say in public what had passed between them and Cardinal Bishop Theobald in private. So his refusal when offered the papal tiara was more than mere form. It was made with complete sincerity. At last my master's time had come. He was elected Pope Clement III in December of the year 1187. I was immediately sent to speak with his old friend Leo de Monumento, and to negotiate a price for our return to Rome. At the beginning of the following Lent, amidst great jubilation, the Pope rode through the streets of the eternal city on his way to the Lateran Palace.

It was as I had hoped and expected. My master dragged the name of the Holy Mother Church deep into the mire of scandal. Seldom before had the Church been held in such contempt by the princes and people of this world. I am proud to say that I played no small part in this achievement. I have presumed enough upon your patience, dearest reader, without listing for you all he did to bring about this blessed state, with me the willing servant in every baseness. One example will suffice.

The fight between those reverent dogs John and Hugh over the Bishopric of St Andrews still dragged on, and was still clinging to my hands like pitch. Soon after my master's election as Pope, John arrived in Pisa full of yet more complaints against Hugh, who had been excommunicted yet again, this time by Urban, for not appearing at the Curia for yet another hearing. I cannot say I blamed Hugh for not coming, for Urban was obviously going to decide in John's favour, and by this time Hugh must have been quite accustomed to the state of excommunication. He was ensconced in the Bishop's palace at St Andrews, with King William giving him every support.

My master, now that he was Pope, would have been prepared to renegotiate matters, if he had been offered suitable gifts, but Hugh and King William did not think this necessary. This was the biggest mistake they could have made. Hugh and the King might still bear a grudge for what my master had done several years previously with the forged letters, but they must learn that they were now dealing not with a Cardinal Bishop but with the Holy Father himself, a fact they ignored at their peril.

On the other hand John was generous, so my master told me to write letters which ordered Hugh to give up his Bishopric. They further stated that, unless he came crawling on his belly to the Holy Father, with appropriate gifts, John would be the unchallenged Bishop of St Andrews in his place. This I did with great pleasure, putting all my skill into their crafting. They were not without effect. Hugh came to Rome the first summer after our return there. However he did not come crawling on his belly, and the only gift he brought was a copy of the letter which he had obtained from Cardinal Roland, formerly Archbishop-elect of Dol. It contained full details of the forgery we had perpetrated in favour of Bishop Jocelin. Sadly Cardinal Roland was no longer with us, as he and all his papers had perished in a terrible fire that had destroyed his house in Pisa during the pontificate of Pope Gregory. Hugh informed us that he had the original letter, with Roland's seal and signature, safely stored away, and he would not hesitate to produce it at a Consistory court.

Of all the mistakes from greed, stubbornness and ambition which Hugh had made in his life, this was the greatest. No one threatened my master with impunity. My master complied with everything Hugh demanded. He absolved him and gave him his blessing as Bishop of St Andrews. Hugh left the Holy Father's presence in triumph.

A few days later I called at his lodgings to collect the original of Roland's letter. I was accompanied by two servants who carried a barrel of my master's best wine, to celebrate the successful end of a long and difficult case. You can imagine how high-spirited and jovial the company was. Hugh and his retinue certainly had good cause to rejoice. At last, after ten years, he was undisputed Bishop of St Andrews. What more was there for his heart to desire? What more was there for his heart to beat for? He gave me the letter and we broached the barrel. It was August, and the air was heavy with heat and corruption. The marsh fever was raging in the quarters of the poor, and the rich were leaving the city in droves. My master had already left for the hills, where I was to join him as soon as I had finished my business with Bishop Hugh.

We drank into the night. I have rarely enjoyed an evening so much. The air was bearable again, like silk against the skin, the wine like silk against my tongue. I did not care about the strange after-taste. In fact, it added spice to my pleasure. I trusted in the antidote which I had taken, as much as others trust in God. Yet my trust was founded on firmer ground, for it was founded on reason and experience. Also, I drank only a few sips of one goblet. As soon as Hugh and his retinue saw that I was drinking of the Holy Father's gift, they fell upon it greedily. The heat was my ally. As I took my leave, I promised I would send a few harlots to them to share their merriment. 'You are the perfect servant,' Bishop Hugh called out contemptuously. I bowed and said farewell, urging them once more to leave Rome without delay, for the fever spared neither high nor low, not even consecrated Bishops. For some drunken reason Hugh and his companions found this funny, and I left with their laughter ringing in my ears.

The next day, o horrible to relate, Hugh and all his company were found dead. It seemed that the fever had moved more swiftly than even I had feared. *Sic transit gloria episcoporum.*

As soon as my master became Pope, he got rid of all the notaries who had worked for Gregory. He could not accuse them of honesty, although that had been their crime. Instead he gave as his reason that they were not suited to deal with the intricacies of negotiating the return of the Curia to Rome. For this he needed Romans, not northern Italians, as most of Gregory's notaries were. He also started to create his own Cardinals, to strengthen his support in the Curia. It was amusing to see the sycophants buzz around us like flies around a dung-hill, flattering, fawning and licking spittle and anything else offered them.

I had taken deacon's orders, and was soon to become a priest. My master offered to make me Cardinal Deacon of St Mary in Aquiro. I knew however that at that time I could serve my master better as his chief amanuensis. As long as I administered my potions regularly, I knew he had a few years to live. I would wait. I was in no hurry. When I thought the end was near, then I would allow him to make me a Cardinal, his bequest to posterity.

I had reckoned without my old friend from my days as a student in Bologna, Lothar. He was distantly related to my master, his uncle my master's closest friend, John de Anagni, the most venial Cardinal of them all. John was so dear to my master that he was made Cardinal of Palestrina in his place. Thus he was given the use of the palace at St Mary Major.

I had not seen Lothar for many years. His uncle presented him to my master, suggesting he join his household, with a view to becoming a Cardinal. He was tall and slender, with the face of an angel, and the most extraordinary eyes, dark brown, downturned, commanding and yielding as the occasion merited, eyes that haunted. My master was enchanted, and asked me to bring him to the painted chamber of his old palace at St Mary Major. I told him it was fruitless, as I had already tried his chastity when we were in Bologna together, and had found it unassailable. So instead my master made him a Cardinal Deacon.

When we met again we resumed our friendship easily, as if the years of separation had never been. We talked and argued about a hundred different things. We both in our different ways, and for different ends, lusted after power, and we would talk for hours about the basis of power and its underbelly, obedience. He saw the power of the Pope as limited and unlimited at once, limited by custom and Canon and Biblical Law, unlimited in that the Pope was not merely the earthly vicar of St Peter, but of Christ Himself. This meant that there were times when the Pope could transcend the Law, and out of his Fullness of Power could create new laws.

It was then that I made the biggest mistake of my life. I revealed to him my vision of a world where faith in the Holy Trinity did not dominate, where the basis of power was shifted from faith to reason. I opened myself up to him very carefully, but he (gentle reader, it hurts me to write this) was too clever for me. He seemed fascinated by the idea, which I placed before him as some dreadful heresy. He encouraged me to tell him more. The warmth and excitement of our renewed friendship, the thrill of the meeting of two great minds, and those eyes, seduced me to claim the vision as my own. Ignoring the prompting of my reason, I shared with him my vision of a Church diminished.

It was at the beginning of Lent in the year 1191, and my master was failing fast. I knew that if I wanted to be made a Cardinal, it would have to be soon. I approached him about it. He coughed and wheezed and said that it had now become impossible. I asked why. He told me that Lothar had betrayed my secret. My master did not care. I had served him well. What did it matter what my motivation had been. But it mattered to Lothar. He had informed my master that if it was ever proposed that I be made a Cardinal, he would betray me to the whole Curia. This would mean certain exile, possibly death. My master said that he was powerless in the affair. He read my thought — how alike were our minds! He told me that Lothar had committed to parchment everything I had told him, and had left instructions with his amanuenses that, should he die suddenly, the parchment was to be read out at Consistory. Thus, like the servant and the king in the fairy-tale, our lives were bound together.

I asked my master why Lothar did not denounce me at once. He replied that Lothar was acting out of friendship towards me, in respect of the fact that what I had revealed to him had been revealed under friendship's mantle. Friendship! A foul and treacherous whore! I asked my master if there was nothing he could do to help me. He shrugged his shoulders and spread out his hands to reveal his palms, empty of gifts, empty of power. I smiled and said that I had been beaten by a worthy adversary. But inside I boiled with rage as fierce as any I have known. For once in my life I had difficulty in thinking clearly. I asked my master for permission to be relieved of my duties for a few days. I wanted to go away and think, although out of habit I used the word 'pray'. He granted my request.

I took a horse and rode into the Alban Hills near Velletri. For three days I rode or walked, stopping only to sleep for a few hours under a hedge or in a wood during the darkest time of the night. I scarcely ate. I examined carefully each future open to me. Each looked bleak. I knew that my master was dying, and with no rich and noble family behind me I could not hope to weather this storm by public confession or recantation. There were too many people at the Curia who distrusted, or envied me and who would be only too glad of this chance to bring me to my ruin. I was known as the left hand of Clement. For those who could not bring themselves to miscry the Holy Father, I was the evil counsellor, egging him on to deeds he would otherwise never have contemplated. There were even some who whispered that I was the cause of my master's poor health, so that I could take advantage of his recurrent helplessness to bring my own wicked plans to fruition. I ask you, dearest one, would I do such a thing?

I had to face facts. My career at the Curia was over, and if Lothar denounced me, which he would do if I moved one step further up on the great ladder, I would be lucky to escape with my life. And if I stayed on in Rome after my master's death? With all hope of high office gone forever, and with Lothar watching me like a hawk, and that hawk would one day become an eagle, I had no doubt about that, all that remained for me was to slip into the service of another powerful man, where I would be a good and faithful servant. I was tired of serving. I wanted to be served. I wanted to command. I wanted power.

So what else was left for me? What else did I want? I had been so sure of my future at the Curia that I had never thought of this before. Where else did I want to go? Wherever I went it would have to be far from Rome, the further away, the higher I could rise again.

I was high up in the hills above Velletri. Night was falling, and the western sky was crimson. The breeze brought to me the smell of smoke from the town's fires. I closed my eyes, and there in some dark cavern beyond my reason I saw the face of that foolish, handsome, simple brother and fellow-countryman, whom I had seduced many years before to please my master. Lust I knew, and knew well how to satisfy it, but love, that we are told garnishes lust like fruit and vegetables garnish meat, making it more palatable to the squeamish, that I did not know, unless it was what I had briefly felt with him. There had been a softness, a sweetness, a joy — what words can Reason find for something that Reason has no part in? And with the sweetness that his memory brought, almost indistinguishable from it, was the longing to go home. I did not trust either the one or the other. My reason told me that it was a kind of love or friendship that had led me to lose my judgement and reveal myself to Lothar. The result had been disastrous. And home: that rough land with its rough King with a pack of Normans baying at his back, and a Church chained to the Lion, for all the Bulls about it being the special daughter of the Holy See. My memories of home were of poverty and squalor. It was the last place on earth I should want to go, and yet, and yet.

At the end of three days I rode back to Rome. I went straight to Lothar to tell him what I wanted. My master could wait. Lothar did not want to see me at first. He was guilty at what he had done, and he asked my forgiveness. He had been torn, he said, between loyalty to me and loyalty to our Holy Mother Church, yet in the end he saw that the good of the Church must override all personal feelings and ties. I did not forgive him, holding on to the little power his guilt gave me. I told him I wanted to stay within the Church, for there was nothing for me outside her embrace. I told him that, although I had not changed one whit of my belief, I would swear by Reason itself that I would no longer work for the Church's downfall. I told him that as surety for my words, I was prepared to be exiled to the furthest corner of Christendom, and kept within the confines of a monastery for the rest of my life. I named the corner, Scotland; and the monastery, the Priory of Inchcolm. I had chosen this place, I said, because I knew and respected the Prior there. I also told him that there in silence and contemplation and the strict observance of the Hours, my soul might change, and I might learn the meaning of the word repentance. I told him that the flesh was willing to make the attempt, even if the spirit was weak, and that as a friend of both myself and of the Church he had a duty to support me in that attempt. He was silent for a long while, pacing up and down the room, looking out of the window, gnawing at his little beard. Finally he said that he would indeed support me, if the Holy Father consented.

Within the week I had in my possession letters for Bishop Jocelin of Glasgow, Bishop John of Dunkeld, and Prior Walter of Inchcolm. The letters informed them that I had sinned exceedingly in thought, word and deed, but that the Holy Father, Christ's vicar on earth, had granted full absolution in the light of a penitent and humble heart. Yes, dear reader, it was my heart that was meant. But the letter unfortunately did not finish there. It went on to say that this indulgence, in the infinite wisdom of his Holiness Pope Clement, was valid only for as long as the bearer of these letters was a brother of the Priory of Inchcolm. If, God forbid, he should cease to be a brother of the the said Priory, then he would have to answer before the Curia itself for the sins for which he was originally exiled.

Now I was impatient to depart. My master, however, begged me to stay with him until the end, which he knew was not far away. He had conceived for me something which, had it not been lodged in a heart and soul so rotten, might have gone by the name of affection. His wits were beginning to disintegrate along with his body. He would often weep like a baby, lamenting that he could not have saved me. It was pathetic to see, so I decided to put him out of his misery by putting him out of the world. He trusted me totally, so I had no doubt that he would drink down the last goblet I offered him. You see, gentle one, I have not entirely ignored the Trinity: three Holy Fathers have I sent to meet their God, a meeting which for all three of them was long overdue.

I left Rome as soon as my master had been buried, and I knew who had been elected to succeed him, the ancient Hyacinth Bobo, Cardinal-deacon of St Mary in Cosmedin. He took the name of Celestine. He was the oldest man in the Curia. My master had brought the name of Pope into such disrepute that they would have elected the uncorrupted corpse of a saint if they had been allowed to. Hyacinth was the next best thing. He was certainly uncorrupted, one of the few Cardinals who could claim that distinction. No one had ever tried corrupting him for years, as he had absolutely no authority, and could be persuaded to appoint a donkey as a Bishop if you told him often and loudly enough that this was canonical. He was not even a priest. They had to ordain him the day before they consecrated him Pope.

Well, they were welcome to him. They deserved him, especially Lothar. Hyacinth was a member of the great Boboni family, who were locked in a fierce feud with the Scotti, and had been for years. Lothar's mother was of the Scotti. Hyacinth might be above corruption, but he was not above family feuds: I have never met a Roman who was. Yet Lothar had one great advantage over Pope Celestine. He was a third of his age.

But what did I care? I was on my way to a new life in a different land. Nor was I alone. With me was my servant Orsino. I had bought him when he was a young boy, and he had grown into a fine, handsome lad. He was totally devoted to me, which I found touching, if contemptible. I can only despise loyalty for loyalty's sake, which I regard always as a sign of a crippled reason. Yet I must admit that I was able to put Orsino's loyalty to great use. Also, although he had a conscience, he had given it into my keeping. He was dumb, which was another great asset. I treated him well, better than most masters treat their servants, and we took great pleasure in each other's bodies. His was hard, well-proportioned, clean-limbed. I would insist that he become a lay-brother at the Priory.

I stood next to Orsino on the deck of the ship which was to carry me from Ostia to Marseilles. I watched Rome grow smaller. I wished I had the power to make the earth open and swallow every tower, every palace, every church, every house, every hovel. I laughed at the vainness of my wish, and turned my back on the coast to gaze out onto the new horizon.

It did not take me long to establish myself in my new home. I liked it well enough at first, but it soon grew tedious. Life was dull, monotonous, predictable. Even my little bear was taken from me. They had renamed him Laurence. We both hated this simpering, holy name. I consoled him by telling him that Laurence had been the name of my mother's most handsome paramour. He smiled at this, and clapped his hands in glee.

For many months it was almost impossible even to speak to Laurence, let alone tryst with him. However, I did manage to arrange things so that the pleasures of the flesh were not entirely neglected.

Everyone seemed to live in the past. When conversation was permitted, which was seldom enough except at the blood-letting, it was all about the days of the fight with the local lord de Mortimer, and the interdict, and the siege, and their Prior's mission to Rome. All things that had happened ten years previously. Had nothing happened since then? I would ask. Yes, of course, was the reply, but not actually to the Priory. Life had run on smoothly and quietly enough since then, praise be to God. Praise be to the Devil of tedium, rather. I decided that it was time my brothers were given less stale topics of conversation. It was a shame to waste precious words on such old news.

De Mortimer's death gave me the first opportunity. It was a stroke of extraordinary luck, and produced both a crisis and a miracle. However, had it not happened, I would have found something else, for I was always on the watch. Reason never sleeps, while faith never wakes up.

The miracle of the blessed martyr Isaac followed seamlessly from the first. Laurence was an excellent shot with the bow. I had had him instructed in the use of all weapons of foot when he was still a boy. Often I would train with him, although my own skill with sword and bow was not great. But through Laurence I doubled that skill. In a world which was ruled as much by iron as by fear of Hell-fire, I wanted to be master of both. Isaac was struck by an arrow as we approached the Abbey at Scone. I had sent Laurence on ahead of us a short time before to announce our arrival, or so Isaac thought. The bow was of a special design, which folded in half, and so could easily be strapped to the back and hidden beneath the habit. Laurence had brought it with him from Rome, where they were skilled in the crafting of all sorts of weapons for sudden, secret striking. Bribing the peasant later was an easy task. St Rufinus is the greatest miracle-worker of all.

I also had my own feud to amuse me, my feud with friendship. I had played with my little Brother much as a cat plays with a very dim mouse, scratching him occasionally so that he would not forget who was in control, but not enough for him to become truly frightened of me. I did not have to worry about him running away and hiding, for I knew that his feet were firmly entangled in the net called friendship. Someone had been filling his head full of those quaint ideas that the Cistercians had once held about special friendship. His lust was deluding him that somehow or other I would be his special friend. Such stupidity deserved to be punished. Besides, he was a constant reproach to my self, for looking into his eyes was like looking into some distorted mirror. I saw there what had led me to share my secret heart with Lothar, and thus to my exile from Rome. I would be doing my little Brother the greatest possible good if I could teach him the lesson that I had learnt too late. But I soon decided that if I could teach someone as soft-headed as he was, it would indeed be a miracle. I looked upon it as a challenge, something to pass the time when I was not busy with other miracles.

Slowly I was gaining power in my chosen house. I had won over both Prior Walter and Subprior Brice. Walter knew some unflattering stories about me from the time before I had left for the schools in Paris, and his opinion of me had not been enhanced by what I had done to our little Brother when they were in Rome. Also, he was the only one who knew of the true reason behind my exile.

Despite all this, he was an easy conquest. The Priory was being run like a bad tavern. The only person who had any clear idea about what their land could produce was the cellarer Brother Henry, and he was as crooked as a Cardinal's crozier. I recognised that from the very beginning. It was a great sport for me to expose his crimes and have him expelled, along with his accomplices, and it greatly increased my standing within the house. However, long before this I had won over Prior Walter by taking off his hands those tasks which he found burdensome. Prior Walter was an excellent leader of men, but a bad organiser. The head of a house of religious, even one as insignificant as Inchcolm, must be good at both. I became his organiser. There is no quicker way into someone's affections than taking away from them unpleasant tasks. There is no more direct way to power than making oneself indispensible. It was something I had been doing for years in the service of Paolo Scolari.

Subprior Brice was a much harder hill to climb. With him I had to play the penitent for all I was worth, for he was quite rightly suspicious of the Papal indulgence which I had brought with me. Penitence was not something that came easy to me, as Reason, although it can acknowledge mistakes, never punishes the spirit for them. The results of a mistake are punishment enough, the consequence of a mistake is the only penance I know. I soon learnt how to play the game, however, even managing to arrange some bodily pleasures under the very nose of my stern confessor. I told you, dear reader, that I was a good organiser.

In many subtle ways I knew how to make life difficult for Brice, while at the same time making life easier for myself, gradually introducing more and better dishes at table, shortening the Hours in church, and so on. I spoke, of course, with the voice of Rome, a voice not easily contradicted. I would always

413

convince Walter of the rightness of a change, then let him fight it out with Brice and his band of saints. Finally Brice resigned in disgust and went off to the woods to live the life of a hermit: the blessed Brice Silvester.

It was my desire to become Subprior, but the time was not yet right. There was an insufferable brother called Andrew, who I knew would become even more insufferable as Subprior. Someone's ruin can be achieved by promotion as well as demotion. Such a one I knew was Andrew. For a long time I had been praising him highly to Walter, and extolling the qualities which would make him the natural successor to Brice. Nor was it difficult to persuade Brice of this, as he had always held Andrew dear, in the same way, I imagine, as he held his hair-shirt dear. I would become Andrew's successor. After a few years of Andrew's tyrannical prying and strictness, they would be glad to have someone like myself, whom they imagined would be lax in comparison. Of course, whether I would really be a lax Subprior was quite another matter.

What I had not yet planned was Andrew's end. It turned out that I did not need to plan it, for he brought it on himself. This was a pity, for had I planned it it would have been a lot less troublesome. But I suppose that was the nature of the man, to be troublesome, both living and dead.

It was the morning of the great harvest thanksgiving service. It was the first decent harvest we had had for years, for the summer rains in the 90's were very bad, and many was the time that Laurence and I longed to be back in the warm, dry south. So we were celebrating in our own way in one of the storehouses at Barnhill Point. Instead of busying himself with the coming festival, our beloved Subprior was creeping around sniffing out sin. Those who take pleasure in denying themselves pleasure can smell it more acutely than a dog smells a rabbit.

Usually Laurence and I trysted in the secret chambers at the back of the storehouses. I do not know who built them, but they were certainly put to good use by Brother Henry for storing his pelf. Prior Walter had ordered them to be walled up. I had overseen the task, making sure that part of the wall could be dismantled, should I wish to gain access to them again. Fortunately little light penetrated to the back wall, and the place of the entrance was well hidden.

That morning I had ignored the promptings of reason, and Laurence and I had lain down in the storehouse itself. We did not have much time, and it was long and wearisome work gaining access to the secret chambers. We locked the storeroom door, sure that the only other key was carefully hidden in the Prior's scriptorium. We were both naked and near the very heights of pleasure when we heard a key turn in the lock. The door swung open and there stood Subprior Andrew. He had at last found the demon of lust he had been so long searching for.

I mocked him, offering him Laurence's nakedness so that he could taste fully the sin and thus know his enemy, perhaps even come to love his enemy, as the Lord enjoined him. All the time I was working out the best, most reasonable, course of action. Andrew was ranting on about Hell-fire and prison and excommunication for me, and death for Laurence. I spoke to Laurence in the base Latin of Rome, which I knew Andrew could not understand. I told him that to save both of us I would kill Andrew, but Laurence would have to disappear, so that the blame would be on him. I said I would pay his journey back to Rome if need be, and see that he did not want for the rest of his life. He shook his head violently and pointed to the secret doorway. I nodded agreement. It would do as a temporary hiding-place. It would give us time to effect his escape. There was a sickle on the floor near my foot. I picked it up and struck Andrew on the neck before he even realised what had happened, so absorbed was he in his righteous indignation. After it was over we locked the storeroom door again and installed Laurence in the secret chambers, but not before we had finished the business that Andrew had interrupted. It gave my lust an extra piquancy with the dead eyes of Andrew watching us, and his blood upon us.

In this way I began my Subpriorship, while my servant Laurence began his life as a troglodyte. For he did not want to leave me, and found it pleasing to live thus, well-supplied with meat and drink, free of the stupid prayers and the harsh life of a lay-brother. I was unsure at first, but his hauntings soon formed a charmed circle around Barnhill Point, making my visits to him more easy, and his detection less likely. And if he was caught, then there was little he could say against me, and I am not my brother's, or my servant's, keeper. Loyalty would have to be its own reward.

It was around this time that I heard the news I knew one day I would hear, although I had not expected to hear it so soon. Lothar de Segni, my former amical enemy and inimical friend, had become Pope and taken the name of Innocent. Innocent! he himself had said about the Papacy that you cannot touch pitch without blackening your hands. Was he trying to fool Christendom with his name, or make them laugh? He certainly made me laugh. I wrote him a letter congratulating him on his newly acquired office. I told him that I had grown out of the foolish, sinful thoughts that I had once shared with him, and grown into the 'fullness of faith'. I was proud of that expression, and knew that it would please Lothar. I also told him that he could see from my newly acquired office, the Subpriorship of Inchcolm, how much I had changed: a man without faith could surely never have been entrusted with the care of so many religious and dedicated souls. I even thanked him for having exiled me as otherwise I might never have come to the ineffable knowledge of the true faith. I finished the letter by asking whether, in his infinite mercy and wisdom, as Christ's vicar on earth, he might consider altering the terms of my indulgence and allowing me beyond the strict limits of my confinement. I did not express myself any more precisely at this juncture, although I knew of course exactly what it was I wanted: I wanted to become a Bishop.

Innocent Lothar never replied to my letter. I had not expected him to. But the letter was not without effect. He decided to investigate the state of my soul. He gave the task to the man who had been the Scottish Benedictines' representative at the Curia for many years, Robert de Berwick, recently created Abbot of Dunfermline. The Pope also instructed him to examine one of my brothers for a second opinion. Robert, for whom I had done many favours in my time as Scolari's amanuensis, informed me of this and asked me which of my brothers I would recommend. I recommended my little Brother, because I knew he would say that I had been impeccable in all my offices, which was true, and I knew he could not betray any of the less orthodox things we had done together without betraying himself. Besides, the fool was still clinging to his broken dreams of friendship with me, and it needed only the slightest warmth from me to bring him running to me wagging his tail like some brainless dog.

The row between King William and the newly crowned King John offered the ideal pretext for me to be called to Dunfermline. I had no difficulty in convincing Abbot Robert that I was now a faithful servant of Christ and the Holy Mother Church, and could be entrusted with duties outwith the Priory, and my little Brother did not disappoint me.

If I wanted to advance to a Bishopric, then I would have to start becoming known at court. I helped avert the imminent war. It was a war no one had wanted, not even the King, so I became the hero of the day, and Queen Ermengard took me to her royal and ample bosom. However, it was not the royal bosom that drew me, but the bosom of the fair Lady Affrica. She enflamed my lust as soon as I set eyes on her. Not many women have had the power to do this. Besides, I had always lived in a world where the only women I met were swathed to the eyeballs in cloth, ancient washer-women, or harlots who shunned the light of day. The world of the court, especially the court of love which Queen Ermengard had established around her, I found an utter delight, and I was seduced by it into making the next great mistake of my life.

I spent two years at the court of Queen Ermengard, hearing the Queen's confession, listening to love-songs, wooing and winning my lady Affrica, and fighting with Richard of the Provender. He was an insufferable and pompous little man, who never forgave me for having displaced him from the Queen's favour.

Ultimately it was not the Queen's favour that I coveted, but the King's. Pleasant as life was at the court of Queen Ermengard, it was the court of the King that held the key to advancement. To become a clerk in the King's chancery was the surest way to a Bishopric, no matter how much Lothar might thunder about his sole and divine right to make and unmake them. The biggest obstacle in my way was the Queen herself. She had found me and made me her own, and as long as I remained with her I could do what I liked, even make love to her favourite lady-in-waiting. This was in fact one of the unspoken conditions of my joining her court.

She was far more jealous of her husband than of any of her ladies. She was also very clever, and she knew that she would need more than loyalty to bind me to her. She tried to set a trap baited with the lady Affrica. When Affrica became pregnant, she thought the trap had closed and I was caught. She told me that no one need ever know, except her most trusted friends, and that the child would be well provided for. However, she told me that there must be no more talk of my entering the service of her husband. This angered me. I asked her what she would do if I did not comply. She said she would expose the shame that I had brought upon her court, and throw both Affrica and myself out of her service. This would ruin both of us. She also said that she would take no responsibility for the child. I said that she was holding an unborn child hostage, and that was sinful. She laughed and said that that was not her problem but the problem of her confessor.

I decided to bide my time, wait until the child was born, then go to the King and tell him everything. He would understand, as he was a prolific begetter of bastards himself. And if the Queen wanted to throw Affrica out and turn her back on the child, so be it. I certainly had no intention of being held to ransom by anyone. Somehow or other I would provide for her, and the child, if they survived the birth. I might even present Affrica to the King as a new mistress. For the time being, however, I would let the Queen think she had won.

I avoided Affrica most of the time she was with child. This was not difficult, as she was often unwell, and kept away from the court. She should have gone to a nunnery to give birth, but she was too ill to travel, and so Abbot Robert allowed her to be under the care of his infirmarer. It was in the infirmary of Dunfermline Abbey that she gave birth to a son. She took a fever and died the day after the birth, but the child survived. Poor brat, I thought, it would have been better if you, too, had died. I came to the infirmary to give instructions for it to be destroyed, but I made the mistake of seeing it, and I was not prepared for the blow that it dealt to my reason. So I left it to fate to decide its future. I arranged for a washer-woman of the Abbey to nurse it, and when it was old enough Abbot Robert promised that he would take it as an oblate.

What then happened proved that fate was crueller to the father than to the son. I requested an interview with the King. Richard, always on the look out to do me harm, heard about this. Not only did he thwart the interview, he also informed the Queen. She was furious. While this was going on, the Papal Legate, Cardinal John de Salerno, arrived at Dunfermline Abbey. The Queen went straight to him to complain about my behaviour. He summoned me to his presence. I had known him when he was a mere clerk at the Curia, and I had always despised him as a greedy lickspittle. He welcomed me like a long, lost friend, which made me even more suspicious of him. He told me that he had been given a special mandate from the Holy Father himself to inquire into how I was faring outside the cloister, with instructions to send me back to the cloister and enforce the original indulgence if there was any hint of scandal. This was more than a hint, he said, looking sad. This sadness was not simply show, and boded ill, for I knew he was grieving not for me but for his purse: it meant that not even bribery could alter this. However, he looked more cheerful when he informed me that, if I had to be sent back to the Priory, he had also to strip me of all office within that house, and to ensure that I never again became anything more than a simple canon. I knew from his cheerfulness that now a bribe would be effective, and so I bribed him. I could just tolerate being confined again to the Priory. I could not tolerate being reduced forever to the status of a mere brother. No, if he had done that, I would have risked everything by going to Rome and throwing myself at the feet of Lothar himself in a spectacular show of penance. The Holy Father, John confided in me as we were parting, had instructed him not to be too harsh on me. I should look upon this as a sign of special favour. I would regard it as a far greater favour if he would forget all about me, I said.

However dubious this special favour was, it was not extended to those who had helped me. Abbot Robert was deposed from office. It was not only because he had allowed Affrica to give birth in his infirmary. He had also enemies amongst his own monks, who thought he was overindulgent in matters of moral laxity. They fed the fires of the Legate's displeasure, not only with complaints, but with fat gifts. Robert, who could be as stubborn as an ox when it suited him least, refused to put one penny into John's greedy hand.

So I was back again on Inchcolm. To add vinegar to my gall Richard was appointed Bishop of Dunkeld. I decided that I would be a thorn in his side, and never allow him to enjoy his Bishopric in peace. His own insolence and pride became weapons in my hand. But I had other, secret, weapons. I had been certain that, tiring of his loyalty and of such a miserable existence, Laurence would have returned to his homeland long ago, or else been caught and killed, or simply died of boredom. But no, he was still there, living as a troglodyte in his secret chamber.

He was the other weapon I used against Bishop Richard. Laurence struck twice, once as the wrath of St Columba, when he slaughtered the Bishop's cattle on Leverith, once as the wrath of Bishop Richard, when he attacked our own lands at Cramond, and killed that insufferable serf Donald, who had been making a nuisance of himself recently, trying to bully some more land out of me, threatening to tell the truth about de Mortimer's burial. I could have outsworn him, but this way saved me a lot of trouble, and felled two dogs with one bone.

It was during all this sport with Bishop Richard that Father Michael appeared. I must have been in particularly playful mood, otherwise I would have got rid of him far sooner, as from the very outset I realised he was going to be burdensome to me. Through St Laurence's ear I knew that he had heard some story about me when he was at the Curia. On the one hand I felt flattered that they were still talking about me there, and it was gratifying to know that the stories they were telling were true. On the other hand I was vexed that it had been Father Michael of all people who had been told.

However, it was watching him and my little Brother together that I found so fascinating. Two friends who had found each other. It was enough to make any ordinary mortal envious, or sick. That fool had learned nothing from me about friendship. What a pity they are not both brothers here, I thought, then it would give me pleasure to teach him his lessons all over again. I would have done many things to have brought them together in the Priory. But there was one thing I was not prepared to do, and that was allow Father Michael to become Prior over me. From St Laurence's ear I knew that this is what he was planning, and so I began to spin my counterplan. But I was thwarted, outmanoeuvred by Father Michael. I must say that the way he got himself appointed Prior over my head was very clever, and my respect for him as an adversary grew considerably. However, so did my hatred, and with it my determination to destroy not only his precious friendship, but also him.

Life at the Priory was made much more tolerable by my acquisition of Brother William. His malicious soul coupled with the most extraordinary artistic talent excited me more than words can express. Since my abortive attempt to leave Inchcolm, my main ambition was not only to become the head of the Priory, but to become the head of a much magnified and beautified Priory. I would magnify it by petitioning for it to be raised to the status of an Abbey, and I would beautify it by building fine buildings filled with frescoes, paintings and statues. If I believed in heaven, I would have said that Brother William was heaven-sent, for through him I realised that both my ambitions could be fulfilled much more easily. No, if I believed in heaven, then I would have said that Brother William was hell-sent.

I still had a great quantity of gold and silver deposited with the Knights Templar. No one knew about this, but it meant that I could arrange grants to the Priory for purposes connected with my building plans. I made sure that no such grants were forthcoming when Father Michael was Prior.

After Walter left, I lost much of my power, but I bore this with great patience and fortitude, for I knew that Prior Michael's days were numbered. With both William and me listening at St Laurence's ear, we were able to follow his plans exactly, which meant that we could lay our own plans accordingly. William had convinced me that Laurence was becoming a liability. He was acting more and more carelessly, and it was only a matter of time before he was discovered. If he was taken alive it could have serious consequences. Laurence had no tongue, but he could still point an accusing finger. I argued that it was very useful having such a secret ally on our doorstep. William countered this by saying that he, William, was worth ten Laurences, and he would yet prove it to me. I laughed and said I did not want William to end up living in a hole, at least not while there was still so much work to be done on Inchcolm. In the end I agreed that Lay-brother Laurence were best released from his miserable existence. Besides, he had long since ceased to arouse my lust.

There was one last deed that Laurence was to do for us, and that was to kill Prior Michael. William was then to make sure Laurence died. This would simply be seen as legitimate revenge on an excommunicate and outlaw.

On the night of the vigil that Prior Michael and his faithful Precentor planned to hold at Barnhill Point, William would lure them up to the door of the storeroom, then tell Laurence that his victims were ready and waiting. This could be done easily through the communication hole to Laurence's chamber. Laurence would certainly get one of them, perhaps both. If by chance he killed only the Precentor, then William was to kill the Prior. William, whose blood was hot with the killing-lust, wanted to kill Precentor Michael as well, but I said no, I would rather leave that to

THE END

Here the manuscript ended abruptly. Martin sat as if stunned, staring at the empty parchment, his mouth open, his eyes glazed. From far away he heard a voice and felt someone shaking his shoulder. With a cry he stumbled out of the gateman's chamber, threw back the bolt of the Priory gate and started running down towards the sea.

His only thought was to be alone. Just to be in the presence of another human being was unbearable. He had to be alone, he had to think, he had to rebuild, rebuild, rebuild. This was the word that was hammering in his head. He felt as though his whole world had been destroyed, everything familiar and dear to him obliterated, and now he had to start again, he had to rebuild his world, or another world, on the ruins of the first.

One thought at a time, he said aloud, as he climbed the steep hill of the east island, sending clouds of protesting gulls whirling into the dawn air above his head. They began to attack, one after another, swooping down on his unprotected scalp. Just like my thoughts, he said to himself. No, more orderly than my thoughts, for at least they are taking their turn. And he laughed, unable to carry the burden any longer.

In a night he had found and lost his father. What was it the old man had said? Life is finding and losing, finding and losing. He felt he had lost without really finding. And he laughed again, for he could not believe how unhappy he was.

For the father he had found had never been a father. What had he said about his birth? It would have been better if the child too had died? Something like that. Then he had never mentioned him again. Perhaps if he had been allowed to finish, perhaps then he would have said one word of — no, not love, for how could a man like Simon de Quincy feel love for anyone but himself? But one word of affection, kindness, praise, even disapproval or anger: anything other than silence.

A gull struck him sharply on the head with its sharp claws. He burst into tears and collapsed, unable to bear the pain any longer.

"Maister Mairtin, are ye aa richt?" It was Malcolm. He had followed the young man across the isthmus and up the slope, for he had seen the distracted look in his eyes and had been frightened for him. "Whit's the maitter? Whit wis in yon pairchment?"

Martin sat up, leant forward so that his head was against Malcolm's chest, and wept like a baby.

Malcolm, completely nonplussed by this behaviour, let him

421

weep. He was hit several times by swooping gulls, but he had had the presence of mind to put on his stout leather bonnet.

Suddenly Martin pulled back and stood up, wiping the tears from his eyes. His one thought now was, Simon would never have behaved like this, weeping in the arms of a servant. How would he have behaved? Then he felt as though the earth was tilting under his feet, and there was nothing to hold on to, for why did he want to be like Simon, since he had hated and abhorred everything he had done?

Then he remembered the old man. It was he who had brought him to this point, it was he who had given him his father, and taken his father away. He would have wept like this, not caring what anyone thought of him. He was brave enough to entrust his story to a stranger, he was brave enough to weep.

"Oh, Calum, ma hairt's sair tae breakin, but it'll mend. Thank ye fur comin efter me, ye wur a muckle solace. A'll be aa richt. A'll awaa tae the kirk. Ye'd better awaa back tae yer yett."

And together the gateman and the young clerk went slowly down the hill towards the Priory, while the gulls screamed triumphantly above their heads.

Even before the bell was rung for Prime, everything at the Priory was in a turmoil of departure. Martin, who had not slept a wink that night, and who was beginning to wonder if he had not dreamt the whole thing, slipped away to the infirmary as the others went in to say the Hour.

"Well, young man," Brother Michael asked eagerly, embracing him, "did you find it?"

"No, Father," he replied. "I found the aumbry, but there was no parchment there."

The old man sighed. "Well, maybe it's for the best. I had hoped, but — thank you for looking."

"But the aumbry was not empty," Martin said. He had almost forgotten the pendant. As he spoke, he drew it out from beneath his tunic and took it off. "There was this pendant. It seems to be a thorn embedded in glass and framed by silver filigree. I think —"

"Give it to me," the old man said, holding out his hand. As soon as his fingers closed round it he gave a cry of joy.

"It is the pendant I received from Abbot Robert. It is a thorn from the Crown of Suffering. But how did it come to be in the aumbry? I thought they had taken it from me after the fire. I thought — but I am not sure. But this is a miracle that you have found it. Have you told anyone?"

"No, Father," Martin replied, "I have told no one. Now you can wear it again."

"No, you must take it, I want you to have it and take better care of it than I did."

Martin refused at first, but the old man was insistent. With trembling hands he tried to put it over Martin's head.

"Everyone thinks it is lost. Take it, and bequeath it to the Abbey of Scone. Tell them to say special prayers for their one-time brother Michael."

Martin saw that there was no point in resisting further. He allowed the old man to place the precious relic around his neck and tuck it back into his tunic.

Then there was silence between them, which Brother Michael finally broke.

"You've come to say goodbye, haven't you?" he said quietly.

Martin nodded, unable for a moment to speak the words of farewell, afraid that if he said even one word, he would have to tell the old man everything. But he had decided to spare him.

"Why do you not answer me?" the old man asked.

"I'm sorry, Father," Martin replied, giving a short laugh, warding off the truth which threatened both of them, "I nodded my reply. I forgot that you — I'm very tired. It was a long search. I did not get much sleep."

"My dear boy, how can I thank you enough? It was a great act of charity, listening to me as you did, with such patience. You will not understand just how great until you are old and alone. I pray to God that you will never have to understand, that you will always have someone you can trust and confide in, no matter how old you become."

The bell which signalled the end of Prime rang out clearly in the still morning air. "I must go," Martin said. "Father, thank you. I will never forget you, or your story. It has been very important to me." His words were as tired as his soul. He knelt down at Brother Michael's feet and guided the old man's hand onto his head. "Give me your blessing," he said.

"Go in peace, and may the Lord be with you always."

"And also with you," Martin added. He rose, kissed the scarred cheek and hurried for the door. "Martin," the old man called after him, "you have been like a son to me. The Lord is merciful, even in death's dark valley."

For the last time Martin went out through the infirmary kitchen. Brother Peter was standing at the fire beside a black pot stirring a particularly disgusting-smelling brew. He fixed Martin with a malevolent eye. "Exonerating evidence! Huh!" he snorted, and turned away.

As Martin walked quickly down the cloister past the chapter house, his nostrils were assailed by a very different, but equally unpleasant smell, the biting smell of lime. They were whitewashing over the horrifying paintings of the martyrdoms which William had painted on Simon's orders. He crossed himself and touched the pendant on his breast.

Martin hung over the stern of the boat watching the island and the Priory of St Columba slipping away behind him. A cloud of gulls hovered over the east island. Is it only this morning that I was up there, he thought to himself in amazement. It is as if it happened in another age, another life.

Already the events of the night felt like a dream. To convince himself that they had really happened he put his hand deep into the bosom of his cassock and felt again the cold touch of parchment. He ran his finger down the long, smooth roll. Five times his finger came upon a cord tied crossways. They were cords which were used to attach seals to charters. At the end of each cord was a stone, gripped firmly in several loops. And threaded through each cord was a gold chain, attached to which was the pendant with the Thorn. Yes, everything was in place.

He looked around. No one was watching. The Archdeacon was sitting just at his back talking to Berengar, who was trying not to yawn. In the bow sat Prior William, glaring at the world and muttering to himself.

A seal popped its head out of the water a few yards astern, looked at Martin with wide, intelligent eyes, gave a disdainful snort, then disappeared as soundlessly as it had come.

In one quick movement Martin drew out the manuscript of Simon de Quincy and the precious relic and held them out over the boat's gurgling wake. He opened his hand and let them fall. With this great sacrifice he would begin to expiate the sins of his father. He caught a glimpse of white beneath the surface of the water, like a fish, or a dead gull, then it was gone, twisting and falling to the depths below.

APPENDIX

INDEX OF CHARACTERS

Notes:
1) The index is not exhaustive but includes all the major and most of the minor characters who appear in the book.
2) All the information in Roman type is historically attested.
3) Any name in CAPITALS has its own entry in the index.
4) References to historical works have been kept to a minimum. There are four abbreviations:

Bower's *Scotichronicon* = The *Scotichronicon* by Walter Bower, abbot of Inchcolm 1417-49, general editor D.E.R Watt, Aberdeen, 1987-

Duncan = *Scotland, the Making of the Kingdom* by A.A.M. Duncan, Edinburgh, 1975.

Inchcolm Charters = *Charters of the Abbey of Inchcolm*, ed. D.E. Easson & A. MacDonald, Scottish History Society Vol. XXXII, 1938.

RRS II = *Regesta Regum Scottorum* Vol. II, The Acts of William I, ed. G.W.S. Barrow, Edinburgh, 1971.

***

ABRAHAM, *canon of Inchcolm serving as parish priest in Aberdour, Fife, during 1160s, until his violent death in 1180. Succeeded by Father SERLO.*

ADA de Warenne, c.1123-78; queen-mother 1153-78; her father was William de Warenne earl of Surrey, one of the most powerful of the Anglo-Norman barons in England, her mother was Isabelle, daughter of King Louis VI of France; in 1139 she married Earl Henry, heir to the Scottish throne. However he died before his father, David I, which meant that Henry and Ada's eldest son Malcolm became King on David's death in 1153. This was Malcolm IV, known also as Malcolm the Maiden, due to his lack of interest in women. He ruled from 1153-66.

It is suggested that the de Mortimers came to Scotland in her train, and that Sir WILLIAM de Mortimer was one of her retainers. *She befriended DUSCATH, and died at Crail,* which was one of her dower lands. Her other sons, besides King

Malcolm IV, were King WILLIAM the Lion, and Earl DAVID of Huntingdon.

AEDH Mac Donald. At loggerheads with King WILLIAM over the earldom of Ross, which title had belonged to his grandfather Malcolm Mac Aedh (or Mac Heth) until the latter's death in 1168, when it reverted to the crown. Aedh was killed at Coupar Angus Abbey in 1186 while he was raiding the lowlands.

AFFRICA, *lady-in-waiting to Queen ERMENGARD, Mother of MARTIN de Dunfermline. Unmarried. Died 1201.*

AJULF, dean of Christianity in Lothian for St Andrews diocese; member of the influential family of Bishop Robert of St Andrews (who died 1159), probably that bishop's chaplain before becoming dean, (See RRS II p. 23, note 33) Kinsman, possibly a cousin, of Bishop JOHN Scot, and one of the many officials of St Andrews who were driven out of Scotland by King WILLIAM at the height of the St Andrews dispute in 1180.

ALEXANDER II, King of Scots 1214-49; son of King WILLIAM the Lion.

ALEXIS, subdeacon and papal legate to Scotland in 1180, where at Holyrood in June of that year he conducted a hearing into the disputed election of JOHN Scot to the bishopric of St Andrews. He decided in favour of JOHN and consecrated him the following day.

ANDREW, bishop of Caithness, a Scot, which was unusual for such a highly placed churchman of this period; perhaps a member of a land-holding family in Longforgan, near Dundee. He had been a monk at Dunfermline, before being appointed bishop in 1146. From then on he spent most of his time at court, witnessing many charters of Kings David I, Malcolm IV, and WILLIAM, whom he supported in his struggles with the Bishop JOHN over the bishopric of St Andrews. He died at Dunfermline in 1184. 'In him monk and curialist combined', Duncan, p. 266.

ANICEA, *wife of Sir WILLIAM de Mortimer, daughter of Duncan lord of Aberdour, member of the old Celtic aristocracy. After de Mortimer's death she married Sir ROBERT de London, who thus became the next lord of Aberdour, since Anicea and de Mortimer had no children.*

ARCHIBALD, abbot of Dunfermline 1178-98; *sided with HUGH* *and King WILLIAM in the struggle with JOHN Scot over the bishopric of St Andrews.*

ARNOLD, abbot of Melrose 1179-89, abbot of Rievaulx 1189-99. One of the envoys of King WILLIAM to Pope LUCIUS III in 1182.

BRICE, *sub-prior of Inchcolm 1175-94.*

CELESTINE III, Pope 1191-98. Giacinto (Hyacinth) Bobo, born in 1106, of Roman aristocratic family; pupil and friend of Abelard; made a cardinal in 1144 by Pope Celestine II, and one of only two cardinals considered by Thomas Becket to be unamenable to bribery (for the other, see LUCIUS III); ·not ordained a priest until the day before his consecration as Pope, at the age of 85.

CLEMENT III, Pope 19 Dec. 1187 late March 1191. Paolo Scolari, member of the Roman nobility, cardinal bishop of Palestrina; he negotiated the return of the papacy to Rome, after many years of exile, and completed the reconciliation process between the Church and the Empire which was started by his predecessor Gregory VIII. Generally regarded as an unscrupulous schemer, Richard I of England called him the Antichrist. *Simon de Quincy joined his household in the late 1170s.*

DAVID, c.1144-1219, earl of Huntingdon, third son of Earl Henry and Countess ADA de Warenne, brother and close associate of King WILLIAM the Lion. One of the hostages for the king at Falaise in 1174, after the king's capture at Alnwick. He was WILLIAM de Mortimer's feudal Lord c.1181, and it was his clerk ROBERT *de Alconbury* who was intruded into the church at Aberdour in that year in defiance of Inchcolm.

DONALD Mac William, grandson of King Duncan II of Scotland, claimant to the Scottish throne and leader of several uprisings against King WILLIAM. It was during one such uprising that he was killed in 1187.

DUNCAN, earl of Fife 1154-1204; justiciar of Scotland north of the Forth, and one of the most powerful of the barons at the court of King WILLIAM de Lion; exceptional in that he was of native, Celtic stock, unlike most of the nobility at King WILLIAM's court, who were of Anglo-Norman descent. He took an active part in the 1173-74 wars between King WILLIAM and King Henry II of England, and was in command of the soldiers who carried out the massacre at the church of St Laurence, Warkworth, Northumberland, during that war.

DUSCATH, see MICHAEL, canon of Inchcolm.

EDGAR, *novice in Jedburgh Abbey 1178, later transferred to Inchcolm, then in 1180 to Scone Abbey. He took the name Michael in memory of his close friend Brother Michael, who remained at Inchcolm. Returned to Inchcolm as Prior MICHAEL in 1210.*

EDWIN, *born in 1120, in his youth a friend of Saint Ailred of Rievaulx. By 1178 he was infirmarer at Jedburgh.*

ERMENGARD de Beaumont, Queen of Scots; daughter of a minor French nobleman Richard Viscount de Beaumont-sur-Sarthe in Maine, granddaughter of one of the many illegitimate daughters of Henry I of England; married King WILLIAM the Lion in 1186, becoming the first queen of Scots for 55 years. She bore him a son, the future ALEXANDER II, as well as three daughters, Margaret (senior), Isabel and Margaret (junior). In 1212 she acted as an intermediary for peace between King WILLIAM and King John (see Duncan, p. 251). She lived until 1234 and founded, along with her son, Balmerino Abbey, Fife, where she lies buried.

FERGUS, *lay brother and infirmary servant at Inchcolm in 1224.*

FLATHBERTACH, *father of DUSCATH, Duncan and GILLE-COLM. He was WILLIAM de Mortimer's chief steward at Aberdour in 1160s and '70s*

GEOFFREY, *precentor at Inchcolm (i.e. leader of the singing in the church and responsible for the priory's manuscripts) from the early 1170s until his retirement in 1202; close friend of Father SERLO. He was succeeded as precentor by MICHAEL.*

GILBERT, chaplain to several bishops of Dunkeld, at least from the episcopacy of JOHN de Leicester. *Present on Inchcolm with Bishop JOHN de Leicester when SIMON became prior there in 1211.* He himself was elected bishop on the death of Bishop HUGH in 1229. He died 1236.

GILLECOLM, *DUSCATH's elder brother, who succeeded his father FLATHBERTACH as WILLIAM de Mortimer's chief steward at Aberdour.*

GREGORY VIII, Pope October to December 1187. Alberto de Morra, born at Benevento c.1110; canon regular then professor of law at Bologna; made cardinal deacon by Adrian IV and cardinal bishop by Alexander III; became chancellor of the Roman Church in 1178.

HENRY, abbot of Arbroath, 1179-1201 or later. Before he became abbot he was a monk at Kelso, the monastery which had supplied Arbroath's first abbot, Reginald.

HENRY (Master), clerk to Bishop JOHN Scot of Dunkeld around 1190, and later archdeacon of Dunkeld. *Mediator between Inchcolm Priory and RICHARD de Prebenda bishop of Dunkeld in 1207 during dispute over Cramond Island (Leverith).* By 1225 his successor WILLIAM de Ednam had taken over.

HENRY, canon of Inchcolm, *he joined the priory as a novice in 1212, and led the rebellion against Prior William in 1224.* By 1228 he had succeeded NIGEL as prior. In 1235 the priory was formally erected into an abbey, with Henry as its first abbot. He resigned in 1244 and died shortly afterwards.

HENRY, de Lochore, canon of Inchcolm, cellarer 1179-1191.

HUGH, bishop of Dunkeld 1214-29, nicknamed the 'bishop of the poor'. When he was still a royal clerk he was known as Hugh de Sigillo, or Hugh of the Seal (see RRS II pp. 31 & 61, note 18).

HUGH, (disputed) bishop of St Andrews 1178-1188. Royal chaplain, he was intruded by King WILLIAM into St Andrews after the St Andrews chapter had elected JOHN Scot in 1178. Deposed by the papal legate ALEXIS in 1180, later excommunicated, he died in Rome in 1188.

HUGH, canon of Inchcolm. He joined the priory in 1195; succeeded MICHAEL as granger in 1198, Sacristan in 1224.

INNOCENT III, Pope 1198-1216. Born c.1160 Lotario, second son of Trasimondo count of Segni, and Claricia, a member of the patrician Scotti family. He was the nephew of Cardinal John de Anagni, who was a friend of CLEMENT III. He was one of the most influential Popes of the Middle Ages. *He was fellow-student and friend of SIMON de Quincy at Bologna University in the 1170s.*

ISAAC, canon of Inchcolm and friend and contemporary of

MICHAEL. Accompanied Prior WALTER and MICHAEL on the royal embassy to Rome in 1182. He died in 1192 near Scone in mysterious circumstances. Later his tomb on Inchcolm became the centre of a local cult.

JOCELIN (Master), archdeacon of Dunkeld, appointed 1172 x 1177; friend of Bishop HUGH of St Andrews, and a staunch supporter of him in his struggle with JOHN Scot over that diocese; accepted from HUGH the church of Dairsie, in Fife, although this was not HUGH's to give away, as the patronage belonged to the priory of St Andrews, not the bishop. When Legate ALEXIS was in Scotland in 1180 he excommunicated Jocelin, cancelled his appointment to Dairsie church, and, restored it to the priory. Perhaps he remained mainly with HUGH until HUGH's final departure from Rome in 1188, and certainly he is notably absent from the records of JOHN Scot after JOHN became bishop of Dunkeld in 1183. He last appeared as a witness to a charter in 1193/94. *He visited Inchcolm in 1178 to investigate the circumstances of MICHAEL's irregular arrival there.*

JOCELIN, bishop of Glasgow 1174-99; started his religious career as a monk at the Cistercian abbey of Melrose; elected bishop of Glasgow at Perth in 1174, in the presence of the king. He was a frequent witness to royal charters and led the Scottish delegation to Rome in 1182 which the king had sent to petition Pope LUCIUS III to lift the interdict from Scotland, and settle once and for all the St Andrews dispute between JOHN Scot and HUGH.

JOHN de Leicester, (Master), bishop of Dunkeld 1211-14, probably some relation to Bishop ROGER of St Andrews, and thus a distant relative of King WILLIAM; archdeacon of Lothian for St Andrews diocese. His election as bishop of Dunkeld was opposed by bishop William MALVEISIN of St Andrews. He died at Cramond and was buried at Inchcolm in October 1214.

JOHN de Salerno, cardinal priest of St Stephen in Celio Monte, papal legate to Scotland 1201-2.

JOHN Scot (Master), bishop of Dunkeld, a member of a powerful ecclesiastical and land-holding family in East Fife; nephew of Bishop Robert of St Andrews, also of Bishop MATTHEW of Aberdeen. The family appears to be Norman rather than native, so it is possible that a sister of MATTHEW and Robert married a 'native', hence the surname Scot. However, there is another tradition which states that he was only distantly related to the family of Bishop Robert. For details see D.E.R. Watt's *Biographical Dictionary of Scottish Graduates to AD 1410* Oxford 1977, pp. 484-88.

In 1178 the chapter of St Andrews elected him to succeed the recently deceased Bishop Richard, instead of waiting for the king to foist the customary royal clerk on them. This did not, however, deter the king from doing just that, the royal clerk whom he chose being HUGH. After a bitter struggle with the king and HUGH, in which JOHN was supported by the papacy, he finally accepted the bishopric of Dunkeld in 1183. However, the struggle did not end there, rumbling on until HUGH's death in 1188. He died in 1203.

LAURENCE, *formerly Orsino, the deaf and dumb servant of SIMON de Quincy, who had bought him in the slums of Rome. He accompanied SIMON to Inchcolm, where he became a lay-brother and was given the name of Laurence.*

LUCIUS III, Pope 1181-85. Born Ubaldus Allucingolus in Lucca, Tuscany, c.1097; a Cistercian monk who was made a cardinal bishop of Ostia and Velletri by Pope Adrian IV in 1159. He was the trusted counsellor of Pope Alexander III, his predecessor, and a leading negotiator of the Peace of Venice in 1177. As Pope he had persistent problems with the Romans. He gave the Rose of Gold to the envoys of King WILLIAM rather than to the leader of the Roman senate, as was customary, in March 1182, just before he was forced to flee Rome, never to return. He died and was buried in Verona, where his tomb is still to be seen. Succeeded by URBAN III, he was one of the only two cardinals whom Thomas Becket (died 1171) considered to be unamenable to bribery. The other was Giacinto Bobo, who later became Pope CELESTINE III. He is the subject of a piece of scurrilous verse recorded by his contemporary Gerald of Wales:

Lucius est piscis rex atque tyrannus aquarum
A quo discordat Lucius iste parum.
Devorat hic homines, hic piscibus insidiatur.
Esurit hic semper, hic aliquando satur.
Amborum vitam si lanx aequata levaret;
Plus rationis habet qui ratione caret.

Which can be roughly translated as:

Lucius in Latin means a pike, the tyrant of the lake,
and between one Lucius and the other the difference is
        not great;
one eats up little fishes, the other eats up men;
one's hunger's sometimes sated, the hunger of the other

has no end,
So if between the two you're sitting on the fence,
remember this: the Lucius that lacks reason has more
    sense.

MALCOLM, *lay brother and gateman at Inchcolm in 1224.*

MALVEISIN, William, royal clerk, archdeacon of Lothian, King WILLIAM's chancellor, bishop of Glasgow 1200-02, bishop of St Andrews 1202-38.

MARGARET, Queen of Scots c.1070-1093, wife of King Malcolm III Canmore, great-grandmother of King WILLIAM of Scotland and great-great-grandmother of King John of England. According to the contemporary English chronicler Roger Howden, King WILLIAM, in the summer of 1199, spent the night at her tomb in Dunfermline, whereupon she appeared to him in a dream warning him not to carry out his planned campaign against England to assert his right to Northumberland.

MARTIN *de Dunfermline (Master), born 1201 in Dunfermline, the illegitimate child of Lady AFFRICA, lady-in-waiting to Queen ERMENGARD. He obtained a degree at the University in Paris. On his return to Scotland in 1223 he joined the chancery of Bishop Hugh of Dunkeld.*

MATTHEW, bishop of Aberdeen 1172-1199; related to JOHN Scot, according to some sources JOHN's uncle (his mother's brother); related also to Bishop Robert of St Andrews (died 1159) possibly his brother, hence his position as archdeacon of St Andrews before he became bishop of Aberdeen. He had to flee the country with JOHN in 1180 after Legate ALEXIS decided in JOHN's favour and against HUGH and King WILLIAM in the dispute over St Andrews. With JOHN he sought King Henry II's protection in Normandy.

MATTHEW, *canon of Inchcolm, sacristan in 1207.*

MAURICE, canon of Inchcolm, witnessed along with Prior Brice, WALTER's predecessor, and WILLIAM, a fellow canon, a charter of Bishop Gregory of Dunkeld to Dunfermline Abbey in the 1160s *(Regestrum de Dunfermlyn, no. 124). Infirmarer for much of the last quarter of 12th century.*

MICHAEL, canon of Inchcolm, witnessed a charter of Bishop Abraham of Dunblane confirming the church of Logy to North Berwick nunnery around 1214 *(Carte Monialium de Northberwic no. 11.) Born 1160 in Aberdour and baptised DUS-*

CATH; became a page, then a squire to Sir WILLIAM de Mortimer; taken to Normandy when his lord was captured by the English at Alnwick; became a novice of Inchcolm in 1178 and took the name Michael; held various offices in the priory including succentor, kitchener, granger, cellarer and precentor. Old and blind, he spent his last years in the priory's infirmary. He told his story, and the story of SIMON de Quincy, to Master MARTIN in 1224. He died at the end of the winter of 1225.

MICHAEL, *formerly Edgar,* prior of Inchcolm in 1210, after having been a canon of Scone, for which see Bower's *Scotichronicon* Book VIII chapter 75, quoted in full under SIMON de Quincy.

NICHOLAS, abbot of Cambuskenneth from c.1195 to c.1207. *Formerly a canon of Inchcolm.*

ORSINO. See Laurence.

OSBERT, abbot of Kelso 1180-1203, before which he was prior of Lesmahago. One of the envoys sent to Rome in 1182 to ask Pope LUCIUS III to lift the ban from Scotland. King WILLIAM took Abbot Osbert's lands, vassals and possessions into royal protection until the latter returned from this mission (RRS II p. 278). Also the king granted him a favourable charter 1180 x 85, witnessed by Bishop HUGH of St Andrews, which might be interpreted as some kind of recognition for the successful completion of the same mission (RRS II, p. 284).

PATRICK, abbot of Dunfermline 1202-1217, formerly superior of Durham. Succeeded the deposed Abbot ROBERT de Berwick.

PETER, canon of Inchcolm; infirmarer in 1224.

RALPH, older fellow squire of DUSCATH in WILLIAM de Mortimer's household in the 1170s.

RAOUL, minstrel and lover of lady ANICEA de Mortimer.

REIMBOLD, abbot of Scone 1198-c.1206, previously cellarer of Holyrood; elected abbot of Scone at Forfar under royal pressure in May 1198 (RRS II, p. 385). Successor at Scone to Abbot ROBERT II, and succeeded by Abbot WILLIAM.

RICHARD, abbot of Jedburgh 1174-92.

RICHARD de Moreville: the Anglo-Norman family of de Moreville took its name from the village of Morville near Cherbourg in Normandy; in 1162 Richard succeeded his father Hugh I de Moreville as constable of Scotland (one of the highest offices in the land), and inherited most of his Scottish lands. His older brother Hugh II de Moreville inherited his father's English lands, and rose fast in the service of the English King Henry II. Hugh II de Moreville was the chief murderer of St Thomas Becket in 1171.

Richard de Moreville was one of the close associates of King WILLIAM excommunicated by JOHN Scot in 1181 for supporting HUGH in the St Andrews dispute; he remained constable until his death in 1190, when he was succeeded by his son William.

RICHARD de Prebenda ('of the Provender'), royal clerk of the provender from c.1170 till 1203. Clerk of the provender was one of the key positions in the royal household, with responsibility for its victualling and provisioning. A relative of King WILLIAM, he was one of his close associates who was excommunicated by JOHN Scot at Redden, Roxburghshire, in August 1181 during the St Andrews dispute.

In 1203 he became bishop of Dunkeld. In September 1207 a commission of inquiry was set up by Pope INNOCENT III to investigate a complaint by Inchcolm that Richard, who had leased the island of Leverith (Cramond island), was withholding the rent and keeping the island in his occupancy *(see Inchcolm charters* no. IX). He died at the episcopal manor-house of Cramond at Easter 1210, and was buried at Inchcolm. *In his latter days as clerk of the provender he was also confessor to Queen ERMENGARD until ousted from that position by SIMON de Quincy.*

ROBERT *de Alconbury,* clerk of David Earl of Huntingdon, in 1180 intruded into the church of Aberdour in defiance of the rights of Inchcolm. For a vivid description of the fracas in the churchyard on the day of his intrusion, *(see Inchcolm Charters,* no. V). He was active in Scotland as a scribe between the years 1172 and c.1185, and his hand-writing is preserved in certain of the charters issued by Earl DAVID, some of which he also witnessed. He was in England from c.1185-96 *and it was here he died of leprosy in 1200.*

ROBERT de Berwick, abbot of Dunfermline 1198-1202. Deposed by the papal legate JOHN de Salerno. *In the 1180s he was the representative of the Scottish Benedictines at the Papal Curia, which was how he came to know SIMON de Quincy.*

ROBERT I, first abbot of Scone c.1163-84. Before that he was a canon of Jedburgh, then prior of Restenneth, Angus. He became prior of Scone in 1162, and soon afterwards the priory was elevated to the status of an abbey. He witnessed the very first extant charter of Inchcolm c.1163-69. As abbot of Scone he was head of the Augustinian Order in Scotland.

ROBERT II, abbot of Scone 1184-98, previously prior of Scone; *nephew of Abbot ROBERT I. He attended the hearing at Holyrood in 1180 in place of Abbot ROBERT, when JOHN Scot was declared bishop of St Andrews.* He resigned office in 1198 as he no longer felt able to carry out his duties, and was succeeded by REIMBOLD.

ROBERT de London, illegitimate son of King WILLIAM and Matilda Ferrers, who later married one Richard de London. Sir Robert held the lordship of Aberdour around the year 1200, after Sir WILLIAM de Mortimer. Also around this time he held the burgh of Inverkeithing. *The lordship of Aberdour came into his possession through his marriage with Lady ANICEA de Mortimer after Sir WILLIAM's death in 1192.*

ROBERT de Quincy: the Anglo-Flemish family of de Quincy took its name from the town of Cuinchy near Béthune in French Flanders. Saher I de Quincy married Maud de Senlis, step-daughter of King David I, and settled in Northamptonshire. His younger son Robert, like so many younger sons of powerful Anglo-Norman and Anglo-Flemish families in England, sought his fortune at the Scottish court, and entered the service of King Malcolm IV. He married Orabilis, a Celtic heiress, and through her became lord of extensive estates in Fife and Strathearn with Leuchars his principal seat. Before the year 1179 he made a grant to Inchcolm of 1000 eels annually from his estate at Strathenry, near Leslie, Fife *(Inchcolm Charters* no. II). He was the most important nobleman from Scotland who we know definitely took part in the Third Crusade, which began in 1189. He probably left Scotland late 1189, but did not arrive in the Holy Land until June 1191. Fighting under the English king Richard I, he became the constable and leader of the English knights. He probably left for home with the bulk of Richard I's forces in autumn 1192, and was back in Scotland c.1194. He was succeeded by his son Saher (II), who was earl of Winchester 1207-19.

ROBERT de Raperlaw (Master), canon of Dunkeld 1214 x 1236. He always witnessed charters alongside archdeacons of Dunkeld. *Amanuensis of Archdeacon WIILIAM de Ednam during the inquiry at Inchcolm, 1224.*

ROGER de Leicester *or* de Beaumont, second son of Robert III earl of Leicester and cousin of King WILLIAM, elected bishop of St Andrews at Perth in April 1189, not consecrated until 1198, died 1202. For a brief period before being elected bishop he was the royal chancellor. See R.R.S. II p. 310.

ROGER de Quincy, younger brother of ROBERT de Quincy. Roger accompanied ROBERT to Scotland, and worked there as chief steward on ROBERT's Leuchars estates. There he fathered a child on a serf. This child was SIMON de Quincy.

ROGER, canon of Inchcolm, succentor in 1207, percentor in 1224.

ROGER, chaplain to Sir WILLIAM de Mortimer; whom he accompanied to Falaise when captured with the king at Alnwick. He took DUSCATH to Mont St Michel in Normandy in the autumn of 1174.

ROLAND, archbishop-elect of Dol in Brittany. He was dean of Avranches in Normandy when he was elected archbishop of Dol in 1177. Because of the fierce opposition of the archbishop of Tours and the French royal family to the existence of an archbishopric at Dol, he was never consecrated. He was appointed one of the papal commissioners sent to Scotland by Pope LUCIUS III in the summer of 1182 to look into the St Andrews dispute, the other being Silvan, abbot of Rievaulx. They failed to bring the affair to a satisfactory conclusion, and the matter was referred back to the Pope. In 1184 Roland was made cardinal deacon of Santa Maria in Porticu, but had been replaced by one Gregory by May 1188. The main supporter of the archbishopric of Dol was Henry II. It finally disappeared entirely in 1199.

SERLO, chaplain of Aberdour, canon of Inchcolm. *Close friend of Father GEOFFREY, Brother Michael's confessor during his early years on Inchcolm, he succeeded ABRAHAM as priest of Aberdour after the latter's murder in 1180, and after ROBERT de Alconbury had been forced to resign he officiated at the funeral mass for Sir WILLIAM de Mortimer in Aberdour church.* He witnessed a charter of ROBERT de London sometime c.1214 (*Registrum de Dunfermlyn*, no. 168).

SIMON *de Quincy* prior of Inchcolm 1211-*19*. The only historical reference we have to him is in Bower's *Scotichronicon* Book VIII, chapter 75: 'And Walter prior of Inchcolm became abbot of Holyrood and was succeeded as prior by Michael a canon of Scone, who died the following year. He in turn was succeeded by Simon, subprior of Inchcolm.' *He was an illegitimate scion of the powerful de Quincy family; born 1158 in Leuchars, Fife, his father being ROGER de Quincy. After studying in Paris and Bologna, he became close adviser to Paolo Scolari, later Pope CLEMENT III; in 1191 he became a canon of Inchcolm; in 1198 its subprior and in 1211 its prior.*

STEPHEN, *canon of Inchcolm, succeeded Brother Hugh as granger in 1205.*

THOMAS, canon of Inchcolm, witnessed a charter of Bishop GILBERT of Dunkeld to Balmerino Abbey at Tibbermore, Perthshire in 1231 *(Liber S. Marie de Balmorinach,* no. 26). He became abbot after HENRY c.1243, resigning in 1258. *He joined Inchcolm in 1206, and accompanied SIMON and MICHAEL to Holyrood in 1208.*

URBAN III, Pope November 1185 to October 1187. Born Umberto Crivelli, of aristocratic Milanese family; of stern and uncompromising character, he was a harsh opponent of the Empire, as his family had suffered greatly in the sack of Milan by Frederick Barbarossa in 1162. He refused to negotiate with the Romans concerning the return of the Curia to Rome. Even in his old age he insisted on riding everywhere, and it is said that he died as a result of a fall from his horse.

WALTER, prior of Inchcolm 1178-1210; he attended the Great Lateran Council in Rome 1179, from where he brought back the charter of confirmation of the priory of Inchcolm *(Inchcolm Charter* no.II*)*. He was in Rome again in 1182 as one of the embassy King WILLIAM had sent to Pope LUCIUS III to try to lift the ban which had been placed on Scotland as a result of the St Andrews dispute. He was in Perth in April 1189 at the election of ROGER de Leicester as bishop of St Andrews (RRS II, p. 308). He appears with relative frequency as witness of royal and other charters from the early 1190's onwards. He was a member of the royal embassy to King John of England in 1199 to ask the new king for Northumbria and Cumbria, which King WILLIAM regarded as his right. He became abbot of Holyrood in 1210 (for the account of his appointment, see SIMON de Quincy). He died in 1215.

WALTER, prior of St Andrews 1160-c.95. Cantor at St Andrews until the death of Prior Robert in 1160, when he was elected prior. He was a supporter of JOHN Scot in the St Andrews bishopric dispute.

WALTER of Roxburgh (Master), archdeacon of St Andrews at the time of JOHN Scot's election as bishop c.1178. He was a supporter of the royal candidate Bishop HUGH in the St Andrews dispute, and witnessed several charters of that bishop.

WILLIAM I, the Lion, King of Scots 1165-1214; son of Earl Henry and Countess ADA de Warenne, grandson of King David I; born 1143; supported King Henry the Younger against the latter's father, King Henry II or Elder, in 1173; captured at Alnwick in July 1174 in the ensuing war, and imprisoned in Falaise, Normandy. This meant humiliating terms for Scotland in the peace treaty, known as the Treaty of Falaise, including the garrisoning of the major Scottish castles with English soldiers, and restrictions in William's sovereignty. The Treaty of Falaise was finally nullified in 1189 by Richard I (in exchange for money, which Richard needed for his Crusade).

King William had several mistresses and a clutch of illegitimate children by the time he married ERMENGARD de Beaumont in 1186 at the age of 43. He had one legitimate son, ALEXANDER, who succeeded him on the Scottish throne. A contemporary Irish chronicle describes him as *garbh*, 'rough, brawny'. Contemporary English chroniclers such as Walter of Coventry comment on his enthusiasm for things French, by which is meant Norman French: French manners, language and culture. He fought several campaigns in the north of Scotland against claimants to the Scottish throne descended from Malcolm Canmore, and representing more traditional, Celtic interests.

WILLIAM, abbot of Holyrood c.1198-1210, the second abbot of Holyrood of this name. *During his period of office the new abbey church was built. He brought WILLIAM de Colchester from England especially to supervise the works.* He was succeeded as abbot by Prior WALTER of Inchcolm.

WILLIAM, abbot of Scone, c.1206-c.1230. *He was formerly a canon of Cambuskenneth, by Stirling, and close associate of Abbot NICHOLAS of Cambuskenneth. He consecrated MICHAEL/EDGAR prior of Inchcolm in 1210.*

WILLIAM, chaplain at Auchtertool, Fife. He witnessed a charter of Bishop JOHN Scot of Dunkeld along with Prior WALTER of Inchcolm between 1189 and 1195 (*Registrum de Dunfermlyn*, no.126). As the church of Auchtertool belonged to Inchcolm it can safely be assumed that he was also a canon of that house. He was possibly also the same William, canon of Inchcolm, who witnessed, along with Prior Brice, WALTER's predecessor, and MAURICE, a charter of Bishop

Gregory of Dunkeld in the 1160s (see MAURICE). *Guest- and novice-master at Inchcolm when MICHAEL joined the community there in 1178. He had moved to Auchtertool by 1189, succeeding a chaplain named Thomas. However he was removed from that charge and brought back to Inchcolm by Subprior SIMON de Quincy around 1205 to be replaced by a vicar.* Such replacements became common in the Middle Ages in parishes which belonged to monastic houses, as they increased the income of the mother house, since a vicar received less payment than a canon.

WILLIAM *de Colchester,* prior of Inchcolm deposed for bad behaviour. Our only reference to him is in Bower's *Scotichronicon* Book IX, chapter 43, under the year 1224: 'William a canon of Holyrood, who had been prior of Inchcolm for some considerable time, was deposed from office on account of his many intolerable excesses. This came about because the whole convent said firmly and unanimously to King Alexander and the bishop that they would all prefer to leave the religious life and return to the world than to put up with him as prior any longer. So the prior was examined on behalf of both the king and the bishop, and on being found all too guilty he left his office, and the priory, albeit against his will. He was succeeded by Nigel a canon and terrarius of Jedburgh.'

WILLIAM de Ednam (Master), archdeacon of Dunkeld, succeeded Archdeacon HENRY by 1225. Ednam is in Berwickshire. *He led the investigation into the behaviour of Prior WILLIAM of Inchcolm in 1224.*

WILLIAM Malveisin, see MALVEISIN.

WILLIAM de Mortimer, Lord of Aberdour, Fife, in the latter part of 12th century. He belonged to the branch of the de Mortimers who were based at Attleborough, Norfolk, and was probably distantly related to the Mortimers of Wigmore, who took their name from Mortemer-sur-Eaulne in Normandy (see *Complete Peerage,* Vol. IX, 1936). The Mortimers of Attleborough were feudal tenants of the Earls of Warenne, and it is very likely that Sir William de Mortimer came to Scotland in the train of Lady ADA de Warenne when she married Prince Henry, King David I's son, in 1139. By 1181 he was a vassal of Earl DAVID of Huntingdon, as de Mortimer refers to him as *dominus meus,* 'my lord', in *Inchcolm Charters,* no.V.
He witnessed many charters of King WILLIAM the Lion 1165 x 1189. He was captured with the king at Alnwick in 1174, and was one of those held hostage for the king at Falaise in Normandy.

His capture at Alnwick is described in a contemporary poem by Jordan Fantome as follows (translated from Medieval French):

William de Mortimer behaved very well that day;
he goes among the ranks like a wild boar,
giving great blows and often taking his share of them.
He found opposed to him a true knight,
Lord Bernard de Baliol, of whom you hear me speak,
who felled him and his charger,
and put him on parole, as is done with a knight.

He appears as a penitent in *Inchcolm Charter, no.V*, in which he humbly begs forgiveness of the canons of Inchcolm for having injured them physically in Aberdour churchyard when they tried to stop him and Earl DAVID putting ROBERT *de Alconbury* in charge of that parish in 1180. In this charter he concedes that he was wrong and that the church of Aberdour belonged to the priory. The gift of half a carucate (52 acres) of land in Aberdour and half the rents of the mill, mentioned in *Inchcolm Charters* no.VI (a bull of Pope LUCIUS III granted 17 March 1182), is usually interpreted as reparation for his 'shameful' treatment of the canons (see *Inchcolm Charters,* p.107).

The legend of the disposal of the body of a de Mortimer on its way to be buried on Inchcolm first appears in Robert Sibbald's *History of Fife and Kinross*, 1710, p.92. According to Sibbald one Sir Alan de Mortimer gave half the lands of his town of Aberdour to God and the monks of St Colme's Inch, for the benefit of a burial-place for himself and his posterity in the church of the monastery. 'Sir Alan being dead, the monks carrying his corpse in a coffin of lead, by barge, in the night-time, to be interred within the church, some wicked monks did throw the same in a great deep betwixt the land and the monastery, which, to this day, by the neighbouring fishing men and salters, is called "Mortimer's Deep". (also quoted by William Ross, *Aberdour & Inchcolm,* 1885, p.10).

There is absolutely no medieval evidence for the existence of a Sir Alan de Mortimer, and it would seem that his gift of half his lands of Aberdour is a folk-memory of the gift of 52 acres and half the mill rent which Sir William made to Inchcolm. It is Ross *ibid*, p.124 who first suggests this, adding: 'It is more than probable that the story which Sibbald tells of Sir Alan's coffin being dropped into the sea between the mainland and Inchcolm — long known as "Mortimer's Deep" — in reality applies to Sir William de Mortimer; for, in his case, the Canons' remembrance of the shameful way in which they had been treated in the churchyard of Aberdour might account for the dead knight being treated with so little ceremony.' *His death occurred during a tournament in 1192.*

WILLIAM de St Pair, monk of the abbey of Mont St Michel in

Normandy in the late 12th century; author of a long poem in Norman French about the history and legends of Mont St Michel. *In 1174 he met DUSCATH and questioned him about his rescue of the little girl Eleanor from the river Sélune, with a view to including the story in his poem.*

GLOSSARY OF SCOTS

The linguistic situation in late 12th, early 13th century Lowland Scotland (excluding South West Scotland) was a complex one, with three languages in common use:
1) Middle Gaelic, the ancestor of modern Gaelic (called 'Scottish' in the novel). This was the most wide-spread of the three, spoken by the bulk of the common people benorth the Forth-Clyde line.
2) a northern dialect of Anglo-Saxon, the ancestor of modern Scots or Lallans (called 'Inglis' in the novel); this was spoken in the royal burghs by the merchants and traders, many of whom were of northern English origin; it had been the chief language of Lothian and the Eastern Borders since the late 7th century.
3) Norman French (called 'French' in the novel), which was spoken in the monasteries and at court by most of the aristocracy, many of whom were of Anglo-Norman provenance.

In the novel I have tried to reflect a little of this linguistic complexity, while keeping it accessible to all English speakers. I have therefore taken advantage of the fortunate situation in Scotland today where we have, besides English, a second language which, with a little extra effort and the help of a glossary, any English speaker can understand: this language is Scots or Lallans. In the novel English, as well as being the language of the narrative, represents Norman French and Inglis, while Scots represents Middle Gaelic. A further consideration in choosing Scots to represent Gaelic is that Scots today has the similar lowly status that Gaelic had at the time of the novel in much of Lowland Scotland.

aiblins perhaps
alow alight, on fire
ayont beyond

bairn child
bauldy bald
beild shelter
ben in, within
bide stay, live
blether chat
bodach old man
bris bruise
brose a thin, watery porridge

cain tribute, portion of rent or other dues paid in kind
caunel candle
chap knock
cheil man, fellow
clim climb
clype tell tales
coggie cup, vessel
coost throw, cast
cuddy horse

dae do
deid-cist coffin
dod piece, lump
dour humourless, stern
dunk dip

efter after(wards)
erse arse

fae from
fash trouble, annoy
feart frightened
fere companion
fleg frighten
fraucht load

gaird guard
gan(g); gaun go; going
gate way, road
geggie show, performance
gey very
gie give
gin if
girnel grange, barn
grabby greedy

greet cry
guid good
gyte mad

hairst harvest; autumn
haun hand
heist hoist
hirple hobble, limp

ilka each
ilkane each one

jalouse suspect

ken know
kirk church
kythe show

laigh low
leal loyal
lees lies
leid language
lithe gentle

mair more
maist most
maun must
mind remember
mirk dark
(the) mornin's mornin tomorrow morning
(the) mornin's nicht tomorrow night
muckle big, great

neb nose
neist next
nor than

pend arched gateway
pickle bit

rape rope
rax stretch
redd save
redd up clear away, tidy up after use
rug pull

saint disappear
sair sore
sauf safe

scretchins scratchings
scunner (v)disgust; (n)horror, wretch
sea-bree sea-fog
seiven-dey week
ser serve
shairly surely
sharn dung
sic such
skelp slap, beat
snuve sneak
speir at ask
speir (n) question
stite rubbish, nonsense
sweir swear
syne then

teinds tithes
thir these
thone that
tillie tiller
toom empty
twaa two
twal twelve
tyne; tint lose; lost

waur worse
wecht weight
whaa who
whaur where
wheen quantity
wiooten without

yett gate
yin one

NOTE ON THE PSALMS

Many of the psalms quoted in the novel, especially those used at the head of each section, are my own translations from the Latin Psalter which was current in the Middle Ages, and which often diverges from the more familiar versions of the Authorised or New English Bible.